THE TANESH EMPIRE OMNIBUS

LEAH R CUTTER

KNOTTED ROAD PRESS

ALSO BY LEAH R CUTTER

Forgotten Gods

A Wind Blown Torment

A Stone Strewn Clash

A Sea Washed Victory

Tanish Empire Trilogy

The Glass Magician

The Desert Heart

The Ghost Dog

The Cassie Stories

Poisoned Pearls

Tainted Waters

Spoiled Harvest

Bloodied Ice

The Witch's Progress

Circle of Air

Circle of Water

Circle of Fire

Circle of Earth

Seattle Trolls

The Changeling Troll

The Princess Troll

The Fairy-Bridge Troll

The Troll-Demon War

The Troll-Human War

The Troll-Troll War

The Shadow Wars Trilogy

The Raven and the Dancing Tiger

The Guardian Hound

War Among the Crocodiles

The Clockwork Fairy Kingdom

The Clockwork Fairy Kingdom

The Maker, the Teacher, and the Monster

The Dwarven Wars

The Chronicles of Franklin

Franklin Versus The Popcorn Thief

Franklin Versus The Soul Thief

Franklin Versus The Child Thief

Huli Intergalactic - Science/Space Fantasy

Origins

The Strawberry Girl

Contemporary Fantasy

Siren's Call

The Immortals' War

CONTENTS

THE GLASS MAGICIAN

THE DESERT HEART

THE GHOST DOG

MAP

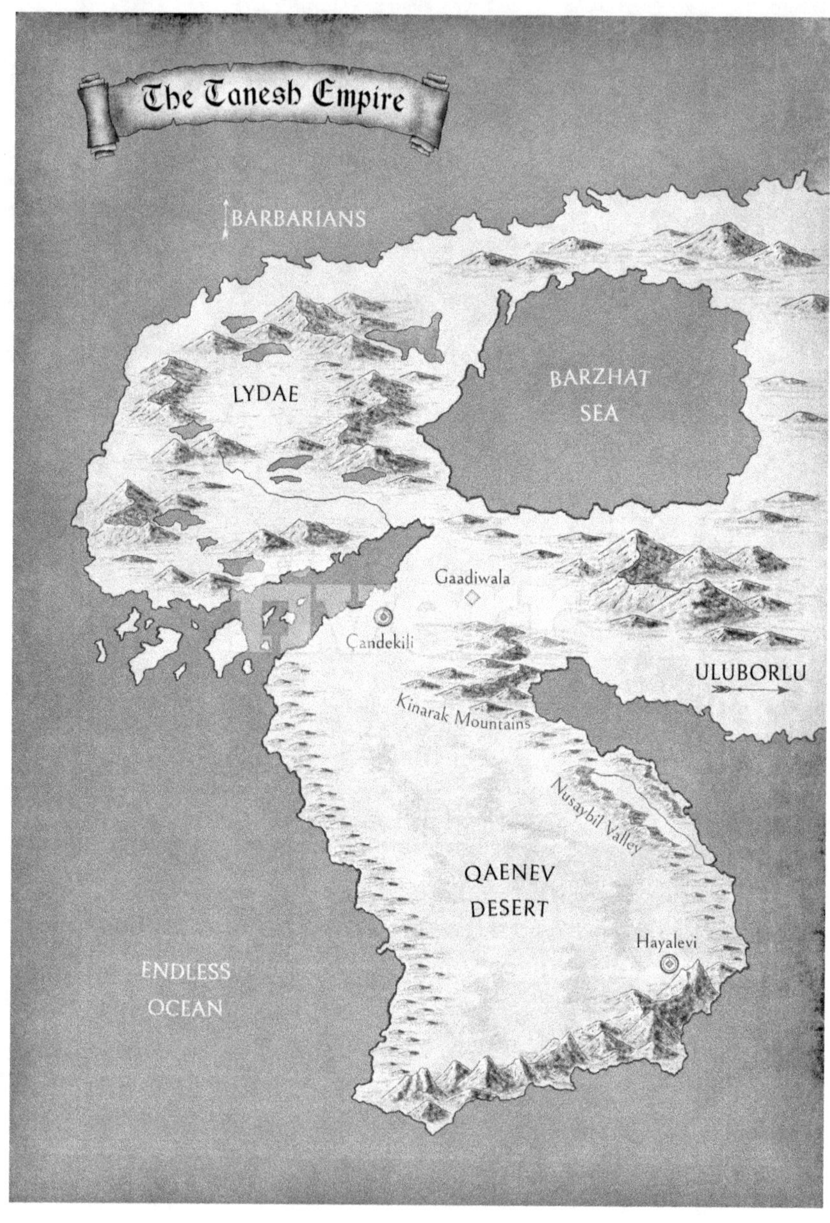
The Tanesh Empire
BARBARIANS
LYDAE
BARZHAT
SEA
Gaadiwala
Çandekili
ULUBORLU
Kinarak Mountains
Nusaybil Valley
QAENEV
DESERT
Hayalevi
ENDLESS
OCEAN

PRONUNCIATION GUIDE

Ç—pronounced as the S in "Sea." TRU-llis (Trulliç)

Zh—pronounced as the S in "Measure." MEER-i-zhah (Myrizhah)

ş—Pronounced as SH. KAR-desh (Kardeş)

ğ—Pronounced with a hard, guttural sound. AH-gkhree-khat (*ağrikat*)

BLOOD CHASE

PARAYAT'S FINGERS SLIPPED AS SHE crawled down the steep roof of the traitor's house.

She started sliding.

Rain earlier had misted the clay tiles, making them difficult to grab.

Parayat dug her bare toes in. Pressed her elbows against the roof. Jammed her fingers between the tiles.

Skin tore. Blood made her hands slick.

She slid faster.

Her foot touched a rain gutter. She slipped her toes into the man-made crevice. Finally! A solid foothold. Bent her knees to absorb the force of her fall. Clutched the tiles with her fingers. Grabbed on tightly.

She stopped.

Hands shaking, blood pounding in her ears, Parayat tried to still her breathing so she could listen.

As a star sister, her magic would hide her in the shadows, her illusions causing lazy guards to look away, not pay attention to her.

She couldn't mask noise.

The stillness of the night flowed over Parayat. Cool red-clay tiles lay under her trembling cheek.

No alarms rang. No shouting men gathered below her, pointing. Nothing but the quiet conversations of women in the next building comforting their babes, the sleepy clucking of hens in the coop on the ground, far below.

The plan had been simple enough. Parayat would slip into the traitor Girsun's house by going from the roof of one house to the next, then in through an open window on the third story. (The doors on the ground level had too many guards, even for Parayat's illusions.) She merely had to scratch Girsun's skin with her poisoned dagger without waking him.

After an hour, Girsun the traitor would be beyond help, dying a painful, messy death.

As the emperor had instructed.

While Parayat's companions, two other star sisters, stayed at a nearby tavern, loudly drinking and playing games of dice and knucklebones, their own illusions making it seem as if there were three of them, giving Parayat an alibi.

A cool breeze tickled the back of Parayat's short black hair, carrying scents from the kitchen set up in the courtyard on the other side of the roof: the roasted mutton and figs Girsun had had for what was to be his final meal, the sour beer they brewed up here in the northern part of the empire, the sweet leavened bread northerners served.

She tested her foothold on the rain gutter. Still solid. Then she forced the fingers of her right hand, then her left, to loosen.

She'd had no idea that the gutter would hold her. She'd grown up in the southern part of the kingdom, where there was never enough rain to warrant gutters. The roofs tended to be less steep as well.

Since coming to the north, doing the emperor's bidding, Parayat had seen more rain these last two months than in her entire twenty years before.

Maybe next time she would just tiptoe across a gutter. It was worth considering.

Under the edge of the roof where she precariously crouched lay a balcony. Though Parayat had welcomed the unseasonal heat, the locals had complained bitterly. It still wasn't warm enough for her, though. Late spring and the winds gave her chickenflesh instead of stirring her blood.

However, the warm weather meant open windows on upper floors and easier access.

Slowly, Parayat bent her knees, awkwardly pressing her side against the clay tile roof.

She lost her balance briefly, catching herself before she tumbled downward, her hands grabbing at the tiles again.

Parayat glanced behind her and down. She gulped. If she fell, it was a long way down to the ground.

It would mean her own messy and painful death.

She swallowed down her fear.

She could do this.

Parayat made herself look again over the edge of the roof.

She could barely see the balcony. Just the wall marking the edge of it. She couldn't see into the balcony itself.

However, she couldn't just jump there. The wall stood in the way. She needed to swing herself closer to the house, then down, inside the balcony wall.

Parayat wiped first one, then the other of her bloody hands on her tight-fitting black pants. Anyone seeing her dressed such would be scandalized. Women were supposed to wear long loose skirts, or even looser pants if they worked a trade. Her shirt would have caused comment as well: sleeveless and black, though not as tightly fitting as her pants. It showed off her wiry muscles, her dark southern skin, the numerous scars from her dangerous career.

A leather belt cinched tightly around her small waist held her usual three knives. She wore additional knives tied to her calves, her back, her side. A blowgun with darts was attached to her left hip, while the poisoned dagger with the obsidian blade stayed firmly sheathed on her right.

After a brief prayer to the goddess Serrat—the mother of all star sisters, the goddess who ruled the desolate places of the world—Parayat made herself move.

She grabbed hold of the gutter between her feet.

Pushed herself off the roof.

Thrust her pelvis forward as her legs fell.

Her legs swung forward into the empty space under the edge of the roof.

The gutter groaned and shook.

Parayat let go.

Her bare feet found the floor of the balcony, just beyond the wall.

But she was off balance. Instead of landing softly, she fell on her butt, the wind knocked from her.

Shaking, Parayat pushed herself into a crouch. She didn't stand, not yet.

She was so close to her target. She had to get to the traitor. Had to do the emperor's bidding. Could not fail the *Padisha-i-Ghazi*.

After taking another deep breath, Parayat stood and looked around.

Not only an open window faced the balcony, but an open door stood there as well.

Had her luck finally changed?

Parayat stopped before she crossed the threshold, peering into the darkness.

Her eyes had adjusted to the darkness of the night, but it was even dimmer inside the room.

A bed lay against the wall to her right. The other dark shapes in the room were probably chests for clothes, an altar dedicated to one or more of the gods, maybe even a nightstand holding a pitcher of fresh water and a basin.

Parayat had never seen people waste so much water before.

Did someone sleep on the bed?

Parayat took a quiet step forward, then froze again when she heard a soft snore.

Yes, someone lay there. And she hadn't woken him or her up.

Just two more steps across the room and she'd be out the door on the other side. Onto fulfilling her mission.

A low growl stopped her.

Damn it! Parayat slowly backed up and out the open door leading to the balcony.

She'd been so close.

A large shape manifested from the shadows, the head easily reaching her waist.

As Parayat backed up, the shape shrank though the growling continued.

Dread suffused Parayat.

Only one type of animal could change size at will.

A blood hound.

"I'm not here to harm the woman," Parayat whispered urgently. "I swear it."

The blood hound had followed her out onto the balcony, growling the whole time, until Parayat's back was pushed up against the wall.

"I'm doing the emperor's will. Like you," Parayat assured the blood hound. "I will not harm the woman."

All the blood hounds looked alike when they were in their more normal state: an average sized dog, the head only rising to her knee, with short, red-brown hair and floppy ears. His nose was black, and took up a disproportional amount of his snout. His eyes were just a shade lighter than his fur.

Blood hounds had been conjured by the emperor when he'd come to power over a century before. When a woman carried a babe of power—either a male magician with his land magic, or a female star sister with her illusions—a blood hound always appeared.

The hound would protect the woman while she was pregnant, thereby protecting the babe. Only someone truly suicidal would attack a pregnant woman with a blood hound present. Their family may or may not recover enough pieces of his body to hold a funeral ceremony.

Once the birth started, however, everything changed. More than one story told of a blood hound killing the mother in order to save the baby.

After the babe was born, the blood hound gobbled down the afterbirth, returning immediately to the emperor, its master. There, the blood hound vomited up the bloody mess. The emperor used the afterbirth to fashion a new scale that he then attached to his great cloak.

When the babe grew up and came into power, he or she could never attack the emperor: They couldn't fight their own blood.

The hound facing Parayat stopped growling. He sat back on his butt, looking for a moment like a normal dog.

Then the hound held out a paw to Parayat.

What did the hound want?

Parayat looked down at her own bloodied hands. The skin was torn all along the edges of her forefingers. She hadn't noticed that the nails had been ripped off of two fingers on her right hand and three on her left. Her thumbs were also a mess. Had she dislocated one?

The hound growled again and shook his paw at her.

Slowly, Parayat held her own right hand out.

Quicker than she could move, the hound darted forward and licked her bloodied fingers.

Parayat's entire arm shook with the effort to keep her hand still.

Those sharp teeth, so close to her fingers. That powerful jaw within grasping distance of her wrist and the delicate veins there.

That tongue—not soft or slimy like a normal dog's, but with a rasp, like a cat's—extending her pain.

Parayat shivered but controlled herself.

She was a star sister. A sister to the goddess of death, Barzhat. One of the emperor's special stars, who did favors and jobs for him, frequently assassinating his enemies.

The pain meant nothing.

The fear was an old friend.

There was power in blood. As a star sister, if she took a blood oath and did not fulfill it, all her sisters would be held responsible until the oath was complete.

The star carved into her left cheek—the one that all star sisters received when they came of age—suddenly pulsed with the pain, as if it hadn't fully healed.

Her stomach turned as the hound finished one hand and held its paw out again.

Would it attack now? Did it know that she was as dexterous with her right as her left hand?

She would do as the emperor's servant bid.

Parayat stuck her other hand out for the hound to lick.

Her right hand throbbed worse than it had been. As if the hound had awoken all the nerve endings. Sending fire shooting down her veins.

Had it poisoned her?

She shivered again.

No.

Adrenaline hit.

As if the hound's saliva had been cultivated like the strongest tea.

Her heart beat faster in her chest. She panted and danced on the knife's edge of pain.

The night grew clearer. Edges that had been fuzzy, hidden in shadows, grew sharp.

"I won't be long," Parayat promised the hound as he finished licking her other hand clean.

The hound merely nodded, then lay down on the balcony, growing as still as a statue.

Hadn't the old kings, who'd ruled before the emperor, once worshiped dogs? Statues like this?

It didn't matter. Parayat had a job to do.

***

Parayat's information about the house turned out to be accurate. She went directly to the traitor Girsun's room.

She wrinkled her nose as she entered. It smelled as sour as she'd thought it should.

With three long strides she crossed the room to where the traitor slept restlessly.

He was an old man, older than she'd expected.

Usually, traitors were young men, angry and easily bribable by barbarians and their gold.

This old man, though, he would be respected.

Possibly the traitor had many accomplices.

Cut the head of the snake off and let the body wither.

No wonder the emperor had wanted Girsun's death to be particularly messy.

Girsun looked like a man of the south, with dark hair and sharp features instead of being blond and broad like the people of the north. He snored slightly, showing a mouthful of perfect teeth.

Of course he could afford good food. He'd probably never been hungry a day in his life. Unlike Parayat and her sisters.

Parayat whipped out the poisoned dagger.

She stopped. Made herself wait.

Not in anger. This wasn't a stab and run job. Though she'd done more than one of those.

Parayat waited until the snores grew deeper. Until Girsun completely relaxed.

Until she could raise Girsun's arm up, exposing the rank hair under his arm, the sweat that still clung there.

With the tip of the poisoned knife, Parayat scratched the underside of Girsun's arm, just the length of her pinky fingernail. The obsidian blade sliced the skin open neatly, the blood beading on the skin.

A spot that would be difficult for him to examine. Something he might let slide if he woke up, thinking it maybe an insect bite.

Slipping her knife back against her hip, Parayat left the room as silently as she'd entered.

The hall shouldn't be more dim than the room, but it seemed that way.

Parayat swayed.

All the excitement drained out of her body, leaving her shaking and weak.

She couldn't stop now.

She had to escape.

In a very short while, she found her way back to the pregnant woman's room.

Was it Girsun's wife? His daughter? It didn't matter.

He was dead.

The hound would see to the woman.

Parayat slipped through the pregnant woman's room, then out, onto the balcony.

"I didn't hurt her," Parayat promised.

The hound nodded.

Parayat climbed back onto the wall protecting the balcony, grabbing onto the gutter, intending to lift herself up, to leave the same way she'd come.

The hound stood up. It looked up at her, waiting until she had a firm grip.

Then it started baying.

W hy in the name of the golden courts of death was the hound telling everyone Parayat was here?

What was the hound playing at?

Parayat's arms shook as she pulled herself up to the roof.

Men shouted beneath her.

"There!"

Parayat didn't have time to stop, to reapply her *blur* illusion, to make herself more difficult to see.

She clambered up the roof, scuttling like a crab across the tiles. At the peak she pulled herself up again, then ran without looking down.

She couldn't fall this time. Men would be waiting for her. It would be an even messier death.

She wasn't sure she could get away.

She had to try.

Suddenly, the blood hound appeared on the keel of the roof behind her, barking angrily.

No magic would hide or disguise her well enough if the blood hound decided to give chase.

No pregnant woman had ever been able to escape from a blood hound. The fastest horse, the smallest boat, the most secret cavern—it didn't matter. The hound would just appear beside her again.

And this hound had Parayat's full scent, her blood in his mouth, baying as if it wanted more.

How was she going to get away when it could magically follow her?

The roof of Girsun's house ended abruptly. Parayat didn't bother slowing but took a running leap onto the next roof.

The men below her shouted. None of them could have made such a jump.

Then again, none of them had trained as she had, for so many years, racing across Knife Ridge.

The expanse wouldn't stop the blood hound, Parayat knew. She raced across the ridge of the next roof.

She'd started here, climbing onto this roof by a room, below. It had been easy enough to slip through the tailor's shop on the ground level, no guards to see or stop her, then up the stairs and through the window of the old blind grandmother, who'd ruined her eyes sewing so long ago.

Could Parayat get away using that same route?

The blood hound stayed on the first roof, still barking.

Parayat took a chance.

She conjured up a shadow of herself, set it to continue running across the roof, leaping onto the next building.

The men below her followed the shadow.

Parayat took a deep breath. Maybe she could get away.

Then the blood hound gracefully leaped from one building to the next, landing on the roof Parayat stayed on.

He started barking again.

The men turned back.

Parayat dropped down to her hands and knees. Where could she go?

She felt herself slipping.

This time, at least, she hadn't been moving. The fall was more controlled.

And she knew that a gutter at the edge of the roof would catch her.

Except this house had no rain gutters.

Parayat's bare feet went off the edge of the roof. She sliced her hands open again by grabbing onto the tiles.

There was the stupid gutter. Under the actual eave of the house, not at the edge of the roof.

Parayat took deep gulps of air.

She looked over her shoulder.

Couldn't see anything below her. Or behind her. Just darkness.

A messy death.

The hound appeared above her on the roof. It howled angrily. Drool dripped from its lower jaw. It had grown in size again until it would have come up to her waist.

Parayat couldn't just let go and trust that she would be all right.

Nothing had ever worked like that in her life.

Instead, she dove for the gutter hanging under the eaves.

It groaned sickeningly loud in her hands.

Metal bent.

The edges pulled loose from the roof.

Parayat dropped down, still holding onto the gutter.

Suddenly she swung out more.

Instead of three stories up, she was only one and a half.

She jumped.

The night wind whistled in her hair. The fall went on forever. Had the hound actually grabbed her, somehow? Carried her away, back to the traitor Girsun's house to stand punishment?

No.

The ground rushed up to greet her.

Parayat landed harder on her right foot than her left. She rolled to absorb the force. Then she pushed herself back upright, ready to run.

Her right ankle wasn't about to forgive her.

The hound stayed on the roof, at least for the moment, baying loudly.

She already heard men rushing around the corner of the house.

She had no choice.

She must run, while the hound gave chase.

Parayat pushed her hand against her side, trying to distract herself from how much the stich there hurt. At least she'd trained running Knife Ridge: though she'd like to tie strips of leather to the balls of her feet to give her better traction, at least she was used to running barefoot.

Any time Parayat slowed, the blood hound appeared behind her, directing the men to her.

It never got close enough to harm her, to tear her limbs off, to rip her throat out.

What game was it playing? Did the hound want her to get away?

Or did it just relish the chase?

Parayat wished she could contact her sisters at the tavern and send them back to the house to threaten the pregnant girl. That way the hound would leave Parayat be.

She took another sharp corner, darting away behind a crooked lean-to. She hadn't been to this part of the city, however, the small shacks and piles of refuge marked this neighborhood as one of the poorer ones.

Could she use the scents here to throw off the blood hound?

If he was a normal dog, she could. But he wasn't using physical scents to follow her. He had tasted her blood, and chased after that.

Still, she had to do something. Even her great strength had drained, her speed dropping.

She'd grown tired of this chase.

Time to play dead, or the men would catch her and kill her.

Parayat took off again, sprinting across the yard and into the next shack.

She *blurred* her face as well as she could as she whirled around the room, stealing a blanket from a poor child, the headscarf from her bewildered mother, as well as a dirty rag.

Parayat would have to remember this place and return in the morning, leaving a coin or two for them to find.

Then she raced out again, going back to the pile of straw she'd found next to a shack that was being built.

Quickly, Parayat wrapped the blanket around a bale of straw. It wasn't as long as a body, but it would have to do. She tied the headscarf around one end, not wanting to give up her own. Then she wiped blood from her torn up skin onto the blanket, the scarf, and down the sides of the straw.

She rolled the rag up into a long bundle, putting it on the ground, next to the straw bale.

Parayat didn't have time to do a full illusion. The darkness of the night would have to help.

The rag became an arm, lying apart from the body, as if the hound had torn it from her.

She created the illusion of a woman lying where the straw bale was, her legs bent under her, as if she'd fallen from a great height. The head rested on the right cheek so the star carved into her left cheek was clearly displayed.

The hound raced up first, sniffing along the edge of the blanket. He nudged at the straw, then looked up, directly at the shadows Parayat hid in.

She raised her chin defiantly.

The chase had been fun.

But it was over.

The hound snorted as if it were laughing at her.

Then it ambled away and sat, giving one last howl as the men came running up.

They saw what Parayat had wanted them to see.

The body. The bloodied hound. The fallen sister.

They gathered together and waited, a few feet away from the "body", until a second group joined them.

"Girsun," one of the men called. "She's dead."

"Thank you," the old man said, coming up slowly.

Had he been with the men the entire time, chasing her?

Parayat stiffened as the old man came into view.

No one seemed too concerned about Girsun. They probably thought his condition was due to his age catching up with him.

They didn't recognize that the waxiness of his skin, the paleness and extreme sweat, was the poison taking hold of him.

He'd be gone long before morning.

Had that been why the hound had chased her? So Girsun would follow, guaranteeing his death?

Or had all the running and chasing been play for the hound?

The hound had already disappeared, going back to his primary duty.

The men left. When they returned in the morning, no evidence would remain that a body or a fight had taken place there.

Parayat and her sisters would see to that.

Parayat moved stiffly through the main room of the tavern in the morning, nursing a cup of special, restorative tea that she'd prepared. She and her sisters needed to be on the road before the rest of the city awoke. There would be rumors about a star sister being chased by a hound the night before. Better they were gone before some foolish guard decided to try to question them.

She froze when she saw a blood hound sitting in the middle of the road in front of the tavern. Staring at her.

Was it the same hound? She wasn't sure. They all looked alike.

The way the hound looked at her though, the way it licked along its snout…it had to be the same dog.

The one who had the taste of her blood in his mouth, still.

The one who probably wanted more of her blood.

For a moment, Parayat considered running.

She'd never get away, though.

And that damned hound *liked* chasing her.

Instead, she pulled herself upright. Stood more solidly on her poor bruised feet.

"I'm leaving," she told the hound directly.

Could the hound hear her? Did it matter?

"And I won't be back," she promised.

The hound nodded and ambled off, looking for a moment like a regular dog.

Then it stopped, looking over its shoulder as if offering a challenge.

Come back at your own peril.

Shaking, Parayat nodded.

She'd never return to this city.

Not unless she wanted another chase.

THE BLOOD HOUND

THE BLOOD HOUND FOLLOWING MYRIZHAH flopped down in the street outside the tinker's shop Myrizhah entered. She knew better than to think the hound would grow bored and leave while she shopped. Even if she tried going out the back, or ran away on the fastest horse, it would still find her. No woman escaped the blood hounds.

Still, Myrizhah couldn't help but stop and glance through the tinker's shop window back at the hound, who lay there in the dusty dirt road like a regular dog. He was medium sized, coming up to about her knee, with short, red-brown hair and tall, pointy ears that stuck on the top of his head. His nose was black and took up a disproportional amount of his snout. His eyes were just a shade lighter than his fur. The hound looked sad and too aware, as if he had seen too many babies die.

No one bothered the hound. Most avoided him, either crossing the street or walking a wide path around him.

Despite his ordinary looks, people could *feel* that he was something special.

Myrizhah turned away, looking back into the shop. It was only lit by the window overlooking the street, making it seem dark and crowded. Hanging from the walls were small brass pans for cooking eggs, large iron kettles for stew, tiny pewter cups given to newborns, and even finely decorated tin squares that could be hung on a wall, merely for decoration.

It was a rich person's shop, despite how tiny and dimly lit it was. It smelled of clean coins, fancy brass polish, and iron shavings.

Myrizhah wasn't rich. But she wanted to give her unborn son the best.

"I see a hound's got your scent," said the tinker, coming out from behind his counter to stand beside Myrizhah. He was an older man with many fine wrinkles around his blue eyes. He wore his white hair to his shoulders while his face was clean shaven, as was the custom here. He had a bulbous nose and flabby lips, with heavy jowls.

It was the type of face Myrizhah had gotten used to here, up north, as opposed to the knife-thin and sharp features of the men she'd grown up with in the south, with their darker skins and full beards.

"Congratulations," the tinker continued.

Myrizhah nodded and reflexively put her hand on her extended belly, as if to protect it. Blood hounds only followed pregnant women whose babies had magic.

It was considered an honor up here, in the north, to birth a baby of power. Something else that was very different from where Myrizhah had grown up.

"Ducca the midwife has declared the baby will be a boy," Myrizhah told the tinker.

"I see," the tinker said, nodding. "You want something to bind him here."

"Yes," Myrizhah said. "A horseshoe made from an ore dug in the nearby mountains."

It was custom both in the north as well as the south to place a horseshoe, the symbol of the Goddess Onnet, on the belly of a woman as she was giving birth, to help draw the baby out. In ancient times, the first letter of Onnet's name had always been carved as the symbol Ω.

A magician's magic was tied to the land, usually close to where he was born. While a magician might have some small power over all the trees, he could do amazing things within his small, local forest. A magician might have an affinity for rock, but he could only perform great magic with the granite mined in a specific range. Same with water workers, who worked best with their personal creek or lake.

This babe had to be tied here so Myrizhah could leave him behind with a clear conscience when she escaped the family she'd been married into and ran away back to the south.

The tinker cast a sly glace at Myrizhah's clothes, obviously calculating her wealth. Then his eyes rested on her belly for a moment and grew softer.

"I'd recommend a horseshoe made from the tin found near the Agrafa pass," he said kindly. Then he grew shrewd again. "Unless you'd prefer something from the silver mine…"

"Tin would do quite nicely," Myrizhah assured him.

Her mother-in-law didn't deserve a grandson who worked with silver or gold, though magicians who worked with metal were rare.

Not that her mother-in-law would have thought such fortune possible. Not from her bad luck daughter-in-law, the one who had already caused the family such grief.

The son she carried kicked suddenly, as if to distract her dark thoughts. Myrizhah couldn't help her gasp. That boy took her breath away, sometimes.

Too bad she would never see him grow up.

"May I offer you a chair, madam?" the tinker said, taking her arm.

Myrizhah stopped herself from pulling away and shouting at the man. No one in the south would ever presume to casually touch her that way.

Instead, she let herself be guided to a guest's chair that was just before the counter. Though the pillow was covered in fine, red linen, it was stuffed with straw, hard and practical.

She refused the tea the tinker offered her, though she did take a cup of cool water.

The boy kicked again. The pain he offered her was almost rhythmic, though she didn't think these were contractions. Not yet. As this was her first child, she had to rely on Ducca the midwife, who told her the babe wasn't due for weeks.

Still, she put down the cool cup and started bargaining with the tinker. Though she might be short of breath, she wasn't addled, and she could still strike a good deal.

When Myrizhah left the shop, her tin horseshoe in hand, she paused for just a moment. It was bright out here, the air in the mountains cooler and drier than what she'd grown up with. The dust in the air smelled the same though, and despite their strange clothes and manners, underneath, the people here were the same too: poor and just trying to get by.

The hound had already risen, giving her that too-knowing look.

It didn't care what her plans were after the baby was born. All it cared about was the babe.

There were stories of hounds who'd "helped" during difficult births, killing the mother but saving the child.

He wouldn't get her, though. This baby would be born with ease.

Then Myrizhah was going to run away. Leave the harshness of the mountains, the softness of the trees, the rich black dirt.

Go live in the desert again.

Even if she died trying.

⁂

Ducca the midwife waited for Myrizhah at the tiny farmstead. It wasn't much bigger than a shack—just a single room with a shelf for her bed and a hearth at the back—but at least it gave Myrizhah a place to live away from the family compound where the rest of her in-laws resided.

Myrizhah knew better than to look around, to hope that her husband had returned from the war. He'd gone off just after they'd discovered she'd become pregnant, with a cheery promise that he'd return in a month, having made his fortune as promised by the *Padisha-i-Ghazi*, the great emperor.

News of his death had made her mother in law, as well as the rest of the family, turn cold to his foreign wife.

Myrizhah understood. They thought she was bad luck.

The fact that she was carrying a son, as well as a magician, had warmed their reception of her only slightly. They were still regularly awful to her, and she wept many hidden tears.

Ducca took one look at Myrizhah then took her by the arm, bringing her closer to the fire.

Myrizhah couldn't help but stiffen. Did everyone have to touch her today?

Ducca was a tiny woman, barely coming up to Myrizhah's ample breasts. Myrizhah always felt like one of the giantesses from the tales standing next to her. However, Myrizhah could also feel the strength in Ducca's hands, how firmly she held Myrizhah. This was no weak, pampered woman.

Ducca wore her blonde hair braided. It shone like gold in the firelight. Just like her husband's had. It had been one of the reasons why Myrizhah had agreed to marry him, to travel so far north, away from her family and everything she knew.

She still hoped his son would have that fine, golden hair.

"This babe is as impatient as you are," Ducca chided. "He's dropped." She reached for Myrizhah's belly, then paused before she touched her. "May I?" she asked.

Myrizhah nodded. Though it wasn't proper for a stranger to touch a woman, this was a midwife. And she did need to know the condition of her charge.

Ducca's strong fingers probed Myrizhah's belly.

Myrizhah kept her mouth closed firmly as she felt the nausea rise.

"The head's down," Ducca told her. "He's coming. Tomorrow or the next day."

Myrizhah nodded, relieved and anxious at the same time. She hadn't finished her preparation. She did have a bundle of travel clothes already prepared. When she'd leave would depend on how quickly she'd recover her strength. If she didn't have to hold the babe, she knew it would be easier to leave him, but she'd never seen a woman just walk away from a birth.

"Have you named him yet?" Ducca asked.

Myrizhah shrugged. She'd told her in-laws early on that it was her people's custom to not speak the name of an unborn out loud, not until after they were born. It was too easy for a curse to be put on the unborn.

It was an old wives' tale. However, Myrizhah didn't believe in curses, not like that. She'd never given the baby a name because she'd never wanted to be that close to the boy.

She was only going to bear him. Then she was going to leave.

Ducca crossed her arms over her chest and scowled. She wore short sleeves that showed off her muscular arms, along with what they called "trous," full pants that looked like a long skirt. She shook her head. "You'll change your mind when the babe is born," she said softly.

Myrizhah raised herself up to her full height. "What are you talking about?" she asked disdainfully.

"You'll come to love the boy," Ducca told her.

Mryizhah merely blinked at the midwife, unsure how to reply. She wasn't going to be there long enough to love him. Then she shrugged. "I'm told that happens," she said.

Ducca nodded. "I have promised to go to Farmer Tiegan's house, to check on his wife. I only promised because I had thought your son was weeks away, not days." She scowled at Myrizhah's belly, as if the boy was purposefully vexing her.

"Go," Myrizhah told her. "I'll be fine."

"I could stop at the main house, get your mother-in-law or one of your sister-in-laws to sit with you," Ducca offered.

"No," Myrizhah said immediately. "Not until the birth is closer," she added when she saw Ducca's shocked look at her strong refusal.

"All right," Ducca said. "I won't be long. I promise."

Myrizhah knew the woman prided herself on her keeping her word. She was always directly honest with everyone. Myrizhah found it off putting at times, refreshing at others.

Ducca had no children of her own. Which may have been why she was so concerned with others having healthy births.

"I have the hound here to help as well," Myrizhah said with dark humor.

Ducca glanced over toward the door of the tiny farmstead. The hound was waiting on the threshold as always, in his usual guard spot.

Before the baby was born, he would protect Myrizhah. That was true of all the blood hounds.

After the baby had started coming was an entirely different matter.

"I'll be back so you won't need his help," Ducca said earnestly. She threw a cloak over her shoulders and hurried out the door.

The room seemed colder without her presence. Myrizhah carefully picked up another piece of wood and threw it on fire. Pregnant women were supposed to be warm all the time, but Myrizhah was cold up here in the north, where the sun was so pale.

Soon, she would be warm again, back in her own southern home. Her family wouldn't necessarily welcome her back with grand feasts of pomegranates and fruit wine—she should stay with her husband's family, even if she found them intolerable. But she hoped she'd be less unwelcome there.

Myrizhah thought she'd spin a little more by the firelight but found her eyes drooping. Instead, she laid down on the tiny shelf and napped, instantly dreaming of holding the tiny tin horseshoe like a dowsing rod in her hands as she marched across endless sands, but the tin had no affinity for the land and it couldn't lead her to water, no matter how far she roamed.

P*ain.*
Myrizhah dreamed of an iron poker shoved into her belly, the pain of it making her cry out.

When she opened her bleary eyes, the pain didn't recede. It took her a moment to place the dark wooden roof above her head, not the canvas of tents or the stucco of the towns.

She was in the north, where it was always cold, with a family who hated her and would just as soon she died in childbirth.

Not that her mother-in-law had said such a thing directly to Myrizhah. However, the woman had refused to pray for her and only said prayers for the unborn son.

He was the only thing of value to them, and only if he turned out to be powerful.

They would all soon find out.

The child was on its way.

Myrizhah had no idea what time it was. Had she been asleep for hours? Or a fraction of that time?

Another rolling wave of pain washed over her. Powerful contractions emanated from her nether regions and up her belly.

Yes, this boy was as impatient as his father had been the first time they'd lain together as man and wife, taking her roughly, then drying her tears and doing it the right way, as a real man should, with tenderness.

There was nothing tender about birth, though.

Ducca had taught Myrizhah a rhyming song to help her to breathe through the contractions.

Myrizhah hadn't bothered to tell the midwife that unlike her northern sisters, she knew how to count far past the fingers on her hand. Still, she tried to hum the song as she slowed down her breathing, getting ready for the first awful push.

Something cold touched Myrizhah's hand, bringing her back from the world of pain. Turning her head took a monumental effort, but she still managed to peer out beyond the edge of the bed.

The hound stood there, dark and glowering.

"Oh no," Myrizhah said. "You don't get to help. I can manage this on my own."

Then another contraction hit and the room grew dark.

Myrizhah knew there was something wrong. She'd seen childbirth before, had held her eldest sister's hand to help ease her through it.

There was too much pain. The blankets beneath her were soaked with too much blood.

Myrizhah hadn't done any stitching for the last four weeks. Nothing should be blocking the birth canal.

But that was how it felt. As if the baby couldn't get out.

Myrizhah cried out as the next wave hit her. She had to do something, anything. Or she might take a knife to her own belly to end this.

Wait. Where was the horseshoe? She'd gone to sleep holding it.

The metal felt cool to Myrizhah's sweating palm. She raised up her tunic and slid the horseshoe onto her belly.

The pain doubled, the horseshoe sticking to her skin as she writhed.

What had the tinker given her? Had he poisoned the metal? She couldn't pull it off—it stuck to her skin as if glued there.

Myrizhah wailed in grief. She had to live. Had to see the desert again. Had to get this baby born.

Coolness touched her fingers again.

With horror, Myrizhah looked to the side.

The hound was there, looming. He had grown bigger than the medium-sized dog he had always appeared to be, and now would come up to her waist, easily. His coat had changed as well, growing black as a curse.

"No!" Myrizhah screamed as the hound grew taller. He placed one paw—now larger than her own hand—on the side of the bed shelf. He lowered his muzzle to her belly, his hot breath easing her pain for the moment.

Myrizhah braced herself for the next part—when the hound tore her belly to bits, killing her in order to save the boy.

Instead, the hound licked her belly, licked at the tin horseshoe, drawing it up in his mouth, much more delicately than Myrizhah would have expected.

Suddenly, Myrizhah could breathe again. The pain instantly lessened.

What had the tinker given her?

A whining noise made Myrizhah look to her right, to where the hound stood.

He had turned the horseshoe, holding the curve so the tin ends stuck out from his mouth like odd-shaped fangs. Then, the hound shook his head. He moved so quickly his head became a blur.

A soft *pop* filled the room when the hound stopped, as though a cork on a barrel of beer had just been loosened.

The horseshoe was no longer tin.

The hound raised himself back up, carefully placing one paw on the bed shelf, then putting the horseshoe back on Myrizhah's belly. It felt cool against her skin and the pain receded another fraction.

Myrizhah craned her neck to see the horseshoe, running her fingers along its smooth surface.

It was now made of clear glass shot through with ribbons of gold and green.

The colors of the old kings. Before the *Padisha-i-Ghazi*, the magician emperor, had come to power centuries before.

Then another wave of pain struck Myrizhah. It was a normal pain, though. Something she'd seen other women bear as part of childbirth.

With a determined cry, Myrizhah pushed, as impatient as the babe to have the birth finished.

The head crowned with her next push. It was too late for Myrizhah to stagger over to the birthing chair so she could at least catch the baby with her arms. Instead, she gave another great push, the shoulders sliding out followed by the rest of him.

It took all the stubbornness Myrizhah had to make herself sit up, to reach for her babe, to awkwardly draw it up across her sore stomach.

The hound licked at the boy's foot, causing him to jerk and cry, drawing in his first breath, letting loose with a healthy wail.

"Shhh, shh," Myrizhah said, cradling the boy's head.

She didn't care for the boy. She couldn't. But she could hold him and comfort him, just this once.

A shadow crossed her sight.

The hound had levered himself up to the side of the bed again, looking down on her.

He seemed to be asking her permission.

Myrizhah collected the boy's feet up higher on her body and gave the hound a sharp nod.

One giant paw reached out and pressed on her belly, hard.

Myrizhah couldn't help but shout with pain once again as her body had yet another contraction. The afterbirth came sputtering out.

The hound moved from the side of the bed to the foot, where he greedily devoured the afterbirth. Then he looked up at her, licking his bloodied chops.

Padisha-i-Ghazi thanks you for your contribution.

Then the hound disappeared, a great wind chasing him.

Myrizhah shivered. She was going to have to clean up this mess, soon. Clip the umbilical cord. Say the prayers to Onnet, thanking her for the live birth, the healthy son.

Then she realized what the hound had said.

He would go directly to the emperor and vomit up the afterbirth. Then the emperor would take a piece of the afterbirth and fashion it into a scale, that would be sewn into the great cloak he always wore.

No magician could attack the emperor in his cloak. They couldn't harm their own blood.

This was why the blood hounds had been conjured. To protect the emperor.

For the hound to speak to her meant that her boy was a magician of great power. That the emperor himself would one day fear.

Then Myrizhah looked down at the boy.

He had both hands clenched tightly around the glass horseshoe, resting his cheek against it.

With a sinking feeling, Myrizhah realized that she was going to have to take the boy with her when she left.

Metal, stone, iron—these were the materials the northern magicians had an affinity for.

Glass—basically sand blasted with such heat that it melted—was a material that only a southern magician could use.

He could only come to power in her lands.

She would have to name him now.

Maybe Alpheais, after his father. Or Trulliç, after hers.

She could decide later.

For now, she could sleep, rest a little, content that she would be going home.

THE GLASS MAGICIAN

CHAPTER ONE

TRULLIÇ

TRULLIÇ FIRST WALKED THE DESERT when he was twelve.

He woke with the dawn, throwing back the heavy sheepskin that had kept him warm during the cold desert night, and eagerly looked around.

The horizon blazed orange and purple, as though it was on fire. No clouds covered the sun's face, of course. Even during the rainy season, this side of the Kinarak mountains rarely saw storms. Streams of sunlight—like fingers—stole across the horizon, tickling the sparse brush on the hill.

Trulliç shook his head. His cousins would tease him mercilessly if they heard him talking like that, mimicking the poetry that Atça, Trulliç's mentor, had insisted that Trulliç memorize.

Below the foothills where Trulliç had camped stretched the Qaenev desert. Trulliç stared hard at it, willing for it to show itself to him.

The sand glittered on the places the early light first touched it, then settled into a pale gold color. It stretched to the far horizon, where Trulliç had been taught grew a foreboding mountain range that dropped abruptly into the endless ocean.

Much closer, but still out a good distance on the flat sands, stood a dark jut of rock. It sheltered an altar to Serril, the god of deserts and desolate places.

The first place Trulliç would officially visit on this, his manhood journey.

Thorn bushes struggled to grow in the border between the true desert and the foothills. A tiny yellow lizard skittered across the sand, popping up out of its hole then racing across to a second hiding place where it would escape the heat of the day. To his left, birds lazily circled the sky, welcoming the dawn.

Nothing else moved. No brown and white sheep grazed for sparse feed. No tiny mice hopped across the quickly heating sand. No caravans made their way along the trade route to the Kinarak mountains, then up the Ladikah pass and to the first town of Gaadiwala.

Trulliç had seen the endless ocean as a small boy. It was one of his first memories. His mother, Myrizhah, still talked of the journey with awe, all that they'd seen, how afraid he'd been of the waves.

He'd never told her what he remembered: How alive the ocean had been, the waves constantly talking to themselves. It had been too loud, too active, too overwhelming. He hadn't been afraid, not exactly. But he hadn't liked it. In fact, it had been the opposite of everything he liked.

Quiet ruled the Qaenev desert. Peace settled into Trulliç's bones. He took a deep breath, breathing in the smell of the dry foothills, the lighter scent of the sand, the air tinged with the precious spices he carried in his pack, of cinnamon and cardamom, of thyme and rosemary, of mint and sage. He'd use the spices either in trade (if he met anyone), or as offerings.

As part of his manhood journey, Trulliç would start his search for his home, to find where he truly belonged, where his magic would be the most powerful.

Magic tied a male magician to a piece of land, whether it was a forest, a lake, a collection of boulders in the foothills, the slope of a mountain, or even an oasis in the desert. While a strong enough magician might be able to affect all trees anywhere, he could only do truly special work with trees growing in his own grove.

Trulliç hoped to find his place, his part of the desert, with his first manhood journey. Atça, his mentor, had warned him that it frequently took several tries, particularly with an area as large as the Qaenev desert. Plus, Trulliç had never dreamed of the desert, something Atça told him was very odd. Normally a magician dreamed often of his home, letting his feet guide him on his manhood journey.

No matter. Trulliç was determined to prove his mentor wrong. His feet would lead him to his home. He just had to watch where they went.

Trulliç quickly gathered up the blanket he'd slept on and his sheepskin, rolling them up and tying them to the bottom of his pack. He shivered in the cool morning air, having slept in just a shirt and unbelted pants. Before he reached for warmer clothes, he patiently rolled up the sleeves on his plain, unbleached muslin shirt, uncovering his hands. Then he rolled his gray pants up around his waist, belting it with a rope. He pulled out his heavy wool tunic, sleeveless and dyed a dull red. When he put it on over the shirt, it hung to the middle of his thighs, too big for him, like all of the hand-me-down clothes he'd inherited from his cousins.

Though this was Trulliç's manhood journey, Myrizhah wasn't rich enough to buy him all new clothes. Mended and recently-cleaned clothes would have to do.

As the heat grew over the course of the day, Trulliç would change out of his wool tunic into a much lighter one that *was* new, a gift from his mentor, made from a stiff linen and striped in gold and green—the pale gold of the desert at first light, and the light green of the hills at the start of the rainy season.

Gold and green were also the colors of the old kings who'd ruled before the *Padisha-i-Ghazi,* the great emperor. Because of Trulliç's studies, he knew that the emperor had ruled for approximately two hundred years (many records had been lost, and scholars argued over the exact date the emperor had come to power). Most of the villagers believed the emperor was immortal, that he'd always been the emperor. They knew very little of the old kings. They easily complied with the latest decree that the emperor be publically thanked at every feast, like he was one of the gods.

Trulliç knew better. He also knew better than to try to say anything to his cousins.

However, Trulliç also had more reason to learn about the old kings than most.

While Myrizhah had been pregnant with Trulliç, she'd bought a tin horseshoe, intending for Trulliç's magical power to be bound to the northern mountains that his father had come from.

Like all women pregnant with a babe of power, a magical blood hound had followed Myrizhah everywhere, intent on protecting her and the child. When Trulliç's birth had started to go wrong, the blood hound had transformed the tin horseshoe into glass.

Myrizhah insisted that meant that Trulliç was a desert magician. Glass was made from sand blasted with such heat that it melted. It was also very expensive, and took a lot of precision and skill to make.

Did the horseshoe mean that Trulliç would be a powerful magician? His mother certainly hoped so. She'd insisted that the tavern her family owned have a horseshoe mortared into the stones above the doorway.

Atça couldn't confirm if Myrizhah was correct or not. Atça, in addition to being the town of Gaadiwala's only magician, also read dreams for the local people. He claimed that no one had ever had any dreams that foretold of Trulliç becoming a great magician. Plus, there were no stories of glass magicians who'd performed heroic deeds, though there was usually at least one magician who lived out in an oasis in the desert.

As no other magicians lived in the Qaenev desert at the current time, it was up to Trulliç to find his home on his own.

The first morning that Trulliç would walk the desert, he planned to travel for a few hours, then wait out the heat of the day in the shade next to Serril's altar. Only the desperate trekked across the sands during the day; most traveled in the early morning and the late afternoon and into the night.

Trulliç broke his fast with one of the travel rolls that Myrizhah had baked for him, made out of cracked wheat, hazelnut pieces, and slivers of dried figs, spiced with mint and nutmeg, all held together with *meslit* syrup, made from the boiled bark of the *meslit* thorn trees that grew everywhere.

Atça had once traded for some honey so Trulliç could taste how similar the two were.

Trulliç understood the comparison but preferred *meslit* and the smoky flavor that came from the wood fires that refined the syrup to the pure honey that his mentor waxed lyrically about. Many poems from the olden days, before the emperor, had been written about milk and honey, two foods that Trulliç really didn't like.

He'd dutifully learned the poems along with the other students. However, Trulliç didn't believe that his tastes would change as he grew older, that he would grow to like the sweeter honey and the softer rugs that Atça sat on.

While Atça was very wise, he was wrong about a few things. For example, how the wolf star traveled across the sky during the rainy season. Not that Trulliç would ever try to correct his mentor. Myrizhah had taught him better than to question his elders.

Finally, Trulliç was ready to start his manhood journey. He put on his wide leather belt, checking his knife, the two bronze coins hidden in a secret pocket, and his horseshoe.

Trulliç, now looking out at Qaenev's endless sands, seeing the boundless desert for the first time, knew that he'd finally come home. This was his place, where he belonged. He felt it in his bones, the sand already singing underneath his skin.

Now, he just had to find which part of it was his home.

Trulliç paused at the edge of the true desert, where the hard stones gave way to open sand. Hot winds blew across the gulf at him, carrying the dry scent of the land. Twisted thorn bushes grew on this side, barely reaching mid-calf, with thin, leafless branches that only the most hungry of goats would eat. Up ahead, still further out than Trulliç had first thought, stood the first station of his manhood journey: the small rock building that held Serril's altar.

This area of the desert wouldn't support a full temple. No water lay under the sands. So what he saw was just a lone, rough building, containing a simple altar, with no priest in full-time attendance of it.

Trulliç would still make the journey to the altar first, then travel to the south and east, to one of the minor caravan routes through the Qaenev desert. He wasn't lazy, like the stories he'd learned about Atyla the scribe who'd tricked his way out of his chores and only pretended to visit the altars of the gods, and instead, kept the offerings himself. Atyla had been punished for his laziness eventually, though Trulliç had still admired his cleverness.

The major caravan routes skirted the desert completely and stayed closer to the mountains that ran along the east and west coasts. Minor routes would follow an oasis trail that only sometimes held water, depending on the season. As Trulliç was making his journey just after the rainy months, water should await him once he found a trail.

Trulliç assumed that his home would be somewhere along one of the caravan routes. He anticipated that he'd always have travelers going through it, kind of like the tavern that his family owned back in Gaadiwala.

He just had to take that first step onto the sands.

Atça, as well as Trulliç's oldest cousin Bekbel who'd also been to the desert, had told him that where the foothills ended and the desert truly began was unclear. The lands overlapped and the border shifted depending on how much rain had come that season, how strong the winds were, and from which direction they blew.

To Trulliç, the difference was as bright as the oil lamps Atça burned in his house during the rainy season, lights encased in glass that no one else in town could afford.

Still, Trulliç paused. This was the start of his manhood journey, right here. Not the visit to the altar just a few hours' walk away. Not leaving Gaadiwala and traveling by himself through the Ladikah pass, making it to the other side of the Kinarak mountains on his own.

Stepping onto the sands for the very first time. That was truly the start of his journey, the start of the rest of his life.

Trulliç reached down for the glass horseshoe held securely against his belt with special leather straps that Atça had given him. Even in the heat of the morning, the horseshoe felt cool and smooth against his fingertips.

Trulliç took one last deep breath, holding in the air of the foothills, the ground behind him.

And stepped forward to find his destiny.

***

The world exploded into being around him.

Trulliç felt as though he'd already walked the length of the desert more than once, his feet knowing how long it would take him to go from the Kinarak mountains to the far coast. He felt the rocky mountains that made up the southern border, the less desolate foothills to the west and east. He tasted the salt in the air beyond them, harsh and hateful to the desert heat.

Trails went through the desert, springs of water that the desert suffered to live. Men, too, traveled across its sands, carrying the precious metals found down along the coast along with spices and exotic birds.

Trulliç felt as though he could find every single caravan, as if he could draw a map of every trail with his eyes closed.

The smell of baked sand suddenly carried many other scents as well, like the sweet palms that grew in the oasis, the secret salt caves that lay buried under the nearby rock, and the musty scent of lizard burrows. Ground-nesting birds cawed sweetly to their young, well hidden by their dusty color. Sand shifted in the wind, a sliding sound as it brushed over the tops of dunes.

Trulliç blinked, surprised. If he felt this much just stepping onto the desert, how much more would he feel when he found his home? His heart would surely burst with the joy of it.

Suddenly, Trulliç understood why the heroes of old broke into song when they made a great discovery, won a colossal battle, or even found their love.

Trulliç wouldn't sing himself, not loudly, not now. The desert left him quiet.

Besides, if his cousins ever found out about it, he'd never live it down.

He still hummed mightily as he took his next step, and his next, and his next, swinging his arms open and free.

———

Trulliç looked up with dismay.

Damn it! Why were the rocks sheltering Serril's altar so far to his left again!

Walking to the altar should have been easy. He could *see* the rocks that held the altar shimmering up ahead.

However, it was as though his feet had a mind of their own. Despite the heat of the sand, the desert enticed him and made him wander without thought.

Trulliç sighed, lined himself up with the rocks, then took a step toward them. Then another.

He looked away on his third step, only to find he'd taken another half dozen or so over the sands without meaning to, not going anywhere near his goal.

Why was he having such problems? It wasn't because he thought that his true home lay in that direction. It didn't lay in *any* direction, as far as he could tell.

Trulliç gritted his teeth and focused on walking toward the rocks again. He was *not* about to fail the first part of his manhood journey. How could he get lost on the way to Serril's altar? It was visible from the foothills!

His cousins would laugh themselves silly if Trulliç had to admit a failure like that.

It took all of Trulliç's concentration, as well as most of the morning, to reach his destination.

The building holding Serril's altar was shoddily constructed. The rocks hadn't been shaved or formed to match. They looked randomly stuck together, as though each came from the bottom of the builder's barrel. The mortar between them looked just as poor, flaking away with every wind.

The temple (though Trulliç wasn't convinced it deserved that name) had three walls connected one to another, like a square U. The fourth wall wasn't connected. Instead, it stood just inside the open doorframe, as if to suggest a door, with a wide opening on either side.

Trulliç bowed his head and stepped inside. At least it was cooler in there. However, he already knew he didn't want to spend much time in the temple. His skin crawled, as if ants covered it, making him twitchy.

Light streamed in from holes in the rock walls. The roof slanted from one side to the other, leaving Trulliç with barely enough room to stand up straight. When he reached his full height in a couple of years, he'd have to duck his head.

Inside the tiny square room a horizontal slate slab took up one entire wall. Nothing indicated that it was the altar, but Trulliç didn't see where else it could be. Sand had blown across the slab, piling up in the far right corner.

With a sigh, Trulliç carefully knelt, then started brushing the sand from the altar.

Underneath the sand, he unearthed two camels that had been left there, made out of twisted branches. Probably someone's offering, asking for a safe journey for their caravan across the desert. They were about as long as Trulliç's forearm and were cleverly made, the ends near the feet tied off with red thread, as well as around the noses. The male had a black stripe down the center of his back, and the other, presumably female, had a similar white stripe.

Trulliç carefully placed the camels back down on the now clean altar, then he closed his eyes, folded his hands in front of him, and prayed to Serril, asking for the cleverness to find his home, for the courage to defend it from all others, and for the patience to let it grow and become all that he'd ever imagined.

When he finished, he dug out his own offerings from his pack. He'd chosen a flat stone about the size of his palm. Then he'd carved a six-sided star on both sides, the symbol of Serril. It had taken him a lot of time and skill to get the stars perfect (and a few nicked fingers when his knife or his concentration had slipped). He'd followed the traditional form and made each star out of two interlocking triangles.

He'd then rubbed a red dye into the lines of the stars to make them stand out. Once the dye had set, he'd painted one side of the stone white and the other side black.

Serril/Serrat was a two-faced god, both male and female.

Serril, the male god, had brought magic to men in the ancient times and been banished to the desert (and other desolate places) by the other gods because of it. Many stories told of how he tricked liars or cheaters into revealing their bad deeds.

As a magician, Trulliç had always worshiped Serril, learned the prayers dedicated to him and celebrated his feast days. But here, in the god's lands, it wouldn't do to forget the other side, the goddess Serrat, who'd birthed the star sisters, the female magicians.

When a babe was born in Gaadiwala who had power, if the child was female, the mother generally walked to the desert and left the babe there, for the star sisters to come and claim as their own.

Sometimes boys were left as well, though generally other magicians didn't take them on. Atça barely tolerated Trulliç living in Gaadiwala, the place of Atça's power.

Male magicians were bound to a piece of land and could do great magic there. Atça claimed that he could always feel Trulliç, like an irritation in his side or an itch he couldn't quite scratch. Still, he had still volunteered to help train Trulliç in all the magical arts.

Female magicians had no such land bond, but their magic was also illusionary. They could trick a caravan into stopping for the night at an oasis when there was none, then steal all their goods. Or fool a man into sleeping with her, so that she might break his vows.

Trulliç had met more than one star sister in the tavern his family ran. He'd rarely talked to one, though. They tended to sneer at him, what they called his paltry magic.

And it was, compared to theirs. He was also just a boy, not a man with his own lands—yet.

His mother or his aunt dealt with the sisters at the tavern. They were less likely to cheat a woman and to pay with coins that changed into stones after they'd left.

But now Trulliç didn't know what to do.

Did he place the white, male side up on the altar when he gave it to the god? Or the black, female side? Which would bring more luck to him? Which would please Serril more?

If Trulliç had only thought! He would have shaved off one side of the stone so it was no longer round. That way, he could place it on its edge and he wouldn't have to decide.

Though Trulliç was tempted to just toss the stone in the air and let it fall on whatever side the fates decreed, he knew that wasn't actually a choice. Atça had chided him more than once for not being more firm or making a decision.

What if Trulliç made the wrong choice? What if he offended Serril/Serrat instead?

Trulliç was a desert magician, after all. He needed to stay on the good side of the trickster god. If that was possible.

In the end, Trulliç placed the male side down, reasoning that Trulliç himself was the representation of male in the desert for now.

He needed the help of the female side, of Serrat the goddess, to keep his eyes clear of deception and illusion and lead him clear along the path to his true home.

<hr>

Trulliç changed out of his warmer wool tunic into his cooler one. He had already sweated through his shirt. The sun blazed outside the rough rock structure holding Serril's altar. The smell of baked sand filled his nose.

He took another sip of the sweet water from Atça's well.

For a moment, he thought it had a milky taste to it before it cleared up to just water again.

Huh. He'd thought that only his feet were being fooled out here.

Then he shivered. Damn it! The sensation of ants crawling all over his skin increased. Chicken flesh raised up along his arms. How could he just sit there and look out on the sands? The desert was there. Just beyond the door. Calling him.

No, he needed to stay here. In the shade. Out of the direct sunlight. At least until the afternoon.

Was it that dangerous out there, in the desert? It didn't look that dangerous. It looked beautiful. The sands invited him to walk on them. The softer winds encouraged him to try. The occasional skitter of a tiny mouse or lizard sounded intriguing, not threatening.

Why should he wait?

He was a desert magician, after all. Surely, if anyone could survive out there, he could.

Trulliç rocked back and forth, trying to recall one of the hymns to Serril, but all that kept running through his head was that he had to go, and go *now*.

He should wait. That would be sensible. His mother would tell him to wait. So would Atça.

But the siren song of the sand kept calling…

Finally, Trulliç couldn't stand it any longer. He shouldered his pack and took another sip of water before firmly attaching the flagon back to his belt. He shouldn't be drinking so much water. He only had three flagons with him. If he wasn't careful, he wouldn't have any water left. He needed to find the oasis and soon.

That was why he was leaving the shelter. So he could go find the oasis. So he wasn't being reckless, despite it being the heat of the day. He was being sensible. Yes. That was how he'd explain it.

Trulliç felt great relief when he stepped on the sands again. His itching skin soothed. He took a deep breath, breathing in the wonderful scents of the desert again.

He'd made the right decision. Despite the sun beating down on him, how the horizon glared.

He could do this.

Trulliç directed his feet to the east. The oasis lay that direction.

But which one? There were so many!

Stop being fanciful. Atça had told Trulliç that again and again. He couldn't really see magic, couldn't really feel it when Atça performed it. Certainly couldn't tell how Atça's power diminished every time he left Gaadiwala.

The nearest oasis stood to the east. All Trulliç had to do was walk that direction.

How hard could it be?

By the time the sun reached its zenith, Trulliç couldn't *wait* to find his true home.

Trudging across the desert sands was *hard*.

Trulliç's cousins had always teased him about how easy his life was. He sat in the hall of his mentor and wrote out poems, learning not just how to read their own Tanesh tongue, but Lydean, the language of the kingdom to the north, as well. He knew his numbers and his fractions. He knew the stars and all the stories of the heroes. (Though if he was honest, he'd learned more about the stars from the goat and sheep herders he'd waited on at the tavern, as well as watching them on his own.)

Trulliç knew that his life was easier than his cousins'. He still carried water from the neighborhood well to the shack he shared with his mother on the edge of Gaadiwala, and on days when he didn't have classes with Atça, Trulliç hauled barrels of beer and ale, and refilled the clay oil lamps, as well as swept and cleaned the tavern. However, the next day, Trulliç went to his lessons, leaving his cousins the hard work again.

Atça had pointed out more than once that Trulliç's life would change dramatically once he came into his powers and found his home. Atça was a town magician, the only one living in Gaadiwala. He lived in a three-story brick house, with real wooden floors imported from Lydae. Thick rugs covered them, soft and comfortable to sit on. He didn't have the regular clay lamps filled with oil and burning a small wick. No, he had expensive glass lamps that burned brightly, making the inside as clear as day.

For now, though, Trulliç kept walking. His feet wanted to lead him all over the place, first to the left, then the right. Was it Serrat's trickery that kept leading him astray? He'd assumed that he should have found the oasis trail by now. He couldn't see anything, though, just sand and more sand.

The sun beat down mercilessly on Trulliç. He'd finally remembered to put on his *chafiyek*, a square scarf folded around his head and tugged slightly over his eyes to shade them. He'd already run out of the sweet water he'd carried from Atça's well. He had to find the oasis trail. He couldn't live without water.

Black spots formed before Trulliç's eyes. Suddenly, he found it hard to breathe. Sweat poured from him, instantly soaking through his shirt and pants.

Trulliç found himself sitting on the ground. He wasn't sure how he'd gotten there. Had he fallen? He pulled his knees up, put his arms across them, then put his head down, struggling to draw in the burning air.

He couldn't remember the prayer to Serril to help guide him. He had difficulty forming words in his head.

It finally occurred to him that he had heat stroke. He'd had it once before, working in the tavern the previous summer.

He needed to get out of the sun, to someplace shady and cool.

But where?

Trulliç struggled to his feet. He swayed, willing the black spots before his eyes to go away. His pack weighed more than a barrel full of ale. He stubbornly adjusted it on his back. He couldn't lose it. To drop it here would mean death, particularly once night came and the temperature plummeted. Bile filled his mouth.

Where could he go? Trulliç scanned the horizon. He didn't see anything but endless mounds of sand. The sun shone down from directly above him. He didn't even know which way was north. He couldn't feel the desert anymore. Looking around, the wind had already blown away his footprints.

Should he go back to town? He didn't want to be a failure.

He also didn't want to die.

His brain cleared a little as he took more deep breaths. He just needed to find shelter. He closed his eyes and tried listening to the desert. Where did the oasis stand? Where was the closest water?

That way.

Trulliç followed his feet. He knew he must be hallucinating because instead of trudging through the sand, he now glided over it, like a gnat skirting across a bowl of water.

Quicker than he expected, a dark outcrop of rocks appeared. Trulliç headed that direction, effortlessly skimming across the sand.

His clothes had dried from the wind, or more likely the water had baked out of them by the sun.

The outcrop shimmered in the heat. Was it real? Or was this an illusionary place, a trap set by the star sisters?

Roughly hewn rocks formed an arch in the middle of nowhere. Beyond that stood another cluster. Like the building holding the altar to Serril, the rocks looked as though they'd been haphazardly placed, one on top of another.

But this wasn't a man made place. The rocks were huge, each taller than Trulliç. Instead of being the gold and brown of the desert, they were an orangeish-red, like the color of the sunset during the rainy season.

Once Trulliç drew closer, he realized they weren't individual rocks but a series of pillars, each oddly carved by the elements. They stood close together, as if they'd sprouted from a single seed.

Darkness beckoned from between them. Trulliç could smell the water they hid.

He made himself walk all the way around the outcrop. It was bigger than the shack he lived in with his mother. The shape was roughly square, with only one opening.

Harsh sand blew against the rocks, as if hoping to wear them down. But the rocks stood stubbornly proud, unwilling to bend or break.

Trulliç walked back to the entrance. The ground sloped down and in beyond the arch. Rough stones filled the path. Coolness breathed out from shadows within.

Could he just sit outside, in the shade of the rocks? Rest until nightfall, then travel again?

Except he needed water. And there was water inside.

Trulliç hit the edge of the arch with his hand. *Ouch*. If this was an illusion, it sure was a realistic one.

Cautiously, Trulliç took a step inside. He instantly felt better out of the sun. The thick stone of the outcrop kept the interior cool.

Like the building around Serril's altar, another tall stone stood just beyond the entrance. Looking back, Trulliç realized that the door faced the west. The stone standing in the doorway protected the interior not just from sand but from the afternoon sun as well.

He stepped around the stone carefully, then paused, letting his eyes adjust. It was darker inside than he'd expected.

Could he raise a light here? Atça had taught him how to create his own mage light, to set a magical yellow fire that floated above his palm.

It had never been much of a light. And it certainly hadn't been useful. It wasn't as if he could throw it and set something on fire with it, though he'd tried more than once when his cousins had teased him.

Trulliç concentrated on his palm, calling the fire within to the surface. To his surprise, the mage light sprang up immediately, much brighter than he'd ever managed before.

Huh. It must be because he was closer to his home here in the desert.

Feeling daring, Trulliç made the small light rise up, illuminating the interior of the rock cluster.

Just a couple of feet in front of him ran a small, clear stream. To his left, the water bubbled out of a collection of rocks, then disappeared again to the right.

Beyond the water lay long slabs of rocks, like rock stairs.

Would there be an altar at the top?

If there wasn't, Trulliç sure felt like making one.

He knelt gratefully at the edge of the tiny stream, then stuck his hand it. Lukewarm water caressed his skin. He cupped it with his palm and brought it to his nose. It smelled clean, not brackish. Plus, it appeared to be fresh running, not stagnant.

Hesitatingly, Trulliç brought the water to his lips.

The world exploded again.

Trulliç woke with cold stone under his back. Darkness filled the room. His muscles ached. His mouth felt as though he'd been swallowing sand. Without thinking about it, he set his mage light to glow beside him.

Then he remembered.

Trulliç sat up, his head still swimming. He'd been laying on the bottom most length of horizontal rock, just past the trickle of water. His pack sat neatly at his feet.

How had he gotten there? Had he climbed there himself?

The smell of water drove him to his feet. He staggered to the creek and knelt beside it again. Then he leaned to one side to look past the guard stone that partially covered the opening to the outcrop of rocks.

Trulliç shook his head. He must still be dreaming. Stars streamed through the air just past the rocks, like they were being blown by a strong wind. The desert itself reflected their light, sparkling like it was made of broken shards of glass, not sand. The night sky above was dark but not foreboding, more like a warm cover, finely woven. He thought he heard the cawing of a desert hawk, but they didn't fly at night. The smell of spices came to him as well, the pungent odors of mint and thyme.

That must mean he could take another drink, right? Since he was still dreaming and his body craved the water in front of him?

He found his right hand already sneaking into the water, his fingers wet.

With a grimace, Trulliç raised his hand to his face and licked off the water.

The world didn't explode again. But he found himself breathing heavily, as if he'd been covered in sand and just shaken it off. He could smell the age of the rocks, how they'd kept this sanctuary for centuries, even before the old kings. The water spoke to him as well, telling him of jewel-encrusted caves just under the surface.

Others had known of this place, nomads and desert people, even the star sisters.

They knew of the jewels, too.

The water was more precious. Digging into the caves would offend the water and kill the trickle.

Better to leave it and be alive than to be rich and dead.

Trulliç tasted the water again, letting it fill all his senses. His mind cleared and he felt as though he could truly think and see for the first time since starting his journey. He felt as though he could taste the minerals in the water, traces of the long underground stones it brushed by.

The stream asked him for a favor.

He could think of no other way to express it. But the idea grew in his mind, stronger, until he felt he must comply.

He rose slowly and gathered up his three water skins. Then he walked to the far side of the stream, just before it went back underground, and rinsed out the three skins.

Curdled yellow fluid poured from them, like rotten milk.

Trulliç shook his head. They'd been filled by Atça from the sweet well he kept behind his house.

Once the water containers were clean, Trulliç filled them with dream water.

Hopefully that would carry him through the next day.

After drinking his fill, Trulliç sat beside the trickling creek, humming a song of gratitude. The water seemed to sing along, playfully reaching up and splashing him once.

When Trulliç finished, the water grew very still. The night took a deep breath and held it.

Someone stood outside the archway.

Trulliç's heart beat hard. The pounding echoed in his ears. Fear filled him.

However, custom dictated that he welcome this stranger. There were far too many tales about the consequences of being a poor host, of not properly taking care of sudden guests who appeared at the door in the night.

Trulliç swallowed, his mouth dry.

"Welcome!" he finally said, his voice cracking. "Please come and share this bounty."

He didn't have any food out—the water filled his stomach completely—but he would still share what he had if the stranger was hungry. Plus, the trickle was a blessing.

Trulliç stiffened when a dog entered.

He set the mage light floating above him to burn brighter.

A blood hound stared back at him from across the tiny creek.

"Where's your charge?" Trulliç asked the dog once he'd drunk his fill at the stream.

The hound looked at him with his head tilted to one side, as if he didn't understand.

Trulliç didn't understand, either. Blood hounds only appeared when there was a pregnant woman carrying a baby of power, either male or female. They had short, dark, brown-red fur, tall ears that rose up to sharp points, a disproportionately large black nose, and eyes a lighter brown-gold color. Their muzzles were long and pointed, like a desert dog's, instead of square and solid, like a northern hunter.

Myrizhah had once told him that the dog who'd followed her had sad eyes, as if he had seen too many babies die.

This dog's eyes were the same.

But where was the pregnant woman the blood hound should be shepherding?

Trulliç gasped. Unless he was pregnant? He couldn't normally be pregnant. Though this was still a dream, right? Maybe he could be pregnant in a dream.

He reached down and probed his belly. It didn't feel any different.

The dog shook his head. He stayed on the far side of the stream and didn't show any interest in the pieces of the travel roll that Trulliç had carefully put out.

Stars still streamed past the door. Beyond them, the desert glistened with its own light. The night sky spread over them, vast and dark and empty.

Trulliç couldn't help but yawn. It had been a long day, strange and tiring. Though if this was a dream, how could he be tired? Maybe he needed to sleep again in order to fully wake up.

In the morning, he'd have to get his bearings. Figure out which way lay the caravan trail. See if he could either find his home or his way back to Gaadiwala.

He could admit that Atça was probably right. Trulliç would need many more journeys across the desert to find his true home.

"Good night," Trulliç told the dog.

He nodded to Trulliç as if he understood.

And maybe he did. The blood hounds were magical. They'd been conjured by the great emperor. After a woman gave birth, the blood hound who'd been following her ate the afterbirth, then went to the emperor and vomited it back up. The emperor fashioned a piece of the afterbirth into a scale and sewed it to the great cloak he always wore.

When the magician had found his or her power, he or she could never attack the emperor. It was impossible for a magician to fight their own blood.

Maybe the blood hound was between charges. But wouldn't he just disappear, then? Go back to the magical ether?

This is just a dream, Trulliç assured himself. It didn't have to make sense.

Atça read dreams. He'd be able to riddle out the meanings for Trulliç when he got back to town.

Trulliç lay down on the stone slab he'd first woken up on.

The dog watched him with soulful eyes. Then he turned three times, like a normal dog would, before also laying down.

Trulliç dimmed the mage light overhead. He left a flicker still glowing. It wasn't that he didn't trust the blood hound, not exactly. Blood hounds would protect the pregnant women they followed, killing any who might harm them.

At least until the woman started giving birth.

Then the blood hound would defend the babe, killing the mother if the birth went wrong, just so the child could live.

Trulliç felt his own belly again. Nothing growing there, not that he could tell.

Had the water made him pregnant? He sure felt full. But it was the richness of the desert he felt, not the stirring of another being inside him.

If he was carrying another soul, it would be the desert. It had found its way under his skin, the sand surging through his blood, his bones like the tough rocks, his eyes as clear as the desert skies.

He had to return to Gaadiwala. His family lived there. Atça hadn't taught him everything he needed to know about magic.

But he would return to the desert. Often. And he would find his home. Would find that special part of the desert that he could claim as his own.

Trulliç drowsed, thinking about the desert, its shifting sands, its cool nights, its blistering days. A soft *plop* made him look over toward the stream, then beyond. There weren't fish in the stream, were there?

The hound rose from where he had been sleeping. He shook himself, like a dog would shake the dirt from his fur after rolling in it.

Trulliç smiled. The action seemed like such a normal dog-like thing. He half expected the blood hound to sit on his butt and scratch his nose with his hind paw when he finished shaking.

But the dog kept shaking himself, twisting faster and faster.

A whirling noise filled the small space. The smell of bitter coal wafted to Trulliç.

What was the dog doing? Trulliç could barely make out his shape anymore—just four legs supporting a gray cloud that grew more white with every passing moment.

The air erupted with a soft exploding noise.

Trulliç sat up, startled.

A black and white dog now stood in where the blood hound had once been. Black patches covered its ribs—too irregular to be called spots. Plain white fur covered its—no, still his—legs. He had short black ears that stood up straight from his head, and smaller black and white spots all along his pointed muzzle.

The dog turned to look at Trulliç.

His eyes were the same impossible blue as the desert sky. Trulliç had rarely seen eyes that color before. Only the traders who came from Lydae had blue eyes, and even then, not very often.

Riyune, the dog seemed to say.

That was his name.

Then he did sit on his butt and scratch at his ear, before turning three times and laying down to sleep.

Trulliç stayed sitting upright. He glanced beyond the guard stone. Stars still streamed across the sand. So this was still a dream, right?

Magicians sometimes had familiars. Atça had told Trulliç about them.

However, that had been more than an age ago. Before the great emperor and the death of the old kings. Before the constant wars with the barbarians to the east that the widows complained about bitterly.

Trulliç shook his head and laid back down on the stone slab. Atça would have to spend a lot of time consulting his books to figure out *this* dream.

In the morning, Trulliç would have to find his way back to Gaadiwala, though he didn't want to. He felt so far out of his element, though. He needed more training—much more training—before he could live out in the desert on his own.

And he hadn't found that part of the desert that would be his home.

I n the morning, Trulliç came all the way to waking. Outside, the sun had already kissed the sands. It looked like a normal day.

The white and black dog, Riyune, still lay sleeping on the far side of the trickle of water.

CHAPTER TWO

NADEEM

NADEEM CAME TO HER POWER earlier than most.

She sat on the dirt floor of the teaching tent, listening to Aunt Haneet tell the story of the great sister Arzhem and how she'd left the corrupt city to walk the desert. All the tent contained was a rug at the front for the teacher. Though Nadeem had been taught how to read and write, most of her lessons involved the great epic poems and memorizing the long history of the star sisters and the Tanesh empire.

Two other girls sat with her in the stuffy teaching tent. Jamak was only a year older. However, at age eight, Jamak thought *she* was going to be a big hero when she grew up. Nadeem would have to call them both "Aunt" after they had their coming of age ceremony, because they were older. Jamak wanted Nadeem to start calling her *Aunt Jamak* now. The other girl, Mojin, was ten, but at least she was nice and wanted Nadeem to use the term "sister," which Nadeem should use for all women her age or younger.

Nadeem hated lessons with Aunt Haneet. Yes, she was only seven, but she already knew most of the words to Arzhem's tale. She much preferred when Aunt Parayat taught them tales. She expected the girls to repeat every stanza exactly as she'd spoken it. It kept Nadeem on her toes, having to listen hard and pay attention, because Aunt Parayat sometimes mixed up the lines on purpose.

Aunt Haneet thought that having an illusion of Arzhem, tall and dark, showing her great tragedy and triumph, would be interesting and keep the attention of the girls. But Arzhem moved so stiffly, and Nadeem could see through the illusion to the wall of the tent beyond. Sometimes she could see Aunt Haneet through Arzhem, which was kind of funny. But Aunt Haneet didn't like it when Nadeem and the other girls giggled.

If only Aunt Haneet would finish! Aunt Parayat had promised to show Nadeem her latest blanket. She'd used a new technique for dying the wool threads, and Nadeem wanted to learn how to make that rich blue, the color favored by the goddess Barzhat.

Nadeem couldn't contain her sigh when yet someone else came to the door of the tent and called to Aunt Haneet. They were never going to get out of here! Aunt Parayat would be taking her afternoon nap by the time lessons were finished. Most of the older women napped in the afternoon, complaining of the midday heat.

Nadeem didn't really understand why. It was hot all the time. The *kabil* of star sisters lived in a desert oasis, all the women together, close to seven thousand souls with no men.

Aunt Haneet stood at the doorway to the tent arguing with someone in whispers. Just past the row of teaching tents stood an open area filled with benches and long tables. While some of the older aunts would eat in their tents, most ate at one of the three dining shifts. The aunts made a point of switching tables and eating with different girls, getting to know all of them.

A large flat area opened up to the east of the dining pavilion, where all important ceremonies would be held, like the coming-of-age ceremony for girls, the celebration of the goddess Barzhat's birthday, or the candle festival that happened midwinter.

North and south of the eating pavilion stretched rows of individual tents, as well as collective tents where the younger girls lived. The kitchen was at the center of the camp.

Though the *kabil* hadn't moved for as long as Nadeem could remember, the star sisters never built permanent structures. They stayed in tents so they could migrate whenever they needed to. Nadeem had already memorized some of the great epics that told of the time of persecution, when the star sisters always had to hide their camps carefully.

Aunt Haneet still talked with someone at the door of the learning tent. Nadeem couldn't hear what they were saying. Maybe they were arguing about the amount of salt used in the goat and cracked wheat stew they would have for lunch that day. Aunt Haneet did love her food. Her round belly and big hips showed that.

Nadeem snickered quietly to herself, but then sat up straight and tried to look innocent when Aunt Haneet scowled over her shoulder at them.

Aunt Haneet wore the same clothing that all the star sisters did: a long skirt made of a light cotton that hadn't been dyed that went to just above her fat ankles; a wide brown-leather belt that held mysterious pouches and the traditional three knives; a dark brown blouse that covered her from shoulders to wrists, though the neck wasn't as high as Nadeem's, and instead showed off Aunt Haneet's big breasts; and a low-cut tunic over it that even Nadeem had to admit was finely made, with thin black stripes between panels of pale red and gold.

Who was bothering Aunt Haneet during lesson time? Nadeem couldn't see who it was. She wanted to ask the other girls, but they were whispering to each other, and Jamak had purposefully turned her back on Nadeem so she couldn't join in.

Nadeem sighed and looked around. The illusionary figure of Arzhem that Aunt Haneet had created for their lessons stood as tall as a woman, fully grown, and as still as a statue without Aunt Haneet's attention on her. What would happen if she turned around and went back into the city that still appeared as a shadowy silhouette at the back of the tent, instead of walking to the desert?

Arzhem stirred, moving her head slowly, looking back the way she'd come.

The two girls beside Nadeem gasped, but quietly enough that Aunt Haneet didn't scowl at them again.

Go back Nadeem ordered the figure.

She sluggishly lifted one foot, then the next, turning around.

Too slow! Nadeem wanted the illusionary figure to walk all the way back to the city and maybe disappear there before Aunt Haneet noticed.

What was making the illusion move so slowly? Nadeem stared hard at the figure. She grew more transparent when Nadeem did so. She could now see everything through Arzhem, including the wall of the tent and even the ropes that held it down.

Ropes. Yes. That was what was making Arzhem move so slowly. There appeared to be ropes tied to her wrists and ankles, and two more tied up to the *chafiyek* she wore on his head, six total.

Six was a special number. All of the star sisters, once they came of age, had a six-sided star made up of two intertwined triangles carved into their left cheek. Each line had its own meaning, which Nadeem had learned so long ago she felt as though she'd always known about them.

Nadeem tugged at the ropes holding Arzhem, but they were too hard to break, like the leather straps that held on her own sandals.

Could she untie them?

Nadeem found the loop in the knots and quickly undid the binding on Arzhem's limbs. She swung her arms wide and moved her feet as if she was taking great strides.

The other girls giggled.

However, the figure of Arzhem still stood in one place. How could Nadeem undo the bindings of Arzhem's scarf? It was like the ropes were tied to her long hair underneath as well. There wasn't a simple, single knot for her to attack.

Nadeem frowned as she concentrated. It was tricky, like picking curved thorns out of wool without breaking the long strands.

The tent disappeared as Nadeem focused on the problem. It wasn't just that there were so many tiny threads. The problem was that they kept retying themselves. How could she undo those knots? She didn't want to shave Arzhem's head. Her hair was too pretty. But that might be the only way she could fully take control of the figure.

"Nadeem?" came a quiet voice.

Nadeem started, coming back to herself.

Shoot. Aunt Haneet stood right there, looking down on her.

"Could you let go of Arzhem please?" Aunt Haneet asked quietly.

Huh. Nadeem had never heard Aunt Haneet speak like that before, like she was talking to a wild hawk, trying to calm it and break it to the fist.

"Sure," Nadeem said, though she wasn't sure exactly what Aunt Haneet had asked. She'd just loosened the ties of Arzhem. She hadn't tied any of her own, had she?

Maybe she had, though. There still appeared to be twisting ties wrapped around the figure's wrists and ankles.

Shrugging, Nadeem willed the ties away.

"Thank you," Aunt Haneet said. "Now, where were we?" She made Arzhem turn, and turn again, and turn again, as if she was lost and didn't know which direction to go either.

"Ah, that way's the desert!" Arzhem proclaimed gleefully, pointing off to the distance.

Nadeem giggled with the other girls. She'd never seen Aunt Haneet be playful before.

Still, all through the rest of the lesson, Nadeem felt as though Aunt Haneet watched her, like a mouse keeping an eye on a poisonous snake.

Two days later, when Nadeem went to the lesson tent, Aunt Parayat sat waiting for her.

"Come in," Aunt Parayat said, gesturing for Nadeem to enter.

Nadeem gladly went and sat in front of Aunt Parayat. Her aunt sat on a teacher's rug—a small, square, braided rug made out of old scraps of cloth instead of the dirt ground.

Good. That meant Aunt Parayat would be leading the lessons that day.

Nadeem didn't know what had happened to Aunt Haneet. There hadn't been any lessons the day before. Had she gotten sick? Or was she still arguing with the stranger who had come to the lesson tent when she'd gotten so distracted?

Aunt Parayat sat straight and tall. Nadeem didn't know if she'd ever grow as tall as Aunt Parayat, but she hoped so. Her aunt wore a smart, sleeveless tunic dyed a pretty shade of blue over a clean white blouse and a brown skirt. Her hazel eyes stared at Nadeem, making her sit up even straighter. Aunt Parayat's nose was long and hooked at the end, like a desert hawk's. The dark skin of her face held many laugh wrinkles, and even now, when she wasn't smiling, showed wrinkles around her mouth and across her forehead. Her headscarf was woven out of blue, black, and white threads, the colors of the goddesses Berzhat and Serrit.

With a wave of her hand, Aunt Parayat closed the door to the tent. "It will just be us today," she said.

Nadeem didn't know if she should be happy or annoyed: Happy that she got to spend more time with Aunt Parayat, who always had the most interesting lessons, or annoyed at how hot the tent would get with the door flap closed.

Then she looked over her shoulder at the tent flap.

Wait.

How had her aunt done that?

The magic of the star sisters was illusionary. They couldn't affect the real world, not like male magicians. Men were trapped in a single place of power, while the sisters could travel to every land, equally comfortable roaming the desert or sailing the oceans.

Had the tent flap really closed? Or was it an illusion?

Nadeem stared, but couldn't tell.

She returned her attention to her favorite aunt. Though all the star sisters were supposed to love and honor each other equally, Nadeem still had favorites.

"Can you tell if the flap is open or shut?" Aunt Parayat asked.

Nadeem shook her head. Though stupid Jamak teased Nadeem when she didn't know something, Aunt Parayat had always said that admitting ignorance took more courage than faking knowledge.

And Nadeem always tried to be brave.

"How about now?" Aunt Parayat asked as she stared over Nadeem's shoulder at the tent flap.

Nadeem looked over her shoulder. She couldn't help her gasp. The tent flap *was* still open! She could see the illusion now, see how the flap looked both open and closed at the same time.

How did her aunt do that? Nadeem really wanted to learn.

"It's open," Nadeem told her teacher proudly. This was going to be so wonderful! Obviously, Aunt Parayat's lesson today was going to be all about illusions.

Aunt Parayat nodded slowly. "While it's not unheard of a girl coming into her power as young as you, it is unusual," she said.

Nadeem tried to keep the smug smile off her face. Given the way her aunt raised a single, beautifully arched eyebrow at her, she knew she'd failed.

"That just means you're going to have to work extra hard to make us all proud," Aunt Parayat continued.

Nadeem didn't like the sound of that. "What do you mean, extra hard?" she asked warily.

"More lessons. Oh, don't look so stricken! They'll mostly be with me and with the other aunts who are also strong illusionists," Aunt Parayat said. "In addition to learning all the stories of our people, the poems of the great heroes and heroines, the feast days and celebrations of the gods and goddesses, and the special arcane knowledge of the star sisters."

Nadeem nodded seriously. It sounded like a *lot* of lessons.

"The other girls will be jealous, you know," Aunt Parayat said in a conspiratorial voice. "Because you'll be learning magic years before they will."

Nadeem sat up straighter and tried to be proud. It would be fun to learn all about magic. To cast illusions. Not that she would try to trick the other girls.

Or at least, not too often.

Yet... "Will I still get to learn about weaving? And dying wool?" She really liked that. She enjoyed the way fibers slipped through her fingers as she spun them into thread on her drop spindle. She also loved learning the different combinations of ingredients that made up various colored dyes, as well as how to set them in the cloth so they'd be permanent.

Aunt Parayat laughed, sounding as young as Nadeem herself. "Of course!" she said, smiling. "I'm glad you want to. After doing magic, dying cloth is my favorite thing to do."

"I will learn all that you will teach me," Nadeem said, finding the ritual words the star sisters gave at the start of a new lesson series, how many of the call and response stories went as well.

"And I am glad to teach you," Aunt Parayat said. "To help you reach your full potential."

Nadeem liked the sound of that.

So maybe *she* could become a great hero, and not Jamak.

A unt Parayat handed Nadeem a long wooden tray filled with three dozen *aǧrikat* shells. "You are now thirteen years old. You have started your menstruation. It is time for you to choose six shells for your coming-of-age ceremony," Aunt Parayat said. "Choose carefully, considering all I have taught you."

Though Jamak and Mojin were older than Nadeem, as Nadeem had the strongest magic, it fell to her to choose the shells for her ceremony first.

Nadeem and Aunt Parayat sat in the familiar teaching tent, just the pair of them, as usual. The black hand-held slates used for learning letters and numbers sat to one side, the precious chalk sticks carefully wrapped in waterproofed leather. Aunt Parayat sat on the teacher's mat, while Nadeem sat on the dirt floor. She kept her back hunched slightly so her head was lower than her teacher's, out of respect. It was easier to do with Aunt Parayat than with some of the other, shorter aunts.

The *aǧrikat* shells were oblong shaped. Each would fill her entire palm. A white, luminous substance covered the inside. The outside of the shell was a mottled gray and felt rough. It appeared to be made out of many layers, with the innermost layer breaking through the outer layers in places. The shells smelled of fresh raw fish.

Nadeem solemnly studied the shells in the tray that she held. The *aǧrikat* mussel came from the Barzhat Sea, where the goddess Barzhat lived. They were extremely rare and hard to come by. They grew along deep shelves in the southeast corner of the sea. Divers couldn't get at them—the only time they were found was after a storm, blown up along the coast.

The goddess suffered men only to sail along the coastlines of the great inland sea, and only when she was in a good mood, her waters clear and blue.

When her mood turned foul, the waters of the sea blackened and all boats ran to the shore.

The goddess drowned anyone who tried to sail directly across the sea, killing them and dragging their souls into her golden court.

Once there, the stories told, all the bad deeds a person had done during the course of their life would manifest as teardrop shaped weights sewn into a vest, weighing the person down. A person had to dance for the goddess and keep dancing until all their weights fell off. Only then would the goddess would give them the true kiss of death and the person would be reborn without sin, their soul clean and light.

When properly prepared, the *ağrikat* mussel caused vivid, wild visions. When not fixed the right way, they were deadly.

If the correct amount of the crushed shell was applied during a star sister's coming-of-age ceremony, it made the magic of a star sister more powerful.

Nadeem examined the shells on the tray. Which ones were the strongest? Which ones weaker? And what did Nadeem want? She knew she didn't have just herself to consider, but the others sharing her coming-of-age ceremony as well.

"May I touch them?" Nadeem asked.

"You may," Aunt Parayat said. She held herself aloof and stern.

Nadeem knew that it wasn't because her aunt was angry with her —in fact, her aunt was very pleased with Nadeem and her progress. But she couldn't influence Nadeem's decision of which shells to choose and could only advise her about the properties of the shells.

Aunt Parayat had been strict about that during all of Nadeem's training, insisting that Nadeem think for herself, come up with her own solution, always questioning what she'd been told, finding new answers to old problems.

So now, it was up to Nadeem to choose the right shells. Though

Aunt Parayat had never said so, Nadeem was aware that this was one of the most important decisions of her life. Did she pick the strongest of the shells, which might enable her to cast stronger illusions? The downside was that the shells could cause her to have permanent visions and make it difficult for her to distinguish between reality and her dreams.

If Nadeem picked the weakest of the shells, she might not reach her full potential. While she was only thirteen, she was already a stronger magician than all but a handful of the aunts in the *kabil*. Aunt Parayat was stronger than all of them, as far as Nadeem could tell.

Outside the tent, the *kabil* of star sisters stirred. The cooks started preparing the evening meal, which wouldn't be eaten until after the sun had firmly set and the temperatures had started to drop. A group of younger girls carefully prepared the ceremonial space to the east of the eating pavilion, sweeping the ground and placing sweet incense in the braziers around the edges of the space, preparing it for Nadeem's coming-of-age ceremony that she would share with Jamak and Mojin.

The other two would choose their shells after Nadeem had chosen hers. So she also had to consider their powers as well, how strong they might become. She shouldn't greedily take all the strongest shells for herself. The tribe must work together if they were to survive. No matter how powerful of an illusionist Nadeem might become, she was nothing by herself. It was only with her sisters and aunts that she was strong.

Or at least that was what Aunt Parayat had tried to beat into Nadeem's skull when she got too proud, or fought too hard to win one of the combats the girls regularly fought with illusionary beings.

Nadeem carefully set the tray on the ground in front of her and picked up one of the three dozen shells. It was slightly smaller, barely covering her palm. The back of the shell felt rough and cool, while the faintly luminous interior felt smooth against her fingertips. The faint smell of fish made her hungry.

Feeling daring, Nadeem lifted the shell to her ear. Could she hear the goddess Berzhat's sad, lonely sighs, as Manisat had?

Nadeem caught her breath when she heard a faint *whooshing* sound. But that was all she heard. It almost sounded like a sigh, but not quite, more like the echo of a long forgotten sigh. Disappointed, she brought the shell down.

When she looked up, Aunt Parayat smiled at her. "I did the same at your age," she confessed, "when the *ağrikat* were presented to me."

That made Nadeem feel better.

The great heroine Manisat had led a huge *kabil* of star sisters in ancient times. At that time, the star sisters were faithful and honored the goddess Serrat, the mother of them all. However, Serrat wasn't well loved. It was difficult to love such a trickster, especially when the star sisters prided themselves on keeping their word and their blood oaths.

Manisat had heard the sad sighs of the goddess Berzhat when she'd picked up an *ağrikat* shell. She'd made her way to the goddess' golden court while she'd still been alive and had promised the goddess that the star sisters wouldn't merely venerate her, but love her. They would welcome her at all their feasts, big and small. A bowl was always left empty at every meal, a welcome place for the goddess.

And sometimes the goddess came, bringing capricious death with her. The star sisters persisted though, in loving the goddess. They'd given their word, and continued to do so at every coming-of-age ceremony, taking a blood oath, binding the star sisters and the goddess of death together.

In return, the goddess promised Marisat and the rest of the star sisters a boon, once in their lifetime, when a woman asked in her truest hour of need.

Nadeem put the shell she'd been holding back on the tray and focused her attention on them again. Which were the strongest shells?

She couldn't tell. Normally, Nadeem saw magic well. Then again, she was used to seeing through illusions, not physical magic.

Were the shells magical, though? Or did they hold some other property? The bark of the *meslit* thorn tree looked brownish red. It could be boiled down and reduced to a sweet syrup. It could also be used to dye wool. However, the wool didn't turn out a dark color but a very pale brown, almost golden colored.

The *meslit* thorn tree didn't have any magic. The golden color it gave to thread was just a quality of the bark.

Nadeem paused, reconsidered, then reposed her question.

Which of the shells held the least amount of the luminous inner substance?

That was much easier to figure out. She would bet that they were the thinnest shells, the ones where the white inner surface didn't rise to the lip of the shell, sometimes the dark grey backs poking through the white.

Nadeem picked out the half-dozen weaker shells and put those to one side.

Then she graded the rest, from what she assumed to be the weakest to the strongest, those that appeared to have the least of the inner white shell to those with most.

She ended up with four piles, with a few in between.

Then she sighed.

Now, she had to choose six.

What would be the best combination? What would help her win? Though this wasn't a contest or battle, she generally thought in those terms.

She chose what she hoped were the three strongest shells—those with the most luminous material—and she put those to one side.

Did she balance those out with the three weakest?

But that would make her merely average, a difficult numerical concept, but she'd finally figured it out after many examples had been given to her by her aunts.

Nadeem wasn't about to be average. She had to be better than average. That was the only way to win.

Instead, she chose one shell from each of the remaining three piles, weakest, next strongest, and next.

This left strong shells for the other girls so they had options as well.

She assumed Jamak would choose the strongest shells, if she could figure out which they were, merely because she always wanted to be the best at everything.

Nadeem tried not to take pleasure when she won at their battles, but she couldn't help it. Jamak had always assumed that she would be the most important star sister and bitterly complained when Nadeem proved that she wasn't.

While Mojin…Mojin would be balanced. She would choose shells from each of the piles. She was smart enough to figure out the difference, of that, Nadeem felt confident.

Satisfied, Nadeem put the rest of the shells back flat on the tray, leaving them roughly grouped in her categories. Then she looked up.

Aunt Parayat didn't smile at her or show any outward signs of what she felt. "You have chosen well, my sister," she said.

Nadeem heard the pride in her teacher's voice. She had done the right thing. She was certain.

<hr>

Nadeem swayed with the beat of the booming drums, the wild wailing of the flutes. Most of the *kabil* still danced on the ceremonial sands behind her, their undulating calls ringing through the desert night.

Sweat covered Nadeem from her scarfless head to her naked torso, down to her bare feet, showing that she was purified and ready.

A huge bonfire burned in front of her, out under the stars. Aunt Parayat stood beside it, along with the other elder aunts. They were naked to the waist, with blue and white stripes in protective patterns drawn across their skin. They wore long skirts with thick leather aprons tied over them and sturdy sandals.

The heat from the fire blasted Nadeem's front, causing more sweat to trickle down between her small breasts, while the coolness of the night tickled her back and raised chicken flesh across her shoulders.

Jamak and Molin stood behind her. The three of them would be scarred together, the shape of a six-sided star carved into their left cheeks as part of their coming-of-age ceremony.

This part of the ceremony wasn't private, but it wasn't done in front of the entire *kabil* either. A girl had to be allowed her tears before she returned to show her new form for everyone to see.

All of the star sisters wore this mark. The goddess Serrat who had born them had such a mark. Plus, the emperor required it. There were only a couple of stories from ancient times, before the times of persecution when the old kings ruled, when the star sisters could choose whether to bear the mark or not. But those stories were told in whispers, passed from older sisters to the younger ones, not in the learning tents taught by the aunts.

Once marked, a star sister could never hide her origin. Few could change their appearance enough to disguise themselves. None could hide the mark after it was set.

Nadeem would never hide the fact that she was a star sister! She couldn't imagine why anyone would. She was proud of being a star sister, a powerful illusionist and mighty fighter.

Aunt Parayat's dark eyes stared at Nadeem from across the flames. She held a large knife, its edge sharper than a desert gale. Rare cherry wood made up the handle: Like most of the desert *kabil*, Nadeem had never even seen a cherry.

But the red wood made it appropriate for the ceremony.

Nadeem stepped forward, past the fire, facing Aunt Parayat. The blue and white stripes across Aunt Parayat's chest and down her arms were done in groups of three, vertical lines to represent Enkat, the goddess of rain, as well as horizontal lines that represented her husband, Xannil, the god of the sun. The single line around Aunt Parayat's torso, at the bottom of her ribs, was for the goddess Barzhat. Aunt Parayat's small breasts were still firm, and Nadeem admired her aunt's wiry muscles. Even though Aunt Parayat was older than most—in her sixties, or so it was rumored—she still was a force to contend with in the physical arena, like wrestling matches.

Nadeem hoped to be that strong and solid when she reached that impossible age.

Aunt Parayat held up the knife, tip pointing toward the stars, then she kissed the hilt. "Do you swear to uphold the honor of the star sisters? To stay true to your promises and your blood oaths? To fulfill the oaths of your sisters and your aunts if they cannot?"

"I do," Nadeem said solemnly. She'd already sworn such oaths in front of the *kabil*.

"Do you swear to love the goddess Berzhat, always welcoming the easy death she brings, not just for others but for yourself as well?" Aunt Parayat continued.

"I swear," Nadeem replied. She'd kissed the statue of the goddess that afternoon in front of the *kabil*, promising not to merely venerate the goddess but to love her unreservedly, as one might love a sister or even a son.

Aunt Parayat stared at Nadeem, judging her, weighing the truth in Nadeem's vows.

Nadeem stayed standing straight and unflinching. This was the most important time of all, in the entire ceremony.

If Aunt Parayat didn't consider Nadeem worthy, she would be in her right to kill Nadeem at this moment. There were many stories of girls who didn't apply themselves, who were judged too lazy to be allowed to live.

Or too powerful and uncontrolled, like the mighty Sahrilla who had too much male in her and could call the desert winds, her magic not just illusionary but real as well.

"I welcome you to the challenge," Aunt Parayat said after a dramatic pause, "the challenge of being a full member of the *kabil* of star sisters."

"Thank you," Nadeem said humbly. "It is my honor." She felt the weight of her choices resting on her shoulders as she stepped forward and kissed the knife held before her.

Two of the aunts suddenly grabbed Nadeem's arms, holding her still and ready to support her.

The first cut of the knife, across the bottom of her left cheek lengthwise, took Nadeem's breath away.

Earth.

That was the base of all life, the basest element of all.

Nadeem breathed through the pain. She'd experienced this much pain before when wrestling with her sisters, learning how to grapple and fight.

The next cut was another long, lengthwise cut, a parallel line at the top of her cheek.

Sky.

The stars above them, where the home of the goddesses and the gods lay.

Nadeem took another deep breath, sweat pouring down her back. She would handle the pain. She would not cry out. She would make her sisters and aunts proud.

Now another cut, going from the base of earth up past the line for the sky.

Water.

Without water, there was no life. It was as essential as earth.

Nadeem swayed when the night breeze touched her ravaged skin. The pain beat like the pulse of the drums in her head.

But Aunt Parayat wasn't finished. She had three more lines to cut.

Nadeem tried to brace herself for the next cut of the knife, trying to recall the songs about the blade's sweet kiss.

All she felt was fire, her blood burning with pain.

The next cut came, from the other side of the earth line up to join the water line, the last cut of the base triangle.

Sand. It wasn't essential. But it was a central element of their lives. Nadeem's *kabil* lived in the desert.

Other star sisters who lived in places other than the desert, used a different line, whether that be mountain, ocean, or even forest.

Wherever the *kabil* of star sisters lived shaped every aspect of their lives. So it had to be included.

Courage. The fifth cut. Coming down from the sky and bisecting the earth line.

Courage in all things, in the face of desert gales or even the fierce joy of the star sisters.

Nadeem took a deep breath, swallowing against her dry throat. Only one more cut remained.

Dream.

She'd asked Aunt Parayat why that was the last cut. Was it because it was the most important? Or the least? It completed the triangles, the ritual cutting.

The star sisters were master illusionists. Could they only create illusions of what they could dream?

Nadeem created the most beautiful, fanciful landscapes.

She still had difficulty mastering the most simple of illusions, a tent flap appearing shut.

Aunt Parayat had merely told her to meditate on it. And Nadeem had, but she'd never been able to figure it out.

Aunt Parayat wiped the blade clean of Nadeem's blood, using a clean, white cloth. The other two would also have their blood on the one cloth, their blood mingling together literally as well as figuratively, before the cloth would be burned in the bonfire at the end of the scarring ceremony.

Then Aunt Parayat nodded at the two aunts holding Nadeem. Their grips on her shoulders and arms tightened.

Nadeem blinked, the pain making her hazy. Wasn't the ceremony over? Except, no. She still had to be given the *ağrikat* mussel shells. She knew they'd been ground into a fine paste after she'd chosen her six.

She'd also assumed that she'd be eating them, next.

Aunt Parayat brought out an oversized *ağrikat* shell. It easily filled both her hands, cupped like a large bowl. Inside glittered a thick, whitish paste.

Nadeem assumed the paste had been made from the *ağrikat* shells she'd chosen.

Aunt Parayat scooped out a small bit of the shell paste.

Instead of asking Nadeem to open her mouth, she reached out and gently applied the paste to the bloody wounds on Nadeem's cheek.

The pain tripled, as if a flaming sword ripped into her skin. Nadeem barely choked back her scream. She didn't mean to flinch and try to pull away from the aunts holding her. She couldn't help herself. It was an animal instinct, to get away from such pain.

She wasn't about to fail at this ceremony, however. She tried to make herself stand still and proud.

Aunt Parayat's firm fingers held Nadeem's chin still while she applied more of the shell paste. The abrasive shells cut open Nadeem's wounds further, slipping into the bloody mess.

Nadeem shuddered, the pain eating at her soul. Tears streamed from her eyes, the saltwater stinging the cuts.

Finally, Aunt Parayat stepped back, satisfied.

"Let your power be full," she said stiffly.

The aunts holding up Nadeem let go of her shoulders. She sank to her knees, shaking.

Then the world exploded and the visions began.

CHAPTER THREE

TRULLIÇ

TRULLIÇ WAITED UNTIL THE SUN had kissed the western horizon before he left the outcrop of rocks.

He'd spent the day inside the rocky outcropping with Riyune. Trulliç had napped when he could, knowing that he'd be traveling at night, trusting that he could follow the stars like the goat herders had taught him. Though he nibbled at the sweet travel roll that his mother had baked him, he found he wasn't very hungry. The water from the stream continued to satisfy both his thirst and his hunger.

Riyune stayed on his side of the little trickle of water. He sniffed at the pieces of the travel roll that Trulliç offered him but didn't gobble them down like a normal dog would have. Riyune seemed quite content to sit and wait out the heat of the day as well.

Had he really first come into the little space as a blood hound? Or had Trulliç just dreamed it? Riyune looked like a regular dog, maybe a little smaller than the ones the herders used, coming up roughly to Trulliç's knee, with a broad head and pronounced eyebrows. Riyune's jaw looked strong, though he had the pointed snout of a desert dog.

However, Riyune's white and black coloring was odd. Most of the dogs Trulliç knew were some shade of mud brown or black.

Plus, those eyes. That searing blue. They appeared as soulful as his mother's when she looked out across the yard, up toward the mountains and the desert beyond.

And yet…Riyune lolled to one side of his butt while he scratched at his neck with his hind legs, like a normal dog. He also grumbled in his sleep, his legs twitching. Beyond telling Trulliç his name, Riyune hadn't spoken or given Trulliç any messages.

Trulliç would have thought that a familiar would communicate more.

Then again, Atça had more than once accused Trulliç of being too fanciful. Atça denied that Trulliç could see magic or someone's power.

Trulliç stubbornly kept trying, however. He doubted himself mightily, but the ability came naturally to him.

Throughout the day, every time Trulliç slept, he dreamed of the desert. Endless sands stretched before him. He tasted the sweetness of cool mists that came at night during the rainy season. He smelled the fear of the tiny mouse hiding while a desert hawk flew overhead. He felt the age of the dunes, constantly shifting in the wind but still solid at their core.

To the east he felt a nearby oasis, a stream that had crested the sands for a patch, feeding the palms and other hidden desert life. It felt different than the place where he rested—more open, easier to find. The outcrop of rock where he currently rested was more aware, as well as more shadowy, and would only show itself to travelers in dire need.

Atça hadn't wanted Trulliç to spend too long in the desert the first time if he didn't find his home right away. The desert was dangerous. No one traveled alone in the desert. It was a sure way for a traveler to find the goddess Barzhat's court, dancing for true death.

That much Trulliç believed, particularly since he'd gotten so sick the day before.

He *knew* better than to try to cross the desert sands in midday, even if it was just after the rainy season and cooler than usual. Why had he gone out in the heat like that the day before? What had made him so impatient? At least his skin stopped feeling as if he had ants crawling all over it.

Had that been part of the dream? Some trick of the god Serril? Trulliç would have to be sure to ask Atça about it.

Still, Trulliç wanted to visit at least one oasis before he traveled back to Gaadiwala. He didn't think the one just to the east was his home. He didn't feel drawn to it, just as he didn't feel as though one particular corner of the desert called to him either.

This time, Trulliç waited until he sensed a change in the air, the desert cooling around him as the sun continued to set. Only then did he tie his sleeping roll to the bottom of his pack, look around to make sure that he hadn't forgotten anything, and take one last, long drink from the water in the creek.

"Ready?" Trulliç asked Riyune.

The dog just looked at him expectantly, as if he had been ready to go all along.

How much did Riyune understand? Trulliç felt uncomfortable talking to the dog like he was a person. How had Riyune found the rocks? Had he really been a blood hound? Trulliç had never heard any stories about blood hounds transforming into real dogs.

However, Riyune had told Trulliç his name. That much Trulliç believed.

Squinting, Trulliç stepped from the small outcrop of rock back onto the desert sands.

A sense of longing filled him. His feet wanted to wander. Why did he want to travel so? It didn't make sense to him. He should be heading toward his home, or town, or something. Not just aimlessly walk over dunes of sand.

Riyune sat next to him, looking up at him.

Obviously, the dog thought they needed to travel together. Or something. Probably looking for easier food.

Trulliç set off to the east, to where he'd dreamed had been an oasis. It seemed easier at night to keep his focus, to make his feet travel in the path he'd set, rather than wandering, though he still felt the tug of the sands.

Riyune walked beside him. However, he frequently looked up at Trulliç, as if waiting for instructions.

Finally, Trulliç told Riyune, "We're going to the oasis to the east."

The dog nodded as if he understood, then walked ahead of Trulliç, aiming a bit more south than Trulliç's original course.

Trulliç stopped and closed his eyes.

Riyune was right. If Trulliç's senses could be believed, the oasis actually lay in that direction.

Trulliç would have corrected his course in a while. Probably.

Disappointment stabbed Trulliç's heart as he trudged along.

Stupid dog knew more about the desert than Trulliç did.

Still, Trulliç couldn't stay disappointed for long. Heat rose from where the sun had beaten down on the sand all day long. Though there weren't any bushes or shrubs for Trulliç to run into, he still paid attention to the shadows, making sure he didn't twist an ankle or something.

The sky turned to a deep purple, the royal cloak of night. Trulliç understood the poetic image better out here in the desert. A few stars winked at him from the east. He could already make out the one the goat herders called the "shepherd's light"—it shone constantly from the east, the brightest star on the horizon. It was just past the rainy season, and the star would stay closer to the horizon for another month or so.

Hawks flew high in the sky, twilight hunters, seeking small game hidden ahead.

When Trulliç looked behind him, he wasn't surprised that the outcrop of rocks where he'd spent the last day had disappeared.

He had a feeling that if he was ever in desperate need again, it would show up wherever he was.

Maybe he was making things up, dreaming too much, as Atça had accused him more than once.

He decided right then that he wouldn't tell Atça about the outcrop disappearing.

Sweet winds blew from the east, carrying the scent of water. Riyune still walked just a few feet ahead, his nose and ears forward, his short, pointed tail wagging slightly as he strode along. His white fur made him seem like a small cloud drifting across the sand.

Or a ghost.

Maybe that was what Riyune was. A ghost dog. Maybe only Trulliç would be able to see him. Maybe he wasn't a familiar at all.

Trulliç looked down at his own dark skin. Was he already dead?

Had he turned into a ghost as well? A ghost dog with a ghost boy, forever trapped in the desert?

He pinched himself. *Ow.* No, he appeared to be real. And Riyune left footprints in the sand.

Whether people other than Trulliç would be able to see the dog was a question that would just have to wait until they returned to Gaadiwala.

E ven in the dimness of the night, the oasis stood apart. Tall palm trees guarded the banks of the tiny stream. Reeds crowded the water, sucking up the moisture with all their might. Not as many *meslit* and other thorns grew here. The air smelled sweet, and the dampness soothed Trulliç's dry throat.

Riyune walked directly to the stream. He stood for a moment at the edge of it, staring into the water. Trulliç realized the dog was sniffing mightily.

Could Riyune tell if the water was bad just by smelling it?

After another moment, Riyune lowered his head and took great gulping laps of water.

Trulliç knelt down beside him, cupped his hands in the lukewarm water and drank as well. Then he sat back on his heels and looked around.

The oasis wasn't large. He could stride across the tiny spot of greenery in a dozen steps. All the life crowded around the water.

After drinking his fill, Riyune lifted his head and sniffed the air.

"Anything interesting?" Trulliç asked after a moment.

Riyune glanced sideways at him, then trotted deeper into the scattered palms.

Trulliç followed, curious.

He smelled the ash before he saw the circle where other travelers had had a fire. It made him smile and draw a breath of relief.

This *was* a real place. Other people had been there. It might even be located on a map somewhere, though Atça didn't believe in maps, claiming that the land changed too often for any of them to be true.

Trulliç had to agree. For all its permanent sand, the desert felt as though it was in flux, as changeable as the seasons and the night sky. Different from day to day, though with deep patterns that Trulliç felt he could tease out, given a lifetime or two.

Trulliç called up his mage light easily again, setting the golden light burning above his head. Though the oasis was tiny, he still felt a touch of regret that this wasn't his true home. He looked around eagerly, but there really wasn't much to see: a few trees, the stream, some bushes. If he listened, he could hear mice scurrying close to the water, and a cloud of gnats, buzzing.

That was it. Just him, alone, in the oasis.

As if reading his thoughts, Riyune came and sat next to him.

All right. Fine. Just Trulliç and this strange dog.

Was that what it meant to be a magician? To always be alone? Was that why Atça had welcomed Trulliç and the other boys that he taught into his home?

At least Atça's true home was a town. He'd always be surrounded by people. Particularly if he did right by them.

Atça only took his fair share of what the town produced, sending the rest on to the emperor. He kept order in the town, and held court once or twice a week, listening to everyone's complaints and meting out justice.

Trulliç's life wouldn't be like that. He'd be alone in the desert, living in his little oasis.

His heart ached with the thought of it.

Sure, travelers would come by now and again. And maybe, once he'd found his true home, he could entice a woman to marry him and come and live with him there, despite it being in the middle of the desert and just the pair of them.

In the meanwhile, he was all alone. Already homesick and tired of adventures.

Riyune whined, as if he, too, felt Trulliç' anguish.

Trulliç just shook his head and sat up straighter.

This was his manhood journey.

He would face his future tall and proud, like a man.

Even if it made him want to weep like a little boy.

Trulliç left the oasis early in the afternoon the next day. The heat of the sun had passed, and Trulliç was determined to make it back to at least the foothills of the Kinarak mountains by the end of the night.

He'd eaten a bit more of his travel roll, though Riyune had turned his nose up at it still. Instead, he'd gone hunting mice, making a nice meal for himself.

So the dog did eat. Trulliç had woken up with Riyune curled up at his side, sharing heat during the cold of the night. He smelled like a dog, that earthy scent that came from always laying in the dirt. He breathed normally as well, and Trulliç was glad for the warmth.

Still, he wasn't sure if he could trust Riyune or not. His appearance had been too strange, even if he did mostly act like a regular dog.

Trudging across the sand was easier the next morning. Trulliç felt he was finally getting the hang of how to cross the sand. He wasn't walking on his toes, not exactly. He did consciously try to keep his feet lighter, so he didn't sink as much. That seemed to be working, as long as he kept part of his attention on it.

The rest of his mind wondered about the desert, where his true home lay, what type of magic he could really do. Atça had insisted that most magic needed to be taught—a real magician performed magic not just in his true land but elsewhere.

It wasn't that Atça hadn't done his best to try to teach Trulliç spells. It was just that Trulliç wasn't a very good magician.

Yet, Trulliç felt stronger here in the desert. His mage light was certainly a lot more powerful. He didn't want to experiment, however. Atça had told him too many stories about mages who had ended up blowing themselves up.

Trulliç still tried a few things. Atça would never know. Like calling up a soft wind that kept Trulliç cooler, even with the sun beating down on the oasis. As well as stretching his senses, seeing how deep the water lay under his feet, if any was there at all.

The winds carried scents Trulliç couldn't identify. Something spicy, not mint, but close. Did Riyune name the scents the wind brought to him? Trulliç couldn't tell. However, Riyune seemed content walking beside Trulliç, while every now and again wandering off to chase some other scent.

The hills rose on the horizon sooner than Trulliç had expected. Had he really only gone such a short ways into the desert itself?

Next time, he would be better prepared. Maybe hire a guide or something.

Though where would he get the money? It wasn't as if he had any skills he could barter. Not like Atça, who read dreams and always told the farmers when the rainy season would start, as well as how long it would be, predicting it down to the day, so the farmers and the rest of the town were always prepared.

Trulliç was just going to have to find his own place in the world.

Someday.

The harsh line demarcating the true desert from the foothills of the Kinarak mountains shown as clearly in the night as it had in the early morning sunlight.

Trulliç hesitated. He didn't want to go back to Gaadiwala. He didn't want to have to tell his mentor what a failure his manhood journey had been. He didn't want to see the look of disappointment on his mother's face when he arrived home so soon. He really didn't want to face his cousins, or their teasing.

But he couldn't stay out in the desert. He hadn't found his true home. Though he felt certain he would always be able to find water, if his senses were to be believed.

Food was another matter. He didn't want to subsist on mice and small prey, not like Riyune seemed to do. Though he'd thought about setting up a cricket trap at one point. If he could find a large enough oasis that supported big enough insects.

Trulliç looked over his shoulder. Riyune had sat down a few feet behind him, butt on the sand, front paws too, head raised high. He had a stubborn look to his eyes, the way he held his jaw.

It was obvious Riyune didn't want to leave the desert either.

"You don't have to go with me," Trulliç said softly. It wasn't as if he owned the dog or anything. Riyune wasn't some kind of purebred that the emperor's court in Atayurtkah kept. He was a desert dog, despite his large snout and unusual coloring.

Riyune didn't reply, of course. Just sat there like a statue made of white stone.

"It was nice to meet you," Trulliç told him.

Maybe the next time Trulliç came to the desert, Riyune would find him again.

Taking a deep breath, Trulliç took the final step over the border, returning to the foothills.

It felt as though blankets had suddenly been put over all Trulliç's senses. He couldn't see as well or as far. His nose only told him about the nearby bushes, not the smells that came on the winds from miles away. His skin ached and his bones felt chilled, as if the desert night had abruptly grown much colder.

Trulliç stopped for a moment. Longing for the desert filled him. He knew if he didn't pay attention his feet would turn him around, march him right out back over the sands.

He belonged in the desert. That much he knew. His mother had been right about that. He was a desert magician.

He had to learn more first, though. About being a magician. About how to survive out on the sands.

About being a man.

Trulliç swallowed against the lump in his throat. He felt worse than when he'd been alone in the tiny oasis, more homesick.

He shook his head and gave a tiny, cawing laugh.

How could he be homesick for a place that he'd never dreamed about before, that he'd only spent two nights in?

It didn't matter. He needed to go home.

Or at least back to Gaadiwala.

Determined, Trulliç strode forward, not even glancing back once, his anger boiling over.

He couldn't live there, in the desert. He couldn't live in the foothills either. He needed to get to the Ladikah pass, where he'd spend the rest of the night, then travel into the town in the morning.

A white wind rushed past, at knee level.

Riyune had decided to join him.

"I'm glad you're coming along," Trulliç whispered. At least for now. Riyune may or may not be a familiar. What he represented to Trulliç was a permanent reminder of the desert and what it had felt like.

Riyune glanced over his shoulder at Trulliç as if to say, *Of course. Idiot.*

Then the dog trotted forward, automatically heading for the trail that led to the pass.

Trulliç didn't feel like a hero on his return journey. He didn't feel like he should break into song.

He still hummed a tiny prayer to Serril, thanking him for his life and his new companion.

Atça seemed surprised when he opened his door and found Trulliç standing there.

"My dear boy!" he exclaimed. "Welcome home!"

Atça still wore his lounging robe made from a pale green silk. No one else that Trulliç knew had any silk, let alone a piece of clothing just for breaking your fast and drinking tea in the morning.

As always, Atça stood tall and proud. White hair fringed his long skull, making his broad forehead seem even bigger. His dark eyes had faded with age to a pale brown that looked golden in the right light, making him seem more magical. He had a large, bulbous nose and fat lips. Because he spent as little time as possible outside, he had the lightest skin of anyone Trulliç knew: Not white like the travelers from Lydae who stayed at the tavern sometimes, but several shades lighter than anyone else. It made Trulliç sometimes want to hide his rough hands and dark skin.

"Thank you," Trulliç said. "May I come in?" Atça liked it when Trulliç used the formal forms.

"Eh? Yes, yes," Atça said. He seemed distracted, staring at Riyune who stood beside Trulliç.

Atça backed out of the doorway. Before Trulliç could take a step forward, Atça added, "Not the dog."

Trulliç blinked, surprised. Then disappointment struck. If Atça didn't want Riyune to accompany Trulliç, it meant that Riyune was just an ordinary dog.

"I won't have that mangy mutt bringing fleas and who knows what else into my home," Atça said harshly.

Trulliç stood still, stunned. Riyune was the cleanest dog Trulliç had ever known. He didn't have fleas, even if he did scratch himself sometimes. And he wasn't a mangy mutt. Trulliç had to chase away ownerless dogs from the back of the tavern sometimes.

Still, Atça was his mentor. With a sigh, Trulliç looked down at Riyune, waiting until the dog turned his face up, those impossibly blue eyes staring into his. "I'm sorry—"

No.

The word came through loud and clear.

Trulliç blinked in surprise. It was only the second time he'd heard Riyune speak, the first being when the dog had told Trulliç his name. Both times, Trulliç couldn't mistake the words for anything else.

Trulliç looked up at Atça. "Did you hear that?" he asked eagerly.

"Hear what?" Atça asked sourly. "Come. Either come in or stay out. Stop letting flies into my house."

Trulliç looked again at Riyune. The pale blue eyes that looked into his didn't say anything else. However, Trulliç knew he shouldn't leave Riyune behind. He felt it as deeply as the sand that sifted through his blood, the memories of the desert heat that still warmed his soul.

"Riyune is my familiar," Trulliç said, willing the words to be true, though he knew they weren't. "He goes where I go. If he isn't welcome, then I'm not coming in."

Fear made the core of Trulliç tremble, but he wouldn't back down. Riyune was too important.

"Familiar? Bah," Atça said. "You've always been too fanciful." He looked critically at Riyune. "There's nothing magical about that dog," he declared loudly.

Trulliç reached down and touched his fingertips to Riyune's warm head. It was the first time he'd voluntarily touched the dog, permitted bare contact between Trulliç's skin and Riyune's fur. Riyune had come and found him at night, both when they'd been traveling as well as in the small shack Trulliç shared with his mother. They'd shared heat in the cold of the night, through blankets, Riyune getting up as soon as Trulliç stirred.

The world didn't suddenly change when Trulliç touched Riyune, as it had when Trulliç had first stepped onto the desert sands.

Still, Trulliç felt the blankets that covered his senses lifting slightly, as if a strong desert wind had blown away the first layer of fog.

Was Atça scared of Riyune? The way he held his mouth, how his eyes narrowed, spoke of fear.

Trulliç shrugged, withdrawing his fingers but still feeling the warmth they'd brought. "Maybe he has magic. Maybe not. He still belongs with me."

Atça pressed his lips together and glared at Trulliç.

That was a look Trulliç was familiar with: That glare which spoke of how stupid Atça thought Trulliç was being.

"Fine," Atça said after another moment. "He can come in. But if he ever messes my rugs, I'll skin him alive."

The thrill of having won an argument with his mentor startled Trulliç. They weren't competing, were they? He'd fought with Atça a few times in the past, with Trulliç always backing down. This was Atça's territory, his true home, not Trulliç's. Besides, Atça was older and wiser, and Trulliç had been taught to respect his elders.

Trulliç stood on the threshold and waited until Riyune looked up at him. "You heard him," Trulliç warned.

Riyune didn't nod or in any way acknowledge what Trulliç had just said.

"I need to be able to trust you," Trulliç added. He knew that Riyune understood. He also suspected that Riyune was the type of dog who knew better than to soil the inside of someone's house, but who might do so anyway out of spite.

Finally, Riyune did the dog equivalent of rolling his eyes as he turned his head to the side.

"Thank you," Trulliç said.

Again, nothing from Riyune. Though if Trulliç were feeling as fanciful as Atça always claimed, he would have said that Riyune did give off a strong sense of smug satisfaction.

Here we go. Trulliç didn't like feeling as though stepping into his mentor's house was more fraught with danger than stepping onto the desert sands.

He still braced himself as he stepped across the threshold.

Nothing happened.

Trulliç looked around the entrance hall of Atça's house, expecting to feel different.

He was in another magician's true home. Shouldn't he feel more magical himself? Or perhaps less magical?

What was wrong with him? Was he really such a poor magician? Why didn't this house ever strike him as magical, though he knew it was?

Dark wood paneling covered the walls in the front hall. Wood that could be used for planks didn't grow in or near Gaadiwala: It all had to be imported. So much wood in a simple room was a sign of extreme wealth.

Two scrolls hung from the walls. The one directly in front of Trulliç held a welcome poem written in the Lydean tongue. The one on his left held warnings and an incantation in Tadnesh against demons.

Riyune trotted over to the scroll to the left and gazed up at it, unfazed.

So maybe Riyune wasn't a demon, something that Trulliç hadn't even considered. Then again, all the demons who both Atça and Trulliç knew about were just from old stories, when mighty foes battled even mightier heroes.

A plain, dark-blue rug made of braided cloth covered the floor in the entrance hall. To the right side stood a cleverly made wooden structure. It was only as high as Trulliç's knees, but it took up half the wall and held many cubbyholes. Trulliç leaned over and untied his sandals, then put them into their usual spot, close to the floor, on the right side.

Atça thoughtfully provided his guests with house slippers made of black felt. They lay jumbled together in a basket woven together out of reeds with a geometric diamond pattern on its side. Trulliç grabbed a pair, wiped the soles of his feet with his hand to make sure they were (mostly) free of dirt, then slid the slippers on.

Atça had already left through the doorway at the back of the front room. Trulliç walked down the hallway next. Atça never bothered to light this hall. It always felt closed in to Trulliç. Sometimes, he would swear the hall grew longer as he went down it. He walked quickly through it. Riyune's claws clicked as he walked behind Trulliç, giving him comfort.

Trulliç knew his mentor's habits and went past the teaching rooms on the right and left of the hallway, and instead walked to the room just past the staircase leading to the upper levels.

The room wasn't much bigger than the front room. However, light poured in from the windows that filled the wall on the left. This morning, Atça had them thrown wide open. The window had two parts: A solid cover that Atça used at night and during the rainy season, as well as a second covering that was made of panes covered in a translucent paper. Trulliç always wondered if the diffuse light that came through the panes was similar to what light coming through tree leaves might look like.

Against the right wall, Atça had many pillows and a comfortable rug for his guests to sit on. Atça himself had settled back in, leaning against the wall and nibbling on a piece of cheese. A brass tray sat on the ground next to him, carrying the remains of his breakfast: A cup that held milky trails of yogurt, a couple of tops from dried figs, a half-eaten piece of flat bread, and the rind of the cheese.

"May I offer you tea?" Atça asked as Trulliç settled himself down, leaning against the wall himself, a comfortable pillow supporting his back.

"Thank you," Trulliç replied.

Riyune stayed close to the door, laying down just inside it, close to Trulliç but out of the way.

Atça poured a small cup of the herbal tea that he drank every morning for Trulliç. It smelled spicy, of cloves and dried *golangie* berries.

Riyune lifted his head and sniffed the air when Trulliç accepted the cup, then lay his head back down again.

Trulliç took a sip, the warm tea clearing his throat.

"Tell me of your great journeys, so that I may learn," Atça said, using the ritual formula that a storyteller sometimes used to gather a greater crowd.

Except that no storyteller Trulliç had ever heard sounded so sarcastic.

He ignored the sting, though. That was just Atça being Atça. He couldn't be genuinely excited about anything.

So Trulliç told him all about his journey, including how Riyune had first appeared as a blood hound. He admitted his weaknesses, such as not waiting until the heat of the day had passed before traveling out on the sands that first morning, of feeling so lonely the second day at the tiny oasis.

Atça merely listened, refilling their cups when needed.

"You have had a great dream," Atça proclaimed when Trulliç finished. "I will have to meditate long and hard to wriggle the meaning out of it."

Trulliç breathed a sigh of relief. His mentor agreed! He *had* had a great dream.

Atça stared at Riyune, considering him carefully, before he shook his head. "Still can't see anything magical about that dog," he said, sounding exasperated. "Just an odd colored dog with strange eyes."

Riyune didn't bother to stir or even to look at them, staying as still as a statue of a dog.

"Maybe that's how familiars work," Trulliç said. He'd been giving this some thought as well, since Riyune hadn't appeared magical at all to him, either. "If a familiar looks magical, then other will know it instantly. They could exploit the familiar. Maybe it would be a weakness in the magician. If the familiar just looks like a normal animal, that protects the magician."

"Perhaps," Atça admitted, though he didn't look pleased. "It is unnerving, though, how still that animal sits."

Trulliç looked over his shoulder at Riyune. The dog lay completely motionless. Trulliç hadn't seen him do that before, but he didn't think it meant anything.

"You have given me much to think about," Atça added, sitting up. "I will spend the day meditating on the symbols from your dream."

Trulliç swallowed down his disappointment. Atça didn't want him to spend the day, learning.

"Thank you for listening to me," Trulliç said, sitting up straighter, then bowing his head.

"Come back tomorrow, no, the day after tomorrow, to hear what I have discovered," Atça said firmly.

"I will," Trulliç said. He didn't add anything like *I will count the hours*. That sounded way too mushy, even in his own head.

Trulliç rose and bowed to his mentor one last time before he left. Riyune followed right behind him on his heels.

What did Atça really think about Trulliç's journey? About Riyune?

It would be at least two days before Trulliç found out. If then. Atça was a master of not answering questions he didn't want to.

Trulliç walked down the dark hallway in his mentor's house, back toward the front hall. Atça would see him in a couple days, tell him what he'd teased apart from Trulliç's journey of the desert.

The hallway grew, as Trulliç suspected it might. If he was being fanciful, as Atça accused him of being, he'd say the hallway didn't like Trulliç, didn't want to allow another magician through.

The light at the end of the hallway winked out. Trulliç stopped, panicked, and looked behind him.

No light there either.

Total darkness.

Trulliç called up his mage light.

It was like trying to do magic through a blanket. Trulliç struggled to bring more magic to his hand, to cut through the darkness with his light.

Riyune's claws clicked in the darkness. Trulliç felt a warm pressure against his calf, where Riyune leaned against him.

The mage light flared suddenly, as bright as it had been in the desert.

Trulliç felt as though he was channeling the energy from somewhere else, not just drawing it from himself. Was it coming from Riyune? Or from some deeper well, further away?

The end of the hallway appeared again, just a few steps away.

Trulliç scurried to the front room, extinguishing his light as soon as he crossed the threshold and stepped out of the hallway. He slipped off the house slippers and grabbed his sandals, tying them quickly.

Riyune waited patiently beside the door.

"Thank you," Trulliç said as he opened the door for the pair of them.

Riyune didn't say, *See? I told you so.*

But Trulliç knew the dog could have said those things, as well as much more. Such as how important it was for Riyune to accompany Trulliç everywhere he went. How Riyune could help Trulliç with his magic.

How Atça, or at least his house, didn't like Trulliç.

Atça had been Trulliç's mentor all his life, had shown him the wonders of magic, taught him what it could be like to be a town magician.

But Trulliç wondered as he left Atça's grand house, what things his mentor had never taught him, had never planned on teaching him.

What things Trulliç now needed to learn on his own.

CHAPTER FOUR

NADEEM

SWEAT POURED DOWN NADEEM'S BACK, though she sat as still as the carved rocks west of the oasis.

Izmet, the star sister Nadeem battled, sat the prescribed three feet in front of her. The pair of them were naked in the center of the ceremonial circle. A small pavilion protected them from the sun overhead. Aunt Parayat and Aunt Karalit watched critically from the sidelines. No one else was allowed to stand close to watch this battle, though several sisters from other *kabils* waited outside, curious.

It was the *panayirat¸* the annual celebration and meeting of the seven star-sister tribes. Everyone spent months preparing for the games: contests to determine the strongest illusionists, the cleverest storytellers, the most inspirational dancers, the finest cooks.

Any girl who had just passed her womanhood training and had been marked could go. Often, mentors brought their most talented protégées to compete in private games.

Like Aunt Parayat and Aunt Karalit.

Both Nadeem and Izmet neared the end of their training. They were both sixteen, the strongest at their age of their individual *kabils*. Izmet was the most powerful girl Nadeem had ever met. She had a deep well of magic that Nadeem found difficult to match.

Above the seated girls two illusionary figures wrestled one another.

Nadeem had chosen her favorite figure—a tall blue-skinned girl with a human body and the head of a desert hawk. Brown and white speckled feathers covered the sleek head and faded out across her shoulders. She also had large golden eyes and a bone-white hooked beak.

Izmet battled using a dog-headed boy with a pointed black snout, soft looking ears that rose up just a little from the top of his head, and pale brown eyes. He had a longer reach than Nadeem's hawk girl and a terribly strong bite. However, Nadeem's hawk girl moved faster, sliding out of any hold the dog-boy put her into.

Both figures bled freely when struck, the drops falling out of the air and disappearing before they touched the ground. Then the wounds healed, the imaginary creatures whole again.

And while Izmet's dog-boy couldn't wrestle Nadeem's hawk-girl to the ground for the count of three, neither could Nadeem get the upper hand. They were too well matched. The battle continued.

When Nadeem had a spare moment to think, her figure circling Izmet's, she wondered if they'd fight for the rest of the day and into the night, only giving up when they'd reached complete exhaustion.

No.

Nadeem had to win.

She always had to win.

Nadeem felt herself grinding her teeth in frustration as the dog-boy slipped away again, out of her hawk-girl's grip. There had to be a way to stake him down!

She knew that she could win if she cheated. She'd have to cause permanent damage, however. Or come close to it. Impale the dog-boy on her hawk-girl's beak. Bleed the illusionary figure dry.

That was against the rules. Just as a star sister couldn't kill another when they wrestled, imaginary foes couldn't permanently damage each other either.

Izmet had considered it once, Nadeem could tell. Had thought about tearing out the neck of her hawk girl, but had pulled back at the last minute.

Was this fight worth breaking the rules? Nadeem would win the battle. Izmet would have the moral victory. Would it count? Did it matter?

Nadeem found her body swaying. She didn't want to cheat. But they'd been fighting since the first light of morning. She just wanted this to be over. Her focus wavered for a moment.

The dog-boy flipped her hawk-girl onto her back. Nadeem felt the hit as if it had been physical, the breath forced from her body by the impact.

With a twist and a flip, Nadeem's hawk girl found her feet again, then stood there, swaying, instead of attacking immediately.

Nadeem was going to lose if she didn't do something quickly.

Lightning fast, Nadeem's hawk girl leaped forward. She feinted with her right hand, as if going to grab the dog boy's upper arm.

When he rolled his shoulder back, out of the way, Nadeem's hawk girl struck with her beak, sinking the hooked end deeply into the soft skin, where neck met shoulder, that spot that a lover might touch, causing chicken flesh to raise across her bare skin.

The hawk girl dropped to her knees, forcing the dog boy down as well. He flailed at her, punches that Nadeem felt but ignored.

He had to go down. Now.

Nadeem flipped them, throwing the boy onto his back, withdrawing the beak and grabbing his wrists.

One. Two. Three.

Done.

Nadeem's hawk girl regained her feet. The cry of victory she gave sounded feeble and hollow to Nadeem's ears, as if the figure was really as insubstantial as she appeared.

Then the battling figures disappeared.

"You cheated!" Izmet loudly proclaimed.

Nadeem took a deep breath and merely stared at the other girl. *So?* "Non-lethal force," Nadeem said slowly. "I didn't tear his head off. I didn't even nick the jugular. He could have lived through that wound."

Izmet glared at her, then turned to appeal to the aunts standing beside them. "She cheated," she said again.

Nadeem sat still and breathed, grateful that the battle was over. She felt dizzy with relief. She looked around, then blinked.

Why was it so dim? Then she realized that she'd been so focused on the battle she hadn't noticed the light changing. She looked out of the pavilion, toward the west. What was the sun doing way down there? Had they really fought all through the day and into the evening?

When Nadeem looked back, she saw Aunt Parayat and Aunt Karalit glaring at each other, as if they'd been the ones battling, not Nadeem and Izmet.

Then again, since they were the mentors for the girls, they had been, in some ways.

"He could have recovered," Aunt Parayat said slowly.

Aunt Karalit nodded, resigned. "Only if he had immediate help," she added.

Aunt Parayat shrugged. "They did battle longer than expected. By attacking as she did, Nadeem saved their physical selves."

"True," Aunt Karalit replied sourly. "We could call it a draw."

"But she cheated!" Izmet complained.

"Yes, and all will know it," Aunt Parayat said, her eyes drilling into Nadeem's.

Nadeem stared back defiantly. She'd won. That was all that mattered.

"I declared Nadeem the winner," Aunt Parayat said slowly.

"I agree," Aunt Karalit said.

"Cheater," Izmet said without a sound.

Nadeem shrugged. She'd won. That was what was most important.

And she was willing to accept the consequences.

Nadeem tried to rest in hers and Aunt Parayat's tent. She'd depleted most of her body fluids during the fight—always a danger when battling using illusionary figures—and still felt light headed, despite the salty tea she'd drunk.

However, she couldn't rest. She paced the dirt floor between their two sets of blankets. Three steps, turn, three more steps, turn. She tried to sit, to rest, but found herself jumping to her feet again and again.

Oil lamps made out of baked clay hung in the corners of the tent, casting as much shadow as light.

She wore a sleeveless tunic that fell to her knees, unbelted so the front slid open as she walked, letting the cooler air touch her heated skin. Nadeem had dyed the linen herself, using the bark of the *meslit* thorn bush. The thread had turned the palest gold, and Nadeem thought it looked good against her dark skin. She wore her hair shorter than most, well above her neck and ears. Generally, only married women let their hair grow long.

The door to the tent stood wide open, allowing in what few breezes the desert night brought. No one would look in, though: Nadeem had finally mastered the simplest yet hardest of illusions—making the tent flap still appear closed. She kept track of that illusion with a thread tucked away at the back of her mind, so she could focus on other things.

Where was Aunt Parayat? Who was she meeting with? Nadeem knew she'd won her battle by a mere technicality. What were the consequences?

She wouldn't be banished, that much she knew. She would have had to commit a much more egregious act for that, like murder. Would they be asked to leave the *panayirat* gathering? When Nadeem had been fighting, she'd been willing to accept the consequences. She'd been too tired to think beyond ending the battle.

Now, with fluids in her and time to think, she worried.

She kept trying to tell herself that it didn't matter. She couldn't survive in the desert on her own forever. But if she needed to do a purification ritual, go into the sands for a week, she could do that.

Finally, Nadeem felt the thread of illusion for the tent flap be cut.

Aunt Parayat entered.

Though Nadeem knew her aunt was only in her sixties, she looked as ancient as the old crone in the Tale of Marisat—the one who'd been dancing forever in Goddess Berzhat's golden court.

Nadeem stopped pacing and crossed her arms over her chest. She stood in the middle of the tent, her legs spread and her weight equally balanced over her feet so she could either take a blow or pivot away.

"Sit," Aunt Parayat directed.

Nadeem stayed standing.

Aunt Parayat merely shrugged. "Or don't." She collapsed on her blankets then rolled her shoulders stiffly.

Nadeem bit her lips together. Obviously, her aunt had been arguing with the others for a while, her whole posture still tense.

But Nadeem knew that Aunt Parayat wouldn't take it easy on her. She saw no reason to be easy or gentle in return.

"You deliberately injured another player," Aunt Parayat said slowly as she flexed her back. She still had wiry muscles through her arms. But she was no longer as flexible as the young girls when they first came in for training, and she wasn't as strong.

She also took longer naps in the afternoon.

If Nadeem had one fear, it was going to wake up her aunt, only to find her gone and already dancing in the goddess' golden court.

"I need to understand why," Aunt Parayat said as she finished working her shoulders and ribs.

Nadeem had so many answers prepared. She knew that would be the first question her aunt would ask.

"I don't know what to tell you," Nadeem said honestly. The restlessness that had driven her to move all evening left, as abruptly as an illusion, the strings cut.

Nadeem collapsed on her own blankets, sitting across from her aunt. She didn't bother with trying to lower her head beneath her teacher's out of respect. This was more important.

"I was hot. Tired. I had to win. I couldn't let the battle go on," Nadeem said all in a rush.

Aunt Parayat nodded slowly. "But you chose this. You weren't delusional, or having visions."

Nadeem shuddered. "No," she said firmly. "I chose the final action, to bleed my opponent dry rather than continue the fight."

"Are you certain?" Aunt Parayat said. "Sometimes your visions—"

"I'm sure," Nadeem said firmly.

Yes, since her womanhood ceremony she'd had visions, more than most.

Violent, dark visions, with her footsteps turning to ashes as she walked across the sand.

However, she'd learned to never drink more than a mouthful of the palm wine served at ceremonies, and to never touch the *igrat* that some of the older aunts drank, claiming it helped ease their aches and pains when in fact, it generally made them gibber and snooze.

Aunt Parayat looked at her closely, then nodded. "That's what I told the others. That you'd made a choice." She paused, then added, "But why?"

"Why did I choose to end the battle? Beyond being tired, being out of patience? Why?" Nadeem asked, her voice raising.

Aunt Parayat nodded. "Yes. Why. Tell me the true reason for the darkness around your heart."

Nadeem sat up taller, her back stiffening. What did Aunt Parayat know? What had she heard?

Nadeem started to shake her head. No, she wouldn't tell her aunt.

But she was already in so much trouble. The sand was already piled up over her head. What harm could another cupful be?

"Why do we battle each other?" Nadeem asked. Instead of shouting the words with the force she felt behind them, she found her voice lowering to a whisper. "What's the point? We battle and prove our worth, but for what? So we can be the best among equals? There has to be a reason. Something else. Something *more*."

All the nervous energy flowed out of Nadeem. There. She'd said it. Those words she'd only whispered to herself on a still night, when no wind could carry them away.

It didn't make sense to her why she had to work and improve and try so hard. It would be years before she was an old, respected aunt. Sure, she could work hard all her life, be a respected part of her *kabil*, but there had to be more. More to struggle for, more reward.

Aunt Parayat had always taught her to question.

She'd never found an answer to this, though.

Aunt Parayat looked at her sadly. "That's what I thought," she said softly, her tone almost matching Nadeem's. "You're restless, more than most. Striving. Questioning." She gave a bitter laugh. "More my daughter than any other."

Nadeem blinked, tears welling up. Aunt Parayat had *never* called her "daughter." Not once. Aunt Parayat was Nadeem's mentor, her teacher, her aunt. Not a friend, a confidant, a mother.

Aunt Parayat nodded, as if Nadeem had just answered a question. "Come!" she called.

Nadeem wondered at the power behind her aunt's tone. If she didn't know better, she would have said that there was something magical about it.

But the star sisters could only do illusions. They couldn't use real magic.

Could they?

A few moments later, the tent flap flipped back and Izmet entered.

Nadeem gasped. What was she doing here?

Out of habit, Nadeem rose to her feet to welcome a stranger to her tent. "Please join us," she said formally. There was no seat of honor, no separate setting.

But strangers *must* be welcomed. Always.

It had been many years since Goddess Berzhat had taken human form and walked among them. But she could return at any time.

Better to always welcome the stranger.

"Thank you," Izmet said.

Izmet and Aunt Parayat exchanged a look that Nadeem couldn't interpret. Why did Izmet seem smugly satisfied? And Aunt Parayat so sad?

Nadeem stood, shocked, when Izmet sat beside Aunt Parayat. She shouldn't do that. Izmet wasn't any older than Nadeem. Surely she knew better? She should sit across from all the aunts, her head lowered in respect. She should never presume to be as important and sit *beside* an aunt. Particularly not one as revered as Aunt Parayat.

"Please, sit," Izmet said, as if this were *her* tent.

Nadeem sat carefully, cautiously. She wished she had belted her tunic, that she had a knife at hand, that she wore strips of leather tied to her feet so could run easily if necessary.

Then she stared defiantly at Izmet. She'd beaten the other girl at the battle that afternoon. Sure, it had been more of a technical win than anything else.

Nadeem could do it again, either physically or with illusions, if the other girl challenged her.

"Oh, go on," Aunt Parayat told Izmet when the girl looked at her again. "I swear she loves the drama of this as much as you do, Nadeem," Aunt Parayat added crossly.

Nadeem sat, waiting. What drama? What was going on?

Wait. What was happening?

Izmet's face began to change.

Nadeem watched, fascinated. Of course, she'd tried to change her own appearance, secretly, away from her aunts and everyone else. She'd figured out how to make the skin of her arms and hands appear lighter, and even how to make her hands appear larger, stretching out her fingers until they were thin and delicate.

There weren't any mirrors in the oasis where Nadeem had grown up. She'd been told she was beautiful by the two lovers she'd had, both other sisters in the *kabil*. She knew she had a small nose, thin lips, and a wide smile. Her eyes were dark brown. The cuts on her left cheek formed delicate scars, darker than the rest of her skin.

She'd never been able to see, though, if she could change her face and disguise her appearance. Most star sisters couldn't.

None of the star sisters had the ability to hide their scar. Though Nadeem couldn't imagine why a star sister would want to hide her mark, that didn't mean she wasn't interested in seeing if she could. It was strictly against the law, though. The emperor decreed that any star sister who hid her mark was to be executed immediately. The rest of the sisters would enforce that rule strictly, stating that they never wanted to return to the times of persecution.

Izmet's skin kept its dark color. Her eyebrows stayed like two wings, thick and solid, over her eyes.

But the color of her eyes changed, from a dark brown to a more faded color, similar to Aunt Parayat's.

Wrinkles sprang up around Izmet's eyes, growing deeper, then spreading like water around the edges of her cheeks and around the corners of her mouth. Darker spots spread across her skin—age spots. Streaks of white sprouted in her dark hair, and her hair suddenly spilled down, caught up in a braid that fell to her waist.

Nadeem couldn't contain her gasp when Izmet's change was complete. "You're not a girl," Nadeem accused her. "You're an aunt!" She looked between Aunt Parayat and Aunt Izmet. "You're the same age," she guessed.

Izmet gave her a sharp smile. "Very good," she said. "Parayat told me you were smart."

The compliment didn't make Nadeem feel any better. "Why the disguise?" she asked. Could any of the other aunts see Izmet's true face?

Aunt Izmet said, "We needed to test you. To see if you had the right instincts."

"I couldn't have won the battle, could I?" Nadeem asked bitterly. "Not without doing what I did."

She wouldn't admit that she'd cheated. Just that she'd been driven to an extreme.

Aunt Izmet's laugh rang through the tent. "She is just like you, isn't she?" she asked, nudging Aunt Parayat.

"Including questioning why the games, why the battles, why isn't there something more?" Aunt Parayat replied.

Nadeem blinked, surprised. Others had these same thoughts and questions? She'd assumed she'd been the only one.

"Have you ever heard of the stars of the emperor?" Aunt Izmet asked.

Nadeem shook her head no. She knew the names of many of the stars in the sky, their history, how the great heroes still watched them from above.

"There are a very select few star sisters who receive special training and work just for the emperor," Aunt Izmet said proudly.

"The *Padisha-i-Ghazi*, the great emperor, himself?" Nadeem asked, shocked.

She'd never even heard rumors of such a group!

"Yes, him," Aunt Izmet added dryly. "The emperor himself."

Nadeem sat back, stunned.

The star sisters worked with the emperor? For the emperor? The stars of the emperor? She remembered the change of prayers during the great feasts, only two years before, where they now had to thank the emperor at every meal. And at least once she'd heard an aunt grumble about the amount of tribute that the star sisters had to pay the emperor, that it had increased every year.

Nadeem didn't say anything, however. She bit her lips together so she wouldn't ask more. They would have to tell her everything.

Aunt Izmet let the silence between them gather weight.

"You passed the first test," Aunt Izmet finally replied. "Would you like to continue? I can't guarantee that you'll become one of the few," she warned, then paused, "though your aunt here thinks you'll be one of the best."

"You were one of the emperor's stars," Nadeem said, turning to her old mentor.

"I was," Aunt Parayat said gravely. "It was an honor."

Nadeem wasn't sure what her aunt meant by that. Her voice held no emotion, as though she was discussing the weather.

Nadeem turned back to Aunt Izmet. "It would be my honor to continue," she said, making sure that she sounded as awestruck as she felt.

Aunt Izmet gave her that sharp smile again. "I'll make sure it is," she purred. "Come. We need to celebrate."

A bag suddenly appeared beside Aunt Izmet. Had it been there all along, just hidden with illusion?

Nadeem shook her head. She wasn't as strong as Aunt Parayat, though she knew that in time, she would be.

Would she ever be as strong as Aunt Izmet? She didn't know. It would be good to test herself, though, and push.

Maybe there was a reason behind all the tests, the struggles.

From her bag, Aunt Izmet pulled out a leather flagon of *igrat*. Nadeem smelled the sour alcohol from where she sat.

"I don't drink—" Nadeem started.

"I know. Parayat's told me," Aunt Izmet said. "If I'm taking you on as an apprentice, this is the next step. To walk you through your visions, see the worst they can become."

Nadeem shivered as if a cold wind suddenly blew through the tent. She'd never purposefully gone hunting her visions, had always felt ashamed anytime she'd had one.

Given her day and how little food she had in her stomach, she suspected any vision brought about by the *igrat* would be overwhelming.

However, Nadeem didn't fear getting lost in her vision world. Particularly not now, when she had so much to look forward to: a new mentor, new training, the possibility of working for the emperor himself.

"Let us walk, then," Nadeem said, sitting up straighter. It was the call of a storyteller to an audience, to get them to travel along the tale's trails with her.

"Let us walk," Aunt Izmet said, raising the flagon and taking the first sip before passing it to Aunt Parayat.

"May you gain wisdom on your journey," Aunt Parayat replied, also taking a drink then handing the flagon to Nadeem.

Nadeem weighed the leather container in her hands. "Let me be your guide," she said as she raised the sour drink to her lips.

Fire water poured down her throat. It burned all the way to her stomach. Nadeem lowered the flagon and coughed, her eyes watering.

Determined, she took another swallow.

Willed the vision to begin.

The sky changed from the soft blanket of night to the purple of an old bruise. Nadeem walked on blackened sand. It crunched under her sandals as though she was breaking tiny bird bones with every step. When she turned back to look, her footprints appeared as white as ash. The air smelled of rotten eggs.

Clouds boiled on every horizon, angry and threatening. The rain they carried would wash the land clean, but the desert wouldn't allow the storm across its border. Every once in a while Nadeem caught a whiff of sweet rain, but she knew she'd never see it.

So it was the desert vision today. Nadeem had visions of other locations as well—a place where water as far as the eye could see came crashing into the shore, chasing her away from the buried chest she needed to rescue. The water itself was composed of tiny, stinging darts that shredded her skin if she let it touch her. Or the forest one, when she raced beneath trees taller than any she'd ever seen, something awful pursuing her. She almost always took a wrong turn and ended up being cornered, the only way to escape to tumble down the mountainside herself.

In the desert, to her right, ran a long wooden barrier. It had rotted in places, the wood falling to dust. In others, it stood taller than her head by several yards. She walked beside it. In the areas where it was still whole, she could tell that it had at one point been round, like the shaft of a great spear.

Once, when she'd reached the end of it, she'd found a huge piece of metal, as big as the entire oasis where she'd grown up.

It sloped on either side, triangular in shape.

Like a spear head.

Beyond what Nadeem called the Spear Mountain lay the heart of this vision place, the desert. A tiny outcrop of rock that sprang up out of nowhere. The rocks looked haphazardly piled, one on top of the other, though they were a single piece. It was smaller than the teaching tent, and only had the single opening.

Gibbering black shapes lived inside the prison created by the rocks, teeming masses of shadows that threatened to tear the world apart. They howled when Nadeem approached. If she wasn't careful, she'd find herself tearing at her own clothes, marking her own skin, their hatred of all living things overwhelming her.

A flimsy red rope was strung across that opening, holding all the creatures in.

In Nadeem's worst visions, she was the one who cut the rope or untied it, unleashing madness on the world.

The creatures would always destroy her first, showing her the ugliness inside her own soul so she would take her own life. Or they'd tear her to pieces when Nadeem refused to believe their illusions.

This vision was more awful than those, however.

As Nadeem neared the end of the Spear Mountains, the darkness came rushing at her.

Someone else was there. He'd already released the black hordes.

Stupid boy. He was obviously a magician trying to rein in the darkness, but his mage light wasn't strong enough to contain the creatures. The shadows cringed, yes, but they didn't stop. Instead, they poured out of the rocks, destroying the boy before he could blast them.

So Nadeem fought them instead. An endless stream of opponents. She was already tired, the day's events blurring into her dream: Her hawk-girl battled beside her, along with the dog-boy, but they were still restricted and couldn't do fatal damage.

Nadeem, however, could kill. She used her knife like it was an extension of her hand and sliced apart the shadows she fought, or cut their throats, or when her knife shattered, broke limbs and clawed out eyes.

It was a battle worthy of songs or poems, but Nadeem lost in the end as she always did, falling under the onslaught of so many creatures.

With a cry, Nadeem woke, finding both Aunt Parayat and Aunt Izmet looking down at her. Worry lined their faces.

"What?" Nadeem asked as she looked from one to the other. She blinked, her eyes gritty with sand. She took a deep breath, smelling her own sour sweat. When she tried to push herself up, she found her head even more dizzy than after the long battle that afternoon.

Aunt Parayat helped Nadeem to sit up, then Aunt Izmet held the water jug while Nadeem took great gulps.

"You went far, my sister," Aunt Parayat said softly when Nadeem finally was able to push the jug away, her thirst sated for the moment.

Nadeem shrugged. She always did.

Wait. Did Aunt Parayat just call her sister?

Before Nadeem could ask about that, Aunt Izmet added, "You walked the dreamlands for more than a day. Went places I couldn't follow." She sounded put out by that.

That was interesting. Could other aunts follow Nadeem's visions?

Dream beside her? Was that what the dream readers did? That was a skill she wanted to learn.

"It was a long time for a vision," Aunt Parayat said. It sounded as though she was scolding Nadeem. "Too long."

Nadeem nodded. She was aware that her visions had not only grown more violent, but stronger as well.

Aunt Izmet sat on the ground beside Nadeem, looking at her sourly.

Was Nadeem not worthy of becoming one of the emperor's stars? Because of her visions? Had she chosen the wrong shells for her coming of age ritual? If only she'd taken the weakest!

But Aunt Parayat had pointed out to her that weaker shells might not have prevented her from having visions—it might have only prevented her from being able to return from the dreamlands.

Aunt Izmet appeared to be reconsidering her offer.

Nadeem held her breath. She wasn't sure what she'd do if Aunt Izmet refused to keep training her. She wouldn't walk the desert looking for the goddess, though she knew other girls who would. There was honor staying at the *kabil* as well.

"It's a good thing you're going to continue your training with me," Aunt Izmet finally said. "One of the first things you're going to learn is how to pretend to drink, and get drunk, while not taking a sip of alcohol."

Nadeem sighed, relieved. That actually sounded like a very useful skill for her to learn.

She couldn't wait to get started.

CHAPTER FIVE

TRULLIÇ

TRULLIÇ WOKE WITH A START. He'd been dreaming of the desert, as he had almost every night since he'd returned from his first manhood journey four years before.

Of course, he never dreamed of his true home. He despaired of ever finding it. His dreams were full of oases, hidden streams, caves that held ancient secrets, foothills that towered over the sands, the cry of the desert hawk filling his ears and sweet dates tickling his tongue.

He'd never determined how he was supposed to live on the sands, either. His dreams didn't show him secret fields of wheat or trees full of fruit and nuts. He couldn't choke down the small rodents that Riyune found so effortlessly, either. If he found a desert hawk chick and raised her by hand her entire life, maybe she could have gone hunting for him, but how could he afford to feed her while she was young? He didn't have the time or the money for such an expensive pet.

Trulliç pushed aside his blankets, sat up and stretched, his shoulders popping. He stood over six feet tall now, taller than most of his cousins. He kind of hoped his latest growth spurt had been his last —it was such a pain being so hungry all the time!

Riyune looked up from where he'd been sleeping, curled up beside Trulliç, his back warming Trulliç's left thigh.

"Yeah, yeah, I'm getting up," Trulliç said. Gaadiwala wasn't big or rich enough to have proper temples with bells to mark all the hours of the gods. They still had the morning bells—bell, really—that had just started to ring.

That was another change since Trulliç had been younger—the bell that marked the morning was no longer rung just for Xannil, the sun god, but also in honor of the emperor.

In a week's time, Trulliç would take another journey through the desert. He didn't know how he felt about that. Or rather, he had too many feelings and couldn't sort them out.

Trulliç stood and threw the blankets back on his sleeping pallet—just a collection of soft sheepskins with the wool still attached that he needed to air out again. He'd worn his plain brown shirt and short pants to bed so he'd stay warm through the cool desert night. Now he threw his workman's tunic over them, its soft gray cotton still clean from the last time his mother had washed it, belting it with the broad leather belt that Atça had given him at the end of the previous year.

After slipping on his sandals, Trulliç picked up two of the four clay water jugs that rested beside the door. His first chore every morning was to walk up the street to the neighborhood well and get water for the day.

His mother still slept in her blankets in the alcove that held her sleeping pallet in their one-room hut, farthest away from the door and closer to the hearth that was never enough on cold winter nights. Their few goods, scattered along the base of the wall. They couldn't afford cupboards or even fine pillows to lean against. They mostly sat on the dirt.

Myrizhah worked until after dark most nights at the family tavern. She wouldn't get up until after he'd gotten the water. Then she would clean herself and go into the tavern and work, baking the flat bread that the customers would eat for that day. It kept her near the fires, where it was warmest. She brought home the leftovers, or the burned pieces if there were no leftovers, for her and Trulliç to have with their supper.

Trulliç hung the two pots over a yoke and trudged down the hill to the well.

Two people stood in line already, with a third drawing her water: Widow Jarkat, who'd lost not one but two husbands to the wars, and so constantly wore the blue-and-black striped scarf of mourning around her neck; Old man Somlekçi, who'd once been Gaadiwala's main potter but whose hands were now too twisted with arthritis to throw pots anymore; and young Erzalat who hauled water out of the well.

Erzalat was a few years older than Trulliç and lived with her parents up in the foothills where they tended a huge flock of sheep. She kept her head covered with a soft gray *chafiyek* to keep the sun and wind out of her face and the sand out of her short, dark hair. Under her light blouse, her biceps bulged as she pulled a full bucket up out of the well. Her mouth was set in a grim line, her jaw hard and square.

Trulliç always assumed that Erzalat could beat him at any wrestling match, and his cousins to boot.

"There's water," Erzalat told the others as she lifted the bucket and poured it into her waiting water jug. "But it's low. And slow in coming."

Fear shot through Trulliç.

Gaadiwala couldn't live without water. The punishment for stealing or blocking another man's stream was death. Atça took all accusations of water theft very seriously. Though he hated leaving town and grumbled the entire way, he'd make the trip out to a farmer's residence to verify claims of water stealing.

Though Gaadiwala wasn't *his* home, not like it was Atça's, Trulliç still had tried to find the water under the town once, like he had in the desert.

It had been *much* harder to find. And then Atça had yelled at Trulliç for wasting his time—until Trulliç found his true home, he could never trust his senses or his magical ability.

Still, Trulliç worried about the lack of water at the neighborhood well. They'd just passed through the rainy season and there had been plenty of rain. The well should be full.

"Can't you do anything?" Widow Jarakat asked, turning to Trulliç.

"Me?" Trulliç asked, surprised.

"You are a magician, after all," old man Somlekçi added.

"But I'm not Atça, the town's magician," Trulliç told them.

Erzalat snorted. "Exactly," she said. She shot a hard glare at Trulliç as she dropped the bucket back into the well. "You're likely to actually help."

Trulliç opened his mouth to defend his mentor, then closed it again. Atça had explained more than once that the town owed him their tithe, that they were unaware of all that he did for them, how he protected them. The tithe had been growing though, both the emperor's portion as well as Atça's.

"Fine," Trulliç said. It would be awhile before he could draw his own water. What could it hurt? He wouldn't be wasting his time, since he had to wait anyway.

Trulliç took a deep breath, closed his eyes, and pushed his awareness under the hard-packed earth.

The smell of rich, wet loam filled his senses as he pushed down. There *was* water below them.

He tracked the cold shaft of the well down into the reservoir below.

Water trickled through the stones into the northern end of the reservoir. Though Atça had told Trulliç more than once that he couldn't believe his senses, it still felt to him as though the water meant for this place had been diverted.

But where was the start of the underground creek? Where had it been blocked off?

Trulliç tried backtracking past the stones, up the small trail of water.

Instantly, he got lost.

Instead of following the main spear of water, he found himself tricked again and again, following the little fingers of water that divided off of the primary stream. He couldn't tell which direction was up, or down, or east, or west. He bumped into the hard rock when he tried to leave the water trail, unable to push through it and rise to the surface.

Trulliç lost all awareness of his body above him. It grew into a faint memory. He'd had fingers once, and toes, but they were long gone. The ground breathed air into him, kept his hungering belly full, drew his attention along, instead of allowing him to float back up, above the ground.

Was this how the hero Arzhem felt when she first left the corrupt city and wandered lost in the desert? Trulliç's feet had meandered every time his sandals had touched the sands, but it had never been as bad as this.

Something hard pinched his cheek. The pain drew his face, his attention, away from the underground water trails and back—ah, there! Back toward the surface.

When Trulliç opened his eyes, his mother stood in front of him. He blinked, surprised.

He was taller than her. When had that happened?

"Are you all right?" Mother asked. Her dark features were pinched with worry.

"Yes," Trulliç said, nodding. *Ow.* Had she slapped him? He put his hand up to his cheek. "What happened?" he asked.

"You got lost in your head," Mother said simply.

Trulliç nodded. It hadn't happened to him for a while, but it had happened before. He looked at Riyune who sat beside his mother.

"Couldn't Riyune help?" he asked. Before, the dog had licked his fingers or something to bring him back.

Mother shook her head. "He came to get me."

"Oh," Trulliç said. Mother and Riyune avoided each other. They both pretended the other didn't exist most of the time.

That Riyune voluntarily went to go get Mother meant that Trulliç had been truly lost.

"Let's get some water," Mother suggested. "Then you need to get to Atça's and tell him what happened."

Trulliç nodded, though he didn't agree.

He didn't want to tell his mentor about how he'd gotten lost in his head again while he'd been looking for water sources, something Atça would chide him for.

All Atça needed to hear about was the lack of water at the well outside of town, so he would hopefully do something about it. And not demand more tribute in payment from the poor neighborhood.

"Have you come with a great vision this morning?" Atça asked Trulliç as he walked into the learning room, Riyune at his heels. "Some new grand prophecy to entertain us with?"

"No, master, I have not," Trulliç replied. He tried not to sulk. Atça was just being Atça, as usual, though it stung every time Atça asked such questions in front of Ordu and Çirmal, the two paying students.

With a sigh, Trulliç lowered himself to the floor beside the others. He sat on bare wood while the other two boys had their own rugs, provided by their families. Riyune lay down just inside the room, next to the door, as if guarding the occupants from any who might enter.

Trulliç had made the mistake once of asking Atça if maybe, since he never dreamed of a single place in the desert, if perhaps the *entire* desert was his home.

Atça had not only laughed himself silly, he'd told the other students about it. They teased Trulliç mercilessly about it, calling him King of the Sands and other titles.

"Since you've decided to join us, even with your lack of stories to entertain us, perhaps you could recite the lines assigned for this morning?" Atça continued.

Trulliç wasn't a paying student. Atça took Trulliç on only because of his magical abilities, no matter how feeble they'd turned out to be.

Fortunately, Trulliç liked the poem they'd been assigned. It told of the hero Lyons, who stole an egg from a stone eagle, then hatched the great rock himself by roasting it in the fires of a mountain of flame—a volcano, or so Atça had explained. Lyons and his eagle then flew to the courts of the gods, where he became their messenger.

Trulliç pushed himself back up to his feet. Atça insisted that they do all their recitations standing. Even if that meant going from seated to standing and back again all day long.

After taking a deep breath, Trulliç recited the next stanza of the poem. He was just getting into the interesting part, where Lyons turned the egg in the coals by using a lever, when he noticed Ordu and Çirmal working hard to keep straight faces, trying not to giggle.

Trulliç found his words tumbling off.

"That's very good," Atça said sourly. "But that's also not where we were in the poem."

Trulliç thought back. Where had they left off?

"Ordu, if you can?" Atça said, sounding bored.

Trulliç sighed and sat back down.

Ordu stood. He gave Trulliç a smug smile, his fat face beaming with satisfaction. Then he started reciting, just two stanzas after where Trulliç had started.

Trulliç recognized his mistake instantly. He'd been thinking about the poem while he'd been walking to Atça's, wondering about the amount of force needed to turn such a heavy object. Since discovering the blocked off trail of water below the well that morning, he'd been wondering what it would take to open up that flow again.

Of course, Atça would deny that the poems he taught had any application to *work*. The poems and songs they learned were to stir the soul, not to teach people how to build or to live more productive lives.

Trulliç kept his back straight and his face neutral as he made himself listen to Ordu, who spoke with a nasal, flat tone. He never added any of the passion that Trulliç felt needed to be in the tale. Ordu would never give Blind Giresul, the market storyteller, a run for his money.

But Ordu was accurate and didn't miss a single, droned out word.

After Ordu finished three stanzas, Atça indicated that he should sit down. "Çirmal? If you could continue to catch Trulliç up?"

Trulliç bit his lips together and didn't say anything. It was just Atça being Atça. Trulliç knew where they were in the poem—he already had the entire thing memorized! He was also aware, though, that he was in trouble for the entire day. Atça would assume that Trulliç hadn't done any of the lessons. Despite the fact that Trulliç *always* did his lessons and never missed any assignments, even when that huge caravan had come into Gaadiwala and he'd spent most of the night working in the tavern with his mother and cousins.

Çirmal stood and continued from where Ordu had left off. Atça had to prompt him a few times when he stumbled over words and phrases, but Atça still heaped praise on Çirmal when he finished.

"For next week, start with the birth of the stone eagle," Atça told the students. "If you think you could remember that, this time?" he directed at Trulliç.

"I will," Trulliç said. "I promise." He really liked that part of the poem as well.

Atça merely raised one eyebrow at him but didn't comment.

Trulliç kept his sigh to himself. He did everything he could to make his mentor proud of him. It never seemed to be enough, though.

He would just have to try harder to please his mentor and his mother, and not be such a disappointment to everyone.

"So why was the King of the Desert late this morning?" Ordu asked as he came out into Atça's back garden. The late afternoon sun still hung on the horizon, but the day had grown cool already. Since the rainy season had just ended, all the flowers along the edges of the garden bloomed. Bees and other insects buzzed, trying to finish their gathering before the hot weather returned. Palms shaded the center of the garden, and the light breezes made it close to perfect.

Trulliç sighed. If only he didn't have to deal with the others! He also wished the paying students wouldn't call him that. But he didn't have any way to make them stop, no leverage. "I had chores," he replied truthfully.

He checked over his shoulder. Riyune lay on the dirt at the edge of the shade, watching everything as always. The dog raised an eyebrow at Trulliç, as if to say it was his call what he wanted to do, to stay and deal with the other students, or to just get up and leave.

"Chores?" Çirmal chimed in, coming to sit on the other side of Trulliç. "Surely you have servants for those kinds of things."

Trulliç shook his head but didn't reply. The paying students *did* have servants, and lived richer lives than anyone else Trulliç knew.

Besides Atça, of course.

"What kind of things did you have to do?" Ordu asked. He sat on the other side of Trulliç.

Trulliç recognized a trap. They didn't actually care about him or anything in his life. They were just looking for another opportunity to make fun of him, something else they could tease him about.

He had to answer them, however. Despite Trulliç's slight abilities at magic, as paying students they held higher rank than he did. On judging days, Atça paid careful attention to rank when he listened to the complaints of the people of Gaadiwala.

Towns that didn't have a local magician had a magistrate appointed by the emperor who did the same thing, listened and held judgment, declaring fines as necessary.

Atça also counted all the baskets of flour, flagons of sweet *meslit*, clay tiles and jugs, pelts of sheep's wool, and everything else the town produced for the emperor, making sure that all the produce was accounted for and the town properly tithed.

Trulliç accompanied Atça one afternoon a week, carrying the books where he kept track of everyone's input. Trulliç didn't like keeping the count, though he could read and write his numbers and letters well enough. There had been too many farmers that winter who were short, who'd offered just about anything not to go into debt.

Atça had been firm, but he'd also tried to be fair, counting extra barrels of palm wine against the family's total, though those didn't make their way to the emperor but to Atça's cellar instead.

The farmers didn't complain to Atça's face about the amount that the tithe had increased every year, but Trulliç still heard their grumbling, particularly when they came into the tavern and had had too much to drink.

"I had to wait beside the well for water this morning," Trulliç told the boys. He wasn't about to tell them about trying to trace the water trails, then getting lost underground. They'd just tease him more, maybe call him the king of the caves or something.

Atça would address the problem. He was good at raising water. He could direct people to the exact location where they should dig their wells.

Gaadiwala was Atça's town, where the magician drew his power from.

However, if Trulliç allowed himself to be fanciful, Atça's powers actually diminished the moment he stepped across the threshold of his house, growing weaker and weaker as he got further from his home.

Trulliç didn't remember how he'd cried and screamed as a young boy when they'd first come to live at the tavern with the rest of his mother's family. However, she'd told the story—often—about how he spent days and nights screaming. Even the horseshoe over the doorway of the tavern didn't calm him, though he supposedly spent a lot of time staring at it as a child.

It hadn't been until Atça had come into the tavern that she'd realized the pair of them couldn't live in the town, that they had to go find a shack out on the outskirts so that Trulliç would have some peace.

Trulliç did remember how he felt like he couldn't breathe. Even now, the tavern still felt all closed in, like there was no air in the smoky main room.

When Atça had taken Trulliç from his mother, he'd calmed down immediately. Then, Atça had taken the boy outside.

As soon as Trulliç could see the stars again, he'd started breathing fully.

That was when Trulliç and his mother had moved to the very edge of Gaadiwala, so Trulliç could see the stars more easily at night. They lived in a mere shack instead of the much nicer rooms at the inn.

Trulliç knew that his mother was just waiting for him to find his true home so she could move back into the tavern.

But Trulliç had disappointed her in that as well.

"Can't you just call water to the surface? Enough to fill your jugs?" Ordu asked reasonably.

Trulliç nodded and lied to the boys. "Of course I can. But who wants a well in the middle of the street?"

Wells needed to be in their proper place. Atça had declared that place to be where the neighborhood well currently existed.

It wasn't Atça's fault that the reservoir under the well was no longer filling properly.

Could Trulliç create a well in his own backyard? Possibly he could call the water to the surface—he'd certainly been able to track it well enough when he'd been out in the desert. That wasn't the same as laying down all the rocks that needed to be placed to create a proper well.

Plus, as his adventures had shown him that morning, if he directed water to his own backyard, he was directing it *from* somewhere else. He'd be the one responsible for the neighborhood well not filling properly.

Erzalat had seemed to accuse Atça of not doing anything, that he wouldn't do anything to take care of their well.

Trulliç had failed when he'd tried, getting so lost.

But maybe if he wasn't right above the water trails, maybe he could stay grounded…

"I don't believe you," Çirmal said dismissively. "If you could call a well, why wouldn't you?"

Trulliç shook his head. Being a magician wasn't all about power, though he doubted the other two boys would understand that. Being a magician was about proper application of power, or so Atça had drilled into Trulliç's head day in and out. It was like the hero Lyons, how he'd applied leverage to turn the stone egg. Just turning the egg over in the wrong direction would have sent it careening down the mountain's edge.

"That's the real reason you were late, isn't it?" Ordu said. "Because your magic failed. As usual."

Trulliç flushed but didn't try to deny it.

"It's okay," Çirmal said, trying to be reassuring. "We know that Atça has just taken you on as a charity case."

Trulliç bit his lips together. He *wasn't* a charity case. Though he could well imagine Atça telling the other boys that.

"Tell you what," Ordu said. "You call up some water, right here, right now, and we'll leave you alone for the next month."

"Week," Çirmal said.

"Month," Trulliç said immediately.

"Deal," Ordu said.

Trulliç knew the boy wasn't telling the truth. He could see it in the way Ordu's skin turned slightly red around his jaw, in the way his aura flared.

Trulliç had tried to describe his ability to Atça, but his mentor had just dismissed Trulliç as being too fanciful, as usual. Atça maintained that Trulliç couldn't trust his vision, all those signals that his magical ability gave him, just as he could only sometimes rely on his senses. Until Trulliç found his true home, he wouldn't be able to calibrate anything he felt or saw, wouldn't know what was real or true.

Trulliç kept his judgments to himself and tried to pay attention to his mentor, but he knew that in this instant, Ordu was lying.

Despite that, Trulliç still agreed to Ordu's challenge. He needed to prove to himself that he wouldn't get lost this time. Particularly since he was just about to go back out to the desert.

If he got lost there, he'd never find his way back home.

"Deal," Trulliç said. He looked over his shoulder, then beckoned for Riyune to come closer.

Riyune didn't quite roll his eyes, but he did stand slowly, stretching his back by placing his front paws on the ground and raising his butt in the air, then shaking himself before he walked over to where Trulliç sat and lay down next to him, the dog's side lightly touching Trulliç's knee.

Trulliç had found that if he started a journey touching Riyune, he tended not to get lost. Or at least as lost.

Then Trulliç reached for his cup of water and poured it over the thirsty ground.

"That's cheating!" Çirmal exclaimed.

"No, it's not," Trulliç said firmly. "It's just always easier to call like to like." One of the reasons why he'd been able to find the reservoir under the ground so easily was because he'd traveled down the rock path of the well. He hadn't just stood in the middle of the village square and tried to direct his senses down under the earth with nothing to guide him.

Water lay in a large reservoir just under the ground in Atça's back garden. Trulliç had found it before. He'd never tried to do anything with it, however.

Before Trulliç sent all his attention underground, he looked at the other students.

Ordu always had a golden aura around his hair, as if he'd come from a bath in the sun. Trulliç didn't know what that foretold, if it meant the son of the richest man in town was destined for riches, or if he would have to find his way in the desert.

Çirmal was the exact opposite, as usual, like he carried his own gray cloud with him. Was he destined for the sea? To live in the rain? Or was it something completely else?

Atça had told Trulliç he couldn't believe what he saw, that it wasn't real.

But Trulliç saw it every time he looked. It *had* to mean something. But what?

Trulliç also saw that it didn't matter to Ordu or Çirmal if he succeeded or not. The boys would claim that Trulliç failed, even if he brought a huge geyser blasting out of the ground.

They didn't realize that this test wasn't about them, but a test for Trulliç against himself.

Could he trace the water without getting lost this time?

Riyune was a solid weight against Trulliç's thigh, warm and comforting. The dog never looked like anything other than a dog. He never had an aura, no matter how often Trulliç checked. The dog wasn't a familiar, though Trulliç still claimed he was sometimes.

Mostly Riyune was just like any other dog. Except he never barked. Never showed his teeth. Always managed to avoid Trulliç's cousins when they would try to kick the dog or if they threw something at him.

Trusting that Riyune would keep him grounded, Trulliç sent his senses down into the cool earth.

Again, he found that layer of clay that lay just under the dirt. He felt it was why the garden grew so well—the water gathered near the roots of the plants instead of sinking further into the thirsty ground.

Further down, Trulliç followed the water to Atça's well. It fed off the main water pool that Trulliç felt spread out under most of Gaadiwala.

He headed north, following the main pool, trying not to get tangled in all the smaller streams that fed the main reservoir. Could he find the offshoot that led to his neighborhood well?

Was that it? It felt familiar, that closed off bladder. Rocks had tumbled into the stream that fed the smaller reservoir, blocking off the flow.

Trulliç backed up along the main stream. When he felt his attention drawn by one of the smaller streams, the steady warmth of Riyune against his thigh brought him back.

Why was it all so distracting? Trulliç wished he could ask Atça about it, but he knew that Atça would tell Trulliç that he couldn't trust his senses, so why was he bothering with this?

Finally, Trulliç found where the main stream of water had been blocked. Another underground chamber had been opened up. It felt new to Trulliç, and it had a regular shape, not the long, skinny, natural shapes of the existing water reservoirs.

Why was the water for his neighborhood well being siphoned into there? No wonder the water at the well had been so low!

He didn't like this new place. The water belonged to his neighborhood well, not to this greedy opening.

Riyune nudged Trulliç's thigh. He caught a sense of urgency from the dog. He didn't have a lot of time.

He still didn't have a lever to nudge the rocks aside. Did he have to be gentle, though?

Trulliç pushed himself into the ground, imaging that he had roots growing out of the bottom of his spine, then with all his force, he focused his will on the rocks blocking the flow of water and *pushed*.

The rocks dissipated into the earth, leaving a large space behind them. But Trulliç wasn't finished. He traced the main trail of water back to *his* well, shoving rocks out of the way so the water had a clear path.

When Trulliç came back to the afternoon in Atça's garden, he found the other two boys had left. Which was good, because Trulliç hadn't actually raised any water up, like he'd boasted he would.

Atça stood over him, his face as thunderous as the first rain of spring.

"How dare you change the water flow?" Atça yelled at Trulliç.

"Everyone needs water," Trulliç said stubbornly. Water rights were important. They caused blood feuds.

But it meant that Atça knew about how low the water level had grown in Trulliç's neighborhood well. *He* had probably been the one who had directed the water elsewhere.

"Are you the town magician for Gaadiwala?" Atça asked angrily.

"No, sir," Trulliç said, shaking his head.

"Did it not occur to you that I might have had a plan for the extra water? That it might have been put to better use in the new area?" Atça said.

"No, sir," Trulliç said. "But—"

"Yes, I know, you've started seeing less water out in your slum," Atça said. "I would have taken care of you as well."

"Really?" Trulliç asked sarcastically, then instantly regretted it.

Atça raised his hand but didn't strike Trulliç like he normally did.

"Go. Now. And do not return until after you get back from the desert," Atça said sternly. "If you come back."

"What do you mean?" Trulliç asked, alarmed.

"You get lost in your head too often," Atça said. "Trusting your *magical* senses instead of paying attention to what's right in front of your nose. I predict the desert will take you before you figure out how to live there."

Trulliç nodded but didn't say anything. He had hoped his mentor would give him more instruction for his time in the desert.

It scared him, though, for Atça to voice Trulliç's deepest fear. He trudged away from Atça's house, his heart heavy.

The desert was his home. But he couldn't live there. Couldn't live in town, either. This hadn't been the first time that Trulliç's magic had interfered with Atça's. And Atça was the town magician. Trulliç had no standing in Gaadiwala. The emperor and everyone would always side with Atça, no matter what Etzalat and the others might think.

What was he going to do?

CHAPTER SIX

NADEEM

A HAND ACROSS NADEEM'S MOUTH brought her instantly out of her deep sleep.

She didn't start, however, or struggle. Her training took over instead—the three long years she'd spent working hard to become one of the emperor's stars. She wouldn't be *the* youngest at nineteen, but she would be one of the younger sisters.

Before Nadeem opened her eyes, she took a deep breath and tried to assess the situation. The hand across her mouth felt small and solid. Strong enough to choke her if that had been her assailant's intent. It smelled of dirt. Blood. And familiar sweat, too.

Çara. The youngest of Nadeem's team of six. The newest member assigned to them by the aunts, still wet behind the ears and unsure of herself, her place.

Nadeem opened her eyes but didn't struggle to get away.

Çara looked scared. The whites of her eyes shone, reflecting the single torch that burned just beyond her. Her mouth looked bruised, and dirt lay in streaks across her forehead, as if she'd brushed away sweat with earth-covered fingers. The left shoulder of her unbleached, plain chemise had torn and flopped down, exposing her breast. Wild curls, tangled with twigs, circled her head.

The cave roof above Nadeem looked the same—full of harsh rocks and beaded stalactites that she always feared would break off and kill her some night. This meant she was still in her own quarters out in the training zone, on the eastern coast of the Tanesh Empire, just east of the Qaenev desert.

Other than Çara's harsh breathing, Nadeem couldn't hear anything. Not the faint breath of wind that generally blew up coast, across the fertile Nusaybil valley and up into the foothills, nor the occasional drip of water caused by the condensation of moisture from sweaty bodies and humid breath, not even the murmuring or gentle snores of her team who lived in the cavern beside hers.

Nothing.

"They're gone," Çara whispered. "Taken."

Nadeem nodded sharply, showing that she was awake and understood. The drugs the aunts had given her earlier that night to help her sharpen her vision hadn't really worn off, but Nadeem wouldn't let that stop her. She aggressively pushed back against the fuzzy feeling inside her head, forcing saliva into her mouth and swallowing past the dryness there.

"When?" Nadeem asked as she sat up. Every muscle protested as if she'd been running and climbing for the last few hours instead of passed out, dreaming.

"Just after you left with the aunts," Çara replied. "Two, maybe three hours ago." Çara shuddered. "Slavers."

Nadeem's breath caught. How had they gotten so far inside the defenses? Who had they bribed? How many of her sisters had been killed?

"I got away. You must go rescue the others," Çara said fiercely. Her eyes held a wide-eyed stare, as if the horror of what she'd seen still lived with her.

"You must go," Çara repeated.

Nadeem looked at the girl closely. Had she been drugged? She didn't appear to be fully herself. Nadeem leaned closer to her for a moment, disguising the movement as a stretch. She didn't smell anything sweet or acidic in Çara's breath.

Then Çara tapped her right knee with her middle finger three times.

It was a signal that Nadeem and her team had come up with, part of their private language so that they could communicate among themselves and not even the aunts would know.

Test.

"I will rescue them," Nadeem said clearly.

She and her team knew that the final test was coming. They were near the end of their training.

Nadeem had assumed that the test would involve all of them from the start. She should have known better and run more individual drills.

But the aunts wouldn't kill the rest of Nadeem's team if she failed. Or actually sell them to the slavers who trolled the coast, looking for innocent girls to cart off to the decadent courts of the east or service the barbarian hoards.

Probably.

"You stay here," Nadeem told Çara as she got off her sleeping platform, stretching as she stood.

What had the aunts given Nadeem to make her so sluggish? This had to be part of the test, to see how Nadeem functioned when she wasn't at her peak.

They'd be surprised at how fast she'd recover. Since assembling her team, Nadeem had taken to building tolerances to most of the soporifics that the star sisters commonly used.

"Tell the aunts what happened if I'm not back by dawn," Nadeem said. That gave her at least three hours to track down the slavers and rescue the remaining four members of her team.

Nadeem quickly dressed in black pants that clung to her legs, giving her more movement, as well as a plain black blouse. She tied a black scarf around her head, low on her forehead to keep the sweat out of her eyes. She chose to tie plain leather strips to the soles of her feet —she might need to climb up or down rocks, so the strips would be better than sandals. Last, but not least, she packed up her knives and blowgun.

None of what she had on was proper or what women generally wore.

However, it was what a star sister wore when she was training or on a mission. Nadeem could always disguise her outfit using her magic if she needed to, to make it appear that she wore something more suited for traditional women.

Çara had already laid down on Nadeem's bed, her eyes closed, her breath regular and deep.

The aunts had probably given her something so Nadeem wouldn't be tempted to ask for Çara's help.

It didn't matter. Nadeem would rescue her team. Bring all four of the others back safe and alive. Even if this was just a test.

However, tests given by the aunts often had a bite. Nadeem was prepared to be bitten as well.

N adeem tasted the night as she stood in the shadows at the entrance of the cave her team used for shelter.

Even this far inland, the air carried more moisture than Nadeem was used to. It felt soft against her cheeks. The aunts didn't set watch fires at night. Though they could have hidden the light easily enough, it was better to train the girls to work in darkness.

Still, Nadeem smelled something burning. She took another moment to glance up, placing the Shepherd's Light—one of the stars that stayed in the east and was generally visible. The moon had already set, but the stars abounded, giving her enough light to see.

Nadeem slipped from the entrance of the cave, heading for the shadows of the grove of *meslit* trees that grew to her left, along the ridge. In the desert, *meslit* didn't grow much past knee height. Here, where there was more moisture, they grew far above Nadeem's head. The thorns increased in size as well—instead of being spindly and not much longer than a thumbnail, they were as thick as a stake and easily the length of Nadeem's palm.

Though Nadeem had her customary three knives, plus a few others, she still plucked two thorns and stuck them at the back of her head scarf. They'd break easily if she tried to use them like a dagger, and their sharp sides made them difficult to hold onto without cutting her hands to shreds. However, the thorns had just enough weight to be used as throwing knives, and accurately too, if one had enough practice.

Nadeem made sure that all of her team practiced.

Just beyond the trees, Nadeem took the path down, toward the valley. A few feet to her left lay the abrupt edge of the cliff. Off that was a short way down to a sure death. To her right, the path stayed open for a bit, then, as it descended, cliff walls rose above her.

Slavers traditionally sailed up the east coast of the Tanesh empire, occasionally storming undefended towns. Mostly they kept their larger ships out in the Uluborlu sea and sailed smaller boats closer to shore, slipping up channels and attacking farms and communities.

The star sisters' training camp stood close to the top of Knife Ridge; a small mountain range that ran between the coast to the east and the Qaenev desert to the west. The slavers wouldn't take the captives west toward the desert. No, they'd go back to the coast.

Nadeem skimmed along the beaten dirt path, glad for her foot coverings. They wouldn't last more than a couple hours before they'd be torn to shreds once she started going across the rocks. Knife Ridge grew along a sharp line. Its stones were black, sharp, and brittle. Many looked like cloth that had been attacked by moths, full of holes.

In a pinch, the sharp rocks could also be used as weapons, but Nadeem hoped it wouldn't come to that.

Far below Nadeem, where the path switched back, she saw a fire burning.

Stupid of the slavers to light such a bright beacon.

A dark shape lay across the path.

Nadeem had no place to hide, so she went for the element of surprise and took off, running as quickly as she could toward the shape.

The shape resolved itself into a prone body. Nadeem recognized the clothes first—a plain tunic, shirt and long full pants—a star sister.

Nadeem's pulse suddenly sounded loud in her ears. Was this one of her team?

She stopped and squatted down next to the body. The girl lay on her side. Nadeem tugged her onto her back while reaching for the pulse at her neck.

Zarahat.

Nadeem took a deep breath of relief.

She was one of the younger girls, not one of Nadeem's team members. She'd probably been guarding the path and had been surprised by the slavers coming up it. Blood covered the right side of her face. No pulse.

May your dance before the goddess be short, Nadeem mouthed silently as she closed Zarahat's one open eye. It was the most common of all blessings. The aunts could have a full service for the girl later, when Nadeem would pay her proper respects.

In the meanwhile, she had to make sure her team didn't end up in the same condition.

Nadeem took off again, skimming lightly along the path, keeping to her toes. She knew she could run like this for half a day, maybe longer if the terrain was mostly flat. She watched the ground carefully. It wouldn't do for her to trip or break an ankle because of some errant rock.

Just around the next bend, Nadeem slowed. There was only a single path up the hills. It zigged and zagged, narrow and steep, with parts where the cliff fell away on one side, while rising steeply on the other.

The star sisters always had it guarded, generally with more than one guard.

If the slavers were smart, they'd hide a guard just past the next bend, someone equipped to make noise to warn the raiders of anyone approaching.

Nadeem stopped briefly, examining the few feet of open space to her left.

One of the things Nadeem had excelled at since coming to the training camp was climbing. She had a great sense of balance and could always find finger and toeholds in the rock. Wrestling continued to be her worst sport: though Nadeem had a long reach with her six-foot height, she didn't have the weight of the other girls.

Nor did she generally exercise the patience to wear down an opponent.

If this was a test—the final test—then the aunts would expect her to use all her skills, both those she was good at as well as all the others she'd trained in.

Without looking back, Nadeem walked to the edge of the cliff. She'd never tried this climb, at least not at this point—she had climbed the face of this rock before, but further up, closer to the camp, and in full daylight.

If she fell—no one would rescue her.

Nadeem took a deep breath and swung herself over the edge. She couldn't see anything, the night and the rock were too dark.

She just had to trust her instincts.

Just as her team trusted her to get them out of this.

Her feet scrambled, seeking out the first toehold with her left foot.

Found it.

Then she lowered herself, finding the next toehold, her fingers digging into the rock.

She trembled, her muscles already exhausted.

Nadeem pushed herself, taking another deep breath to calm her fear, focusing on the task at hand.

She could defeat this rock. Rescue her team. Finish this test triumphant.

Become one of the emperor's stars.

***

Nadeem looked over her shoulder again. It was so hard to judge just how far above the path she was! She cursed the aunts again.

But she couldn't find any more toeholds in the rock. The cliff face had been sheared off, like a fine sheep's coat. Nadeem knew if she landed on something or didn't have solid footing, she'd tumble down the rocks and land broken at the bottom. If she pushed out too far, she wouldn't land on the narrow path below her, and would instead tumble off and keep falling.

She opened her jaw, making sure she wasn't clenching it. She needed to be loose for this. With one last large exhale, she pushed off, dropping down.

The fall went on for much longer than Nadeem expected.

Or maybe she just so scared that time seemed to stretch and expand.

Impact.

Nadeem's ankles twinged. She rolled, absorbing the shock. Forced herself to a stop.

The path was very narrow here. The cliff's edge going down lay inches away.

Nadeem took a deep breath. Stood.

Her ankles still hurt, but she hadn't broken or sprained them either.

Stop shaking, she ordered herself.

Her knees felt weak and her head swam.

At least two toenails had broken off in her climb, and a fingernail had split. The skin on the tips of her fingers had been sliced open by the sharp rocks. Nadeem had stopped more than once to suck the blood away, shaking her hand to dry it quickly.

She couldn't afford to lose her grip.

Focus.

Where was the slaver's fire?

Nadeem couldn't see it from her vantage point. She still smelled it, off to her right.

She checked her knives, her blowgun, the thorns still stuck into her scarf. Then she took off along the path again. The night felt more quiet to her, the light of the stars dimmed. How much time did she have before dawn? The climb had taken her longer than she'd expected.

Fortunately, after a short while, Nadeem passed above the raiders. She dropped to the dirt, then crawled to the edge of the cliff to look down.

The raiders had camped at a broad spot. The path ran straight along the climbing rock face, but there were several feet between it and the edge of the cliff going down. The place they'd chosen would be easy to defend, both from above and below the path.

They'd banked their fire, but Nadeem could still see the embers, still smell the smoke.

Where was her team being held? Nadeem couldn't see enough of the camp to determine how many raiders waited for her. Half a dozen? Maybe more?

She decided the slavers would place her team as close to the edge of the cliff as possible. That way, there would be one less direction for them to escape, unless they decided to throw themselves off and kill themselves.

It also meant the raiders could easily intimidate their hostages by threatening them with the cliffs below.

Could Nadeem get past the raiders, then climb up the cliff to rescue her sisters? Not before dawn. She could climb down the bit of rock just below her, so she could avoid the guards on the path at the next bend. But then she'd have to climb up another cliff face, and if she remembered correctly, it was more sheer than the one she'd just negotiated.

Nadeem made herself wait and watch for another hundred heartbeats. No one stirred at the camp. The guards must be the only ones awake, and they were on the path, above and below the camp. No one stood guard in the actual camp itself.

That would make it easier.

Nadeem didn't care what happened once she'd freed her team. They could fight their way out. They'd trained well and hard and were good enough to defeat two dozen untrained men, even if they carried swords and whips.

After another hundred heartbeats, Nadeem slipped over the next cliff edge. If this was the final test, the aunts were certainly putting her through her paces.

Nadeem's muscles trembled as she found the first toeholds. She couldn't see. She was going to fall. Going to fail.

No.

Nadeem found the next finger-hold. She balanced on her left foot and swung her right across the rock, banging her knee.

But she found a tiny ledge, a place where she could stand and breathe for a moment.

Then she forced herself to continue, her heart pounding hard in her ears.

She felt like saying a blessing every time she found the next toehold, every inch she traveled closer to the ground.

This time, there were holds all the way down the rock.

The smell of feces rose as Nadeem got closer to the path. Ugh. She tried to move to the side, and barely managed to avoid stepping in a huge pile of shit.

The slavers had been using the wall for doing their business. Were these men barbarians? Why didn't they dig a proper latrine? Or were they just too lazy to do so much work for a single night?

Nadeem stayed crouched down next to the wall, forcing herself to adjust to the stench. She didn't cover herself in their filth, though she considered it for a moment. Then she realized they wouldn't be smelling anything over their own filth, so it really wasn't necessary.

No star sister had enough talent to make themselves invisible. Nadeem was as good as most, though, when it came to being unnoticed.

The guards standing at the top and bottom of the path would be watching the dark carefully, so she wouldn't be able to slip by them.

Hopefully, though, she could get up close enough to rescue her team without being seen.

Nadeem put her hands wide in front of her, willing the flesh to *blur*. The edges along her spread fingers grew less distinct. Anyone trying to spot her would have more difficulty figuring out exactly where she started and where the night ended. Then she scurried across the path, heading directly for their fire.

Three mounds circled the banked embers: one pack and two bodies.

A mule brayed into the quiet night. Nadeem crouched down and froze.

No wonder they'd been so bold, climbing up Knife Ridge. Pack animals would make it much easier to cart away unwilling victims.

Nadeem would still bet that they'd been paid—and paid well—by the aunts to enact this test. And Çara had known it was a test. She'd probably gotten away before the slavers had made it too far down the path, before they'd camped for the night. Slipped away before anyone had realized she was gone.

The slavers didn't realize the death that awaited them. Even if Nadeem failed, the aunts would still never let them leave the ridge alive.

It must have been some bribe to have gotten them there…

Focus. Nadeem had to get to her team and get them out of there first. Then she could worry about how the aunts had arranged all this. It seemed awfully elaborate for a final test.

Nadeem stayed crouching and waddled across the open space, moving slowly but steadily. The snores (as well as the stench!) of the slavers rolled over her, but she willed it not to stay with her.

Pay attention to the night. The soft sighs. The smell of the fire.

The smell of her team.

There. To the right.

Nadeem had guessed correctly—the other four members of her team had been placed close to the edge of the cliff. Bound tightly with thick ropes. Gagged. Unconscious. Bruised and beaten.

Galbril. Duzhen. Yalovreen. Nikzhar.

Nadeem went first to Galbril. She was the wrestler of the team, big boned and strong as a mule. Stubborn as one, too. She'd been the first one that Nadeem had been paired with by the aunts, the first of their team.

Nadeem woke her like she'd been woken, a hand over Galbril's mouth, though she also pinched the other woman's nose.

The eyes that opened looked startled and crazed, moving from side to side rapidly, trying to take everything in at once.

When Galbril's eyes finally slowed, staring straight at Nadeem with sanity again, Nadeem lifted her hand off. She untied the gag and used her first knife to saw through Gabril's bindings around her wrists.

When Galbril had rubbed circulation back into her hands, Nadeem handed her a second knife so she could free Duzhen. Another wrestler, though not as big as Galbril. She had the best sight and often scouted for the team, seeing traps and illusions that the other missed. Gabril had asked for Duzhen to be partnered with them, and after watching her win more than one sprinting contest, Nadeem had agreed.

Duzhen woke more quietly, her eyes immediately focused on Nadeem and burning with anger.

Despite the seriousness of the situation, Nadeem felt a smile cross her lips for the first time that night. The only thing that kept Duzhen from spouting obscenities and cursing all the gods was her gag.

Nadeem waited another moment, getting an eye roll from Duzhen before she undid the gag. Duzhen would either wait and start her cursing later, or she'd begin right away, but silently.

Gabril went to work freeing Duzhen's hands while Nadeem woke the others.

Guards, Nadeem signaled them once they'd were ready. She pointed up and down the path.

Gabril nodded. *Ten more*, she signaled.

Nadeem nodded. A dozen men in all, then, at least. She pointed to Nikzhar, then indicated their strongest illusionist should take out the guard going up the hill.

Nikzhar nodded, then grimaced and shook her head. She motioned for Nadeem to come closer.

"My leg is broken," she whispered against Nadeem's ear.

Nadeem looked down, alarmed.

Wait.

Nikzhar's legs looked fine. They weren't covered in bruises or swollen.

Nadeem reached out and pushed against Nikzhar's left thigh.

The girl didn't cry out, but she did gasp. Her eyes welled with tears. "I'm sorry," she whispered. "Just leave me behind."

"But your leg isn't broken," Nadeem whispered back.

"Yes, it is," Gabril said.

Nadeem looked at the wrestler, then looked back at Nikzhar.

Her leg now bore massive bruises and had swollen to twice the size it should have been.

Nadeem cursed silently.

How much of this test was actually real? How much of it was merely an illusion, cast by a group of aunts working in concert?

How much could Nadeem ignore? How much did she have to play by their rules?

The roaring of a barbarian slaver from behind her answered her questions. At least for now, all she could do was fight.

Nadeem dodged the blow of the ugly, hairy slaver in front of her, then used her momentum, turning, to lay a solid blow across his ribs.

But the stupid barbarian didn't go down.

Nadeem had the reach on him. She could dodge most of his blows. But he was frighteningly strong.

Her team wasn't doing much better. They all fought to the best of their abilities, Nikzhar using a stolen bow to keep at least some of the barbarian hoard at bay.

But more slavers kept coming. Nadeem knew it wasn't right. There weren't that many men to start with. The others just appeared, though.

The aunts had to be behind this. It was an unwinnable battle. Just like the first one that Aunt Izmet had designed to test Nadeem, to see if she was willing to go beyond the rules and join the emperor's stars.

A desert hawk cried out above Nadeem's head, distracting her.

Thunk. The barbarian landed a solid blow against Nadeem's ribs.

They didn't crack. But she knew she couldn't take much more. She'd started weak, and the fighting had only weakened her further.

The hawk, though. It was her personal totem. The symbol of her team. Her favorite illusionary fighter.

If this battle wasn't real (despite how her ribs hurt, her legs trembled, her ragged fingertips bled) then Nadeem should be able to call up her hawk-girl.

"Cover me!" she shouted to Gabril as she took two steps back, withdrawing from the melee.

She could do this. She could find the thread. Pull them out of this illusion. Before they all suffered permanent damage or died.

Nadeem focused back on Nikzhar's leg. It looked broken, swollen, and bruised. Nikzhar's face was pale, sweat running freely from her forehead and down her back. She watched the battle with ultimate concentration, before she hefted another knife into the fray.

It didn't matter if she took out her mark or not. Another barbarian would just step up.

Nadeem turned away from Nikzhar. She couldn't let herself get distracted by guessing if the girl's leg was actually broken or not.

Instead, Nadeem raised her head and her arms toward the sky. "Hawk sister!" she cried. "I call to you. Come join our battle. Fight with us toward glorious victory!"

A desert hawk's warning cry echoed across the sky.

She would not come closer. This wasn't her fight.

Desperate, Nadeem changed her call. "Transform me! Give me your golden eyes! Your bone-breaking beak! The feathers that protect and defend you!"

A stillness passed through the air above Nadeem, like an impossible cloud crossing the eye of the sun in the middle of the desert.

Nadeem started to change. Her bones grew lighter as she expanded. Blue skin traveled from her outstretched fingertips and up her arms. The world grew sharper and the day grew brighter.

Instead of giving words of thanks, Nadeem issued a great, loud *CAW!*

When Nadeem turned back to the battle, she realized she towered over the others. With graceful movements, she reached out and one by one touched the heads of her team.

Gabril turned into the mule fighter she resembled, her braying laugh echoing out over the valley as she landed a solid kick on the barbarian in front of her.

Duzhen took on the features of a mountain cat, spitting and hissing at her opponent, still cursing in her own way.

Yalovreen surprised Nadeem. Instead of becoming more like the lizard creature she generally fought illusionary battles with, she grew a great set of butterfly wings, colored every shade of blue, from the palest white-blue to the darkest blue-black.

Spiked wings that could slice an opponent in two.

Even Nikzhar changed, her leg mending itself as she rose up, her skin growing woody and covered in thorns—a walking *meslit* tree, set to do as much damage as she could.

The barbarians gasped, as if they shared a single breath.

Then they surged forward, ten, twenty, thirty or more.

Nadeem gave her cawing battle cry again.

It didn't matter how many opponents they faced.

Now, they could win.

"No one has ever figured out the final test was an illusion so quickly," Aunt Izmet said proudly, squeezing Nadeem's hand. "In fact, most of the teams have to be tested more than once before they pass. How did you do it?"

Nadeem stirred sluggishly, searching for the words. Every muscle hurt. Her fingertips actually had been torn to shreds by her great climb. That part of the test had been real. She would have died if she'd made a single misstep.

The aunts had expected her to fight her way through the guards to her team. Not to avoid them and go around.

Nadeem lay in Aunt Izmet's tent on a well-cushioned pallet stuffed with feathers, with soft furs propped up behind her to help her sit. Diffuse sunlight lit the brown cloth, making the tent seem more open and airy. Not only did the tent flap stand propped open, Aunt Izmet's tent had window openings as well, letting the cool afternoon breezes in.

"Nikzhar's leg wasn't broken," Nadeem finally said. She slowly reached for the tea beside her, taking a deep sip. Her lips had split open, and all the exposed skin on her face and neck had blistered and burned—she and her team had evidentially fought the aunt's illusions in the bright sunlight for far too long.

"Interesting," Aunt Izmet said. "I'll have a talk with the council later to see what happened."

Nadeem shrugged. It would never occur to Aunt Izmet that the problem had been that the aunts had underestimated Nadeem and her team.

Aunt Izmet believed too much in her own power and the power of the emperor. She didn't question things like Aunt Parayat had taught Nadeem.

It made Nadeem uncomfortable sometimes, the unquestioning loyalty that Aunt Izmet demanded, that Nadeem tried to give.

The battle had been glorious, and one that poems should be written about.

But no one could hear the details of it. It was part of her secret training.

A question nagged at Nadeem's fuzzy brain. She had to take two more sips of the sweet and salty tea before she found the words. "Did I pass?"

Aunt Izmet's grin answered her. "I already have your first assignment. From the emperor himself."

Aunt Izmet's voice took on a fanatical fervor that it often did when she talked of the emperor.

Nadeem had learned to parrot the tone back, but Aunt Parayat's voice, questioning everything, still sounded at the back of her mind.

For now, though, Nadeem didn't have to question. She'd passed. It was enough.

"Good," Nadeem said, as she lay back down.

She'd finally made it. She was one of the emperor's stars.

There was that voice again. Aunt Parayat. Warning Nadeem about being careful what she wished for.

Today, Nadeem decided she couldn't be happier that one of her wishes had finally come true.

CHAPTER SEVEN

TRULLIÇ

TRULLIÇ SAT ABOVE THE DESERT. Riyune sat beside him. Trulliç had brought sticks and a heavy piece of brown tent cloth in his pack, then built an impromptu lean-to, so he sat in the shade on the final Kinarak foothill, before scrub and dirt transformed into sand.

The desert called to Trulliç. It promised soft paths for his feet, sweet dates and cinnamon bark, an endless blue sky to bring joy to his heart.

The desert lied.

Trulliç knew as soon as he stepped one foot onto the sands, he'd be lost. He'd wander, drawn on by the promise of shelter or water, only to have the desert laugh cruelly at him.

Maybe not this trip, but perhaps the next, or the one after that, the desert would take all of Trulliç, strip his skin from his bones, greedily drink his blood, absorb all of him into itself and then go looking for its next victim.

The desert didn't give life. It only took.

Trulliç now understood the bards in the marketplace who sang of a cruel mistress, who stole their hearts and then didn't return their love.

Trulliç couldn't look away from the desert. Even when he closed his eyes he still saw its golden sands spread out before him. If he wasn't careful, he'd wander from his camp straight down the hill.

But why should he go into the desert this time? It was his fourth trip since his initial manhood journey. He was sixteen. He wouldn't find his true home. Despite all his dreams of the desert, it never showed him the same place twice.

Maybe it was finally time to put aside boyhood dreams and fancies and grow up, like Atça always told him. Stop daydreaming about the desert, face the reality that he would never become a powerful magician. His glass horseshoe was just another trick, an illusion cast by the blood hound. Trulliç needed to accept that he would only ever do small magics on the fringes of another magician's territory.

Trulliç angrily pressed his palms against his eyes, pushing out the tears welling up. He wouldn't cry, not for the desert. It was his true home, he couldn't deny that.

He'd never be able to live there, though.

He gave himself the rest of the day to watch the sands, to dream of tiny lizards who scuttled from one rock to the next, to listen to the desert hawks and their lonely cries, to taste the sweet water from hidden rivers, to feel the scorching winds and the abrasive sand they carried.

When the sun was on the far horizon, Trulliç finally stood. He rolled up the cloth and sticks, carefully tying them to his bag. After one long last look, his eyes sweeping all the way across the sands, he firmly turned his back on the desert and started back up the hill.

An eerie, high-pitched noise came from behind him.

Was that the desert calling to him? Was she finally ready to show him all her secrets, give him the ability to live on her sands?

But no. It was merely Riyune, whining.

Trulliç had never heard Riyune make a sound. The dog never barked or growled.

"I'm not going," Trulliç told Riyune. He kept his attention focused firmly on the dog, not even sneaking a peek at the golden sands that still beckoned at the foot of the hill. "I can't."

Trulliç sniffed but didn't let any more tears come. He was done with his mourning for his true home.

Time to move on.

Riyune whined again, looking from Trulliç to the desert and back again.

"You can go if you need to," Trulliç said softly. He'd miss Riyune terribly, he knew. The dog strengthened his magic and was always there when Trulliç felt alone.

Riyune had come from the desert. He belonged there, more than Trulliç.

Trulliç had never believed that Riyune was his familiar. In the ancient stories, the familiars interacted more with their magicians, talked plainly, and cast their own magic.

Riyune had never done any of those things.

Plus, Trulliç believed that he'd feel some sort of bond with Riyune if the dog was truly his familiar. He'd never be able to suggest that the dog just go.

Riyune sat stubbornly in the path, growing perfectly still, as if he'd turned into a statue. Trulliç had seen him do that more than once.

Would the dog stay frozen this time? Or just disappear, like a ghost?

"I can't," Trulliç said again. He figured Riyune would know what he meant.

Though it broke his heart, Trulliç turned away from the desert and started walking up the hill.

Riyune didn't whine again.

After twenty steps, the dog also hadn't joined Trulliç.

A second ache settled in on top of the first wrapped around Trulliç's heart.

He was on his own, now.

He didn't drag his feet, or start walking more slowly.

He'd made his decision like a man. He would have to face the consequences on his own as well.

When Trulliç reached the top of the foothill, he was tempted to turn and look back. But he knew he wouldn't see the desert from there—the path wound back and forth up the steep hill to the pass. He did pause and breathe for a moment. His mage light shone above his head, giving him enough light to continue walking

Just ahead he knew there was a small shelter where he could spend the night before he walked back down the other side to Gaadiwala.

Suddenly, Trulliç's mage light flared.

He looked up, startled.

A white streak flew past his legs.

His heart beating hard, Trulliç looked down.

Riyune sat in front of him, looking as though he'd been waiting there all along. He nodded once to Trulliç, as if to say, *Come on, then.* Then he turned and trotted down the path, toward the shelter.

For the first time in a few days, Trulliç felt his heart grow lighter.

It would be hard, he knew, turning his back on the desert as he had.

Perhaps, though, his journey forward would be a bit easier with a friend by his side.

***

Atça looked like the cat who'd just gotten into the cream when he opened the door and saw Trulliç standing there. He wore his green silk morning robes. "Didn't even step on the sands, did you?" he asked.

Trulliç shook his head, ashamed. "I would have gotten lost," he said. Atça had even said that was what would happen to him. "I decided not to get lost," Trulliç added, looking up. Instead of stopping at home, he still had his pack on his back, coming straight from walking down the pass.

"So you're leaving the desert for good?" Atça purred.

"For now," Trulliç told him firmly. He didn't think he could ever leave the desert for good. She was in his heart, her sand in his blood, her rocks adhering to his bones.

Atça gave him a sour look at that. He cross his arms over his chest and stared at Trulliç for a few moments.

Would his mentor reject him? Because he wouldn't completely refuse the desert?

"I see you still have that mangy mutt with you," Atça added.

Trulliç nodded. He wasn't going to tell Atça of how Riyune had almost left him.

Riyune would leave him, someday. That much he knew.

At least it wasn't now.

"I may, just may, have an assignment for you," Atça told Trulliç after another long moment. "Come back at dusk."

Trulliç nodded, then backed away when Atça firmly shut the door in his face.

An assignment? So maybe Atça had forgiven Trulliç for messing with the water flows under Gaadiwala?

Trulliç took a deep breath, relief trickling over him.

He knew he was still on Atça's "troublemaker" list.

But maybe if he did well with this assignment, he could get back into the good graces of his mentor.

Trulliç dreamed he was walking over a sand dune when the ground started shaking and the sand started skittering away.

It took him a moment to realize he'd been asleep and his mother was shaking him awake. He brushed the sleep from his eyes and swallowed against a dry throat.

"What happened?" Mother asked, pushing aside his blankets and looking at his body and legs. "Are you hurt?"

"No," Trulliç said, pushing himself up to sitting. "I...I couldn't stay. In the desert."

Mother went from frantic worry to icy stillness. "I see." She sat back, pushing herself away from Trulliç. She still wore her *chafiyek* scarf covering her gray-streaked hair, the blue and gold one that she'd received from her husband so many years before. Her gray tunic bore smudges of soot from the ovens she worked behind the tavern, and the sleeves of her plain muslin blouse were tied up and out of the way.

"What are you doing home?" Trulliç asked. The light through the door was still bright, still daylight. Normally, Mother didn't get home from the tavern until it was dark, and frequently after it was night.

"Someone saw you in town," Mother said. "Asked me how your journey had gone."

"Oh," Trulliç said. He felt like squirming, but Mother didn't like it when he did that. "I did go talk with Atça already. He may have an assignment for me."

"An assignment?" Mother asked. She pursed her lips together in disapproval. "A *job*?"

"Yes?" Trulliç said, unsure of what Mother was unhappy about now.

"So instead of going into the desert to become a real magician, you've decided you're content with being another magician's lackey?" Mother asked angrily.

"That's not fair," Trulliç said hotly. "I can't live in the desert. Can't find my home. I need to do *something*."

"Did you even try?" Mother asked.

Trulliç sighed. She wouldn't understand. He would have gotten lost if he'd set foot on the sands. Never found his way back. The desert would have absorbed him, eaten him alive.

"I had such great hopes for you," Mother said quietly, turning away. "All those miles I walked with you strapped to my back. Telling myself that it would all be all right if I could just get home."

Trulliç nodded. She'd told him her heartache more than once. It wasn't his fault that he wasn't a better magician, more powerful.

Mother shook her head. "'Children will lead their own lives'," she said. "My mother told me that before I went north with Alpheais, your father." She pushed herself up, brushing off her long skirt. "I thought I knew what she meant. I didn't realize it might mean that they would choose *not* to live."

With that, Mother swept out of the door.

Trulliç stayed where he was, trying to breathe. It wasn't that Mother had taken all the air out of the tiny shack with her, but it suddenly felt closed in and confining.

Mother had talked more than once about how Trulliç had howled when they'd first reached Gaadiwala, how he couldn't stand to be indoors. It was why they lived outside of town.

Trulliç threw back his blankets and strode out of the shack, standing in the yard, the chickens scattering in front of him, then settling down again quickly to their quiet clucking and scratching.

Riyune appeared beside Trulliç, as if summoned. He stood with his head cocked to one side. What was he asking?

"I can't," Trulliç whispered. He realized he was standing with his back directly to the desert, that it stretched out behind him, calling to him, even over the foothills and through the pass.

Trulliç reached down for the glass horseshoe that he always carried, that emblem of his birthright.

Was it, too, a lie?

The smooth glass brought him no comfort, as well as no hint of his destiny. He clenched it tightly in his fist. Raised his hand. Shook with anger, disappointment bitter on his tongue.

Then he made himself lower his hand.

He would not throw the glass horseshoe across the yard, send it skittering through the chicken poop and dirt.

Instead, he secured it away again. Best to keep it out of sight.

There was nothing magical about the talisman. Atça said it was plain glass. Trulliç believed him.

Trulliç still held onto it. Maybe as a promise that one day there would be more for him. That the desert would welcome him, tell him her secrets, not just consume him and keep him all for herself.

That there was hope, as fragile as the glass might be.

Evening stole gently across the sky, darkening the clear blue to a softer color, then turning slowly to black. Trulliç felt odd, walking through the town as the lights went on in people's houses. He heard children crying for their dinner, old men saying evening prayers as they knelt before altars, young women chasing the chickens back into the yard.

He knew that the town would soon sleep. Not much happened in these neighborhoods after the sun fully set. The tavern would keep going for a while, full of the first travelers of the spring and good ale.

Atça opened the door before Trulliç knocked, issuing him into the house. Trulliç paused momentarily to change out of his sandals into house slippers before following his mentor.

They didn't turn into the learning room, or the front sitting room. Instead, Atça led Trulliç to the meeting room, where he sometimes held private court with rich merchants and farmers who could pay his fees.

Trulliç hadn't been in this room often. It smelled of sweet frankincense burning on the altar to Serril in the corner. Wood covered the walls, of course. Shelves, also made out of wood, held Atça's many folded books, as well as scrolls and maps. A rich red-and-gold rug covered the floor. In the center lay many pillows and backrests, so guests could lounge comfortably.

Maybe Mother would be less disappointed with Trulliç's choice when he told her about this meeting. Then again, she'd probably just make a snide remark about bribes and cheap whores. She'd already made her displeasure known about Trulliç doing an assignment for Atça.

Atça already had his tea set ready. The pungent odor of mint, cardamom, and fine black tea wafted toward Trulliç as he sat. Riyune stayed near the door, as was his habit. But instead of laying down and sleeping, he took on his statue pose, legs in front of him as if ready to accept offerings.

Atça looked at Riyune, then back at Trulliç. "I swear he does that just to disturb me," the old magician muttered.

Trulliç bit his lips together to hide his smile. Riyune had never hidden from Trulliç just how much he didn't care for Atça. He'd never made a mess on Atça's fine carpets or chewed any of the pillows. But he'd make sure he lay just exactly where Atça would trip on him. As well as turning completely motionless when it was just Atça and Trulliç.

Riyune was wrong to not like Atça. Atça had been Trulliç's mentor and teacher for a long time. Without him, Trulliç would have been lost the first time he'd stepped on the sands. He owed his teacher a lot.

"How may I serve you?" Trulliç asked after Atça had served the tea. The bitter taste washed through his mouth, leaving his senses clear.

Atça looked at Trulliç seriously. He wore his judging robes, fine black and blue silks, the color of the goddess of death, Berzhat. A golden girdle around his waist held the ceremonial dagger of office, presented to Atça by the emperor himself. Pearls from the far away sea encrusted the dagger's sheath, and fine silver covered both ends.

"What I am about to tell you can never leave this room," Atça told Trulliç.

Trulliç stiffened, sitting up straighter. "I swear to never tell a soul," he promised.

Atça nodded after staring at Trulliç for another moment, giving his words weight. "I've discovered a conspiracy. Of magicians. Against the emperor."

Trulliç swallowed against his suddenly dry throat. Magicians? Fighting against the emperor? They couldn't win. The emperor protected himself against all magicians by using the blood hounds to collect the afterbirth of every magician, then made himself a great cloak of scales from them.

No magician could fight against his own blood. In ancient times, the times of the old kings, weaker magicians were required to give the stronger magicians who lived nearby a vial of their blood.

Atça had never asked Trulliç for one. He'd assumed it was because he was such a weak magician Atça didn't need the extra protection.

"How may I help?" Trulliç asked. He would fight this beside Atça. Maybe this was his destiny!

He shook himself. No. He didn't have a grand destiny. He was a failed magician. He could only do his tiny part.

Hopefully it would be enough.

"I want you to travel to Çandekili and meet with Yerkoyliç, the town's magician." Atça leaned closer and whispered, "It's rumored that he's one of the ringleaders."

Trulliç blinked, confused. Why would Atça be sending him into this snake pit?

Atça leaned back and took another sip of his tea. "I want you to see how true this Yerkoyliç is. How loyal."

Trulliç nodded. He could probably do that, though he wasn't sure.

"And to deal with the matter, once you make your judgment."

The room suddenly grew very hot, as if the summer sun had just crept back over the horizon.

Atça wasn't looking at Trulliç anymore, but at Riyune.

The dog continued to do his impression of a statue.

Except—was that a glow coming from him?

No. Trulliç had to have just imagined that. Let his overly fanciful nature take over.

Then Atça turned his attention back to Trulliç. "So how is your dear mother?"

Trulliç knew that Atça wouldn't say another word about the matter. He wouldn't be so direct as to say how he intended Trulliç to deal with the matter.

But Trulliç knew.

If Yerkoyliç was not faithful, it would be up to Trulliç to kill him.

"You're going where?" Bekbel, Trulliç's oldest cousin, asked as he carefully tipped one of the dozen barrels of beer that crowded the cellar over onto its side. It came up to his mid-chest, made out of precious wood, reinforced with metal bands. A huge cork about the size of Bekbel's hand stayed connected solidly to one end.

Bekbel's muscles strained through his thin work shirt as he struggled with the barrel. The shirt was made of gray muslin and came down to mid-thigh. He wore loose brown pants and plain straw sandals. He had the same nose as Trulliç, small and sharp. His dark eyes didn't miss much, and his tongue was always biting.

"Çandekili," Trulliç bragged. He shivered despite himself. The rough rock walls kept the cellar cool even on the hottest days. It smelled musty, not like clean dirt, stale even though rinds of cheese were aging on racks along one side and the barrels of beer lined the other. "Atça wants me to meet with the town magician." He wasn't about to tell anyone that he was supposed to kill this other person.

Bekbel gave a low whistle. "Some secret magician's meeting, hmmm?" he asked.

"No, nothing like that," Trulliç assured him, lying through his teeth.

Bekbel nodded. "Right," he said, obviously not believing a word Trulliç had just said. "Little light here?"

Trulliç raised his mage light higher, sending the golden ball to float above Bekbel's head. Trulliç noticed with surprise that he was almost as tall as his oldest cousin. Bekbel was five years older, the oldest son of his mother's sister, and had always been one of the tallest cousins.

When had Trulliç gained that much height?

And what was he going to do about Yerkoyliç? What if he turned out to be in a plot to harm the emperor? Trulliç had never really considered killing someone. How was he going to do this? How could he make Atça proud of him?

"Sorry?" Trulliç said when he realized that Bekbel had asked a question.

"I said, is that why your mother's so angry? Because you're going to Çandekili?" Bekbel asked as he tipped over another barrel onto its side.

"She's just…disappointed in me. That I'm not living up to my destiny or something." Trulliç couldn't disguise the bitterness of his tone.

Bekbel nodded. "I remember one night last year, when your mom and mine got really, really drunk."

"Wait, you're talking about my mother? Myrizhah?" Trulliç asked, clarifying.

"Yup. They didn't know I was there. They were both bragging about their sons, trying to outdo each other." Bekbel paused, considering. "Of course, my mother had more to brag about than yours."

Trulliç snorted. "Of course." He'd never been good enough for his mother, for Atça, for anyone.

"It was before your third trip to the desert," Bekbel said. "And your mom was sure that that time, you'd find your home. And that she'd be able to escape Gaadiwala and the tavern and everyone and go live with you in the desert."

"Really?" Trulliç said, surprised. His mom had never even hinted that she wanted to live somewhere else.

"My mom teased her about shaving her head and becoming a nun or something," Bekbel said. "But your mom—she's always had dreams. Bigger than yours. Why else would she go off with some stranger she'd just met and get married?"

That made sense, actually. That his mother would want more than Trulliç, more than anyone else. "Well, I'm afraid I'm just going to disappoint her," he said, trying to swallow down his bitterness.

Bekbel shrugged. "Maybe. Maybe not," he said. "She might just go off and live in the desert without you. Or at least that's what she's threatened Grandma with."

Myrizhah had never gotten along that well with her mother. Then again, Trulliç hadn't known his mother to get along with anyone. She was too quick to speak her mind, too fast to storm out in anger, too slow to forgive. Atça had warned him that Trulliç would have to be careful around her, and would have to leave her behind someday.

Trulliç knew Myrizhah hadn't merely threatened to go live in the desert. If she'd mentioned it, that meant she already had a plan in place and was just waiting until she could put it into effect.

He swallowed around his pain.

Mother would abandon him. Particularly since he wasn't off doing his own magic, but doing the bidding of another magician.

"Hey, it's all right," Bekbel said. He was suddenly standing beside Trulliç.

"I'm fine," Trulliç said bravely. He noticed his mage light had dimmed considerably. "Let's get these barrels upstairs," he added.

"All right," Bekbel said slowly. "But you know, you have family, here in town. If you ever need anything."

"Like I would need help herding goats or something," Trulliç said.

"Might find an attractive one," Bekbel teased.

Trulliç helped Bekbel roll the first barrel to the foot of the ramp leading up, out of the cellar. While Trulliç helped physically push the barrel, he also applied his magic, making the barrel lighter so it rolled up the ramp with ease.

After they'd gotten the second one up the ramp and into the courtyard, Trulliç left his cousin and walked over to the ovens back there, to see what other work his mother might have for him since he was leaving the next day.

All the while, a single question rolled around and around in his head.

Would you help me go kill a stranger?

Trulliç couldn't ask his cousin that. Couldn't ask any of his family. Could only hope they wouldn't hate him if he failed.

Or worse, if he succeeded.

Trulliç noticed the weather ridge right away. In a very short distance the scrub changed from scraggly and wide spaced to taller and fuller. The leaves grew from finger thin to palm sized. The green of the leaves didn't change, and continued more gray than green. But grasses sprang up beside the bushes, as bright as the one season when Gaadiwala had had so much rain everything bloomed at the same time.

Then flowers started showing, hooded with bright yellow and white petals, followed with open-faced pink and gold flowers, then tiny pink and red clusters, and others, more flowers than Trulliç had ever seen. And not growing in gardens! But covering the ground. He couldn't name half of them.

Bees buzzed beside the road, along with flies and crickets. As Trulliç walked, he even passed a hidden pond that held belching frogs.

The closer Trulliç got to Çandekili, the more crowded the trade road grew. He passed at least three caravans with a dozen or more camels slowly ambling along. Other merchants ambled along with large packs on their backs.

When the trade road crested a slight rise, Trulliç got his first real look at Çandekili. He'd thought that it wasn't that much larger than Gaadiwala—he was wrong. It stood, walled and proud, in a green valley. He could barely see from the front gates to the back. How long would it take to walk from one end to the other? Half a day? Maybe more?

Stone houses cropped up like weeds, though the ones at the

center appeared to be on some sort of a grid. The roofs slanted either one direction or another, making the placement of the houses seem even more random. Dark brown and reddish rock made up most of the houses, though there were a few yellowish ones as well, and closer to the center of the town, some of the rock had been whitewashed.

The grand house in the very center of the town shone in the morning light, reflecting it as if it were coated in gold. Was that Yerkoyliç's house? Probably. Other large buildings stood beside it, though it was at least a story taller than them.

To the right, just inside the gate, stood an open square. Trulliç assumed that would be the marketplace. But what was that other open area, just inside the gates?

Suddenly, Trulliç was even less sure about his mission. Obviously Yerkoyliç was a powerful, important magician.

How could Trulliç even think about questioning his loyalty?

Or possibly kill him?

Trulliç stepped inside the gate of Çandekili with trepidation. He knew what Atça's magic felt like. He'd grown up with it. He didn't remember a time when his own magic wasn't influenced by it.

Yerkoyliç's magic had a sweeter flavor than Atça's. It felt lighter, too. Trulliç couldn't tell if it was stronger or weaker. Those didn't seem to be the right terms, either. Instead, Atça's magic felt dry, like the packed dirt that made up the streets of Gaadiwala, and it was as solid as the rocks of the foothills. Not laced with *meslit* syrup, but the fires that refined it, more smoky than sweet.

While Yerkyolic's magic felt like a garden, full of jasmine, gardenias, and other fragrant flowers. Instead of hard rock, there were soft breezes and fertile earth. It felt busy, too, like all the bees and ants and other insects that worked constantly all through the spring.

Houses crowded close to the street, looming over Trulliç. He took deep breaths, though the smell of so many people crowded close, so many fires and different smells, made him want to gag.

He told himself that there was enough air. He just had to keep breathing, despite how closed in everything felt.

The people here were different, as well. They seemed better dressed than the people in Gaadiwala, though they had the same look to them: tall, thin, with dark hair and dark eyes, wearing tunics over long-sleeved shirts. Some of the women wore full pants, though many wore long skirts. More than a few had aprons on. Almost everyone wore headscarves, though most were of flimsy material, not heavy enough to protect them from the sun.

No one bumped into Trulliç, or each other. He still felt hemmed in by so many bodies. He could count over a dozen nearby, with a dozen more scattered in the street in front of him and behind him.

Trulliç looked away from the crowd and up at the houses. Banners hung from the walls of every third one or so. He recognized the sandal maker, the lamp maker, as well as the oil merchant. He nearly stopped at the tinsmith's store, wanting to look at the horseshoes for babies.

A banner with a barrel painted on it adorned the next building, though the front windows and the door were closed. Was that a tavern? Why weren't they open yet?

Though Trulliç didn't see anyone looking at him—they must be used to strangers here—he still felt watched. Was it Yerkoyliç? Did he know that another magician had come to his town? Though Trulliç was only a minor magician, at best. He was probably too insignificant to be noticed.

He didn't know if that made him feel better or not.

Trulliç glanced down at Riyune. The dog clicked as he walked, his nails scraping the stones. Anyone else looking at Riyune would think he was a normal dog, walking along, just with unusual coloring and very strange eyes.

Trulliç knew better, however. Riyune was tense. Nervous. On guard, his head up, looking around, trying to keep track of everything around them.

"It'll be all right," Trulliç said softly.

He didn't need to see Riyune to know how the dog rolled his eyes at him.

The magic Trulliç felt swimming around him suddenly surged. It was like walking along a path and happening across a large flowering bush. Everything seemed brighter suddenly, and the smell of flowers was briefly overwhelming.

Trulliç stopped to sneeze, once, twice, three times.

When he looked back up, a large man hurried down the street toward him. Trulliç hadn't seen many of the emperor's guard—they rarely made it to such a small village as Gaadiwala. They had come a few years back, though, to collect the town's tribute to the emperor.

This man had the same look to him, built broad like a building, head shaved, all muscles. He wore a red-and-black striped tunic, and now that Trulliç had thought about it, he'd seen others in that same tunic, those same colors.

That answered that question.

Yes, Yerkoyliç and his magic did sense Trulliç. And had sent someone to deal with him.

CHAPTER EIGHT

NADEEM

NADEEM KEPT THE LOOK OF disgust off her face with ease, pretending instead to listen with great care to Aunt Izmet and her instructions for Nadeem's first assignment as one of the emperor's stars. They sat in Aunt Izmet's tent in the training camp, sipping tea in the cool evening. Soft breezes came up from the coast. The smell of spices came with them. Occasionally the *thunk* of knives hitting a target from the range next door wafted in.

It had taken Nadeem most of a week to heal from her final test to the point that she felt as though walking from her cavern to the eating tent no longer made her want to take a nap. It took a second week before she had regained her strength and felt as though she could try running or climbing again.

Luckily, Aunt Izmet had taken pity on her and brought her a small drop spindle she could use while still seated. Nadeem had always liked the feel of the thread slipping through her fingers, growing long and smooth as she spun thread from coarse hunks of wool.

Nadeem took another sip of her tea despite the revulsion rolling through her stomach. Aunt Izmet had sweetened it with *meslit,* but it still had a bitter aftertaste on the back of Nadeem's tongue.

She'd expected her first assignment to be easy. Though Nadeem had trained hard for three years to win her spot among the emperor's stars, she was still new. She accepted that, took the ribbing the older aunts gave her about being wet behind the ears as good naturedly as she could.

But this? Killing an old man in his sleep, so his death looked natural? Where was the honor in that? She hadn't expected they'd be rescuing orphans or looking for lost sheep in the Kinarak foothills. She had expected to be sent into battle somewhere, maybe in the barbarian lands to the north or east.

The emperor still fought the northern barbarians. Surely there was something that Nadeem could do that would be more useful than this assassination.

Aunt Izmet frowned at Nadeem as if she could read her thoughts. "This is strictly a political move by the emperor," she said sternly. "It isn't personal."

Nadeem contained her snort at that. Everything was personal. She'd learned that as a young girl at Aunt Parayat's feet. Her aunt had always insisted that Nadeem look beyond the first layer, to the second, or third face that lay beyond.

They were supposed to be masters of disguise, after all. What good was her magic though, if she couldn't see through to the true heart of something?

Did this man, Malik, have friends who were too powerful? Had he refused to pay some tax of the emperor's? Was he too popular? Nadeem was going to have to learn all she could about her assignment. She was already justifying her research in her head, all in the name of doing a thorough job, in case one of the aunts asked.

Layers upon layers of illusion and lies.

Aunt Izmet added, "It is for the glory of the emperor that you should be chosen for this task."

"For the glory of the emperor," Nadeem repeated, perfectly mimicking Aunt Izmet's fevered tone.

Surely there would be some glory in it, right?

"You'll take Gabril and Duzhen with you," Aunt Izmet said.

"Have they already been told about the assignment?" Nadeem asked, curious.

"They have. In separate briefings," Aunt Izmet assured her.

Why wasn't her team being briefed together? Was it so that secret information could be given to Gabril and Duzhen? Things that they were being told that they'd never tell Nadeem? Additional assignments that they'd also be expected to fulfill while on the primary one?

Nadeem was certain it was another damned test.

She'd passed the big one. She could pass all these little ones as well.

"We'll leave in two mornings' time," Nadeem said as she put her tea to the side. "Thank you for trusting me in this matter. It will be done."

Aunt Izmet nodded. "You'll need to swear it."

Nadeem paused and blinked. Star sisters took their oaths seriously. If a sister took an oath, all the rest of them were bound to uphold it. "Really?" she asked, surprised. "Surely this is a private matter, and not for all the sisters?"

Aunt Izmet nodded. "There's a special oath, just for the emperor's stars."

That made sense. So if she failed, it wouldn't be all of the star sisters who would be held responsible for fulfilling her oath, but just the emperor's stars.

Nadeem wouldn't fail, however.

Aunt Izmet pulled out her ceremonial dagger. It had a red wooden handle with a black obsidian blade. Had it been made from the rock near here?

"I need your blood oath, that you will take care of this matter for the emperor," Aunt Izmet said, handing the knife to Nadeem, handle first.

Nadeem weighed the blade in her hand. It was well balanced. Sharp. The stone would be brittle, given how thin it was.

"I swear to you that I will kill this man, this Malik," Nadeem said. "Or die trying. I give my oath on that."

After kissing the tip of the blade, Nadeem turned it, then sliced a fine cut along her left palm that stung only a little. Beads of blood sprang up along the cut. Nadeem swiped her finger along the blood, held it out to Aunt Izmet.

Instead of daubing the blood onto a ceremonial cloth, or directing

Nadeem to smear it back on herself, marking her forehead or cheeks, Aunt Izmet leaned forward and took the proffered digit in her mouth, sucking the blood off.

Nadeem held herself very still. No one had ever done this before. Her revulsion suddenly came back, her stomach rolling.

"I take the blood of your oath upon myself," Aunt Izmet said. "I, or one of my sisters, will succeed if you fail."

Though Aunt Izmet spoke in a neutral tone, Nadeem couldn't help but wonder if there was more to it, if there was an acknowledgement that Aunt Izmet was already convinced Nadeem would fail.

Nadeem met with Gabril and Duzhen out in the training tent after breakfast the next morning. She had no illusions that the aunts weren't somehow listening in.

Or that one of the other two wasn't going to report back on every word that was said.

She still didn't want Çara or the others listening in to the details of their first assignment. It would be up to them to face their own assignments in the future, and they were likely to be very different.

Plus, Nadeem wasn't sure how she felt about the assignment now that she'd had a night to sleep on it. She'd been disgusted at first, but she'd managed to come up with a few scenarios that explained away her hesitation. Perhaps he was a powerful man but corrupt, and so needed to be dealt with surreptitiously. Or perhaps he was a traitor to the great emperor, and by dying would kill an entire conspiracy.

That morning, under the long tarp, Nadeem had set up targets at the far end for knives. Though she didn't believe in throwing away her only weapon, throwing knives could be used as a good stealth defense. She was more accurate with a blowgun, so she wanted to practice with the throwing knives.

The day had dawned with summer heat, despite it still being spring. She wore a dull red and green striped tunic without a blouse underneath, along with a pair of very loose pants that gave her full movement. She didn't expect to have to wrestle with either Gabril or

Durzhen, but she wanted an outfit that would let her flow and move and do whatever needed doing.

She felt as though she would need that ability a lot in the upcoming days, the ability to change and flow and move as necessary.

Malik lived in the town of Koruli, just north of Gaadiwala on the trade route coming out of the desert. The town was a little smaller than Gaadiwala, and though it had a better water source, it was less important because it had no magician.

Nadeem had readied three targets so all of them could practice at the same time, then take breaks and watch each other, critiquing movement and stance. "You've all been told about our first assignment by the aunts, correct?" she asked as she threw her first knife.

It made a nice *whump* as it hit the target. However, it landed in the fourth circle out. There were five rings around the center. Nadeem would have to do much better. She must still be tired. That must be why she hit so far out.

She took a drink of her tea, pausing while the others answered. She'd made it sweet that morning with a large dollop of *meslit* syrup, needing the extra energy.

Gabril replied. "I have," she said. She threw her first knife, which landed on her target in about the same location as Nadeem's. She wore a similar outfit to Nadeem's, just a tunic and pants, though she'd tied her hair back with a band instead of a standard *chafiyek*.

"Yeah," Durzhen said. "Completely stupid if you ask me." She threw her knife with precision and hit the exact center of the target. She wore all black that morning and moved like a shadow, her gray eyes cloudy.

Nadeem pressed her lips together so she didn't grin too hard. Of course, Durzhen would have spoken her mind not just to Nadeem, but probably to the aunts as well when they'd told her of the assignment.

"I can kill someone one from halfway across a goddamned town and make it look like an accident," Durzhen continued. "Where's the challenge in that?"

"It is to not be seen," Gabril said solemnly. "To come into town as ourselves and leave as ourselves, with no one suspecting our involvement."

Nadeem nodded. That was part of the challenge, particularly when dealing with a smaller town. Strangers would get remarked on. Remembered. Particularly a group of star sisters.

"We could stay a couple of days after the death and spread rumors of other deaths that happened in the night," Nadeem said.

"I agree," Gabril said. She threw another knife that landed in the second circle, much closer to the bullseye. "We need to make sure that no suspicion lands on us, or our other sisters."

Durzhen snorted and threw another perfect bullseye. "Townspeople are always going to suspect us. 'Where the sisters go, trouble follows'," she said, obviously quoting someone.

Nadeem wondered when Durzhen had heard such a thing. She believed it, however. The aunts always warned them about outsiders, and taught how little the star sisters were trusted, despite their blood oaths and kind deeds, the number of children they took in that the townspeople abandoned. She'd never met her own birthmother. She'd been raised in the *kabil* of star sisters.

This assignment would be the first time she'd experience such prejudice firsthand.

She took the time to throw her own knife, again landing in the fourth circle.

She really needed to practice more.

"There are soporifics," Nadeem said slowly, "that in large enough doses are lethal."

Gabril grimaced. "And anyone with a lick of knowledge would know those and be able to trace them back to us. No, we need something else."

Her next hit went way off the mark, barely nicking the target.

"All we have to do is smoother him," Durzhen said. "He's an old man. Old men die in their sleep all the time."

Nadeem's third knife landed on the outer ring of the target, exactly where she'd intended for it to go. She nodded. "True, old men do just die. But I don't think it will be that easy. Otherwise, why would the aunts send all three of us?"

Gabril grinned. "They're sending me so I can look after the two of you and make sure you don't get into too much trouble."

Nadeem believed that. Either the aunts had told Gabril that was her responsibility, or she'd just taken it on herself as one of her duties, as she generally did. She was

"Yeah, well, I'm supposed to keep y'all on the straight and narrow. Make sure you honor your oaths. As if," Durzhen said.

Nadeem didn't have to see Duzhen's expression to know just how hard she was rolling her eyes. She always pushed the limits set by the aunts. If she could figure out a clever way around a problem, she would go that way, even if it involved more work, rather than do what was expected of her.

"And you?" Gabril asked after throwing another knife that was very close to the bullseye. "What is your task?"

Nadeem blinked. Aunt Izmet hadn't given her a specific task in the group beyond killing the old man. "To keep an eye on you two, of course," she said.

"Of course," Gabril said, her eyes narrowed.

She obviously thought Nadeem had lied and had some other task that she'd been given, like the pair of them had been.

Anyone who had not worked with the other two as closely as Nadeem had for years would have missed the look that Gabril threw Durzhen. It was subtle and done while Nadeem lined up her next shot, supposedly all her attention on the bullseye.

Gabril seemed to be saying, *See? I told you so.*

What really made her angry was when Durzhen nodded in agreement, just the slightest incline of her head, but enough to get her point across.

They both thought Nadeem wasn't true to them, that she was aligned with the aunts, that there was more to this assignment than they were being told.

No matter what Nadeem told them, they'd never believe her.

Nadeem threw her next knife, then blinked, surprised when it hit the center of the bullseye.

Seemed all she needed to do to be accurate was to get very angry.

She was going to have to remember that.

The sun touched the western horizon as Nadeem, Gabril, and Durzhen came through the Ladikah pass. They needed to hurry if they wanted to make it to Gaadiwala before full night had set in. They'd traveled along Knife Ridge going north as far as they could go, then bought camels for crossing the first part of the desert, going west. At the Manisal oasis, they'd sold the camels and set off across the last part of the sands on foot, heading directly toward the Kinarak mountain range.

Mint kissed the air as they walked down the rough pass. A herd of someone's goats brayed at them as they passed. Gabril and Durzhen walked behind Nadeem though the path had widened out so they could walk abreast.

They wore "town clothes" today, long skirts and loose blouses in black, with colored tunics, their headscarves equally bright. They also had wide leather belts with knives prominently displayed, sturdier sandals than most, and heavy backpacks. They'd never be mistaken for anything other than star sisters, however, given their scarred cheeks.

Durzhen kept the rear position and watched behind them as well as past Nadeem's shoulder. Gabril moved like a walking mountain, solid and steady. Despite how none of them fully trusted the other, Nadeem was still glad they were there with her. Nothing had been said on their eight-day journey to make her think that either of her two sisters had changed their minds about her—she was just glad that neither of them thought they should take it upon themselves to kill her in her sleep.

They probably already knew just how difficult it would be to surprise her, even when asleep.

Was working with distrust part of the first assignment? Yet another test of the aunts? Nadeem had finally decided that it must be. Though a star sister wasn't anything without her other sisters, perhaps each emperor's star needed to shine on her own.

Gaadiwala spread out below the them as they crested the last foothill. The buildings didn't seem organized, but set in random clusters. Was there a purpose to the sprawling town? Did every neighborhood grow up around a well? Gaadiwala didn't have a river flowing through it for houses to sprout along. There must have been a thousand souls living there.

Only one or two of the stone buildings were taller than a single story, and no wall protected the town. Pounded dirt made up the streets. Nadeem was glad it was past the rainy season: Gaadiwala must turn into a sea of mud when the rains came.

The shacks they passed at the outskirts of town had chickens in the yards, but that was their only wealth, Nadeem was sure. Only a few of the shacks had chimneys for fires to keep warm, she didn't see any rugs covering the floors and only rough, stained, and torn cloth over the doors or windows.

No one in the *kabil* of star sisters lived so poorly.

And Gaadiwala had a magician! Why didn't he do better for his people? The emperor should have done something about this man, this Atça.

Maybe that would be her next assignment, after they'd taken care of Malik.

The three of them kept to the shadows, passing a group of old men standing around a well, drawing their water together, then further into town, where the houses grew closer together. Rock walls made up all the buildings and many of the roofs. The town was stone rich, but wood poor.

Why didn't the magician encourage more trees to grow? Surely he could do that.

Nadeem considered going to the magician's house, at least walking by it. However, she already knew what she'd see: a rich palace, probably mostly made of wood, that outshone every other house around it.

It was a disgrace that Atça be allowed to live with such wealth while the rest of the town lived in such squalor.

Nadeem nodded to herself. Yes. The next time they passed through Gaadiwala. If their mission was successful. She would have words with this Atça.

Finding a tavern wasn't difficult. While there weren't many, they were all located in the same area, on side streets just off the market square.

After the three of them had looked at all the taverns that Gaadiwala held, Nadeem led them back to the tavern that seemed to have the most women working in it. It had a horseshoe embedded in the wall above the door—was that the name of the place? The Horseshoe Tavern? Or was it just for good luck? The ends of it faced down toward the ground, so it still resembled the symbol for the goddess Onnet.

The front windows of the tavern stood wide open to show the rickety tables and stained pillows covered in dust and other travelers' sweat. Would they have a courtyard behind the tavern where Nadeem and her companions could stay for the night? Could they rent a couple of tables and sleep on them?

"Come on," Durzhen said after Nadeem had stood there looking for a few long moments. Durzhen pushed past Nadeem and walked up, through the door.

Nadeem looked back at Gabril, who merely shrugged. "She is hungry," Gabril said.

Nadeem nodded.

She still hesitated.

It wasn't that she was scared. Not exactly. But it was the first time that she'd ever gone into such a place. She'd just wanted to make sure that she was making the right choice.

"All right," she said eventually. She hadn't promised the aunts that she'd look after the others. But that was her responsibility, right?

So she squared her shoulders and marched into the tavern as if she was marching into battle.

The noise of the place reminded Nadeem of a star sister ceremony, or even the *panayirat*, when the seven star-sister *kabils* all met once a summer. There seemed to be over a dozen conversations going on all at the same time, with everyone trying to shout over each other.

The smell of the chicken and garlic soup they were serving made Nadeem's mouth water. The unleavened bread she spied seemed fresh baked that day as well.

Durzhen waved to them from a table against one of the walls. Nadeem counted nine other tables scattered across the room. They all stood only a foot or so off the ground, surrounded by pillows for guests to sit on or lean against. At least fifty people were crowded into the space. All locals—no, there were a few other travelers there.

Nadeem carefully picked her way through the crowd. Any man who looked up far enough to see her face looked away quickly.

Fools.

The women who were serving gave them quick smiles and nods. Nadeem could tell they were busy, and patiently waited until a tall, proud woman came up to serve them.

"Welcome, stranger sisters," the woman said. "I am Myrizhah. How may I help you?"

Stranger sisters? Nadeem had never been called that before. But it made sense. The traditional greeting was always "Welcome, stranger." That this woman also labeled them sisters might mean that she felt more of a kinship with them.

Nadeem spoke up before Durzhen could say something impolite, as she usually did. "Thank you, sister," she said with a smile. "We need food, if your kitchen is still serving. And someplace where we can unroll our bedrolls for the night."

"Certainly," Myrizhah said. "The courtyard is generally reserved for you and your sisters, if you'd like. The merchants have already claimed the tables." She kept her face perfectly solemn as she said that, but Nadeem could tell how little she thought of the men.

"We have at least three bowls left of the soup, as well as bread, and either beer or *igrat*." Then Myrizhah quoted a price that Nadeem was certain was at least four times what the locals paid.

Durzhen couldn't contain her snort.

Nadeem glared at her, then shrugged and sat back, indicating that Durzhen should do the bargaining for them.

One of the things that Aunt Parayat had always emphasized with Nadeem was to let others do what they were good at.

What would Nadeem be considered good at after this first assignment? Killing? Or was there more to it than that?

Myrizhah showed them the courtyard after most of the guests had left the tavern for the evening. She had dark circles under her eyes, as if she'd been awake too many hours.

And maybe she had—it was fully night, now. She had a small lamp that she used to show them where to lay their bedrolls.

"Thank you," Nadeem said, pressing a small coin into her hand as she was leaving. "Can you tell me what the horseshoe on the sign outside means?" She hadn't heard anyone calling the tavern by that name, and had remained curious all night.

Myrizhah grimaced. "It was supposed to be a sign of our good luck," she said, her bitterness evident. "Instead, it's just a reminder of broken dreams. Good night," she added, firmly turning away.

Nadeem didn't know what Myrizhah meant by that. How had a tin horseshoe represented dreams?

Gabril spoke, her words floating across the quiet dark. "It's a custom to place a horseshoe on the belly of a pregnant woman, so the channel will open and the birth will be easy."

Nadeem nodded to herself as she rolled out her blankets. She'd heard that. The star sisters didn't practice such beliefs, but she knew that the horseshoe could also represent the goddess Onnet. "Birth gone wrong?" she wondered.

"Who knows? Who cares?" Durzhen slurred. Either the girl had actually drunk all the beer they'd been served, or she was good at faking being drunk. Nadeem hadn't tried too hard to see beneath the face she wore.

The courtyard itself was paved with wide, flat stones, making it a hard but smooth surface. The smell of the ovens still lingered in the air. Above them, stars filled their sliver of the sky, what was visible between the houses all around them.

A child cried briefly, followed by a soft lullaby. An old man snored fitfully. Chickens clucked in their pen.

Nadeem was the furthest she'd ever been from her *kabil* and the oasis she'd been raised in. She had never been to such foreign lands, with so many people. She didn't understand how anyone could live with their neighbors so close, almost breathing the same air.

She suddenly understood the great hero Arzhem and why she left the corrupt city for the sparseness of the desert. Though the air here was dry and the stones as harsh as the rocks of home, it still was too closed in.

For the first time, Nadeem questioned her choice of becoming one of the emperor's stars, particularly if it meant that she'd always have to live in places like this.

The morning would bring new light. It would be up to Nadeem to find her way with it.

Nadeem, Gabril, and Durzhen were up and had left the tavern just as dawn arrived. It wasn't that far to Koruli—perhaps half a day's walk—but they needed to stop and disguise themselves before they arrived.

The wide road ambled to the north across stony foothills and brambles that supported goats and sheep better than men. At least it felt more open to Nadeem, who'd dreamed of being buried in a box under the desert, tortured with the knowledge that the open sands were just a few feet above her head.

They passed a flock of beautiful, long-haired *nadjil* sheep, the shepherd watching them carefully from the top of a small hill. They were taller than usual sheep, reaching almost up to Nadeem's waist, with white faces while the rest of their coat was black. This herd had weathered the winter well and had fat bellies and many lambs. They were rich men's sheep, valued for their straight, long hair. Nadeem had only ever been able to afford a small bit of fiber from a *nadjil* sheep once—the oils in it had left her hands soft for an entire day.

The problem with the *nadjil* sheep was that they needed better food. The more common *ivesil* sheep could eat like a goat and live on brambles and thorns. *Ivesil* sheep also had fat tails, broader than Nadeem's outstretched hand. Only a stupid farmer would trim their tails: The sheep stored water reserves there that enabled them to live through the dry season.

Their wool was coarse, though, with shorter hairs, making it harder to spin and work with than the *nadjil.*

Nadeem sighed and didn't think about what it would take to raise *nadjil* sheep where she lived. Though that might be one of the advantages to living in a town, even one as poor as Gaadiwala, if she had regular access to such wool.

Both Gabril and Durzhen noticed Nadeem's preoccupation with the sheep but they didn't comment on it—Durzhen, as far as Nadeem could tell, had no hobbies, while Gabril loved to work leather, making beautiful braided belts.

Just past the flock the road turned abruptly to the west. Up ahead, Nadeem could tell that it would turn back again, zigzagging around some border that no longer existed. To the right there appeared to be a small outcropping of rocks.

"Durzhen," Nadeem called, pointing.

Durzhen nodded and took off at a dead sprint.

She'd probably been bored with just walking.

When she got about halfway to the rocks, she turned around and gave an all clear sign.

Nadeem and Gabril followed quickly.

The rocks turned out to be just what Nadeem had hoped—a resting spot for travelers that few still used because of the way the road now turned. A merchant or caravan would have to know the rocks existed if they were traveling late at night.

But it was the perfect place for the three of them to rest and to disguise themselves.

They couldn't hide the fact that they were star sisters, or that there were three of them, though they'd debated that. Instead, they could hide their ages. Elderly women would be granted more respect and wouldn't be commented on as much as younger women.

They'd still reach Koruli by early afternoon.

But it wouldn't be the same three star sisters who'd been in Gaadiwala. Instead it would be three venerable aunts.

The rocks had at one time contained a small altar, though Nadeem wasn't sure for which god. Had it been for Enkat? The goddess of rain? That would make sense in such a dry place. Or had it been for Innis, the god of fertility? All that remained was a small cup carved out of the side of one of the walls to hold offerings.

Nadeem poured a few drops of water from one of her flagons into it, just for luck. The other walls were made from stone and falling apart. No roof covered the small temple.

"Here," Durzhen said, pointing to the foot of one of the walls. "No one from the road can see us."

"Thank you," Nadeem said as she sat. "I will go first," she added. "Then Gabril, then Durzhen. We can be the mirror for one another."

It was a practical choice. She was the strongest illusionist among them and would take the least time.

Gabril sat down facing her. "I will be your mirror."

Nadeem nodded her thanks, then held her hands out in front of her. It was always easiest for her to start with her hands, imagining the age spots that Aunt Parayat's hands now held, how veiny they looked, the thin skin, the wrinkles, the bones that stood out.

Nadeem's skin lost its youth and hardness. The callouses across her thumbs and forefingers from blade work softened and disappeared. Age took over as the veins stood up against the backs of her hands. What might have been freckles now spread and multiplied as age spots.

Old age marched on, up past her hands and her wrists, encircling her forearms. Muscles withered and wrinkled skin took over.

Then Nadeem went to work on her face. She faded the color of her eyes to a softer brown, like Aunt Parayat's. Her hair thinned and lost its glossy brown color, going gray and mousy. She felt the wrinkles forming across her broad forehead, around the edges of her mouth and the corners of her eyes. Her skin stretched and she lost youthful weight, the bones and veins now showing.

When Nadeem looked up, Gabril stared at her intently. "Ears," she said after a moment.

Nadeem nodded, shrinking her ears down a little, making them more pale as well.

"Perfect," Gabril said after another moment. Then she shook her head. "I don't see how you can change so quickly and become someone else."

"Practice," Nadeem said with a shrug. "Start with your hands, something you can see."

Gabril nodded and began.

It wasn't until much later that Nadeem realized that *practice* wasn't actually what helped.

It was her focus.

She wasn't becoming someone else.

Just a different version of herself.

CHAPTER NINE

TRULLIÇ

THE MAN WHO APPROACHED TRULLIÇ called out, "Hold, you!"

Trulliç stayed where he was, shocked and scared. Why did this man want him to stay? The man looked like one of the emperor's guards, more broad and muscled than even Muratil, Gaadiwala's blacksmith. The guard had a shaved head, meaty hands, and a bulbous nose. His dark eyes glared at Trulliç as he approached. Dark skin glistened in what little light came down to the street between the buildings.

"You need to stay here," the guard said firmly.

At least he didn't tower over Trulliç, but they did look each other directly in the eyes.

"Why?" Trulliç asked. He glanced down at Riyune. The dog looked more curious than scared. "Why do you want me to stay here?"

A crowd had already gathered around them. Trulliç's skin crawled from all the eyes staring at him, taking apart his poor sandals, his travel-stained pants, his sweaty shirt. At least his tunic was new. And kind of clean. Sort of. It was the same tunic he'd worn on his original manhood journey, so many years before. At least now it only fell to just past his waist instead of to his mid-thigh.

"Yerkoyliç has asked that you stay here until he can finish his business at the palace and come to meet you," the guard explained.

That brought a collective gasp from those around them, followed by a flurry of mutters.

Did Yerkoyliç never leave his palace? Or did he just never greet traveling magicians?

Trulliç didn't know. But if he thought about it, how many magicians would be traveling through Çandekili? Most magicians were either born near the place of their magic, or they traveled just once in their lifetime to get to their home.

He was the only magician he knew of who was homeless. No magicians had ever traveled through Gaadiwala, at least not that he was aware of.

"All right," Trulliç said, trying to be amiable. "Though it would have been my pleasure to go to the great magician instead."

The man merely grunted. He'd delivered his message. He wasn't planning on doing any more conversing.

Trulliç was fine with that. It gave him a chance to look at the people around him.

His first impression had been that the people here had a lot more money than those in the poor village of Gaadiwala. Almost everyone he saw made that apparent.

First of all, they wore clothes with colors, not the dull browns and grays of Gaadiwala, but reds, oranges, blues, and greens as well. Many of the merchants he saw had embroidered vines, leaves, and flowers on their tunics. The women, too, had similar motifs embroidered on their belts, headscarves, or blouses.

What did they think of Trulliç? They seemed to be more curious than hostile. Did they understand why he was being held? Was it just for being a magician in another magician's territory? Or was there some other law or custom that Trulliç didn't know about that he was breaking?

At least Riyune continued to be calm, sitting beside Trulliç, not touching him but close by.

Finally, a high-pitched wailing flute sounded off in the distance.

The guard turned to Trulliç and said, "Yerkoyliç comes."

Trulliç found himself standing up straighter and tugging at his tunic. He wished he could have at least washed his hands before the other magician saw him.

The crowd good-naturedly grumbled as they were moved out of the way by other guards, clearing a path. All the guards looked like the one standing near Trulliç—big-boned, with the same tunic.

That spoke of a lot of money, for someone to be able to afford to dress their guards all in the same clothes. Trulliç had never even heard of such a thing.

Finally, Yerkoyliç himself appeared.

He only came up to about Trulliç's shoulder, if that. His round face looked boyish—possibly due to how fat it was. His nose melted across the middle of round cheeks, below beady eyes. Even his chin barely stuck out, overshadowed by his flabby lips. A gold and white *chafiyek,* finely made and more for show than for actual shade from the sun, covered his head. His dark skin was lighter than Trulliç's as well, possibly from spending all his time indoors.

While the people who'd been watching Trulliç had all looked rich, the magician was obviously much, much richer. His vest was made out of the finest linen. The same embroidered vines, flowers, and bees decorated the vest, though the figures on his were outlined in gold thread that caught the sunlight. He wore fine white pants that looked as though they'd never touched the dirt. His shoes looked more like house slippers, red velvet and gold. Trulliç was surprised he'd worn them here, in the streets.

"Hello! Hello!" Yerkoyliç called as he approached. "My good magician! Welcome!"

The people still surrounding Trulliç gasped and murmured. Had no one suspected him of having magic? Had they all assumed he was some sort of criminal?

Yerkoyliç walked closer, then bowed his head to Trulliç. "What brings such a powerful magician as yourself to my humble abode?"

Trulliç bowed his own head in return. "I am Trulliç. I have been sent here to see you by the great magician Atça."

That caused even more murmurs and whispers. Three magicians, all working together! Trulliç had to admit that even in the old stories he'd never heard of such a thing.

His statement also appeared to catch Yerkoyliç off guard. But he recovered quickly, clapping his flabby hands together. "Wonderful! Wonderful!" Then he paused, nodding. "It is my honor to welcome you to Çandekili, to the city of my heart. But, tell me…" He paused, thinking.

"How may I serve you?" Trulliç asked. He could tell that Yerkoyliç wanted to ask him something. And as a guest, it was up to him to be as polite as possible in return for the warm hospitality being offered him.

"It's nothing. Just a trifle. But…did you see the wards at the city gate?" Yerkoyliç asked. He seemed confused.

"Wards?" Trulliç asked. He thought back. "I didn't see any wards, though I could tell, of course, when I crossed into your territory. Your magic is strong and sweet," he added.

That seemed to please the crowd. It was true, though. Yerkoyliç's magic did seem strong and very sweet, perfumed with flowers. Whereas if Atça's magic had a scent at all, it was smoky.

"Ah, ah, all right," Yerkoyliç said, rocking back and forth. He seemed perplexed. "You didn't see them at all?"

Trulliç shook his head. "Would you like to walk back to the gate and show them to me? So that I might see them the next time?" he asked. He really wasn't sure what Yerkoyliç wanted.

"No, no, that's too much to ask of such an honored guest, such as yourself," Yerkoyliç said.

It was clear to Trulliç that Yerkoyliç really wanted to go back to see his wards, to see what had gone wrong with them.

"Please. I insist," Trulliç said. "I would love to see your wards. You must show them to me. And your spectacular magic." That way, the next time Trulliç went to another magician's territory, he might know that magician's wards. They might be an indication of a magician's power.

"Would you?" Yerkoyliç said. He seemed very anxious. "It isn't that I would expect such paltry wards as mine to affect such a great magician as yourself. They do, however, work nicely on the star sisters, who tend to bypass Çandekili as a result."

"I see," Trulliç said, though he didn't, not really. Were these wards supposed to stop him from coming into the Çandekili? "Don't you trade with the star sisters?" He knew they brought precious spices and other goods from the desert. The merchants in Gaadiwala bought them and then moved them up along the trade routes going inland.

"No, no, we have no need," Yerkoyliç said. "Your merchants in Gaadiwala and other places keep us well stocked in spices."

He turned toward the gate and indicated that Trulliç should walk beside him. When Riyune fell into place as well, Yerkoyliç said, "I see you have a familiar as well."

Trulliç said, "He's a good companion," not accepting or denying Yerkoyliç's statement.

"Trulliç, you are a *powerful* magician, indeed," Yerkoyliç said firmly.

"No, no, you are the powerful one here," Trulliç replied truthfully. Çandekili belonged to Yerkoyliç. Every stone seemed to recognize the man. It felt as though the houses loomed in closer as he walked by. The people, too, reflected Yerkoyliç's spirit—happy, content, busy.

Trulliç wasn't sure what that said about Gaadiwala and Atça, how poor they were, how colorless, how dull they seemed.

"What causes you to travel so far from your home?" Yerkoyliç asked as they walked.

"Atça sent me," Trulliç said. "He's been my mentor and my friend." He really didn't want to admit that he was a homeless magician. Not when he finally saw the possibilities awarded to a magician who had found his home.

"Atça's also a powerful magician," Yerkoyliç said. "You are lucky to be able to count him as both friend and mentor."

"I am," Trulliç said fervently. "Though I am merely a traveler here, I hope that you might deign to show me some of your wisdom and learning as well."

Yerkoyliç gave Trulliç a large grin. "We have much to learn from each other! I am looking forward to it."

"Me too," Trulliç said.

And he found to his surprise that he was looking forward to working with the jolly magician.

He also found himself fervently hoping that Yerkoyliç's loyalties remained true.

Trulliç and Yerkoyliç reached the city gate quickly. The guards turned away the crowd who had followed them, telling them to go back about their business. Trulliç knew that he'd be the topic of all conversations for the next week: his dirty clothes and broken nails, how Yerkoyliç had greeted him, was Riyune actually a familiar or merely a dog.

Yerkoyliç stepped across the threshold of the gate. He didn't go gray like Atça did when he traveled outside of Gaadiwala. But Trulliç could tell that the fat, puffed-up man deflated slightly just outside of his city.

Would he ever go gray? Trulliç wasn't certain. Yerkoyliç's bright colors would fade the further away he got from Çandekili. However, Trulliç would bet that the other magician would always have some color to him.

Yerkoyliç turned to his right, walking a few feet to the west along the city wall, then stopped. Solid gray and brown stones, mortared together, made up the wall. None of the stones were larger than Trulliç's head. The wall itself rose up only a few feet above Trulliç. It was thick enough that a man could have walked along the top of it. However, no platform ran along the top. Dried bushes and grass grew along the base of the wall, kept short by goats and other livestock being brought to market.

No houses stood outside the wall on this side. As Trulliç had descended the road down to the city, he thought he'd seen some houses outside the wall to the north. Were those for guards? Or were those for people who couldn't afford to stay in the city?

So close to the wall, Trulliç thought he could see some of the magic there. He knew that Atça would tell him to stop being so fanciful. However, if what Trulliç was seeing was true, then the magic wasn't in the stones themselves, as he would have expected. No, the mortar held bits of magic. When Trulliç looked more carefully, he thought he could make out tiny pieces of blue, red, and green stones mixed into it.

Atça would have strengthened the rocks, made them harder. Yerkoyliç had strengthened what was in between the strong stones.

"There, do you see?" Yerkoyliç asked. He waved his hand toward the wall.

Trulliç shook his head. Because of the magic in the mortar, the wall itself appeared very smooth, the rocks perfectly aligned, almost like baked bricks. However, that was all Trulliç saw. He didn't see any words written on the wall, or some sort of magical shield.

"Hmmm," Yerkoyliç said. He thought for a moment, then stamped his foot close to the base of the wall.

Vines suddenly shot up the walls, quickly reaching waist height. Thorns dotted every branch and stem, and the green leaves looked as sharp as knives. They buzzed as though they were alive with bees, ready to attack. Flowers budded up next, then blossomed into star shapes with five petals, each looking as though merely brushing against them would cut a person to shreds.

"Are these the wards I was supposed to see?" Trulliç asked, amazed.

"Yes. Sort of," Yerkoyliç said thoughtfully. "As you approached the city, you should have seen these, or an image of them. When you got close enough, you should have triggered them. They should have sprung up on their own."

"That's impressive," Trulliç said, marveling. If he'd been walking on his own without owing a duty to Atça, would he have just walked away from Çandekili if these vines had sprung up as he'd drawn near?

Possibly. Though his mother had sometimes accused Trulliç of having more stubbornness than sense. He might have walked into Çandekili on his own anyway.

"I know it's a horrible imposition for me to ask yet another favor," Yerkoyliç said slowly.

The other magician still seemed puzzled. "No, no, not at all," Trulliç said. "What can this poor guest do to help you?"

"Try to touch one of the vines. I don't want you to actually touch it. Don't hurt yourself. But merely put your hand out," Yerkoyliç said.

The fat man stared hard at Trulliç as he slowly reached out toward one of the vines.

Nothing happened.

"See?" Trulliç said, relieved. "I'm not a powerful enough magician to warrant such defenses."

"No, that's not it at all," Yerkoyliç said, looking carefully at Trulliç. "It's because you're too strong. You overpowered them."

Trulliç shook his head, not believing Yerkoyliç. "You're mistaken," he said.

Yerkoyliç tilted his head to one side and gazed for another moment at Trulliç.

Underneath the jolly exterior, Trulliç caught a glimpse of a truly intelligent mind examining him. Atça got that same look sometimes when Trulliç performed what little magic he could under Atça's roof.

"As you say," Yerkoyliç said after a bit. He glanced from Trulliç to Riyune and back before his mask slipped back on and the jovial magician was standing in front of Trulliç again. "Come!" he said, indicating that Trulliç should walk beside him. "We shall walk along the wall of the city and contemplate the defenses. Maybe you can assist me in strengthening them."

"Gladly," Trulliç said. "Though I doubt I can help."

"No matter," Yerkoyliç said. "Let us walk."

Trulliç felt a stab of grief. What would have happened if he'd been mentored by Yerkoyliç? How would his life had been different? Would he have been able to find his home?

Then Trulliç put away his doubts. Atça had been good to him. Helped him. Taught him everything he could.

Trulliç couldn't contain his rising excitement, however, at the thought of being able to learn so much more from the happy magician beside him.

"I love my city," Yerkoyliç started out as they began walking around the outside of the city wall. "Çandekili truly is the home of my heart."

"I can see that," Trulliç said. From what little he'd seen, the city was a reflection of the man: happy, busy, a little self-indulgent.

Rich.

Trulliç didn't know what that meant about the relationship between Atça and Gaadiwala.

Then again, Atça's power had always seemed to center more around his personal home rather than the town itself. If Trulliç's fanciful imaginings could be believed.

"What does the great Atça want with such a poor magician such as I?" Yerkoyliç asked.

Trulliç knew he couldn't tell Yerkoyliç the truth. "He recognizes that you are a powerful magician, much more powerful than you claim." He held up his hand when Yerkoyliç would have protested. "I have seen it myself."

Trulliç still didn't know if Yerkoyliç was stronger than Atça or not, or if he was just that different of a magician.

"So Atça is interested in exploring a future, stronger alliance between the pair of you," Trulliç lied. He hoped this would get Yerkoyliç to talk about loyalties.

Plus, if Yerkoyliç was true, maybe Atça would be interested in such a relationship.

"To see how two such powerful magicians might better align their powers and their interests, to better their people," Trulliç continued.

"But wouldn't that be against the wishes of the emperor?" Yerkoyliç said, obviously shocked, stopping in his place. "What exactly are you proposing?"

"What do you mean?" Trulliç asked, confused. When had the emperor said that magicians couldn't form an alliance? He knew of no such decree. Otherwise, how could Atça have mentored him? Or how could any older magician teach any younger magician?

Yerkoyliç looked carefully at Trulliç. "You truly didn't know," he said quietly. "The emperor has been sending out more decrees, every month now, it seems," he added sourly.

Trulliç nodded. He'd noticed that. Atça was always receiving scrolls and messengers from the emperor, much more so now than when Trulliç had been younger.

Had Atça forgotten to mention this one to Trulliç? Or had the message arrived after Trulliç had left Gaadiwala?

"Earlier this year, the emperor let it be known that he needed to approve of any alliance between magicians," Yerkoyliç said. He looked over one shoulder, then the other, to make sure that no one had approached and was listening to them. "If one read between the lines, one could easily make the assumption that no magician was to contact another. It was part of why I was so surprised to find you here."

"I see," Trulliç said. Surely, Atça had known this. Why had he sent Trulliç to meet with Yerkoyliç? What kind of reception had he expected the other magician to give Trulliç?

Yerkoyliç nodded at Trulliç, as if coming to a decision. "You said you were mentored by Atça, correct?"

"Yes," Trulliç said slowly.

"And have you found your home? In the desert?" Yerkoyliç asked.

"How did you—" Trulliç started, then cut himself off. "No," he said softly, shaking his head. "I haven't."

"How did I know your home is in Qaenev?" Yerkoyliç said, smiling. "You smell like sand, dry and coarse. Hot winds blow around you. Even the widest street of my city hems you in."

"Yes," Trulliç whispered. He didn't ask how Yerkoyliç knew. It was the same ability that Trulliç had, the one that told him about Atça's power, Yerkoyliç's.

The ability was real. Those thoughts and feelings that Trulliç had wasn't just him being fanciful.

Atça was wrong.

"I've searched for my home," Trulliç admitted. "But it hasn't shown itself to me."

Yerkoyliç nodded. "That's too bad. I couldn't imagine being uprooted from Çandekili. It's too much a part of me."

"You were born here?" Trulliç asked.

"I was," Yerkoyliç said proudly. "By the time I was walking, the streets were bending to my will. There was already a city here, but no magician."

"I was born far to the north, in Lydae," Trulliç told him. "My mother brought me back."

"She knew you were a desert magician?" Yerkoyliç said amazed. "That's marvelous!"

Trulliç nodded. What would have happened to him had he been raised beneath the mountains of Knassia? Where everything was green, and it snowed in the winter? He couldn't contain his shudder.

Yerkoyliç started walking again, curving around the city wall. Trulliç walked beside him. The other magician appeared to be lost in thought.

"I will be honest with you," Yerkoyliç said suddenly. "I was afraid that you might be here to challenge me. To take my city away from me."

"By Serrat's star, no," Trulliç said, horrified. "Not that it isn't a lovely city," he added hastily. "But—"

Yerkoyliç laughed. "I understand. It isn't yours. You have no interest in it at all." He paused, then added, "But I will also admit that I have a special interest in the desert."

"Really?" Trulliç asked. "Why?"

Yerkoyliç paused again. "Have you ever heard of the desert heart?"

Trulliç shook his head.

"Of course, you know the story of Forit?" Yerkoyliç asked.

"She was Innis' wife, and the fairest of the gods," Trulliç said. He found himself standing straighter, as if he was reciting for Atça. "During the great battle between the darkness and the gods, before the forming of the world, she sang such a beautiful song that the darkness revealed its heart to the gods. Innis pierced the heart with his great spear, killing the darkness. But the only way Forit could draw out the heart was by binding the heart of darkness with her own, and so she died as well."

Her body fell and became the earth. Her teeth became the mountains, her fingers became the many rivers, and the place where her heart had been became the desert.

As the gods and goddesses grieved, their tears fell on her prone body.

Her freckles, the only imperfection about her, became humanity. The darker freckles became the people of the south, the lighter blemishes became the people of the north.

"There are stories that her heart still exists in the center of the Qaenev desert," Yerkoyliç said.

Trulliç hadn't heard of such myths. He found himself biting his tongue so that he wouldn't accuse Yerkoyliç of being fanciful.

He made the decision right there and then to *never* accuse someone else of having too much imagination.

"Wouldn't her heart be infected with darkness?" Trulliç asked.

"That's what some say," Yerkoyliç admitted. "But others say that after all these years, she'd be cleansed of it. Or would have purified the darkness."

"What would you do with such a remarkable item?" Trulliç asked, wondering. That sort of power would be truly amazing.

Yerkoyliç shrugged. "What couldn't you do? But it would take more than one magician to find it."

Trulliç thought back to the start of their conversation. "Is that why the emperor doesn't want any magicians to align together? Because he's afraid that they'll find the heart?"

"Before he does, yes," Yerkoyliç said softly.

"Why would the *Padisha-i-Ghazi* want the desert heart?" Trulliç asked, bewildered. The emperor already had so much power! He controlled the lands from the northern Kingdom of Lydae to the southern tip of Tanesh, beyond the Qeanev desert. The people thanked him at all meals, now. Bells rang in the morning for him. Workmen now added his symbol, a rounded scale with a sharp tip, to every building and well.

But he was always at war with the northern barbarians who were trying to expand beyond the southern kingdom of Lydae. Did he think that he could win if he had more power?

Or did he want even more than just the barbarian lands?

"Who could say what such a one as the emperor could do with such an item?" Yerkoyliç said. "But we've strayed into such serious topics! We should talk of lighter things. Tell me of your remarkable mother, your training, your desert."

Trulliç nodded and happily changed the topic, telling Yerkoyliç of the Horseshoe Tavern, his cousins, his life.

All the while wondering just where Yerkoyliç's loyalty lay.

Trulliç waited in Yerkoyliç's outer room, as requested. Pillows in every color Trulliç had ever seen or imagined littered the floor. A silver tea service waited in one corner. A basin with a pitcher stood next to the doorway, so a guest could wash their hands when they arrived. The faint scent of flowers suffused the room—a heady odor of blossoms that Trulliç didn't recognize.

Curtains hung against the far wall—probably hiding the door to the inner rooms. Trulliç peeked behind them but didn't touch the carved wood he saw there—if he wasn't being fanciful, he'd say the doors were well warded with magic, and that Yerkoyliç would instantly know if someone entered.

Riyune had already settled in, laying in front of the door like a statue. Trulliç found he couldn't sit and instead paced the room.

His stomach still rumbled, uneasy from the great feast he'd just had. He hadn't even heard of half the dishes they'd served—like hen's tongue soup, or red lamb stew—and he wasn't used to so much fat, either.

The conversation had been stilted at dinner. Trulliç had felt shy in front of so many rich merchants. They all wore better clothes than his, rich with embroidery and fine linen. He'd felt out of place in his old tunic, the one striped gold and green like his glass horseshoe, that he'd worn for his manhood journey.

He yawned, tired from the long day, the stress of being in a strange magician's city, of trying to determine Yerkoyliç's loyalties.

The guild masters had certainly been careful about praising the emperor for his bounty. However, there was an edge to their words that Trulliç still hadn't deciphered.

"Ah, there you are, my young friend!" Yerkoyliç said, breezing into the room. He seemed full of energy, as if the night was still young.

He wore the most beautiful red vest in the style of the northern merchants—shorter, ending just at his waist, and with buttons up the front—embroidered again in gold thread, with the same repeating motif of flowers, vines, birds, and butterflies.

"Come, come!" he said, gesturing for Trulliç to follow him. "I want to show you something."

Yerkoyliç led Trulliç through the curtains, the doors opening easily for Yerkoyliç without him having to touch them. Riyune walked beside Trulliç into the room.

The inner chamber was even more grand. Tapestries showing the great palace, the walls of Çandekili, even a map of the city itself, hung there. Jewels had been woven in with the threads. Soft rugs covered the floor, all decorated in patterns of flowers and vines.

Against the far wall stood yet another gauzy curtain hiding more doors. Probably leading to Yerkoyliç's bedroom, Trulliç guessed. Beside it stood a small altar with a black-and-white cloth covering it, embroidered with a familiar zig-zag symbol—the symbol of the god Serril.

A square, sunken area made up one corner of the room, a place where guests could lounge and easily talk. In the opposite corner stood a bookshelf, similar to the ones Trulliç had seen in Atça's house. Scrolls, small statues, precious gems, and other knick-knacks covered the shelves.

The shelves caught Trulliç's attention and held it. He found himself walking toward them without asking. Riyune walked beside him.

A cleverly made wooden box maybe ten inches on a side, while slightly deeper, stood on the middle shelf. The wood at the corners interlaced, showing that two sides were made from a dark, almost blackened wood, while the other two sides were made from a wood so pale it looked white.

No top covered the box. Trulliç gasped when he looked inside.

Sand filled the box.

Not just any sand. Sand carried from Qaenev. Sand that came from the heart of the desert.

Trulliç turned to look at Yerkoyliç. "What are you doing with this?" he asked.

Was the box magical? Or had Yerkoyliç done something to make the sand, itself, magical?

"Ah, I knew you would understand the specialness of my project!" Yerkoyliç said, beaming. "I knew you were the one!"

Trulliç turned back to the box, fascinated by the sand. Memories of the desert overwhelmed him. Heat flushed through his body. Hot winds stirred his hair. He smelled baked earth and sweet palms.

Sand grated against Trulliç's fingertips as he dipped his hand into the box. He couldn't help but scoop up a handful, feel it slip easily through his fingers.

Longing filled his heart. Oh, how he needed to go back!

Riyune leaned against Trulliç's leg, returning him to the room.

Trulliç swallowed against a suddenly dry throat, stepping back, away from the seductive box.

"What *are* you doing with that?" Trulliç asked, repeating his question firmly. A regular box of sand shouldn't have affected him that way.

Yerkoyliç had done something to it. Something that had enhanced the true essence of the desert, captured it in that single cubic foot of sand.

"Searching for the desert heart," Yerkoyliç said. He took a quick step closer to Trulliç. "We *must* find it before the emperor!"

"Why?" Trulliç asked, puzzled. Wouldn't it be a good thing for the emperor, who was so powerful, to have the desert heart? To bring more glory to the Tanesh empire?

Yerkoyliç came closer still, lowering his voice to a whisper. He smelled of the sour beer he'd drunk during dinner, of faded and spoiled flowers.

"The emperor doesn't just want to conquer the northern barbarians. He wants to rule, everywhere."

Trulliç strained to hear Yerkoyliç's next words.

"He wants to become a god."

Trulliç bit back a bitter laugh. The emperor was already almost a god, never seen but always in people's minds. Just because he now had formal prayers didn't mean that people hadn't been praying to him, or using his name to curse, for a long while.

"Don't you see what that would do the empire?" Yerkoyliç asked.

Trulliç shook his head. So what if the emperor wanted to become a god?

"You think the wars with the northern barbarians are bad," Yerkoyliç said. "All the good men we're losing. What do you think will happen when the emperor declares war on the gods?"

Trulliç shivered. What happened if the gods turned their backs on the people? If they started working actively against them? How many would die? Would the empire survive? Or would the gods blast it to nothing, desolating all the land?

"We must stop him," Yerkoyliç insisted.

Calmness overcame Trulliç.

He knew where Yerkoyliç's loyalties lay.

And Atça had told him what he must do if Yerkoyliç wasn't true.

"You're wrong," Trulliç said bravely, though he wasn't sure he believed it. "The emperor will take care of us. Protect us."

Yerkoyliç gave a bitter laugh. "You are so naïve," he said. "Why do you think the prayers have changed? That the emperor's symbol is being added everywhere?"

"But the gods won't destroy us for a single madman's quest," Trulliç reasoned.

Though he didn't really believe it himself.

"I'm not willing to take that chance," Yerkoyliç said. He raised his fat chin in defiance. "Are you?"

"Yes, I am," Trulliç replied.

The flowers and vines in the rugs started to stir.

"Too bad," Yerkoyliç said. "We could really have used a desert magician."

"Yes," Trulliç said. "Too bad."

Then he attacked.

Trulliç knew he should be more afraid.

Yerkoyliç controlled everything in the room. The rugs. The walls. The tapestries.

Yet, Trulliç's heart beat strongly with excitement.

Yerkoyliç had made a huge mistake.

He'd enchanted sand from the Qaenev desert. Brought it into his inner chamber.

And sand was Trulliç's element.

Vines sprang up around Trulliç's feet, winding around his calves and holding him tightly. Riyune whined, a sound Trulliç had never heard, and bit at the vines constraining him. The cloying scent of flowers filled the air, making Trulliç gag and cough.

Without thinking, Trulliç grabbed a handful of sand with a magical fist.

Atça had never taught him such a trick. He wondered if Atça even knew it.

"Let me go!" Trulliç commanded.

Yerkoyliç sneered. "You're just a dumb errand boy. You have no idea of the stakes you're playing with."

Trulliç couldn't help but agree.

However, he was determined not to remain ignorant.

With a punching motion, Trulliç threw the sand at Yerkoyliç. It hit him squarely in the center of his fat face.

"The sand will always win," Trulliç intoned as Yerkoyliç started choking, the sand making its way down his throat. "It is mightier than all of us. It overtakes all kingdoms, all who dare to build there. It will always overcome."

Yerkoyliç fell to his knees. The plants around Trulliç's legs began to wilt. He tore himself free.

"How—why—" Yerkoyliç choked out. His face turned as red as a poppy.

Trulliç couldn't brag about Atça at that point. Couldn't even proclaim that it was Trulliç's loyalty to the emperor that drove him.

"The desert is mine," he whispered fiercely.

If anyone was to find the desert heart, it would be him.

The walls of Yerkoyliç's room faded. The tapestries on the walls dropped their gems with loud thunks. The pillows unraveled, spilling their straw onto the floor.

Riyune ran to the door of the room, then stopped and turned back, looking at Trulliç.

Though he didn't hear Riyune speak, Trulliç still knew exactly what the dog said.

Come on. We've got to get out of here.

Still, Trulliç walked back to the shelves and grabbed the box of sand. The palace would fall in on itself.

Sand—any part of the desert—should never be trapped that way.

Then Trulliç ran, ignoring the body that was already starting to rot.

Trulliç ran behind Riyune, trusting that the dog would get him out of the palace, then out of the city.

Rugs turned to dust as he ran over them. Paint spilled from wall murals as the life that bound them faded. The floor felt solid, but he wondered how long the building would last. The stench of rotten flowers made him cover his nose and mouth with his headscarf, hoping it would help him breathe.

The few people Trulliç passed in the hallway seemed dazed. One woman leaned against the wall openly weeping, reds and blues from the mural staining her arms, her face, as if she were melting, too.

A buzzing noise followed Trulliç, sounding like an angry swarm of bees. No one was behind him when he looked back.

He nearly stumbled on the mound of dried grass that suddenly sprouted in the middle of the hallway.

Was the city disintegrating? Turning back into a grassy plain? Yerkoyliç had been born in the city, to the city, and had touched every part of it, welded it tightly to himself.

Guilt struck Trulliç. He told himself that Yerkoyliç was a traitor to the emperor. The fat magician had been trying to grab the power of the emperor for himself. He'd deserved what he'd gotten, to be choked on the sands of the desert, the heat killing all his plants and flowers.

It still made Trulliç feel bad to see Yerkoyliç's people suffering.

The floor tilted suddenly. Trulliç tumbled, but he didn't drop the box of sand he'd been carrying.

He was going to lose his travel pack, his clothes and sleeping roll.

No one would notice him, though. There would be many refugees on the road.

Trulliç concentrated on running. Riyune led him down a back staircase and out into the courtyard.

From outside, Trulliç saw the damage better. The corners stayed more upright, while the center floors sagged, as if the great palace was melting.

Fire blossomed in the ovens next to the outdoor kitchen, as if angrily celebrating its freedom. Hens ran around here and there, nearly tripping Trulliç twice.

Guards stood at the gate to the palace. One recognized him. "You —magician! You can't leave!" he shouted. "You must stay! Help Çandekili!"

Trulliç paused. He knew he couldn't stay. People would eventually accuse him of killing Yerkoyliç.

However, could his magic help?

He put out his hand, fingers widespread, trying to stabilize the wall. The magic wasn't in the bricks, he remembered, but in the mortar.

Flashes of blue sparked in the wall.

For a moment, the wall stood straighter, as if it might hold.

Then the mortar turned to sand. The stones trembled.

"Run away!" Trulliç cried as the wall started to come apart.

His magic was too different than Yerkoyliç's. He couldn't help the city, or the people there.

All he could do was run, make sure he got out before the city collapsed in on itself.

Trulliç had been right—there were many refugees on the road. No one looked twice at him or Riyune. He just seemed another homeless traveler coming from Çandekili.

His only possession was the box. He would ask Atça how Yerkoyliç had enchanted it, how he'd managed to bring the soul of the desert to such a small patch of sand.

However, Trulliç doubted that Atça knew how.

A nearby farmer had set up some fires along the edge of his fields so the refugees might at least have someplace warm to spend the night.

Trulliç avoided the fires. Someone might recognize him, identify him.

Mark him as the killer he was. Though no judge would even fine Trulliç for killing a man who'd proven himself disloyal to the emperor, he didn't want to risk the rage that Yerkoyliç's people might have against his killer.

Instead, he made himself walk further into the night, away from the groups of people wailing and mourning. He sat with his small box between his legs, Riyune curled up next to his side.

The box produced the warmth of a fire, the heat of the desert escaping out of its open top.

Though maybe that was just its reaction to Trulliç and his shivers.

He found himself reaching into the box, scooping up a bit of sand, then letting it slide out of his fingers.

Despite his fear that someone would recognize him, accuse him of Yerkoyliç's death, Trulliç found a great calm descending over him.

The desert did that to him. Calmed him. Made him feel more powerful as well.

How bright would his mage light be if he had one hand in the desert box?

Stronger than ever, he suspected, though he didn't try it just then.

Yes, he was really going to have to ask Atça how Yerkoyliç had made such a box.

And why Atça had never bothered making one for Trulliç.

CHAPTER TEN

NADEEM

NADEEM LED GIBRIL AND DURZHEN down the hill toward Koruli. She walked with a stout stick now, using it rather like a cane, as if she needed aid walking. Their pace had slowed considerably as well.

Just under the surface of her companions, Nadeem felt their impatience. Hadn't they practiced being old? Nadeem was tempted to walk even slower or to take yet another break.

However, now wasn't the time to test them. They still had secrets they hadn't told her, missions within missions.

Koruli had been built in a valley with the main part of town at the foot of the surrounding hills, though many houses dotted the slopes. Instead of tight neighborhoods like Gaadiwala with shacks crouched around each of the available wells, the buildings were more spread out.

The twisting street coming out of the hill surprised Nadeem. Had they originally been built along sheep tracks? Loose stones covered the route they followed. Nadeem wouldn't have tumbled—she was more sure footed than that—but she still went slowly. This was an unknown trail. And they were all supposed to be old.

In the center of town, a single street held the marketplace. It wasn't very long or extensive. Just a few shops. The farms here made do without buying many goods.

Then again, they had the water so they could grow more crops and animals.

Only a single inn stood at the end of the market street. A burlap cloth painted with a brimming cup was the only indication of what they served.

"Hello?" Nadeem called as she stepped out of the dusty street and into the dim room. The air stank of spilled beer and strong *igrat*. Half-a-dozen small tables littered the floor, with dissolute pillows and cushions surrounding them. Rough stones lined the floor, so at least the guests didn't have to make a choice between bug-ridden pillows or dirt.

A large fireplace stood to the right, large enough for three men to stand in, upright. It was cold now, but would probably give adequate heat during the winter months.

An older man poked his head through the door in the back of the room. He stood tall and round with a great belly. White whiskers curled around his chin, though under his nose was clean shaven. The top of his head, too, appeared clean shaven, with more white curls hanging down around the edges of his scalp.

"Ah! Good sisters!" the man called, as if he was happy to see them.

The way his eyes narrowed and his mouth turned down told a different story.

"Welcome, welcome," he said, hastily wiping his hands on a rag. "How may I help my honored guests?"

"Do you rent rooms?" Nadeem querulously inquired, sounding much like old Aunt Hareet with her quavering tones.

"I do, I do," the man said. "I am Erkiç," he added, bowing his head. "I would be happy to give you shelter for the evening."

And to take us for every coin you can, Nadeem realized.

No matter. They were here on the emperor's business in this tiny town, come to kill one of their elders.

Aunt Izmet would say there was no greater glory.

Nadeem still had her doubts.

The beds in the room were about what Nadeem had expected: straw mattresses that needed to be restuffed laying on rusting iron bedframes; stained pillows that still bore the drool marks of the former guests; a window slit that maybe a lizard could crawl through but no breeze.

At least the room was large enough that the beds didn't take up the entire space. Plus, two of the sisters could stand abreast in the aisle between the beds on the longer walls.

"Now what?" Galbril asked as she sat heavily on the bed to the right of the door. Of the three, it probably was the most defensible.

It gave a warning creak.

Galbril winced but didn't get up. Her old age mask slipped away from her, melting like dust in the rain.

Durzhen dropped her bag onto the bed against the far wall. "We wait until dark. Then we go find this Malik. And kill him." Her mask faded less quickly.

Nadeem shook her head. "You two stay here. I'm going out to scout the town first. See if I can find Malik before this evening."

"I would be the better scout," Durzhen pointed out.

"How long would it take for you to age again, dearie?" Nadeem asked, using Aunt Haleet's tones.

Durzhen pressed her lips together. "Too long," she said, gesturing toward the window. "You took too long getting here. It will be night soon."

"We needed to be believed," Nadeem said, "by all who saw us."

"Then, old mother, I wish you luck in your hunt," Durzhen said formally.

"Thank you," Nadeem said. "I'll be back before it's full night."

Quickly, she escaped the room.

What were the other two up to? What was this tension she felt between them? What were they really supposed to do?

Nadeem put all her doubts behind her. She kept her old lady mask on as she went through the main room of the tavern and out the door, back onto the dusty street.

She bowed her head to those she passed, a casual greeting, making sure she was seen as an old woman, a star sister, traveling through their town. She walked to the main well, then into one of the side streets.

When she was certain no one watched her, Nadeem *blurred* her hands, her appearance, so that no one would easily follow her.

Then she walked back into the market, needing to hear and learn all she could about this Malik.

Before she killed him.

———

Nadeem found an old mother sitting out on her front stoop, enjoying the last of the sun before it set between the hills. It was the last row of buildings before the start of the hills. The rock walls of the house looked sturdy and well-maintained, though the wood framing the door and windows was well-weathered. The people who lived there weren't poor, but they weren't rich, either. Chickens scratched in the yard behind a low rock fence. Not only the usual herbs and stew vegetables grew in the garden, but beautiful blue delphiniums and white daisies as well.

The old woman wore a *chafiyek* that had been carefully embroidered with vines and butterflies, once a brilliant green and red but now faded. Her brown tunic and soft blue shirt showed the same care and age, carefully mended holes done in different colored thread.

The old woman sat on a wooden bench with a large basket of fiber at her feet and two long-tined combs in her hands. She carded the wool, humming softly, arranging the fibers to be all in one direction so they could be spun.

Nadeem hadn't been able to hear any gossip about Malik at the market. She couldn't really start any conversation if no one could see her. And she had to be careful about asking about him.

Still, fiber work had always been something she enjoyed.

Before Nadeem dropped her *blur*, the old woman said, "Greetings, stranger."

Had Nadeem made some kind of unconscious noise? How had the

old woman known she was there? She hadn't been able to see her. She still sat with her eyes closed, basking in the sunlight.

"Hello," Nadeem said, keeping her voice gruff and old. "What fibers are you working?"

"Ah," the old woman said, nodding. She picked up an already carded hunk from beside her on the bench. "*Nadjil*," she said proudly.

Nadeem fingered the soft fibers. She'd rarely gotten to work with *nadjil*. It was too expensive, and those sheep couldn't survive the desert. "It's beautiful," she said honestly. "You could spin fine thread from this."

The old woman cracked a wide grin that showed gaps in her teeth. She finally opened her eyes. They were completely covered with white film.

No wonder the old woman had known Nadeem was there! She was blind and had sensed Nadeem in other ways.

"Ah, it will," she said. "Come, sit with an old woman for a while. I am Tonyal."

"Haneet," Nadeem said. She sat down with a soft sigh, still acting the part as if she was an old woman, too.

They sat for a few long moments in companionable silence, enjoying the sunshine. Scrub, green with spring, covered the hills in front of them. The bushes would turn brown as the summer gained its head. A path led from the house, up between the hills: narrow, just wide enough for a single person, probably leading to richer houses further up the valley.

Finally, Tonyal put down her combs and fished around in the pocket of her apron. She pulled out a small drop spindle, handed it to Nadeem with a chunk of fiber. "Here," she said. "I can tell you want to."

Nadeem laughed softly. She always found spinning thread so soothing.

The long shaft was made from a slender piece of wood, smoothed out through use and age. It wasn't any thicker around than her pinky finger and was about the length of her forearm. Three notches had been carved at the top to help guide the thread. The round whorl at the bottom could comfortably fit in Nadeem's palm. It was made out of baked clay, painted white and blue with a similar pattern of vines and butterflies as Toyal's headscarf.

Nadeem hadn't carried a drop spindle with her. Maybe the next trip away from the *kabil* she would.

"Thank you," Nadeem said, honored. She recognized this as Toyal's personal drop spindle, the one she'd probably carried with her since she'd been a young girl.

Then Toyal handed Nadeem a hunk of soft fiber. Not too much—just a touch, to do a small bit of spinning.

Nadeem knew that as an honored guest she could ask for more, but she wouldn't take the old woman's livelihood away. This fiber would spin into fine thread and could be sold for a lot at the marketplace.

Nadeem spun a few inches of thread from the fiber with her fingers, enough to wrap around the spindle below the whorl. She hefted the weight of the spindle—heavier than she was used to. It would spin too fast if she wasn't careful.

Carefully, Nadeem smoothed out some more of the fiber, twisting it back and forth between her fingers, before she finally let go of the spindle.

It dropped smoothly, spinning out thread from the fibers as she guided it with her fingers.

"Just lovely," Nadeem murmured after a moment. The fibers spun very nice thread. It would be strong and not break easily.

Toyal sighed. "You *are* just a traveler, then," she said sadly.

"I am," Nadeem said, surprised. "Who did you think I was?"

Toyal gave a cackling laugh. "Don't take this wrong, but you smell like the desert and death," she said. "I know that I'll be dancing in the goddess' court soon. I'd been hoping I might rate a visit from her first."

Nadeem controlled her fear. She didn't stiffen or react. "Really?" she said casually.

How could the old woman have known?

"Or maybe everything smells like death today," Toyal said sadly. "I've been away from my home for so very long."

"You weren't born here, in Koruli?" Nadeem asked, surprised. Most people rarely traveled; they were born, lived, and died all in the same place. Merchants traveled and some craftsmen and women, but that was it.

"I was born in Çandekili, west of here," Toyal told her. "Left as a young, foolish girl, following my heart. Never went back after I was married. But Narlis has been gone now going on three long years. It's time I followed him into the goddess' court. I'm surprised that I lasted this long."

"I see," Nadeem said. She wondered what it would be like to have a husband, to stay in one place, to be married and happy with a family.

She had her sisters, her *kabil*, her missions and training.

She wouldn't trade that for anything.

She dropped the spindle again, spinning fiber into fine thread.

"So tell me of your town," Nadeem said after another long moment. "What has kept you here?"

Toyal talked of her three grandchildren and four sons, how hard they worked, the large number of flocks of sheep that they kept. She mentioned many names that Nadeem didn't bother keeping track of, instead just losing herself in the flow of the story.

Nadeem perked up, though, when Toyal mentioned Malik. Something about the harvest not coming in?

"What happened?" Nadeem asked, interrupting the old woman's ramblings.

"Three? No, four years ago. When the rains didn't come. Malik helped out the famers who couldn't make the emperor's tithe," Toyal said. "Paid it himself, he did."

"Why would he do that?" Nadeem asked sourly, as if she'd heard bad things about the man.

"Malik's been as constant as the hills, helping those in need," Toyal said defensively. "Paying our debts. Never asking for more than a man can give." She lowered her voice. "Don't know as to how we would have survived without him. Koruli might have been abandoned, the town scattering, if people couldn't pay their debts."

"But the land's good here," Nadeem said. "You've got water and wells. Good scrap for sheep."

Water had always been such a concern in the desert. Any year that got less rain in the rainy season was a bad year. She remembered four years ago. It had been the summer before she'd gone into training. The star sisters planned better than most, so there hadn't been famine. But people had been hungry.

"Ah, you're from south of here, aren't you?" Toyal said cannily. "Concerned about water. All the people from the south are." She heaved a sigh. "It's true, though, what you say. We got good wells. But if we can't pay the emperor his due, we'd be slaves. People here are stubborn. They'd leave the town and go elsewhere rather than not be free."

Nadeem controlled her shiver. Was that why she was to kill Malik? To destroy the town?

There must be a good reason for it. The emperor had commanded it.

Or maybe the old woman was wrong. The people here would stay.

"The townsfolk wouldn't go to other towns, would they?" Nadeem asked, putting surprise into her voice. Most people were too settled.

"Those with a craft would," Toyal insisted. "Though the young men—always so stupid—would probably just go off to war. Thinking they could gain riches that way."

Nadeem nodded. In the *kabil,* she hadn't heard the aunts talk much about the wars. Plus, the star sisters rarely kept their sons, so didn't have to worry about sending them to be part of the emperor's troops.

"Fighting for the emperor is an honor," Nadeem said firmly. That was what she was doing. Aunt Izmet would expect such a response from her.

"Aye, it is," Toyal said. "But if everyone is off fighting, who will tend the sheep? Grow the grain? Tan the leather? Have more babes?"

Nadeem grunted, neither agreeing or disagreeing.

It was an honor to serve the emperor. To do his bidding.

Even if Aunt Parayat's voice at the back of her head was questioning even that.

Nadeem left Gabril and Durzhen at the inn, loudly complaining to the innkeeper about needing more wood for the fire, more hot water for their tea, more bread with their meal. A few locals had joined them for dinner, treating them with varying degrees of respect: On the one hand, they were old and strangers, therefore due respect. On the other hand, they were star sisters, who were never trusted because of their ability to cast illusions and trick people.

Nadeem felt confident that Gabril and Durzhen would be able to maintain the illusion that there were three of them, giving her an alibi. Not that she would need one: The assignment had been to make Malik's death look natural.

Before Nadeem left the inn she stripped off her tunic, blouse, and skirt. Underneath, she wore tight black pants that would have scandalized anyone who saw her. Women weren't supposed to wear tight clothing. However, the pants allowed her greater movement. Her shirt was sleeveless, also black, showing off her wiry muscles and dark skin. In her belt around her waist she had the traditional three knives, plus others tied to her calves. She had her blowgun attached to her left hip. The headscarf she wore was also black, and held sharp poisoned needles.

The town was dark. Very few lights shone through the windows. The community worked during sunlight hours and slept at night. It wasn't as if there were traveling storytellers who had set up for the evening in the marketplace, or even a band of players putting on shows.

And Koruli was so small that probably only happened at the height of summer, and not even every year.

For now, Nadeem waited just outside the door of the inn as her eyes adjusted. She still wouldn't be able to see much, she knew. The stars didn't shine very brightly that night, and there was only a half-moon.

Still, she felt confident that she could make it to Malik's house. The innkeeper had volunteered that information when Nadeem had exclaimed that she'd heard about some of his good deeds that afternoon, speculating that he must live in a palace in the hills.

The innkeeper had been quick to explain that Malik kept a modest house in town, and lived within his means. Particularly since his wife had died that winter.

At Nadeem's disbelief, the innkeeper had insisted on drawing her a map, using the charcoal end of one of the sticks from the fireplace, sketching on one of the smooth stones on the floor, so that in the morning Nadeem could go and see for herself.

The house was only two streets away, down to the cross street leading west off the market street, past the large garden, then up two doors on the right. From what little Nadeem could see, the houses weren't that fine. Sure, they were mostly two stories, but they weren't grand or overly large.

Chickens clucked at her from the large garden. She understood that three of the nearby families all owned the land together—all sons and daughters from a wealthy merchant who'd insisted that the land not be divided. They'd fought for a while, then finally agreed to raise chickens and grow a few vegetables there. As they all had their own houses nearby, it was a good arrangement, much more civilized than running harsh walls and dividing up the land so small that it couldn't serve any purpose.

Malik had supposedly brokered that deal as well.

Either Malik had bribed all the good people of the town into thinking he was a hero sent from the gods, or he really did have a generous heart.

Nadeem assumed it was actually a bit of each. He also provided most of the *igrat* the town consumed at its midsummer feast.

The house before Nadeem stood dark and foreboding. She made sure that she blended well into the shadows as she stepped forward.

The front window, of course, was latched from the inside. She didn't try the door, assuming that it was locked.

To the casual observer, the stones that made up the front of the house would have appeared smooth, with few cracks.

Nadeem walked close to the wall, then looked directly up.

Just out of her reach above her, the rocks stuck out a ways.

With a great leap, Nadeem grabbed hold of the ledge, her toes finding holds along the way.

The wall had been well constructed, and there weren't as many holds as she'd expected.

Still, it didn't take her long to climb up the wall, reaching a window well above the ground.

No latch held the window shut. The wooden cover swung open easily. She lifted it up above her head and held it there.

Nadeem stuck her head in the room and waited, listening, breathing in the quiet of the house.

Good pork had been cooked that night, a rich man's feast with sweet carrots and fennel. The house itself was still. She didn't hear any steps or breathing.

It was too dark to see much. There appeared to be hunks of furniture in the room, maybe a desk under the window. An office, perhaps, where Malik conducted his trade.

Nadeem pulled herself up and through the window. She didn't want to put a foot on the desk—it might not be strong enough to take her weight, even as slight as she was—so she jumped into what she believed was an open space, landing on her hands and summersaulting gracefully.

Then she stopped again, listening. Had anyone heard her? Suspected that their castle had just been violated?

But she didn't hear anything besides the muffled sounds of the night.

Nadeem walked quickly across the room for the door in the corner. She opened it an inch and peeked out.

The hallway was well lit, which surprised her. Was Malik still up? Entertaining guests, perhaps?

Nadeem waited, but she still didn't hear anything. Didn't smell anything beyond rich leather polish and perfumed pillows.

Nadeem stuck her head out a bit further.

The office she'd climbed into had been at the end of the hall, built out of the corner. To her right stood an open doorway, as well as a closed one further down. To her left the staircase opened up.

Malik would be up here, in his bed. Hopefully alone. Which room, though?

Nadeem *blurred* herself. She couldn't turn herself invisible, unfortunately. And there weren't many shadows to blend into in this brightly lit hallway. She still made it as difficult as she could for the eye to track her.

The floor was made of dark wood, scarred and old. Nadeem walked silently along it. She only had leather strips wrapped around the balls of her feet to give her traction.

Just before the open doorway, Nadeem paused again.

She didn't hear anything inside the room.

She took another step forward.

Peeked inside.

Just inside the door an older man sat on the floor, leaning against pillows.

"I don't see you," the man said carefully. "But I know you're there. I've been expecting you."

Nadeem stiffened, surprised. How did he know she was there?

The man nodded to himself. He pushed himself up slowly, using a solid cane, showing his age. He had long white hair that he wore in the northern style, cut around his shoulders and curled under. His large bulbous nose proclaimed him from the north as well, though his thin, long face and darker skin spoke of southern origin as well. Perhaps his mother had been from this south, while his father from here.

No one had mentioned that during their praises of the man.

"Please, won't you come join me?" he asked, turning his back and walking further into the room.

Nadeem didn't bother asking if he was Malik. She assumed he was. A servant or someone playing the part of the rich merchant wouldn't have this confidence.

She cut the thread of illusion surrounding herself. It didn't really matter if he knew she was there, if he saw her.

He'd be dead before too long.

And she had too many questions.

"Why did you expect me?" Nadeem asked as she stepped into the room, stepping around the pillows.

Malik poured himself a large mug of water, then did the same for Nadeem. "I've dreamed of three stars streaming across the sky," he said, "coming from the far east. After they passed over my house, it burst into flames."

"What do you think the dream means?" Nadeem asked, freezing.

"Three star sisters came into town this afternoon," Malik explained. "We haven't seen your kind in a decade or more. And you arrived from the east. So I assumed that you are the three stars I saw crossing the sky. As for my house burning—I figured that meant that you were here to kill me."

He peered at her closely, at her black sleeveless shirt that allowed her free movement, the tight black pants that others would consider indecent. The knives tucked into her belt, her blowgun and darts attached to her hip.

"A stranger coming as you did, crawling up the wall of my house and in through a window, isn't here to share dinner and break bread," he added.

Nadeem nodded. She should have known that such a great death, ordered by the emperor, would trigger a warning dream.

Next time, she would be more prepared.

Or at least that was what she promised herself.

That there would be a next time.

That she couldn't fail at this.

<hr>

Nadeem took the glass of water Malik had poured for her, then toasted the man when he raised his cup. However, she'd learned over the past three years how to fake drinking, so didn't bother to actually take a sip.

The room had no bed in it. It appeared to be another study. A small bookshelf sat against the far wall. Had this at one point been the room for one or more of his children? A painted wooden doll still sat on the shelf between the scrolls and small boxes sitting there.

Under the window stood a low writing desk, for kneeling behind. Rich pillows leaned against the other walls. This was a more intimate meeting room, where deals could be struck informally. A different kind of office than the one Nadeem had come through.

Bright clay lamps, hung from the ceiling, lit the room well. A single glass lamp stood on the writing desk. Expensive but practical.

Malik lowered himself back down to the ground, leaning heavily on his cane. It was made from a solid piece of black wood, with a silver head in the shape of a snake.

Strange symbol for a man of such power. None of the gods were represented by a snake.

Nadeem glanced around the room again before she sank down gracefully, showing off her youth and agility. No altar was tucked away in any of the corners.

Stranger and stranger.

"I was born here, in Koruli," Malik started. "My mother came from the north."

Nadeem nodded. She'd assumed that was the case.

"Things were different, then," he said.

Nadeem didn't roll her eyes, but she wanted to. He was starting to sound like Aunt Haneet and the others, who constantly complained that children didn't understand, that things had been so much better when they'd been young.

"The emperor had less power, then," Malik continued.

That made Nadeem sit up a bit straighter.

Maybe Malik really was a traitor. Maybe she could kill him without guilt.

"The people don't resent the prayers that have been added," Malik said softly. "Or that his symbol is now added to all buildings."

Nadeem nodded. Of course the people shouldn't resent such things. The emperor had been good to them. The years, fruitful.

"Only some of us ask about the meaning of such symbols," Malik said. He picked up his cane and held it toward her.

The snake head was finely made, of course. The skin was covered in tight scales, carved out of silver.

Each scale looked like the emperor's symbol.

"Where did you get this?" Nadeem asked. She reached out and touched the cold silver, running a finger along the bumps.

There wasn't anything magical about the head of the cane.

It still made her shiver. There was something…off about it.

Something unnatural. She'd never seen such a thing before. Were any of the *kabil* aware of this sort of thing? Something that was, but was not, magical?

"From the emperor, himself," Malik said. "To thank me for helping the town."

"I see," Nadeem said. "And now, as your repayment for such kindness, you incite the people of Koruli against him?" she asked archly.

"No, no," Malik said, shaking his head. He gave her a rueful grin. "I exhort them to follow his edicts. To pray to their gods. To do their duty. And this watches me, makes sure I do."

Nadeem shook her head. "It isn't magical," she told him. "I don't sense any magic in it at all."

Malik blinked, obviously surprised. "Really?" he said.

He picked the cane back up and examined it briefly.

Then he shoved it at her.

Nadeem blocked the cane automatically.

Malik smirked at her. "You wouldn't defend yourself so violently if there was nothing about this cane that unsettled you."

Nadeem shrugged. "I might have. You moved quickly. I'm trained to defend myself."

"As all the star sisters are," Malik said, nodding. He paused, then added, "I know you've probably taken a blood oath to take my life."

"I have," Nadeem told him gravely. "You will not leave this room alive," she added.

She didn't see any reason why she shouldn't be honest with him. "If there is something you need to tell me, some confession you must make, I would make it now," she said. She didn't know where this conversation was going. She didn't like the edges of it, though.

Malik nodded. "I've made my peace with Enkat and Xannil," he said.

That surprised Nadeem. That he followed the goddess of rain and the god of the sun, as opposed to Innis, the god of fertility, whom most merchants followed.

"Did you know that Xannil is portrayed as a happy god in the north?" Malik said casually.

Nadeem shook her head. She hadn't heard of that before. Xannil was an angry god, sullen, often jealous of his wife Enkat, hiding her so no rain came.

"You should travel to the north sometime," Malik told her. "Listen to the people there, to the priests and their gods. See how the emperor is viewed." He held up his cane again. "The snake god that's slithering his way into their hearts."

Was Malik implying that the *Padisha-i-Ghazi* was becoming a snake?

Then she remembered his symbol. It looked like the scale of a snake. And the great cloak that the emperor wore, composed of scales made from the afterbirths of all the magicians and illusionist.

What kind of power did that cloak give him?

He'd already lived a long, long time. Longer than any man. Almost two hundred years, if the scholars were to be believed.

Was he immortal?

Was he like a god? Growing more godlike every year?

Nadeem opened her mouth to ask another question when she noticed Malik had grown pale, suddenly.

His mouth gaped, hanging open like a dead fish's.

Then he slowly tumbled to his side.

Nadeem leaped to her feet, turning toward the door.

Gabril and Durzhen entered silently.

"What have you done?" Nadeem asked angrily.

They looked at each other, then back at her.

"We've completed the assignment, as we swore to do," Durzhen said, putting away her blowgun.

"The question is, what were you doing?" Gabril asked.

Nadeem looked over at the body, then back again.

The poison had already killed Malik. It would putrefy his body next.

"Learn all you can about your enemy," Nadeem instructed them. "Wasn't that one of the first things we were taught?"

"No," Durzhen said, shaking her head. "Do your duty. That always came first."

Nadeem swallowed back any more words she might have said.

Silently, she cursed Aunt Parayat's voice, that questioning tone she heard at the back of her head.

Aunt Izmet had taught obedience first.

Unquestioning obedience.

Nadeem had never learned not to question.

Now, she had to learn how to keep asking questions, but at the same time, stay alive.

"You know, his death was supposed to look natural," Nadeem told the other two sourly. "There's no way to hide that he's been poisoned."

At least Durzhen looked guilty for a moment.

Gabril spoke up. "You were supposed to smother him in his sleep. Not talk him to death," she said.

Nadeem had always assumed that her team was as curious as she was about everything.

Now, she realized how little they questioned her direction.

They'd never thought for themselves, though she'd always tried to get them to. Instead, they just followed her.

Blindly.

She cursed silently. She'd always considered herself a good leader.

She knew better than to blame Malik for stripping that away from her as well.

"He was expecting me," Nadeem said quietly after a few moments. "I couldn't have surprised him. Couldn't have smothered him in his sleep." She paused, then added, "What would you have done?"

"Strangled him the moment I walked into the room," Durzhen said firmly.

"But he'd had a dream about us coming," Nadeem said.

"So?" Durzhen said hotly.

Nadeem sighed. "A command from the emperor to kill a man is an important event," she explained gently. "Big enough that someone may dream of it. If I hadn't stopped and asked and talked with Malik about that, I wouldn't have that useful bit of information for the next assignment."

"Oh," Durzhen said. She pushed her lips together as if she wanted to dispute what Nadeem said.

Nadeem held her peace and didn't say anything more. She knew she was right.

"All right," Duzhen said stubbornly. "I guess that's useful. For the next time."

"But what are we going to do with the body now?" Gabril asked.

Nadeem nodded. She was the one responsible for their training.

Or their lack of it.

"We burn the place down," she said.

Malik had said that the stars had left his house ablaze.

Everyone had gathered at the inn that morning, before Nadeem and the others had made their way back down to the main room.

Seemed there had been a terrible fire at Malik's house.

Luckily, the walls had been thick enough to contain the fire, and it hadn't spread beyond the house.

It appeared he'd been drinking his own *igrat*, which people knew he did from time to time.

Since his wife had died, he had been drinking a bit more.

But this time, he'd drunk too much. Had been careless with one of his fancy oil lights.

Or at least that was the story people were telling each other.

"It's a shame," Nadeem said truthfully.

Malik had been a good man.

But the emperor's will had to be done.

And Nadeem, still wearing the appearance of an old woman, had a better, more stout stick to walk with as well. A cane with a silver snake head.

CHAPTER ELEVEN

TRULLIÇ

TRULLIÇ CARRIED THE BOX ALL the way back to Gaadiwala. Though the box was small, just a little bigger than his outstretched palms, the sand in it made it heavy. He found early on that he didn't have to take the full weight of the box, that he could magically float it and just appear to be carrying it. He tried once to have it floating just behind him. While he could do that, he didn't want other people to see it, for them to realize he was a magician. He didn't want to run into refugees from Çandekili and have them remember him, or accuse him of killing Yerkoyliç.

Gaadiwala looked dim in the late afternoon light. Trulliç missed the colors of Çandekili, the colors of the hillsides with rain. It all seemed gray to him.

He decided that while his people would not be as gaudily dressed as those in Çandekili, they would still wear colors. The houses would be more colored, too. Not just rocks and bare dirt.

He could almost see it in his mind's eye, this town on the edge of the desert, with golden-sand colored buildings and flags flying everywhere, palm trees and tall *meslit* thorns growing along twisting streets.

Was that his home? Or was he just being fanciful?

No. He'd made the decision to not call anyone else fanciful.

He wasn't being fanciful either.

Those square towers. Those gold and green striped flags. Those sweet smelling dates.

Those were real.

He would make it so.

Was it too late to go directly to Atça's house?

Trulliç decided he didn't care.

Atça needed to explain too many things.

Riyune followed eagerly behind. Trulliç could tell the dog seemed…happy, perhaps. Not smugly satisfied, but content.

He didn't feel any of the guilt Trulliç felt about killing Yerkoyliç.

Trulliç wasn't certain the dog could feel guilt about anything.

He assumed that anyone who saw him in town and recognized him would tell his mother that he'd come back.

He would go to the tavern next.

Atça's house also seemed gray, cast in shadows. It still looked grander than all the houses around it, three stories of finely milled stones, set beautifully together.

Trulliç had once thought it was the finest building he'd ever seen.

Now, he wondered if even poorest slums of Çandekili had been better.

He knocked on Atça's door and waited.

The old magician came quickly. He seemed surprised to see Trulliç. "My boy! Welcome!" he said. He peered at Trulliç, at the box he carried, then glanced quickly at Riyune and away again. He wore a tunic striped black and blue, the colors of Barzhat. It hung loosely on him, unbelted, going down to the start of his thighs, with a blue pair of baggy pants and an off-white shirt.

"Do you know what this is?" Trulliç demanded, hefting the box toward Atça.

Atça gave him a cold smile. "Of course. That is a land box."

"Why didn't you make one for me?" Trulliç asked. He couldn't help the pleading note in his voice.

"My dear boy, the emperor outlawed those decades ago," Atça said smugly. "I take it you took this one from Yerkoyliç?"

Trulliç nodded mutely.

"I suppose that he might have claimed that he wasn't breaking the law, since he made a land box for land that wasn't his," Atça said, speculating. "However, if any of the emperor's guards find *you* with it, they're likely to kill you outright."

"Oh," was all that Trulliç could say.

The box *was* powerful. It did make his magic more powerful. He didn't feel as strong as he usually did when he stepped across the border into the desert. It still increased his power dramatically.

"Why does the emperor want magicians to be weak?" he asked. But he knew the answer already.

The emperor didn't want any of the magicians to challenge him.

A group of magicians, all with land boxes…they might be strong enough.

Or they might not be.

Not if the emperor became a god.

"Has anyone seen you with the box?" Atça asked archly.

Trulliç shrugged. "Just the people here," he said. "But none of them would know what it is. What it means." Plus, they were his people, the people of Gaadiwala. They wouldn't report him to the emperor's guards when they came through.

Would they?

"Maybe. Maybe not," Atça said with a shrug. "You can't keep it here, in Gaadiwala."

Trulliç sighed and nodded. What was he going to do with the box? He didn't want to give it up. Couldn't just leave it someplace.

Was he going to have to take it back to the true desert? To release the sands there?

Atça seemed to consider for a moment, before saying, "You can come in. But you must cover the box. And you should never use it here, in Gaadiwala."

Trulliç turned to Riyune to see his reaction to Atça's request.

The dog nodded once, as if agreeing.

"All right," Trulliç agreed.

He stepped across the threshold of Atça's house.

He felt Atça's magic immediately. He'd sensed threads of it after he'd crossed the border into Gaadiwala, the stirring of Atça's power. But the house was the center of it.

While Yerkoyliç was all flowers and bees, Atça was stone and dirt. Hearty in ways Yerkoyliç wasn't.

They were both strong.

But Trulliç had killed Yerkoyliç, had proven himself stronger.

Was it possible that Trulliç was also stronger than Atça?

That remained to be seen.

Trulliç relinquished the box to put on house slippers. His power immediately faded. He took his tunic off and covered the top of the box with it before he picked it back up, wrapping the cloth around it fully.

He couldn't help his sigh of relief, how happy he was with desert power flowing back over him.

Atça made a sour face at him. It was obvious that he'd been hoping that Trulliç would ask for something to cover the box with, something that Atça could have then used to control the box somehow.

Trulliç shivered when he considered that Atça might have tried to poison the sands.

No. Atça could never touch the box or the sands inside.

Trulliç followed Atça into the study. Atça had obviously been working there. Scrolls lay out on the writing desk. A half-full cup of tea sat beside it. The lights all flared brightly as Atça stepped into the room, making it seem as bright as day.

Atça poured Trulliç a cup from his own tea service, then indicated that Trulliç should join him, leaning against the best guest pillows done in red and gold.

Trulliç remembered Yerkoyliç's patterns. How everyone who could afford to had vines, flowers, and butterflies embroidered on their clothing. What were Atça's patterns or motif? Did he have any?

Trulliç sipped his tea and looked around the room. Riyune had taken up his usual place by the door, sitting as still as a statue.

There. Patterns of stripes.

Now that Trulliç thought about it, he realized that very few people he'd seen on the road wore stripes. It wasn't uncommon. However, it wasn't as common elsewhere as it was in Gaadiwala. Almost everyone in the town wore some sort of stripes, generally a striped tunic, though some of the richer merchants also had striped shirts. Many of the women wore striped headscarves.

Pleased, Trulliç looked back at Atça, who stared at the covered land box.

"What was Yerkoyliç doing with a desert land box?" he asked.

Trulliç didn't see any reason not to tell Atça. "He was looking for the desert heart."

"Really?"

Trulliç didn't like the satisfied, smug smile that Atça gave him.

"What did he tell you about it?" his mentor asked. He tried to sound casual, but he failed miserably. He was very curious about what Trulliç knew.

"That it was Forit's heart, still alive in the desert," Trulliç told him honestly. "That the emperor is also searching for it, to become a god. That the other magicians—and he was part of a group—wanted to find it first."

"So they could use it themselves, I imagine," Atça said sourly. He gave a dramatic sigh. "Those fools! They could have been working *for* the emperor, instead of against him."

"What do you mean?" Trulliç asked, surprised.

"Don't you see? If the emperor is searching for the heart, that means it must exist," Atça said.

He almost seemed excited. It was very strange.

"We should find it first. So we can present it to him, as a gift," Atça continued.

Trulliç stiffened. He bit his lips together so he didn't automatically disagree.

It sounded like a bad idea, either way. Either the emperor would use it to become a god and throw all of the empire into war with the rest of the gods, or the heart would still be corrupted with darkness. Releasing such a plague on the world would also be a bad idea.

"Just think of the reward the emperor would give for such a prize!" Atça continued.

"Maybe," Trulliç said. If such a thing existed, it would need a strong magician to hold it. Right?

Or maybe they just needed to find it. Then the emperor could come and claim it.

"As a desert magician, I would think you should consider it your duty to find the desert heart for the emperor," Atça said in his lecture tones.

Trulliç shook his head. He didn't agree.

"Does it even exist?" Trulliç asked. "Haven't magicians been searching for it for years? And wouldn't the emperor have found it already?" He didn't think this was a good idea at all.

Atça pursed his lips and thought for a moment. "You're right, it is a very old legend, that the heart still exists." He paused, then added, "But it is also part of the story that the old kings knew of the existence of the heart and hid it for millennia."

"That doesn't mean it exists," Trulliç said. "That's just another excuse for why people never found it." For all of Atça's flaws, he always had tried to get Trulliç to think and not just accept whatever was presented to him.

Atça nodded. "That's a possibility. Or it could be that their magic is finally draining out of the world and the heart can finally be found."

"And you want me to go looking for it," Trulliç said dryly.

Atça gave him a wintery smile. "Oh, I doubt that you'll be able to find it. It has been lost all these many ages. And you can't even find your own home!" He chuckled.

Trulliç took a deep breath. That hurt. Despite how true it was.

"I do need to go back into the desert," Trulliç said slowly. "I need to release the sands in the land box."

Atça looked at him curiously. "Can't you just break the box?"

Trulliç studied the small box sitting beside him for a moment. Despite being covered, he still felt the sands there, calling to him.

The box itself wasn't magical. The sands had been enchanted, though.

"No," he said. "That would just spill the sands out, have them uncontained. They wouldn't lose their magic. Not for a while."

He'd been surprised that the sands had maintained their magical abilities after Yerkoyliç had died, since his city had fallen with his death. Trulliç had assumed that all of the magician's works would die with him.

"You might seek a guide, you know," Atça said. "To help lead you through the desert. Maybe one of the star sisters who frequent that tavern of your family's."

Trulliç blinked. "That's a good idea," he said seriously. "Thank you." Then he grimaced. "I have no way to pay such a guide, though."

"When you find one, send them to me," Atça said. "I will pay their fee. That way, I can honestly tell the emperor's guards that I helped destroy the land box."

"Thank you," Trulliç said.

It wasn't until much later that evening that he wondered what else Atça might tell the emperor's guards.

Particularly if Trulliç didn't do exactly as Atça requested and go looking for the desert heart.

<hr>

Trulliç wasn't surprised to find his mother waiting for him in the small shack they shared. He knew enough people in Gaadiwala had seen him arrive that afternoon and that they'd tell her.

"Well?" she asked as he came through the door.

Trulliç nodded. "Hello, Mother," he said. He walked over to his sleeping roll at the back of the one-room shack and put down the box. Riyune came in after him and settled down next to the box.

"Where's your pack?" Mother asked.

"It was destroyed when Çandekili collapsed," Trulliç said honestly. "I had to get out of the palace alive. Leave it behind."

Mother stared hard at him. "Was it really that close?" she asked, disbelieving.

"The floors were starting to disintegrate under my feet," Trulliç told her. "The murals on the walls were melting."

Would Gaadiwala survive Atça's death? Probably. Atça wasn't as involved with all the parts of the town, hadn't formed it in his image, not like Yerkoyliç had fashioned Çandekili.

Mother nodded, as if she agreed with where Trulliç's thoughts had gone. "And what's this?" she asked.

Trulliç uncovered the box, taking his tunic and tossing it to the side. Then he lifted the box with his magic and flew it over to where his mother stood.

Mother stood very still. She didn't take a step back, as Trulliç had expected her to. She didn't seem startled, either. She looked at him, then looked inside the box.

"Sand?" she asked.

Before he could stop her, Mother reached her hand into the box and drew out a handful of sand. It slid evenly through her fingers back into the box.

Trulliç knew his mother didn't have any magic. The sand didn't react to her as it did to him.

It still recognized her.

Trulliç wouldn't be surprised if the sand, the desert, didn't claim his mother as one of hers, a child of the sand. He knew that Myrizhah had made trips to the desert, that she'd walked the desert every year, like he did, though at different times of the year from him.

"What is it?" Mother asked again.

"A land box, according to Atça," Trulliç said. He sighed. "The sand has been enchanted. It's as if the desert, or the spirit of the desert, lives still in this sand."

Mother nodded. "I can feel it. It soothes my heart, my aching bones."

Trulliç blinked. He'd never really thought about his mother having aches and pains like an old person.

But his mother wasn't young anymore. Gray streaks ran through her long black hair. Wrinkles gathered around her eyes. Her knuckles were obvious, the skin seemingly thinner now across the backs of her hands, showing blue veins as well.

"Where did you get this? Did Atça make it for you?" Mother asked.

Trulliç shook his head. "Yerkoyliç, the magician in Çandekili, had made it." He grimaced. "You can't tell anyone about the box," he warned. "The emperor has forbidden them."

"Ah," Mother said, nodding. "What do you intend to do with it?"

"I must release the sands in the desert," Trulliç said. "To just break the box and dump them out anywhere else would be foolish."

Mother nodded. "What happens when you place your glass horseshoe in the box?"

Trulliç blinked, surprised. "I never thought of doing that."

"Try it," Mother said.

Slowly, Trulliç undid the glass horseshoe that always hung from his belt. The glass felt cool and smooth in his hand as always.

Gingerly, Trulliç reached into the box, laying the horseshoe down on the sand.

Nothing happened.

Trulliç looked up at Mother. "Nothing," he told her.

Her face fell.

Trulliç bit his lips together. He couldn't help being such a poor magician, such a disappointing son.

Then Trulliç reached back into the box, grasping the horseshoe again.

He gasped.

There, just at the corner of his vision, he could see that same town he'd seen earlier that day. With desert all around it, though it wasn't centered in the desert. The desert ended nearby.

Tall, square pillars made up the corners of the town's walls. Many of the buildings were square as well. Golden sand-colored stones made up the walls. Flags and banners flew from the top of every roof, in every color imaginable. Finely paved streets ran between the houses and through the markets, not straight but as curved as the desert winds, with dates and figs growing in the gardens. Great statues of dogs guarded the gates.

"What is it?" Mother asked.

"I think I know where my home is," Trulliç said eagerly. He described what he saw.

Mother shook her head and gave a bitter laugh, then she quoted:

"In Osmerli you will die—in front of buildings of colored sand
    From each roof banners fly—like wings of birds sailing from
a mighty hand."

Trulliç put his hand over his mouth. "No," he whispered, shocked. But she was right.

The poem was from the times of the old kings. When their greatest warriors went to battle against the emperor. When had Mother learned it?

The emperor had laid waste to the entire area, causing a sandstorm to swallow the grand city whole, calling rock out of the earth to choke off the Pirazizil River that fed the oasis.

The city had been located at the southern tip of the Qaenev desert. The emperor had crossed the entire desert in a day to battle the old kings.

"But I see it," Trulliç told her. He grasped the glass horseshoe tighter in his hand. "I know where it is." That was probably why he'd never found his home. He'd needed to travel much, much further across the sands.

Mother nodded. "Do you believe this to be your home?" she asked quietly.

Trulliç answered her honestly. "I don't know. I've seen the city now, twice. But I've seen so many places in the desert." So many secret spots that also called to his heart.

"You should go to Osmerli, then," she told him.

"Will the emperor let me raise the city again?" Trulliç asked.

Mother gave him a tight smile. "His blood hound enabled your birth. I think he would have you make your city."

Trulliç didn't know how to answer that. Didn't know how to respond when she added, "And I will join you there."

Though Trulliç had a better idea where his home in the desert might be, he still thought that Atça's idea of finding a guide was a good one.

The Qaenev desert was huge. Though the emperor crossed it in a day, it would take them most of an entire season. And luck would have to be on their side, with good water and no storms.

How could Trulliç prepare for such a journey? Would he have to cross over the top of the Qaenev desert first, to the far east, then down the ridge of mountains there, keeping to the coast, and then cross over again into the desert when he got to the far south? It was the only way that he knew would work. Though the mountains to the east of Qaenev weren't small or easy to cross, the ones to the west and along the coast there, were known as being particularly foreboding.

It would take a long, long while to get there. But Trulliç was determined to at least have a guide for the first part of the journey, across the wide top of the desert. Then he'd find a second one after he'd made his way to the tip of the continent.

It hurt that he no longer had a decent pack. That he'd lost his sheepskin and sleeping roll.

But if he was going to be gone for a very long while, he could just take everything from his home.

He didn't know how he'd pay for such a long journey. But maybe he could work with one of the caravans that traveled the coast, from north to south.

As long as he managed to stay away from the slave ships that ran there.

Trulliç walked with his mother into the Horseshoe Tavern early that morning. He left the land box in the shack, trusting that no one would bother it. Though his mother had some sort of affinity for the box, he didn't believe anyone else in all of Gaadiwala would take a second look at it.

Not unless Atça told them of it.

As Trulliç would at least tell his mentor that he was searching for the desert heart, he didn't think Atça would turn on him. Would report him to the emperor's guards for holding contraband.

At least, not yet.

Trulliç's cousins seemed happy to see him, demanding to know of his adventures along the road. They'd all heard the news about Çandekili, and Yerkoyliç.

The speculation was that the emperor had had the magician assassinated, that one of the blood hounds had done it. Strange dogs had been seen roaming the palace just before the magician's death.

Trulliç managed to contain himself and not look at Riyune.

The dog maintained an innocent air that Trulliç didn't quite believe.

Trulliç spent the day working at the tavern, cleaning the old attic and carting barrels with his cousin Bekbel.

It wasn't until later that night, after supper, that Trulliç saw her.

It wasn't uncommon for star sisters to stay at the Horseshoe Tavern. Generally they traveled as a group, in twos and threes, but it wasn't uncommon for one to be traveling by herself.

The star sister who sat alone appeared to be about his age. She had a small nose, thin lips, and dark brown eyes. Her hair was short, shorter than most—cut far above her neck. She didn't bother wearing a headscarf inside, though it sat bunched up on the table next to her, a lovely dark green color with gold thread running through it. She wore a tunic similar to his own, dyed a light, golden-sand color with dark stripes of black and blue running through it. It was done in the southern style, open all the way down the front, merely tied together at the waist with a brown leather belt as wide as his outstretched hand.

She had knives in her belt, of course. And probably other places as well.

Trulliç could tell she was a powerful illusionist. She practically glowed with power.

And with dark rage.

He nearly didn't go up to talk with her. She had a thunderous air that warned off most. The other diners at the tavern sat away from her, farther along the rough benches, giving her a wide space.

"Can I get you anything?" Trulliç asked as he came up.

Stormy eyes glared at him. She considered him for a moment,

blinking. "No, magician," she said slowly. "But you are not the town's magician, are you?" she said after another moment.

"I am not," Trulliç said. He took that as good enough of an invitation as any and sat down directly opposite her. "My home is in the desert. Far to the south."

She nodded. "Then what are you doing here?"

Trulliç grimaced. "My family is here. That's my mother," he said, pointing her out. "I'm saying goodbye," he added, realizing that it was true. This was probably one of the last nights that he'd be here. "I'm looking for a guide."

"Guide?" the woman asked, puzzled.

"Someone to lead me across the top of the desert," Trulliç said. "The sands…they tend to confuse me," he admitted.

"I see," the woman said, nodding, though she still looked perplexed.

"I know the star sisters sometimes guide the caravans across the sands," Trulliç added.

She gave him a tight smile. "And you'd like to hire me?"

Trulliç nodded and held his breath.

The star sister's anger flared for a moment, then damped right back down again. She quoted him a price.

Trulliç swallowed. That was a lot of coin.

But he didn't have to agree to the price. He'd let Atça bargain with her. All he did was say, "Let me take you to my mentor. He'll be the one paying."

She nodded once at him. Held her hands out, palms open, the way the desert people greeted each other.

"I am Nadeem."

<hr>

It surprised Trulliç how tall Nadeem was when she stood beside him. She'd seemed shorter when she'd been sitting. Then again, she'd been hunched over her tea, as if she was one of his aunts trying to keep warm during the winter.

Nadeem stopped when she saw Riyune come up next to Trulliç.

She looked for a moment at the dog, then at Trulliç, then back again. "What is that?" she asked.

"He's my familiar," Trulliç said.

"No, he isn't," Nadeem said.

Trulliç blinked, surprised. "How do you know?" he asked.

Nadeem looked between them again. "There's no connection between you," she said after a bit. "If he was your familiar, I should be able to see some sort of ties or something. But there's nothing."

"So he just looks like a normal dog?" Trulliç asked, curious. Yerkoyliç had certainly believed him when he'd said that Riyune was his familiar.

Nadeem shook her head. "That isn't a normal dog."

"Do you see him as magical?" Trulliç asked. Maybe Atça was wrong!

"No, not really," Nadeem said. "He casts a strong shadow," she eventually added.

Trulliç didn't understand what that meant.

"He sits there, like a regular dog," Nadeem told him. "But the shadow he casts is extra strong. And long."

Trulliç vowed to look carefully at Riyune's shadow the next day in the bright sunlight. He'd never noticed such a thing.

He didn't know what that meant.

"So what oasis are you from?" Trulliç asked as they left the tavern together.

Nadeem looked at him strangely. "Why do you think I grew up at an oasis?" she asked.

Trulliç bit down his apology. He was *not* being fanciful. He knew it. Instead, he shrugged. "You have that look. That feel," he said. "Of a desert person."

Nadeem nodded. "So do you," she said. "I grew up in Lhadara, to the east."

Trulliç knew she lied. The Lhadara oasis was too small to support a *kabil* of star sisters.

He didn't question her, though.

He had enough secrets of his own. Like the land box that sat beside his sleeping pallet covered with blankets in the shack he shared with his mother. He could *feel* it. Not as loudly as the desert when he stayed near her. But loud enough that he no longer worried about someone taking the box. Even if it was stolen, he'd still know where to find it.

He did wonder, though, if she'd grown up in the Kardeş oasis. It was rumored that a large *kabil* of star sisters lived there and kept it permanently hidden.

He'd dreamed of it once, which was the only way he'd known about it.

Twilight was just starting, casting a purple hue to the sky. Stars had started to come out to the east. The moon was already halfway through its journey, just a sliver, almost new.

People in Gaadiwala looked strangely at Trulliç and Nadeem. Then again, they always did. He could just imagine the gossip already starting back at the tavern. Though if anyone was stupid enough to say anything to his mother, well, they deserved what they got.

"I grew up here," Trulliç told Nadeem. "In Gaadiwala."

"How do you like it?" Nadeem asked him. She seemed actually curious, not just being polite.

"It's difficult," Trulliç admitted, "as a magician, to live in the town of another magician."

Nadeem nodded. "He's not very strong," she said.

Trulliç didn't defend his mentor. "But he's always here," he said instead.

"That makes sense," she said. "And he's the one who will pay my fee?"

"Yes," Trulliç said.

"Determined to get rid of you?" she asked.

Was she teasing him? That sure sounded like something one of his cousins would say.

"You know how it is with mentors," Trulliç said lightly. "Always disappointed no matter how hard you work." He hadn't meant the words to come out as bitter as they'd sounded.

"My mentor…" Nadeem paused for a long moment. "I think she'd be proud of me. But it's complicated."

To that, Trulliç couldn't add anything more.

Atça opened the door wide when Trulliç knocked. He wore one of his striped tunics, gold and red, with a gleaming white shirt and black pants. He looked at Trulliç, then at Nadeem, one eyebrow arching.

"Atça," Trulliç started. "I have found a guide who has agreed to take me through the desert." He didn't bother spilling out the rest of his plan to his mentor.

He would tell Atça later all of what his journey would entail.

Maybe.

"Nadeem, may I introduce Atça, the magician of Gaadiwala," Trulliç said formally. "He is my mentor and has volunteered to pay your fee."

Trulliç didn't bother mentioning any amount. The pair of them could haggle about it.

He wasn't sure which of them would get the better deal.

"Ah, thank you, my son," Atça said. "It is truly an honor to meet one of the star sisters," he said, addressing Nadeem.

"The honor is mine," she murmured.

Trulliç felt himself bristle at her words. She'd used the proper form and the words sounded correct, but they had an edge to them that didn't sound right.

Like she was actually mocking the old man or something.

Atça didn't reply but merely nodded. "Come in, come in," he said, holding the door open wider.

Trulliç let Nadeem enter first.

When he would have followed, Atça held up his hand, stopping Trulliç.

"No," Atça said. "This bargaining should take place without you here. Trust me that she and I will come to a mutual agreement."

With that, Atça shut the door in Trulliç's face.

Trulliç rocked back on his heels. Anger washed over him.

How dare he? It was *his* journey. *His* path across the desert.

But Atça was paying. It was his money.

With a sigh, Trulliç turned away.

Riyune sat in his path for a moment, as if questioning why Trulliç was leaving.

"Come on," Trulliç told the dog. "I'm sure Nadeem will tell us all about it."

Riyune gave Trulliç a classic dog eye-roll, but trotted beside Trulliç as they made their way back to the tavern.

Trulliç knew that Nadeem wouldn't tell him anything that she didn't think was appropriate. The star sisters were very strict about their oaths.

Hopefully, there was nothing about this bargain that she would keep from him.

CHAPTER TWELVE

NADEEM

NADEEM DEPARTED FROM HER SISTERS just before they reached Gaadiwala.

They'd spent the morning walking north from Korbul to maintain their story of three elderly star sisters on a training journey. When they cut back south, they lost their disguises and gave the town a wide berth before finding the trail south again.

Nadeem had kept an illusion around Malik's cane so it appeared to be a stout stick tied to her bag. Though the cane wasn't magical, not in a sense that she understood, it still took to the disguise well. She had to maintain the tiniest thread to hold it in place.

The late afternoon sun warmed her *chafiyek*. She was glad for the scarf's length, protecting her neck. She wore one of her favorite tunics. She'd dyed all the thread to be used before one of the aunts had woven it together: the light, golden-sand color coming from *meslit* bark, the black from the nut of the logwood tree, and the blue from desert crickets.

It wasn't solid in the front but split, held together with her wide belt. She wore a gauzy blouse underneath, thick enough to protect her from the sun but cool enough to let breezes in, as well as a pair of loose, baggy pants instead of a long skirt.

The three of them had been quiet all during their walk. Nadeem led, wondering how she could teach the others to question, if that was even possible. She'd had the advantage of Aunt Parayat her entire life. The others hadn't.

How else had she failed her team?

Would she even to be allowed back into the training camp?

"Nadeem," Gabril called from behind as she neared the crossroads. Just before Gaadiwala the trail split, going roughly in all four directions.

Nadeem stopped and turned back.

Gabril and Durzhen stood shoulder to shoulder just a little ways down the hill.

Would she ever be able to stand like that with them again? Or had she lost her team as well?

"We go on our next assignment from here," Gabril told her.

Nadeem nodded. "I see," she said, though she didn't. Not really.

They'd been given another assignment? More tasks for them to do, before going back to the training camp? Or sent back to their own *kabils*?

Why hadn't she been given another assignment? Aunt Izmet had actually told her to take her time returning. Nadeem had assumed that the others had been told the same thing, that they'd travel together, slowly retracing their footsteps, maybe going off and having an adventure or two along the way.

Instead, the other two were leaving her. She'd have to travel on her own.

It wasn't uncommon for star sisters to travel alone. Still, Nadeem felt as though a sharp blade had severed the ties between them.

Nadeem swallowed down the hurt.

She'd failed them.

She willed away the shock and pain that probably was plainly showing on her face.

"I wish you well, my sisters," Nadeem said, bowing her head low. And she did.

"Much success in your journey, too," Gabril said, also bowing.

"Until we meet at the golden halls, or before," Durzhen added.

So. It was a final goodbye. The last wasn't generally said casually—only when someone was going on a long journey and possibly wouldn't be returning.

"Until then," Nadeem said. She gave them one last bow then deliberately turned her back on them and continued up the hill toward Gaadiwala.

If they were going to attack her they should have done it earlier, before they'd given her any warning.

Now, she'd never trust them again.

Nadeem studied the young man standing in front of her. He was obviously the son of the woman who had served her. He had the same long chin and thin face. But his bulbous nose came from a father from the north, and his eyes weren't as dark as his mother's or his cousin's.

He had power. She'd marked him from the moment she'd stepped into the tavern. She'd never met a magician before.

But this wasn't his home. He seemed rootless. Like a storm billowing and blowing, just looking for a place to strike.

He was as tall as she was, though a bit younger. He might grow taller still.

She was surprised when he invited himself to her table and sat down. She'd deliberately given off an air of *don't touch*. It had been remarkably effective.

But he also had power and so wasn't automatically scared of hers.

It puzzled her that he was looking for a guide. When he said that he was from the desert, that his home was in the desert, everything came together. That storm he carried. The dry winds.

Why would he get lost in the desert? It didn't make any sense. How could it overwhelm someone who was a native? Even if he'd been raised in the town? Surely it was close enough that he'd visited. Why had he never found his feet?

The dog, Riyune, didn't make sense either. He was like the cane she carried, tied to her pack. Not quite what he seemed.

He wasn't a familiar. Though Nadeem had never met another magician or seen a familiar, Riyune didn't belong to anyone other than himself.

His shadow was as strong as he was. Even in the dim light of the evening, it walked beside him. Nadeem didn't understand how or why, but just told Trulliç honestly what she saw.

Trulliç led her to the house of the town's magician, Atça.

The old man had a miserly soul, more grasping than Aunt Haneet.

This had been the man who'd raised Trulliç. Responsible for teaching him. Mentoring him.

Suddenly, Trulliç's inability to find his own feet in the desert made a lot more sense.

Nadeem took off her sandals as requested by the old man. He wore a striped tunic similar to her own, though his stripes were wider, and the colors of the goddess Barzhat, blue and black.

She looked around the front hallway. She'd never seen so much wood in one place before.

Instead of impressing her, it made her question why more trees didn't grow in Gaadiwala. Couldn't they get the water? But surely Atça should have been able to raise it.

The hallway leading to the back of the house made Nadeem put a hand on her knife at her waist. Spiders lived there in the corners of the ceiling, spiders she couldn't see but felt, nonetheless.

The formal sitting room that Atça led Nadeem to had more wood, of course. Shelves covered in scrolls that she wished she could ask about. This miser would collect fascinating things, of that she was certain.

Atça directed Nadeem to sit in the place of honor. Nadeem took it without the usual dance of initially refusing.

It wasn't that she was in a hurry to get out of this place. But a way of indicating to Atça that yes, she was that much further above him. Her rank was indeed that much higher, that she should naturally take the place of honor.

"Have you been enjoying your time in my town?" Atça asked after he served what Nadeem had to admit was a fine cup of tea. His tea service was made from polished silver, ornate and obviously not from the region.

"I'm just passing through," Nadeem told him. She'd really only seen the tavern, as well as walking in and out of the town. She remembered her initial impressions of Gaadiwala, how poor it seemed despite the fact that they had a magician.

Her opinion hadn't changed.

"Trulliç asked for me to be a guide for him across the desert," Nadeem said after a moment. She knew that she should spend more time inquiring after her host's health.

She didn't have the patience for that.

But Atça just nodded. "Yes," he said slowly. "Tell me, what do you think of that poor boy?"

Nadeem opened her mouth and shut it again. It was one thing to tweak the town magician's nose.

It was another to tell him to his face just how poorly she thought of him and his teaching.

"He's lost," she said honestly. "Still searching for himself."

"I agree," Atça said. "And dangerous, too," he added. "Did you hear about Çandekili? There's a rumor that Trulliç actually killed the magician there."

"Ah," Nadeem said, nodding as if she had, though she hadn't.

She was pretty certain that the rumor had started with Atça, and that he would spread it far and wide.

"I'm worried about the boy," Atça confessed.

Nadeem merely smiled at him, encouraging him, instead of snorting in laughter.

Of course Atça was worried about Trulliç.

Trulliç was a more powerful magician than Atça, though the boy didn't know it, and Atça wasn't ever going to admit it. This "mentor" had probably told the boy often enough that he was a pitiful excuse for a magician, specifically so he'd never find his true power.

"He's a danger, not just to himself but to others as well," Atça said.

Reluctantly, Nadeem agreed. Trulliç was a storm waiting to happen, lightning looking for a post to strike.

"You know, it might be better if Trulliç didn't return from the desert," Atça said.

Nadeem blinked, surprised. "And what would you suggest I do?" she asked.

A vague hint about death was never enough, not for a star sister. If she was to take another assignment, another blood oath, then it needed to be spelled out. And then judged whether the death would be right or not.

"I'm sure you can take care of it," Atça said breezily with a wave of his hand.

"If there's something you actually want me to do, you need to tell me outright," Nadeem said. "Otherwise…there's too much room for misinterpretation."

Atça paled and swallowed hard.

Nadeem retained the silence. Either let the fool say what needed to be said or this job would pass, too.

"Trulliç needs to die," the old man finally whispered.

There it was.

Nadeem nodded, thinking it through. Aunt Parayat had told her that others would approach her, asking her to enact their petty vengeance.

She did not have to fulfill any request someone made, particularly when it came to taking a life. It was always up to her whether or not to do such a deed.

Did she agree with Atça that Trulliç needed to die? Was he that much of a danger?

She'd seen the wild look in his eyes. How tightly wound his power was. That strange dog whose eyes were the color of the sky.

Trulliç had been raised by a bitter old man who hadn't taught him to think, hadn't taught him grace, hadn't taught him anything but grasping control.

An old man who probably gave out punishment before teaching the moral of any lesson.

Yes, Trulliç would explode one day if he never found his feet.

"What if he finds his home?" Nadeem asked. That would probably settle Trulliç down, though she didn't know. She'd never dealt with magicians before.

Atça gave a dramatic shudder. "That would be worse."

"Why?" Nadeem asked.

"I only raised him for this long because I thought I could help him," Atça whined. "But he's gotten headstrong recently. Independent. Started listening to trouble makers." Atça leaned over and said urgently. "He's no longer loyal to the emperor."

Nadeem blinked, surprised. Trulliç didn't strike her as the type of young man who would lead a rebellion.

"He's going to find the desert heart," Atça continued. At Nadeem's questioning look, Atça added, "A very powerful artifact. I was the one who told him the legends of it, thinking that he could gift it to the emperor. But he's determined to use that power all on his own. It's why he wants to go to the tip of the desert. He claims his home is there, but he'll never find that either."

Atça seemed pleased that Trulliç wouldn't find his home, of course. He would never wish for another to be happy or productive. That wasn't his way.

"These are grave charges," Nadeem said. "I cannot just take your word on it. Not when a life hangs in the balance." Though she might have failed her first assignment, that didn't mean she'd take another, an easy job, without question.

That seemed to throw Atça off. "But you must!" he insisted. "The boy needs to be dealt with."

Nadeem believed that. Atça wanted the boy out of the way. And Trulliç might truly become a danger someday.

"All right," Nadeem said slowly. "If I determine that Trulliç is false, then he shall die by my hand."

Nadeem pulled out the knife in the sheath at the center of her back. It had an obsidian blade that was brittle and would break or chip easily against bones or a hard blow.

But it was also her sharpest knife, and the one traditionally used in a blood oath.

Nadeem held out her right hand, the knife steady in her left.

Slowly, Atça held his own right hand out.

Nadeem didn't smile at him. It wasn't necessary for her to take his blood as part of the oath. However, most outsiders didn't know that.

And this was a serious enough matter, the taking of a life, that Nadeem felt Atça's blood should be on the line as well.

Nadeem drew a swift line across Atça's palm. The blood beaded up immediately. Then she cut her own hand.

Before Atça could draw back, Nadeem intertwined their fingers and pressed their bleeding palms together.

"As our blood mingles, so shall our will and our words," Nadeem said formally. "I swear by the blood that this shall be done."

Atça stayed perfectly still for a long moment before he finally nodded.

"So shall it be," he intoned.

"Good," Nadeem said. She released Atça's hand and licked off her palm, just to watch the look of disgust cross his face while he struggled to be polite.

"Now, let's talk price," Nadeem told him as she picked up her tea.

Nadeem's blood oath weighed heavily on her soul. Had she just committed to foolishness?

Atça could now claim a blood oath with all the star sisters. He couldn't twist the words of the oath—there was power in the blood. If he claimed the oath, going to another star sister to get her to fulfill it, they would know exactly what she had promised to do.

Of course, Atça didn't realize that. He would claim that she promised something else.

Anyone he went to would straighten him out immediately, however, so Nadeem wasn't worried.

She spent the evening at the tavern watching Trulliç. Surely Atça was twisting the truth when he talked about Trulliç being a rebel, no longer loyal to the emperor.

Yet, when the evening prayer was said before the meal thanking the emperor for his bounty, Trulliç grimaced and didn't even bother to mouth the words, while the others spoke fervently around him.

They were to leave the next morning. It was obvious to Nadeem that Trulliç was saying goodbye to people that he didn't expect he'd see again.

His cousins, aunts, and uncles, however, didn't appear to have the same understanding. They all thought he was just taking another short trip into the desert.

Trulliç arranged with Nadeem to meet her in the early morning at the tavern. He arrived before the dawn when the world was still gray and indistinct. The cool air wouldn't last. They'd get to the Ladikah pass by noon and would stay there for the rest of the day, not traveling down the far side of the Kinarak mountains until the next morning.

They would camp on the far side of the mountains overnight and wait there through much of the day as well, not traveling across the desert until it was cooler in the evening.

They could, of course, just stick to the border and not cross desert sands at all. That would take much more time, however. And though Atça had paid Nadeem generously—much more money than he'd wanted to—he hadn't paid for her to take an extra month of travel.

Trulliç carried a strange box, each side a little bigger than his large, outstretched hands. It was wooden, well made, and enchanted.

When Nadeem looked at it, then up at him, he shook his head mutely.

After they'd left Gaadiwala, Trulliç said, "It's a land box. It was made by Yerkoyliç, the magician from Çandekili."

"What's it for?" Nadeem asked. She'd never heard of a land box before.

Trulliç stopped and turned, floating the box over to her.

Nadeem stiffened. She'd never seen Trulliç do magic. Yet it came effortlessly to him.

It made sense that his magic was more powerful out of Gaadiwala, where it no longer was overshadowed by Atça's.

And they were closer to the desert as well.

Inside the box lay sand. Desert sand.

How did the box hold essence of the desert? Nadeem marveled and reached in.

Though the morning was still cool, the sand held in the heat of baked sands.

"Yerkoyliç created it so he could look for the desert heart," Trulliç said casually.

"You took it from him," Nadeem said, looking back up at Trulliç to watch his face.

"I did," Trulliç said gravely.

Nadeem blinked, surprised.

It seemed Atça was correct.

Trulliç had killed Yerkoyliç. But why?

"And now you're looking for the desert heart?" she asked.

Trulliç grimaced at that. He still responded, "I am."

"Tell me about it," Nadeem said as Trulliç gathered the box back to himself.

Trulliç nodded and turned, walking again. As he walked he recited one of the great poems about the birth of the world, Forit's death, the tears of the gods creating all people.

Nadeem fell into an easy step behind him. He had a good voice for telling stories, a nice rhythm, and was interesting to listen to.

After he finished the poem, he told her of the legends, of how Forit's heart still existed in the desert, purified of the darkness. Of how the emperor wanted this heart. Of how the magicians were also trying to find it.

"And you?" Nadeem asked after a moment. "What would you do if you found this heart?"

Trulliç gave a bitter laugh. "I don't know," he said softly. "Leave it where it is, if I can."

Nadeem nodded and didn't ask any more.

Possibly Atça was correct about that as well—that Trulliç was no longer one hundred percent loyal to the emperor either.

She watched Trulliç stop on the border between the foothills of the Kinarak mountains and the true desert.

Deep purple sky spread out over the dark sands. The heat from the day still rose from the baked earth. Stars peeked out at them, the moon just new.

"Why are you stopping?" Nadeem asked Trulliç.

"This is the border, here, between the scrub and the sand," he said.

Nadeem came to stand beside him. They'd had a good travel day. They'd learned many of the same epic poems and battles. Nadeem's favorite story was also Lyons, the one who'd raised a stone eagle from the stone egg. She'd gotten the inspiration for her favorite illusionary fighter from him.

She looked carefully at the earth where Trulliç pointed. She didn't see the difference between the two lands. It wasn't fully sand, it wasn't merely scrub, but a combination of the two.

A lizard popped up nearby, then scurried and dove for another hole in the ground when it realized it wasn't alone.

"Here?" she asked, stepping across the border.

Trulliç nodded mournfully.

"You can come across," Nadeem told him.

He looked like an addict, hungering for his next drink. She'd seen a few—aunts who needed their nightly *igrat*. They didn't tend to live long once they'd reached that stage.

"It will be all right," Nadeem said softly, though she didn't know for certain what would happen once Trulliç stepped onto the sands.

She put her hand on her right hip, wrapping her fingers around the hilt of the knife there.

He wouldn't attack her, would he?

He'd be surprised at just how fast she could move if he did.

With a shuddering sigh, Trulliç stepped across the border.

Nadeem saw the change immediately.

Trulliç had always been about her height. She now realized that he constantly hunched his shoulders. Suddenly, he stood up straight and tall, and probably had at least two inches on her.

His shoulders broadened as well. Instead of a boy, a man now stood in front of her.

A powerful man.

His dog, too, transformed, though the change was more subtle. He grew more spindle-legged and gaunt, like a feral dog. All his features grew sharper as well, his nose longer and more angular, his ears more pointed, his tail thinner and shaped like a blade.

Trulliç looked at Nadeem and smiled. "You glow like the moon," he said softly, "though with more colors. Light blue and pink. Luminous."

Nadeem wondered if the aura he saw had come from the *ağrikat* shells.

"This way," Trulliç said, turning and walking east.

The box now floated behind him, tagging along like a lonely, dark cloud. The magic from it had spiked as well.

Trulliç's feet barely touched the sand as he glided along. When he looked down, he stopped, making an effort to walk normally. But as soon as he lost focus, he glided again, like a desert wind. Nadeem would have to run to keep up with him if he didn't slow down.

He'd be able to go miles and miles at that pace and never tire. He looked as though the very sands fed him.

Nadeem shook her head, confused at the change. It was obvious to her that he belonged here.

Then she thought for a moment.

Atça.

Trulliç had asked Atça about his true home.

And Atça had lied to him.

"Wait," Nadeem finally said as Trulliç raced ahead.

He looked back. Even in the dim light she saw his guilt.

"I just…wander when I get here," he said as he came back. "That's why I needed you for a guide."

Nadeem shook her head. "Tell me the real reason why you're looking for the desert heart," she said.

Trulliç blinked, surprised.

"If it's here, if it exists, it belongs here," he said plainly.

"Even if the emperor is looking for it? Even if he wants it?" she pressed.

Trulliç bit his lips together and looked away for a moment, then looked directly back at her, his eyes boring into hers.

"He can't have it," Trulliç said. "It's mine." Then he gave a bitter laugh. "It isn't as though I'll be able to find it," he added. "I can't even find my true home."

Nadeem shook her head.

She didn't have to tell him. She shouldn't. She'd sworn a blood oath to end his life if he was not loyal to the emperor.

But the emperor had had her destroy a town. Probably to create slaves of its people.

He wanted an army of fanatics like Aunt Izmet.

Not questioning thinkers like Aunt Parayat.

"What is it?" Trulliç asked.

It was so obvious. Anyone would be able to see it.

Anyone but a student of Atça's.

Riyune stared hard at Nadeem. It also seemed that he, too, wanted her to say something.

If the dog could have spoken, he would have said something.

Nadeem beckoned Trulliç closer. She held out her right hand to him.

Puzzled, Trulliç held out his hand in return. It felt hard and hot in hers, like a rough rock baked long in the sun.

"Don't you see?" Nadeem asked, gesturing in front of her, at the sand, the wide open space before them, the stars spilling across the heavens, the sand reflecting the faint glow.

"See what?" Trulliç asked.

"This is your home," Nadeem told him.

Trulliç automatically shook his head. "No," he said. "Atça said—"

"Atça hired me to kill you," Nadeem told him. She kept their fingers intertwined, but opened up the palms, so he could see the cut that had nearly healed. "He wanted you dead before you figured out that your home is the entire Qaenev desert."

"No," Trulliç said. He sounded heartbroken. "It can't be! How could I live here? What is there to eat?"

"Are you hungry?" Nadeem asked seriously.

"No?" Trulliç asked, sounding uncertain. "But surely I still need water."

"What direction is the closest water?" Nadeem asked.

Trulliç automatically pointed.

"You see?" she said.

"But—" Trulliç stopped when Riyune came up and butted his head against his other hand. He shivered, hard.

The land box thumped, falling to the ground.

"The desert *is* my home," Trulliç whispered. "It's always been my home."

"Your home is the entire desert," Nadeem told him again. "All of this."

Trulliç nodded, his eyes still staring off into the distance. "I can feel it. All of it. The borders. The sands." He paused and turned to her. "The Kardeş oasis of the star sisters."

Nadeem stiffened. How did he know of that?

Of course. Her home was now part of his property, the area he controlled.

No wonder Atça wanted Trulliç killed. Particularly if he was no longer loyal to the emperor.

"My city is in the south," Trulliç said. His voice still sounded as though he talked in a dream. "Osmerli," he added.

The city of the old kings. Before the coming of the emperor, over two hundred years before.

"Go," Nadeem said, releasing his hand.

"But—" Trulliç turned back to her, though she could tell it was already calling him, his body listing to the south.

"Go," Nadeem told him gently. "I'll be here when you return," she lied.

She knew that if she placed a single foot on the sand, he would be able to find her. She would have to leave the desert, and soon, if she wanted to hide from him.

Trulliç turned away, then turned back. He took both of her hands in his and kissed the fingertips softly. "Thank you," he said. "If you hadn't told me…if you hadn't insisted on it, I might never have figured it out."

She nodded. Of course he wouldn't have been able to figure it out. She hadn't spent that much time in the presence of men, but it seemed to her that most couldn't see beyond the tip of their noses.

"Thank you," he said again. Then he disappeared, his dog a white blur behind him.

Nadeem stood alone in the desert, just the land box beside her.

She knew that he ran to the south to raise his great city. It would be a marvelous sight, the pillars rising out of the sand. That soon caravans would make it a regular stop. The star sisters, too, would come to pay homage.

Before the emperor attacked.

In the meanwhile, Nadeem had her own work to do.

⸻

Nadeem paused, blade in her hand. The moon lifted its face high above the desert, though it didn't shed much light. She knelt comfortably, admitting that she'd not be able to do this standing, not by herself.

If she was truly brave enough, she'd take her own life. She'd betrayed the emperor, failed at her first assignment, then broken a blood oath to take the life of one who would oppose the emperor. She'd failed her sisterhood, failed in her dreams.

She could no longer call herself a star sister.

But she wasn't ready to dance in Barzhat's golden court. Not yet.

Plus, she had too many questions that Aunt Parayat had to answer.

Nadeem kissed the tip of the blade, then put it against her left cheek. With a steady hand, she sliced open the star that her aunt had cut there. Her greatest pride. Her mark of sisterhood.

Nadeem didn't know how many cuts she needed. She couldn't cut the star out of her cheek. That, too, would be against the wishes of the emperor.

But she could scar it. Make it hard to identify. Destroy the symmetry of it, the delicate lines, until all that was left was a mess of lines.

Tears streamed down Nadeem's face as she cut away her identity.

Finally, when her hand shook with the pain and effort, she reached down and grabbed a handful of sand from the land box. Then she pushed the hard grains against her burning cheek.

The first time her cheek had been cut, the magic of the *ağrikat* shells had been pushed in.

Now, she took on the magic of the desert.

The world exploded as the sand sank into her blood.

And Nadeem dreamed.

THE DESERT HEART

CHAPTER ONE

TRULLIÇ

TRULLIÇ SKIMMED ACROSS THE DESERT, his feet rarely touching the burning sands. He moved as fast as a storm, whirlwinds of sand following in his wake. The white blur of the dog Riyune kept pace with him, staying easily at his side.

Color had burst across the landscape with the rising sun—the peerless blue of the sky and the golden sand that stretched out to all horizons. Trulliç didn't bother teasing out the scents and tastes of every place he passed—the sour, brackish water from a slowly drying up spring, the desiccated remains of a lizard as long as his arm, the taste of iron from the red rocks.

He promised himself that he could come back and explore later. That he would take the time to walk every inch of his newly-discovered home—the great Qaenev desert—and learn all of its secrets and delights.

Anger washed over him. Atça, his mentor and the town wizard of Gaadiwala, had lied to Trulliç. Laughed himself silly when Trulliç had asked if it was possible that the entire desert was his home.

Trulliç would go visit him later and demand answers.

For now, Trulliç needed to get to the southernmost tip of the great desert, to find the foreboding mountains that rose up from the flat land and separated the desert to the north from the endless ocean to the south.

There, he could raise his new city on the foundations of Osmerli, the city of the old kings.

A normal caravan would take months to travel the entire length of Qaenev, and they would have to plan carefully, following the oasis routes when they could, then traveling to the eastern border to continue their journey along the hills there, where they could reliably find water.

Of course, then they'd have to be careful of the slaver ships that plied the coast, catching travelers and ambushing towns unaware.

Trulliç estimated that he would cross the long length of the desert in just three days. Once he'd learned how to pace himself, how to apply his strength correctly, he knew it would take him less than a day. However, during this trip he stopped frequently to sip at streams, to marvel at each and every oasis he discovered, to watch the tiny desert mice hop away from Riyune or elegant, yellow snakes undulate across the dunes.

He discovered that he didn't need to change clothes now. He could wear the same light-weight, gold-and-green striped tunic both in the heat of the day as well as during the colder nights. His plain gray shirt never grew crusted with sweat despite his exertion, his brown wool pants remained comfortable, and sand never bothered his feet in his sturdy leather sandals either.

As he crested another rise and saw the marvelous sands spread out before him, wonder washed away the remains of Trulliç's anger. He'd found his home. The land where his magic was the strongest.

Male wizards, so-called land magicians, were always tied to a particular geographic location. Most had merely a grove of trees, a small pond of water, or even an outcropping of rock. There were ancient tales, of course, of magicians strong enough to affect all trees or all lakes, though they'd only be able to do special magic in their home.

As far as Trulliç knew, no magician had as large of an area as he did to call his own.

The star sisters, on the other hand, could travel everywhere across the Tanesh empire and beyond, and still have the same amount of magic. They were illusionists, not land magicians. Their magic didn't affect the real world, though they certainly could fool anyone into thinking so.

Trulliç felt his heart bursting with joy again. Nadeem, the star sister he'd hired to lead him through the desert, had pointed out the truth to him. Had explained how he belonged in the desert, belonged to the desert, and nowhere else.

What would he have done without her? Would he have survived? Or would he have wandered into the desert, lost and afraid, and let the sands eventually consume him?

He suspected that might be how he died someday—walking into the sands and letting the desert have all of him.

Not yet.

The land changed as he sped along, pure sand giving way to rocks, dirt, and gravel. Scrub now appeared again, thorny plants that only the most hearty of goats or sheep could nibble on. Up ahead, Trulliç felt the edge of his domain, the terribly sharp cliffs with their knife-like edges. Beyond them lay the hateful ocean, the opposite of everything he loved.

He'd seen the ocean once as a child. His mother had thought he was afraid of the waves, that they might carry him away. He had been afraid, but not because he'd thought the waters were out to get him. Rather, it was because they were so alien, wild and constantly moving. The air felt wrong. The sound of the waves grated on his ears. He'd been sickened by the salty smell.

The desert, on the other hand, was still. Peaceful. Quiet.

Trulliç slowed his pace, then slowed further, until he was merely a man again, walking over the sand, not a great magician racing like the wind.

Riyune appeared beside him. He had the same long, pointed snout of a desert dog, though his ears were floppy, not pointed. White fur covered most of his body. Black patches lay across his ribs, too irregular to be called spots. He also had black ears, and smaller black and white spots all along his muzzle.

Only his eyes proclaimed him as something different. They were the same impossible blue as the sky above them.

Trulliç had rarely seen eyes that color before. Traders who came from the northern kingdom of Lydae occasionally had blue eyes. According to his mother, Trulliç's father had had that color of eye, though he'd died before Trulliç had been born.

Nadeem had said that Riyune had a longer, more solid shadow. Under the brilliant desert sun, Trulliç turned to study his constant companion. He'd once thought Riyune was a ghost, given the odd way he'd first appeared to Trulliç.

However, Trulliç didn't see anything unusual about the dog, who now sat on his butt and scratched his nose with one of his hind legs. Then Riyune stood and shook himself like a normal dog.

Trulliç couldn't help but shiver when Riyune pierced him with those overly bright eyes. Though the dog had only spoken to Trulliç a few times over the years, Trulliç still couldn't help but think that the dog said now: *So? Get on with it.*

"I don't suppose that you could have told me that the entire desert was my home? You know, earlier?" Trulliç asked. Waves of anger crashed over him again.

Riyune didn't bother replying. Instead, he looked at Trulliç, then out over the rocky plain they stood before.

Trulliç sighed. Riyune would likely never answer him. But Trulliç felt certain that the dog had known.

Would Riyune have stopped Trulliç from dying out on the desert sands if he'd gotten lost before he'd found his home?

Trulliç liked to think that was the case. However, he didn't honestly know. Riyune had first appeared to Trulliç as a blood hound. The blood hounds shepherded pregnant women, protecting them if they were carrying a child who had magic.

Was Riyune still just protecting Trulliç until he birthed whatever it was that the dog waited for?

Trulliç would have to ask Nadeem later. She might know about such things, as she was a star sister. And a woman of great power.

He felt connected to her, though he didn't know exactly where she stood on his desert. But he felt certain that he would be able to find her later. Scoop her up and bring her here, to his city.

Trulliç turned to face the open plain. It sat broad and flat, the hills still some distance away, a mere smudge on the flat horizon. Rocks and sand covered the area along with low, green-gray scrub. A quiet squeak from a desert mouse told Trulliç that the nights here would be cooler, probably winds blowing off the far ridge and billowing into the valley.

When the emperor had destroyed Osmerli, the city of the old kings, over two hundred years before, he'd blocked the water that ran from the great Pirazizil river in the east all the way to Osmerli. The oasis trail had run from the border to the city along that constant stream. Nothing taller than calf-high scrub and thorn bushes grew there now, not the tall cottonwoods, palms and figs Trulliç had seen in his dreams.

Nothing remained of the great stream on the plain.

Beneath it, however…

Trulliç pushed his senses under the ground, searching for the ancient riverbed.

There. Right there.

Sand and great stones lay in its path. The banks themselves had been blasted as well, the oasis trail waters no longer able to run true. The ground felt different, not sand but clay and packed earth as well.

Trulliç paused and looked over the great plain. He could *see* the towers he wanted to raise. Tall and square, golden-sand colored, with green and gold banners hanging from every corner. Crenulated walls ran between the towers, and solid guard houses stood underneath. To the west lay a broad market, selling every type of spice and exotic goods.

Sparkling fountains and wells were situated everywhere, so that even the poorest wouldn't have far to walk to fetch water.

With a sigh, Trulliç turned away and started skimming over the sands again, heading toward the Pirazizil river. It would take a caravan at least half a day to travel from the eastern border to Osmerli, but Trulliç knew it wouldn't even take him an hour.

While he could raise the rocks of the city, build a home for travelers and other seekers, what good were fancy buildings and beautiful open courtyards if there wasn't any water?

———

Trulliç stopped abruptly when he reached the border of the desert. Riyune stopped beside him.

It wasn't obvious to anyone but him, he knew. The land held the same shrubs and scaly thorns on either side. Sand blew constantly from one edge to the other and back. The air smelled the same, full of the musty *meslit* trees and hard-baked earth.

The border cut as sharp as a knife as far as Trulliç was concerned.

He'd only so recently come to the desert. Found his home. Less than four days had passed.

He was loath to leave it again so soon.

Was there another way?

Just beyond the scrublands lay rocky foothills. Trulliç raised his head like Riyune would and sniffed the air.

Did water lay just over those hills? Nestled between those rocks?

He reached out his senses past the desert border. It felt like pushing against wet wool. He could barely see anything, while behind him the desert called to him clearly.

Stubbornly, Trulliç pressed on, forcing his senses underground, seeking the old waterway.

He'd guessed right. The old river did lay amongst the jumble of rocks. It had been diverted by the emperor. Instead of turning to the west and running across the sands, it now turned east.

Huge boulders blocked the old river path, each easily the size of the shack that Trulliç used to share with his mother.

Could he blast them away? Destroy them with his magic?

Possibly. But it would take so much effort. The river ended on land, not in the desert.

Trulliç shook his head when Riyune, who sat next to him, looked up at him with his head cocked to one side, obviously asking what the problem was.

Atça would have pushed the rocks aside. His magic was like that, solid and unyielding.

There had to be another way.

Trulliç walked alongside the border of the desert, heading north, paralleling the river. There had to be some other way to get water to his city. How deep did he have to go to find another river or well?

The first time Trulliç had walked the desert, six years before when he'd been twelve, a secret cavern had shown itself to him. It had contained sweet water. He understood now that all travelers could find this oasis if their need was desperate enough.

And if the cavern judged them worthy.

The cavern had tapped into waters hidden far under the sand, in jeweled caverns. Other travelers had known about the jewels. If they'd gone digging for them, they would have offended the water. It would have left them on the sands to die.

It was always better to be alive than rich.

Could Trulliç just find water near the city site? Could he go deep enough to draw it up?

That didn't feel right. And he couldn't just create water. It had to come from someplace.

The spot where he would raise his city didn't sit on top of a great reservoir.

The water had come from the river. And that river flowed on land that wasn't his.

How could he get access to it without killing what was there? Stealing another man's water was a killing offense.

Trulliç found his feet still walking north, a thread drawing him along. He kept most of his senses pushed underground, seeking something other than sand and rocks. Only a small fraction of his attention watched the golden sands, skirted the scraggly bushes that had recently had their leaves chewed off by a nearby herd of wild goats, felt the solid heat of the sun shining down on the black-and-white checkered *chafiyek* that covered his head and neck and kept the bright light out of his eyes.

Just ahead, Trulliç felt movement. He paused. A dark brown lizard popped up near his feet then scurried over to another hole.

There. A trickle of water coming from the great river. It pooled and died just across the border, in his desert.

The nature of the land there was different. More clay to hold the water in.

Without thinking, Trulliç reached out his senses, then drew back. Ewww. Clay felt slimy against what could be thought of as his magical hands. Sand felt much cleaner.

But sand was also greedy. It drank down whatever water touched it, not allowing it to pool or travel for long distances.

This trickle started in the emperor's lands. But it came to Trulliç's of its own free will.

The emperor couldn't block it without declaring a blood feud or a great war.

Something Trulliç hoped to avoid for as long as possible.

If he went back to where the Pirazizil had been originally diverted and destroyed the rocks there, he'd be tweaking the nose of the emperor. The emperor would be forced to save face and deal with Trulliç immediately.

If, however, Trulliç could tap into an already existing flow of water without affecting those who were downriver…maybe the emperor wouldn't attack him just yet.

Trulliç sunk his senses under the ground again, reaching for the clay.

It didn't respond as well as sand to his touch. Wouldn't stretch and form the pathway he wanted. He couldn't transform the sand to clay either.

Frustrated, Trulliç came back to himself. Riyune sat beside him as if standing guard. That made Trulliç feel better, that no one could attack him while his attention was elsewhere.

It didn't help solve his immediate problem, however.

There had to be some way to divert the stream. Grow it and bring the water to his city.

But how?

Trulliç paced back and forth on his side of the border, growling at the stubbornly uncooperative clay just beneath his feet. The sun had sunk low on the horizon. Already the sand had started releasing its heat. Desert hawks circled above him, twilight hunters looking for any movement they could pounce on.

How was he going to divert the water? He'd followed it upstream a significant distance. A huge reservoir sat under the river. If he tapped into that, then diverted part of the stream, no one would be the wiser. The farmers downstream and to the east of him wouldn't lose their water.

While Trulliç could blast a path through the sand, he needed to start it here. He also realized that just opening up a path through the sand wasn't good enough. He needed to build a riverbank of clay, earth, and rocks so the water wouldn't immediately sink back into the desert.

Trulliç found his fingertips had snuck down, past his waist, to where his glass horseshoe hung.

When his mother Myrizhah had been pregnant with him, she'd bought a tin horseshoe to help ease the birth. However, the tin had burned her belly when she'd placed it on her skin.

The blood hound tending her had magically transformed the tin to glass shot through with ribbons of gold and green, the colors of the old kings.

The horseshoe had always been Trulliç's symbol. It didn't have any great magic in itself. It promised grander things, however. Glass came from heat-blasted sand. Instead of her boy having an affinity toward the metal tin and the tin mines near where his father had come from, he needed to return to the desert instead.

Glass. Trulliç slid his fingers across the smoothness of the horseshoe.

The clay didn't really like him.

But sand—and glass—did.

Trulliç grinned, plucking the horseshoe from its ties.

Why not?

First, he sent a quick prayer to Enkat, the goddess of the rain and water, asking for her help. Then, using two hands and holding the horseshoe like a dowsing rod, with the curve aimed toward the ground, he pushed his will under the earth. He pulled at the remaining heat of the desert behind him, blasting it deep into the sand.

Glass formed in its wake.

The glass seemed thick to Trulliç. Not the sort used in the fancy lamps Atça had had, but instead heavy and impure, studded with dirt and rocks.

Trulliç pushed the glass out until it became a great rounded road under the earth, wide enough for a large caravan to trundle down the center of it.

Then wider still.

It didn't take much for him to encourage the water to start flowing in his direction.

Then he had to race ahead, pushing the glass road along until he reached the old riverbank.

Trulliç paused as he built a curving bank, setting the water to run along the old trail.

The water itself helped him push aside the great boulders blocking the path. The clay came together more easily now, reforming the banks so the river's course would hold true. It grew to about four feet across. Trulliç set his glass road far beneath it, taller than man, so the water would stay cool.

Stars came out, twinkling on the new river. But Trulliç wasn't finished. He nudged the water along, glassing over some of the worst of the divots in the earth so it would flow smoothly, quickly, into his city.

Long after the moon had set, Trulliç felt all strength flowing out of him. While the sand could bolster him, the water sucked away his magic and power. Plus, he seemed to be more powerful when the sun was up, less so at night.

It was a vulnerability he would have to hide so another magician— or more likely, the emperor—couldn't use it against him.

Trulliç let the water flow into the sands at the edge of the great plain. Tomorrow he would raise the towers and fountains of the city, instruct the water where to flow.

For now, he lay down beside the riverbank, listening to the water gurgle and sing to itself while he dreamed of sand-wrapped blankets and talking stars.

T rulliç woke and stretched. Dawn had cleared the sky of the few clouds that had drifted across the borders. His arms and hands were as sore as if he'd been pushing and hauling barrels of beer all of the previous day. He sat up and rolled his shoulders. They too felt stiff and sore, the coldness of the night having crept into the muscles.

A warm spot pressed against his lower thigh. Riyune lay on his side, still dreaming, his paws making abortive movements.

Trulliç hesitated, then slowly reached down and brushed his fingertips against the top of Riyune's head, sliding them against the soft, warm fur.

The day immediately came into sharper focus. Trulliç sat up straighter, his aches and pains fleeing. The sand took on additional colors, gold and red and even blue hues, while the water turned the blackest black, cold and viscous.

Just past the river, Trulliç saw the ghostly outlines of buildings. Golden square towers boxed in the broad expanse. Toothy walls ran between them. He heard the echoes of long forgotten trumpets and the rumblings of large merchant caravans. The braying of mules and the calling of date sellers. The sweet incense burning to the various altars dedicated to the gods and goddesses: Innis and Serrat, Enkat and Xannil, Onnet and Barzhat.

And a dark altar where no light burned, dedicated to the former goddess Forit. She who'd died to save all that was light from darkness and chaos. Her body fell and became the earth. Her teeth became the mountains, her fingers became the many rivers, the place where her heart had been became the desert.

As the gods and goddesses grieved, their tears fell on her prone body.

Her freckles, the only imperfection about her, became humanity. The darker freckles became the people of the south, the lighter blemishes became the people of the north.

Trulliç blinked and shook his head. The mirage slid away.

So did Riyune, moving apart from Trulliç. The dog stood and stretched like a normal dog would, paws down and butt in the air, before he stretched forward as well.

Where had that vision come from? Had it been the past that Trulliç had just spied? The former city of the great kings?

Or was it a sign of the city to come?

Why had the emperor destroyed the old kings? Was it just so he could take their land?

Or had it been because the old kings wouldn't show the emperor the way to the desert heart? Where Forit's heart still lay, entangled with the darkness and chaos that came before time?

Trulliç, like everyone else, had just assumed the emperor had wanted to take over the kingdom.

Now, he wasn't so certain. Particularly not after seeing the dark altar and the thread of magic that flowed from its blackness.

Riyune wouldn't answer his questions, that much Trulliç knew. Or he'd get the equivalent of an eye roll from the dog.

Sometime, though, Trulliç would need to know.

* * *

Trulliç made the decision to start small. Though he felt he could raise a great city, what was the point? No one would live there. Not yet. And the thought of living in a town composed of empty buildings filled him with dread.

Did he call people to him, once he'd built them a place to live? Would they come on their own? He had no idea how that worked. Yerkoyliç had been born in his city, the streets bending to his will as a small child. Atça, as well, had been born in Gaadiwala, the town he controlled.

Since Trulliç could claim the entire desert as his own, he really wasn't certain what to do with the people already living there. He wasn't about to banish them. Or to draw them here, to the city he was raising. Not until there was good trade.

He'd have to figure that out later.

Trulliç took a sip of the cool water from the waiting river. It seemed poised, ready to be directed further. Riyune, too, drank his fill. He'd caught a couple small mice for his breakfast.

Trulliç merely had to breathe in the desert air to be filled. Though he knew he'd miss eating, strictly speaking he didn't need food when he had sands beneath his feet.

And he'd miss tea. That was the first thing he needed to bring here, to…

What was he going to call this place?

Trulliç Town?

He couldn't help the giggle that escaped. No, that wouldn't do.

Trulliç held out his right hand.

Then paused.

It didn't look right. That bare hand raised in the air.

After another moment, he reached down and unstrapped his glass horseshoe again.

There. That looked right. Felt right.

Though he knew the horseshoe by itself had no magic, it appeared to be able to channel his own, give him a tighter focus.

Trulliç raised his hand again, directing it at the flat plain just past the new river.

Stones tumbled together. Then grew larger, as other rocks amalgamated. Stone met stone, squaring off, building higher and higher. The sound of a great sandstorm filled the area. Trulliç tasted the dust in the air. His heart beat hard as the tower assembled itself. He merely directed it. The stones seemed to have a will of their own. They belonged together. Like magnets, they attracted each other. They clanged as they touched, deep booms that reverberated through the open air.

Large openings formed, ready for the glass windows Trulliç would will into place later. The building itself wasn't too wide, maybe thirty feet on a side. A doorway opened at the base. Long slabs of stone flew into the building through the open windows, attaching themselves to the walls as stairs. The top opened and blossomed, forming its own crenellations.

Trembling, Trulliç lowered his hand. He was still tired from his work the night before. Plus, he didn't really want to raise more than one building. Not yet.

He did direct the water to flow over to the black stone he raised for the fountain out front. He shaped it into a pretty circle, three feet around and two feet deep. The water murmured quietly to itself as it swirled. He knew that someone like Atça would have raised a splashing fountain. And maybe Trulliç would do that for other watering holes.

For his own personal well, though, the constant sound of the tinkling water would have been too much of a distraction.

He strapped his horseshoe back to his waist and looked up at the tower. It stood three stories tall, the walls square and true. The color was exactly the same as what he'd seen it in his vision, golden sand that would change as the light did, growing more red with both the sunrise and the sunset, turning a much darker purple at night.

Banners, he knew, would come with time.

And people.

Trulliç walked around the end of the river and toward his tower. It all seemed like a dream.

Maybe that should be the name of the town. Hayalevi. The dream house.

The name floated from him, carried on the winds, up and away, to the edges of his land.

Those who lived in the desert wouldn't have to ask the name of the great city. Its name would live with them, follow them into their dreams.

Would they come to live with him? Trulliç couldn't answer that. But he hoped they might.

Trulliç paused on the threshold of the great tower. The stones he'd raised had gained more mass than he'd realized. The doorway stood a good three feet deep. This would keep the interior much cooler than the exterior.

Did he want to put in an extravagant wooden door? Something he could easily lock? No, that didn't make sense to him. Wood would never become a natural element to him, not something he could work with.

Did Atça have an affinity toward wood? Trulliç doubted it. His former mentor had used a tremendous amount of wood in his house as a sign of wealth, nothing more.

Would Atça had become a stronger magician if he'd surrounded himself with a material that he did manipulate well? That would have sustained him better? Like hard dirt or stone?

Possibly. But that wouldn't have been as grand. Atça needed his ego fed more than his magic.

Trulliç stretched his hand out toward the ground and *pulled* at an ancient rock that he felt buried there. It wasn't the same as the golden walls he'd built. Instead, if felt colder and sharper.

The stone crested the floor, rising only a foot above the dirt there. Then it stopped, stubbornly resisting Trulliç's command.

The black rock looked fragile, with many tiny holes eaten into it. When Trulliç applied a lick of heat to it, the surface smoothed out, becoming like black glass.

Trulliç used both hands and tugged at the rock. Slowly it slid from the earth, rising up to the height of the opening for the door. It stood about two feet inside the tower.

With a wave of his hand, Trulliç set his fire across the entire stone. The divots, pockets, and tiny holes on the surface disappeared. Trulliç felt the rock *settle*. It stood solid and firm, giving him privacy but still allowing people access.

The rock had an awareness to it, alive in a way Trulliç couldn't explain. It would act as a guardian for his door, alerting him whenever someone crossed the threshold.

He didn't know if it would keep an attacker from entering. He had the feeling that it would try to turn away any who meant him harm.

Riyune looked up at Trulliç and nodded, as if he approved.

If Trulliç was being fanciful, as Atça had always accused him of being, he'd say the dog was impressed.

Then Trulliç reminded himself that Atça had been wrong. The things that Trulliç had felt he could do, the magic he wanted to perform, were actually real.

He had to get out of the habit of doubting himself, his abilities.

This was his land. His home.

He was only limited by his imagination and his strength.

He was never going to worry about being *fanciful* again.

With a grin, Trulliç stepped forward, around the guard stone, eager to explore his tower.

His true home.

CHAPTER TWO

NADEEM

NADEEM WOKE IN THE DARK, unsure for the moment where she lay. Cool sand grated against her fingertips, the earth hard against her back. She lay still for a moment, gathering her senses to her. She smelled water—heard it bubbling somewhere close to her left. The air smelled of minerals and old rock, dry but not musty. When she blinked her eyes, she realized that light did enter the space where she lay, a small amount from her right, two long lines, like a lamp shining from behind a tall rock.

It took another moment before Nadeem pushed herself up to sitting. Her left cheek, where her star-sister scar had once proudly been carved, flared with pain. Nadeem closed her eyes for a moment, taking a few deep breaths, forcing herself to ride out the agony and not cry out.

When Nadeem opened her eyes again, she realized she was in a cave of some sort. Rock walls surrounded her. The dirt and sand floor beneath her felt cool, as if it hadn't seen the heat of the day. To her left burbled a tiny stream.

Goddess, she was thirsty. She lurched to her side but thought better of standing. Instead, she crawled to the water.

It felt lukewarm against her skin, not as cold as she'd expected. She brought her wet fingers to her nose. The water didn't smell brackish or bad. Maybe a tinge of iron from the rocks below, but that was it. As her eyes adjusted to the dimness, she realized the tiny stream flowed across the floor of the cave, rising up from just inside the wall to her left, then diving back underground on her right.

Greedily, Nadeem licked her fingers, then cupped her hand and brought more up.

The pain in her cheek suddenly diminished, as though one of her aunts had laid a cool salve over it. Nadeem opened and closed her mouth, testing her limits.

Yes, the pain had greatly gone down. How had the water done that? She wasn't certain she cared—the relief from the constant pain felt too good.

Feeling daring, Nadeem leaned over the stream and splashed water directly onto her wound.

She gasped. The pain hadn't receded that much. Still, as the water dripped down her cheek and across her neck, she felt better. The water healed her, somehow.

Would the wound always physically hurt? That she didn't know. She'd taken her knife and cut through the existing scar on her cheek, then rubbed enchanted sand into it, sand that carried the essence of the desert.

Where was the box? Her knife? Where was she, for that matter? Who'd brought her here?

She found she thought much more clearly now that she'd had some water, the fog from her visions rolling away.

She still wore the same clothes she'd had on before: a long-sleeved, loose, gray-colored blouse to protect her skin from the desert sun, baggy brown trousers instead of a long skirt that most women wore, and a sleeveless tunic, woven with blue-and-black diamond shapes. Her matching *chafiyek* lay on the dirt beside her. Sturdy leather sandals still covered her feet.

In front of her, beyond the small trickle of water, lay horizontal slabs of stone. Like a sleeping place. Or an altar. Rough-hewn rock made up the walls behind the slabs and on either side.

Turning, Nadeem saw the space wasn't very big, maybe ten feet square. Opposite the stream lay the opening to the cave.

Then she blinked.

Was she not awake? Still dreaming?

Slowly, Nadeem crawled toward the opening.

A rock stood just inside the rough stone doorway, blocking the opening while still allowing light and air to pass through.

Just past the doorway stood the open desert. Nadeem had fallen in the scrublands. Not this far onto the sands.

Stars streamed across the night sky, making it as bright as twilight. She couldn't count the number of stars she saw. Watching them fly across the sky that way made her dizzy.

Golden sands spread to the dark horizon. The ground glittered with its own light, as if pieces of glass reflected the shooting stars above it. Nadeem reached a hand across the threshold, scooped up a palmfull of sand, then let it slide out.

She felt every grain of sand against her skin, as if each was alive. It felt cool as well, sending chicken flesh across her shoulders. She shivered.

What was this place?

Nadeem had had visions her entire life, many more since she'd first been marked as a star sister, six years before when she'd been thirteen, at her coming of age ceremony. The *ağrikat* shells rubbed into the open wound had caused her visions to grow deeper and wilder.

This wasn't a vision, however. Nadeem couldn't say how she knew that, just that she did.

But she wasn't actually in the Qaenev desert, either. This felt like an in-between place, neither here or there.

What would happen if she left the comforting enclosure and wandered the desert? What would she find? A way back to the world?

Or an entrance to the realm of the gods?

She didn't know.

The stream called to her, tugging her back further into the shelter. She knew now that it wasn't a cave built into the side of a hill, as she'd first thought. In the morning she'd take a walk all the way around it. It was probably just an outcropping of rocks.

Nadeem drank more of the lukewarm water. It satisfied her as much as a full feast.

When she was finished, she pushed her hand into the water, digging her fingers into the rocky bed.

A vision overcame her, stealing her sight.

Underneath the rocks lay a great, bejeweled cavern. She had the impression that if she dug out just one of those gems, she'd be rich the rest of her days.

But going digging for them would offend the stream, the rocks… this place. It would leave her in the desert itself and let her die of thirst.

Nadeem nodded as she withdrew her hand. Other travelers had used this cavern, called it to them during their greatest need. They also knew of the gems and jewels and had all decided that it was better to be alive than rich.

After another long drink of water, Nadeem pushed herself up to standing. She swayed, every muscle depleted. Why was she so weak? By destroying her star sister scar, had she drained all her strength?

Nadeem listened, listing, as the stream and the rocks told her to go lay down. Regain her strength. Sleep on the stone slabs.

For a moment, Nadeem resisted. She wasn'y going to lie back down on the ground again, damn it!

Then she swayed again, almost falling over.

The cavern had done her no harm so far. She wasn't just being stubborn, but stupid, a fine line that she'd crossed many times before.

Slowly, carefully, Nadeem stepped over the trickle of water and sat down on the bottom slab. It felt wonderfully cool under her fingers. She yawned, then stopped her yawn partway.

Her cheek was no longer on fire. The pain had withered tremendously.

What was this place?

Nadeem didn't know, but she was going to have to ask Trulliç.

If she was ever allowed to leave this place.

Nadeem woke as the sun rose, the light creeping around the guard stone that stood in the opening of the cavern. She looked around as the light grew brighter.

The rock wasn't solid. Instead, it looked as though it had grown into walls, the stones merging one into the other. The creek itself stayed the same, just a tiny trickle of water. Nadeem looked more carefully at the stone slab she'd slept on—it was just a plain, irregular, long piece of rock set into the wall. Three others lay stacked above her. It would be easy to climb from the bottom to the top.

She nearly giggled at the thought. The place slept four, but no more.

Stretching, Nadeem's muscles in her arms and back pulled, still slightly sore, as if she'd climbed and fought a lot the day before.

And maybe she had.

Nadeem swallowed against the bile that had suddenly filled her throat.

Before she'd gotten to the cavern, or it had come to her, she'd been lost in her visions.

The vision told of endless war. The black gibbering darkness of her dream place had been loosened on the earth. The very gods themselves fought it, while the emperor had been corrupted and fought against them, spreading filth.

She'd fought long and hard beside two-faced goddess Barzhat, the goddess of death. Each of the goddess's twelve arms held a long knife, and her four legs danced as she killed all who came upon her. Both her blue face and her black face cried golden tears that turned into the weights the dead wore.

But even the goddess couldn't hold out against the darkness.

Nadeem had had to kill Barzhat after she'd been corrupted. The fight had been to the death of both parties though, and Nadeem had fallen a long, long time, as long as it took for a star to fall from the sky into an endless pit.

Nadeem shivered. That hadn't been her only vision after she'd removed her star sister sign. But that one had been the most powerful.

With trembling fingers, Nadeem reached up and touched her

cheek. The skin felt rough, the edges of her scarring apparent. It was sensitive, too, sore like it was bruised.

Slowly, Nadeem made herself stand. She stretched. Yes, her muscles still hurt, but it was a good ache that showed she was recovering. She bent over and touched her toes, then did a few more stretches in place.

She wasn't up to full strength, that much she knew. She was still recovering from…something.

She took another step and knelt by the water. Two mouthfuls made her mind clearer.

She stared at the water. It wasn't magical. She couldn't see any hint of magic flowing through it.

Yet, it was still special.

Nadeem walked over to the opening looking out over the desert. The foothills weren't that far away. She was possibly only half a day's walk to the scrublands.

How had she gotten here?

Now she saw that her pack had come with her. It sat next to the opening of the door. Had it been there the previous night and she'd just missed it? Possibly.

Or possibly not. She hadn't been in the actual desert the night before.

She eagerly tore into one of her travel rolls made of crushed walnuts, cracked wheat, chopped figs, and held together with *meslit* syrup and a paste made of dates.

Only after she'd finished eating (and had drunk her fill of the sweet water) did she do an accounting of her belongings.

The magical box that had held the essence of the desert in its enclosed sands—the land box, as Trulliç had called it—was no longer with her.

Same for the cane she'd carried from Koruli. She'd been sent there to kill Malik, her first assignment as one of the star sisters who reported directly to the emperor and did jobs for him.

She'd failed that task miserably. One of her former teammates had killed Malik instead, and they'd had to burn down the house to hide the evidence so the death would appear to be natural.

Nadeem still wondered if by killing Malik they'd killed the entire town of Koruli, turned it into a slave camp for the emperor.

Malik had received the fancy walking stick as a gift from the emperor himself. Fine black wood made up the base of it, while the top of it held a silver head in the form of a snake.

Nadeem had taken it with her, casting a heavy illusion on it so that it would appear to be a stout walking stick.

Where had the box and the stick gone?

Nadeem wasn't sorry that the land box had disappeared. She had a feeling that Trulliç would find it and use it.

The stick though….It wasn't magical, not like herself or Trulliç. There was still something to it, something that wasn't quite right.

When she got to the foothills, she'd have to backtrack and see if she could find it.

From the position of the sun, Nadeem knew the outcrop of rocks faced directly west. She debated leaving at that point, walking to the foothills.

But she knew that though they didn't seem that far away, it would take hours to reach them. No one traveled in the direct heat of the day in the desert. Except madmen and fools.

Nadeem, for all her mistakes, still wasn't a fool.

She walked back to the water, taking another long drink as well as filling her own water skins.

Then she laid back down on the bottom most slab and napped, recovering her strength.

She had a feeling she'd need it.

With twilight came gentle breezes, licking Nadeem's scarred cheek. It still hurt but not nearly as much as it had. A ghost of pain to remind her of what she'd done.

At some point she'd have to find a mirror to see what she now looked like. She'd attempted to disfigure the star that had been carved by Aunt Parayat at her coming of age ceremony. She knew she'd managed at least a few long cuts bisecting the existing lines. Then she'd tried to carve a curving line through the mess as well, though her hand was shaking so much at that point she wasn't sure how well she'd succeeded.

Nadeem took one last long drink of water from the tiny stream. Then she bowed her head and thanked it for its hospitality, as if it had been the most generous host.

And in some ways, that was exactly what had happened.

She also sent a quick prayer to Serrat/Serril, the two-faced god/goddess of desolate places and the primary goddess of the star sisters. She didn't know who else to pray to besides Barzhat, the goddess of death, who was also beloved by the star sisters.

Nadeem couldn't call herself a star sister anymore, however. She'd disfigured the star on her cheek.

She would have to figure out who she should pray to. Maybe Enkat, the goddess of rain. Except that her bountiful curves and the way she let her husband Xannil hide her away, had never sat well with Nadeem.

Maybe she should start praying to Onnet. Yes, she was the goddess of childbirth. She was also the goddess of the hunt.

But who or what did Nadeem hunt? What was she going to do once she left the desert?

Aunt Parayat had been her initial mentor and had taught Nadeem to question everything, even the emperor himself.

Nadeem decided that she would travel to Kardeş, the hidden oasis of the star sisters, and demand answers from her aunt this time, not more questions.

But first, she had to make it out of the desert.

Nadeem knew that as soon as she set foot on the sand, Trulliç would know where she stood. It was probably the only reason why he hadn't already come to fetch her—because she still was in that in-between place.

She knew she couldn't hide from the desert magician forever.

She just had no idea how to face him. How to face her failure. He would remind her of everything she'd lost.

No, not yet. She couldn't see him, not yet.

Still, Nadeem couldn't stay in this place forever. The stream was an incredibly polite host and wasn't making her feel as though she had to leave quickly.

But a good guest didn't overstay her welcome.

Sitting beside Nadeem's pack she found her belt with its traditional three knives, along with the other weapons she generally carried. Without thinking she strapped her equipment back on, all her knives, her blowgun and darts, even a long *meslit* thorn. She hadn't felt naked without her weapons, but she felt better carrying them again.

Nadeem shouldered her pack. Its comfortable, familiar weight made her feel better, even if she hadn't regained her full strength yet. She wouldn't be able to run for half a day with her pack on flat ground, not yet.

It was only a matter of time before she did, though.

Nadeem stuck her head out of the shelter and looked again at the scrublands to her right. Would Trulliç come after her right away? Maybe. Maybe not. It would depend on how much work it would take him to raise his city.

Not very much, she suspected. Then he would come looking for her.

"Thank you again," Nadeem said over her shoulder to the stream. Then she stepped outside onto the sands.

Cool night winds swirled up, then died back down. The stars were just starting to peak out from the dark sky. Nadeem turned first to her right, intending to walk all the way around the outcropping of rock.

From the outside, the rocks still appeared to be grown together, one place on top of another, in tall spires. But no gap lay between each segment.

Malik's cane leaned against the wall about halfway down the northern wall of the cavern. Nadeem couldn't have seen it from the front entrance.

Why was it there? Why hadn't it appeared beside her pack? She was certain it had been tied to her pack earlier—she'd found the straps.

Gingerly, Nadeem reached for the walking stick, as if the snake head might suddenly come alive and bite her.

The wood of the cane felt slippery against her palm, as if it had been greased with pig fat. She'd never seen anything magical about the stick, but she'd known that it was special. Different.

Now, it felt like it belonged in that in-between place she'd just left.

However, the stream had not welcomed it. If she had to guess, she would say that it barely suffered the cane's continued existence. It hadn't destroyed the cane because she had been the one carrying it.

Why was the cane so offensive?

Nadeem set the tip down beside her, probing the sand.

She hadn't left a solid footprint behind her. The sand around the outcropping of rock wasn't that soft.

However, what little mark she'd made as she'd walked disappeared, as if the cane sucked away all traces of her.

Curious, Nadeem took two more steps out, away from the outcropping of rock. Then she deliberately poked at the footprints she'd left behind in the softer sand.

They disappeared.

Nadeem had wanted to get out of the desert so she didn't have to face Trulliç. As the magician of the great Qaenev desert, he'd be able to find her anytime she set a foot on the sands.

With the cane, she could walk the desert freely.

What was the cane, exactly? How did it erase her steps? Why did that offend the stream and the cavern so much?

Questions and more questions.

Would Aunt Parayat provide Nadeem with any answers?

Nadeem hoped to. For her aunt's sake. Because Nadeem's knife was sharp, and she wouldn't hesitate to use it if it put her at an advantage.

Nadeem took a deep breath when she passed over the border of the desert and onto the true scrubland.

Normally, the border was indistinct. The same thorny bushes with scraggly leaves grew on both sides. Sand mixed freely with dirt. Winds blew this way and that.

However, Nadeem could tell. She suspected the border wasn't as distinct for her as it was for Trulliç. He'd know exactly where the edges of his land ran.

But now, she had more of an affinity toward the desert as well. Her mangled cheek told her, if nothing else. Pain stabbed her anew as soon as she stepped over. Not the debilitating pain of before, though she suspected even this ache would lessen.

It would never go away. Not until she placed her feet solidly on warm sand again.

To be safe, Nadeem still walked a ways north of the border. She didn't want to make it easy for Trulliç to find her.

The cane in her hands didn't change once it left the desert. The wood still felt greasy, and the silver head remained cold against her palm.

Now that she was off the sands, however, Nadeem cast a heavy illusion on the cane, making it appear as a stout walking stick. She *blurred* her own features, too. She couldn't make herself invisible— none of the star sisters had that ability. She could make it difficult for the eye to track her. With this disguise, she could walk directly by a man and he wouldn't notice her.

Nadeem looked carefully at her outstretched hands as the edges grew indistinct.

Then they turned darker. She became more like a shadow.

Nadeem stiffened. She'd never had that ability before. Did it come from the desert sand she'd rubbed into her mangled wound?

Had she picked up some of Trulliç's abilities? The power of the sands?

None of the star sisters could cast magic like the land-based magicians. All her magic was illusionary. Though she had been one of the strongest illusionists in her *kabal* of star sisters, she'd never heard of one having the power to become a true shadow.

Had she gotten stronger still?

Gleefully, Nadeem started to run across the scrub. She knew she didn't have the strength to go miles and miles at this speed, not with a full pack. She still felt tired from her visions and trials.

But life wasn't all about revenge, unanswered questions, and pain.

There was still joy to be found, too.

Nadeem stayed in the shadows and carefully counted the number of horses and camels the caravan traveled with. She wouldn't steal from a caravan that needed all of its pack animals.

However, several of these went unburdened and had stayed so for the last two days. She assumed that meant the animals were going to the large market in the next town to be sold.

She'd also heard the men's whispers at night, around the fire, of the new magician and how the desert had come alive, aware in a way it had never been before.

Hayalevi. The town the desert magician had called forth.

Nadeem wasn't certain how many days had passed while she'd been in that in-between place in the cavern. Maybe a week had gone by since she'd last seen Trulliç.

He'd claimed the entire desert as his own, though. And that included any and all who lived in the desert. They shared his dreams, though she did not, protected by the emperor's cane.

While not everyone in the caravan wanted to travel the length of the Qaenev desert, the leader of the caravan had already made up his mind to go to this new place. He bragged about making (yet another) fortune there.

In the meanwhile, Nadeem planned on "buying" one of his animals. Though she could walk and run all the way to Kardeş, going overland on camel would be easier and quicker.

She'd spent time sitting quietly with the animals the previous evening. They had seemed to accept her, smelling her presence though they couldn't really see her.

She'd never steal from a caravan, not even one as well outfitted as this one. Never take food from someone else's plate. You never knew when you might become the beggar, asking for another's forbearance. Though other star sisters might cheat an unpleasant inn keeper or tavern host, that had never sat well with Nadeem.

She had coin. She could pay.

The defenses around the camp were laughable. The two guards

they'd set weren't trained, and though they did stay awake all night, they didn't regularly walk the perimeter.

Did the merchants trust that no one would rob such a large caravan as theirs? Or did they think the animals, themselves, would set up an alarm if a stranger drew near?

She walked between the animals, looking for the one who would carry her without question. One of the male camels had caught her eye —he was young and had great strength. He also seemed more lazy though, and would require a firm hand.

One of the females might be a better match for her. The camel she had in mind had a sweet temper—well, sweet enough for a camel. She wouldn't be as strong as the male or go as long. But she wouldn't need so much minding, either.

Nadeem started walking between the male and the female camels, still unable to decide.

She froze when the leader of the caravan left the main fire and walked over to the horses. He murmured in the ear of the first horse, then stroked the mane of the second, also talking to it.

What was he saying? He appeared to be talking to each of them.

Nadeem waited until his back was turned before she moved closer, confident in her disguise. The man wouldn't be able to see her directly, not as indistinct as her magic made her. Plus, she had added more shadow to her skin, blending further into the night.

"Tomorrow you'll find a fair hand to guide you," the man assured the mare he currently stood next to. "Maybe a farmer who will let you walk his fields." Then he moved to the next mare. "And you! You will have a handsome stud or two, already lined up. Now, don't be bashful. You'll have beautiful colts, strong and mild-tempered."

Nadeem smiled. He seemed to know each of the animals and had already figured out his sales pitch for them.

"And you," he added as he turned.

Who was he addressing? He appeared to be facing the darkness.

"The stranger who visits my crew in the night and makes my charges uneasy. Come out of the dark and be an honored guest at my fire."

Nadeem grew very still. He obviously couldn't see her. He directed his speech to a blank spot in front of him while she stood a few feet to his left. She breathed very shallowly, willing him not to notice where she was.

After a few moments, the man added, "My men think you're a ghost who's come to haunt us. I think you're flesh and blood. Come and sit by our fire, so that I might win some bets." He grinned. "I'll even share the payout with you."

Nadeem kept herself under strict control, not moving, barely breathing, though a smile threatened to break out.

The merchant intrigued her. He would be considered handsome by most, with a tall, broad forehead, a large, hooked nose, and eyes that twinkled with intelligence. His skin was darker than most, though his lips and the palms of his hands were pink. He wore a finely made sleeveless tunic, slit down the center in the southern style, and belted over loose trousers, a plain shirt, and solid sandals.

After a few more moments, he shrugged. "Or don't. Stay in your shadows, play your games. Just don't hurt my horses or camels. They will fetch a nice price at the market tomorrow."

With that, the man turned and marched back to the main fire, his back tall and proud, unafraid of whoever stood behind him.

Nadeem waited, counting her heartbeats.

Should she go up to the man's fire, as he'd asked? Appear in the light and demand to be treated as an honored guest?

He couldn't hurt her. None of them could. She was almost back up to her full strength and speed.

Why not take advantage of his offer? She could always disappear anytime she wanted to.

Besides, she had planned on buying one of his animals, leaving coins behind.

May as well do the bargaining face to face.

With a grin, Nadeem stepped away from the animals. She kept her illusions up around her until she reached the edge of the firelight.

No one noticed her. She was pleased at how well her magic hid her.

Then she stepped forward, dropping the threads of her magic as she came into the light.

The men around the fire gasped. A couple rose, reaching for their weapons. The head of the caravan waved them back down.

"Greetings, honored guest," he said as he stood. "I am Levent. Be welcome at our fire."

"Thank you," Nadeem said, taking another step forward. "I am Nadeem, a traveler of the desert."

The men closest to her, on her left side, seemed perplexed, but they waited for Levent's word. Good. They were as well-behaved as she'd thought.

"Not a star sister?" Levent asked, curious.

Nadeem turned her mangled cheek toward him. "Not any longer," she said firmly.

That shocked the entire crew.

No woman that Nadeem had ever heard about had turned her back on the rest of the star sisters. She didn't know if that put a price on her head or not. She wouldn't be surprised if it had.

"I see," Levent said eventually. He nodded to himself, then continued. "You are welcome as an honored guest," he said firmly, addressing the crew around the fire as much as her. "We will share water, food, fire, and shelter with you," he added, using the traditional phrase.

Then he paused and grinned at her. "Though you've caused me to lose some of my bets, traveler."

He put an emphasis on that last word.

Nadeem nodded. He'd probably bet that she was a star sister.

"Perhaps you have something of interest for me to buy, merchant," Nadeem said. "After we share fire, water, and food."

She had always been planning on buying a travel animal from him.

"It will be my pleasure," Levent assured her. "Please, come, sit beside me and tell me your tales, so that I might learn."

"Gladly," Nadeem said, walking around the fire to the honored spot next to him. A servant appeared out of the dark and placed a clean rug on the ground, along with a new pillow.

Nadeem nodded in thanks, then sat with the rest of the men. Only now did she realize how hard her heart pounded and how dry her mouth had gotten.

They were just men. She could handle them.

But she was no longer a star sister. Had declared herself merely a traveler.

At least they'd seemed to accept her.

Levent clapped his hands. "Food! And water for our honored guest!" he called out.

There would be no stories, no talk or bargaining, until his guest was properly taken care of. Levent was taking his responsibilities as a host seriously.

But then, there would be many questions they would ask. Only some of which she would answer.

For a moment, she regretted her decision to come and sit at the fire.

Levent smiled warmly at her. He was curious, handsome, and intelligent. He'd work to make sure his guest stayed at ease.

Maybe it would all right.

CHAPTER THREE

TRULLIÇ

Trulliç raised his glass horseshoe to the next opening on the second story of his tower. Sand swirled up. The heat blasted his front, making him grin, as the sand solidified into clear, thick glass. It partitioned itself so the bottom section easily slid away, letting the breezes in.

Trulliç laughed with delight. This was how magic was supposed to be! Easy, clean, and joyous.

He took a deep breath, trying to let go of the anger that kept rising. Atça had lied to him, many times over. His former mentor had insisted that magic must be *taught*, that it wasn't a natural ability. That Trulliç could never trust his senses when it came to magic. That Trulliç was being *fanciful* whenever he thought he had some magical abilities.

Soon, Trulliç would go and demand answers from his former mentor.

And a reckoning.

For now, he had one more story of his tower to explore.

He'd kept the first floor as a mostly open space where he could greet people and hold meetings. He stubbornly pushed away the small voice that questioned who he would meet with. People would come to Hayalevi. He was certain of it.

He wasn't destined to live all alone in a great city on the edge of the desert, like some hero from a tragedy.

On the second floor, Trulliç had added additional walls, dividing the space so that guests would be comfortable there.

The stone stairs leading up to the third floor looked the same as the first set—made of long slabs of irregular rock. They reminded him of the pieces of stone that he'd seen in the cavern that had shared its water with him, so long ago, during his manhood journey. The gray rocks had wear patterns on them, as if they'd sat under dripping water for decades. They still held his weight firmly as he stepped up them and through the hole leading to the top floor.

It smelled differently up here. Trulliç paused before he took the final step onto the floor. What was it?

A sweet spice teased his senses. Cinnamon, maybe? Or figs, perhaps?

Trulliç took the final step up.

It was the sweet smell of the desert, her song made into perfume. It lifted his spirits, banished the rest of his anger. Whatever power he'd used that morning was instantly replenished. Actually, he felt stronger now than he had when he'd first woken.

A box sat in the corner of the room.

Even before he reached it, Trulliç identified it.

It was the land box, the box that had been with Nadeem. The box that held enchanted desert sand that Yerkoyliç had created to aid his search of the desert heart.

The box itself was nothing special. Plain wood stained a dark brown, though well made, with interlocking corners. It was perhaps ten inches along each side, and maybe a foot deep.

How had Yerkoyliç made it? Atça had said the land boxes were forbidden. They gave a magician too much power.

Trulliç believed it.

Magicians were land based. Once they left their home, their power diminished.

With a land box, however, a magician could carry a bit of their home with them. Keep themselves strong.

Maybe even challenge the emperor.

The great *Padisha-i-Ghazi* was famous for the long cloak he wore. Each scale in the cloak had been fashioned from the afterbirth of a magician or star sister. Someone with power couldn't fight their own blood. Thus, the emperor protected himself from those who could possibly be stronger than he was.

However, if a group of magicians attacked, and each with a land box…

Trulliç shook his head and pushed those thoughts to the side. The emperor would hopefully accept Trulliç, his power, and his land. Trulliç didn't want to fight the emperor.

Hopefully, the emperor would feel the same way about Trulliç.

Trulliç reached a hand into the box, letting the glowing sands slide through his fingers. He'd originally planned on bringing the sands to the desert and releasing them from their bonds.

Now, he wasn't sure.

The sand didn't feel trapped or constrained. It didn't mind being where it was, sitting in a box away from the rest of the desert. It had more awareness than the rest of the land. Trulliç wasn't certain what exactly he could do with the sand in the land box.

He'd have to experiment and see.

Trulliç paused for a moment. Why was the box here? Where was Nadeem? He couldn't feel her.

She'd left the desert. Though she'd said she'd stay and wait for him.

Trulliç snorted. No, she wouldn't wait. Nadeem didn't *wait* well. He'd only known her for a very short time, but he knew that patience wasn't her strong suit. And it had been, what, a week or more, since he'd left her.

Where had she gone? Not back to Kardeş, the oasis of the star sisters. He'd know if she walked on the desert.

She would come back to him. She had to. He had to reward her, thank her for..well, everything.

Trulliç turned away from the land box and looked over the third floor. He only built a few walls, dividing the space, leaving most of the entire floor open. This would be his study, where he slept and dreamed.

There was one more floor to explore, however. A much smaller staircase led to the roof. The stones there were more like bricks, baked and regular.

From the top of his tower, Trulliç felt as though he could see everything. To the south lay foothills that gave way quickly to the forbidding mountains that guarded his realm from the endless oceans.

To the east lay the closest water as well as the nearest oasis trail. Just past the border in that direction lay towns and people—the emperor's people, but people nonetheless.

To the west lay a lot of desert before the hills began again. More oasis trails curved there, following rivers that still ran in the heat of the summer.

And to the north—sand and more sand. Most of the desert filled that direction, going to the horizon.

Which direction would the people of his city come from?

Trulliç didn't know. But he'd come up here every day to see if he could spot anyone coming.

Trulliç spent much of his time in his tower. He didn't want to add banners, not yet. Though he'd seen what they'd looked like before, when this had been the city of the old kings.

He knew his banners would be the same colors, with thin stripes of green and gold. Like the ribbons of color that made up his glass horseshoe.

But there wasn't really much else for him to do here. Not until some other people came.

He'd already planned out where the streets would to. How the fountains would be laid out. The smaller alleys for those who felt they needed to hide. The wide-open markets.

When Trulliç walked across the flat plain, he could see all the buildings in his mind. Riyune walked beside him sometimes. Other times, the dog went off on his own to follow an interesting scent, or to pluck a hidden mouse or small lizard from the dirt to snack on.

Everyday, Trulliç found himself wandering back to his tower as the sun climbed directly overhead in order to go rest in the shade. No one traveled during the heat of the day.

However, Trulliç didn't feel the heat as he once had. It baked his bones, making him feel loose and alive, but he no longer sweat like he had. He didn't really need to hide in the shade like most people else did.

Again, the wash of anger over the lies Atça had told him.

Agitated, Trulliç paced his room in his tower.

What should he do? He knew he should go walk around the boundary of his territory, the entire desert. He wasn't sure how he needed to strengthen it, just that he needed to. And he'd promised himself more adventures, to go walk every inch of sand and learn about all the life hidden there.

What he really wanted, though, was people. Someone to talk with. How long had it been since he'd spoke to someone? A week? Two?

Trulliç sighed and sat in the center of his room. When he'd been on his first manhood journey, that had been one of his fears. That he'd be stuck living in the desert without any people, only occasional travelers to keep him company.

Riyune nudged his leg.

"I know you're here, but I'm sorry, you're not enough," Trulliç explained. Unless the dog was suddenly willing to talk with him?

But Riyune gave him the dog equivalent of an eye roll before he deliberately walked over to the western window.

"What, do you see something?" Trulliç asked. He eagerly jumped to his feet and looked out.

He couldn't see anyone coming.

Trulliç sent his senses out, feeling his way. No one walked across the desert to come greet him.

However...

An oasis sat tucked away just this side of the western mountains.

A permanent oasis. One that had a small village enclosed inside of it.

Trulliç grinned.

So maybe no one had been able to get to his grand city yet.

That didn't mean he couldn't go visit the people of his land. He didn't have to wait until they came to him.

He could go to them.

Before Trulliç left, he raised one more small building. It stood solid and separate. Just a square room with a guard stone. He left the inside dark and shaded, a resting place for travelers.

In it, Trulliç built two altars.

The first was an altar to Serrat. He'd always been the god that Trulliç prayed to. He was the god who'd brought magic to mankind so he could win a bet with the goddess Onnet. He'd been banished from the land of the gods as a result, and was considered the god of desolate places, like the desert and craggy mountain peaks.

Trulliç dedicated the second altar to Serril, Serrat's female side. The god was frequently represented with two faces—one female, one male. In stories Trulliç had learned as a child, the god could take on either form, and appear as either a man or a woman.

Serril had given birth to the star sisters. She had a birthmark in the shape of a star on her left cheek, which was why the star sisters marked themselves the same way.

The first altar, Trulliç colored the stones black, so people would know it belonged to Serrat. The second, he made the stones white.

But what should Trulliç offer his god? To both aspects of him?

Trulliç reached down to the sand beneath him and lifted up a handful. Then he compressed it with his other hand, as if the sand were clay. Trulliç sang a song of thanksgiving as he pressed the sand together harder and harder. The heat that rose from between his cupped hands refreshed him, drying out his skin.

When he released his hands, a small glass ball floated in the air before him. The glass was black and smooth, like a pearl from the Barzhat Sea. He sent it to sit on the altar for Serrat.

Then Trulliç did the same for Serril, forming a small white glass ball and setting it on her altar.

The glass balls didn't glow, which Trulliç found disappointing.

What had he done wrong? They should be a light to all who came into this tiny temple.

When he took a step back, he realized they didn't need to glow.

The sand underneath both altars glowed—a soft, golden light—while the glass balls loomed, protecting the altars.

Whoever came here to pray would automatically recognize this as a holy place. Maybe sometime a priest would come and properly sanctify the altars, though given how the space felt, that might be unnecessary.

Only after Trulliç left the small temple did he realize that he'd broken one of the emperor's recent commandments. Any new building needed to have a small scale-like shape added to its foundation to represent the emperor. Many new buildings were now dedicated to the emperor.

Trulliç reached his hand out to form the shape in the wall of the temple, then drew it back.

Yerkoyliç had claimed that all the recent proclamations from the emperor were because he planned on becoming a god.

People now thanked the emperor at every meal, as if he was responsible for the bounty they were about to enjoy. New buildings had to bear his mark. Bells in the morning rang in his honor.

Trulliç walked away before he despoiled the temple to Serrat/Serril with the sign of the emperor.

This was *Trulliç's* land. His territory. Yes, in the grand scheme of things, it was part of the empire as well.

But Trulliç wasn't about to deface his property with another man's mark.

Not until guards arrived and told him that he must.

The village of Ishmirli held maybe thirty families, so about one third of the size of Gaadiwala, where Trulliç had grown up. They were mostly shepherds or traders, tending the caravans which came through, either on their way to the coast or coming from there. The village had a single inn located in the north-east corner of the tiny market square.

Though Trulliç could have sped across the sands and arrived there well before sunset, he took his time gliding over the land, paying attention to the life he encountered—the nests of mice, the skittering lizards, the desert hawks and smaller birds.

He also marked the edge of his border, where the desert ended and the foothills of the mountains began.

He didn't feel the need to defend that border. First, someone would have to sail the endless ocean, then scale the foreboding cliffs to approach the desert from that direction. There were much easier options. He decided to focus on those.

The Qaenev desert was huge. Trulliç didn't know how many miles across it stood, how deep the sands ran north to south. Though Atça hadn't believed in maps, didn't trust them, he'd still shown Trulliç a recent map drawn by the emperor.

Though the emperor had much more land both to the east of the desert as well as the entire kingdom of Lydae in the north, the desert still made up a large part of the empire. Possibly as much as a quarter of the total land space, if that map was to be believed.

Though the emperor claimed the Barzhat Sea as his as well, Trulliç knew better. That belonged to the goddess Barzhat, who only sometimes suffered men to sail along the edges of the water. Trying to sail directly across was a sure way of finding the goddess's golden court, to dance before her until she gave the final kiss of release so a soul could be reborn.

Trulliç arrived in the village of Ishmirli just as twilight started. It was still spring, not full summer, so the sun set earlier than usual. Plus, he was much farther south than his home village of Gaadiwala. The sun set even earlier than he was used to.

The market stood empty, the merchants already in their homes. Trulliç didn't pass anyone on his way to the tavern. Maybe in the morning there would be more people around.

Trulliç remembered how poor Gaadiwala had seemed, particularly after he went to Çandekili, the town Yerkoyliç controlled.

Trulliç didn't want his villages to be as poor as Gaadiwala.

However, there were already people living here in Ishmirli, people who had already established their routines. He didn't want to completely disrupt them by suddenly changing their wells or streets. Maybe in the morning he could bring the town together, find out what their needs were.

The tavern had a painted sign hanging in front of it—a goblet made of stone, brimming with red wine. Interesting. The Horseshoe Tavern, the tavern his family had owned, served beer primarily. Wine couldn't grow in the region, but wheat and other grains could.

Trulliç sent his senses further, beyond the village to the west. Ah. There were valleys on the very edge of the desert that would produce good grapes. Clouds and rain from the ocean would roll over the hills there, making it a green place.

Stepping inside the dim room brought many memories of his family's tavern. The rough wood tables, the clean but worn pillows scattered across the stone floor for guests, even the fireplace on the side, large enough for three men to stand in.

An older gentleman stood just beyond the stone counter that lined the back of the room. "Can I help you?" he asked. His white hair hung long around his face in the custom of the men from Lydae, though his skin was dark and his meaty hands proclaimed him as someone from the south. He wore a simple tunic made of plain brown cloth.

He paused for a moment, then took three hesitant steps forward, peering at Trulliç.

"I feel I should know you," he said softly. He blinked, then shook his head. "Sorry. Please forgive an old man whose wits are wandering. I didn't meet you, except, perhaps, in a dream."

A spike of joy pierced Trulliç. Maybe the people of the desert would know him! Everyone in Gaadiwala knew Atça.

"I am Trulliç," he said simply.

The man gasped. "The great magician!" he said, taking a step back. He gasped again. "Stay—stay right here. I'll be right back!"

The man took off through the open door.

Trulliç looked around the empty room, then down at Riyune. "So I guess I should just serve myself?"

The dog gave him an expression that could easily be read as, "Duh."

Trulliç snorted but didn't go behind the counter. He could smell the sour beer they brewed here, the remains of the flatbread they served.

What he really wanted was some good tea. Hopefully when the man got back, he'd serve Trulliç some.

A fter a short while the man came rushing back in the tavern. "You're still here!" he proclaimed gleefully.

Trulliç nodded. "I am." Had the man thought he'd just dreamed he'd met the great desert magician?

The tavern keeper stepped to one side and beckoned for someone else to come in.

A thin, short man entered. He had dark, thick hair that he kept oiled, in the older tradition, the ends touching the red and black *chafiyek* he wore loosely around his neck. His face had a permanent dour expression, with disapproving eyebrows and miserly lips. His dark eyes greedily sucked in Trulliç and everything he wore, discounting Riyune immediately.

"Ah, my good friend!" the man said, coming forward. "I am Gökel, the headman of this village. Welcome!"

Trulliç stood back up and bowed his head, keeping his hands at his sides. He didn't want to touch this man. He'd never really liked touching anyone.

Maybe this Gökel was a good leader, though Trulliç doubted it. He probably was the type who exaggerated the amount of tribute due to the emperor, skimming the best of it off the top and keeping it for himself.

Still, Trulliç was a stranger here. He didn't want to cause any trouble. He just wanted to meet the people of his domain. Get to know them.

And hopefully, help them.

"Brugral! Wine for our famous magician! And make it your best!" Gökel said as he came forward, ordering around the poor tavern keeper.

"Tea, please, if you have it," Trulliç insisted. He'd tasted wine—his family's tavern had served it whenever they'd acquired some barrels of it, which hadn't been too often. Sometimes, Trulliç had drank the sour beer they brewed, though he'd never developed a tasted for it.

Since arriving in the desert, he'd found what he missed most was the dark tea Atça had always served him.

Come to think of it, Yerkoyliç had also served Trulliç a delicious tea.

Was that what magicians preferred to drink?

"Have you eaten?" Gökel asked. "How can this poor host honor such an important guest?"

Trulliç blinked, surprised. Wasn't this Brugral's tavern? Or did Gökel consider the whole village his?

"Please, sit," Trulliç said, indicating one of the nearby tables, "and tell me your tales so that I might learn."

It was the traditional greeting a crowd might give a storyteller, or that a host would give a guest. However, Trulliç truly wanted to know more about Ishmirli and the people of his realm.

Brugal came over to where they sat with a platter of fresh flatbread, some finely rendered lard to spread on it, along with sliced onions and a small container of salt and spices.

"The tea will be along as soon as the water has heated," he said breathlessly. "Please, enjoy these humble refreshments in the meanwhile."

Trulliç would bet that Brugal had just served them his own dinner.

"Thank you," Trulliç said, trying to catch the man's eye to convey that he really was grateful. He wasn't sure he'd eat more than a mouthful—he didn't need to eat. But it would have been horrifically impolite of him to tell the tavern keeper that he wasn't hungry.

Gökel reached immediately for the bread and lard. Then he paused and pushed it toward Trulliç. "Here, eat," he said gruffly.

Was Gökel always the first one to eat? Trulliç had known families in Gaadiwala where that had been the case, where the head of the household ate first, then everyone else.

"Thank you," Trulliç said, amused. He would gladly break that tradition—that the highest ranked person ate first—but he also wanted to make sure that Gökel realized that Trulliç did outrank him now.

Trulliç spread the fine lard on a small piece of flatbread, added onions and a sprinkle of salt and spices. It smelled heavenly, just the faintest hint of pork remaining in the lard, the salt mixed with mint, oregano, and sage.

Brugal scurried away before Trulliç could thank him again.

Gökel watched Trulliç take his first bite before he served himself. At least he knew his manners.

"The humble village of Ishmirli is honored by your presence," Gökel told Trulliç after taking his own first bite. "How may we serve the great desert magician?"

Trulliç sighed and put the bread down. This wasn't how he wanted this meeting to go. He just wanted to come and be around people. He wasn't used to being an important person.

Suddenly, Atça taking students made more sense to Trulliç, plus why he'd agreed to teach Trulliç in the first place. Everyone else would treat Atça like an important person, not like a regular villager.

At least with his students, Atça had the opportunity to actually talk with someone as familiarity made conversations with his students less stilted.

Trulliç paused, considering. "The question is, how may I help you? The village of Ishmirli is in my territory. What do you need?"

Trulliç didn't like the greedy look that filled Gökel's eyes.

"We are a poor village," Gökel said.

Trulliç didn't snort. Gökel sounded like a storyteller in the market when he took on the wheedling tones of a shifty farmer.

"We need more money," Gökel said. "And more rain for our pastures."

"I am a desert magician," Trulliç said dryly. "I can't control the rains. Or make coins out of sand." He paused, then added, "I can build better roads so it's easier for travelers to reach Ishmirli. If there are reservoirs or aquifers under the earth, I can build more wells." He wasn't about to offer to build new houses for everyone in town, though he suspected that he could.

He also had an affinity toward glass. He could produce better lamps for the people, make them plentiful, as well as glass windows.

Gökel sniffed, as if that wasn't good enough.

Brugal appeared before their table again. While Gökel ignored the man, Trulliç asked, "Yes? What is it?"

"There's a well on the northern side of the village, next to the path to Suluvanti, that has been failing…" Brugal said hesitatingly.

"You'll have to show me in the morning," Trulliç told him, giving him an encouraging smile.

"Those people have just wasted the water there," Gökel said disparagingly.

Brugal shrugged and walked away.

"It's those people from the other side of the valley," Gökel said. "They don't belong here. Maybe you can get rid of them."

Trulliç blinked, surprised. Why would he say that? Trulliç would think that Gökel would want more people in his territory, more people that he could rule over.

Then again, he didn't know the feuds in this area. Maybe there had been fights about water rights in the past.

There was just so much to learn!

"Tell me more," Trulliç said.

No matter how Atça might have accused him of being the slowest student he had, Trulliç knew he wasn't stupid.

And though he might not know everything about Ishmirli, he could learn.

⁂

The tea Brugal brought Trulliç was truly wonderful. It smelled faintly of cinnamon and citrus, though the tea itself was black and rich. Trulliç suspected that yet again, Brugal had provided him with supplies from his own private stock, and that regular patrons of the tavern weren't served such fine tea.

In the morning, Trulliç would have to ask Brugal where bought the tea from. Trulliç would like to keep some for his tower, for the mornings when he really wanted tea.

For now, Trulliç tried to pay attention to everyone Gökel had a disagreement with. The head of the village didn't appear to like anyone. Every single person in town had slighted him at one point.

He'd seemed to assume that now that Trulliç was here, that the desert magician would get all the villagers to fall into line and do everything that Gökel demanded.

Trulliç had sat with Atça many times when he'd held court, listening to people's complaints, then casting judgments that Trulliç carefully kept in Atça's ledger books.

Did Trulliç need to set up that sort of system? A traveling court, with Trulliç going to various towns and villages and listening to their complaints?

He sighed inwardly. He supposed he should do that, though he hoped that most people could settle their own disputes.

However, he also realized that a village like Ishmirli wouldn't be able to mete out their own justice. Not with a headman like Gökel. Trulliç had developed a true antipathy for the man. How did the rest of the villagers stand him?

More importantly, why? It wasn't as if Gökel had some sort of magic and could provide the people here with a better life.

Throughout the evening, other villagers had come into the tavern for a quick drink or a word with Brugal. They'd all come to see Trulliç, he knew. However, none of them would approach the table where he sat with Gökel, afraid to intervene.

Finally, after Gökel whined about yet another slight, this time by Widow Handen, who appeared to eek out a living by tending sheep in the northern valley, Trulliç asked, exacerbated, "Who hasn't done you wrong in Ishmirli?"

Gökel sniffed. "I don't know what you mean," he said.

Trulliç shook his head. "Tell me about the good people here," he said plainly.

Gökel shrugged. "Everyone has their good and bad points," he said.

"True," Trulliç admitted. "But you can still tell me something good," he insisted. "Tell me something that has delighted you in the last few days."

"Life isn't always fun and games," Gökel growled. "There's hard work to be done. A man's duty."

Trulliç looked at the man sitting next to him. Trulliç knew he looked just a boy in comparison—after all, he'd just turned eighteen.

He wasn't completely naïve, however.

And Gökel seemed to have forgotten his place, had stopped acting like a generous host at some point during the evening. He'd begun to believe that this was still his village, not Trulliç's.

Trulliç bent down, glancing over at Riyune who sat perfectly still, like a statue, next to him.

The dog was no help, as usual.

Then Trulliç scooped up a bit of sand from the floor and spilled it onto the table.

Gökel didn't seem to notice, was still ranting about how no one appreciated him. Including Trulliç, evidently.

Trulliç had had enough.

The edges of the wood table had been slicked over, softened by many hands and bellies rubbing against it over the years. The center of the flat surface felt more rough. Trulliç carefully slid his finger across it, through the small pile of sand. The table probably wasn't rough enough that he'd get a splinter. Probably.

"Enough," Trulliç said, interrupting Gökel.

"What do you—" the man sputtered.

"I said enough," Trulliç growled as he drew a circle in the sand with his finger. "I'm not here to punish people at your whim."

"Then what are you here for, boy?" Gökel sneered. "What can you do for the fine people of Ishmirli? If you can't make it rain and you can't give us more coin?"

Riyune suddenly pushed his head against Trulliç's knee. Words didn't come through clearly, not like on the other two times when the dog had spoken to Trulliç.

The feeling was still there. The urging for Trulliç to just do it. Riyune would be there, would support him.

The words fell from Trulliç's lips before he could stop them. "I could get rid of you," he said softly. "I think the fine people of Ishmirli might thank me for that."

The sand he'd drawn up onto the table sprang up into a mini-whirlwind, not much taller than the span of Trulliç's palm.

"Oh, really?" Gökel said. He didn't seem frightened of the magic Trulliç was performing. Maybe he'd been expecting something more grand. "And what? Replace me with old Brugal, there?" Gökel laughed, a high, nasty sound.

"Yes," Trulliç said simply.

"I dare you," Gökel said.

When Trulliç didn't reply, Gökel snorted in derision. "I didn't think you had it in you. You're just a boy, trying to fill a man's role."

Trulliç nodded. "You're half right. I am still learning how to be a man. But I know my role."

He was the desert magician. He needed to take care of his people.

The fine people of Ishmirli needed a much, much better headman.

He could help with that.

Trulliç cupped his hand around the mini-whirlwind and casually threw it at the man sitting next to him.

Gökel started choking.

It was so easy—far too easy—for the rage inside of Trulliç to leap up and join the sand already choking the man. For Trulliç's anger to add winds that pushed the sand deeper down the man's throat.

After a few long moments, Gökel stopped choking and fell to the side. Trulliç called up more winds to pick up the body and carried it far out into the desert, where it would feed the creatures there, the hawks and mice, the snakes and lizards.

Brugal stood shocked, as still as a mouse before a desert hawk.

"And what will you do with me?" he asked, his voice breaking.

"Do you want to be the village headman?" Trulliç asked in return.

Brugal gave an obvious gulp. Then his eyes grew more shrewd. "Maybe."

He nodded his head toward the open door.

Trulliç realized belatedly that other villagers had been standing there. Watching. Judging.

"You've scared them but good," Brugal told him. "And you still scare me."

"That wasn't what I meant to do!" Trulliç said, horrified. What had he done?

Brugal was right, though. One of Trulliç's first acts as the desert magician had been to kill someone.

That wasn't what he'd intended to do, not at all. He didn't want his people to be afraid of him, tiptoeing around him, scared that they would be the next to die.

"I've been listening to you all night. I think you have a good heart." Brugal paused, then added, "And that we can work together."

Trulliç nodded slowly. "How can I make it up to them?" Was it possible to show them that he wasn't a scary, vengeful magician?

Brugal finally smiled at him, his first true smile of the evening. "Honestly? Between you and me? You already made a good start by getting rid of that braggart. He was the headman here because his father had, and his grandfather before that. His son would have tried to assume the same role, though I don't think people here would have stood for it." Brugal put his hands on his hips and regarded Trulliç. "However, you've also done great damage by listening to him first. We'll have to fix that in the morning."

Trulliç nodded. He'd be happy to work with Brugal on that.

To fix this mess he'd just made.

CHAPTER FOUR

NADEEM

NADEEM HAPPILY RODE WITH THE caravan for a week. But now it was time for her to continue her journey on her own. She checked the bags strapped to Banut, her sweet female camel, making sure they were tight but not too tight. Darkness had just kissed the sky, hiding the clear blue with night. Only a few stars twinkled on the horizon. The air felt softer here, along the oasis trail, since they no longer traveled across hot sands.

She wore the traveling clothes she'd picked up at the first town the caravan had visited. She was dressed like a merchant, actually—with loose black pants and a short, navy-blue tunic over a light-weight, white blouse. Her *chafiyek* lay around her neck, a finely woven cloth with blue, black, and white squares. Tough leather sandals with thick soles that she could easily run in covered her feet. A heavy cloak was tied to Banut's back for when the night grew chilly. Along with what appeared to be a stout walking stick, though Nadeem could still see the snake-headed cane at the heart of the illusion.

"Must you go?" came a quiet voice to her left.

Nadeem didn't startle, though she hadn't known anyone was there. However, she'd been expecting Levent's visit.

"I must," she said simply as she buckled the pack on Banut's right side. "There are things I must do."

Namely, go and visit Aunt Parayat in Kardeş, the hidden oasis of the star sisters. To find out if there was already a price on her head for turning her back on the rest of her sisters. For not fulfilling her oath to Atça.

To see if she could get her wily aunt to answer some of Nadeem's burning questions.

Levent came closer, standing beside her. He put a reassuring hand on Banut's flank. The merchant had a way with animals. Though Banut hadn't been nervous, she shifted her stance so her legs were wider and she appeared to relax further.

He wore his usual merchant's outfit, a tunic slit down the center in the southern style made out of dark green, over brown loose trousers and solid sandals. His black hair curled slightly around his face, giving him a younger smile.

"When will I see you again?" he asked plainly, though his tone held a caressing note.

"When the gods will it," Nadeem replied, giving him the usual response that storytellers did in their tales when lovers parted. He'd been her first male lover. Gentle and different than the women she'd known. She hadn't decided yet which she liked better, male or female, or if she'd ever choose. Both had their advantages.

Levent's smile broadened. "I shall count the days," he said, continuing the litany. Then he grew more serious. "I am on my way to Hayalevi, to see the great towers of the desert magician."

"Trulliç," Nadeem told him. "I will go there too, someday."

When she could face her failure. When even his name didn't put her ill at ease.

Levent tilted his head to the side. "You know him?" His eyes narrowed.

Oh goddess, he wasn't jealous, was he? They'd made no promises to one another, no vows or bonds. Nadeem had been warned that men would be like this.

"Of course I know Trulliç," Nadeem said, putting as much disdain into her voice as she could. "He's the magician of all of Qaenev," Implying that all desert people would know him.

Levent nodded slowly. "But you aren't a star sister anymore," he said.

Nadeem shrugged. "I grew up in an oasis." She was still of the desert, would always think of herself that way. More so now that she'd rubbed enchanted sand into her mangled cheek.

The wound still hurt now and again, a brilliant flare of pain that always caught her off guard. If she wasn't careful, she'd gasp when it struck instead of maintaining a stoic mien.

The pain had grown less and her skin had started healing.

Her affinity toward the desert had grown greater.

Trulliç could accurately point in the direction of the closest water, no matter where he stood on the sands. Nadeem had begun to acquire that ability. If water ran miles and miles away, she might not be able to smell it on the air.

If it was closer, though, she could walk in a straight line to it.

She knew that other desert creatures had the same ability, to always be able to sense water. Humans were the only ones not gifted that way. They needed to learn where the oasis rivers ran.

Nadeem knew where they lay now, without a map.

Levent smiled at her and shook his head. "No, you knew Trulliç from some other time. Before he became the desert magician." He paused, then sighed. "I hope that you will tell me, someday."

Nadeem shrugged again. Her past was her own. Levent had hinted before that he'd like to know what had happened to her, why she'd turned her back on the star sisters and labeled herself merely a traveler, now.

While Nadeem was happy to share her bed with him, she didn't feel the need to do more than that.

"Be on your way, then, mysterious stranger," Levent said as he bowed his head and stepped back. "May our paths cross again before the next rains."

Nadeem looked over her shoulder at him. "I do thank you for your most excellent hospitality," she said seriously.

"It was my pleasure," Levent said, giving her a sweep bow this time. "And I hope to see you in the spring in Hayalevi. Even if at that point I'll just be a plain merchant while you'll still be a mysterious stranger on even more mysterious business, dealing with the desert magician and no one else."

Nadeem couldn't help her shiver. Levent may be right. Once she finished with her individual business with Aunt Parayat, she might have to go to Hayalevi.

To warn Trulliç that he, too, had even more of a price on his head.

Nadeem swung her foot up into the mounting stirrup, then pulled herself over Banut's back. Most needed mounting blocks, but Nadeem had trained herself to do without.

"Safe journeys and easy water," Levent called up to her.

"Good trade and easy water for you, too," Nadeem replied.

She paused for a moment, then shrugged. What did it matter if Levent saw her do magic? He would keep her secrets, she knew. Even if he told anyone, who would believe a merchant's wild tales?

Nadeem lifted her hands up in front of her and *blurred* her fingers, making the outline of her skin indistinct. Then she lowered her hands to either side of Banut's neck and did the same thing.

She heard Levent's gasp, but she wasn't done yet.

She added shadows to them both. Darkening them. Hiding them. Making them part of the night.

Levent stood perfectly still, aware that he'd witnessed a rare display. No star sister would ever have changed like that in front of a stranger.

And anyone who was not of the *kabil* was considered a stranger. No matter how familiar they might be.

Then Levent gave her a third bow, low and held deeply for a moment. "Until I see you again. At your wish, obviously."

Levent turned and walked back toward the camp, still shaking his head.

Nadeem smiled. It had been a pleasant interlude to ride with the caravan at dawn and dusk, to lay with Levent during the heat of the day, to not worry about destinies and blood oaths for a while.

It was time for her to get going though, back to her life.

To gather up the remains of it, see what she had left, and travel forward again.

Nadeem waited in the shade of a boulder, Banut seated beside her, watching Kardeş. Or rather, watching the guards. She was familiar with the pattern they ran: two obvious watchers who let themselves be seen now and again, with a third secreted away that none could see. Someone patient enough to wait through two changes of guards would eventually note the third.

Or perhaps not. She was well hidden and never joined the other two, even when she was relieved of her duty.

Few had that patience, however. Fewer still would have found Kardeş in the first place.

A caravan following the oasis trail that stretched north and south of Kardeş would pass far to the east, not noticing where the water split. Even if they managed to stumble upon the second stream, the star sisters kept the oasis itself hidden. Even to Nadeem's eye, the bushes that marked the edge of the oasis all shimmered, giving the appearance of a mirage. If the guards spotted anyone coming, the entire village would simply vanish.

Nadeem waited until the end of the next shift of guards, just as dusk approached, when the watchers would be tired and bored, not guarding as carefully, before she made her move.

She'd already strengthened her own illusion, blurring her edges and hiding her face in shadows. She cast further illusions on Banut, keeping her hidden by the rocks. The camel wouldn't move but would stay where she was, at least for a few hours.

Nadeem tied the snake-headed walking stick to her back. Carrying it was the surest way of hiding her steps from Trulliç. She had no idea if it would help or hinder with the star sisters. She suspected neither—they weren't of the desert, no matter what she'd told Levent.

Not like she was.

Taking a deep breath, Nadeem pushed herself up to her toes a few times, stretching out her calves. Anxious anticipation settled deep in her belly.

Could she slip into the oasis undetected? The star sisters' home?

The most heavily defended place in the entire empire, save that of the emperor's palace itself?

Only one way to find out…

Nadeem took a few more moments to stretch, then started her race across the open sands, going as fast as she could, her heart singing with the joy of the wind.

———

Nadeem could admit to herself that she was disappointed when nothing happened when she stepped into Kardeş. The oasis wasn't separate from the desert.

She realized that she'd been hoping that there would be as distinct a border between the oasis and the desert. That the star sisters' home was somehow different from the other villages and towns in Trulliç's domain.

It wasn't, however.

Trulliç could still find them, appear in the middle of their tents. And they wouldn't be able to turn him away.

Nadeem crouched down next to a large cactus and paused. No alarm sounded. No one had seen her. She took a deep breath of relief. The smell of the village filled her, the sweet scents of the cooking fires and the sweat of girls, spices, and sheep.

Now, where would she find Aunt Parayat? Dusk was fast approaching. Hopefully she'd be in her tent, where she'd napped through the heat of the afternoon.

If she was still alive. That had always been Nadeem's fear, that at some point her aunt wouldn't awaken from one of her naps.

Nadeem rushed there as fast as she could. Nothing had changed, at least not in the three plus years she'd been at the training camp on Knife Ridge. The cooking tents still sat to the east where the tallest trees stood, the area in the oasis that would cool the soonest in the afternoon. Next to them lay a wide open area with many long tables and benches, where the sisters would gather together and eat.

The teaching tents lay to the north of there, and the private tents of the teachers lay to the south.

While the younger sisters stayed mostly in communal tents, the aunts generally had private ones. Some still chose to live together, old friends who couldn't bear to be separated, in groups of three or four.

Aunt Parayat had always lived apart, at least as long as Nadeem had known her.

Nadeem had to pause while a group of laughing aunts walked past her, heading toward the cooking tents. They walked arm in arm, comrades.

A pang of jealousy went through Nadeem. She would never enjoy such sisterhood, not ever again.

Then she steeled herself. It was better this way.

The tent flap for Aunt Parayat's tent stood open. There was something off about it. But what?

Ah. That was it. There was an illusion cast around the opening. Most would see the tent flap as closed.

Wait.

Before, it had been so easy for Nadeem to cast illusions of grand warriors and throw herself into battle. The small, mundane things had always been so difficult.

Had her aunt grown so much weaker that Nadeem had to look twice in order to even detect the illusion?

Or had Nadeem grown impossibly strong?

She suspected the latter, but she didn't have time to make certain.

With one more deep breath, Nadeem slipped inside the tent.

It looked the same as it always had: a small square, about twelve feet on a side, with a few personal possessions. The brown tent fabric had always made the space feel cooler than the outside. The sand floor had two thick, large rugs on it, beaten clean regularly so the black-and-blue braid was visible. A distaff full of fiber, ready for spinning, stood next to a pile of baskets containing small balls of yarn.

At the back, Aunt Parayat had a fluffed mattress full of down feathers that she slept on. She'd woven her blankets herself, so they had unusual geometric patterns and odd colors as she'd experimented through the years.

Nadeem smelled the lanolin of the wool and realized that scent, as much as anything else, told her that she was home.

Her aunt lay on her mattress, still napping, her torso naked while her hips and legs were covered with a thin sheet. Many more lines crossed her face than the last time Nadeem had seen her. Her soft pink mouth was open, making her look unbelievably vulnerable. White curls surrounded her head. Her arms still had muscles, but the tanned skin sagged with age.

Before Nadeem could reach out and touch her aunt, make sure she was still alive, Aunt Parayat opened her eyes. The faded brown stared directed into Nadeem's.

"Hello, Nadeem," Aunt Parayat said very quietly. "I've been expecting you."

***

Nadeem withdrew to the far side of Aunt Parayat's tent while her aunt sat up, stretched, and slipped on a light-weight tunic to cover her nakedness. The tunic had been woven recently from unbleached thread, with hints of black, brown, gold, and green running through it, specks of color that hadn't coalesced into a pattern.

Would the weavers change their patterns now that Trulliç had found his home? His colors would be gold and green, that much Nadeem knew.

Aunt Parayat walked up to Nadeem, holding out her hands in greeting. "It's good to see you," she assured the younger woman.

They grasped arms like comrades at war, clasping each other's forearms tightly. Nadeem felt assured that her aunt's arms still felt like steel despite how soft her skin had gotten.

But her aunt had also shrunk in the past three years. Nadeem had never been taller than Aunt Parayat before this.

"It is good to see you as well," Nadeem told her former mentor.

"I have little to offer you here," Aunt Parayat said, indicating the tent. "Beyond fresh water and hungry ears."

Nadeem smiled. It was one of the calls a crowd made to a storyteller, offering to quench his or her thirst while they dealt with a different sort of need.

"I'm not sure you'll be happy to hear what I have to say," Nadeem said. She raised her head then turned it slowly, so Aunt Parayat could see her mangled cheek. "I am merely a traveler, now."

The words hurt. Much more than Nadeem had ever imagined they would.

Aunt Parayat still held onto Nadeem's arms fiercely. "There are worse things," she said darkly. "Much, much worse."

Nadeem's relief made her knees buckle.

"Though you are no longer of the *kabil*," Aunt Parayat said as she led Nadeem to the side, indicating that she should sit in the place of honor, "I still declare you friend."

"Thank you," Nadeem whispered, her sudden tears choking her words. "I am honored by your friendship."

"Sit," Aunt Parayat said.

When Nadeem would have protested, Aunt Parayat pointed to the pillows. "Guests of honor sit there. And they show respect to their elders by following their requests. Particularly old women who have little patience."

"Yes, ma'am," Nadeem said as meekly as she could, sitting quickly.

"We don't have much time, I'm afraid," Aunt Parayat admitted as she sat beside her former student. "While I will engage with you, many would declare you a traitor."

Nadeem nodded. Aunt Izmet, the one who'd trained Nadeem to be one of the emperor's stars, would have killed her rather than talk with her.

But Aunt Izmet believed in following all orders fanatically, rather than questioning.

"Did you dream of me coming to see you?" Nadeem asked. If her arrival had prompted her aunt to dream of her, others may have shared the same dream.

Aunt Parayat shook her head. "No. I just know you well enough. You would return when Aunt Izmet's teaching and training failed you."

"Why did you send me off with her?" Nadeem asked, though her aunt hadn't pushed her that direction. Not really.

Aunt Parayat's quiet laughter filled the tent. "As if I could have stopped you," she said. "No, you were destined to become one of the emperor's stars from the moment you took over Aunt Haneet's lesson, showing such strong magical ability when you were so young." She paused, then added, "It was why I took on your lessons personally. So that you might have a chance against the brainwashing Aunt Izmet would try to give you."

"The questions," Nadeem stated. "Always asking questions." Her aunt had never let anything be. She'd always had questions, and then more questions, for Nadeem, forcing her to think beyond what she'd been told.

"Exactly," Aunt Parayat said. "It was my fervent hope that encouraging your questioning nature would inoculate you."

"Against what?" Nadeem asked. There had to be more to her aunt's schemes. There always was. Plans within plans.

Aunt Parayat reached up, moving so slowly Nadeem didn't flinch when her aunt touched her chin and gently turned her face so that she could see the mangled mark there. "It glistens, you know," Aunt Parayat said quietly before she dropped her hand. "A faint glow of magic. Like a male magician might have."

Nadeem stiffened. She knew she'd grown powerful, that her magic possibly had expanded beyond mere illusions.

Normally, a star sister would be killed if they'd grown that strong. It wasn't natural.

She grimaced. She'd become an abomination.

"Stop that," Aunt Parayat said, pinching the flesh on Nadeem's arm hard enough to make her wince. "You aren't a pariah. You are something different."

Nadeem waited, willing her aunt to give her a clue as to what she should become. What trails were open to her now.

Aunt Parayat dropped her gaze to her own hands, grasped tightly in front of her. "The emperor," she said after another long moment, "is evil."

Nadeem blinked, more startled than if her aunt had suddenly declared herself pregnant.

"Why would you say that?" Nadeem asked finally into the chilled silence.

"I've met him," Aunt Parayat said, turning her gaze from her hands to Nadeem. Her eyes burned with a fever Nadeem had never seen before. "He thinks he's a god, or can become one. He will destroy not just the Tanesh empire, but the entire world. You must stop him."

"How?" Nadeem asked. "I can't attack him. He has my blood." Like all babies born with power, a blood hound had followed her mother around and gobbled up the afterbirth, carrying it to the emperor for him to fashion a scale from.

Aunt Parayat's eyes narrowed. "Your blood is not the same as it once was," she said simply.

Nadeem didn't know how to respond to that. Her aunt was correct.

But how could she challenge the *Padisha-i-Ghazi*? The great emperor himself?

"You stay here and rest," Aunt Parayat said, rising. "I will bring you food for your continued journeys."

Nadeem swallowed hard. She would admit that a part of her had hoped that she'd be welcomed here in Kardeş, and that she'd find a place among her sisters.

She should have known that her mentor would have other plans for her. A destiny to fulfill. Yet another blood oath, though one that shook her to her core.

Some part of her nearly giggled as part of an old call-and-response song drifted through her head, of how a woman's work was never done.

And neither was hers.

***

Nadeem slept fitfully on Aunt Parayat's down-filled mattress, her dreams filled with visions of the end of the world, as always.

Only this time, she fought not only the darkness but the star sisters as well.

The emperor had infected her former sisters with his darkness. They danced to their deaths under her blade, laughing and unconcerned about the sweet kiss of night. Their sweat and blood covered Nadeem. Each drop that touched her cheek weakened her, draining away her magic, until nothing remained except her will.

She became her sword at that point, the steel directing her, dancing on its own, until the goddess Barzhat picked her up and wielded her.

But eventually, even the goddess stumbled during the onslaught.

There were just too many of the sisters, with an endless army marching over the sands.

After she died, Nadeem's soul flew over the sands to the edges of the star sister army. She saw in horror that the aunts marked the cheeks of all who came to them with brands of fire—old and young, men and women alike. The first touch changed them into girls, star sisters given knowledge and power without earning it.

The abomination woke Nadeem. She sat up, still shivering.

The tent had grown dark, the night pressing in on all sides. A simple clay lamp illuminated the room. Aunt Parayat sat patiently beside the mattress where Nadeem lay.

"You went deep," Aunt Parayat told Nadeem as she handed her a water skin.

Nadeem merely nodded, ashamed. She'd always been reluctant to share her visions, humiliated that they controlled her instead of the other way around.

Since she'd rubbed the desert sands into her cheek, they'd grown worse. Deeper. Longer. And always about the death of the world.

"I couldn't walk beside you," Aunt Parayat told her. "Tell me what you saw, so that I might learn."

Nadeem took another drink of water instead of immediately answering her aunt. What could she say?

"Please," Aunt Parayat said as she settled herself into a cross-legged pose. "Share what you have seen."

"The end of the world," Nadeem whispered, afraid to speak the words out loud. "Always. The end of the world. Gibbering darkness set loose by the emperor. Corrupting people. The star sisters. Even the gods."

Aunt Parayat nodded. "The emperor seeks the desert heart," she said. "The heart that tamed the darkness."

"That was what Trulliç said," Nadeem replied, not surprised that her aunt knew.

Aunt Parayat tilted her head to one side. "Trulliç," she breathed out. "Ah. That explains much of your change."

Nadeem waited while Aunt Parayat considered her anew. When it seemed that her mentor wouldn't say anything more, Nadeem added, "Atça, Trulliç's mentor, hired me to kill Trulliç if it turned out that the boy was disloyal to the emperor."

Aunt Parayat shrugged. "That is your business, and yours alone. Both the judgment and the deed. As you are no longer a star sister, it is not possible for you to fulfill a blood oath."

Nadeem stiffened. "Atça may call for another to fulfill it, then."

"That would be his right," Aunt Parayat said. "Would you fight the next star sister who came to kill Trulliç?"

"I wouldn't have to," Nadeem said with a tight smile. "She wouldn't get ten feet into the desert without Trulliç knowing. And he could defend himself."

"Is he that powerful?" Aunt Parayat asked, curious.

"Not yet. But he will be," Nadeem assured her. Even if she wasn't there to knock some sense into him, maybe that dog of his would.

Nadeem reached just past the sleeping mat and picked up the snake-headed walking stick. She cut the illusion to it and handed it to her aunt.

Aunt Parayat gasped when she grasped it. "Why do you carry this cursed thing?"

"It was a gift from the emperor, given to the man I'd been assigned to kill, as part of my first mission," Nadeem told her. It pleased her that she wasn't the only one who didn't trust the magic embodied by the cane.

"Did you kill him?" Aunt Parayat asked.

Nadeem wasn't sure about the casual tone in her aunt's voice. Obviously the question held much more importance than her aunt wanted to let on.

"I did not. I failed," Nadeem replied, her words still tasting bitter. "My team had to do it instead."

Aunt Parayat leaned forward and squeezed Nadeem's arm. "Good," she said. "I have too many souls weighing me down when I reach the goddess's golden court. It is better for you not to have any."

Nadeem nodded. Aunt Izmet would have told her that since the emperor had ordered the killing, the weight of the soul would be balanced against the emperor's wishes. That she wouldn't have been burdened with it after she died.

There were many things that Aunt Izmet said that Nadeem no longer believed.

"Still, why do you carry this, then?" Aunt Parayat said, handing the walking stick back to Nadeem. "It feels cursed, like it carries dark deeds in its heart."

It always amazed Nadeem how slippery the wood felt, as if it wasn't really of this world. "It hides my steps from Trulliç," she said. She wasn't sure why Aunt Parayat said it was cursed—that wasn't the feeling she got from it at all.

"You need to show him this," Aunt Parayat told her firmly. "He needs to know that the emperor can hide himself from the desert magician. Could possibly disguise an entire army marching across the sands."

Nadeem gasped. She hadn't considered that aspect of the walking stick or thought about more than just her need.

She shook her head. All her training was failing her. Her teachings that always made her consider the entire *kabil* and not just herself.

"So are you just going to sit there and feel sorry for yourself?" Aunt Parayat's voice came through Nadeem's haze with the sting of a whip.

"I don't want to kill the emperor," Nadeem whispered, speaking her heart's ache.

"Then don't," Aunt Parayat said with a shrug. "You merely have to stop him from acquiring the desert heart. From loosening that gibbering darkness on the world that you've always had visions of."

Nadeem swallowed against a suddenly dry throat.

Her aunt was correct. Nadeem didn't have to actually kill the emperor. All she had to do was to stop him. Somehow.

"You don't have to do it by yourself," Aunt Parayat said gently. "You have friends who can help. Like Trulliç."

Nadeem shook her head. None in her team would help—they'd all fallen into Aunt Izmet's trap, would only listen to her. They would consider Nadeem a traitor. None here in Kadeş would call her friend either, besides Aunt Parayat.

Was Trulliç a friend? She'd been hired to kill him, after all.

Maybe he wouldn't hold that against her. She had told him of his true home.

"I will stop the emperor," Nadeem said, aware that her words, no matter how quietly spoken, rang like a blood oath through the empty space of the tent. "He shall not have the desert heart."

Aunt Parayat gave her a proud smile, the same a mother would give a daughter after the birth of her first son.

Though Nadeem had no idea how she would fulfill her oath, she knew it was the most important one she'd ever taken. Even if it involved no blood.

CHAPTER FIVE

TRULLIÇ

TRULLIÇ SLEPT FITFULLY UNDER THE stars outside the tavern, next to the cold kitchen ovens. Brugal had offered Trulliç his own room in the tavern. However, Trulliç couldn't sleep in a room. He suspected that he'd never be able to sleep inside ever again. He needed to be able to see the stars. More now than ever before.

The strange smells of burnt bread and the sounds of people around him kept him awake. He almost left more than once, wanting to step outside of the village just so he could breathe again.

But he'd already done so much damage by killing Gökel. The people were afraid of him. What would they do if he didn't spend the night but disappeared and reappeared? Would more stories of him grow, stories of him going off and killing other village headmen?

Hopefully his people wouldn't always be afraid of him. He wanted for people to treat him like how the people in Çandekili had treated their wizard, with respect but also with great fondness.

If only Atça had let Trulliç come into his power sooner! Maybe Trulliç wouldn't have started out his rule on such bad footing.

Before the dawn filled the sky, Trulliç went to sit on the front stoop of the tavern. Brugal came downstairs shortly afterward. He seemed surprised that Trulliç had already risen.

"What can this humble host offer such an esteemed guest?" Brugal asked.

"Merely some more of that excellent tea," Trulliç replied. "And tell me where you got it, so that I might purchase more." Trulliç didn't have much money on him. He hoped that the people in the market would barter for glass lamps or windows instead.

"I will take you to the stall this afternoon," Brugal promised. "This morning, however, if we could go north of town to look at that well?"

"Of course!" Trulliç said, grateful that he might be able to make up for his early impression.

After Brugal brought the black spiced tea, they stayed seated on the front step. Brugal greeted everyone who walked up by name and introduced them Trulliç. It felt casual and friendly, much more how Trulliç had wanted to meet people. Riyune stayed seated beside him, acting like a normal dog, reaching out his head to sniff offered fingers, scratching himself, even yawning and rolling in the dirt from time to time.

Brugal told the people who came by that he and Trulliç would be heading up toward the northern-most well in a little while, and that they'd be in the market that afternoon. Many rushed off at the news.

Trulliç hoped there would be easy water near the well. That he'd be able to show the village that he could do something positive for them.

And not just kill.

Though the village of Ishmirli was richer than Gaadiwala, it was still a small, poor village. Gökel hadn't been lying about that. The huts had more wood than the ones in Trulliç's hometown. The people used it for making fences, tables, and benches. Trees were more readily available from just over the hills. Plus, cottonwood grew near the stream that ran east of Ishmirli.

The streets were all dirt and sand, not gravel. Spring grass covered the nearby hills, bright green but already browning. Scrawny chickens scattered in front of them or called from their yards. No other dogs dared approach Riyune, but even from a distance Trulliç could count the ribs in their skinny sides. Goats and sheep bleated from nearby pastures, tough scavengers looking for their next meal.

Trulliç tried to get a sense of how the houses were laid out. In Gaadiwala, they were all clustered around the wells. In Ishmirli that seemed to be part of it, but the neighborhoods also seemed to be dictated by families: first one small hut added onto a larger house, then another, and another, until it became a sprawling compound.

A crowd of people followed Trulliç and Brugal as they walked north along the main street. This was the path traders would take, going from the port to the south to the larger towns and villages to the north. Trulliç cleared the path of sharp stones as he walked, pushing them unobtrusively into the dirt. Not just so it would be easier for him to walk, but so that all who walked would find the path clear.

He wasn't sure if anyone noticed. He wasn't about to call attention to it, however. Let the people discover it later, marvel at his passing. It was the least he could do.

The well stood at the top of a small rise. Huts clustered to both the right and left of it, beyond the road. Trulliç recognized that the people in this neighborhood weren't as well off as those closer to the center of the village. They hung plain bolts of cloth over their doors instead of proper wood. The stone walls needed attention, the spring rains melting the mortar. No chickens squawked at them, and the children all ran away as they approached.

The well itself had originally been built out of fine brick that had cracked with age. A stone trellis had been built above the well with a rusted winch for lowering and raising water buckets.

Past the collection of huts the track ran straight and true. Trulliç turned and looked back over Ishmirli. He'd have to visit Gökel's compound later—he assumed that was the larger set of houses off to the east. The market could be seen as well, an open area surrounded by a cluster of buildings. The other taller buildings probably held temples that he should also visit.

"This is the well?" Trulliç asked Brugal in a loud voice so everyone who had followed them up the hill could hear.

"It is. Can you fix it, magician?" Brugal asked in return.

"I will try," Trulliç promised the man.

He beckoned for Riyune to come closer.

People who hadn't seen the dog before or realized that Trulliç traveled with a companion, gasped as Riyune came walking up.

Riyune gave the equivalent of a doggie eye roll, then he sat beside Trulliç and did his statue imitation. It didn't bother Trulliç when Riyune froze that way, though he was aware that it unnerved some people.

Trulliç tentatively reached out his hand and touched his fingertips to the top of Riyune's head, feeling Riyune's warm, smooth fur.

All the land came more alive. Trulliç felt more connected to it, the sand and the dirt, the scrubby trees and the small life. He wasn't as aware of the people in front of him—just had tenuous ties to them. Would those grow stronger? He hoped so.

Why did that always happen whenever Trulliç touched Riyune's fur? Why did the desert dog create such a strong connection for him?

He would have to try to figure that out at some other point.

For now, he had a job to do.

Trusting that Riyune would keep him anchored above ground, Trulliç pushed his senses under the ground, diving down the shaft of the well and into the water below.

It was obvious to him that the water levels had dropped and the reservoir had started to dry up. Why?

Trulliç easily navigated the branching stream that fed the water table. No other source pulled at the water, not that he could find. The reservoir was just old and tired. Not enough spring rains had fallen to refill it, not just for this past year but for several seasons. No new streams had formed to fill it.

Disappointment washed over Trulliç. He nearly gave up at that point. He couldn't cause the rains to fall, to bring water where there wasn't any. However, he didn't want to disappoint the village. Particularly not after he'd made such a blunder the night before.

He caused his awareness to flow back to where he'd started, just under the well. Instead of following the obvious path, he pushed deeper into the earth. Maybe under the original reservoir would be a secondary source, another spring.

Riyune leaned against Trulliç's leg, up where his body still stood.

Was Riyune following along? How did the dog do that?

It took Trulliç a moment to figure out what the dog had seen.

There. Not directly under the well, but to the south. A large untapped reservoir. And it was already part of the village. He wouldn't be taking another man's water.

It didn't take much power to push aside the strong boulders and hard-packed clay, then to cause the body of water to flow his direction.

Trulliç heard the water bubbling in the well even as he drew his awareness back into his body.

"There's water again!" Brugal proudly announced.

The people gave a ragged cheer. Trulliç wondered why it wavered so. Was it because they were afraid of him?

He peered at the gathered crowd curiously. They didn't seem afraid of him. Rather, they seemed shocked. Had they not believed that he could do such a thing?

But they knew him. He was the desert magician. They were his people.

A young woman broke free of the crowd and came forward. She wore a clean but faded tunic of dull blue over a full black skirt, her *chafiyek* the only piece of clothing somewhat new and a pretty green. She had the long hair of a married woman, braided over her shoulder, with an infant tied to her back.

"May I?" she asked, hefting her water jug and pointing with her chin toward the well.

"Please," Trulliç said, stepping to the side.

She lowered the old bucket, splashing it into the water, then drawing it out. She then cupped her hands and offered Trulliç the first drink from the well.

Trulliç wasn't sure why this felt like such an important ritual. But he lowered his head and drank from her palms.

The water was just water. Plain, cool, refreshing. It wasn't like the water from the cavern that had cleared away all his bad dreams, opened up the desert to him.

Still, it made Trulliç laugh delightedly, particularly after the woman then lifted her hands and drank as well.

The woman blushed and bowed her head. "Thank you, Trulliç," she said softly. "We needed the water."

Trulliç turned back to the well. He rebuilt the bricks, hardened the stone trellis. The well would stand for a long time, now.

"Are there other wells that need repair?" Trulliç called out.

"Gökel's sure doesn't," a man said. The people around him laughed rudely.

Trulliç nodded. Gökel had probably only kept his own well in good repair. "I'll visit them all," Trulliç promised.

That brought a stronger cheer.

Trulliç looked over at Brugal, who shrugged. "We'll do that next," he said.

A parade formed, in front and behind them, as they made their way from one well to the next. Not all the wells needed more water or better access to the reservoirs beneath them. They did all need some repairs that Trulliç gladly did, strengthening walls and bricks, trellis and buckets.

No one offered him water again. It made him strangely sad that no one else claimed such familiarity with him and instead held him at arm's distance.

That was all right. The people here would get to know him. They would grow more comfortable with him and would come to understand that he wasn't always to be feared.

<hr>

As the afternoon drew long shadows from the buildings, Trulliç led Brugal and the villagers who still followed them to the edge of Ishmirli where the foothills faced the desert to the east. Trulliç breathed in the open air, the scents of the sand, his chest loosening for the first time in a day.

"Stay here," Trulliç told Brugal as he walked a few steps away, drawing closer to the desert. He turned to face the villagers.

Then he unstrapped the glass horseshoe that he wore tied to his belt.

He realized that he didn't need to tie it to himself anymore. The glass horseshoe was part of him, now. It would follow after him, bobbing along in the air like a small dog if he ever dropped it.

It was good to know that he couldn't lose it out here in the desert. It was too important, too much a part of him, though it still had very little magic in itself.

He held up the horseshoe, drawing everyone's attention to it. "Mothers use horseshoes to draw out their babes," he said loudly, aware of the legend he built. "My mother had planned on me to stay in the north, where my father was from. She bought a horseshoe made of tin from one of the local mines."

The people stirred, their feet shuffling, almost as one. Even in the dimming light they knew what he carried wasn't tin.

"The blood hound who attended her transformed the horseshoe from tin to glass," Trulliç said.

The crowd gasped quietly.

"Let me share my gift with you, now," Trulliç said. While the water and the wells had been good, important, the people needed to have his token as well. Just as the people in Yerkoyliç's city had emblems of flowers, birds, and bees, his people needed to understand glass.

Trulliç turned his back on the villagers and raised both of his hand over his head. The horseshoe tugged at his finger. He released it, allowing it to float above his head.

Great sheets of sand built in front of Trulliç, wave upon wave of them. He blasted them with heat and magic, forcing them to collapse down on themselves, forming hundreds of glass balls. Ones that fit in his palm and clear with just a single ribbon of gold or green. Solid black marbles not much bigger than the tip of his pinky. Large balls bigger than his head and striped in different colors.

The balls bobbed in the air, then started to disperse. Most flew toward the villagers. Trulliç heard people laugh with delight as they snagged their own glass ball from the air.

Some of the balls burrowed under the sand. Trulliç understood that they would stand guard on the borders of Qaenev, challenge those who would challenge him.

The rest flew past the villagers in attendance. Trulliç knew they'd find their way into the homes of the people of Ishmirli who weren't attending him.

Everyone would have glass in their homes. Not just the balls, but lamps and windows as well. Trulliç would make sure of it.

He felt the villagers more solidly, as if they'd suddenly become part of the land. His heart swelled with joy as they cheered.

He was truly the desert magician, now.

It didn't surprise Trulliç that the woman who'd offered him water from the first well appeared outside the tavern the next morning before the sun rose. She had the infant tied to her front now, along with two young boys in tow, maybe five and eight years of age.

They all had packs tied to their backs, *chafiyeks* around their necks. The littlest one also carried a stout walking stick.

"I am Seydat. We are going to Hayalevi," she announced.

Trulliç nodded, still not completely surprised. He considered the young woman in front of him. She'd not lived an easy life. Her hands showed strength and wear. She wore the same clothes from the day before, a plain blue tunic over a full black skirt. Clean but faded and patched, hand-me-downs from someone.

A warm spot grabbed Trulliç's attention. There, between her breasts, hung a teardrop shaped piece of glass. She'd strung it on a piece of leather. Though he couldn't see it, he still knew that it matched his own horseshoe, clear glass with gold and green stripes running through it.

Curious, he looked more carefully at the children. Tucked into their packs were small glass balls. Only the infant didn't carry his sign. Trulliç felt no connection to the baby, either. Was the boy too young? Or was it something else?

Seydat appeared to be waiting for Trulliç to say something. Finally, he nodded. "I would be honored to have you," he said seriously. "Though there isn't much there, yet," he warned.

That made Seydat smile. "Yet," she told him. "But there will be."

Trulliç wasn't sure what made her so certain. He was willing to believe her, however.

"Ah, just you?" Trulliç asked, unsure how to delicately inquire about her lack of husband.

"Just us," Seydat said, raising her chin defiantly.

Obviously not a story he was going to get anytime soon.

"That's good!" he said enthusiastically. "I can—"

Another pair of villagers walked up and stood next to Seydat. They were older people, stubborn and strong. "We would go to Hayalevi as well," they announced.

"All right," Trulliç said, surprised. He'd felt no strong connection to this older couple, though they both carried his emblem. They hadn't walked with him the day before, though he wasn't certain how he knew that.

Throughout the morning, more people arrived at the tavern, until Trulliç had a group of eighteen adults, seven teenagers, and five children, all ready to go with him. Some had come with goats, chickens, and sheep.

Trulliç honestly wasn't sure how he was going to feed all these people. How would they occupy themselves? His city wasn't ready yet!

He wasn't about to turn anyone back, though he warned them all about how the city was still in the process of coming alive.

Close to noon, Trulliç felt as though all those who had planned to come had already shown up. Anyone else would have to make their own way to Hayalevi.

Trulliç marched back to the foothills with the group strung out behind him. More villagers had joined them, though they weren't planning on making the entire trip.

Would this sort of parade happen everywhere he went?

Hopefully, over the years people would get more used to seeing him and would treat him with less formality.

Trulliç gathered the group of people who would accompany him into a tight pack, standing closely together.

"Ready?" Trulliç asked them solemnly.

They nodded as one.

Trulliç reached for the thread of connection he felt with every person and wrapped them all tightly around his hand. He picked up the animals, too, collecting them together.

Then he called up a great cloud of sand, sliding it under their feet.

As one, they all took off, gliding toward their new home. Trulliç felt his heart might burst with joy. He had his people! Or at least a few, at any rate.

It didn't matter that most of them were poor or didn't have families.

More would come.

T rulliç settled everyone on the main floor of his tower while he went out to build the rest of his city. The travelers were all glassy-eyed. He wasn't sure why. They seemed shocked to be there. Or maybe it was because his city only contained the single tower, along with the fountain and the altar.

Trulliç strode from his tower, determined. Then he faltered and stopped. Looked around the great flat plane.

What should he build first? He saw what his city would eventually become. But what buildings should he start with? Who should he build for first?

He wanted to build something for Seydat and her children. He couldn't see what, though. What she would want. She should be first. But he couldn't imagine what she wanted.

He turned back toward the tower, only to find Seydat walking toward him. She didn't roll her eyes at him, though that was the feeling he got from her. She'd been the first to recover from their journey, instructing her children to get more water for everyone from the black stone fountain just outside the tower.

"What do you want for a house?" Trulliç asked.

Now Seydat did roll her eyes at him. "You must build the temples first," she instructed Trulliç. "And the fountains and the wells. Then let the other structures come."

Why did she insist on that? Trulliç wasn't sure. However, he did know that his tower hadn't been complete until he'd built the temple to Serrat/Serril.

Grateful for the instruction, Trulliç started raising temples.

He couldn't place the gods too close together—they'd be jealous of one another. He also couldn't make one temple better than the others. As he envisioned the buildings, he realized that all of them needed to be humble places. Intimate. The temples he built were merely altars for the most part. The people closest to them would maintain them. Not priests.

Eventually priests would come. And he'd have to build them houses and their own altars as well.

Trulliç walked toward where he envisioned the market square, wanting to start there. He wanted his people to be prosperous. So he first built the temple to Innis, the god of fertility, in the south western corner of the square. He carved a great spear over the doorway so Innis's followers would know him. Dark stones made up the temple walls, a dark and sober place, fit for a dark and somber god.

Trulliç set up the temple to Enkat on the opposite corner of the market. She was much loved of storytellers and scholars, as well as farmers and shepherds, as her dance brought much needed rain. Trulliç carved her altar out of the far wall of her temple, while he left the middle of the room open, the ground covered with fine, fresh sand, so dancers and performers could perform as well as worship there.

The temple to Xannil was farther away, on the eastern edge of Hayalevi. It took Trulliç a moment to realize that he'd placed it exactly where the sun would touch the great plain first most days during the summer. The sun god's temple was another dark place as he was a jealous god, hiding away Enkat his wife so the rains didn't come. Trulliç built a small alley with open lean-tos next to the temple, where fortune tellers and dream readers would come to ply their trade.

Barzhat got her temple in the north of the city. The goddess of death's altar had a light, airy feeling to it as Trulliç punched holes through the roof, opening it to the sky. It, too, had a fine sand floor for people to dance on, practicing the steps they'd give for the goddess one day.

Onnet's temple drew Trulliç to the west. He meant to make it like all the others, but the stone walls formed in the shape of a horseshoe and he chose not to fight them. He made cozy seats for crones to sit and rest their bones, as well as places where young, pregnant women could come and gossip. It was one of the few buildings he added colors to, green and orange stones lining the edges of the main doorway.

When Trulliç finished, he felt the pattern of the altars around him. They weren't balanced. The temples to the east and west held those edges of the city. The market square held down the southwest corner. His tower and Serrat/Serril's temple sat directly in the center of Hayalevi.

But he needed one more sacred place. To the east and north, to balance the marketplace temples.

Trulliç let his feet guide him, wandering across the river, past his towers, and east. A small building pushed at him. Smaller than the temple to Serrat/Serril, than all the other temples. About the size of the altar Trulliç had visited first as part of his manhood journey so many years before.

Riyune suddenly appeared at his side. The dog pushed up against his leg so Trulliç could see better.

A small, dark spot appeared on the sand in front of Trulliç. He felt the stones under the ground, calling to him. They wanted to be freed.

Trulliç raised his glass horseshoe and tugged at the rocks he felt there. With a sigh of relief, the stones pushed out of the cold ground, forming together, basking in the sunlight.

Trulliç knew that no matter the time of day or how hot it got, the air inside the littlest temple would always feel cool. The rocks themselves remained rough, as if scalloped by the wind and nothing else.

The temple bore no mark. No symbol to tell people who they worshipped there.

There wasn't even an altar inside, just a void where an altar had once stood.

Trulliç turned his back on the temple to Forit after he raised it, refusing to walk into it.

However, he knew that even though he'd never visited the place, that wouldn't matter. The temple, and the missing altar, would always haunt his dreams.

<hr>

The rest of the houses came easily after that: squat one-story rambling buildings for the older people, ones with more stories for the younger people. Trulliç built a shared compound for the goats, the sheep keeping to themselves. Yards with stone fences for the chickens. The huts all had glass windows. Trulliç found the shapes inside of himself, square and solid, the walls mostly red and golden. Rooms divided onto other rooms, giving people more space, more privacy.

He also discovered that trees came with the buildings, tall date trees and palms, fig trees and cottonwood. He didn't know that they lived under the earth with the stones, but they shot up as he constructed the buildings and boulevards. *Meslit* thorns came, too, along with bushes and flowers. Even tough grasses sprang up near the waterways and at the base of the fountains.

Fields would come soon. They'd never bear that much, but there would be enough grain to feed the few who lived in Hayalevi now.

Trade routes needed to be established, and soon.

After he'd settled everyone, he came back to his tower to find Seydat and her children waiting for him. She'd prepared tea for him, brewed exactly how he liked it, sweet and strong.

"Thank you," Trulliç said, accepting a cup gratefully. "I need to build you a home," he said seriously after he'd allowed the tea to clear his throat and refresh him.

Seydat smiled at him and shook her head. "You need someone to keep you organized," she said seriously. "To greet your guests, settle them into the city when you're away on business."

Trulliç blinked, surprised. "I do?" he asked. He had never thought he'd need an assistant. Though that was what he'd been to Atça in many ways.

But Gaadiwala had been a tiny village, maybe one hundred families.

Hayalevi would grow to many times that size, given time.

"I don't know how to pay you," Trulliç said seriously, giving voice to his greatest fear. "I can raise houses, build fountains for the oasis water, even grow some desert plants. But I cannot create coins out of the air."

Seydat nodded. "You can give me a place to live, a purpose for my life. An education for my children so that they can have a better existence. Coin will come as the people do, paying you for your glass and goods."

"All right," Trulliç said slowly. He hadn't expected anyone to pay him for creating glass goods. He paused, then added, "You will have to see to your own food. I...I'm not going to be hungry. Often." He gulped, then finally admitted, "Ever."

Seydat seemed surprised at that. "You don't need to eat?" she asked, incredulous.

"I don't think so," Trulliç told her. "I'm never hungry." He had had a few bites to eat while at Brugar's tavern, out of courtesy, but for the most part all he'd had was tea.

"Then it won't matter that we don't have much coin presently," Seydat told him firmly. "Now, you need to build me a small room, off the side of this tower."

Trulliç made to push himself to standing, then he shook his head and settled back down.

"No," he said, surprised at himself. Most of Seydat's ideas had been correct. He was more than willing to admit that. "You need a separate place. A place of honor."

She shook her head but he held up his hand to stop her before she spoke. "You are a single woman with three children. You need a space for your family that is your own. Apart from your position." He didn't add that she also needed to be away from him. As much as he loved having other people around, he still needed the ability to be alone.

Seydat tilted her head to the side and looked at Trulliç with disbelief. "You are naïve," she said softly. "My association with you is my status."

"For now," Trulliç said. "But you will have your own place among my people."

Seydat shook her head but only said, "We'll see."

When Trulliç finished building Seydat's house—a large building with two floors, directly next to his tower—he insisted that she and her children go and stay there while he rested.

Trulliç wasn't tired. The sun and the sand continued to energize him. He just needed some quiet. He walked all the way to the top of his tower and looked proudly over Hayalevi. True, there weren't many buildings there. But he'd add more as more people came.

The sun hung low in the western sky, the coolness of the evening already creeping in. Trulliç breathed in the night, trying to calm his rising anger. The rage had slowly haunted him all day, growing greater as he'd created his town.

Why hadn't Atça done more for the people in Gaadiwala? Was he actually that weak of a magician? Yerkoyliç had held all of Çandekili in his palm. He hadn't built all of the buildings there—the town had existed before he'd been born—but he'd strengthened them. Made them taller and richer.

Yerkoyliç had still made Çandekili a place to be proud of. And it had died with him. Trulliç knew that the stones he raised would stay standing even after his death.

What was wrong with Atça? Was he really that miserly with his power?

And why hadn't Atça told Trulliç that he was the desert magician? Why had Atça lied to him all those years?

Trulliç had never dreamed of the desert as a young boy, though magicians always dreamt of their true homes. Why had Trulliç never seen this place?

Had Atça put *agafi* in Trulliç's water?

Trulliç remembered first walking the desert when he'd been twelve. The water skins had been filled with water from Atça's sweet well.

He remembered how the cavern that had found him had insisted that he dump those skins out, fill them with pure water instead.

Had the skins been full of *agafi*? Was that why Trulliç had gone wandering that first time across the sands? Had almost died?

The rage built like a summer storm, quick and overwhelming.

Trulliç cast himself from the top of his tower out onto the sands, heading directly north. He became a howling wind, swirling up and up, taller even than his tower. Dust, heat, and small rocks flew like arrows from his path. Lightning crackled around him. The smell of death flowed with him.

Why? *Why?* WHY?

Trulliç howled and cried as he raced across the desert. The heat of the sun couldn't compare to the white hot fury of his rage.

He'd been lied to. Tricked. Fooled. His entire life.

Atça still lied about him, Trulliç felt certain.

Hell, Atça had hired Nadeem to *kill* Trulliç.

Enough.

Trulliç didn't have to suffer Atça any longer.

He would go and confront his former mentor.

Now.

INTERLUDE

TRULLIÇ BLEW DOWN ATÇA'S DOOR, his desert winds howling, raging around him. He stomped into the front entrance way, sneering at the wood there.

He remembered when he used to think that Atça was the richest person alive.

The hallway, the house, the entire town, seemed so closed in. Trulliç couldn't imagine ever living someplace ever again when he couldn't see the stars.

"Atça!" Trulliç yelled. "Get out here!" The entire house shook with the power of his voice.

Atça walked out of the darkened hallway leading to the rest of his house. He wore his typical black and blue striped tunic, with a shirt so white it looked like bleached bones. His pants were solid black, but he had bare feet instead of house slippers. He stood tall and proud before Trulliç, his dark eyes glaring.

"How dare you enter my house like this!" Atça roared. "You are not the master here."

"You know better than to challenge me," Trulliç warned him.

Atça suddenly looked uncertain.

"I found my home," Trulliç said. "It *is* Qaenev. The entire desert."

Trulliç couldn't help but still feel wonder. The sands. The rocks. The hidden places. The oasis. His new city. All of it.

"I know," Atça said sourly.

"You knew? You knew that my home was the desert? Why? Why didn't you tell me?" Trulliç demanded.

That was the real reason why he'd come to confront his old mentor, his tormentor. To demand answers about how Trulliç had been trained. The lies Atça had maintained.

"It wasn't my place," Atça maintained steadily. "You needed to find out on your own."

"You kept me weak," Trulliç accused Atça. "Tied to your side."

"I kept you alive," Atça told him. "How do you think the emperor would have felt about a magician who claimed the entire desert? He would have had you killed outright when you were a babe."

"You did try to kill me," Trulliç said. He believed Nadeem's oath. That Atça had hired her. Thank all the gods that she'd broken it.

Atça shrugged. "You were no longer useful," he said.

"Malleable," Trulliç countered.

Atça shrugged again.

"I never dreamed of the desert when I was younger," Trulliç said. He remembered the first time he'd walked the desert when he'd been twelve. The vision from the stream, making him pour out what remained of Atça's sweet water, the flagons Atça had filled from his well. "Did you feed me *agafi*? All the while I was younger? So I'd never dream of the desert?"

That was the one question Trulliç dreaded asking.

The one he knew he must. Had his mentor fed Trulliç a potion that would give him dreamless sleep?

Atça pressed his lips together for a moment as if he wouldn't answer. Finally, though, he nodded. "I did."

"Why?" Trulliç asked. He hated how his voice cracked, how he sounded so heartbroken.

Atça had betrayed him. From the very start.

"I knew you were a desert magician. *The* desert magician. If you dreamed too young of the desert, you wouldn't have survived," Atça said. He sounded as though he was trying to be reasonable. "Tell me.

How overwhelmed you might have been if you'd started dreaming of the entire desert when you were seven. Trying to take it all in."

Trulliç paused. Could he have handled it?

"Your mother came to me when you were that age," Atça said. "Told me of your nightmares. You weren't sleeping. I decided to let you live and to merely stop your dreams, so you wouldn't wander into the desert when you were too young and be consumed."

"You should have stopped giving me the *agafi* sooner," Trulliç told him. "Before I walked the desert the first time."

"You were too fanciful. Seeing magic. Living in poetry," Atça sneered. "How could I have known?"

"You poisoned my water the first time I walked the desert," Trulliç said.

Atça shook his head. "No. I merely gave you much more of the *agafi* so you might survive."

Trulliç bit his lips together. Atça told the truth as far as he could tell. His old mentor probably just hadn't realized how the extra *agafi* would affect Trulliç or make him wander the desert in the midday sun.

"Why did you keep me alive?" Trulliç plaintively. It was the one last question he had. Since Atça had seemed to know just how powerful Trulliç would get one day, why hadn't he done his duty to the emperor and killed Trulliç outright when he was just a babe? Defenseless?

Atça gave a barking laugh. "You will go after the desert heart on your own one day," he predicted. "Keep it. Use it." He shook his head. "I had hoped, when you'd been younger, that you might have brought it to your old mentor out of gratitude."

Trulliç blinked, surprised. *That* had been why Atça had kept him alive? So that he might gain the full power of the desert heart and use it himself?

Of course, Atça was that greedy. He always kept all of the power, the wealth of Gaadiwala to himself.

"What is the desert heart? Really?" Trulliç asked. He didn't believe that it was Forit's heart, still intertwined with the darkness from before the creation of the world.

But Atça just laughed again and shook his head. "You'll have to find out for yourself. If you can get it before the emperor kills you."

"How much does the emperor know about me?" Trulliç demanded.

"He knows you're no longer under my control," Atça sneered. "Not since you killed Yerkoyliç. I've informed him of how dangerous you are, how you're no longer loyal."

"But it was *your* idea to kill Yerkoyliç! Your plan!" Trulliç said, his anger building.

He never would have left Gaadiwala if Atça hadn't given him the assignment in the first place.

Atça gave him a wintery smile. "That might be viewed as a mistake," he said haughtily. "Or as an opportunity. No one will ever believe you that it wasn't your idea, that you weren't so desperate to find your own home that you thought you'd try to take Çandekili first." His smile grew colder. "Oh yes. The emperor has heard all about you by now. I've made sure of it."

"It was your last mistake," Trulliç said.

He understood much better now the relationship between a people and their magician. How strong or weak they could become. He had his own city. Not many people, but they were coming.

Gaadiwala would only be slightly worse off without Atça. But in many ways, they'd be stronger as well without this greedy monster constantly bleeding them dry. He'd be happy to make his case in front of any judge, or pay any fine.

From his side, Trulliç drew a handful of sand out from a small bag and cast it at Atça.

He'd also learned a lot from the land box. Like how to carry enough desert with him when he left.

The sand flew directly into Atça's face before he could defend himself. He choked on it, falling back into the darkened hallway. Hacking and dying loudly.

Trulliç left before the house collapsed around him.

He would spend a short time here, and talk to the people of Gaadiwala, tell them what had happened, what was to come.

Then he had to get back to the desert.

To be ready to greet the emperor's soldiers when they arrived.

CHAPTER SIX

NADEEM

NADEEM GLIDED ACROSS THE SAND on her new-found power, like a stone skipping across the water. She could maintain her speed only for a short while, then she would land and walk for a while.

She knew this was how Trulliç traveled, only he never had to stop. It filled her with both joy and dread. She loved the freedom of how she moved but feared what it meant that she was becoming.

As Nadeem slowed, she felt her pack pushing at her, tugging her back toward earth.

The only thing in her pack that felt heavy when she ran was the snake-headed stick she carried. The pull of it was what slowed her down. Its shadow needed to touch the ground.

Nadeem stopped and looked around. The main body of the desert lay to her right. She still skirted the edges, following an old oasis trail. Summer had already come to the desert, the short spring exhausted. Small thorns and bushes lined the path she followed. She would have to get out of the sun soon before it reached its zenith. The air carried just a hint of water, but mostly just iron-touched baked rocks.

After taking a surprisingly sweet mouthful of water from one of the skins she carried with her, Nadeem took off again. She resented every time she had to stop, however, she couldn't leave the stick behind. Not like she'd left her sweet camel Banut, giving her to Aunt Parayat to sell in exchange for the goods she carried.

The next oasis was just ahead. Nadeem would push herself to reach there before full day. Then rest until evening and travel some more.

It wouldn't take her long to reach Trulliç's city—Hayalevi. If she could somehow sell how she traveled, she knew merchants such as Levent would buy her services in a heartbeat. Being able to cross the desert quickly would put him at a great advantage.

Then again, Levant might choose to travel slowly, to give fate the chance to offer him treats. If he moved too fast, he might miss something, something important.

Nadeem didn't think she'd miss anything. Except possibly Trulliç if she didn't keep hurrying along.

She had to get to him before the emperor or his guards did.

Though she didn't know how she knew, she still felt it in her bones.

The emperor was on his way.

Nadeem paused on the slight slope that lay just to the west of Hayalevi. She whistled quietly to herself.

It had been a little more than a month since Nadeem had last seen Trulliç.

He'd been *busy*.

Neighborhoods took up every corner of the town. Empty spaces still lay between them. In her mind's eye, Nadeem could already see the buildings crowding out the open areas.

A tower stood in the center of the city. Nadeem knew that would be Trulliç's tower. It was the highest building in the city. Nadeem suspected it always would be. Even the guard towers that Trulliç would eventually build wouldn't be as tall.

The water course she followed ran deep and smooth, the water like black glass. She figured she'd imagined that there was actually glass at the bottom of the river, though now, seeing the city and all the glass windows, maybe she had actually sensed it.

Dawn was just approaching, long fingers of light stretching their way from the hills to the city below. People already stirred, and the smell of fresh flatbread wafted toward her. To the south of the city lay fields of grain, small but fruitful. Closer in stood an orchard.

None of this had been here before Trulliç, Nadeem was certain.

But then, he hadn't known he was a desert magician.

She could only shake her head as she made her way down the hill.

The door to Trulliç's tower stood open. However, a large black rock stood just inside the opening, a guard stone. Nadeem recognized it as similar to the one that had blocked the opening to the cavern that had found her, protected and healed her.

The stone felt cool and smooth to her fingertips, like black glass, though she could see the pits in the rock.

"Hello?" Nadeem called as she stuck her head around the corner.

A young woman sat nursing an infant in the corner. An older woman sat beside her, spinning idly on a drop spindle. They both wore tunics that were a surprising gray color, like soft clouds, though the young woman had green and gold ribbons tied into her long braid, and the older woman wore a *chafiyek* made out of the same colors.

The room itself was plain and bigger than Nadeem expected, easily able to hold two dozen people. The glass windows had been tinted with blue to keep the bright sunlight out. A pile of pillows lay stacked in the corners, along with some rolled up rugs, ready to be pulled out when guests arrived. Glass lamps hung from the ceiling, making the room quite bright.

Tall, evenly spaced stones made up the walls, like bricks made by giants, each about the height of Nadeem and three times as wide as she was tall. They were the same red-gold as most of the city, as if baked out of burnt sand.

"Hello, traveler," the young woman said, nodding her welcome. "Please, come sit with us. Rest after your long journey." She indicated the spare guest rug sitting beside her.

The older woman stared at Nadeem. "I know you," she said quietly.

Nadeem blinked, startled. "Do you?" she asked, challenging, as she stepped further into the room.

The older woman gasped quietly when she saw Nadeem's mangled cheek. "I do. I served you tea in Gaadiwala, at the Horseshoe Tavern. You and your two…sisters."

Nadeem held herself still. This woman *did* look familiar. Nadeem remembered her now. Her face appeared slightly less bitter than it had, her look a touch more friendly.

And she still shared the same bones as Trulliç. A relative, probably his mother.

"I am merely a traveler," Nadeem told them clearly. She was no longer a star sister.

"You are still welcome," the older woman told her. She even gave Nadeem a small smile, though it looked as though the action was unfamiliar to her. "Come. Sit. Rest. Would you like water? Tea? Food?"

Nadeem knelt on the blue-and-black braided rug beside the women. It was awkward, but she didn't want to remove her pack. Not yet.

"Water, tea, would be welcome," she said. "And possibly some flatbread. Nothing fancy."

The young woman finished suckling her babe and pulled him with a sleepy protest from her breast. "Not fancy is what we do here," she said with a smile as she tied the infant to her chest. "I'll let you two catch up," she added with a wink as she briskly walked from the room.

The older woman tilted her head to one side to study Nadeem. "How did you find Hayalevi?"

"It was in my dreams," Nadeem told her truthfully. "But I also need to see Trulliç. I bring grave news."

The woman nodded. "He will return before the end of the day. He strengthens the borders of the desert against the coming of the emperor's guards," she said frankly. "I am Myrizhah," she added.

"Nadeem," she said. "Thank you for your hospitality," she added.

Myrizhah gave her a soft laugh. "It isn't much. We're still fighting to make ends meet, to have enough bread and food for everyone. Water is plentiful. And glass. Not much else."

Nadeem nodded. "I saw the buildings as I came through the town, from the west. Did Trulliç make all the glass?"

"He did," Myrizhah said proudly. "As well as raised all the buildings, the roads, the trees and the fields."

"Trulliç has finally come into his own, then," Nadeem said.

Myrizhah laughed softly and shook her head. "No. He is still young. Still learning. If he can survive the next few years, then maybe…" Her voice faded and she looked into the distance.

Nadeem looked puzzled at Myrizhah. "Maybe?" she asked softly.

"Don't pay attention to an old woman's ramblings," Myrizhah said. "Did you meet my son when you were in Gaadiwala?"

"Yes," Nadeem said.

The other woman came back with a tea service unlike any Nadeem had seen before. The cups were polished glass, clear with gold rims and green bottoms. Stray traces of color ran through them. The teapot, as well, had been made from glass.

When the younger woman set the tray down, Nadeem realized everything was made of glass: the tray, the plates, the holders for the salt and lard, the small bowl with picked onions, even the knife.

"Fine work," Nadeem said as she picked up the knife. Though the glass pieces would be difficult to transport, they would bring a hefty price at any of the markets.

"It comes from Trulliç's heart," Myrizhah said. "But it's cold."

The women exchanged a look. They both worried about him.

Could the younger woman be Trulliç's wife? No, she probably was married to someone else, probably a relative. Trulliç could create a town but not a babe in merely a month's time.

She felt uncomfortable at the touch of relief that came over her when she realized Trulliç was still unattached.

All the women ate a bit, drinking a fine citrus tea and chatting about the rains that they needed, the way people arrived in the city every day, and Nadeem's journey across the sand.

When Nadeem had eaten her fill, Myrizhah asked, "Do you need a room? Or would you like to set up a tent near the market?"

She clearly intended for Nadeem to be on her way, no matter what news she said she carried.

Nadeem thought for a moment. "I need to see Trulliç," she said softly.

Myrizhah shook her head. "I'll tell him the moment he arrives—"

Nadeem took her pack from her back. She pulled out the emperor's snake-headed stick, then walked with it to the edge of the door.

It tugged at her. It didn't like Trulliç's tower. It wanted out.

Too bad.

The guard stone stood just inside the entrance to the tower. Nadeem placed the stick on the far side of the stone, then walked back into the room.

A whirlwind sprang up in front of the guard stone. The sand on the floor circled up in small sandstorms. The smell of baked rocks and harsh storm winds flowed into the room.

When everything died down, Trulliç stood there. Riyune stood beside him.

"Nadeem!" Trulliç said excitedly, taking two steps toward her.

Then he stopped. Frowned.

Turned back toward the door and stuck his head around the guard stone, staring at the stick waiting ominously for him.

"What is that evil thing?" he asked, his tone grown as cold as a winter storm.

"A present from the emperor," Nadeem told him. "Gifted to the man I was assigned to kill."

Without warning, Nadeem found herself carried to the top of the tower. She knew steps flowed beneath her feet. She couldn't have stopped, though. Nothing in her training left her prepared for this type of magic.

At the clear opening on the top of the tower, Nadeem caught her breath and surged to her feet. She planted herself firmly in the bright sunlight. If she could have, she would have pushed roots down into the earth so that Trulliç could *never* do that to her again.

Trulliç stood beside her, glowering. The stick floated in midair, off the edge of the tower. Riyune had evidently wisely stayed below.

"Don't," Nadeem told Trulliç. He obviously intended to blow it into a million pieces.

"Why not?" he asked, frost coating his tone.

Nadeem nodded. She'd hoped that by finding, and founding, his city, that Trulliç would have spent his rage.

She'd been wrong. He'd grown much, much more angry.

Maybe she should have killed him when she'd had the chance.

"Did you know I was coming?" Nadeem challenged him. "Did you feel my footprints across the desert?"

Trulliç slowly shook his head.

Nadeem marched over to where the stick still hovered, poised for its destruction. She boldly reached out and grasped it, ignoring how slippery the wood still felt, how she was no longer on stable ground but reaching far over the edge of the tower. She still gripped it, determined, off balance, her own anger building.

No matter how well trained she was, Trulliç could still send her tumbling to her death in an instant. And the idiot just might do it.

"And now can you find me? With senses other than your eyes?" she asked. She tugged on the stick, trying to bring it closer. To get a better stance.

It stubbornly stayed floating in the air exactly where Trulliç had placed it.

Trulliç narrowed his eyes at her. He blasted sand at her, but it slid around her, the edges of the storm caressing her.

Nadeem held on.

"But how?" Trulliç finally asked her, his anger fading. "Why does that hide you? Why can't I reach you when you're touching it?"

Nadeem shrugged. "I don't know. But do you think you could let go of your anger long enough to help me figure this out?"

Trulliç blushed, his tanned skin growing much darker. "I can," he said softly. He drew the stick back across the edge of the tower, letting go of it so that Nadeem could take its weight again. "I'm sorry," he said.

Nadeem nodded. That would have to do for now.

He'd never survive the upcoming battles if he lost himself in rage, however.

And Nadeem wasn't sure that she had the time to teach him.

***

The young woman appeared at the top of the stairs after a few moments. "Tea?" she asked Trulliç.

"Please, Seydat," he said, still staring hard at the stick Nadeem held.

"Is that your wife?" Nadeem asked after the woman ducked back into the tower. Nadeem knew she was flouting custom by asking so directly.

She also figured Trulliç wouldn't mind.

"No," Trulliç said, still distracted. "She's my assistant. And you met my mother, too. Myrizhah?"

"Ah," Nadeem said. The other woman downstairs. That explained much. Both the woman's previous bitterness and her current worry.

Trulliç reached one hand out to touch the walking stick, then hesitated. "May I?" he asked, finally looking up at her. Then he blinked.

"What happened to your face?" he asked. His own mien instantly grew dark and stormy.

"I am no longer a star sister," Nadeem said, raising her chin defiantly. "I am merely a traveler now."

"Who did that to you?" Trulliç said, the storm approaching again all too quickly.

"I did." Nadeem subtly widened her stance in case Trulliç decided to blast her.

"You did that to yourself? Why?" Trulliç asked. He seemed truly confused.

Nadeem wasn't sure how to answer him. He was at the heart of her failure. "I can't live by their oaths anymore," was all she replied.

"Are you here to kill me?" he asked, tilting his head to one side.

Nadeem gave a bitter laugh. "As if I could." Though Nadeem had never met another land magician, she knew Trulliç was the strongest of them all.

"Atça is dead," Trulliç told her. "I killed him."

Then why are you still so angry? Nadeem didn't ask that. She suspected Trulliç didn't know.

"So you have no oath to fulfill, not in regards to me," he boasted.

"That isn't how it works," Nadeem said. "Killing the oath maker doesn't erase the oath."

"Not even if both parties are dead?" Trulliç asked softly.

Nadeem couldn't help but wince. Technically, he was right. She was dead, at least as far as the star sisters were concerned. So was Atça. If he'd never asked another star sister to fulfill the oath…

Still, Nadeem shrugged. "We'll see," she said. No matter what the *kabil* of star sisters might eventually decide, Nadeem still knew what she had done, as well as what she had chosen not to do. Only Barzhat could judge the weight of her deeds.

Trulliç continued to stare at Nadeem's mangled cheek. "You used to have a different aura," he said eventually. "Light blue and pink. Pearlescent. It's changed. There are more colors in it now. More gold and green."

"I am a desert creature," Nadeem told him. "Like you."

Trulliç finally gave her a true smile. "Really?"

Seydat poked her head above the staircase again. "You should come inside, Trulliç," she said. "Make your guest more comfortable," she added sternly.

"Oh. Oh! Sorry," Trulliç said. He seemed chastened. "I am most comfortable outside, in the bright sunlight," he explained. "I do know though, that other people aren't. Please, come with me inside, into the shade, where it's cooler."

Seydat gave him a nod of approval.

Nadeem couldn't help but smile to herself as he escorted her down the stairs.

Trulliç was trying to do the right thing. And it appeared he had some good help.

But there was still so much for him to learn. For him to figure out.

And there wasn't much time.

Nadeem and Trulliç circled each other warily.

They had walked out of the city, past the flat plain and the gravel, onto the sand itself. Night stretched from the east, though the sky in the west still burned orange and red. Stars floated above them. The desert hawks had finished their hunting, their cries fading. Cool breezes floated around them, carrying the sweet smell of dates.

After they'd spent time talking in Trulliç's study, they'd come out here. Trulliç had left the stick in his mother's care, though she'd complained about how slippery the wood felt when she'd touched it. They'd left Riyune behind to guard the stick as well, though the dog had seemed indifferent to the stick.

Nadeem had insisted that they leave the city, though, so she could start training Trulliç how to fight.

Her real intent was to make him learn how to battle without losing his temper.

Generally the first lessons were all about falling. A girl had to learn how to fall without hurting herself.

However, Trulliç didn't have the patience for that. So they'd started immediately with wrestling.

Trulliç's green-and-gold striped tunic already showed his first falls. Though he had a longer reach, he didn't have her training.

Or her speed.

He should have been faster than her out there on the sand. Was he holding himself back? Or did he not know how to apply it? He could run, yes. Skim over the desert faster than a falling hawk. But he couldn't move his arms or hands as fast.

After Nadeem had knocked him on his ass for a third time, she asked in exasperation, "Didn't you have any brothers and sisters? Cousins you fought with?"

Trulliç shook his head. "Only child. I had cousins, but I didn't spend that much time with them. I had lessons with Atça instead."

Even in the dim light, Nadeem could see his expression grow darker.

That was why Trulliç knew the old poems and could recite them. It had been part of his training.

Of course, Atça hadn't considered training the body to be as important as training the mind.

Nadeem easily blocked his next attempt to grab. "What, are you afraid to hit a girl?" she taunted. She slid out of his hold and twisted around him, tripping him so he stumbled.

"No!" Trulliç said. "I could pick you up and throw you to the very edge of the sands with my magic," he growled.

"But if someone got through your magical defenses, you'd be helpless as an infant," Nadeem sneered. "Hell, even a star sister who hadn't had her initiation could kill you."

Trulliç barred his teeth and rushed at her.

Nadeem sidestepped his awkward attempt and spilled him onto the sands again.

"And they will be coming for you," Nadeem told Trulliç. "Not initiates. But trained stars. Ones fanatically dedicated to the emperor. How will you stop them?"

With a roar, Trulliç tried to grab Nadeem. He missed.

"Or do you only fancy yourself a great warrior?" she asked. "Are you still just a boy?"

Nadeem knew the instant before Trulliç grabbed her with his magic that she'd finally pushed him too far. Or at least far enough that he could accidentally kill her.

She suddenly found herself spinning in a whirlwind, abrasive sand cutting her cheek, the wound there sending spikes of pain. The floor of the desert lay far beneath her feet. Cooler winds caressed her.

The storm died down as quickly as it started, the winds silencing themselves. Nadeem found herself poised like a great eagle, ready to plunge to her death.

She opened her arms and closed her eyes, welcoming Barzhat's embrace.

Trulliç's voice sounded right in front of her face. "Why?" he asked plaintively. "Why are you doing this?"

Nadeem opened her eyes. They both floated high above the desert, at least as high as the top of Trulliç's tower. The sands spread below them like a jeweled carpet below her. She hadn't expected the sand to sparkle in the night. Or was that part of Trulliç's magic? She smelled the water from the oasis trail leading into Hayalevi. Felt the far border of the desert fading into hills to the south. Tasted the cool sweat of her fear.

"You must learn to control yourself," Nadeem told Trulliç. "If I can get you to lose your temper so easily and make mistakes, so will the emperor's guards."

Trulliç sighed. "I'm not sure how," he admitted. "I go racing out across the desert almost every night. A storm of death. Trying to blow it away."

Nadeem nodded. "Does that help?"

"Sometimes," Trulliç replied. "Sometimes not."

That didn't surprise Nadeem. "You must face your anger," she told him, "and defeat it. Or it will destroy you and everything you've built."

"I told you. I already killed Atça," Trulliç said darkly.

"But that didn't help," Nadeem pointed out. "You need to overcome his lies."

"How?" Trulliç asked, sounding much younger than his eighteen years.

Nadeem's own anger surfaced. She had her own failures to face. The lies she'd been told to overcome. "I don't know," she told him coldly. "Just do it. Or we're all lost."

Trulliç nodded sadly. Slowly, they began to float back down to earth. But not straight down. Nadeem felt as though she was a feather floating on a breeze, drifting slowly to the ground. She found her breath catch, and her heart filled with wonder at the gentle journey.

Trulliç landed a few feet away from her, looking back toward the city. "What will happen if I fail?" he asked.

"Your city will be blasted back into the sands. Your people killed. Your name will be used as a curse," Nadeem said. "Or worse. The entire world will fall when the emperor makes his bid to become a god."

The gibbering darkness of her visions unleashed on the world. Those who could stop it becoming corrupted by it instead. All the light and goodness destroyed.

"Why are you here?" Trulliç demanded. "Really? What is your mission from your aunts?"

Nadeem sighed. But it was easier talking to him this way, listening to the quiet of the desert, feeling the peace of the night, rather than talking in earnest to one another.

"Aunt Parayat said I must stop the emperor," Nadeem said.

"Kill him?" Trulliç asked sharply.

"Just stop him," Nadeem said. "I've yet to kill anyone."

Trulliç gave a bitter laugh. "And I've killed three men so far. With more to come, I'm sure."

The quiet came over them again. "We will stop him," he assured her. "One way or another."

Nadeem couldn't help but smile. "Or die trying."

"May your dance for Barzhat be short," Trulliç said, giving her the traditional reply.

"Yours too," Nadeem said. "Should we go back to the city?"

Trulliç nodded. "Sure. I want to—" He paused. Stiffened.

Grew angry again.

"What is it?" Nadeem asked.

Trulliç looked over at her. His eyes burned like hard diamonds. Sand whirled around his feet.

"The emperor's guards. They're here."

CHAPTER SEVEN

TRULLIÇ

DESPITE THE GROWING NIGHT, TRULLIÇ still went immediately to "greet" the emperor's guards.

He knew he wasn't at full strength. Had the guards arrived at the border after sunset in order to take advantage of that? Or was it just a coincidence?

Trulliç didn't believe in that sort of luck. Particularly not where the emperor was concerned.

He brought Nadeem with him, in part because she'd insisted, but also because he hoped she would keep him from doing something stupid.

Like just killing all of the guards offhand. Because he could.

Trulliç wasn't sure why the guards approached the desert from the west. Surely it would have been faster to approach them from the direct north? That was where Atayurtkah lay, the emperor's grand city. When would the emperor send people from the city? It had been a little more than a month since Trulliç had founded his city.

Maybe these guards had been stationed to the north, in Lydea, and had sailed down from there.

Trulliç remembered Yerkoyliç's dismay when the magic in his

town's wall hadn't automatically reacted to Trulliç's presence. At the time, Trulliç had assumed it was because he was such a poor magician.

Now he wondered if his own magical power had been so great it had overwhelmed Yerkoyliç's defenses without Trulliç even realizing it.

However, the emperor's guards had set off the wards that Trulliç had been strengthening all around the border of the desert. As Trulliç and Nadeem neared where the guards stood, Trulliç couldn't help his smug smile.

Two dozen guards stood just past the border of the desert, shuffling their feet uneasily.

In front of them, on the desert side of the border, floated a large array of glass balls. They varied in size from the length of Trulliç's pinky to larger than his head. Colors ranged as well—from midnight black to clear, deep violet to brilliant yellow.

The glass balls all floated about the same height as a man's head. Anytime a guard shifted, the balls did as well, looming and threatening so the guards couldn't cross into the desert.

The balls didn't form an impenetrable barrier. They did act as a warning, telling any visitor that they were about to step into a magical place owned by a powerful magician.

Now that Trulliç was here, he could make the balls explode, and the glass shards would automatically aim for the eyes of the guards, blinding them. One of the bigger balls could kill a man by driving deadly glass spikes into his heart.

The guards all wore similar outfits, the leather of their chest plates dyed red with a great golden emblem in the center of each. It took Trulliç a moment to realize that it was a snake's scale—the symbol of the emperor.

They wore short leather aprons that hung down to their knees. Underneath, depending on the season, they wore either long wool trousers or shorter, lighter weight, cropped cotton pants. Their sandals were solid leather, hearty and well worn.

They all had shields tied to their backs, but they didn't carry the same weapon. Some had bows, others had knives and swords, still others had whips and long pikes with wicked bayonets. They stood as a unit despite their different fighting implements. They'd probably trained together for a long while.

Trulliç touched ground inside the border so the mass of floating glass balls stood between him and the guards. Nadeem stood at his side. Just behind him, Trulliç felt the white streak that was Riyune, racing to meet them.

Riyune would probably be upset that he'd had to get there on his own. But he wasn't about to miss out on all the fun.

Trulliç stepped forward, causing the balls to clear a space for him in the center while forming a more solid line on either side. "I am Trulliç," he announced. "This is my desert."

Nadeem stepped forward as well, standing at his left side, while Riyune appeared at his right. They both bristled at the group, strong and capable.

Trulliç was not alone. It was a novel feeling, one he wasn't used to. It made him feel both proud as well as uncomfortable.

An older guard stepped forward, though keeping to his side of the border. "I am Marius," he said. "I am the head of the local garrison at Erdinet, come to meet the desert magician, at the command of the emperor."

Marius was obviously from the northern kingdom of Lydae. He had a bulbous nose and wore his hair in the longer, northern style. Though it was too dim to see clearly, Trulliç would bet that Marius had light-colored eyes. He stood a head shorter than the guards around him, but he looked solid and well-muscled.

Trulliç paused, considering. Erdinet was a seaport, located on one of the southern most islands of the kingdom of Lydae. Had the soldiers sailed from there? If so, then their approach of the desert from the west would make more sense.

But why had the *Padisha-i-Ghazi* sent *this* group of soldiers? There had to be something special about them, a reason why the emperor would trust them with contacting the new desert magician.

Trulliç peered more closely at the men. They seemed hardened, more weary and bitter than the soldiers he'd seen passing through Gaadiwala. Their weapons were worn, well used.

"Welcome to my desert," Trulliç said belatedly. "I am honored by your presence."

"We have talked with villagers along the oasis trail. More than one has dreamed of your great city, Hayalevi," Marius continued. "We would like to see it, to report to the emperor of the wonderful addition to his empire."

"Ah," Trulliç said. He knew that the emperor's guards would come to investigate his city. But what did they truly expect to find?

"You will be welcome there," Trulliç said. He waved his hand, causing the glass balls to sink directly back under the sand, set to warn of the next travelers.

"Are all to be greeted thusly?" Marius questioned as he and his men stepped across the border.

Trulliç pushed his senses out, focusing on the men's steps, seeking their feet.

The guards didn't have the same feeling as the cane did, that void or darkness.

But there was something…shifty…about them.

There was much more to this group of guards than what met the eye.

Trulliç was going to have to keep a very good watch on them, using all his senses.

"Only large groups will awaken the desert's natural defenses," Nadeem said, stepping forward when Trulliç didn't reply.

"Natural?" Marius asked, his head cocked to one side.

"Do you think that the desert magician isn't natural? That this isn't his true home?" Nadeem challenged.

"No, no. You misunderstand," Marius replied. "It is very obvious that all of this is his home. However, it is still part of the empire. He will need to pay tariffs and taxes, like everyone else."

Marius gave Trulliç a challenging look. Did he expect Trulliç to disagree?

"Of course," Trulliç replied. "I would welcome a visit from the emperor as well."

Trulliç didn't know if the soldiers believed him or not. He wasn't sure it mattered.

The emperor, or at least his representatives, had arrived.

Trulliç had to ensure they were well taken care of.

Or he would be facing the emperor, sooner rather than later.

"Are you ready?" Trulliç asked his new guests. The night was growing longer and he was already tired. Nadeem and Riyune still bolstered him, standing on either side. The guards formed a tight group before him. Quiet filled the desert, only the soft wind speaking.

"For what?" Marius asked.

"To go to Hayalevi," Trulliç said. He would have preferred to leave the guards there and make them walk the entire way to the city on their own. But he knew that would be rude. Seydat, as well as his mother, would yell at him for not treating his guests better.

Nadeem probably would have left them all without food or water, given the angry glares she shot their way. He wasn't sure if it was this group of guards or all of those in the emperor's employ that caused her to react like that.

Riyune, on the other hand, seemed resigned as only a dog could be.

"What do you mean?" Marius asked, confused.

"I will take you to Hayalevi with me," Trulliç told them.

"With magic?" Marius asked.

Trulliç paused. It appeared to be an important question to Marius.

"Yes," Trulliç replied. "Unless you want to walk all the way across the desert on your own?"

The men shifted, uneasy. The soldiers who carried swords put their hands on the hilts, while others gripped their pikes more tightly.

"We would like to see that," Marius said firmly, as if instructing his men.

"You are in for a treat," Nadeem said.

Trulliç glanced at her, curious. She gave him a quick smile. "Though it is unsettling at first," she added.

Trulliç reached out and gently touched all the men in front of him with desert winds. These weren't his people. He couldn't gather them in. Not like Nadeem and Riyune. They weren't desert creatures.

These men were foreigners, carrying foreign weapons. And he still couldn't figure out what made them so shifty, as if they did but didn't stand directly in front of him.

However, none of them had hidden away anything like the emperor's walking stick. Trulliç could ascertain the position of every man, where he stood, what he carried.

It wouldn't be difficult to disarm them. To cause all their weapons to fly away into the heart of the desert, for winds to scour their blades until nothing remained.

That would be rude as well. To remove all the support the guards relied on. What they felt protected them.

Trulliç wondered if they realized that the only thing that protected them once they stepped into his territory was his good will and the rules of hospitality.

With gentle winds, Trulliç lifted the group of guards, buffering them from the abrasive sands. He tried to make the start of their journey as placid as possible, so he didn't frighten the men.

They all wore stoic faces, determined not to show any emotions, though Trulliç smelled their fear, bitter and strong.

Only Marius appeared not to be afraid. He leaned forward, facing the winds. Though he also tried to keep his face grim, he couldn't help the smile that broke out now and again.

Trulliç kept their pace slow and even. They traveled much faster than any man or horse could have, but not as fast as a storm wind.

It would take them the rest of the night to arrive in Hayalevi. They'd arrive just after dawn.

Then there would be more questions. More awkwardness. More fencing with these "guests." What did they really want? And how much would the emperor demand for his tithe? Trulliç wasn't rich, and he was loathe to ask his people for money.

Hopefully Nadeem would help keep Trulliç from blowing the guards to pieces when they angered him, as they were sure to do.

In the meanwhile, he glanced over at her. She had her eyes closed, her arms and her head thrown back, as if she flew across the sky on unseen wings.

Riyune sat as still as a statue. The white of his fur glowed, making him seem ghostly.

Trulliç looked forward and let the happiness in his heart bubble up, filling himself with the sheer pleasure of the cool night and the unique feeling of having friends supporting him, all too aware that there was likely to be little joy in the coming days.

Dawn had touched the great plain by the time Trulliç carried them to the edges of Hayalevi. The day promised brilliant warmth, the sky a searing blue.

Trulliç felt sorry for the guards, watching them wilt as the heat took hold. The sunlight invigorated him. He felt like a plant sometimes, just needing sunlight and water to live. Nadeem, too, looked refreshed, as if she'd just spent the night sleeping on a feather mattress instead of traveling across the desert and back.

Riyune gave him a great dog yawn and shook himself, but didn't leave after they touched down. Was he tired, too? Trulliç thought the dog's steps appeared to be dragging, but he couldn't tell for certain. He wouldn't be surprised, though, if Riyune slept through the heat of the day, as he generally did.

"Welcome to Hayalevi," Trulliç told the guards as they stood and stretched, shaking their heads. "If you'll come with me to my tower, I can give you refreshments and find you a place to rest for the day."

Marius nodded, stepping forward. "That would good," he said bluntly. Then he gave Trulliç a smile. "It was a magnificent flight. Magical. Thank you for that."

"You're welcome," Trulliç said, pleased.

The rest of the soldiers didn't appear to share Marius' wonder or enjoyment. They stamped the ground, obviously happy to be standing solidly on the earth again.

"Follow me," Trulliç said as the men gathered together.

"Did you, ah, raise, all of this?" Marius asked as they drew closer to the first buildings.

"I did," Trulliç affirmed.

He didn't like the greedy look that appeared in the soldier's eyes.

"Raising rocks and stones is easy," Trulliç continued. "But rocks and stones won't feed my people. Crops—trees—those are hard. I can't raise coins out of the ground." He'd learned a lot more about people's greed since he'd had to kill Gökel.

Marius nodded. He looked thoughtful.

Trulliç hoped that would put a dent in the soldier's appetite for taxes, though he doubted it would help much.

Was that why Atça had kept the buildings in Gaadiwala so poor looking? So the town wouldn't be so heavily taxed?

Trulliç didn't think that his former mentor would have considered that aspect of taking care of his people. As for Trulliç, it was too late now. He'd already started building his city. Plus, he wanted Hayalevi to appear as magnificent as it could. He intended to be proud of his city and its people.

"Tell me about raising the city," Marius said.

Trulliç told him about seeking water first, making sure to emphasize that he wasn't stealing water from anyone else. He talked of raising his tower, pointing out the glass that filled every window of every building they passed. Then he repeated Seydat's advice about creating the temples first, how they anchored the city.

"What building did you dedicate to the emperor?" Marius asked.

Trulliç didn't believe the man's innocent tone. "I haven't yet," he confessed, lying. "I was hoping that one of his representatives might help me plan something appropriate."

Marius seemed content with that response. However, he walked directly over to the next building they passed—a small square hut with an enclosed stone wall to keep the chickens in the yard. He peered intently at the base of it.

Trulliç knew who lived there—he knew everyone in his city. This small house belonged to a poorer couple who were childless. They'd had Trulliç create an altar to Innis inside the hut, taking up one entire wall, so they could pray to the god daily.

However, Trulliç didn't believe that Marius wanted an introduction to the people living inside. He dreaded having to ask, but knew that he must. "Is there something wrong?" he inquired when Marius continued to stay where he was and not make an effort to rejoin them.

"Where's the emperor's sign?" Marius asked. He pointed to the golden scale that covered his own red-leather chest plate. "All new structures should bear the sign of the emperor."

"Really?" Trulliç asked, acting surprised. "I didn't know that."

At the hard look Marius shot him, Trulliç merely shrugged. "Gaadiwala was such a small village and had so few new buildings."

Marius grudgingly nodded. "So you might not have known."

Trulliç turned, ready to keep walking, but Marius stayed stubbornly where he was.

"Yes?" Trulliç said. "Is there something else?"

"Can you add the mark now?" Marius asked directly.

Trulliç peered at the soldier. The question struck Trulliç as rude. However, he didn't think he could call the man out about his manners.

In addition, Marius seemed to already know the answer. He knew that Trulliç could shape anything in the buildings of his city.

"I can," Trulliç said. "But not now," he added when Marius appeared to be wanting him to do it immediately. "I've been awake all night and have expended a great deal of magic. I need to recover before I take on such an important task."

Marius pressed his lips together, as if biting back his words. Did he really want to challenge Trulliç on this? How much did the soldier know about magicians? How the land supported them, strengthened them? Marius wasn't magical himself. Trulliç would bet his own mother's life on that.

However, there was still something off about the man. Still something very different than with the other soldiers.

And Trulliç wasn't completely lying. He had expended a great deal of magic that night, flying to the edge of the desert, carrying them all back. Just before dawn he'd been quite tired.

Marius didn't need to know that it wasn't merely the land, but the sun itself, that strengthened Trulliç.

Finally, Marius seemed content to let it go. "Fine," he said as he walked away from the hut, rejoining his men. "But we should see to that first thing, placing the emperor's mark on all the buildings raised in Hayalevi."

Trulliç nodded, swallowing against a dry throat. He didn't want to mar the beautiful stone he'd raised.

He knew, however, that he didn't have a choice. Not if he wanted to maintain some semblance of peace between himself and the emperor.

T rulliç didn't know if he should be amused or horrified by his mother's reaction to the soldiers. She changed her demeanor from gracious desert host to tavern server in the blink of an eye. It wasn't that she treated their guests with disrespect. But her smile lost all its warmth, her tone became crisp and curt, and she held herself in such a way that she discouraged any familiarity.

The soldiers didn't know any better and so treated her with kindness, particularly when Trulliç introduced her as his mother.

The inside of the tower stayed cool even as the temperature outside rose. The men seemed grateful to be inside, out of the direct sun. Nadeem had left them there, claiming exhaustion, gladly taking up Seydat's offer of a place to stay. Riyune came and sat next to Trulliç like a regular dog, lolling on his side, resting his head on his paws and soon snoring.

Seydat and Myrizhah served them all sweet tea, flatbread, onions, and lard.

"Where do you get your salt?" Marius asked Trulliç, lifting the dish with salt and spices that were traditionally sprinkled on top of everything else.

Today Seydat had used a mixture of cumin, mint, and fennel with the salt. It had a sweet aftertaste that Trulliç liked, though as usual, he found himself eating out of habit and politeness, not because he was actually hungry.

Traditionally, salt came from towns along both coasts. However,

Trulliç had no coastline to claim as his own. Mountains and foothills ringed the desert on all sides, not ocean.

"To the south," Trulliç grudgingly admitted. "There's a small salt flat." He'd been astonished to find it. At first he'd thought the sand was just colored white. It wasn't until he'd tasted it that he'd realized it was salt.

"Ah, very good," Marius said. "And the herbs?"

"From the fields just south of the city," Trulliç said.

"But we're in the desert!" Marius exclaimed.

Trulliç shrugged. Though the land to the south was much less arid than the rest of the desert, it was still *his*. "The mountains just beyond the fields provide some coolness. Rain flows over the tops and down the slopes."

"You'll have to take me there," Marius said.

While Marius' men were all too well trained to actually groan at the thought, Trulliç still could tell that they weren't enthusiastic about traveling more that day.

"Later," Marius added.

"Of course," Trulliç told him. "I'd be happy to take either just you, or you and some of your men."

Marius nodded. "What sort of caravans do you get through here?"

Trulliç found the question strange. "The city hasn't existed for much more than a month. We aren't on any regular caravan routes yet."

Marius' gave a look that showed how little he believed that. Maybe it was because the city had so many fine buildings that would have taken men many years to build.

Trulliç continued on. "Plus, it's the end of summer. Not many caravans are traveling this far south. Come spring, I expect to see quite a few." He hoped. He wanted his city to become a vital trading center, though he wasn't sure exactly how to achieve that.

"Maybe," Marius said slowly, his look of disbelief still firmly etched across his face.

Trulliç wondered how Marius was judging Hayalevi and if that just put another black mark against the city.

After the men had finished, Trulliç was the first to stand. "Come, let me make you a shelter where you can spend the rest of the day."

Marius stayed seated. "I think this is a fine place to stay," he drawled. "Don't you agree?" he asked the men.

Several nodded sleepily.

"Really, it wouldn't be a bother to build you all shelters," Trulliç said. He was desperate to get them to leave, to have his tower back to himself again.

"This place is fine," Marius said, his hard eyes belying his seemingly easy posture, how he stayed loose and leaned back.

Trulliç didn't know what to do. On the one hand, he needed to provide for his guests. That was his duty as a host. On the other hand, the guests shouldn't insist on staying in the house of the host if there was another place for them to go, if a suitable other location had been provided for them.

However, Trulliç didn't want to call the soldier out on his manners. Marius had been perfectly polite up until then. Trulliç tamped down on his own ready anger. While he could easily kill Marius and all his men, that wasn't the answer.

At least, not yet.

Myrizhah came into the room. She placed her hands on her hips and scowled at the men. "Shoo! All of you." She glared at Marius. "This is a place of business," she said primly. "All guests are greeted equally. Not made to squeeze in between you group of lollygaggers. Now go. Trulliç will provide you with adequate shelter."

Trulliç bit his lips together to prevent himself from grinning. He'd heard his mother use that exact same tone with patrons of the tavern who'd had too much beer or wine.

"Now, ma'am—" Marius started.

"Did you hear me, young man?" Myrizhah questioned, her voice like a whip.

Marius automatically sat up straighter.

Trulliç would bet that Marius' own mother sounded exactly like that when calling him to task.

"Yes, ma'am. I heard you," Marius said slowly.

"Then you will be on your way," Myrizhah said firmly. "Don't you want to watch the desert magician at his work? Calling forth the great stones from under the earth?"

"We do," Marius said, though he didn't stir. He wasn't beaten, not yet.

However, Myrizhah wasn't finished with him either.

"Then you will get up. Now. And accompany him," Myrizhah told him, her tone brooking no gainsay.

Marius at least was smart enough to know when he was beaten. "Fine, ma'am," he said, slowly rising. "We will leave your place of business."

Myrizhah merely sniffed at him, obviously disapproving of his slow capitulation.

Trulliç suspected that if the soldiers had done something equivalent in the Horseshoe Tavern, his mother would have cut them off, insisted on payment immediately, then kicked them out and not let them return.

The rest of the men complied, their displeasure apparent in every move.

Too bad. Myrizhah was right. This *was* a place of business, and they had no right to occupy it and disrupt what went on there.

"Thank you," Trulliç told his mother as the soldiers started to file out.

She peered at him, still upset, then sighed, her anger melting away. "You have a good heart, son," she said softly. "But I fear it will lead you astray."

Trulliç wasn't sure what she meant by that, but he wasn't about to ask. He'd never been that close to his mother. She'd always seemed so disappointed in him. She did appear to be prouder of him now, though he felt as if he hadn't gained her full approval.

Not yet.

Trulliç trudged out of the tower, following his guests. He knew that whatever building he raised for them would have to marked with the emperor's symbol.

He hated the idea of marring his beautiful stone with the emperor's mark. But he knew of no way around the decree.

Maybe he could talk with Nadeem, to get her to create illusions of the mark on the buildings, spells that would disappear when the soldiers left.

He doubted that would work. Marius, or one of the others, might be able to discern the difference.

Still, he decided to at least ask Nadeem about it.

Before he went ahead and just killed all the soldiers anyway.

***

Trulliç led the guards through the great market square (that was still mostly empty), past the temple to Innis, to an open area of land. To the north of them flowed the oasis trail river. Far to the south stood the fields.

After consulting with Marius, Trulliç built a three-walled structure for the soldiers, kind of like a large lean to, the kind normally built for goats or sheep. However, Marius insisted that was the structure he and his men were used to.

The long side of the building faced south, with a three-foot thick wall to keep out the worst of the sunlight. The east and west walls were also thick and solid, while the northern side was open, allowing in air and whatever breezes might stir. It could easily hold two dozen men.

The roof slanted from the open, high, northern wall down to the shorter, southern one. Marius insisted on plain dirt for the floor. Directly out from the northeast corner of the building, Trulliç raised a small well, using the smooth black stones that melted together like glass. On the opposite corner, he built an outhouse with a single bucket.

A line of long, thin windows ran across the tops of all the walls, just under the eaves. Trulliç covered them with a glass mesh: easily broken, but it would keep birds and bugs out, and allow breezes to come through.

Marius didn't seem impressed with anything that Trulliç did, though his men oohed and ahhed as the stones rose up out of the ground, forming themselves into bricks. Marius did seem to appreciate the well, particularly as it filled with water immediately.

But he looked dissatisfied when Trulliç finished.

Before the soldier could say anything, Trulliç asked, "Should I put the emperor's mark in the center of the roof? There?" He pointed to the open, northern edge. "That way everyone can see it."

Marius nodded slowly. "That would do."

Trulliç called up a piece of light-gray slate, fashioning it into a scale that looked exactly like the one on Marius' chest piece, then attached it to the building.

It looked like a turd on his beautiful work.

Marius appeared to appreciate it, however. "Nice," he said, nodding. Then he looked around. "How about a fence? Or a wall of some sort?"

Trulliç raised a short stone wall surrounding the area, giving the men a larger than normal yard, big enough for a dozen camels. With the wall came fig trees and a small garden of herbs.

It always surprised Trulliç when plants rose up with his stones. As if they, too, had just been sleeping under the ground, waiting for his call. He never felt them with the stones. They always came on their own. Still, he tried to act as if they'd been planned all along.

"Can you raise chickens as well?" Marius asked as he walked over to where the tiny lavender and rosemary bushes that grew beside the stone wall that enclosed the soldiers' building.

"Sorry—you'll have to buy your own," Trulliç said dryly.

Marius grunted as he brushed his fingertips across the tops of the plants. "Can you raise plants anywhere?" he asked. He seemed genuinely curious.

"No," Trulliç said. "There needs to be water. I've brought water to this place. And you're located close enough to the oasis trail for things to grow here. In the center of the dessert, where there's nothing but sand? I couldn't raise anything green or growing."

"But you could direct water there," Marius pointed out.

Trulliç shook his head. "Only if I stole it from someone else. And I would never do that."

Marius merely nodded, obviously thinking.

"I will meet you later this afternoon, then," Trulliç said, stepping back. "You need time to rest. As do I."

He didn't actually feel tired at all. The sunlight invigorated him. But he wasn't about to tell Marius that.

Marius opened his mouth as if to disagree, then thought the better of it. "Fine. This afternoon. Do you have a bell that rings the hours?"

"Not yet," Trulliç said. Bells were rung by the priests of Innis. Local people took care of the temples at this time. Hayalevi hadn't grown big enough to support priests.

"Then I will meet you here at two hand-spans," Marius said, turning and squinting toward the west.

It was the oldest way to tell time—by specifying the number of hands spans from the bottom edge of the sun to the horizon.

"I look forward to it," Trulliç lied as he hurried away.

He didn't know what Marius would insist on Trulliç doing when they met again.

He knew, however, that he wouldn't like it.

CHAPTER EIGHT

NADEEM

Nadeem gratefully took Seydat up on her offer of a quieter place to stay while the soldiers all gathered on the ground floor of Trulliç's tower. Though Trulliç could probably take care of himself if the soldiers offered any threat, Myrizhah would be the one to make sure they kept their manners.

After drinking a little sweet tea and eating some flatbread, Nadeem found herself surprisingly restless. She would have thought she'd be tired. She hadn't slept the previous night. The flight had been like a dream, with the golden, cool desert spread out beneath them and the black sky like an overstuffed quilt above. She'd caught the scent of musty desert mice, tantalizing traces of hidden springs, and the clear smell of dates somewhere in the far distance.

Nadeem found she couldn't sleep now. Not because she was afraid of her dreams, but something still niggled at her, bothered her, about the soldiers.

She sat up on the soft pallet that Seydat had given her, cleverly woven out of reeds from the oasis river, and listened. Seydat and Myrizhah still served the guards in the tower just next door. Seydat's two older children played in the yard behind the house. Chickens roosted there, giving quiet coos of contentment.

The room was very plain, the walls made out of the tall, thick stones that Trulliç built. Nadeem reached out and brushed her fingertips against the rock. It felt cool and dry, like the softest sand. The wound on her cheek gave a warning tingle, then went back to sleep.

Nadeem couldn't see any magic in the walls, though she was certain that a trace still remained. It didn't surprise her—this tower was Trulliç's heart, the epicenter of his power. Would the other buildings in Hayalevi give her the same feeling? Probably.

An open, glass-covered window stood far above the bed, with a matching one on the other side, so breezes might blow through the small room. Glass lamps hung from all four corners. The room was only as long as the bed, and maybe three times as wide, with a pounded dirt floor. A very nice braided rug lay in the center of it, colored brown and green.

Nadeem looked at her own hands and *blurred* the outline of them, making them indistinct. She knew that the eyes of anyone looking directly at her would slide off. Then she made herself darker. Though she didn't feel hollow, that appeared to be the effect. Just an outline of her hands and her arm remained. She looked like a shadow of herself. Against any dark background, she couldn't be seen.

No other star sister had this power, Nadeem was certain. Aunt Parayat hadn't proclaimed her an abomination, however.

Nadeem slipped out of her room, heading directly back to the tower. She arrived just as Marius announced that they would stay right there.

Nadeem had to bite her lips to hold back her giggles when Myrizhah rebuked him. Served him right. Who did he think he was, to disrupt their household that way?

It was obvious, though, that Marius expected for Trulliç and Myrizhah to meekly obey his wishes. She imagined that most of the citizens in the empire did just that.

The soldiers knew better than to try that sort of thing with the star sisters. Or perhaps the emperor had ordered them to pay the star sisters more respect, since some of them did special jobs for him.

Would the emperor send some of the special stars out after the desert heart? If so, how would Nadeem stop them? And then stop the next group the emperor sent? And the next?

The only way she knew to get the emperor to change his mind about acquiring the desert heart would be to destroy it before he could acquire it.

Or to kill the emperor.

But how? Now that the first group was here? How to stop them?

Nadeem had no doubt that Marius's true mission wasn't to see Trulliç but to find the desert heart. Hopefully Trulliç had figured that out as well.

Nadeem flitted from shadow to shadow, following Trulliç and the soldiers through Hayalevi, the market square, and finally, the place where Trulliç started to raise a great building for the soldiers to stay in. No one saw her. No one even looked in her direction, though she passed directly in front of more than one merchant calling out their wares.

She eagerly watched Trulliç start his new building. What a wonder —how the stones flew out of the earth and merged together. They changed color as they melded, the hues darkening into a brownish red. The smell of magic lay thick against the back of her throat, acrid and harsh like *igrat* that hadn't been allowed to age. Her cheek tingled, verging on painful, as magic winds caressed it.

It surprised Nadeem how ugly the mark of the emperor looked that Trulliç put on the building. It seemed completely out of place. Everything else Trulliç had raised or set his hand to had a grace and beauty to it. Why did this scale of the emperor's feel so different?

Nadeem stayed where she was after Trulliç hurried away from the soldiers. He didn't appear to notice her as he passed.

He could find her, she felt certain of that. Her magic didn't hide her from him. Only the emperor's stick had done that.

Instead, she drew closer to the soldiers, intending to spy on them. It was something she'd learned from Aunt Izmet, how important it was to learn about the enemy, study their strengths and weaknesses.

Plus, she was still certain that they were more than they seemed, and that they would immediately start searching for the desert heart.

However, the soldiers didn't appear to be doing anything out of the ordinary. They unpacked their packs, some settling in to sleep, while a couple began patrolling the stone wall set around their camp. Two others left, heading for the marketplace, coming back with chickens, bread, and some vegetables, obviously intending on starting their evening meal soon.

What was she missing? She couldn't see anything different about the soldiers. Couldn't determine their true nature. Didn't sense anything magical about them.

Patience had never been her strongest virtue. However, Nadeem settled down to wait in the shade. The soldiers would make a mistake and reveal themselves to her.

Then she could prepare.

Through the heat of the afternoon, the soldiers lazed around their camp. They didn't do *anything* that Nadeem found suspicious. Instead, a few started cooking their evening meal, others slept, while others sharpened and prepared their weapons, and a couple patrolled.

Nadeem remembered the hidden watcher of the Kardeş oasis. No one could hide here. The number of soldiers was too small, too easy to count. They weren't even behind four solid walls, merely a shelter of three, so everything they did could be seen.

More than one of the inhabitants of Hayalevi walked by the soldiers' encampment, obviously curious themselves. As far as Nadeem could tell, they didn't see anything out of the ordinary either. The people from the city stayed well away from the short stone wall that separated the soldiers from everyone else. Were they afraid of the emperor's soldiers?

After a couple of hours, Nadeem stood up from where she'd been sitting, stretching her legs. She wished for a moment that someone else could spell her, so she could walk around a bit. Sitting and waiting always wore at her.

"There you are," she heard someone quietly say from around the corner of the building. Someone obviously speaking directly to her.

Nadeem turned and walked that way, out of sight of the soldiers.

Trulliç stared at her, seeing her despite her shadows. "You've grown strong."

"Thank you," Nadeem said. She didn't see any point in denying it—her magic was much stronger than it had been.

"Like your aura, your magic has changed, hasn't it?" Trulliç asked, studying her. "You still cast illusions, but they're different, aren't they? It took me a while to find you, though once I figured out what I was looking for, it grew easier."

Nadeem merely nodded. She still wasn't about to tell Trulliç about rubbing the enchanted desert sand into her wound.

Trulliç glanced over to where the soldiers still did perfectly normal things. "I've been watching them too," he said. "But I can't tell what they're up to."

With a sigh, Nadeem admitted, "Me either. But they're here to find the desert heart," she added, warning him.

Trulliç stiffened for a moment, then he nodded. "That hadn't occurred to me. But I think you're right." He gave her a lopsided grin. "They aren't just here for me, are they?"

"They are not, young man," Nadeem said, using a prim auntie voice, teasing him.

Trulliç grinned at her. "So Mother told me as well."

"Your mother is wise," Nadeem said, meaning it.

Trulliç nodded, looking at the soldiers again. "I wanted to ask you about something." He paused, considering. "Is it possible to mark the buildings with an illusion of the emperor's mark? So that the soldiers are satisfied, but I don't have to permanently change the stone?"

Nadeem thought for a moment. It surprised her that he didn't want the emperor's mark on all of his buildings. Then again, given how ugly the one was on the soldier's encampment, maybe it wasn't that surprising after all. Did he hate the emperor that much?

"I could mark some of the buildings," she said slowly. "But I couldn't mark all of them. That's too many threads to keep track of." Her magic didn't permanently affect things. She couldn't cast an illusion and then walk away. She had to keep a tiny bit of her attention on any piece of magic she did if she wanted it to remain. While she'd been trained to track half a dozen small spells, much more than that and she'd lose track, so the illusions would disappear.

"That's what I thought," Trulliç said. He sighed.

"What is it?" Nadeem asked. Why did he not want the mark of the emperor in his town? Did he think himself separate from the emperor? Above him?

Should she have killed him as a traitor? Except she, herself, wasn't the most loyal to the emperor anymore either.

"I don't want him here," Trulliç whispered urgently. "I'm afraid that those marks will give him power over my city."

Nadeem's eyes widened. She hadn't considered that. "I don't know if that's how his magic works," she said slowly. Could the emperor reach out through his mark?

There was the legend of Lynds, who'd been able to reach all the star sisters through the mark they carried on their cheeks…

"Then what am I going to do? I know Marius will insist that I mark every building tonight," Trulliç said. His eyes grew colder. "I don't want to fight him, but I will."

Nadeem understood what Trulliç actually meant—that he'd kill the soldiers rather than give in to their demands. And that wouldn't be good for anyone.

"Is it possible for you to put a very shallow mark on the buildings? Something that would blow off in a day or so? I can follow along and make them seem as though they're more deeply set in the stone, at least at first," Nadeem volunteered.

"That would work," Trulliç said, nodding.

"Let's go try it," Nadeem said. She hadn't ever worked with a land magician before, trying to combine their magical skills. She suspected no star sister ever had.

Hopefully, it wouldn't be the last time they worked together. Because Nadeem really wanted there to be a song or story about them someday.

When the sun was two hand spans from the horizon, Trulliç presented himself at the soldiers' camp. Nadeem walked beside him, undisguised. Riyune kept pace as well.

Nadeem still wasn't sure what to make of the dog. He pretended to be an ordinary dog most of the time.

She'd seen him watching her with knowing eyes too many times, however. He reminded her of a blood hound, one of the dogs who shepherded pregnant women. She'd seen one in Kardeş when she'd gone to visit Aunt Parayat. But his coloring was all wrong, and Trulliç wasn't a pregnant girl.

At least as far as she could tell. She nearly giggled at the thought. Trulliç shot her a worried glance, but she merely smiled and kept it to herself.

The soldiers hadn't done anything other than what was expected of them for the rest of the afternoon: sleeping, guarding, preparing, cooking.

"Ah. Welcome, friends!" Marius said, greeting them both. He paused for a moment, looking curiously at Nadeem.

She raised her chin defiantly.

"I had thought you to be a star sister," Marius said. "Was I mistaken?"

Nadeem smiled coldly at him. "I am merely a traveler, now. I've given up my oaths."

"I see," Marius replied, his tone disapproving. "I've never heard of such a thing." He paused, then asked, "Does the sisterhood know?"

"I've seen and spoken with the aunt who raised me," Nadeem told him truthfully. "And she gave me her blessing."

Marius narrowed his eyes at her but didn't reply.

Trulliç spoke up. "Would you like a tour of Hayalevi now?"

Marius nodded, though he didn't stop staring at Nadeem. "Yes, please. We'd like to start with the temple dedicated to Innis."

Was that the temple that all the emperor's soldiers worshipped at? His symbol was a spear, and he was renown as a great warrior. She would have thought that they'd worship Barzhat, or Onnet, even.

But some of Marius's men did carry spears. It was as good of a place as any to start. And it was the temple closest to them.

Of course, not all of the men accompanied them. Only about half a dozen, with the rest of the two dozen staying behind, guarding the camp. Though Nadeem doubted that any of the people in Hayalevi would bother the soldiers. They didn't seem scared of them, not exactly. But she'd watched them all stare while at the same time never getting close enough to call out a greeting.

Would the streets ever be jammed with people? Nadeem didn't know. Trulliç had implied that at some point they would be. She couldn't see it.

Or maybe she couldn't see herself living in any crowd for too long.

Innis's temple had a spear fashioned out of black, smooth stone over the doorway. The temple was located in the southwest corner of the market square because Innis was also the god of good fortune and money, and tended to be the god favored by merchants and caravan owners. The dark stone of the building made it stand out from the red-gold that Trulliç generally favored.

Before they went inside, Trulliç made a great show of waving his hand over the cornerstone, carving the emperor's mark there. Nadeem silently made the mark appear as though it was carved deeply into the stone, instead of being barely scratched on the surface.

"Good," Marius said, approving when Trulliç finished. "The emperor will be well pleased."

Trulliç gave him a pleasant smile.

Nadeem hoped she was the only one who could smell the burning anger on him.

A few of the soldiers went inside to pray and make offerings. They chanted in beautiful, rich tones, singing a hymn Nadeem had never heard before about the fruitfulness of all things, the harvest, the hunt, and the home.

Next, they went to Onnet's temple, west of Innis's. Nadeem smiled when she realized it had been built horseshoe shaped. She and Trulliç went through the show of making the emperor's mark on the light-colored stone next to one of the benches set into the wall for the crones or for pregnant women to come and rest.

They visited the rest of the temples, the men making offerings, singing hymns, even dancing a few steps at both Enkat's temple as well as Barzhat's.

It was only as they were on the way back from Barzhat's temple that Marius stopped letting Trulliç lead. He turned and went back east another block or so. "What's that place?" he asked, pointing to a dark, cold building.

Nadeem shivered. She hadn't seen the small enclosure before. It was as though Trulliç had carved stones from the night sky and made a building.

Or from a nightmare.

How had Marius known about it? Nadeem would have sworn they hadn't passed it before.

"That's Forit's temple," Trulliç said slowly.

Marius stood, waiting.

Had Trulliç meant to skip it? The guard had specifically asked to tour all of the temples in Hayalevi.

How had he known about this one? It wasn't a usual temple. In fact, it was the first one Nadeem had ever even heard about.

Nadeem didn't like this temple. Why had Trulliç built it? The rocks felt out of place, as though carted in from some foreign land. They didn't have the smooth appearance of the rest of Trulliç's walls, instead looking like a giant with sharp fingernails had carved holes in the sides. No symbol of the goddess marked the outside walls.

What was Forit's symbol? Nadeem wasn't certain.

Marius stood next to the entrance of the temple, obviously waiting for Trulliç to set the emperor's mark in the cornerstone, as he had for the rest of the temples.

Trulliç glanced at Nadeem and shook his head. He didn't want her help with this one?

Nadeem kept her face smooth, not showing her confusion. She still stood beside Trulliç, just in case.

Winds swirled under Trulliç's direction, buffing smooth the cornerstone. He carved the same stylized snake's scale that he'd used on the other buildings. He stared hard at the stone, his hand extended, the muscles clenched as if he pressed against a solid wall. It was difficult to see the symbol, until Trulliç filled the outline with golden sand.

Marius just grunted. He didn't make any effort to enter the temple.

As Nadeem watched, the sand started spilling from the outline Trulliç had just carved.

After just a few moments, the wall reverted to its original pocked look.

"What is this?" Marius asked. He seemed more angry than puzzled.

Trulliç sighed. "This rock won't take any mark. Not mine, not the emperor's."

"Show me," Marius said. He appeared to be challenging Trulliç.

However, for once Trulliç didn't appear to react with anger. Instead, he shrugged, and put out his hand again.

Taller winds sprang up. Instead of merely touching the cornerstone of the temple, sand smoothed away a three foot high section. Into the center of it, Trulliç carved a curved shape.

Then Trulliç scooped up a handful of sand. He cupped his other hand over it.

Heat blasted out, making Nadeem take a step back. The white light that shot out from between Trulliç's cupped hands made her blink.

Trulliç pulled the light between his hands, as though it were taffy, then curved it.

Nadeem realized that he'd formed a horseshoe out of golden glass.

Trulliç floated the glass horseshoe through the air, pressing it into the carved mark on the wall.

It stayed there, shimmering for a few moments.

Then the glass darkened. Turned black. Dissolved into the wall as the mark disappeared.

Trulliç turned to Marius and shrugged. "The stones won't take anyone's mark," he said.

Marius grunted, staring at the wall.

Why did Trulliç raise this temple? Use these rocks?

Obviously, Nadeem was going to have to ask him about it later.

After a few more moments, Marius himself went into the temple. Trulliç and Nadeem followed him. The rest of the men stayed outside.

Were they scared? Or was it just because the temple wouldn't hold more than three or four comfortably?

Nadeem shivered in the cool air as she stepped across the threshold. Her cheek gave a warning tingle of pain, then subsided. One of Trulliç's glass lanterns burned in the corner inside the temple, hanging from the ceiling, suspended on an iron chain. It smelled of sweet incense, heavily spiced, though Nadeem didn't see any burning.

In fact, she didn't see an altar on the far wall. Just a gaping hole where the altar should be.

She looked questioningly at Trulliç. "This is the temple as it insisted on being built," he said defensively.

"I see," Marius said. He looked as though he'd just been handed a goblet of soured wine. "Just a placeholder? Not a proper place of worship?"

Trulliç shrugged. "The stones insisted on being built this way. I would have done more for the mother of us all."

Nadeem nodded. He was right. A temple to Forit should have been large and grand. When she'd fallen, her body had built the earth. Her blemishes had become all the people.

Yet, no one worshipped her, or built temples to her, even. Was it because she was a dead god and couldn't assist her followers? There were many hymns thanking Forit for her sacrifice, as well as holy days dedicated to her, but no temples or priests. She didn't demand anything from her followers, so she had none.

Marius crossed his arms over his chest and stared at the hole where the altar should be. Nadeem tried to see if there was any magic associated with that void, but she couldn't see anything special. If she had to guess, she'd say that the stones themselves held traces of magic. But she couldn't see what.

Marius finally nodded to himself, uncrossed his arms, and started singing a hymn of thanks to Forit. He had a surprisingly clear tenor, not the voice that Nadeem had expected.

Trulliç joined in after a few words. His voice blended well with Marius's, being a bit lower.

Hastily, Nadeem found her place and sang as well.

At the end of the hymn, Marius bowed his head, then turned and strode from the temple, as if he couldn't stand being in there any longer.

Trulliç followed quickly behind him.

Nadeem stayed for a few moments more. Their song echoed in her ears, as if the walls had clung to the noise and still reflected it.

Had the magic of the stone increased? Or decreased?

Nadeem shook her head, telling herself not to be fanciful. The walls were exactly the same as they had been when she'd walked into the temple.

Still, she was glad when she stepped outside again, into the warm air.

Trulliç and Marius discussed plans for an evening feast. They both acted as if nothing had happened.

Nadeem found her eyes being drawn back to the temple repeatedly.

There was something about that place. Something important.

Something that Marius knew and wasn't about to share with either of them.

⸻

Nadeem struggled to stay awake. It had been a long day preceded by no sleep the night before. She stifled her yawns and stayed focused on the temple of Forit. Watching the soldiers wouldn't tell her anything.

Somehow, Marius had known about this temple. Were there other soldiers that she'd missed? Or someone in town who worked with them? Maybe someone else who carried a cane, like the one she'd brought to Trulliç? Perhaps one of the merchants who'd passed information to them when they'd gone to the market for their dinner?

Trulliç had agreed to keep his attention focused on the soldiers and their encampment, while she stayed outside the temple.

Though the feast had lasted long into the night, Nadeem felt certain that the soldiers wouldn't stay and talk about taxes the next day, as Marius had promised.

Instead, they would seek out something at the temple. Do something.

Nadeem sat in the darkest of shadows next to the temple. No one could see her. The only way Trulliç would find her is through his magic, tracing her steps on the sand.

She wore tight black trousers and a black tunic, so she could move easily and fight. Instead of sandals, she wore mere strips of leather tied to her bare feet, again so she could run and fight. She had the traditional three knives of the star sisters tucked into her belt, along with blow darts and other weapons.

Trulliç had asked to watch her cast her illusions. Nadeem had nearly said no, but she'd let Levent watch when she'd left him. So she acquiesced, and let Trulliç watch her *blur* herself.

When she'd finished, Trulliç had merely smiled at her and said, "You are a marvel," before he'd walked away.

What had he meant by that?

Nadeem shook her head. She had to pay attention to what was in front of her. Nothing else.

The night air felt soft and cool around her. She heard the scuttling of mice and lizards taking advantage of the dark. Occasionally she heard the soft plunk of fish in the oasis trail river just past the temple. The smell of the heavy incense from inside the temple floated out to her now and again, though nothing sweet burned inside the temple itself. She assumed the scent came from the rocks themselves.

The night had mostly passed and the sky to the east began to have a slightly gray cast to it when Nadeem noticed movement.

Damn it! Had she fallen asleep?

No, that wasn't it. It was because mere shadows moved in front of her. Not men.

She blinked her eyes, making sure she understood what she was seeing.

The soldiers weren't as dark or as hollow as her. Her eyes didn't slide off their forms, as watchers did when she *blurred* herself.

They still weren't easy to see. She'd only noticed them because they'd moved. If they'd taken more time, creeping along, she might not have seen them at all.

Maybe because they hadn't been challenged all the way to the temple, they'd thought themselves safe.

Where was Trulliç? Had he been fooled? He must have been.

Nadeem waited until the three men had gone inside the temple before she moved herself. Quickly, she reached the door and peered inside.

The soldiers—Marius and two others—had already stripped off their disguises. They seemed weighted down with weapons, packs, and bags, as if they planned on being gone for a long time, crossing an inhospitable country.

Marius put his palms together and lowered his head, praying for a few moments. Nadeem realized with a start that he prayed to *the god emperor*.

She couldn't help her shiver.

It was so wrong for the emperor to want to raise himself up to the level of a god! She wasn't worried about the people rebelling from such a thing, but the gods' reaction.

She'd had so many dreams of the coming battles. Were they about to come true?

Marius's eyes glowed red when he finished his prayer and looked up.

Nadeem froze.

Marius was *not* magical on his own. He wasn't a magician. He certainly wasn't a star sister.

Instead, he appeared to be a conduit for someone else's magic. Able to channel magic from someone far away.

Nadeem would bet that the person's magic Marius channeled was the emperor's.

With glowing fingers, Marius reached up and tugged at his breastplate.

No, at the emperor's golden scale embossed on his armor.

Marius peeled the scale off his chest. A plain, merely painted scale lay underneath.

Using both hands, he pressed the scale against the far wall of the temple, that hole where the altar should be.

A sizzling noise filled the air. The foul scent of burning sulfur replaced the sweet scent of incense.

The dark hole widened. Lengthened. Until it was roughly man-shaped.

Beyond the opening, stars streamed. Nadeem nearly gasped when she realized it looked like the land outside of the small cavern that she'd rested in, the one that had rescued her after she'd mutilated the star sister mark on her cheek.

The men quickly marched through the gaping hole.

Nadeem hesitated. She had to go get Trulliç. Tell him what she'd seen. Though a part of her wanted to immediately go after the men.

She turned to run.

Before she got three steps more soldiers appeared out of the dark. They paid no attention to her, if they even saw her.

They ran as well, through the door of the temple. Out the back, to that other land.

Nadeem *raced* to the soldier's encampment.

No one remained there.

Trulliç sat against one of the buildings, fast asleep.

"Trulliç!" Nadeem said, kneeling next to him and shaking him.

Trulliç shook his head slowly. His mouth lolled, and his eyes didn't open.

Damn it! He'd been drugged.

When? During the feast, perhaps.

Nadeem had only pretended to drink the beer and wine that had been presented, as Aunt Izmet had taught her.

It hadn't occurred to her tell Trulliç not to have any. And Riyune lay fast asleep as well. Had he been drugged, too? Did the drugs that affected Trulliç affect his dog as well?

"Come on," Nadeem said, pinching Trulliç's cheek hard.

That at least got his eyes open. "The soldiers have all gone," Nadeem told him as he blinked groggily.

"Wha—" Trulliç said. He obviously was trying to fight off whatever they'd given him, shaking his head.

Deliberately, Trulliç placed one palm on the sand beside him and the other on Riyune's back.

Winds swirled up, creating small dust devils of sand.

Angry, heated winds carrying the smell of a dark storm pushed against Nadeem's back, making her cheek ache.

Trulliç blinked at Nadeem as the winds died down, sober. "Tell me what happened," he said plainly as he stood up. Riyune also stood, shaking his head, and then the rest of his body, hard enough that he nearly fell down.

Nadeem tugged on his hand. "Get us to Forit's temple first."

Trulliç nodded. He turned his own hand over so his burning hot, hard fingers intertwined with hers. They rose into the air and blew to the temple, racing faster than Nadeem had ever moved. It made her breath catch and her heart sing despite the dark deeds done that night, that they were about to go do.

As they stepped inside Forit's temple, the opening vanished.

Trulliç reached out with his hand. Could he reopen the portal?

He shook with the effort, but the stones resisted him.

The soldiers were gone, without a trace.

And they had no way to follow them.

Or to stop the emperor from bring death and destruction to them all.

CHAPTER NINE

TRULLIÇ

TRULLIÇ SHOOK HIS HEAD AND made Nadeem tell her story of the soldiers again. He couldn't feel them anywhere on the desert sands.

Trulliç stood with Nadeem outside Forit's temple, the dawn about to break. People were already up, the women baking bread in the cool of the morning, merchants preparing for their morning shoppers, roosters complaining loudly about the coming light.

"How could Marius channel magic?" Trulliç asked again. He didn't understand how the emperor had done that with the soldier. Was it a talent that all magicians had? Or was it something that only the emperor could do? Or was there something different about Marius?

Trulliç was viciously glad that he'd barely scratched the emperor's mark in all the buildings. He felt certain that his gut instinct had been right, that somehow the emperor could touch all of Hayalevi through those marks.

Trulliç would later go and destroy all of them, make sure his city remained apart from the Tanesh empire.

"I don't know how Marius channeled magic," Nadeem said, frustrated. "We have to go after them!"

"How?" Trulliç asked. "Where did they go?" The soldiers had

obviously gone…somewhere. But where? He'd barely caught a glimpse of that other place before it had disappeared.

Nadeem paused, pressing her lips together. Trulliç waited. Finally, Nadeem said quietly, "I may know where they went. And how to get there."

"Really? Where? How?" Trulliç said, surprised. Creating magical doorways to other places didn't seem like star sister magic at all.

Nadeem took a deep breath before she answered. "There was a cavern that appeared out of nowhere. It was made out of rocks that looked like they were just piled on top of each other. Inside, there were shelves for sleeping and a small stream of clear water."

Trulliç held himself very still. It sounded like the place that he'd discovered on his first manhood journey. Or rather, the outcropping of rocks that had found him. "Go on," he said.

"I don't know how to get there," she said, shaking her head. "It just kind of appeared. I know, that sounds stupid. It had a guard stone just inside the door, like your tower does."

Trulliç nodded. It did sound as though they were talking about the same place.

"Beyond…beyond the door," Nadeem said, her voice falling to a whisper, "at night, the stars streamed across the sky. The soldiers went somewhere that looked the same. With the stars racing that way."

"Yes!" Trulliç said excitedly. "I've been to that cavern. It exists."

"Oh!" Nadeem said. "I was afraid I'd just dreamed it."

Trulliç nodded. "Me too," he said. "But I think it's real. There were gems—"

"Buried beneath it!" Nadeem said. "And if anyone dug for them—"

"The water would have been insulted and gone away, leaving them to die," Trulliç said.

"So it is real," Nadeem said, relieved. "But how do we get there? Or how do we call it?"

"I had the impression that it only came when one had great need," Trulliç said slowly.

Nadeem seemed thoughtful at that. But she nodded, agreeing.

What had been her great need? Had it been after she'd taken a knife to her cheek and removed the star sister's mark? Was that what had changed her magic? Going to that cavern? Or had it been something else?

"We need to call the cavern," she told him.

"You need to rest first," he told her.

"But—"

"The stars only streamed at night," Trulliç interrupted. "It does us no good to call the cavern now. We also need packs. And supplies."

"Fine. You're right," Nadeem said grudgingly. "But how are we going to call the cavern to us?"

Trulliç shrugged and said, "I am the desert magician." Hopefully the cavern would recognize him.

And their great need.

After Trulliç got Nadeem settled and resting, he went out again into Hayalevi, Riyune at his heels. He didn't need to rest, not like she did, not during the day. The sun energized him. Once the sun went down, he'd be tired. He'd try to nap later that afternoon.

For now, he had things to clean up.

More people were awake, merchants opening their windows or front doors so people could come in. Children screeched and raced along the street, playing a game of tag. A small herd of goats bleated as they meandered along, being herded toward the market place. The smells of fresh tea and cinnamon from someone's breakfast wafted through an open window.

The people of his city all had a smile and a "hello" for him, though no one tried to stop him and chat. He hoped that was because they could see he was busy, and not because they were afraid of him.

He went first to Forit's temple, but nothing there had changed. The black walls still felt cold, the sand on the floor undisturbed, as if no one had entered, the back wall blank and empty, a hole where the altar should be.

No foreign mark marred the walls on the outside either, where Trulliç had tried to place one earlier.

Pleased, he went to Barzhat's temple. Blue glass filled the windows, and a single line of black glass stood over the lintel, the symbol of the goddess. The temple was one of the few round places in the city, but that was how the stones had come out of the ground. Fine sand covered the floor, good for dancers and those who wanted to practice the steps they would give the goddess when they arrived at her golden court.

The mark of the emperor on the cornerstone was barely visible. Trulliç buffed the stone with sand and wind, clearing away the snake scale easily.

Trulliç breathed a huge sigh of relief. He'd been afraid that the rock would have been permanently infected by the mark, and that the emperor would already have a foothold in Trulliç's city.

Riyune seemed pleased as well, nodding at Trulliç as if he approved.

Trulliç visited the other temples in the reverse order that he'd traveled to them with the soldiers the day before. It filled him with satisfaction that he could easily clear the mark from all the cornerstones.

Last, he went to the building he'd raised for the soldiers. The large, pale-gray scale of the emperor's mark in the center of the roof appeared to catch the sun like a beacon. It made Trulliç shiver.

He'd never destroyed a building before. He wasn't sure where to start. Did he just sink the rocks beneath the ground? What about the fence and the plants there? Should he just leave the lean to, and tell the merchants they could have it for goats and other livestock?

Riyune leaned against Trulliç's leg. He had that feeling of acceptance again, that whatever he decided would be all right.

Trulliç peered more closely at the building. His ready anger came, fury at what the soldiers had done.

Not only did they trick him, they'd abused his hospitality. They'd drugged him at the feast he'd held in their honor.

He wrenched the gray stone scale from the roof of the building with some effort. He hadn't attached it that firmly. It felt to him as though the scale had grown roots and had started to infect the rest of the roof.

He sent stone flying high in the air above the city. If he could he would have sent it all the way to the emperor's court.

Instead, he focused his rage on it.

The stone exploded with a loud bang.

Trulliç called up winds to carry the dust and shards far into the foothills to the south, not wanting them to touch the interior of his city.

Then he reshaped the building. Made it smaller, less grand. Turned the well out front into an animal trough. Changed the latrine in the back into a compost heap. Opened the stone wall up, so it had many gates.

The earth greedily swallowed the remains of what the soldiers had left behind. After a few moments, no trace of them remained.

Trulliç found himself still breathing hard, his cheeks flaming, his blood pounding in his temples. How dare they? He coughed up his disgust and spat, unable to do more.

He wouldn't destroy a perfectly good building. The emperor and his soldiers couldn't make him that angry.

When he looked around, he realized that he had an audience. The people standing there gaped at him.

He could smell their fear.

Damn it! He kept doing the wrong thing. Soon, all his people would leave Hayalevi.

Riyune leaned against his leg again.

Trulliç's anger drained away.

His people weren't afraid of him.

They were worried about the emperor and what he would do next.

———

Trulliç stood on the top of his tower, the sun beating down on his head. He *breathed* in the desert air, smelling the baking sands and the far off salt flats. Winds stirred restlessly around him. He didn't see anyone in the streets below—everyone napped during the heat of the day.

Nadeem still slept as well. Trulliç envied her. Her dreams seemed sweet, not full of the anger and terror of his own. Riyune had stayed with her, laying down in front of her doorway as if guarding her.

Trulliç had one last thing to do before he also napped. Myrizhah and Seydat had already prepared their packs for them. Trulliç couldn't tell them how long they'd be gone, so the two women had spent the morning buying and baking travel rolls.

Water was their main concern. If the other side held true desert, Trulliç felt certain he could find water for them.

He had no idea what the other land held, though.

The emperor's stick floated in front of Trulliç, held by his winds. The silver snake's head glistened in the bright light.

The constant rage burning in Trulliç demanded that he sacrifice this thing. Break it into thousands of shards and hurl it far into the heart of the desert.

His hand shook as he fought to control his anger.

The emperor's symbol that he'd placed on the soldier's former building, yes, that deserved to be destroyed.

This walking stick, though, needed more care.

It still felt slippery to Trulliç. He had no other way to describe it. Whenever he tried to place it in his mind, to feel its place in his city as he could every stone and grain of sand, the stick slipped away, like a snake leaving its skin behind.

He didn't understand it. He didn't know what type of magic had made it.

And until he could learn more about it, he wouldn't just destroy it.

He knew they couldn't take the stick with them. Nadeem had told him how the cavern hadn't allowed the stick inside. But he also didn't want to just leave it here where it could do mischief.

He could, however, isolate it.

Trulliç loosened the glass horseshoe tied to his belt and held it in one hand. The stick remained floating in the air on his winds.

If Trulliç was being fanciful, he'd say that it felt to him as if the stick had just grown very still and wary, like a mouse hiding before a desert hawk.

More sand raised up in the air, swirling tightly around the floating cane. The acrid smell of magic flowed over Trulliç, chasing away the scent of the desert.

Light flashed from the silver snake's head, like a warning signal.

Trulliç's hand holding the glass horseshoe shook as he called forth more sand, more heat, more light. Angry storm winds howled around him. Lightning sizzled and crackled. The whirling sand grew as bright as the sun.

Trulliç refused to look away, letting the heat bake him dry of care and fear.

The stick stayed solid in itself, refusing to be transformed. Trulliç could break it. He couldn't change it.

Good thing that wasn't what he was trying.

With a soft *whump* the storm collapsed in on itself.

The winds trailed softly away.

Three inches of glass now encased the emperor's walking stick. It was primarily clear glass, with swirls of green and gold twirling through it, like Trulliç's horseshoe.

Now Trulliç felt the walking stick. Or rather, the glass around it. He could place it easily with his magical senses, not needing to rely on his sight to find it.

The stick remained exactly as it had been. But muted. No power trickled from it. No sense of its slippery nature. No light or magic.

Trulliç didn't think that the glass encasing the stick would hold it forever.

But for now, it would have to do.

***

Trulliç marched confidently over the sands. The sun hung barely a single hand span over the horizon. Riyune strode bravely beside him.

Or at least that was how Trulliç hoped he appeared. Or how people might sing of him, someday.

He was certain that Nadeem rolled her eyes at him behind his back. Riyune did frequently as well, though the dog hid his amusement less.

Trulliç had carried Riyune and Nadeem far into the heart of the desert itself. Sand spread all around them, as endless as the ocean that surrounded the Tanesh empire itself. Nothing stirred on the surface, though Trulliç knew that snakes, lizards, mice, and other small creatures lay resting in their hiding places, awaiting the cooler evening.

He wore his manhood tunic, the one that Myrizhah had bought him new for the first time he'd walked the desert. Under it, he wore a loose, unbleached shirt and baggy brown pants. His sandals were new, made out of solid leather and tied up the front, like the soldiers', instead of merely strapped to his ankle.

Food, a heavy travel roll, and as many skins of water as he could carry stuffed his pack. He figured Riyune could find his own food, as the dog frequently hunted mice and small animals.

He didn't bother carrying any weapon other than his eating knife. Nadeem had more than enough weapons for the pair of them. Possibly enough for a small troop of fighters.

She wore clothes that wouldn't necessarily be considered proper: tight black pants that didn't disguise the muscles in her legs, a black tunic belted just as tightly across her chest, and a sheer blouse. She wore knives on her belt, more knives strapped to her calves, her loose blouse sleeves hid darts, and her *chafiyek* held throwing stars.

Trulliç assumed she had more weapons hidden elsewhere. He didn't really want to know.

She also carried a pack full of food and water, almost as heavy as his own.

Trulliç wasn't sure how to call the desert cavern. He didn't think songs or praise would do it. The cavern knew its own worth, and wouldn't be swayed by flattery.

Could he convince it that his need was dire? Not his need for food or shelter, but for finding the soldiers? He wasn't certain.

Still, he strode up a slight dune, spread his legs wide in a solid stance, and sang out:

O sweetest water! What a welcome home!

He ignored how Riyune shook his head and rolled his eyes. Trulliç knew he had a good singing voice. He'd adapted a hymn for spring, welcoming the rains.

But the cavern didn't suddenly appear, even after he'd finished singing all three verses.

Nadeem merely nodded at him, as if congratulating him on his effort. "Can you feel the cavern anywhere?" she asked.

Trulliç closed his eyes and shoved his senses underground. Why hadn't he thought of that?

He pushed down on his anger. He couldn't think of everything. That was why he had help. No matter if her simple question had brought him back to the time when he doubted everything, when he was still a landless magician studying with Atça.

No water rested under the surface here. Only sand, rocks, and more rocks. No hidden sweet river.

He came back to himself and opened his eyes. "I don't feel it anywhere near here. Or anywhere out there, either," he added, gesturing to the desert around them.

"Ah," Nadeem said. She looked out at the horizon, then looked back at him. Her gaze felt heavy. "Songs won't work, I don't think. Nor dances, either."

Trulliç slowly nodded. She was probably right.

He was such a failure, destined to die here in the desert, his life bleeding away while the soldiers pillaged the desert heart.

"Try using blood to call the cavern here," she said.

"What?" Trulliç asked, blinking. Blood? What did she mean by that?

Nadeem drew out one of her knives—the one with the black blade. He felt a kinship to the knife. It was made out of obsidian.

"The cavern comes in times of great need," Nadeem said as she drew closer to him. She kept the blade in her right hand, while she held her left palm out toward him. "We are not dying. We have food. And water. But the world will die if we let don't stop the soldiers and the emperor claims the desert heart."

Trulliç nodded. She was right.

"I swear to do everything in my power, and beyond even that, given the help of the gods, to stop the emperor from laying waste to all the lands," Nadeem said. "This is my new oath. By my blood, I swear."

With a quick, clean cut, she sliced open her left palm. The blood welled up instantly. Nadeem made a fist, then shook her hand, once, twice, three times, scattering drops of red onto the golden sands.

Then she handed Trulliç the hilt of the knife.

He swallowed against a suddenly dry throat. He didn't want to actively go against the emperor. He still had hope that perhaps the emperor would just leave him be. Live and let live.

His mother would call him a foolish boy for such a hope.

Trulliç glanced over at Riyune, who watched with solemn eyes. He didn't seem inclined to take the same vow himself, but he also didn't seem to oppose Trulliç doing so.

With a shuddering breath, Trulliç took the knife and sliced open his palm.

The pain was a minor thing.

The heat of his blood mingling with Nadeem's took his breath away. What was she?

She cleared her throat, calling him back.

"By the full power of the desert, I swear to stop the emperor from desecrating this place, and the worlds beyond," Trulliç said, the words flying from him unheeded. "By my blood, I swear to pursue this, to the end of my days."

Like Nadeem, Trulliç made a fist to bring the blood more quickly to the surface. Then he shook his hand as well, scattering drops.

"There," Nadeem said when he looked up.

On the northern horizon stood a dark outcropping of rocks that hadn't been there just moments before.

"Our need is great," Trulliç told her as he handed back her knife.

Nadeem gave him a tight smile. "Let's hope our will is great enough to match it. Come on."

She took off toward the cavern, running down the slope of sand.

Was she whooping? Like a young girl?

He shook his head, then raced after her, letting joy fill his heart.

They were about to do desperate deeds.

It suddenly made more sense to find delight in the moments in between.

<hr>

The cavern appeared the same as the first time Trulliç had seen it. The rocks felt as though they'd been haphazardly piled one on top of the next, then melted together. The tall stacks of rocks grew close together, like shoots of grass. Just inside the open doorway stood a guardian rock. He realized now that it was carved from different stone—granite, perhaps.

The outside of the cavern was roughly circular, but not exactly. More like someone's fis, laid on edge, with points sticking out. Long pieces of shale, roughly put together, covered the roof.

Both Trulliç and Nadeem walked all the way around the cavern before stepping inside. The air just beyond the guard stone felt cooler and softer. Trulliç immediately set his mage light glowing in the center of the room so they could see.

Trulliç couldn't help but smile at the soft trickle of water that he heard. He would have to ask Nadeem, but they might empty out all their water skins and refill them with the water from the cavern, even if there wasn't anything magical about it.

Nadeem already knelt next to the stream, bathing her cut hand. "Here." She directed him to do the same.

Trulliç shivered as the lukewarm water caressed his skin, the stream tasting his blood.

"We are still sworn," Nadeem whispered. She appeared to be talking to the stream.

After another moment, she stood, stretching, then took off her pack. "We'll be here for a while, until it's fully night," she told him.

Trulliç nodded, drawing his hand out of the water. The line across his palm had already closed up. Just a thin white scar showed.

Nadeem asked, "Was this your first blood oath?"

"Yes," Trulliç said. "I've never had to take one before. But it wasn't your first blood oath, was it?"

Nadeem laughed softly. "No. Far from it. I had thought the oath to kill you would have been the last one I took. But I was wrong." She stretched out on one of the upper shelves, relaxing.

Trulliç dropped his eyes back to the water. Nadeem was very…

distracting, dressed as she was, now wiggling and making herself comfortable that way.

"What was your great need?" Nadeem asked after a few moments. "That brought you into the cavern the first time?"

Trulliç stood. Now that Nadeem appeared to be settled, he could settle in himself. He stepped over the stream and lay down on the very bottom shelf, stretching out.

He told her about his manhood journey and walking the desert the first time. About Atça drugging his water with *agafi*, not realizing (or not caring) that it would make him feel so restless.

"I met Riyune here, too," Trulliç added. He turned his head, looking over at the dog who lay on the far side of the small stream, looking as ordinary as he ever did. "He first appeared as a blood hound. Though that might have been a dream."

He heard shifting above him, as if Nadeem, too, had turned to look at the dog. "He has the same shadow as a blood hound," she said softly.

Riyune lifted his head, growing as still as a statue. He stared hard at the pair of them, as if judging the best way to rip out their throats.

Careful! Trulliç wanted to cry out.

But Nadeem just laughed. "Made me wonder if you were pregnant or something," she said lightly.

Trulliç heard Nadeem shift again, rolling onto her back.

"Wake me when the star show starts," she said sleepily.

Trulliç knew that in moments, Nadeem would be asleep. It must have been part of her training, to sleep wherever and whenever she had the chance.

He sighed and looked back at Riyune, who'd gone back to being an ordinary dog.

What was Riyune, exactly? Who was he?

Coming back to the place where Trulliç had first met the dog just raised more questions, not answers.

Trulliç dreamed.

He knew he wasn't awake because his mage light had changed from yellow to a deep purple, casting long shadows through the cavern. From where he lay on the bottom shelf, he could barely see around the guard stone. In the dream, the guard stone still stood, but it had grown transparent, just a gray mesh that he could see through.

Riyune had stayed on the far side of the stream before Trulliç had gone to sleep. Now the dog rose, shook itself and went to stand in the doorway.

A thin howl filled the air.

Trulliç *had* to be dreaming. Riyune never barked. He certainly didn't howl.

At least half a dozen figures floated across the sands.

In that way of dreams, Trulliç knew that these were the ghosts of the dead kings, those who had once ruled Osmerli, the city that had stood in the desert before Hayalevi. They had tall crowns that had grown jagged and sharp, like brittle stone. Their eyes shone black in their white faces. Long silver hair made up their beards.

They looked as gaunt as starving men. The closest reached out to touch Riyune's head with skeletal fingers, blessing him.

Trulliç couldn't hear what the old kings said. Their counsel for Riyune came to him as hisses and swishing wind. They carried the smell of old incense, weak and sour. He tried to raise his hand, to ask them what they wanted, but sleep had shackled his wrists to the rock he lay on.

The guard stone grew more solid as Riyune stepped back around it. The dog dropped beside the stream, collapsing into sleep, his gentle snores filling the small space as if he'd never left it.

Trulliç sighed. He'd wished he could have talked with the old kings. See if they had any advice for how to fight the emperor. But maybe his next dream would bring him to them.

He let sleep carry him away again.

A soft *plop* woke Trulliç. He started, the sound out of place. Nadeem had already leaped down from her shelf, knife in her hand. She stood and stretched, laughing.

"Riyune thinks we've slept long enough," she told Trulliç over her shoulder.

Trulliç looked past Nadeem to the dog who tried to look innocent and not as though he had a couple more rocks ready to cast into the stream in order to wake them.

Nadeem grabbed her pack and walked to the opening of the cavern. She gave a low whistle.

"What?" Trulliç said. He got up and went to the opening, peering out beside her.

Stars streamed across the black sky. Golden sands spread out before him, like a soft carpet. The smell of salt and smoke floated by, carried on a wind, here and gone.

Nadeem quickly tied all her weapons to her, then slipped on her pack. "I'm going scouting," she told him. "If I'm not back in an hour or so, see if you can make it back."

"But—" Trulliç said.

"If I can't make it, you probably won't be able to either," Nadeem told him firmly.

Trulliç sighed. She might be right. "Safe trails and easy water," he told her. It was one of the traditional farewells that people gave each other.

She gave him a brilliant smile. "Good winds and easy water," she told him. Then she slipped out of the cavern onto the shining sands.

Trulliç knew that his mage light hadn't wavered. The cavern was just as brightly lit as it had been a moment before.

It still seemed dimmer, the shadows darker, without her there.

Riyune sat beside Trulliç as they watched Nadeem walk away from the cavern. The dog looked up at Trulliç expectantly.

"She told me to wait," Trulliç explained.

Riyune seemed to be wanting more.

"So we wait. At least a little while," Trulliç added.

Riyune looked at Trulliç, then back out, over the sands. He looked as though he would chase after Nadeem in a heartbeat if only Trulliç would give the word.

Trulliç made himself wait. Watch.

The figure on the sands grew smaller.

Abruptly, Nadeem disappeared.

Trulliç surged to his feet. He swallowed against a dry throat. "She said to wait…" he said.

He looked again at Riyune.

Though the dog didn't say anything, didn't actually speak words, his look certain spoke volumes.

Go after her. Idiot.

"You're right," Trulliç said. He slipped on his pack.

Paused.

Turned back toward the center of the cavern. "Thank you for your hospitality," he said plainly. "For the wonderful fresh water and safe bed."

He didn't know if the cavern heard him, if the stream understood, but he would be a poor guest if he didn't thank his host.

Then he slipped out of the cavern, onto unknown sands.

CHAPTER TEN

NADEEM

THIS PLACE WAS, BUT WASN'T, the same as the desert in Nadeem's visions, the ones she'd had since she was little, before her initiation ceremony, even.

The ground remained soft glittering sand beneath her feet. She still feared it would turn to crunchy ash, filled with the tiny shards of burned bones. The sky streamed with stars, lights leading her path. Gentle winds tickled the back of her neck, carrying the smell of briny water. The sand, too, flowed along.

Loneliness filled her. Even at the heart of the desert, where few animals or insects lived, she still felt part of *something*.

This place was isolated. Nothing lived here. Not even the tiniest of biting flies.

It didn't surprise Nadeem when she turned back that the cavern had disappeared. Nothing living remained on this landscape.

Nothing but her.

There was no way back to her home. Her desert. Her old life or her sisters.

Trulliç would have to find his own way. Just as she would.

Nadeem turned forward again, willing to follow the stars.

Nadeem pushed herself to run, forcing one foot in front of the other.

The sand fought her, making her sink down. Sticking to her feet, gritty against her skin.

Though the air stayed calm, it felt as though she battled great winds, full of the sour smell of her own sweat.

She struggled, trying to glide as she had in the Qaenev desert. While she couldn't go as fast as Trulliç, surely she should be able to run here.

The land accepted only walking, however.

Panting, Nadeem slowed and started moving at a slower pace. Her steps became easy again.

Though this was a desert and it was related to the Qaenev, it wasn't the same. She didn't have the same power here.

Trulliç probably wouldn't have the same amount of magic here either.

Nadeem had no idea how long she'd been walking. The stars streamed over her head—she couldn't tell if it was still the middle of the night or close to dawn. She smelled briny water on the winds, so she knew she could refill her water skins.

So she couldn't run. Nadeem stopped and turned around, looking back at the way she'd come.

Even just standing still bothered this place. It wanted her to keep going. Everything *flowed* in a single direction—the sand, the stars, the winds. She was only supposed to go one way.

Stubbornly, Nadeem tried to retrace her steps. She found herself sweating in the cool night air, her legs trembling with the effort, cursing like her old teammate Duzhen. It made her smile until she realized just how alone she was again.

Reluctantly, Nadeem turned and went the easier direction. The land was too big to fight on her own.

Suddenly, a white blur raced past her.

Nadeem stopped, reaching automatically for one of the knives at her belt.

Riyune sat in front of her. He glared at her, daring her to try to harm him.

Nadeem replaced the knife slowly. She remembered Riyune at the cavern, when he'd grown fierce and still, a predator debating whether to kill his prey now or later.

She didn't trust this dog. If he was a dog. He appeared skeletal in this land, more like fur-covered bones than flesh and blood.

But if Riyune was here…Nadeem turned.

Trulliç walked briskly across the sand. He wasn't floating like he usually did.

Nadeem scolded herself for her small heart that he couldn't move that quickly here either.

"How did you get so far?" Trulliç asked. He seemed angrier than usual. "Why did you disappear?"

"I didn't," Nadeem said. She felt her own anger brewing. "I just walked. Following the desert."

"Oh," Trulliç said, deflating. "I thought…I thought you'd just left. Abandoned me."

"Why would I do that?" Nadeem asked, truly puzzled. "You're the desert magician. We're in a desert. It isn't the Qaenev, but surely you have some power here. Why would I throw that away?"

If the light had been better, Nadeem would have bet that Trulliç blushed.

"I thought…I just thought—"

"You just let Atça back into your head," Nadeem told him.

Trulliç looked down at the ground, ashamed.

"Look, I've already had to point out to you that you were the desert magician," Nadeem said. "Don't make me have to beat some sense into you this time."

"You sound like my mother," Trulliç said. He sounded horrified.

"Your mother is a wise woman," Nadeem told him seriously.

"She is," Trulliç said. He paused, then added, "She thinks I have a good heart. But she's worried that it isn't enough."

Nadeem firmly kept her lips pressed together so she wouldn't say anything.

From the look Trulliç gave her, she knew he heard the words

anyway. That she, too, was worried that his good heart wouldn't be enough at the end.

Dawn came all at once in this strange land. Stars streamed in a midnight sky until all of a sudden, the sky lightened. It was as if someone had lit a lamp, causing the sky to brighten.

Nadeem shivered in the abrupt heat. It unnerved her, how quickly the night had passed.

It also meant that later, night would leap upon them without warning.

Trulliç seemed just as unsettled walking beside her, but he didn't say anything. They just kept going. Riyune kept pace with them, moving in a strangely direct manner. Normally, dogs would go off chasing scents, straying in front of them then trailing behind.

But Riyune seemed just as determined to get where they were going without additional forays.

The horizon changed abruptly, as if they'd just climbed a hill and could now see off into the distance. Instead of clear blue, the sky grew gray and dark.

Nadeem feared what was coming next.

"Doesn't smell like a storm," Trulliç told her, pausing.

"I've dreamed of this place," Nadeem quietly admitted.

Trulliç raised an eyebrow at her.

"It's where the end of the world occurs," she told him.

He nodded. "It feels like the end of the earth, doesn't it? As if nothing lays just beyond those clouds."

"So lonely," Nadeem said.

Trulliç cleared his throat, as if he was about to argue. Then he shook his head. "Let's make sure it isn't the end," he said firmly.

They started walking again, into the great unknown.

The sand changed as Nadeem feared it would, covered in ash and tiny bones that cracked as she walked. She was glad she had on proper sandals and not just strips of leather tied to her feet.

Trulliç grimaced as he walked. He tried to lift himself up, but the effort to do so wasn't worth it.

The land wore at Nadeem's soul. To the right lay a great wooden wall, tall as a two-story house. It curved both at the top and the bottom, though, as if it weren't a solid block, but a rounded piece.

Like the handle of a great spear.

"We're getting closer," Nadeem told Trulliç. She wanted to run. To race toward that death she knew was waiting for her, fighting an endless stream of gibbering darkness. To go and dance in the goddess's court before the rest of the world did, before it all came crashing down.

She also wanted to drag her feet. To delay the end and keep breathing the sweet desert air as long as possible.

Trulliç put up his hands in front of him. "I'm trying to see if I can feel anything different," he explained to her. "All I feel is death."

Nadeem nodded. As a star sister, she'd agreed to love Barzhat, the goddess of death. She'd invited the goddess to all of her meals, welcomed her into her heart.

This place should have felt like home, in a way. But it was the farthest thing from it that Nadeem could imagine.

Riyune stopped abruptly, causing Nadeem and Trulliç to pause as well.

Figures moved on the far horizon. They resolved into a group of men, maybe a dozen in all.

"The soldiers," Nadeem said.

"Aye," Trulliç replied. He looked over at Nadeem. "Do you think you could hide?" he asked.

"I can try," she said. She stared at her hands, willing them to *blur*.

Slowly, oh so slowly, the outline of her skin changed. She felt as though she fought the very air to make the illusion work. Her cheek ached, pain beating in time with her heart. Sweat broke out along her back and slid down her hair, under her *chafiyek*.

"Don't," Trulliç told her after a few moments.

Stubbornly, Nadeem kept trying to complete the effect, to be not only blurred but hollow.

"Don't waste your strength that way," Trulliç said after a few more moments.

Panting, Nadeem lowered her hands. Trulliç was right. The land wanted her as she was, not changed.

Maybe that would give them an advantage, though. If she couldn't change, maybe Marius couldn't either.

"Can you do any magic here?" Nadeem asked Trulliç.

He shrugged. "Some. I can find water. I can raise rocks. And I can create glass," he said. "But all at great effort."

"Let's hope it's enough," Nadeem said.

In the end, it wouldn't be Trulliç or his heart that would be tested. It would be hers.

The soldiers stood in four solid lines, facing them as they approached. The foul smell of rotting blood filled the air. Dark clouds stretched over them, unnatural, a storm that would never bring rain.

Nadeem's breath caught when she realized that a small outcropping of rock stood behind the soldiers. It looked the twin of the cavern she and Trulliç had called to get to this place.

She's seen something like it before in her visions. Once it had held back the darkness brewing inside with a thin red string.

Here, a great gray guard stone stood just outside the entrance, blocking the way.

Whatever was inside the cavern sickened Nadeem, making her stomach knot and clench.

Marius stood in front of the guard stone. He'd drawn the emperor's mark in black charcoal on the gray stone. He paid no attention to his visitors. He held his hands out, obviously trying to channel magic through them onto the large mark.

He shook with the effort. Acrid magic swirled around him. A dingy layer of fog undulated at his feet.

However, he didn't appear to be very successful. The stone in front of him resisted his efforts to break it.

Nadeem was shocked at Marius's appearance. He seemed hollow, as if all the efforts he'd made here had started eating at him from the inside out. His cheekbones stood out on his face, and his skin hung loosely from his skull, as if he'd lost a great deal of weight. His eyes burned black with rage. The muscles on his arms had shrunk, and wrinkles covered all his skin, as if he'd turned into an old man overnight.

"Grab them," he ordered his soldiers.

Nadeem laughed. She pushed Trulliç behind her and easily took out the first three soldiers. Did they know nothing about the star sisters?

She didn't expect Trulliç to be able to fight, but a great wind howled past her, knocking over another two soldiers.

Even Riyune joined in, harrying one of the bow bearers, tearing the skin and muscle just above his mid-calf sandals.

Nadeem laughed again as she spun, slicing skin as easily as she did air. She felt as though Barzhat had come to visit, lending Nadeem the goddess's strength and grace. She moved as easily as her hawk girl did when she'd been fighting illusionary battles with her sisters.

Pivot. Slice. Block. Duck. Kick. Kill.

Was this the dance that the goddess would demand from Nadeem when she entered her court? Nadeem had never killed before, but these men didn't seem real, despite the fact that their blood now coated her hands, her nose was full of the stench of their spilled bile, her ears still rang with their angry cries.

"No! Stop!" Trulliç called.

She glanced back at him. He stood alone. No one threatened him.

She turned back to the soldier standing in front of her and speared him with her knife, stabbing his neck and driving her blade to the hilt into his skin.

When she stepped back, he dropped slowly, collapsing like a falling leaf.

Trulliç came rushing up to her. He seemed really angry. "What?" she asked defensively. She'd just saved their lives. Hadn't she?

He merely pointed toward the outcropping of rock.

Marius hadn't joined the fight. He'd gone back to where they'd first seen him, hands extended, trying to magically blast through the guard stone.

Only this time, the magic was working.

Nadeem swallowed down her bile when she realized that Marius was *using* the deaths of his soldiers to power his magic.

Black clouds rose from the fallen men, wafting toward Marius, making his mage light stronger.

Who used the dead to make themselves stronger? Nadeem had never heard of that type of magician before.

Then she shivered, realizing that *this* was the power of the emperor. This was why the kingdom of Tanesh had constant wars.

The emperor needed to feed off them.

By loosening the desert heart and that gibbering blackness on the world, the emperor would become the strongest being on earth.

He would become a god. Possibly, the only one remaining.

Trulliç called up mighty winds, trying to disrupt the flow of power from the dead soldiers to Marius, but the magical draw was too strong. A physical wind couldn't stop the energy Marius drew from the soldiers.

Riyune raced around, looking possessed, leaping up in the air and trying to bite the black clouds. His mouth grew bloody, as if he was biting glass.

Nadeem couldn't see any way to disturb the streams of magic flowing to Marius. The emperor's mark in the guard stone glowed with a sickly yellow.

All she could do would be to stop him.

She drew her first knife and threw it directly at the center of Marius's unprotected neck. The armor dipped there, probably to help cool the soldiers off.

Barzhat still guided her hand.

The knife sunk into Marius's skin. He gave a terrified wail as he dropped down. The magic he'd been channeling blew him to pieces with a loud splat.

Nadeem hurried over to where Marius had been standing, avoiding the large gory mess that covered the ground.

The guard stone still stood. But it trembled mightily.

The heart of the rock had been cut out. Darkness loomed just on the other side.

It was only a matter of time before it broke and the world was consumed by nightmares.

N adeem dropped another rock in front of the cavern door. She and Trulliç attempted to reinforce the guard stone.

Their pitifully small pile of rocks wouldn't impede anything, however. This place didn't accept *change*. It wouldn't have surprised Nadeem if after another night of streaming stars, all the grudging rocks that they'd moved would have gone back to their original places.

Trulliç couldn't raise another guard stone in front of the one standing. No rocks could be called out of the ash here. He called rocks from the desert that surrounded them, but they came unwillingly into this place.

They had to do something. Cracks now ran from top to bottom of the guard stone. Something on the inside of the cavern wanted out.

Now.

"I don't think this is working," Nadeem told Trulliç as he struggled to lift a great boulder with his magic.

He sighed, dropping the stone to the ground with a soft *whump*. "I agree," he said. "Do you have any other ideas?"

Nadeem looked at him. Then back at the guard stone. "You said you'd enclosed the emperor's walking stick in glass," she said slowly.

Trulliç nodded. "I'm not sure how long it will last. That stick is… slippery. But it will hold for a while."

"You could try encasing the guard stone in glass," Nadeem said.

"That might work!" Trulliç said excitedly. "I'll start with a thinner coating of glass, then build it up."

Even if that didn't work long term, it would at least give them some time before darkness fell and the stone broke.

Trulliç stood before the door. Nadeem shivered when she realized that he'd adopted the same stance as Marius had.

Ash and sand swirled up, dancing in front of the stone. It wouldn't be a clear glass, she knew.

After a moment, the sand fell back. Trulliç stood, panting, as if he'd just run a mile or more.

"Let me try again," he said. This time, held his glass horseshoe in one hand, pointing the ends of it at the guard stone.

The sands and ash swirled up again. Heat also blasted forth.

"Careful!" Nadeem warned. She didn't want him to break the guard stone with his magic.

Trulliç merely grunted. The heat didn't lessen. However, he did take a step backwards, bringing the heat with him.

Light sprang up, bright enough to make Nadeem's eyes start watering. She blinked, looked away, then forced herself to keep watching, even if it was out of the corner of her eye.

A great glass wall formed. Swirls of ash ran through it, like long lines of dripping mud.

Nadeem caught her breath. Would it hold?

Slowly, the glass encased the guard stone. It was easily as thick as her arm, obscuring the gray stone behind it.

When Trulliç stepped back, Nadeem drew a breath of relief. The stone would hold.

A booming *crack* rang out.

The glass shattered, falling to pieces at the foot of the guard stone.

The rock bulged ominously.

They were running out of time.

"How did Forit bind the darkness?" Nadeem asked Trulliç as they stood in front of the ruins of their attempts.

The bodies behind them stank, putrefying in the dim light. Night would fall soon.

And so would the rest of the world.

"She sang such a sweet song that she coaxed the darkness to expose its heart," Trulliç replied, as if reciting a lesson. "But the only way to entice the heart of the darkness was to use her own. Innis didn't realize that he was killing his wife when he stabbed the darkness."

Nadeem nodded. "Sacrifice," she said solemnly.

That was what a blood oath really represented. The sacrifice one was willing to make.

"Blood and death broke the guard stone," Nadeem announced, standing up and walking closer to it. "Only blood and death will heal it."

Trulliç looked pale under his tanned skin. "Yours?" he asked. His voice squeaked.

"You need to go back and fight the emperor," Nadeem told him firmly. "I can't do that. I can only stop him, here." As she had sworn to do. He would never get through the guard of her heart.

"I can't," Trulliç said. He rose finally and came over to her. "I just…Why?" He trembled where he stood, looking as though a strong wind would knock him over.

Nadeem took out her sacrificial knife, the one that she's used to swear a blood oath to Trulliç. "If you don't do it, I'll do it myself," she promised him.

This close to the guard stone, she felt the darkness clawing at her back. It welcomed her death and wanted to consume her.

She could not allow that to happen.

She would stand guard here instead, until the end of days.

"The only way to keep the guard stone alive is to renew it," she said. She sounded more sure of herself than she felt. "It needs another sacrifice."

Trulliç swallowed, still bothered. "Can't it be someone else?" he whispered.

She looked into his haunted eyes. Trulliç had killed before. Hell, he'd even twisted the necks of more than one of the soldiers with his winds, ending their days.

"You have a good heart," Nadeem said deliberately.

Trulliç flinched.

"Now you must be strong enough to do what needs to be done," she said. She held the knife out to him, pleased that her own hand didn't shake.

"No," Trulliç whispered. He stared at the knife in horror.

When he looked up, tears streamed down his face. "Don't make me do this."

"Then I will do it myself," Nadeem said, reaching for the blade.

Trulliç snatched his hand away surprisingly fast. "I don't want to sacrifice you," he said, looking away, as if afraid to show her too much by looking at her.

"It's the only way to save the world," Nadeem assured him.

She knew she was right. Felt it like the goddess's embrace, deep in her bones. There was no going back for her. Only forward, into the sands.

She wrapped both her hands around his, the one holding the knife. Then she brought the blade forward so it kissed her breast.

"It's sharp enough to go straight in," she told him. "It won't take much effort at all."

Trulliç gave her a crooked grin. "That's what you think," he said. His eyes bored into hers. He cared for her. More than she'd realized.

More than they could ever explore.

"I'll say hello to the goddess for you," Nadeem said. "Make sure your own weights aren't too heavy."

The stone behind her gave a resounding crack.

"Now!" Nadeem ordered Trulliç. She tried to force his hand holding the knife closer, the tip of the blade breaking her skin.

"No!" Trulliç wailed. He began to press the blade in.

A white whirl snatched Trulliç's hand away.

Riyune held the blade in his mouth.

Then he tossed it into the air, like he frequently tossed mice up, by their tails, to swallow them whole for his dinner.

Only the blade struck his open mouth, ramming down the back of his throat, the tip shoving its way through the fur of his neck.

Nadeem shook, horrified.

Why had Riyune sacrificed himself that way?

She felt bad that her next thought was: Would it work?

Trulliç raced over and knelt down next to his fallen companion. Tears streamed down his face. "Why?" he asked, sounding heartbroken.

Nadeem shook her head. She didn't know.

The dog was already dead by the time she drew closer.

The guard stone shook. The foul scent of darkness wafted out, smelling like rotting reeds and long forgotten pain.

Nadeem helped Trulliç lift Riyune's lifeless body. The knife fell to the ground with a startling clang as it hit the rocks.

Nadeem let it lay where it fell.

They carried the dog's body to the guard stone, lifting it up, placing it over where Marius had carved the emperor's mark.

As they pressed Riyune against the rock, his body dissolved *into* the stone.

Nadeem kept pushing. She felt like a baker, kneading a stiff dough, trying to force it into an unfamiliar shape.

When they stepped back, the guard stone stood firm. Trickles of Riyune's blood flowed out from where the door had been wounded. The shape his body formed wasn't a dog's body, but it wasn't a snake's scale either. It looked more like a cloud waiting patiently for more to gather so it could bring the rain.

The sky above them suddenly cleared. Evening had gathered, with brilliant oranges and purples to the west, over the shank of the spear. Stars appeared. They danced in the darkening heavens before they started flowing.

Away from this place. Back the way Nadeem and Trulliç had first come.

They could go back now. The desert heart was safe again. Not only was the guard stone safe, it had its own guard dog now.

EPILOGUE

TRULLIÇ

TRULLIÇ LAY UNSLEEPING IN THE cool cavern. He had no idea how long he and Nadeem had walked across the desert, the stars showing them the way, the sand and the winds blowing them along. It hadn't felt as though it had taken as long, though.

Was this place another incarnation of the cavern that held the desert heart? Or was it one and the same place? Had it felt Forit's great need and sacrificed part of itself to her?

Trulliç truly didn't know. He suspected none of the great poems or stories even hinted at such a thing.

Nadeem lay on the shelf above him. They hadn't talked much during their walk. He wasn't sure what to say.

How did he feel about her? He wasn't sure if it was love. The great sage Borceli had declared love would lift his heart like a feather and swirl it on the winds. But that wasn't quite how he felt.

Instead, it was more like she was a part of his heart, like the desert and the night winds. That killing her would have broken him completely.

Or maybe he was already broken. Because he would have killed her if that had meant saving the world.

If he'd had to kill her, he also knew that after he'd dealt with the emperor, he would have joined her in Barzhat's golden court. There would have been nothing left for him to live for.

Not even the desert winds.

Why had Riyune sacrificed himself? Was it so that Trulliç wouldn't have to kill Nadeem? That didn't make sense. Trulliç didn't think that Riyune liked Nadeem all that much.

Nadeem had seen too much of Riyune's true nature, Trulliç felt certain.

He sighed and tried to make himself more comfortable on the cold stone shelf. The small creek beside him burbled now and again. Outside, he knew the stars still raced across the sky, heedless of what went on below.

A soft sound made Trulliç stiffen. He looked over toward the guard stone.

A white shape nosed its way into the small cavern.

Trulliç gasped.

He heard Nadeem gasp as well, obviously awake.

It looked like Riyune. It had that same white and black-spotted fur, the long snout and thin tail.

He could also see *through* the figure, to the bones.

Riyune had returned as a ghost.

The dog didn't appear to notice the difference. He turned three times on the far side of the stream, as if smoothing the ground for his bed. He flopped down, resting his muzzle on his paws. He gave a great yawn, then closed his eyes.

Trulliç could still see *through* the dog. He was but wasn't there.

When Trulliç looked up, he saw Nadeem's head poking over her sleeping shelf. Her huge eyes held questions he couldn't answer. He merely shrugged.

Would the dog still be there in the morning? Would he be a real dog by then?

What was Riyune? What had happened out there on the desert plain?

And what would the emperor do now?

For now, Trulliç could only sleep and hope his dreams held at least some of the answers he needed.

THE GHOST DOG

CHAPTER ONE

TRULLIÇ

TRULLIÇ DREAMED OF THE OLD kings. He traveled east across the desert, toward the grand city of Osmerli, the capital of the old kings that the emperor had destroyed over two hundred years before. Hayalevi, the new city that Trulliç had raised, now stood in its place.

Thick walls surrounded Osmerli, eighteen feet tall and three feet wide, made of cold gray granite quarried from the mountains south of the city. Banners flew over the western city-gate entrance. Trulliç's banners were similar: gold and green stripes against an off-white background. He'd deliberately made his different, however, by adding a black horseshoe to the center, to represent the glass horseshoe that had been created at his birth.

However, in the dream, while his banner flew next to the ones of the old kings, the edges of his were tattered and the horseshoe in the center looked like a broken circle, while the banners of the kings appeared brand new.

The buildings were similar between the two cities: beautiful walls built out of rust-colored stone. Thick, too, in order to keep out the desert heat or hold in the warmth of a winter fire. Fine lattice work and glass covered the windows. Embroidered gold and green blankets hung in front of the open doorways, every traveler a welcome guest.

Trulliç whirled around the city like a dust devil, visiting each temple. The buildings were in the same places as the ones he'd raised, though in Osmerli they were much grander.

The first was the temple dedicated to the goddess Onnet and had not one but two side courts for dancers and performers. Fine white sand covered the circular performance space, and bleachers carved out of yellow stone surrounded the courts, each able to hold over one hundred people. Though neither court was full at the time, Trulliç still felt a pang of jealousy knowing that his small temple had yet to draw so many followers.

The market square was bursting with merchants selling exotic wares, like carved wood from the land of the Uluborlu far to the east, dried grapes from the kingdom of Lydae to the north, the finest salt from the coastal regions, as well as tapestries, well-made leather goods, finely spun wool, and more. Additional caravans entered the city hourly, their camels piled high with goods, the sheep and goats they drove of the highest quality.

Trulliç knew he just had to be patient. People would come to his city. It would swell with their stories and songs.

He didn't have time, though. Not before the emperor attacked.

But the dream continued, taking him by the cool temple of goddess Enkat who brought the rains, then out to where Xannil greeted the dawn, then circled back to the dark spot where Forit's temple stood.

A simple red ribbon was strung across the entrance to Forit's temple. Strong magic pushed everyone away from the spot. Still, wilted flowers lay at center of the opening, placed there by couples long separated as well as lovers with broken hearts.

Then Trulliç spun outward to the colorful blue and black temple of the goddess Barzhat who welcomed and judged those who died. A group of star sisters—female illusionists—were camped there, a *kabil* traveling on their way to the *panayirat*, the annual celebration and meeting of the seven star sister tribes. They practiced throwing knives at man-shaped targets, dummies stuffed with straw. Trulliç didn't look closely enough to see the faces they'd painted on their targets, too afraid that he might see his own there.

Finally, he traveled inward toward the heart of the city. The smaller temple of Serrat/Serril stood guard there, the two-faced god who inhabited the desert and desolate places, both black and white, the trickster who'd brought magic to mankind.

But the temple was dwarfed by the palace of the kings. While in Hayalevi, Trulliç's tower was easily the biggest building, here in the city of the old kings, it was only the size of *one* of the palace's towers, and there were six of them, three along each side of the palace walls. In between the towers stood huge buildings, gardens, stables, fountains, trees—like a mini-city within the greater city.

Trulliç wondered if he should build a palace just as fine one day. However, he was the only desert magician. Maybe he needed merely a single tower.

Had there been six kings? One for each tower? He couldn't recall any poems that listed their names or how many kings there had been. The history, what little there was of it, merely mentioned that there had been more than one.

All the books about the old kings had been lost when the emperor had destroyed the city, killing the kings and their descendants.

Something tugged Trulliç to the right, as though the dream was responding to his thoughts. Maybe he was missing a truth about the dead kings.

Trulliç gasped as he came around the edge of the building.

Grand steps made out of red tile with geometric designs, diamonds and circles, embossed on the front led up to the entrance of the tower. Long platforms jutted out from the building on either side of the steps.

Trulliç willed himself to slow, then finally stop, so he could examine the statues.

A huge dog carved out of stone lay on each platform. Each of the dogs was about the length of three men and the height of two. Each dog's front paws were stretched out in front of it with the hind legs curled at the back, the head upright, the tops of the floppy ears raised, as if listening.

These didn't appear to be just any kind of dog. No, these looked like blood hounds, the beasts conjured by the emperor to escort a pregnant woman who carried a babe of power. They were carved out of cool, white marble, struck through with black.

Trulliç had the uncomfortable feeling that the statues watched him and had judged him unfit to enter.

A rumbling growl erupted as soon as Trulliç set one foot on the stairs. Stubbornly, he brought up his other foot, climbing, daring the dogs to do their worst.

Trulliç shook as the statues began to move, the rock grinding against itself. The noise set his teeth on edge. He took another step, determined to go meet the kings of old, though the stairs now seemed endless, the steps rising forever up to the sky. The smell of the ancient desert, those parts rarely seen by man, washed over him, full of dry baked sand and bleached bones.

One of the marble blood hounds jumped down onto the steps in front of Trulliç. The ground shook under Trulliç's feet. He stopped, startled, his heart pounding.

However, the statue was no longer huge—instead, it had shrunk down to the size of a single man. It shook itself, looking remarkably like a dog shaking sand from its fur, then it started to rise up on its hind legs.

Trulliç gasped. The form of the dog elongated. What was it changing into?

Fog suddenly poured in, hiding the living statue. Trulliç felt himself yanked backwards, traveling rapidly out of the city and over the sands, only to be dumped onto the hard ground, waking with a start.

Trulliç gasped, finding it hard to catch his breath. Fear and horror gibbered in his mind. He shook his head and made himself sit up.

He was still in his tower, the one he'd raised in Hayalevi. The coolness of the night would be stolen by the heat of the day soon, the sky beyond his window already lightening. His room stood mostly empty: a simple chest in the corner to hold his few belongings, a wooden bookshelf that was already collecting ancient books of poetry he'd found at the market, the straw-stuffed pallet he slept on with his sandals beside it. In the corner, the snake-headed staff made by the emperor glowered behind its thick case of glass.

Try as he might, Trulliç couldn't remember the poem that had mentioned how the old kings had once worshipped dogs. He knew there had to be one, as he had such a clear memory of it.

If Trulliç hadn't killed Atça, his old mentor, Trulliç could have asked him. Atça probably would have remembered as he had a much better mind for that sort of thing than Trulliç. He'd also studied for decades more than Trulliç had.

Riyune stirred against Trulliç's leg.

Trulliç glanced down. He couldn't help but shiver again when he realized just how much the coloring of the stone dogs matched the one laying against his leg.

Once Trulliç and Nadeem had left the cavern in the middle of the desert, Riyune had turned back into a dog, no longer just a ghostly shape with the bones showing, a figure they could see through.

Riyune only appeared to be dead in the land of myths.

However, even in the midday sun, Riyune cast a light shadow, as if he were no longer solid. In addition, Riyune had stopped eating and drinking. He still did normal dog things like sit on his butt to scratch at his neck with his hind legs, and he always circled three times before he laid down, as if flattening the area before he slept.

In the dim light of the morning, Trulliç saw Riyune raise his head and stare over his shoulder. Then the dog nodded once, as if saying, *Yes.*

It brought Trulliç back to his original question.

Had the kings of old merely worshiped dogs who happened to resemble blood hounds?

Or did the old kings have the ability to transform into the shape of a dog?

Before the dream had been snatched away, had that been what the figure in front of Trulliç had been changing into? Going from dog to king?

<hr>

It had been two weeks since Trulliç had stopped Marius in the myth lands, two weeks since Riyune had sacrificed himself to close the guard stone only to return as an almost normal dog. Well, what went for normal when it came to Riyune.

Two weeks since Nadeem had stepped up to the brink of death, welcoming it the same way that the star sisters welcomed the goddess Barzhat, with open arms and love.

Two weeks since Trulliç had realized that he had feelings for the former star sister. Feelings that still confused him.

Feelings that he was certain Nadeem didn't return.

But then again, Nadeem hadn't fully returned to the land of the living, either. She remained distant, as if she'd been encased in cool glass, always looking out but not really there anymore.

That morning, Trulliç found Nadeem in the back kitchen with Myrizhah—his mother—and Seydat—his secretary, for want of a better term, the young woman who kept him organized. The three women worked in a comfortable silence, not bothering each other with questions or inane commentary.

Trulliç had recently realized that everyone in Hayalevi had grown more quiet since coming to his city. It wasn't a somberness that infected his people, but rather the peace of the desert.

The kitchen was much larger than a single family's hearth. It had a large handpump in the far corner for bringing water up into a basin, two iron stoves for cooking, as well as a large fireplace for roasting.

Nadeem stood next to one of the stoves. She broke a piece of dough off the mound in front of her, flattened the piece between her hands, then threw it into a sizzling pan, grilling the flatbread they'd serve that day, both for themselves and to any guests who arrived.

Trulliç levitated a warm piece of flatbread from the pile that Nadeem had finished cooking just before she flopped down the most recently finished piece.

"Hey!" she said. She made to snatch at the piece of bread still floating in midair, then turned to glare at Trulliç. "You could wait until I was finished."

"Where's the fun in that?" Trulliç asked, teasing.

He was aware of the sad look Myrizhah shot him. She knew too much of her son's soft heart and could probably guess the extent of his feelings for Nadeem. As well as the state of Nadeem's hard heart.

Nadeem's glare softened and she rolled her eyes at him before returning to her task. She wore an outfit more like Myrizhah's and Seydat's than like a star sister: a bluish-white blousy shirt the color of a hazy sky under a green-and-white striped sleeveless tunic that fell to her knees. Unlike the other women, though, Nadeem wore tight black pants made of some sort of stretchy fabric that gave Trulliç far too many ideas about all the muscles in Nadeem's legs.

Though Nadeem was no longer a star sister, she still wore a wide brown leather belt that held mysterious pouches and the traditional three knives. He was certain that she had other weapons hidden on her body. She'd cropped her dark brown hair even shorter than usual, almost as shorn as a spring sheep. Though he couldn't fault her for it. Generally only married women wore their hair long. Both his mother and Seydat wore their hair down past their shoulders, held back by a *chafiyek*, a square scarf that was worn over the crown of the head but could also be rewrapped over the face and mouth to protect a person from sand and sun.

"Any word yet?" Myrizhah asked, as she did every morning, looking up from the other stove where she was standing. Seydat walked over to the corner and poured fresh water from the basin there into the bowl she was mixing. Trulliç knew that despite how she kept working, she was completely focused on the conversation.

Trulliç sighed and replied to his mother. "None of the caravans have any news of the emperor or troop movements," he said.

"They're coming," Nadeem told him.

"I know that," Trulliç said. He took a deep breath, trying to control his ready rage. He'd made some progress over the last couple of weeks, but he knew he was missing something, a crucial step to help him get over his anger so it wouldn't get the best of him during the middle of a battle.

Trulliç watched his mother stir a pot that contained a thick chicken soup flavored with mint and oregano that would be served to any guests who came that day.

He knew she wasn't to blame for how Atça had treated him. How could she have known? How could anyone other than another magician have understood just how poorly Atça was training Trulliç?

Only someone with power would have realized how Atça's lies were twisting Trulliç and his abilities.

Myrizhah had done her best, carrying a newly born babe from the northern part of the Kingdom of Lydae where he'd been born all the way back south, through the entire Tanesh Empire, home to Gaadiwala, the village on the edge of the Qaenev desert. The trip had taken her years, and Trulliç had been able to walk as well as talk by the time they'd arrived.

Though Myrizhah rarely spoke of her journey now, he remembered her telling travelers about it at the Horseshoe Tavern that his uncle owned. He knew that she'd edited the tale, only reciting the good parts.

Not the parts that Trulliç remembered: the endless walking, how starved they'd both been at least half the time, how desperately hot and cold it had grown on the road.

No, his mother had done everything she possibly could have to give Trulliç the chance for a good life. She'd come to the desert, gotten Atça to mentor him, raised the money for Trulliç to go to school instead of working like his cousins.

A fine strand of hair slipped out of Myrizhah's *chafiyek*. Shock rocked through Trulliç's body when her realized just how gray his mother had grown. He swallowed against an uncomfortably dry throat.

His mother had always seemed undefeatable to him, a desert rock that withstood torrential spring rains, punishing summer suns, as well as roaring winter storms.

As she pushed her hair back, she seemed to feel his eyes on her. She turned to look at him, the question in her eyes clear. Did he need something from her? Anything? Everything?

She was always willing to do whatever she could to help him. Which included smacking him when he most deserved it.

He smiled at her, feeling something loosen in his chest, a band across his heart that he hadn't realized had been there.

Then he shook his head. No, he didn't need anything more from her.

She'd done her best by him. She'd always done her best.

And he could forgive her for Atça.

***

Trulliç traveled to the northernmost part of the Qaenev desert later that morning. Riyune raced at his side, able to keep up despite how Trulliç just *flew* across the sands.

The old Riyune wouldn't have been able to move at such speeds. Admittedly, the dog had never been normal, but since dying in the myth lands, he was even less so now.

Trulliç helped Nadeem as they traveled, loaning her more fleet feet so she could race beside him. She didn't enjoy being carried at great speed, but she accepted his help while she mostly moved on her own.

The pair of them were visiting a village up here to see if any of the caravans that had come from the north during the last couple of weeks could report on the emperor's troop movements.

Trulliç knew that the emperor was coming. He'd bring a grand army with him, intent on destroying Hayalevi and killing Trulliç. The emperor had already sent his guard, trying to free the desert heart from the myth lands so that the emperor might become a god.

He would usurp the goddess Barzhat. All death would feed him. He'd sup on the souls of those who died, possibly killing them forever.

Barzhat merely judged those who died, giving each a vest with teardrop-shaped weights on it, the weights representing the bad things that a person had done while they were living. Then the person had to dance in the golden court of Barzhat until all the weights fell off and the soul could be reborn.

Trulliç had to stop the emperor. He'd sworn a blood oath to protect the land.

He still didn't know how.

Finding out how many troops the emperor intended to bring to the desert at least felt as though he was doing *something*. Discovering which direction the emperor was intending to come on his invasion also seemed to be right.

However, Trulliç had never fought a great battle or commanded troops. He'd read a lot of poems and stories about such battles, but he didn't have any experience. Hell, he didn't even really have *guards*. His magic was enough to defend him in the desert.

Trulliç had to stop the emperor and his bid to become a god as well as to destroy Hayalevi. Somehow. Hopefully without killing anyone, because the emperor would only grow stronger with each death.

The town of Egreliki was inland from the sea but along the main trade routes. The garrison that the emperor had sent two weeks before wouldn't have passed through the town, as it was south of where they'd first entered the desert. It lay ensconced in the Yerminil peaks, foothills in front of the town protecting it from the desert, while close enough to the Higli mountains to catch the rainfall that came over the mountains.

The town itself had been built close to an oasis, so many of the buildings were actually made of wood, a rarity for desert towns. The normal red brick had been whitewashed, making Egreliki shine in the morning sunlight.

It made Trulliç proud that he had such a beautiful town in his land. He was glad he wore a more formal tunic, striped in gold and green, along with brown pants that Myrizhah had insisted he change into (since they were clean) as well as a new, off-white muslin shirt, and his sturdy leather sandals.

They touched down just at the edge of town, at the base of the foothills where the land gave way to proper desert. Trulliç wasn't certain why Egreliki was part of his territory, as the heart of the town didn't sit in the desert, but he had no doubt that it was, indeed, his.

He pushed his power down deep under the ground, seeking water and wealth as Nadeem and Riyune waited beside him.

Ah. That was why this town was also his. The water that kept it alive originated in an aquifer that had its toes in the desert. The water rights were his, which meant the town was as well.

Water meant life. Trulliç had always known that. He shook his head as he felt his emotions grow heated.

Atça had been planning on bankrupting the poorer parts of Gaadiwala, in particular where Trulliç's family lived, just so the magician could make himself more rich.

Trulliç ground his teeth, remembering how ineffective he'd been at stopping the magician at first. How he'd gotten lost under the ground because Atça hadn't given him the right training. How Atça had lied to him all those years.

Nadeem laid a hand on Trulliç's arm, bringing him back to the surface. He threw a grateful smile at her, though shame and fear swam in his belly. He couldn't afford to get lost like that!

Atça was dead. Trulliç had killed his former mentor.

But Atça's death still hadn't been enough. Would never be enough.

Trulliç couldn't do anything about that now, though. Instead, he pasted a smile on his face to greet the small group of people coming down the main path away from the town and out toward the desert. He needed to at least play the part of a great magician and not a trapped, angry boy.

"Greetings!" called a fair voice.

Trulliç blinked, surprised. He'd assumed the mayor or other official would be there. Not a woman.

Then again, she had the short hair of someone unmarried. Maybe she worked for the mayor? She wore pants like a man, though the color of burnt orange and very baggy. Her blouse was the color of the finest desert sand, golden and rich, while her sleeveless tunic was forest green with stripes of much lighter greens running down it. Her *chafiyek* was also striped, yellow, red, and orange.

The people behind her were just as colorfully dressed. He knew instinctively that they'd stand out like spring flowers against the white walls of the town. They had the dark skin of the desert people, with dark eyes and hair.

"I am Zehra," the woman said as she led the group forward. "I am the mayor of Egreliki. Welcome to our town! We are happy that you decided to honor us this morning."

Trulliç blinked, surprised. A woman mayor? He glanced for a moment at Nadeem. Well, why not? His mother was certainly capable of running not only a tavern but an entire city. If she'd stayed in Gaadiwala, she could have easily been in charge of the entire village after Atça had died.

If the men would have let her.

"I am Trulliç," he said belatedly, bowing his head.

Zehra gave him a knowing smile, as if she realized where his thoughts had gone. She was probably used to such judgments by men.

"This is Nadeem, a traveler, and my best friend," Trulliç continued, indicating the woman standing on his right.

She raised her chin and turned her head slightly, so that at least some of the people gathered saw her mangled cheek where a star sister was usually marked with a star cut into their flesh.

He didn't bother introducing Riyune, though Zehra did give the dog a questioning glance.

"What can I do for the desert magician?" Zehra asked. "Besides provide him with the best hospitality that a town can offer?"

Trulliç smiled. It was a bit forward of her to ask what he needed before offering him hospitality. Then again, that seemed to be her nature.

"I need to talk with any caravans that have recently arrived. Particularly from the north," Trulliç said.

Zehra nodded, her face suddenly serious. "It's the emperor, isn't it?" she asked quietly. "He's coming. With troops."

"How do you know?" Trulliç said, surprised. Most of the towns people he'd talked with, as well as the caravans, had no idea.

The people in Hayalevi knew, though. They shared Trulliç's dreams and fears too often.

Zehra frowned. "I felt you coming to our town," she said. "So I knew to be here to greet you. I've dreamed of the great battle you had with the emperor's guards." She threw a glance at Riyune. "Of your sacrifices." She took a deep breath, then looked at him with unguarded eyes. "All the sacrifices we're going to have to make."

Trulliç blinked. This woman had no magic. She wasn't a star sister. She didn't have power on her own.

But she seemed more sensitive than most, and the tragedy her eyes held tore at Trulliç's heart.

"I'm sorry," he whispered, though he didn't understand the details. Just that the town would be engulfed by the guards, possibly destroyed.

Zehra shrugged. "I'm not afraid to dance in Barzhat's golden court.

My life has been short but sweet, and I've tried to do the right thing. But my people…" Her voice trailed off in sadness.

"If I brought them to Hayalevi, would they be safer?" Trulliç asked.

Zehra shook her head. "Most won't leave. This is their town, where their roots are strongest. And many more would stay just to fight."

Trulliç shivered, knowing that the woman spoke the truth. He could feel the wave of support for him, the desert magician, swelling.

"How long do we have?" Trulliç asked. Maybe he could get more men here. Or raise guards. Or maybe walls around the city. Something, anything, to protect his people.

"Three days," Zehra proclaimed, easily pronouncing his doom. "The emperor will wash against your shores in three days."

Trulliç stood stoically still, not letting himself gasp, though her words felt like a solid blow.

Three days? How could he get ready? He didn't even know what he needed to do in order to be ready. He found himself panting, his heart beating rapidly.

Then he paused, making himself take a deep breath, peering curiously at Zehra. *Wash against your shores.* What an odd way to talk about a desert state.

"I will do everything in my power to be ready," Trulliç said solemnly when he realized that she was waiting for him to say something. He couldn't promise more than that. He still didn't know what he was going to do.

"Thank you," Zehra said. "Now, I have a boon to ask of you."

"If it's in my power to grant, it's yours," Trulliç said. He couldn't deny his people anything.

"Give me this hour to enjoy the hospitality of my town," Zehra said. "Nothing more."

"Gladly," Trulliç said, though as they started walking back up the hill leading from the desert to the town, he realized that he'd been lying.

He felt a pressing need to get back to Hayalevi. Raise walls, defenses all the way around the entire border of the desert. Do something, *anything*, other than to sit with strangers and drink tea and eat flatbread slathered in lard.

But he smiled the entire time he was there, chatting easily with everyone, telling of Hayalevi, the secret places of the desert, what it felt like to travel so fast over the land, how he'd originally stopped the emperor's garrison with glass balls that rose out of the sand.

About halfway through the meal, Trulliç realized how focused Zehra was on him. She was very attentive, filling his cup, lightly touching his knees when she leaned closer, how she teased him subtly.

It finally occurred to him that she might want to bed him. He flushed at the thought. She smiled at him and touched his leg again.

If the circumstances had been different, he might have accepted. But Nadeem sat on his other side, a distant presence that still felt as solid as a mountain. Not that he'd made any offer to Nadeem. He was too afraid she'd reject him. And then where would they stand?

Plus, the emperor was coming. Trulliç didn't have a night to spend with Zehra, even in pleasure.

Three days was all he had.

He had to make the most of it.

CHAPTER TWO

NADEEM

NADEEM SAT IN SILENCE, WATCHING Zehra and her party at a distance.

The breach felt impossible to cross. It was only a few feet of sand, but Nadeem knew if she tried, the distance would grow longer and longer with each step.

Zehra wanted so badly to sleep with Trulliç. And maybe that would be the best thing for the boy, to get more of his emotions out of the way, give him some release.

It wasn't as if Nadeem had given him any encouragement or even hope of a relationship in the future. She couldn't promise him a future. In fact, she was pretty sure that death had just been postponed. She'd be back, ready for Barzhat's embrace, in three days' time.

It didn't make sense to her to fight her way back to life. Not when the emperor was coming. Not when an untrained boy was supposed to be leading the battle. Not when the myth lands still called to her in her dreams every night, clamoring for her soul.

Riyune lay just behind Trulliç, as still as a statue. Trulliç had told Nadeem of his dream the night before. She could easily imagine a carved figure laying in the same position as Riyune did, guarding the steps of the towers of the old kings.

As if hearing her thoughts, Riyune slowly turned a stoic face toward her. Then he deliberately cocked his head to the side, looking for all the world like merely a puzzled dog.

Nadeem laughed once, briefly. The man sitting beside her—Ebrhard? Ecklin? E-something—shot her a quizzical look.

Nadeem just shook her head, keeping her commentary to herself.

Riyune had his own secrets. Just as she had hers. Though the laughter had felt good…

Nadeem shivered and pulled herself back.

No.

She would stay separate. Apart. Until the world ended.

In just three days' time.

All the journey back to Hayalevi, Nadeem thought about teasing Trulliç by imitating Zehra. *Oh, Trulliç, how strong you are! How wonderful your magic is!*

But that would mean stepping across the gulf, interacting with Trulliç more than Nadeem felt comfortable with.

They'd told Myrizhah and Seydat about Zehra's dreams of the emperor arriving in three days. The other women grimly nodded.

"Should we prepare for siege?" Myrizhah asked, breaking the deadly quiet that had consumed them all.

"That would mean raising walls all the way around the city," Trulliç said. "Osmerli had a great wall, and it didn't save them. Plus six kings."

"I could go to the Kardeş oasis and ask the star sisters for help," Nadeem offered to Trulliç. "I don't know if any will come. They are dedicated to the emperor. They might try to kill me. But some—some will come with me."

The thinkers would follow her, not the fanatics. Plus, the star sisters were desert creatures, like Nadeem, like Trulliç. Their loyalties would be divided.

Every time Nadeem had made the offer to go recruit the star sisters over the last couple of weeks, Trulliç had declined. He didn't want the star sisters here. They weren't truly his people, at least not all of them.

Now as the time for the battles drew near, he finally acquiesced. "Bring them," he said. "Those who would be loyal to me. Who wouldn't betray me to the emperor."

"The number is likely to be small," Nadeem warned.

Trulliç gave a bitter laugh. "It will be worthy of a song," he told her. "If any remain to sing it."

Nadeem nodded. Trulliç was right. They were always going to be outnumbered. All that remained was that they died in honor.

The gap between them felt a little wider suddenly.

"I will return soon," Nadeem promised.

"Take Riyune with you," Trulliç said.

"What?" Nadeem asked, startled. How could she? It wasn't as if she could tie a leash around the ghost dog. Or even a collar. And it wasn't as if Riyune would willingly travel with her.

Trulliç had turned and addressed the dog directly. "You need to go with Nadeem. Make sure she gets to Kardeş fast and returns even more quickly with whomever will follow her."

Riyune gave a great dog sigh, then cocked his head to one side, as if questioning what Trulliç wanted.

"Protect her," Trulliç added. "Like a blood hound with his charge."

Instead of responding, Riyune stood and stretched like a dog, butt in the air and front paws out, then he stood straight up and shook himself.

He glanced again at Trulliç before walking beside Nadeem, then collapsing beside her with a loud *huff*.

Riyune knew exactly what Trulliç had asked. Nadeem was certain of it. Did he act like such a dog in order to throw the humans off his scent? Or was being a dog his nature as well? Not merely a false disguise he wore?

"Thank you," Nadeem said, first to Riyune than to Trulliç.

She didn't know if she could get anyone other than Aunt Parayat to follow her. But even at her great age, her aunt would be fantastic help.

Even if it meant dying in the process.

Myrizhah packed a simple bag for Nadeem with traveler's food, like the log-shaped rolls made out of cracked wheat, hazelnut pieces, and slivers of dried figs, spiced with mint and nutmeg, all held together with *meslit* syrup, as well as salted meat and more nuts.

The flagon Nadeem carried was small for such a journey. Then again, like Trulliç, Nadeem knew she could always find water in the desert.

She kept on the same outfit she'd been wearing earlier, a more traditional whitish-blue blouse under a gold-and-green striped sleeveless tunic, her wide leather belt with the three knives, but matching it with the black leggings of the star sisters so she could run and fight without hindrance. She wore a black-and-white checked *chafiyek* that she'd wound over her nose and mouth so that it would be easier for her to breathe the desert air as she traveled.

Nadeem and Riyune stood next to Xanil's temple, near the eastern gate of the city. It was only a simple archway, not a formal gate for a walled city. During the past two weeks since they'd come back from the myth lands, caravans had started arriving. They entered the city from the east, as it was only a short distance from the border beyond the desert sands. Plus, the path followed the bubbling Pirazizil river, so they would always have water.

The western gate was far less frequented, as the travel to there from the lands outside the desert would take more than a week's time. In addition, while a string of oasis lay along the trail, water wasn't always guaranteed, particularly during the summer months.

"Ready?" Nadeem asked, glancing down at the dog sitting beside her.

He looked up at her, his bright pink tongue lolling to one side.

Nadeem rolled her eyes at him. It was hard to accept that Riyune was both a dog as well as something else sometimes, particularly when he acted so much like an animal.

"Let's go," Nadeem said.

Nadeem raced out of the eastern gate, Riyune at her side. She felt her feet lift higher, her speed increasing.

So it seemed that the dog had the same ability as Trulliç to grant her speed.

Had he always had this capability? Or had it only developed once the dog had been killed in the myth lands?

Nadeem didn't know or really care. This was a trip for the ages. She wished she could take on her favorite illusion form, that of a great hawk with blue feathers, and fly across the land. She gave a great cawing cry.

The rocks and sand blurred as she speeded along. The wind cut at the wound on her cheek that would never heal. She smelled her own sweat as they curved to the left, cutting up the trail leading to the lands beyond the desert.

Suddenly, Nadeem felt her feet slowing. She tried to push on but was out of breath, as if she struggled against deep sand.

She came to a stop and glared at Riyune. "What is it?" she asked, wary.

Riyune stood like a white marble rock, his gaze fixed on something ahead.

Nadeem squinted her eyes against the bright sunshine. A caravan was making its way down the trail.

She recognized its leader. Levent, the trader that she'd spent a sweet time with, many lifetimes ago.

Her heart lurched and her stomach dropped. Panic washed through her for a brief moment.

She did *not* want to continue her relationship with him. She didn't really even want to see him. He would try to bring her feelings back to the surface, to make her live again.

Then she laughed at herself. Levent couldn't make her do anything she didn't want to do. He'd never had that ability.

Instead, Nadeem raced toward him and the rest of his crew, eager to see him again.

Levent's black hair still curled around his face, giving him a smile younger than his twenty-eight years. His dark eyes were filled with joy looking on Nadeem. His caravan had grown smaller over the time he'd been traveling, probably selling everything he could before making the journey across the desert to Hayalevi, being unsure of water or welcome.

"Greetings, traveler!" Levent called gaily as he easily slid down the side of his great camel. "So good to see you again!" He strode broadly up to Nadeem, his arms held in front of him, his hands open wide.

"Good to see you, too," Nadeem said, clasping wrists with him like the soldiers did.

"I told you I was on my way to see the city of the great desert magician," Levent said with a broad wink. "Not that I was merely hoping to run into you as well."

"Trulliç is here," Nadeem said. She hesitated, then added, "He's preparing for war."

Solemnity took over Levent. A hard edge appeared as well, his jaw tightening, his eyes growing harsh. "I know. I've shared the dreams of the desert magician. I'm here to offer my services."

"Thank you," Nadeem said, relief making her knees weak. "Thank you, thank you, thank you."

"You are most welcome. And where are you off to?" Levent said. He glanced at her, then at Riyune. "Surely this isn't the creature you're riding?"

Nadeem couldn't help but laugh at Riyune's outraged expression. "No, but he does help me fly," she said.

Levent gave her a curious look but she didn't have time for more explanations.

"Go see Trulliç. Tell him that Nadeem sent you. That Nadeem… will vouch for you," she said.

"Are you certain you want to make that claim?" Levent asked. He'd returned to his serious mien again.

"I am," Nadeem said. Whatever else Levent might be carrying, he'd always had a good heart.

"Very well," Levent said. He stood up even straighter, as if a soldier presenting himself for inspection, then he bowed his head to her. "For you, I will offer Trulliç all my services. Including being a former captain in the emperor's army."

Nadeem stiffened. She hadn't realized he had a military background. Except maybe she had known, at some level.

Levent didn't walk. He marched.

"Again, a thousand thanks for your offer," Nadeem said. She pulled one of the smaller obsidian knives from her side. "Trulliç should know you speak the truth, but if he needs convincing, give him this."

Levent took the blade reverently with both hands. "I look forward to returning this to you when next I see you," he said.

Nadeem nodded. She did, but didn't, look forward to their next meeting. While he was a delightful man, charming, intelligent, and inquisitive, he was also a painful reminder of the gap between where Nadeem existed and the life on the other side.

"Riyune!" she called, turning toward the dog.

Riyune gave the equivalent of an eye roll, then stood up from where he'd been sitting at her side. He shook himself, the sand flying from his white fur. Then he snapped his jaws together, as if asking, *Are you finally finished?*

"See you in Hayalevi!" Nadeem called as she started to race away.

She risked a single glance back after just a few moments, when the caravan had already retreated into the far distance. She could just make out Levent staring after her like she was some sort of mythical creature.

And maybe she was. She still hoped that maybe someday someone would sing songs about the great works that the desert magician and the former star sister had done.

But for now, she had to go persuade as many of her sisters as she could to join her and Trulliç and stand against the emperor.

Before it was too late.

Nadeem didn't bother stopping at the border of Kardeş, though she knew she should. She flashed by the guards, both those hidden in the foothills as well as the two obviously standing in her path.

She had to admit she admired the ingenuity of the two main guards, as well as their training. They knew that they'd never be able to catch the wind speeding toward them. Instead, they stood stock still, then abruptly pulled a hidden rope between them, meaning to trip her as she passed.

The rope snapped on impact. Both guards fell back, having leaned too much of their weight on the rope.

Nadeem wanted to tell them that it was all right, she wasn't going to harm the sisters, but she didn't have time. Instead, she continued her racing steps, Riyune a white blur beside her, as she approached Aunt Parayat's small tent. She didn't bother slowing until after she was inside.

The world reeled as Nadeem came to a halt. She'd grown too used to everything moving in a blur. Everything seemed darker as well. The evening had already fallen, and there weren't many lamps lit in the tent.

Aunt Parayat sat on her teacher's cushion, her tea beside her. She seemed startled to see Nadeem. "I'd expected death to come racing toward me that way," Aunt Parayat said dryly. "Not you. At least, I presume you are not death."

Nadeem shrugged. She hoped she wasn't bringing death to the star sisters she recruited, though she knew there was a good chance that she was.

Aunt Parayat didn't rise, but she did hold out her hands in greeting. "It's good to see you," she said warmly. "Please, share what little hospitality I have to offer."

"Thank you," Nadeem said. She looked over her shoulder at Riyune. Since dying in the myth lands, he'd stopped eating or drinking. Had expending so much energy, running himself halfway across the desert while aiding Nadeem's speed, given him an appetite?

The dog gave her a huge yawn, then sat down directly in front of the opening to the tent, obviously content to sit there as the guard.

"That's a strange creature you travel with," Aunt Parayat said, peering intently at Riyune.

Nadeem shook her head. Her aunt didn't know the half of it. "What do you see?" she asked, curious. Aunt Parayat was stronger than most, particularly when it came to seeing through illusions.

"I see—"

One of the guards whom Nadeem had raced by suddenly came into the tent.

Riyune stood and barred the way. For the first time ever, Nadeem heard the dog growl. It was the sound of a deadly predator, much larger than its victim. The noise made the hairs on the back of her neck rise up and set her blood racing.

The dog suddenly grew larger as well. Instead of being the size of a regular dog, its back rising level with Nadeem's knee, now Riyune was the size of a fierce lion, his back level with her waist. And Nadeem wasn't short.

Only the blood hounds had the ability to change size that way.

"Put your weapon away, Mojin," Aunt Parayat directed in a harsh, commanding voice.

Mojin? Nadeem looked at the girl with great curiosity. She'd shared her coming of age ceremony with Mojin, chosen the *ağrikat* mussels deliberately so that as a warrior, Mojin would remain balanced.

Had it worked? What was the girl like now?

Mojin looked startled, but she slowly slipped her knife back into her belt. She wore the traditional all-black outfit of the star sisters, tight fitting so that she could move quickly and fight without impediment.

Only then did Riyune settle down, shaking himself once and shrinking back down to his natural size before laying down and resuming his guard position.

Nadeem noticed that he was still between Mojin and her, that he could still protect the rest of the tent from his position.

"Ma'am," Mojin said. She swallowed hard. "We saw *her* race toward your tent. We got here as quickly as we could."

"You did your duty as well as you were able," Aunt Parayat said. Nadeem could hear the prideful smile in her voice. "You were just faced with something you couldn't have stopped. That no one could have stopped. The desert wind, itself."

Mojin stiffened. "Yes, ma'am," she said. She cast a look at Nadeem, curiosity mingled with fear. "Don't I know you?"

"We were sisters, once," Nadeem admitted. She turned her face so that Mojin could see her mangled cheek.

The heat of Mojin's stare made Nadeem's cheek pulse with pain briefly.

"I see," Mojin said, though it was obvious she didn't understand in the least.

"Guard the entrance to my tent as diligently as your previous post," Aunt Parayat instructed. "See that no one disturb us. Not even another desert wind."

"Yes, ma'am," Mojin said stiffly before turning and marching out the door.

"We don't have much time before the others come and demand answers," Aunt Parayat said. "Mojin is a sweet girl, strong and warm. She will do her duty and turn them away, but they will overwhelm her in the end. What do you need?"

Nadeem's heart gave yet another hard beat in her chest, as if trying to remind her that she was still alive. She stifled her response.

Not now. Not yet. Maybe not ever would it be time for her to fully join the living.

But still, she couldn't help but feel a great rush of gratitude toward her former mentor who didn't ask Nadeem what she wanted, but would happily give her whatever she needed.

"Star sisters," Nadeem said bluntly. "As many as you can recruit. To help defend Hayalevi from the emperor."

"That's a tall order," Aunt Parayat said. "Most are fanatically dedicated to the emperor. They've already received recruitment orders to come and fight for him."

"How many will go and fight with the emperor?" Nadeem asked. Even if none of the star sisters came with her, learning that number may help Trulliç in his fight.

"At least a quarter," Aunt Parayat said.

"Of all the *kabils*?" Nadeem asked, horrified. That would mean thousands of star sisters.

"No, just of Kardeş," Aunt Parayat said.

That still meant hundreds of trained fighters on the side of the emperor.

"Why not all the *kabils*?" Nadeem wondered out loud.

Aunt Parayat snorted. "Because he's as arrogant as any man. He thinks he doesn't need them. He barely put any effort into recruiting the women here."

"Really?" Nadeem asked. It actually made sense that the emperor wasn't afraid of Trulliç. He'd been emperor for at least two centuries and fighting wars for much of that time, while Trulliç was an untrained, untested boy, still.

"He'll pay for his arrogance," Aunt Parayat said darkly.

Arguing voices could be heard just beyond the tent door.

Riyune gave a quiet, warning growl.

"You need to be gone," Aunt Parayat said. "I give you my blessing, but we'd end up spending days arguing with the others if they saw you."

"Meet me on the eastern hill at dawn," Nadeem said. "With all you can persuade."

"I will," Aunt Parayat said. "It won't be many," she warned.

"Every blade will help," Nadeem said, nodding. She'd always known that she wouldn't be able to bring an army of trained fighters with her, though she desperately wished she could.

Aunt Parayat rose gracefully to her feet. "Now, go. I need to deal with these idiots. I will see you at dawn."

Nadeem nodded. "Riyune," she called.

The dog stayed where he was, though he did glance over his shoulder at her, as if asking, *What now?*

"This way," Nadeem said. She picked up an edge of the tent, cleverly hidden by illusion. All who passed thought Aunt Parayat's tent was firmly staked down.

The dog sniffed, then stood and shook himself. He gave Aunt Parayat a doggy grin, showing all his teeth, then moving as fast as a blur, raced out of the tent without looking back.

Nadeem rolled her eyes. "At dawn," she said one last time before she also raced off into the cool night.

***

Patience had never been one of Nadeem's virtues. Still, she waited for the dawn with something akin to it. Riyune napped beside her. Evidently he was similar to Trulliç that way and seemed to be more energized by daylight than by starlight.

Mice quietly rustled in the grass near her feet. Nadeem listened carefully for the cawing of a hawk or the soft hoot of an owl. Those sorts of noises would be out of place at this time of night. Though they might sound natural, the calls would be made by star sisters approaching her, groups signaling their readiness.

Winds carried the smells of Kardeş to Nadeem: the watch fires, the scent of sweet girl sweat, the water from the oasis. Would Riyune catch the scent of any attackers before they appeared out of the darkness? Nadeem wasn't sure.

Her legs ached due to all that she'd asked of them today. She stretched them while she waited, tightening the muscles then releasing them, flexing her toes then making them into fists. She'd drunk all the water she'd brought, knowing that she could easily make a trip to an unguarded part of the oasis if she needed more.

And maybe she should get more before they left at dawn.

How many would her aunt bring? A dozen, perhaps? Or maybe only a handful? Nadeem had no idea.

That the emperor wasn't taking Trulliç as seriously as he should may be in their favor. Perhaps the emperor would overplay his hand or extend himself like a beginning fighter, leaving a vulnerable side unguarded.

Nadeem didn't know. She had battled many times before in small groups. She'd learned at least some strategy when it came to fighting with larger armies, but she had no actual experience either.

She hoped that Trulliç would at least listen to Levent, particularly when the merchant handed over Nadeem's blade. Surely Trulliç wouldn't be a complete idiot about it and wouldn't instantly be jealous of Levent and not want to work with the man.

Nadeem counted heartbeats as the stars moved slowly overhead. She even laid down for a bit, flat on her back so she could see them better. The sand felt cool, welcome against her skin. The pounding in her cheek subsided as if the desert winds were a cool balm. The smell of the nearby *meslit* trees, a sweet spicy smell, washed over her.

Would she be able to rest like this once she was dead? Or would Barzhat cause her to dance forever and ever for breaking a blood oath?

But the oath had been wrong. Nadeem might occasionally have regrets about not fulfilling it, worrying about Trulliç and his anger. However, killing him wouldn't have made anything right.

Would Riyune have stopped her from killing Trulliç? She honestly didn't know.

She'd heard the story of the blood hound who'd created the glass horseshoe that was Trulliç's symbol. Could see it suddenly in her mind's eye—a much younger Myrizhah crying on her birth bed, the hound as large as a small horse beside her, shaking and shaking the tin horseshoe until it changed into glass.

Had there been other babies in the past who'd been promised as the desert magician? Had none of them gotten as far as Trulliç and actually claimed their territory?

Nadeem had the impression there had been. Other babes who hadn't been protected, who'd stayed in one place too long until the emperor came after them. Or the ones who'd been lost the first time they'd stepped into the desert, overwhelmed by the enormity of their land.

Nadeem sat up with a start. Had she been dreaming? What strange questions went chasing through her head, what odd visions.

She suddenly realized her right hand was warm, warmer than it should be. She curled her fingers slightly.

Warm fur slid across her skin.

With horror, Nadeem slowly turned her head.

Riyune now lay against her leg, as she'd seen him do often with Trulliç. Her hand had found his side.

She didn't remove her fingers, but instead scratched the dog carefully, like other people did with regular dogs.

Riyune gave a contented sigh and stretched out further, pushing himself more firmly against her leg.

Whatever Riyune truly was, his dog nature was part of it, not something forced on him.

Nadeem gave him another skritch before laying back down, content to share warmth, if even for a single night.

<hr>

Nadeem was up before the dawn, waiting nervously on the eastern ridge. Aunt Parayat had to come. Even if it was just herself. Someone would show up. Right?

Riyune seemed grumpy that morning, as if he resenting getting up in the cool, pre-morning air. He didn't growl at her, not exactly, but he did let her know his displeasure by moving particularly slowly.

The eastern sky lightened with long fingers of pink clouds reaching out. Nadeem kept to her hiding place, making herself wait. She had to be sure that whoever did arrive wasn't part of a trap, so she stayed hidden, out of sight.

When would Aunt Parayat come? Why couldn't Nadeem hear anyone approaching? Surely her aunt would have been able to persuade at least one or two.

Slowly, oh so slowly, the moments passed by. Nadeem kept checking over her shoulder to judge the position of the sun. It felt as though it was climbing backwards, just to thwart her.

Finally, though, the first rays raced across the land.

Nadeem heard the call of a desert hawk, once, twice.

That had been the signal Aunt Parayat had always used when she'd been training Nadeem.

Then a loud, shrieking whistle broke through the morning quiet.

Nadeem started but resisted surging to her feet and giving her position away. That had been the call of her class, of Mojin and the others, how the aunts would call all the youngsters back to their lessons.

Who had Aunt Parayat brought with her?

Nadeem crept toward the crest of the hill.

Down in the valley on the opposite side she saw dozens of star sisters grouped together, silently waiting. Possibly hundreds stood hiding in the predawn.

Young ones. Old ones. Cooks from the camp. Even those who traveled as merchants for the *kabil*, gathering goods for them.

Nadeem swallowed down the lump in her throat. Her feet itched to run away. She was leading all these fine sisters into death.

But the goddess of death was their friend. She'd welcome them, one and all.

At the front of the line stood Aunt Parayat. She looked as stubborn as a *meslit* tree, but as old as the hills themselves.

Nadeem knew that she'd never see her aunt like this again.

No matter.

At least Aunt Parayat would have the opportunity to die in a battle worthy of the old saga. Of this, Nadeem was certain.

CHAPTER THREE

TRULLIÇ

TRULLIÇ TURNED THE OBSIDIAN BLADE over in his hands once again. He knew it was Nadeem's knife even before the stranger, this Levent, told him. It carried her scent, that promise of quick death and even less sufferance.

"She gave this to you," Trulliç said, repeating himself.

It was obvious that Nadeem trusted Levent. But why? Was it because he was tall and handsome, charming even Myrizhah? Clever, too, given the wordplay he'd exchanged with Seydat. Or was it because of his military bearing? The discipline at the man's core that he carefully hid with an easy going smile?

Levent was dressed as a merchant in a loose striped tunic and baggy pants, all in shades of brown, with a *chafiyek* of gold and green. His proud nose stood up from his face and would have given him an arrogant air if not for his charm.

"I appreciate your offer," Trulliç said as he reluctantly handed the knife back to Levent. They sat at the base of Trulliç's tower, the merchant having been greeted and given hospitality by Myrizhah and Seydat before they bothered Trulliç and told him that he had a visitor. "You know the odds we face, yes?"

He wanted to take up Levent's offer of help so badly. But it wouldn't be a fair exchange. What could Trulliç offer Levent in return for his knowledge, and probably, his death?

Myrizhah came back into the room with tea. The calm mint scent flowed over Trulliç as ten thousand questions bubbled inside. Who was Levant? What did he mean to Nadeem? Were they involved?

Trulliç didn't have a claim on the former star sister. Yet his insides twisted at the thought that she'd given herself to this merchant and not to Trulliç, despite the fact that Trulliç hadn't asked her for anything more than her friendship.

Levent smiled at Myrizhah and thanked her for the tea, taking an appreciative sip before replying to Trulliç. "I think I understand the odds. All those who share the dreams of the desert magician do. The emperor is coming with an army of thousands, hardened veterans of foreign wars. We will have scant hundreds to meet him, untrained volunteers."

Trulliç nodded and sipped at his own tea. The sweet taste fought with the bitterness he felt. So much that he had planned for his city, his people! Would all his dreams be chased away by the desert winds in a few days? A storm called up by the emperor himself that Trulliç couldn't battle?

"We have some advantages, however," Levent continued as if he was unaware of Trulliç's thoughts. "For one, we have the desert magician. He can control the sands, the wind, maybe even the weather."

Trulliç bobbed his head from side to side. It was true, he had called up great storms when he'd been most angry.

"For another, we are actually here in the desert itself. While the emperor has traveled these lands, it's been a great while. He's surely forgotten some of what the desert herself will teach us," Levent said.

Trulliç blinked, surprised. He'd been aware that the emperor coming to his territory would give him an advantage. He just hadn't been sure how to use it.

Plus, he kept going back to that phrase that Zehra had used, about the emperor washing against his shores. What did that mean? It had to be a clue about how to fight him.

"Third, you are inexperienced," Levent said before he paused and took another long sip of his tea.

Trulliç stiffened. It was the truth. He finally asked, "Why do you consider my inexperience a bonus?" when Levent didn't say anything more.

"Because the emperor will underestimate you," Levent said seriously. "He will only bring as many men as he thinks he needs to crush you. He won't expect you to be able to put up any serious defense. He's been unopposed by his own people for so long that he'll just assume victory."

"Have you met the emperor?" Trulliç asked.

Levent hesitated, then nodded. "Aye. Once." His eyes took on a faraway look. "The emperor came to see the troops as we returned from Lydae, after putting down a brief and foolish rebellion. The emperor spoke to us, thanking us for our duty." Levent shook his head. "He stood there in that great cloak of his, speaking of honor and how proud he was of all the slaughter we'd committed."

Trulliç wanted to ask about the cloak. It was made from the afterbirths of all the magicians and star sisters so they could never directly oppose him.

Instead, Trulliç asked the question that Levent seemed to need to hear. "What happened after the emperor spoke to you?"

Levent seemed to still be in his own head. His voice dropped to a whisper, thin and strained. "The emperor killed all the prisoners we'd taken. With his magic. He strangled them all, stealing their breath and life away." Levent shuddered. "It wasn't a cruel death, their ends came quickly. But I'd promised them a fresh start if they'd just turn away from the rebellion and return to the empire. I broke my word."

"No, the emperor didn't honor your word," Trulliç pointed out, instantly seeing the flaw. Surely Levent understood that he wasn't to blame.

Levent gave Trulliç a sad smile and shook his head. "No. I knew I was lying when I made those promises. The emperor had already warned us to take no prisoners. I knew better. But I couldn't stand to kill all those people myself. I wanted to be able to sleep at night."

"Did it help? That the emperor killed them, and not you?" Trulliç asked, curious.

Levent gave a sharp bark of laughter. "You're a sharp one," he said. "No, no it didn't. Not at first, anyway. It was still my fault. Still my responsibility."

He turned to look at Trulliç, his eyes now focused as a hawk's after spying its prey. "Watching the emperor kill those people, though… how he changed while doing it…I don't think the emperor is fully human anymore," he said, his voice going back to a whisper.

"He lives on the death of others," Trulliç said quietly.

"You know?" Levent said, surprised.

"I guessed," Trulliç said. "When we battled his guard in the myth lands and prevented them from stealing the desert heart, the main guard, Marius, grew stronger as we killed his companions."

Levent nodded. "There were rumors of that as well, of the primary leaders of an army, the generals and such, being able to channel the emperor's magic. And his madness." He shuddered.

"So how do we stop the emperor? Without killing anyone and feeding him?" Trulliç asked, going back to the question that haunted his days and nights.

"I wish I knew," Levent said. "I can help organize what men and women you have. Help you shore up your defenses. But as for fighting magic…that's got to be your call."

Trulliç nodded. "I accept your help," he said.

He'd had a momentary sprout of hope, that maybe Levent could tell Trulliç the secret he needed in order to win the war.

But no. Trulliç still had to discover that part himself.

And soon.

<hr>

The night was over half gone, and Trulliç still couldn't sleep. He worried about Nadeem and if she'd be able to persuade any of the star sisters to join them. He worried about his mother and how long she'd live even if they survived the war. He worried about his people, what a war would do to them, how it would change them.

He glowered at the emperor's staff that still stood in the corner in its thick coating of glass. He imagined it laughing at him, taunting him to just give up now. The emperor had defeated the six kings. What hope did a singular desert magician have?

That made Trulliç sit up. How *had* the emperor defeated the six kings? Everyone always assumed that since the emperor had won and there were no songs or stories about the war, that the victory had come with an easy, single battle.

Had it been a protracted struggle? Had the six kings almost been victorious except for a bad piece of luck or an ill wind?

Trulliç pursued that line of reasoning. The kings could possibly change into dogs. Or maybe they were actually great dogs who could change into men. Had the emperor struck at just the right time, in mid-change? Had they been trapped and unable to fight?

Then what? Why did the blood hounds of the emperor resemble the dogs of the kings of old?

Or maybe…maybe the emperor hadn't destroyed the kings. Maybe he hadn't been strong enough to do so, despite what the legends said.

Maybe the emperor had been forced into a different arrangement. Maybe he couldn't kill the kings. Maybe he just made them serve him in their dog form.

It was a horrifying thought. The emperor had been in power for two centuries. Had the kings been enslaved all that time? Serving their most hated overlord?

Was this the emperor's final chance to kill them? Kill Trulliç and kill the kings at the same time? Get to them through Riyune?

Atça would accuse Trulliç of being fanciful, a word that Trulliç had truly grown to hate. And maybe he was being fanciful, spinning out tales like any marketplace storyteller. But he knew that the blood hounds and the old kings were connected. And Riyune had first appeared as a blood hound in the cavern before he'd changed shape into the white and black dog.

Trulliç found himself pacing across his room. He wasn't about to sleep like this.

He knew his mother would tell him to rest, preserve his strength.

He didn't need to go racing out in the desert. She didn't understand how the daylight refreshed him, not sleep.

With a great howl, Trulliç became a whirlwind of rage and flew out of the tower, off his balcony and onto the desert below.

Storm clouds gathered over his head. Lightning raced him. The smell of baked sand and sudden death washed out from him. He howled with the wind, blasting stones apart.

Why had Atça betrayed him? Lied to him about everything? Abused him and his magical power?

He knew why. Atça had been born greedy. He'd never have enough power, enough money, enough status. He was always grasping for more, as well as pointing out to everyone around him how much he had.

Damn him. Damn him! DAMN HIM!

Trulliç's anger super-heated the sand around him, causing it to explode outward in shards of glass and stone.

Trulliç found himself on his knees, weeping in the center of the aftermath. The sand spread out in waves all around him, as if it was too ashamed to be near him.

He was too angry to cry properly, to mourn for what could have been, as only a few tears fell from his eyes and splashed onto his hands.

Would his anger be enough to stop the emperor, though?

Somehow, he doubted it.

As dawn came, Trulliç ate a small bit of flatbread while Myrizhah, Seydat, and Levent formed plans. He had very little to offer except in terms of logistics. Sure, he could move people wherever they needed to go. Water wouldn't be much of an issue as he could always raise wells. Food was more of a concern as he learned that an army marched on its stomach. But Seydat and Myrizhah had already started to deal with that.

Could Trulliç cut off the emperor's supply chain? Not when they traveled outside of the desert. Once they crossed the border, though…

Trulliç thought he heard someone call his name. He sat up

straighter, brushing away the few crumbs that had landed in his lap. He wore the brown pants again, as they seemed clean enough to him. But to please Myrizhah, he'd put on yet another tunic, this one made from a cloth that had been dyed green with gold stripes embroidered into it.

Then he thought he heard something again.

Was that Nadeem? Calling his name?

Trulliç ignored Myrizhah telling him that he couldn't just leave as he got up, walked around the guard stone of the tower, and looked out.

There. Nadeem *had* been successful. She had a few hundred star sisters with her. But if Trulliç wanted their help, he had to transport them to the city and then to where the fighting would be the worst.

"I'll be right back," Trulliç called over his shoulder as he disappeared. He could only imagine the puzzled faces he left behind.

Truly his heart flew as fast as his feet, racing toward Nadeem. She might never return his feelings, but she was worthy of all his attention.

It took him less time than usual to reach where Nadeem and her charges marched down along the western trade route, possibly only an hour. The caravans the star sisters passed all stopped and stared. Few outside of the star sisters themselves had seen so many gathered together in one place.

The star sisters themselves sang fighting songs as they marched. Or they tossed deadly knives back and forth. Some even had drop spindles and spun wool as they walked.

Most wore their habitual black, immodestly tight outfits, though a few of the older aunts wore colorful tunics and *chafiyeks*. Plain leather strips covered their feet, giving them purchase on rough rocks.

The column slowed as Trulliç approached. Nadeem wasn't walking in front. Instead, she was about a third of the way back, walking with an elder woman who held herself stiff and proud.

"I am Trulliç," he announced while waiting for Nadeem to come forward. The star sisters at the front of the line nodded stoically at him and stood ready, bearing deadly pikes. Would they attack him if he tried to move among them? They had that look.

The old aunt beside Nadeem sniffed as she drew near, as though she weren't impressed. Still, she told him, "I am called Aunt Parayat. These are my sisters. They are here to fight for you, for the desert, for the goddess Barzhat."

Trulliç suddenly understood why so many of the star sisters had come to serve him. The emperor wanted to become a new god of death. He'd steal away the power of their beloved goddess.

"Thank you," Trulliç said, bowing low. "I am truly honored."

He straightened up, only to find Aunt Parayat looking at him expectantly. "Well? Let's get going!" she instructed him, sounding as imperious as Atça.

"Yes, ma'am," Trulliç said, biting down on his anger. This was someone who meant a lot to Nadeem. He couldn't just blast her for what appeared to be her nature. He needed this old woman, even if she reminded him of his former mentor and tormentor.

Trulliç closed his eyes and reached out with his senses. He found all the star sisters there on the road, felt their cool strength and slippery magic. "Stay steady and strong!" he called out in a booming voice. There was no other warning he could give them before he caused them, as a large group, to all rise above the ground.

Then, just because this Aunt Parayat had demanded that he get going, he sped them all away to his city, going much faster than he had with the soldiers.

Hopefully Nadeem would understand and forgive him.

"That was quite an experience, young man," Aunt Parayat said. Her dark skin didn't hide how her cheeks glowed. Her eyes sparkled with excitement. "How exhilarating!"

Trulliç wasn't sure what to say in return. He'd expected to be scolded, that was what Atça would have done. Not praised, with several of the women looking as though they wanted to do it again, right now.

"I'm glad it suited you," Trulliç said. And he was, mostly. Maybe a tiny part of him was disappointed that the sisters hadn't been scared.

Then again, maybe he should have considered what he knew of their training.

A trip through the air was no different than scrambling up and down the cliffs along Knife Ridge. Or even winning their long illusionary battles.

"You may have to take another ride soon," Trulliç finally said as he turned toward the main tower with Aunt Parayat and Nadeem beside him. Riyune trotted after them, looking as satisfied as any dog after a successful hunt.

Aunt Parayat just looked at him with a single arched eyebrow.

Really, she looked more imperious than any of the queens and great heroines he'd read about. And she had been Nadeem's mentor? No wonder Nadeem had such a cool edge to her sometimes.

"The emperor will probably attack from the northwest," Trulliç said. "That's the direction Zahra saw them coming in."

Aunt Parayat shook her head. "That will be the first wave," she said. "He will split his troops as he has in the past. It's easy for him to do a two or three pronged attack, as he can coordinate with his generals using his magic."

Trulliç felt himself rocking back. More than one front? But he barely had enough people and resources to protect the first!

Maybe that was what Zahra had seen. That her town would fall as Trulliç directed his forces elsewhere.

He shook his head. He *hated* this. People were going to die. Innocent people. Good people. *His* people. And there wasn't any way he could save them all.

<hr>

Aunt Parayat and Myrizhah got along just fine, as Trulliç knew they would. He was more interested in how Nadeem would react to Levent working as Trulliç's primary military commander.

However, nothing but friendship appeared to flow between the pair of them. That as well as admiration. Levent appeared to greatly respect Nadeem, as he should. He instantly charmed Aunt Parayat as well, the pair of them comparing notes about the wild antics in their pasts.

Nadeem sat at her removed distance, slightly amused, watching them all. Trulliç had hoped that Nadeem might come all the way back and not be so far away after visiting her star sisters, but she seemed as distant as ever.

It made Trulliç wonder if Nadeem would ever come fully back. Or if she'd deliberately sacrifice herself during one of the battles.

What could he do to stop her? There wasn't time!

At least Trulliç felt as though he was making progress on his side of the war. People were being divided up. Fighting orders were issued. The star sisters would split up into three groups leading his people, the ones who'd volunteered to join the war.

And more people continued to pour into the city. Normally, Trulliç tried to greet everyone who came. But now masses arrived like a swollen river. He had to leave the war council to go raise more buildings for his people to live in.

One of the star sisters, a young woman named Kalil, asked Trulliç about knives and weapons. She was petite, shorter than most of the other star sisters. Her hair was brown and her eyes were hazel, like his. Was she of mixed birth? Her mother of the desert and her father from Lydae?

"I work with rock and glass," he explained. "Not iron or leather."

She bent her head to the side and regarded him. Then she pulled out her obsidian blade. "This is glass, isn't it?" she asked.

Though Kalil tried to sound innocent, she missed her mark by a long shot. Someone had set her up for this. Had it been Nadeem? Or maybe Aunt Parayat?

But she was right. He could arm his people with glass. Balls they could throw that would explode when they struck anything, as well as obsidian blades.

Why hadn't he thought of it? Instead, he'd been trapped, helpless, as he had been all his life.

"I will make you blades," he told Kalil, trying not to grind his teeth in anger.

It was *not* her fault. He shouldn't be angry with her. Or even at the emperor, really. This had been his problem all along.

"How many blades do you need?" Trulliç asked, trying to modulate his tones. The star sister had taken a step back in the face of his ready rage.

"As many as you can provide," Kalil said. "If they're well balanced, we can use them as throwing weapons."

Trulliç nodded and continued to try to think of the weapons he might be able to form. "It would take too long to form arrows from obsidian arrowheads," he said.

"If you could form shards, we could use them with slingshots and have a longer range," Kalil said.

"Good, good," Trulliç said. "I'll need to go to the foothills south of here—the Yalçin mountains—to get the materials. Then I'll be back and you can direct me how to shape them."

"Do you need help?" Kalil said.

Trulliç couldn't help but smile at the gleam in her eye. Another of the star sisters who'd truly enjoyed the ride that morning. "No," he said softly. "I would just have to carry you as well as all the materials."

He didn't bother telling her that in the bright midafternoon sunlight, he was at his peak for strength. However, he needed some solitary time. He suspected he wouldn't get much time alone over the next few days.

Only two more days before the emperor attacked.

Trulliç shook his head and whirled away, no longer paralyzed by the fear that had held for far too long.

Trulliç looked down from the tops of the foreboding peaks of the Yalçin mountains. The desert spread out to the north in front of him. On a clear day, he might be able to see at least halfway across it, though the heat would cause the ground to shimmer like a mirage.

The air blew cold up here, carrying strange scents of frozen rock and rain. Hawks let themselves be carried for miles on the mixture of winds, their cries thin and feral.

Behind Trulliç, just past the cliffs, the ocean pounded the rocks. He couldn't hear the sound, but he felt it deep in his bones, how the water wanted to tear down the mountains and destroy the desert.

He hadn't meant to come all the way up here. His original plan had been to stop in the foothills. The heights had drawn him, though. He'd learned to always carry a pocketful of sand, something to help power him when he stepped away from the desert.

Crossing out of the desert lands felt different this time compared to the time he'd gone north, back to Gaadiwala. That time a light shroud had fallen on his senses, as if he lived in a haze. His thoughts hadn't been as precise. Even the pocketful of sand had only cleared his head somewhat.

Up in these foothill, Trulliç still knew he was no longer in the desert. However, his senses weren't as clouded.

Was that because the area up north was so much closer to the emperor and all the land he'd proclaimed as his? While technically the desert belonged to the emperor, Trulliç knew the truth. It was his, and his alone.

These mountains felt unclaimed to Trulliç, owned by neither the emperor nor the desert magician. He wasn't about to try to take them, however. It didn't make any sense to expand his lands this way. Particularly when these mountains couldn't provide his people with food.

Obsidian, on the other hand…

To his left stood a tall mountain that had blown its top off. Instead of rising into a peak, it was bowl shaped, with one side rising higher than the other, as if formed by a drunken potter.

Black obsidian rocks lay scattered across the entire valley beside Trulliç. Many had salt-white crystals blooming on the sides. It was the equivalent of a gold mine.

Perhaps the star sisters would like to claim this area, mine it in exchange for providing Trulliç protection.

For now, he couldn't try to make that sort of deal. That was for the future.

Because he was determined there would be a future.

Trulliç hurried down into the valley. He picked up a piece of obsidian, then nearly dropped it when he realized how much heat it had absorbed from the sunshine. After he cooled the rock off with a wind, he picked it up again.

Though it looked like a rock, Trulliç recognized that at its core, obsidian was actually glass. He reached out with his senses and started tugging all the loose obsidian on the plain toward him. He stopped quickly when the pile reached the size of a small hut. He didn't want to be greedy.

He was *not* greedy. Not like Atça.

There was still plenty of obsidian left behind in the valley for others to find and pick up. He had no claim on this land. In fact, he might just tell the star sisters about it and tell them they should use it, free of charge.

He was *not* greedy like Atça.

Still, Trulliç took a few more moments to run to the far end of the valley where the land started going up steeply again. The rock formations here were odd. It took Trulliç a moment to figure out what they reminded him of. The rocks that made up the cavern that led to the myth lands had the same appearance, of one rock haphazardly placed on top of the next.

They looked strange, as though some mighty hand had slopped the rocks together. What had caused this? Were they put there by the gods?

Trulliç stopped in front of one that had a manlike shape. Beautiful obsidian decorated the tops and edges.

It seemed more than familiar, though Trulliç was certain he'd never been here before. Had he dreamed about this place?

Trulliç's breath caught in his throat. His heart suddenly started hammering. He found himself panting. The sun beat down on him, making his head swim instead of bringing him more life.

No. It couldn't be.

Trulliç was aware that it was only his imagination that made the stones in front of him look similar to Atça. But they did. The rock formation had the same tall and proud appearance. White crystals clung to the fringes of the stone that would be the skull, like Atça's white hair. A smooth, broad portion made up the forehead, with a large bulbous nose jutting out. Dark pits where stones had fallen out, made up the eyes.

Without thinking, Trulliç blasted the rocks with an abrasive desert wind. However, through luck (or maybe by direction of the gods) the wind merely scoured the rocks, smoothing out the part that would be the body, making it appear like the figure had just put on a robe.

Trulliç stood panting with effort. He couldn't keep doing this, reacting with anger over nothing. Atça no longer had any power over his life.

Atça was *dead*. Trulliç had killed him.

But seeing this figure, even if it only had a rough resemblance to the original, had pushed Trulliç back to the place where he was just a small boy being lied to, fighting every day to maintain himself, his sense of magic and what was true.

Trulliç dropped to his knees. He couldn't fight Atça, or rather, Atça's ghost. It was like fighting the wind. Atça's influence and the memories were constantly there. They would never go away.

How could Trulliç stop feeling like this, though? Stop going back to that little boy who could never do enough to please his mentor? That child who could never do enough, be enough?

How could he free himself?

Tears started streaming down Trulliç's face.

He couldn't have freed himself from Atça's influence. Not before he did.

He *had* been just a small boy. And while Myrizhah couldn't have saved him, Trulliç couldn't have saved himself earlier either.

He'd done the best he could.

Trulliç wailed his grief, his cries echoing off the nearby mountain tops. He'd been a boy. A little boy. And he'd been abused by his mentor. His magic twisted and aborted.

He couldn't have saved that little boy. He could only let the past stay there, behind him, while the man moved forward, protecting the boy forever more.

Trulliç didn't know how long he wept and raged. When his tears finally slowed, he felt as hollow as a glass ball. He swayed with the slightest breeze, exhaustion overwhelming him.

Finally, slowly, Trulliç looked up. The figure didn't resemble Atça as much now. It looked more like an oddly shaped man.

Trulliç pushed himself up to standing. He still felt as though he tilted to one side, unable to be fully upright just yet. Though he felt empty, he also for the first time, felt more light as well, as though his feet could travel faster, farther. He knew he no longer carried as much of the past with him, sewn to his clothes like Barzhat's golden weights. He'd cried the tears necessary to release them, finally.

Should he leave the figure as it was? Make it look more like Atça? Less so?

In the end, Trulliç decided to leave the figure as it was. He may need to come and talk with this Atça at some point. Or maybe throw rocks at it.

He'd always know that it was here, though. He'd have to make sure that the star sisters didn't touch it, that this pile of rocks was sacred to Trulliç.

Trulliç looked around again. The mountain with the top blown off still rose high above the plane. Obsidian rocks littered the valley. Birds dove down to the softer places below. The smells the air carried were mixed and rich, carrying a wetness from the ocean.

Everything looked the same. That seemed wrong. It should look different.

Except that Trulliç knew that just *he* had changed. He'd been reformed, somehow.

Trulliç found himself straightening up, his back growing tight and rigid.

The emperor be *damned*. While Trulliç had had a lot to fight for before, now, with the chance of a new life, free of some of the influences of his past, he had even more to fight for.

And not just fight, but win.

CHAPTER FOUR

NADEEM

NADEEM DREAMED OF THE OLD kings. She stood on the sidelines as court started for the day. Six proud thrones were arranged in a semi-circle at the front of the room, to her right. Each throne was gilded in gold, studded with snowflake obsidian and rubies. Great banners hung on the walls, one behind each chair, with a different embroidered symbol: bouquets of white calla lilies, a tall Ibis, a fierce lion, a great Orca, a distant mountain at sunset, and a series of circles, one inside the next.

Why were there no dogs? Or did the banners represent something different and not the kings themselves? Maybe the families they came from?

Strain as she might, Nadeem couldn't get a good look at the kings. It was as if fog filled the space where the men might have sat.

She found herself gasping when she turned her focus back toward the crowd. The people here were rich. No one in this crowd had missed a meal recently, as shown by their round, full faces and meaty hands. Their clothing was rich as well, finely spun and embroidered. Many had the coloring of the desert people, dark and familiar, though she recognized a few merchants who'd come from Lydae, blond men and women with faint blue eyes.

A group of women moved from the sidelines up toward the dais. Nadeem found herself gasping again when she finally recognized this group as star sisters. They moved with the same grace as Nadeem's sisters, their bodies well trained.

They wore black, as her sisters did. But that was where the resemblance ended.

These star sisters were completely covered from head to toe in bulky robes. The *chafiyeks* they wore were also black and were wrapped around their faces so that just their eyes showed. Each wore a sparkling circlet of silver, with six stars dangling across their foreheads.

Were they marked with a star as well? Or were their cheeks smooth?

Without the star sister mark, they would be able to completely disguise themselves. No man would be safe. He would never know if the woman he hassled could turn around and kill him with the flick of her wrist.

Despite how they were covered, Nadeem found herself envying them. As just their eyes were visible under their bulky robes, they would be well hidden forever.

The star sisters had always been secretive. Maybe, however, they hadn't always lived completely apart from the rest of the world.

Would her sisters rejoin the world if given a chance? She knew that some might leave the sisterhood. They'd get married, have children, and fade into the background, be regarded as completely normal women.

Until need rose and their true nature revealed itself.

Nadeem couldn't imagine such a fate for herself. But for the new ones just joining, would they have a different coming-of-age ceremony? Could they live without the mark?

Before Nadeem could ask one of the star sisters here, she found herself plucked out of the dream and placed back in her small room.

With a sigh, Nadeem collected herself. The room remained the same. Her pack sat in the corner, still packed so she could leave at a moment's notice. A small picture of a cat drawn in charcoal by one of Seydat's children was still tacked to the wall beside the small glass-covered window. Her sandals lay at the foot of her bed, placed so that she could easily slip them on if she needed to escape quickly.

Though most of the star sisters lived in tents, in temporary structures, Nadeem had still settled here in a building made of stone. However, everything about the room screamed that it was temporary. Aunt Parayat's tent had more personality, with her small loom in the corner, a basket holding wool that needed to be spun, her teaching matt, and even her clothes.

But Nadeem couldn't stay here, could she?

She shivered, recognizing what had woken her so sharply from her dream.

The thought of there being a tomorrow, of something after the war.

There would be no after the war for her, beyond the golden court of Barzhat. She couldn't allow herself to even think of that.

***

Nadeem watched Aunt Parayat subtly take over the war council. She doubted even Levent noticed. But Nadeem knew he approved as his body language changed and he started to defer to her like a soldier would treat his general.

It was skillfully, masterfully done. Nadeem shared a secret smile with her aunt when she'd just made yet another decision directing the course of the battle.

Panic struck Nadeem as her aunt looked away. Surely Aunt Parayat didn't expect Nadeem to do something similar? That would be too much like coming forward into the world of the living.

No, this was wrong. Nadeem didn't panic. She'd rarely even been afraid. What was happening to her?

Nadeem excused herself and left Trulliç's tower. She pushed herself into the shade and leaned against the solid bricks, taking deep breaths. She needed to get ahold of herself. Was she coming too far back? She didn't want to! She sweated through her loose blouse and tunic. The soles of her feet felt sticky in their sandals. Her stomach churned. Was she getting sick? What was wrong?

When Nadeem looked up, she found that Riyune sat quietly at her feet looking up at her. She couldn't read his expression. Was he curious? Worried? Hungry? The council had feasted on roasted chicken for lunch, and he'd turned his nose up at any bones they'd thrown his way.

Nadeem glanced around the immediate area, expecting Trulliç to be standing just a few feet away, his eyes saying more than his lips ever would.

No one paid any attention to her, though. The people of Hayalevi went about their business with an urgent air, everyone preparing to go to war in two days. A merchant with a large cart piled high with blankets bustled off toward the market, while three workmen went the other way, intent on their discussion of catapults.

Nadeem pushed herself off the wall of the tower and went back inside. But Trulliç wasn't there either.

Strange. Why would Riyune be there without Trulliç? Where was he?

The council all looked up at her arrival. "What news?" Myrizhah asked harshly.

Nadeem blinked. "I don't know what you mean." Why would they expect her to know anything?

Still, that feeling of foreboding and panic washed over Nadeem again.

Something was wrong. Something was very wrong.

Aunt Parayat kept her sharp eyes on Nadeem while she addressed the rest of the group. "We know that the emperor will attack Egreliki in two days' time, perhaps less. We suspect that will be merely one of the forks of his battle plan. Has he already started his attack elsewhere?"

All the blood rushed out of Nadeem's head, leaving her woozy. Was that what she was feeling? Was that why she panicked? Was the desert in danger? Would she feel that, being a creature from here?

"Where's Trulliç?" Seydat asked quietly.

"I thought…I thought he'd be here," Nadeem said. "I've never seen him separated from Riyune before. Except when Trulliç told Riyune to follow me."

"Does the dog know where Trulliç might be?" Levent asked, curious. He knew there was something special about Riyune, having seen how fast the dog ran beside Nadeem. But Levent hadn't fully accepted how different Riyune was, being the most surprised when the dog had snubbed the bones he'd been thrown.

"If Trulliç was in the desert, he'd know if the emperor had attacked," Nadeem said firmly. "He's left the desert."

"Why would he do something foolish like that?" Myrizhah said, her voice harsh and stern, as though she were addressing the boy Trulliç had been and not the man he was becoming.

"I don't know," Nadeem said. "Maybe the emperor hasn't arrived."

The disbelieving looks from everyone made her feel guilty for speaking such an inane hope out loud.

"I'll go find him," Nadeem said. Surely that was something she could do.

"Please," Aunt Parayat said. "Without the desert magician, all our hope is lost."

Nadeem turned and strode out of the tower. As she expected, Riyune followed her, then sat expectantly looking up at her feet.

"We need to find Trulliç," Nadeem told the dog seriously. "Right now."

Riyune lolled his tongue out the side of his mouth as he considered her.

"Please, help me find Trulliç," Nadeem said, speaking more plainly.

The dog appeared to roll his eyes at her and stood up. He committed himself to a huge yawn, his jaw nearly splitting, before he gave himself a great shake. Finally, he looked back at Nadeem, as if asking, *Are you ready?*

Nadeem rolled her eyes at the dog. "Yes. Let's go."

With a nod, Riyune started running south.

Nadeem followed on fleet feet, hoping they'd get wherever they were going in time.

Nadeem had never been in the Yalçin mountains before. They reminded her of Knife Ridge. The stones here were just as jagged. Wild *meslit* bushes grew as tall as trees, with thorns that would cover her entire palm. Birds flew high across the plain, riding the winds. The foothills had more rain than the desert, so there were more bushes. However, hot desert storms still scrubbed the more delicate plants from the face of the hills.

It would be a good place to train, as Nadeem had out on Knife Ridge with her old cohort. However, none of her team had come to fight with her. Not that she'd expected they would. They'd all have been recruited by the emperor and would fight for him, instead.

Up Nadeem went, chasing after Riyune, further away from the desert. She found her breath catching as they climbed. Riyune didn't slow down, but Nadeem felt herself tiring.

Was she that much of a desert creature that she could only thrive there? She knew that since she'd rubbed the enchanted sand of the desert into her mangled cheek, her magic had changed. Did she only draw her power from there now? Instead of being a star sister and able to travel and cast illusions throughout the entire Tanesh empire? Was she now bound like a male magician?

No, she should be able to cast her illusions here. It was just her other abilities, her fleet speed and how quickly she could find water, that would lessen away from the desert.

Should she carry a bit of sand with her everywhere she went, as Trulliç had advised her to do? Possibly.

She shook her head.

Only if she survived the coming battles. Only if she chose to.

Riyune climbed a winding trail, disappearing around the next bend ahead of her.

Worried, Nadeem pushed herself to close the distance between them faster.

The hill flattened out into a great empty valley. Trulliç stood about midway across, a huge collection of stones beside him. Riyune sat at his feet, looking back at her. Even from this distance, Nadeem could see the dog's impatience.

Trulliç hurried across the valley to Nadeem, his hands out. "What happened? Are you all right?"

Nadeem stepped forward automatically, taking his hands and clasping them like soldiers and old companions would. "I'm fine," she assured him. "But there's something wrong."

She quickly explained Aunt Parayat's fears that the emperor was attacking using a pronged attack, and that the war had already started.

Trulliç shook his head. "No, even here I would have felt him moving across my land."

"Are you sure?" Nadeem said. "What if his troops were protected, or carrying implements like the emperor's cane?"

Trulliç's expression grew stormy. "We will stop him," he said simply.

Strange. The rage that normally blew off Trulliç didn't follow his statement. He was angry, yes, but stubbornly so. Not like a storm. More like a well-protected city.

Nadeem suddenly became aware that she was still holding onto Trulliç's hands. They felt stone hard and warm in hers, the skin roughened by the desert sand. "What happened to you?" Nadeem asked. She tried to let go of Trulliç's wrists, but he held on.

He gave her a bitter laugh. "I threw myself at the rocks," he said. "Crashed myself to bits so I could be reborn."

Nadeem blinked. Of course. How like a poet, which really was Trulliç's soul. "I'm glad," Nadeem said. She tugged lightly at Trulliç's hand, willing for him to let her go before she made him.

"But what about you?" Trulliç asked, still sounding maddeningly calm. "How will you come back?"

With a quick twist of her wrists, Nadeem freed herself. It seemed that Trulliç hadn't been holding on that strongly.

"No," she found herself saying. She wrapped her arms around herself, hugging herself tightly. "No," she said again. She couldn't come back, just to let go again.

"There won't be much to continue with, if you're gone," Trulliç said quietly.

Nadeem found herself shivering, as if cold winds had sprung up and were caressing her.

"I need you in my life," Trulliç continued. "I want you by my side. Now and always."

Nadeem shook her head. "You don't want me," she said, her voice sounding as harsh as the sand scoured rocks. "You want some idea of me."

Trulliç laughed, the sound lighter and freer than she remembered. "I don't believe that's true," he said. "But even if it is, I still love the you that you'll become after the war."

Nadeem shivered again mightily. After the war. That was the problem, wasn't it? There was no after the war for her.

Aunt Parayat would accuse Nadeem of a failure of imagination. She couldn't see an after the war for any of them.

"Come back to me," Trulliç said softly. "Come back to the world. There is much goodness here, much to love. Even if you don't, can't, love me. Even if you want to stay out on your own or find your solace with someone else. Return to me. Please."

No one had ever asked Nadeem to be with them. Her old team, the star sisters she'd trusted with her life, had turned their backs on her, betrayed her, would kill her given the chance.

"I can't," Nadeem said, her voice cracking. She couldn't trust this, couldn't trust Trulliç. "At least, not yet."

"Thank you," Trulliç said, his voice warm and filled with contentment. "You've at least given me hope with that 'yet'."

Nadeem shook her head and finally turned away from the rock wall to face Trulliç again.

She could see the changes, how tall he carried himself now, his back unstooped and his shoulders relaxed. His face had fewer worries, even with the coming war.

"We need to get back to Hayalevi," Trulliç said.

"Why did you come here?" Nadeem asked. "Surely it wasn't just to break yourself into a million pieces."

Trulliç laughed again, the joyous sound carrying around the bowl of the valley.

Nadeem suspected that she could get used to the sound of that laughter.

"I came up here to gather obsidian for the star sisters," Trulliç said, indicating the pile of stones she'd first found him beside. "This land is unclaimed," he added, indicating the entire ridge. "It doesn't belong to the desert. It really doesn't belong to the emperor, either. I don't know if you can feel the difference, but I can."

Nadeem thought for a moment. Yes, the mountain she stood on wasn't part of the desert. She knew that because she wasn't as strong here. But it felt cleaner than the other parts of the empire she'd visited. Was that just the fresh winds blowing off the ocean? Or was it something different?

"I want the star sisters to own it," Trulliç said seriously. "I know, I know, it isn't much to look at. You can't really survive up here."

Nadeem snorted. How little he knew of the resourcefulness of the star sisters. There were plenty of small creatures they could eat hidden in the rocks, rain catchers they could create for the morning dew, how the branches and leaves of some of the nearby scrub would sustain a body.

Trulliç gave her a puzzled look but went on. "However, you could mine the obsidian up here. Possibly use it for trade."

Nadeem nodded slowly. He was right. She looked out over the valley. Did all those rocks contain obsidian? If they did, that represented a fortune for the sisters, right there. Plus, they could conduct rigorous trials here in addition to the Knife Ridge training area.

"Why would you give this to us?" Nadeem asked.

"I'm not," Trulliç said adamantly. "It isn't mine to give. It is no one's land. However, I wouldn't object if the star sisters claimed it for their own."

Nadeem appreciated the distinction. Plus, if the star sisters took over these foothills, it would give Trulliç peace of mind, as he wouldn't have to defend this border.

Then again, there wasn't much to attack here. The only access to these mountains came from ships crossing the endless ocean. They'd have to find a port, then scale foreboding cliffs. Anyone who made such a journey would be an opponent worthy of the star sisters.

"I'll let the main council know," Nadeem said. "They will have to decide for all the *kabils*."

Though she couldn't imagine them turning the proposition down, not with all that obsidian just laying around, free for the taking.

"And the other?" Trulliç asked.

What other? Nadeem looked at him curiously.

"You'll let me know if you decide to be my companion? My love? My wife?" Trulliç said, his voice quiet but firm.

"I will," Nadeem said, feeling herself still shaking inside, though her body remained steady, not betraying the strong emotions clashing through her.

What had Trulliç said about breaking himself into a million pieces against the rocks up here?

Nadeem hadn't broken completely apart. But she'd started the process. A crack had formed in her protective shell, that distance she'd been holding everyone at since nearly dying in the myth lands.

And though she could patch that hole back up, for the first time she wasn't sure she wanted to.

***

Nadeem enjoyed racing down the mountain with Trulliç more than she should have. But it was fun to glide so fast between the rocks, to tease Trulliç by racing ahead, then letting him catch up. The winds blew easy against her face. Though her cheek ached, it was a good pain, like the kind her muscles had when she'd been training long and hard.

Everything changed, though, once they reached the desert proper. Trulliç's face grew serious. Nadeem saw the man behind the boy, how he would mature over the years. He didn't have as handsome a face as Levent's. Trulliç had the tall, proud nose of the people of the desert, their darker skin, eyes and hair as well. His thin lips could be very stern or very playful.

It was an intelligent face. His body was long and hard after living in the desert, all the water squeezed out of it. But underneath it all, he still had the soul of a poet.

Could Nadeem live with a desert poet the rest of her life? That would possibly be easier than with a desert magician. Maybe someone would write songs about the mighty deeds they did together.

Nadeem could be content with that.

Still, Trulliç hurried toward Hayalevi, his great pile of stones flying with him. He went first to Barzhat's temple where the star sisters had camped.

As soon as he touched down, several of the guard ran forward. "Take these," he said. "Shape them quickly. I'll be back to help if I can."

Then he turned to Nadeem. "I can't tell for certain," he said slowly. "But the emperor, or at least some of his guards, may be here. They're well disguised. But something is wrong."

"I'll go inform the council," she said, turning.

"Good. Gather a third of the defenders and bring them here in an hour's time," Trulliç said.

"Where are you going?" Nadeem asked. Trulliç appeared to be walking right beside her, hurrying back toward the magician's tower.

"I need to go master a cane," Trulliç said with a grimace. "Or destroy it."

"Good luck," Nadeem said, and she meant it.

Trulliç appeared to transform into a dust devil as he raced away, a spinning collection of sand and wind.

The old Trulliç wouldn't have been able to do anything with the emperor's cane.

This one, however, might have the patience and deep roots within himself to withstand the emperor's slippery magic.

CHAPTER FIVE

TRULLIÇ

TRULLIÇ DID NOT GIVE HIMSELF time to think. He raced up the stairs of the tower and into his room, gathering up the glass-encased staff and throwing himself the rest of the way up to the top of the tower.

Sunlight beat down on Trulliç's head, warming his soul. He planted his feet wide, feeling as though roots shot down from the base of his heels through the soul of the tower, and into the desert below. The stones connected him and his strength. He smelled the baking fires and felt a memory of hunger, how his mouth had once watered for his mother's fine flatbread fresh from the stove.

But that was no longer him.

He studied the case, looking at the cane with great curiosity. He knew it was dangerous. When he broke the glass, the cane would regain its power.

Could it call its master to it? Or even worse, channel its master's power so that the emperor could blast dangerous magic through it?

Possibly. That was why Trulliç had encased the cane in glass in the first place, so that the errant magic couldn't slip through.

He also realized that he'd merely neutralized the cane. He hadn't stopped it, not really. Like everything else in his life, it had been waiting for him to do something more.

The emperor was coming. Trulliç had to be able to stop him, stop his magic.

The cane would be a good test.

A movement caught Trulliç's eye.

Huh. Riyune had joined him. Why had the dog stayed behind earlier that morning when Trulliç went up into the Yalçin mountains? Had it been to protect Nadeem? Or had the dog realized that Nadeem was going to have to fetch him?

Trulliç truly didn't know. But Riyune being here made him uneasy. Trulliç wasn't sure why.

He glanced between the glass case floating in the air above the tower and the dog beside him.

They cast the same sort of wavy shadow. Neither of them were solid things with solid lines.

What magic would fill Riyune when it came time? Was he, too, a vessel for channeling something powerful from beyond?

Trulliç smiled softly at himself when he heard Atça's voice accusing him of being too fanciful. He knew at other times that he'd get angry at the reminder, but for now it just made him shake his head and push his former mentor away.

He could deal with Atça's ghost later. Again.

For now, Trulliç had to focus on releasing the cane and blocking its magic. Hopefully Riyune wouldn't get in the way.

Trulliç expanded his senses, wrapping them more firmly around the glass case floating in the air. The glass itself was heavy and thick. It had a sheen in the sunlight that reminded Trulliç of the fountain in the courtyard, the splashing water casting the same shimmer.

Inside the case, Trulliç couldn't feel the cane at all. He could see it with his eyes, he knew it was there in front of him. But he couldn't find it. The cane felt…slippery. As though it wasn't really there but somewhere in between the world and its place of origin.

Maybe Trulliç could just blast the cane back to where it came from. But that didn't feel right. The emperor could just call it forth again.

No, Trulliç had to *block* the cane from getting through.

But how?

***

Trulliç called up all his defenses. To the right of him, a wind storm swirled in on itself, ready to lash out and carry the cane far past the desert, even beyond the Yalçin mountains and to the ocean. Another storm full of crackling lighting, hunched together on Trulliç's left, the power strong enough to damage the tower itself if Trulliç wasn't careful.

He'd even borrowed the largest caldron he could from Seydat, carrying it up to the top of the tower and filling it with water, willing to drown the cane if he needed to.

Beneath where the cane floated, Trulliç had already heaped a small hill of sand, hoping that would at least help him capture the damned thing.

His preparations finished, Trulliç sent a brief prayer to Serril, the god who'd brought all magic to mankind, both the men and the women. He was a trickster god and difficult to appease. But Trulliç felt as though Serril approved of him as the desert magician, as well as the people of his city, those he'd brought into the desolate places. Maybe the god would help Trulliç fight the emperor as well.

Of course, the goddess that Trulliç really needed to invoke was Barzhat, as she stood the most to lose if the emperor won. But Trulliç had never worshipped her and it felt false to suddenly start now.

Trulliç untied the glass horseshoe he always carried with him. It had helped him in the past with his greatest magic. It really didn't have that much magic in and of itself, but it helped him focus.

For now, Trulliç narrowed his attention on the glass surrounding the cane. He knew glass, knew its flaws and its strengths, the heat needed to make it flow like the sweet *meslit* syrup, the length of time needed to cool so it wouldn't crack.

The glass melted around the cane, reforming into sand and rock below where the cane floated. Heat radiated out from the sand, making it too hot for even Trulliç to touch, but he took a step forward anyway. The warmth seared his face. He was forced to deflect it before it actually burned him.

However, that extreme temperature didn't melt the wood or the silver of the cane. Whatever it was made from, it wasn't normal. Or perhaps stronger magic protected it.

Trulliç called up a soft, chilling wind. The sand crackled as it cooled, sounding like glass breaking.

Finally the temperature lowered enough that the cane appeared to awaken. Magic slid from the thing. Trulliç knew the cane still floated in the air in front of him because he could see it. That was the only sense that told him where the cane existed. Though it did exude a slipperiness, as though it was made from oil. Maybe he could hone in on that feeling when he tried to detect those with such magic.

Trulliç turned his attention to the top of the cane, the silver head of the snake. Each scale of the small figure looked like the emperor's leaf symbol. What was that snake made out of? It stayed still, but it still seemed to waver in the heat.

Then Trulliç focused on the body of the cane. The wood just below the head of the snake seemed almost normal. If he turned his magical sense to just the wood, he could almost feel it, as if it were closer to him than the snakehead.

A silver cap tipped the bottom of the cane. Like the top, Trulliç found he couldn't sense it with his magic.

Were those two parts of the cane actually connected to some other place? Like how the cavern connected this world to the myth lands, did the cane connect this world to someplace else?

But where?

Trulliç wrapped his sand around the head of the cane. It slid off, as though trying to pile around a steep hill. He tried winds next, but the winds just blew past the cane as if it wasn't there.

And still the cane exuded a power that made Trulliç's skin crawl.

Trulliç caused the cane to turn upside down, then he thrust the head into the water. The cane didn't notice it at all. If Trulliç felt like being fanciful, he'd say that the cane laughed at him.

Trulliç brought the cane out of the water and thrust the top of it into the sand.

Ah. There. He could finally *feel* something. Grains of sand rubbed against the wood of the cane, scraping at the black dye. The silver tip was hidden far below. Trulliç couldn't feel it, not exactly, but he could feel *something*.

Why did the sand appear to drown the cane, while the water didn't?

He remembered Zahra's odd phrasing again, about the emperor crashing against his shores.

Trulliç knew he didn't have much more time. The first wave of his volunteer army were about to go out and greet the wrongness that he felt, close to the Kinarak mountains, near Gaadiwala.

Of course, the emperor would strike there first. He should have thought of that. The emperor didn't merely slaughter the men and women of the places he conquered, he also destroyed their dreams.

Did he think that by hurting the people of Gaadiwala that he would hurt Trulliç? Did he not understand that they weren't his people? After he'd killed Atça, he'd given them the choice to come with him to the desert. Only a couple dozen had made that decision, most of whom were part of Trulliç's immediate family—his aunts, uncles, and cousins. The rest had stayed in Gaadiwala.

Killing the people who'd remained in the village Trulliç had been raised in would make him angry, yes, but no more angry than any of the other deaths of the innocents.

No, when the emperor reached Egreliki and killed the people there, that would hurt much more.

Trulliç drowned the cane in sand. Something in the sand, like the glass, neutralized its power. Not completely. It still maintained its oily nature. But its call felt distorted, as though the sand tainted it.

He didn't trust the sand to hold the cane, however, so he locked it back up in glass. Thicker this time, clear and wavy. Then he caused the case to go shooting across the sky into the true desert, then down into the ground, burying it deeply in the sand, away from any water or true rock.

He would have to fetch it back up later. For now, it was safe enough. He wouldn't have to deal with a foe at his back while the emperor's forces attacked him from the front.

Riyune hadn't done much of anything while Trulliç had experimented with the cane. It was almost as if the dog had merely come to be a spectator without any commentary.

Did the old kings not know how to deal with the emperor either? Had they been hoping that Trulliç's magic would be enough?

Or had Riyune been here to kill Trulliç if the emperor had taken him over? If his dreams of the old kings had been true and not just his imagination, Trulliç hadn't been the first desert magician they'd tried to help.

And he wouldn't be the last.

Riyune accompanied Trulliç to the temple of Barzhat, where the star sisters and their charges had gathered. Very few of the men looked like hardened warriors, though several of them did have an edge that told Trulliç they were truly people of the desert. Some of the women who weren't star sisters had that same roughness.

The desert wasn't kind or forgiving. Too often a single mistake would lead to death. The nights of the desert could freeze, while the sunlight blasted and burned.

The people of the desert reflected that, their eyes like hawks studying the horizon for storms or bandits, their noses keenly tuned to any trouble.

They were *his* people. The stillness each held was reflected in Trulliç's own soul. He recognized the depths of their feelings and their cares.

The star sisters were a different breed. The promise of death bound them together, their training and excellence shining through. They weren't as still as the desert people, and much of their roughness had been smoothed away.

Yet they were here, fighting for him, as well as for their goddess.

Myrizhah stood there with the group. She didn't mean to go with them, did she? But no, she was just seeing to some last minute provisions.

"Thank you," Trulliç said to his mother, stepping up to her.

"For what?" she asked, looking harried, as if she'd planned on hurrying away and now something was stopping her.

"For doing everything that you could for me," Trulliç said. He took her hand and squeezed it.

Myrizhah blinked for a moment, surprised. Then she shrugged. "It needed doing," she said simply.

"Aye," he said, letting go of her hand. "Still. Thank you."

Myrizhah looked at him, puzzled. She seemed to realize suddenly that he was different than before. She gave him a small smile. "Your soft heart may survive yet," she said. Then she was off, back to the tower and the war council, back to keep the home fires burning.

Trulliç found himself the natural center of things as the crowd circled around him. "I don't know what we'll find out there, at the edge of the desert," he said. "I suspect it's part of the emperor's troops. They'll be walking in plain sight, using magic that lets them hide from the desert."

That brought an angry grumble from everyone. The desert shouldn't be trifled with that way.

"There will be hundreds of them. Maybe thousands. Trained warriors, with swords, arrows, pikes and shields," Trulliç explained. "I don't know if we'll be able to stop them or just slow them down. But," he continued, his voice turning hard, "they are not my people. They don't belong here. They are not part of the desert. If that means we must kill them all, then we must."

An angry growl from the entire crowd erupted around him.

Trulliç would rather not kill the soldiers coming with this wave. He knew that their deaths would only strengthen the emperor.

However, his people needed a victory as well, just to show them that it was possible. His war council had decided that the other parts of the army would get different instructions.

This group, the ones led initially by the desert magician himself, would cause the most causalities. They would receive the most as well, being the tip of the spear.

All of the people surrounding Trulliç carried some symbol of his, whether a glass marble buried deep in a pocket, a small amulet made of glass, or even a glass shard sharpened and ready to be used like a knife. The star sisters all had pieces of obsidian with them, making them easy to find.

"Then let us war on those who would invade us!" Trulliç called, using a booming voice aided by the desert winds.

The cry that rose up deafened him.

With the sun still beating down on his head, Trulliç effortless lifted his people up as one.

And flung them toward battle.

As Trulliç had suspected, the emperor's soldiers weren't trying to walk stealthily. It was easy to spot them from more than a mile away, high in the sky. Why they walked across the desert in the bright sunlight, he didn't know. Maybe it was because they were unlikely to meet other travelers at this time, or maybe they were just that arrogant, thinking the sun wouldn't beat them.

However, Trulliç and his group were able to hide. The star sisters kept them disguised, and the guards never looked up.

Trulliç gulped dryly when he saw the lines of the soldiers stretching on and on.

He hadn't been exaggerating when he'd said there would be thousands of the emperor's men for every hundred of his own.

The group traveling with Trulliç stayed eerily silent, as quiet as the desert night. Trulliç didn't know that such a large group of people could be so noiseless. Then he realized it was because they were reflecting his own mood, the fierce rage that held him still.

Trulliç set them all down in a valley. The soldiers would come this way, marching in a ridiculously direct line. None of the trade routes were that straight, then again, they followed the course of whatever river ran deep beneath them.

It didn't take long for Trulliç to hide the first third of his people under the sand. They had reeds they could use to breathe and were used to staying still. They would start the ambush.

He wished he had more time to pray for them and their souls.

They were likely to carry the brunt of the attack. He suspected most of them wouldn't survive.

Then he whisked the star sisters away, placing them past the end of the line of soldiers. It would be likely to confuse the soldiers and to make them think that a much larger army attacked them if they were forced to fight at both ends of their line.

It frightened Trulliç when he realized just how many men they were facing. Well over two thousand. He needed to stop this breach. These men carried large amounts of magic. They had that same slippery feeling that he'd felt from Marius and his squad. He wasn't sure what they could do. Would they channel the emperor? Draw on strength that was not theirs? Once they started dying, would the survivors grow stronger?

That was part of the reason why Trulliç led this attack. He needed to learn as much as he could about the emperor and his forces, as quickly as he could. And while he wanted to bury all the soldiers in sand and not let them attack, his war council had advised him to let the battle play out. He would lose people, yes, but he'd gain information in exchange.

It wasn't a fair exchange. After much arguing, Trulliç had agreed to it.

He'd also insisted on being there at the start. So he could bear witness to the sacrifices his people made. Aunt Parayat had agreed and had insisted on it as well. Trulliç needed to be there to give his people hope so that they'd fight for him.

The star sisters were trained to fight and die. His people had never had to fight anything greater than a winter storm or maybe drought, mighty forces on their own, yet not the same as battle veterans.

Trulliç cast the last third of his people along both sides of the emperor's army. They'd commit more scattered attacks, dashing in out of nowhere, taking out a single soldier then whirling away again. The soldiers wouldn't know what hit them and wouldn't know where the next attack would be coming from.

Riyune stayed with this group, something that surprised Trulliç. He'd expected the dog to stick by his side.

But as soon as Riyune touched the desert sand, he grew in size, his spine easily reaching Trulliç's waist. He seemed to shimmer in the bright sunlight, an unearthly glow. He growled deep in his chest, a menacing warning that sent shivers down Trulliç's back.

Something that Levent had said stuck with Trulliç. *Fear is in the mind of the enemy's commander.*

And Trulliç intended to push those seeds of fear deep into his attackers.

<hr>

Trulliç felt the first death as if it were his own.

He'd stayed up and away from the start of the battle. He floated above the attack, getting a bird's eye view of the battle. He'd wanted to be closer to the ground, but he'd acquiesced at the insistence of Beyzha, one of the star sister "aunts" who'd stayed with him. She'd battled beside the emperor's soldiers at one point in her long life and could give him advice about their tactics. It was important that he protect her because her insights after the battle would be as useful as his own.

She didn't seem that old to Trulliç. Her dark skin didn't hold many wrinkles, and her body was as muscular as a man's. Her eyes, however, gave away her age, holding secrets and pain in their dark depths. She dressed in all black, a tight outfit that allowed her movement. In addition to her knives, she carried a bow with arrows tipped with obsidian heads.

It had been exciting to see his people suddenly rise up out of the sand. They slayed the soldiers nearest them without too much commotion.

Then the soldiers started to cry out orders. The enemy was in their camp, beside them, surrounding them.

They quickly changed formation. Instead of being a long line, they clumped together, shields out and locked in place.

Trulliç saw his opportunity and took it before Beyzha could say anything or warn him against it. He sent a rolling ball of wind down, knocking the soldiers aside like a child's game.

The opening he'd created was quickly filled with his warriors, surging like a spear into the gap.

They died just as quickly, their blood mingling with that of their foes.

The soldiers tried to band together again, but Trulliç continued to harry them with his winds, knocking them aside whenever more than four had gathered together.

His people weren't winning, though there were too many bodies, too much blood, too much confusion for him to say for certain.

However, the soldiers were halted, at least for now, and that was what counted.

Beyzha pointed Trulliç's attention to the north, further back along the line. He flew them that way.

As they traveled, one of the men pointed skyward towards them.

Beyzha shouted, "I have us hidden! They must be tracking us through magic." She sounded angry that they'd seen through her illusion.

Trulliç nodded. He'd expected many of the soldiers to have magic, possibly even be fueled by the emperor. He darted to the far side and looked back.

A group of eight soldiers had broken off the main group and were loping after them.

"You keep going," Beyzha said. "Drop me off here. I'll take care of them."

"No," Trulliç said stubbornly. "Your report is needed by the war council."

"Then you better drop those soldiers before they reach you," she warned.

Trulliç nodded. He'd been thinking about Zahra's comment for a while now.

He reached out and felt for the sand just in front of the running soldiers. It softened with his touch, growing deep and fine. Too soft to hold any weight on top of it.

The first soldier started to struggle as soon as he set foot on the patch. The second and third followed along, not realizing the trap they'd fallen into.

The others, however, easily ran around the area that Trulliç had created.

"Do that again!" Beyzha said, obviously impressed.

A muffled booming sound occurred, followed quickly by two more. Sand erupted from where the three men had been buried.

The sand was streaked with blood, as well as the slippery magic of the emperor. Trulliç hurriedly gathered it all together and sent it flying across the desert, across the border, so it couldn't taint the land here.

He shared a glance with Beyzha. He shouldn't try to bury these men. Maybe others, who had less magic. But not these.

Beyzha fired her arrows at them and took out two more, but ran out of arrows before she could drop the others.

Should Trulliç kill the soldiers who kept coming outright? Except that these were the emperor's special men. Either they would draw power from each other's deaths, or their deaths would fuel the emperor.

Trulliç blasted the oncoming soldiers with bouts of harsh winds, bowling them over and sending them back into the rest of the melee. He would trust that Beyzha would watch for him, warn him if they were coming near again.

In the meanwhile, Trulliç concentrated on how the side battles were going.

Not so well.

The soldiers had dug in quickly, hiding behind pikes and shields. It was impossible for his people to get to them. The soldiers were too well organized.

How were they able to form up so quickly? Or was that part of the emperor's magic as well?

Trulliç didn't send winds to disrupt the men. Instead, he gathered together a ball of sheer energy. It was similar to lightning, but it only contained magic.

What would happen when he dropped that on the soldiers?

The disruption was obvious. Though he'd struck toward the middle of the group, the ends shuddered as if they'd been hit, too.

Trulliç followed up with another blast. It appeared to travel through the men, the energy leaping from one to the next where they had locked their shields together.

It was equally obvious this wasn't part of their usual playbook. They weren't used to being attacked this way. They didn't seem to have any idea how to fight something that attacked them as a whole.

The soldiers were used to fighting, however. They broke apart quickly, each man at the ready to defend himself.

Trulliç's people and some of the star sisters joined the fight now.

But for every man they took down, the soldiers took down three of Trulliç's. His people just weren't trained that way. The slaughter sickened him. The smell of gore would follow him into his nightmares. Not the cries of the soldiers, however. His people remained quiet, almost silent, as they killed or died. Only the soldiers cried out.

He could drown all the soldiers in sand. Use winds to carry them far, far from his lands. He could distinguish them from his own people.

But then what? They'd just come back. Stronger, sneakier than before.

He had to stop all of them from coming. Before he lost more good men and women.

***

Trulliç did a quick pass over the end of the line of soldiers. Unsurprisingly, the star sisters had been very effective. While a few stragglers remained behind, most of the bodies strewn across the sands weren't wearing black.

It didn't take much to bury the corpses and blow the sands clean of their blood. The bodies of the star sisters he kept to one side. He wasn't sure what the women would do with their dead, but he wanted to give them the option of gathering them up for their own services.

As Trulliç dropped the last of the soldiers into the sand, he realized that their corpses weren't as heavy as the sisters' bodies. He explained his experience to Bayzha, who agreed that he could step down, out of the air, to go and examine one more closely.

Trulliç felt more at peace with his feet on the ground. While he was still connected to the desert when he flew above it, it wasn't the same as walking across the sands himself.

He hurried over to the closest body. Bayzha stood guard, her eyes constantly scanning the horizon for any threats.

Trulliç turned the body over with a wind, not wanting to touch it himself. Then he gasped.

The man's eyes looked as though they'd been burned out of their sockets. His face was gaunt as well. Even his hands appeared skeletal.

The next body Trulliç reached for appeared more normal. Then, his face started to cave in on itself. Whatever soul or life or essence that had remained with the body was being sucked away.

Damn it! The emperor was still reaching into Trulliç's lands. How could he disrupt this flow?

It was proof that the emperor was growing strong even as his men died, as Trulliç had suspected would happen.

He threw up glass around the body. That seemed to break whatever connection the soldier had to his master.

Should he encase the entire area in glass? Would that stop the emperor in his tracks?

But no. When he turned back to the soldier, he saw that while encasing the corpse had slowed the progress of the magic, it didn't cut the emperor's magic off completely.

What could he do? What would stop the emperor?

Trulliç shattered the glass around the body, as the man was already dead. Then he ignored the horrible putrefying stench the corpse was starting to give off and focused instead on the armor of the soldier.

Like Magnus, the soldier wore a leather chest plate, dyed red, with a great golden snake's scale in the center of it. He also wore a short leather apron that hung down to his knees, over a shorter, lighter weight, cropped set of pants.

Magnus had been able to remove the snake's scale from the center of his chest. The emperor had focused his magic through it. Could it also be used to suck the remains of a man's life from him?

Trulliç raced down the line, looking for an uncorrupted body. When he finally found one, he reached down to tug at the emperor's mark in the center of the man's chest.

Then he snatched his fingers away as magic burned through the air.

"The chest plates!" Trulliç yelled at Bayzha. "We need to remove them!" He wasn't sure why the one he'd tried to touch had attacked him and burned his fingers. Maybe it was because it sensed another's magic.

The problem with using a wind was that it wasn't delicate. He couldn't tear the chest plate off without tearing a man to shreds. And he wasn't even sure he could touch the chest plates physically.

Bayzha came running toward him.

Before she got close, a spear flew out of air.

If Bayzha hadn't been running, with her back toward the rest of the line, she might have been able to catch the spear or at least deflect it.

Instead, it caught her square in the middle of her back. Her arms flung out, as if she was trying to fly away. The spear's momentum carried her forward. She fell onto her face, looking like a pinned bird.

The three men from earlier came into sight. They saw Trulliç. Two immediately started shooting arrows toward him, while a third sent yet another spear.

Trulliç easily defended himself from their thrown attacks. He didn't let them come any closer but blasted them again with strong winds.

This time they didn't get bowled over. They seemed ready and caught each other before they fell further away.

The three of them remained locked together, two behind the first man.

His face grew terrible, as if it were made of wax and melted. His eyes burned with a brilliant gold fire. Fangs shot out of his mouth, already bloodied. His hands turned into great claws.

The man roared loud enough that Trulliç felt it in his bones. He found himself frozen with shock.

The creature, for he could no longer be called a man, gave a terrible, hypnotic cry as he started loping forward.

Trulliç shook and tried to free himself. There was something about the cry, something about the magic he'd just witnessed, that held him still.

The part of his mind not scrambling madly to free himself wondered briefly if this was what had happened to the old kings, if the emperor had frozen them against their will.

The two men who'd been supporting the creature dropped to the desert ground, blackened husks, their life and all matter sucked away. Not even their bones remained, just ashes.

Ashes. Dust. Sand.

While Trulliç couldn't move his limbs at all, he could still call the sands and the winds.

He *blasted* the creature running at him.

As he expected, his attack didn't knock the thing off course.

But it did slow it down.

Trulliç refined his attack and sent out sands and tearing winds again. He couldn't levitate the creature away—like the cane, while Trulliç could see the creature, he could barely sense him. The monster's power was coming from someplace else, someplace that Trulliç couldn't reach. However, Trulliç could stop the transfer of power.

He focused on the scale burning bright in the center of the thing's chest, gathered his power together, then pushed out with all his might.

The heat of the sand rushing from him burned his fingers. It pushed back the *chafiyek* he wore over his hair. Nearby bodies crisped to ash all around him.

The great glob of glass that Trulliç had generated found its target. It smacked right into the creature's chest, hot enough to annihilate bone.

And, it seemed, strong enough to counter the emperor's magic.

The creature stopped. Trulliç heard the cry of a man this time and not a beast. The liquid glass *burned* his chest, immolated the emperor's symbol.

The man cried again, dropping to his knees.

Now it was Trulliç's turn to run forward, trying to get to the man before he crumbled away.

The heated glob of glass smoldered on the remains of the man's chest. The emperor's symbol glowed brightly underneath it, as if trying to warn him away. Trulliç levitated the glass up, encasing the snake's scale.

Could he cut it completely off from the power of the emperor? It wasn't as strongly built as the head of the snake on the cane.

He added another layer of glass to the floating symbol, turning it in the air as he blew out and spun the glass. Green and gold stripes found their way into case, though Trulliç didn't knowingly add them.

The shape took on the form of a stylized heart, bulbous and full, containing the symbol of the emperor.

Trulliç felt the anger swirling from it. The emperor was trying to get at him, at his prize. He couldn't afford to be studied closely. Trulliç might learn too much.

The symbol stopped trying to suck at the magic surrounding it. Instead, power began to pour out of it.

Trulliç couldn't cut the leaf off from the emperor's power. They were too in tune with one another. Or maybe it was because this piece had come from the emperor directly, himself.

With a strong wind, Trulliç cast the encased symbol high into the air. The glass exploded as it reached the cooler temperatures up above him, shards and small spikes raining down.

Trulliç hadn't thought about dropping glass on his enemy like heavy rain, though he now realized he could do it and could kill a large group that way.

But at least he finally had an idea how to stop the emperor from using the deaths of his soldiers to power himself. As well as a possible method for defeating the fighting army.

The star sisters needed to focus on the symbol of the emperor that every soldier wore. Would it be possible to tear the scale symbol off the fighting soldiers? Trulliç could tell his people to do the same. Without the emperor's symbol powering them, the soldiers might lose much of their training. Hell, maybe even half their strength.

They might become beatable.

After burying the bodies that remained and wiping the desert clean of their intrusion, Trulliç rose back up in the air.

His ragged army couldn't stop this group of soldiers from continuing. They'd all die trying.

However, he'd slowed this group down.

As Trulliç flew overhead, he gathered up his people, drawing up the wounded as well. The soldiers who remained didn't know where their enemy had disappeared to, or where they were going.

The soldiers would be delayed, but that was all, while they regrouped and tended to their own wounded.

Then they'd start their trek again.

Eventually, they'd reach Hayalevi.

CHAPTER SIX

NADEEM

NADEEM STOOD AT THE BACK of the gathering of the war council, listening to Trulliç's report. She'd seen the horrifyingly small number of the army who'd returned.

And Trulliç hadn't even been able to stop the soldiers' attack but merely to slow them down.

"Why didn't your border defenses stop them?" Levent asked.

Nadeem found herself nodding. She'd seen the glass ball rise up out of the desert and stop Magnus' group from crossing over to the sand.

"When I visited the city of Çandikili, the city's defenses didn't react to my presence," Trulliç said slowly. "I assumed at the time it was because I was such a minor threat. Now I wonder if my magic was so strong it overwhelmed those defenses."

Nadeem heard the plain truth in Trulliç's voice. He wasn't bragging.

Breaking himself into a million pieces on the rugged rocks of Yalçin had truly changed him. The old Trulliç wouldn't have been able to admit to his own power.

"Could you have killed them all?" Aunt Parayat asked. "Once you located them?"

"Yes, but that wouldn't have been enough," Trulliç said adamantly. "If I drown them in sand, they'd explode out of it and taint the land. If I speared them with glass shards, the emperor would still have used their deaths to grow stronger. If I built a great glass wall around them after they were dead, that would slow down the emperor but not stop him. He and his men would keep coming."

"Maybe you can hold the men in sand, and the star sisters could then come and strip them of their emblem?" Seydat suggested.

"Maybe," Trulliç said slowly. "When I tried to pull the emperor's symbol from the chest of a fallen soldier, it burned my hands."

"We tried as well," said one of the star sisters who'd survived the battle. "It had the same effect. Couldn't touch it. We could carve the breast plate off the man, but it was like removing the hide from a goat. Magic seals the armor together. It won't come off easily."

Nadeem tried to pay attention to the rest of the questions, the ideas that everyone tossed into the ring. Trulliç could stop the armies at the border, but he couldn't stop the emperor. And he was wasting lives when he did so, lives that the emperor then fed on.

They could fight like this for years, with the emperor just sending troops into the desert, men willing to die on their own home soil. Though the desert was different enough from the rest of the empire that it probably felt foreign to them.

They had to bring the emperor here. While Trulliç could build a huge glass wall to keep the soldiers out, it also would keep all his people in. The desert people needed to trade with those outside the desert. Isolating themselves wouldn't work.

But how to bring the emperor here? Or at the very least, protect the people who already lived here?

She'd sworn to do everything in her power to stop the emperor from laying waste to all the lands. Trulliç had sworn a similar blood oath.

There had to be something more that she could do.

But what?

At the end of the evening meal, Nadeem helped Myrizhah gather up the dishes. Although Myrizhah could have directed anyone else to do it, she still insisted on doing it herself. "Gives my hands something to do," she said.

Nadeem understood that. It was why she'd volunteered to help. She needed to do something, anything. The war council had come up with some new ideas, but Nadeem wasn't very hopeful.

Tomorrow would be another skirmish with the emperor's soldiers, probably the second prong of his attack.

And more would die.

Nadeem paused when she picked up the one plate that still contained a full serving of thick goat stew with flatbread and tiny onions. Who hadn't eaten? Even Trulliç had taken a few bites, more to make the others comfortable than because he needed the food.

With a start, Nadeem realized that Myrizhah had set a full place for the goddess Barzhat. It was custom for the star sisters to do so. It was how they showed their love for the goddess, by including her in all the family meals, not just the feasts dedicated to her.

"Why did you set a place for the goddess Barzhat?" Nadeem asked as she followed the woman back into the large kitchen area.

Myrizhah shrugged. "I've done it often enough when I served star sisters, when I worked in the tavern," she said. "And we're preparing for more deaths. It seemed like the right thing to do. To invite the goddess here, to share bread with her, in the hopes that she'll judge our warriors lightly."

"Thank you," Nadeem said. It was a touching gesture.

It also gave her an idea.

"Where's Trulliç?" Nadeem asked as they finished rinsing off the plates.

"At the top of his tower, I'd imagine," Myrizhah said. "Studying the stars." She paused, then she added, "He seems changed. More relaxed."

Nadeem paused, trying to figure out how best to explain it to his mother. "He went through a trial on Yalçin mountain," she said.

"Good," Myrizhah said, nodding. Then she speared Nadeem with a hard look. "May we all survive our own individual trials."

Nadeem knew the woman was talking about Nadeem's issue, still living a half-life.

There wasn't anything she was willing to do about that, however. Not until after the war, though now she very much doubted there would be an after the war for her.

Nadeem climbed to the top of the tower. She didn't bother announcing herself or knocking. Trulliç would have barred her from coming up if he didn't want to see her.

He stood at the far edge of the square opening, looking north over the desert. Riyune lay on the ground beside him, imitating a statue, with his front legs out and his back legs curled under him. The dog didn't even blink when Nadeem came up the stairs.

Stars filled the sky to over brimming. The air was cool up here, carrying the smells of roasting goat. She heard the murmur of the people below, a soft, soothing sound.

Trulliç turned as Nadeem crossed the space. He wore a simple muslin tunic striped with green and gold, his black-and-white checked *chafiyek* tied around his neck. He smiled sweetly at her. He kept his hands stiffly at his sides, though she knew he wanted to reach out and touch her.

Would she ever welcome his touch? Or even get used to it?

Nadeem walked silently to the edge of the tower and looked out. Night covered the desert, and the stars only showed a small slice of her beauty. Still, the sand appeared to sparkle, even from up here.

"I have an idea," Nadeem said quietly.

Trulliç turned to face the desert, seeming to understand that it was going to be easier for Nadeem to address it, and not him, directly.

"We—I mean the star sisters—welcome the goddess Barzhat into our lives and hearts," Nadeem said. "We are meant to love her, truly love her. To greet her with joy no matter what form she takes."

Trulliç nodded. He looked worried where this conversation was going.

Nadeem continued anyway.

"In exchange, a sister can ask a single boon from the goddess at the sister's time of greatest need," Nadeem said. "The goddess may or may not grant it. Usually she doesn't. The need is rarely great enough."

"Go on," Trulliç said, still looking worried.

"We are at our hour of greatest need," Nadeem said. "I plan to cross over to the myth lands and ask for Barzhat's help. Not just for fighting the soldiers, but to stop the emperor from taking the goddess' place."

"I see," Trulliç said. He sighed, as if a great weight had just settled onto his shoulders. "I don't want you to go," he said. "But I won't stop you, either."

"Thank you," Nadeem said. That was all she could ask for.

"And afterward?" Trulliç asked, his voice challenging. He turned now to face Nadeem. "What happens after the war if all is not lost?"

Nadeem nearly laughed. She should have known she couldn't talk to Trulliç without him bringing this up again.

"I will deal with you honestly, Trulliç," Nadeem said. She could promise him that. She took a deep breath. She'd felt fear a few times in her life, that fluttering feeling inside her chest that took her solid center away. She pushed it away, as she always did.

"I like you, Trulliç," Nadeem said softly. "I like the man you're becoming. So much more than the clueless boy I always wanted to smack."

Trulliç chuckled and had the grace to look chagrined. "Good," he said. "I'm glad. However, I can hear a large 'but' coming."

"I go to embrace the goddess," Nadeem said. "Maybe to dance for her, to beg for her favor. Like your trial on the mountain, this will change me."

Trulliç nodded solemnly but held his tongue. He really was growing up.

"I don't know if there is any coming back from being with the goddess," Nadeem admitted. "I don't know what exactly will happen."

"I see," Trulliç said. "Though I don't, not really. No one knows what happens when we deal with the gods intimately."

He thought for a moment before he finally added, "Come back to me when you can. If you can. You will always have a place here."

"Thank you," Nadeem said. "Both for being willing to understand, as well as for the offer."

Trulliç gave her a crooked smile that made him look more rakish and less vulnerable. "Wherever you want to stand—here by my side, in my bed, or across the room—you will always be welcome."

Nadeem blinked, surprised. Trulliç was growing up. "I don't know what will be," she said softly. "I cannot make any promises. I will not be foresworn."

The silent word *again* echoed between them.

"Before you go then, let me apologize," Trulliç said.

"Whatever for?" Nadeem said, confused. What had he done that he felt the need to apologize?

"When we were in the myth lands. You were willing to sacrifice yourself to close the door to the desert heart," he said.

"Yes," Nadeem said. She still felt confused. There hadn't been any other choice.

"I didn't want to take your sacrifice," Trulliç said. "If I could have chosen myself, I would have. But you were right. The desert magician needed to live on, to fight the emperor."

"And?" Nadeem asked, her natural impatience building.

"I would have taken your life," he confessed in a small voice.

Nadeem snorted in derision. "There's nothing to forgive," she chided him. "We were both driven by need. I know you would have chosen differently if you'd had a chance."

"I just didn't want that standing between us," Trulliç said stubbornly. "I didn't want you to think I held you in less regard."

Nadeem shook her head. "You've been reading old love poems again, haven't you?"

Trulliç opened his mouth to deny it, but then closed it again. He shook his head and looked down at his feet.

Nadeem couldn't tell if he was blushing or not, not in the starlight.

"It's all right," she assured him gently. "I was ready to die."

"You still are," Trulliç said, his voice holding a harder edge.

"So are you," Nadeem shot back.

"I would, if that would save the desert," Trulliç said after a moment. "But I don't believe I'll be faced with that choice. I want to live. I want to have a life with you."

Nadeem held silence between them like a wall of glass. She would *not* respond, "Me, too," as much as a part of her really wished to.

She had yet to embrace the goddess. Dance for the goddess of death.

The quiet of the desert surrounded Nadeem as she slowed. Stars cast an eerie glow on the sand. Maybe it only sparkled when Trulliç was there. She didn't hear even the rustling of wind, smoothing sand into ridged waves. The coolness of the night gave a dusty smell, making her think of places long forgotten.

There were still many hours before dawn. The night held its reign firmly.

Nadeem knew she was still on the edges of the ancient desert. She didn't have time, or Trulliç's speed, to get to the heart of the Qaenev. Still, she'd gotten to a place where man rarely traveled, as the caravans always came along the trade routes that outlined the sand.

Without hesitation, Nadeem pulled her obsidian knife from her belt. It had served her well in the past.

She'd already taken a blood oath to stop the emperor from desecrating the lands. Did she need to swear a new oath? Or just reaffirm the one she'd already taken?

Nadeem knelt on the cool sand. It felt solid under her legs, as though cast from hard stone. With a quick motion, she sliced open her left palm. Blood sprang up on either side of the peeling skin. Nadeem placed her hand down on the sand, ignoring the pain of the wound.

"I still stand by my oath to do everything in my power to stop the emperor from laying waste to these lands," Nadeem called out into the still air. "Now, my need is greater. I ask for the help of the gods to stop the emperor once and for all."

Though Nadeem didn't feel a great wind, she heard it swishing around her. She glanced to the side. Was something coming?

When she looked forward again, she saw the cavern immediately in front of her. The dark rocks still looked misshapen, piled haphazardly on top of one another. The opening felt as though it had been carved out of solid night, black and cold. She couldn't see through it to the guard stone.

Nadeem rose gracefully to her feet. She bowed her head low to the outcropping of rocks. "Thank you for coming," she said. She crossed the few feet necessary to reach the cavern, finally able to see inside. She paused before crossing the threshold, then deliberately reached across the opening and placed her still bleeding palm on the guard stone.

The coldness of the stone made her gasp. It hurt as well, sending shooting pains from her palm, circling her wrist, and up her arm.

Nadeem stubbornly refused to draw back, though. She gritted her teeth and kept pressing her weight against her palm.

Gradually, the pain decreased until she felt as though she had a normal wound. When Nadeem pulled her hand away and looked at her palm, she couldn't help but gasp.

The skin had already closed and healed. However, the scar cut a wide swath across her palm, white and shiny even in the dark night.

Was this the last blood oath she'd ever take? Was that the significance of the large scar?

Or was it just the greatest one?

<hr>

The cavern looked the same as it always had when Nadeem edged her way around the guard stone. The light from the stars outside gave enough light for her to see. A bubbling stream divided the cavern floor in two. Beyond, on the other side, were stone shelves for travelers to sleep on. She wondered why there were always four. Did the cavern never take more than that?

Grateful for the water, Nadeem knelt down beside the stream before she crossed it. First, she deliberately dipped her left palm into the water. A shock went across her palm, reminding her of rubbing against a wool blanket in winter then touching something else. She cupped her hand and took a deep drink. The water refreshed her and calmed her, like the first spring waters pouring off the mountains.

Then she splashed water on her cheek. The coldness made her gasp, but as always, the waters soothed the constant ache she felt, as if she'd applied a salve to the ravaged skin.

Would her cheek ever completely heal? She doubted it would. Magical desert sands kept the wound open. It never bled, and Trulliç had told her that it looked as though the skin had healed. Nadeem knew the truth, though she'd never tell Trulliç how much it hurt.

After standing and stretching, Nadeem stepped over the stream and lay down on the first stone shelf. She knew that for the cavern to move, she had to pass into dreamtime. Fortunately, her years of training as a star sister had given her the ability to fall asleep whenever she had the opportunity.

You never knew when the next time to sleep may come.

After a brief, timeless time, Nadeem woke. Even without turning her head she knew that the stars streamed across the sky outside. The cavern had taken her to the myth lands.

Though Nadeem didn't know how much time had passed, she still took the time to stretch, to prepare her limbs for great exertion. She didn't know what physical challenge she would face, but she assumed it would be daunting.

She was calling on a goddess, after all.

Refreshed from her nap and her time in the cavern, Nadeem stepped eagerly out into the cool desert night. The sand here sparkled, more than even when Nadeem stood with Trulliç, as if precious gems were scattered across her path. Stars streamed across the sky. Watching them, tracking them too closely, would make her dizzy. The air smelled sweet, as if a caravan carrying incense had just passed.

Without traveling there to make certain, Nadeem still knew exactly which direction lay the cave that held Forit's heart. She was equally sure that wasn't where she needed to go. The goddess Barzhat, while being the judge of death, wasn't going to found close to where Forit had made her greatest sacrifice.

Nadeem turned her back and walked the opposite direction. She didn't know if it was correct, but she had to go somewhere, now that she was here in the myth lands.

How would she know when she'd arrived at the right place? Was there a temple dedicated to Barzhat here in the desert?

No, there wouldn't be. Barzhat's golden court lay under the sea, not the sand.

Still, Nadeem marched in the direction she felt was north, trying to find the right spot, a place that felt appropriate, that she could dedicate to the goddess.

Nadeem didn't have to travel very far. Or at least it didn't feel like she'd traveled a long way from the cavern, though when she looked over her shoulder, she couldn't see it.

Dunes of sand rose up on either side of her, creating a natural bowl. The ground felt more smooth here, like the fine sand of a performance space. Nadeem walked to the center of the impression and turned around. Behind her, another dune blocked her sight. When she turned forward again, she realized that only a small path led the way out of the depression.

It was like a circular arena, with a single way out.

Or like a trap.

Still, this felt like the right place.

Nadeem stood in the exact center and sang out one of the star sisters' usual greetings to Barzhat:

O great goddess! We welcome you!
Come partake of our hospitality!
Your place is with us
At the heart of our gathering
O great goddess! Please join us!
You are always welcome
In whatever form you may take
At the heart of our family!
O great goddess! Our love knows no bounds!
We will always clamor for your return
Please sup with us
Your place is always ready

Nadeem paused and listened after she finished. She didn't hear any response. No winds suddenly sprang up. The goddess' tinkling anklets didn't sound in the air.

She should have known it wouldn't be as easy as that.

As part of her training, Nadeem had learned dances to the goddess, practice for when you arrived in her golden court. She started off with a few steps of that, but stopped herself after only a few moments.

That wasn't right, either. Those steps were too fancy, too prepared. The goddess needed Nadeem to dance from her heart.

There had been a training sequence that Nadeem had learned. It was a series of blocks, jabs, punches, and kicks. It felt more appropriate to her, a dance of death.

Nadeem started by placing her palms together and bowing her head to the north, the direction of the goddess. Then she started deliberately moving. First a slow block with one arm, followed by an equally slow punch with the other. Step, step, low block and pivot. Sweeping kick, heel kick, block, block, block.

By the time Nadeem finished the sequence, she found herself sweating despite the cool night air.

The goddess hadn't come. But Nadeem felt as though she was on the right track.

She went through the fight sequence again, moving with a fraction more speed. Then again. And again. Her dance of death sent her hands flying, her feet kicking, her body swaying as she blocked unseen opponents.

She couldn't add magical speed to her dance. Though this place resembled the Qaenev desert, it wasn't, not really. The myth lands demanded that a person be just as they were, without special abilities or really even magic.

Still, Nadeem had been training for long enough that she was able to almost move at a blur as she danced and sweat freely under the streaming skies.

A shuffling sound filled the area. Nadeem didn't break her dance but let it carry her naturally around.

A dark figure had appeared on the edge of the bowl, seated, as if watching a performance.

Nadeem's heart was already racing with the effort of her dance. She still felt it lurch, and her breath grew short.

Was that the goddess? Had Nadeem been blessed with her presence?

Then a second figure appeared. And a third.

No, it wasn't the goddess. Nadeem danced on. Fear fluttered around the edges of her skin. Were these warriors that the goddess would make her fight? They were darkly clothed, like star sisters.

How close would death come this time for Nadeem? Would she finally step fully into its sweet embrace?

More figures filled the arena, silently watching. What were they waiting for?

While the desert gave Nadeem great power, she still knew that she would falter before long. She was still human, and she couldn't dance forever. Not like she would when she finally came to dance in the real court of the goddess.

Finally, Nadeem stumbled after a kick, her legs too tired to draw back fully and place her foot properly. All the exhaustion that Nadeem had tried to forget came slamming down on her, weighing her down as heavily as one of the goddess' teardrop-shaped weights would after Nadeem died. She still struggled on, throwing yet another punch, then doing a sweep with her legs.

No, wait. That was the wrong place. She'd skipped ahead.

Where should she start? She turned and blocked again, but then couldn't remember what followed next.

She was going to have to start from the beginning, at that slow place.

A bell rang out, clear through the night air, as if signaling the end of a match.

Nadeem froze where she stood, though she panted heavily. Sweat covered her skin. She blinked, trying to clear her vision.

A whirlwind of blue sand stood at the only opening to the bowl-shaped depression where Nadeem had been dancing. Was that the goddess? Nadeem stared, trying to make out the goddess' two faces, one blue, one black, or even her four arms. Some of the paintings and statues showed Barzhat with twelve legs, though Nadeem had always imagined the goddess with merely two.

Streaks of lightning went out from the sandstorm. They buzzed by Nadeem, making all the hair on the back of her neck stand up as well as the hair along her arms. The bolts struck the figures sitting there, passively watching like stones.

Nadeem shivered as the first stirred, as though waking. The darkness shrouding the figure dissolved. Nadeem found herself looking at a star sister, her cheek proudly marked for all to see. She wore a sleeveless black tunic tied tightly around her waist, tight black stretchy leggings that would allow her to move, as well as heavy black sandals.

The only color on the woman was the great golden teardrop that appeared attached to the front of her tunic.

Nadeem turned back to the whirling sand storm in front of her. "Who are these women?" she asked out loud. Her voice sounded tinny in the night air.

The women themselves answered her. "We are star sisters, long deceased." The chorus of their voices barely sounded above the shifting sand. "We have one last dance for the goddess before we are reborn."

Nadeem suddenly understood. The golden teardrop each woman wore was the last weight given to them by the goddess, the last deed they needed to atone for before the goddess would grant them true death. The women would fight the soldiers of the emperor until the goddess judged that they were worthy. Then, the teardrop would fall from their bodies and they would disappear to be reborn elsewhere.

"Thank you," Nadeem said, addressing the whirlwind that was slowly fading. "I am forever in your debt. I will always welcome you with a warm embrace."

Was that laughter she heard in reply? The goddess seemed happy to accept her gift.

Nadeem turned to address the dark forms seated around her. "Thank you, star sisters, for giving the people of the desert your last dance."

A murmur went up among the women. Had they only now realized that Nadeem wasn't really a star sister?

One of the figures suddenly sprang up beside Nadeem. Though she was merely a shade, Nadeem could still tell that she'd at one point been one of the desert people due to her darker skin, large nose, and tight curls that fell around her face.

The figure held out her hand. Across her palm lay one of the golden teardrops of the goddess.

"Take this," came the whispered command.

Unwelcome fear spiked through Nadeem. She wanted to refuse. She didn't want to touch this weight, to bring her own time dancing before the goddess any closer.

But she'd come this far. She'd sworn to do everything she could, and with the help of the goddess, maybe she could stop the emperor.

With a steady hand, Nadeem reached out to lift the weight from the star sister's palm.

The cold of it burned her fingers, burning away what life Nadeem had felt. She shivered but she didn't drop it. Instead, she took the weight and pressed it against her own chest, saying, "I gladly embrace you, Barzhat."

Ice shot through her blood, freezing her solid. The world took a step back, and Nadeem felt as though she watched everything again from a distance.

She had been taking steps, albeit small ones, back toward the land of the living.

Now, she'd gone back to the world of the dead, to the half-life she'd had before.

Trulliç was going to be well and truly angry, despite the help she brought.

It was too late. Nadeem had asked the goddess for help. And Barzhat had indeed given her a great boon.

It was up to Nadeem to pay the price.

CHAPTER SEVEN

TRULLIÇ

TRULLIÇ CONTAINED HIS ANGER, THOUGH he wanted to rage and storm across the face of the desert when Nadeem returned.

Yes, it was marvelous that the goddess had decided to help, gifting them with the shades of star sisters. Trulliç didn't know what their abilities would be, but he assumed they'd easily be the match of any of the emperor's special soldiers.

But the price…He didn't want to pay the price of Nadeem's soul.

He didn't have any choice. The decision had been hers, as it always had been.

Instead of raging, Trulliç thanked Nadeem profusely. Polite, formal words that expressed at least some of his relief. Then, instead of disappearing back into his tower as he wanted, he remained on the ground level, listening to the latest battle plans as they were being formed by the war council.

"We know that the emperor will strike again soon," Levent said. "Possibly today. But where?"

"Midway between Egreliki and Gaadiwala?" Trulliç guessed. "Just south of Çandikili, to the west?" The attack against Egreliki wouldn't happen until the next day. It made sense that the emperor would split the difference between where he'd sent his first line of soldiers and the third.

Trulliç hadn't gone to check on the survivors of Gaadiwala, if there were any. He knew it was partly out of cowardice, as they'd be right to blame him for the fate that had fallen on their heads, as undeservedly as it might have been. He hoped he could help the villagers after the war, but he couldn't focus on them right now, as much as he might want to. Plus, there was only so much he could do for people outside of his land.

He hated this pressure of time. It felt so unnatural, not how the desert moved at all.

"He might attack there," Aunt Parayat said, nodding. It was obvious she knew the geography of the Tanesh Empire and didn't need to consult a map. "His men could also be coming on ships, and attack closer to Nusaybil Valley, which would be closer to Hayalevi as well."

Was that what Zehra had meant by the emperor crashing on his shores? Or was it that the emperor would strike out at Egreliki from the ocean, instead of overland?

"The main city of the emperor, Atayurtkah, is north and slightly east of Gaadiwala," Trulliç said. "If he sent his out his troops from the main city at the same time, one could have marched directly to Gaadiwala, while the other could have gone to the coast and sailed down the coast from there."

"That actually makes more sense," Aunt Parayat said. "Particularly if the emperor did send men from the main city."

"Why would he stop at Nusaybil Valley? Why not sail directly to further down the coast to the port that's closest to Hayalevi?" Seydat asked.

"He'd be able to pick up more star sisters near Nusaybil," Aunt Parayat said. "More trained troops."

That froze Trulliç's soul. The first group hadn't contained any star sisters, just soldiers. He didn't want to set sister against sister.

He had no choice. The ones fighting for the emperor had chosen the wrong side, that of a mere man intent on overthrowing their goddess.

"I think we can all agree that the emperor's sent men along the coast and is expecting to land as close to Hayalevi as he can," Myrizhah said, looking around the war council.

"Then why attack at the top of the Qaenev desert first?" Trulliç asked, confused.

"To get you to spend men and energy," Levent replied. "The emperor, for all his power, isn't a land magician. It's difficult for him to do what you do in terms of logistics. And he's never had to fight anyone with so much land or power."

"He still killed so many of my people," Trulliç said. He felt his cheeks grow darker, flaring with rage. He was able to control his anger so much better than before. However, the deaths from earlier made him truly upset.

"I'm sorry you lost so many good men," Levent said softly. "But we gained so much knowledge from that first battle!"

"The emperor gained knowledge as well," Trulliç pointed out.

"He didn't learn the full extent of your power," Aunt Parayat said flatly. "You've yet to show that."

Trulliç blinked, surprised. While on the one hand he had been holding himself back, on the other, surely the emperor already knew? Then again, had the emperor ever dealt with a true desert magician before? Maybe that hadn't been the power of the six kings…

"It was good that the emperor was able to overcome your defenses near Gaadiwala," Levent said with a sharp nod. "Let's make sure that he continues to underestimate you."

"No," Trulliç said, the power in his voice surprising even to him. "If the emperor continues to just send his men to die and bleed my people, I'll never be able to win or to defeat him. We will only end this war when we end the emperor."

The uneasy silence around the room made Trulliç shiver. Did they all think he'd fail when he faced the emperor?

"You can't attack the emperor," Aunt Parayat said, pointing out the obvious. "His cloak protects him from you. From all the star sisters as well."

Trulliç shrugged. "The emperor won't be in his court when he comes to Qaenev. He'll be in the desert. And he'll finally face the full power of the desert magician."

"Do you really think you'll win?" Myrizhah asked.

Trulliç wasn't certain if that was wonder he heard in her voice. "This is my land," Trulliç said, keeping his tone low. "I won't let anyone take it from me."

Hadn't he expressed that clearly before? Evidentially not, based by the rustle that went through the room. Even Riyune looked up, as if surprised.

"Then we should plan on a fourth attack," Aunt Parayat said, her words cutting through the unease. "The second will occur possibly after Egreliki, closer to Hayalevi. After both are crushed, the emperor may grace us with his presence. We should be prepared for such an honored guest."

Trulliç nodded, truly impressed by the amount of sarcasm the older woman managed to drip through her words.

Would he really have a day's rest between attacks?

Or, as he'd feared, would the next attack, so close to Hayalevi mean that he couldn't split his army, and therefore would have to choose to let Egreliki fall?

The entire city waited restless as time passed and the next attack didn't come. The troops were gathered and told to stay near the gather point so that Trulliç could easily fling them into harm's way.

Sunlight burned bright in the mid-afternoon. Most people napped, or at least tried to, under what shade they could create. Trulliç blew cool breezes over them, though he couldn't sweeten their dreams.

Relief and dread came with the falling of night. Maybe they would have one more day to live. Or maybe the emperor would attack at midnight, when Trulliç's powers were at their weakest.

Many of those waiting spent the early part of the evening singing. Some even performed ritual dances, practicing for their meeting with Barzhat.

Trulliç went with Nadeem out beyond Barzhat's temple, just north of the city, where the true desert began again. The stars shone down coldly over the glittering sand. Trulliç's soft heart was intent on breaking as Nadeem walked silently beside him, not sharing words with him. She'd grown so silent, *as silent as a grave* his poet's heart pointed out.

How could he bring her back to him?

Nadeem stopped at the top of a small rise. She pressed one hand against her chest, where the golden tear-drop of the goddess had nestled beneath her skin.

Trulliç winced at how pressing against her chest appeared to hurt her, though she would never have complained. (Just as she never complained about the wound in her cheek, though Trulliç knew it still bothered her as well.)

With her other hand, Nadeem reached out into the darkness. She made a fist and pulled, the muscles of her arm straining.

Dark shapes popped up above the sand, growing like misbegotten shadows.

"Star sisters," Nadeem said, as if she was explaining to Trulliç what he saw. "The emperor has not yet come. Tomorrow you will be called to your task by the desert magician. Obey him as you would me."

Trulliç blinked, startled. Why would she have to say that? Or were the star sisters likely to not listen to him?

"Thank you," Trulliç said, first to Nadeem, then to the gathered crowd of shades before him. "You will get to do great deeds tomorrow, defending the desert from invaders."

A soft sigh went through the crowd, as if relieved to find out their task.

"Is it possible to send them to Egreliki?" Trulliç asked Nadeem as they walked back toward Hayalevi, the spirits all gone back to their resting places.

"I don't think that's wise," Nadeem answered slowly. "It's better for them to stay here and defend the city. Particularly if Aunt Parayat is right, and the emperor stopped in Nusaybil Valley."

"Can't the star sisters here take care of them?" Trulliç asked. He wanted to be able to save the shining jewel of a city.

"I wouldn't ask them to," Nadeem said firmly. "They have enough to deal with, fighting against the emperor. They shouldn't have to fight their own sisters as well."

Trulliç sighed, defeated. She was right. It wasn't fair of him to ask the star sisters to fight their own. Not the living ones, at any rate.

"Then I will send more star sisters with the army going north to Egreliki," Trulliç said.

Nadeem shrugged. "You're sending them to their death, either way."

Trulliç couldn't help but shiver at the coldness in her voice. "Then they'll be able to fulfill their greatest duty, won't they?" he asked, unable to hide the bitterness he felt.

"Yes," Nadeem said, replying very seriously. "Exactly."

Obviously, she didn't understand that there could possibly be anything wrong with that.

The old Nadeem would have.

T rulliç woke with the dawn, as usual. He made himself smile though he knew that Atça would have smacked him for being so fanciful, believing that he could feel the first of the sun's rays as they struck the desert.

Atça had just been so wrong about so many things.

Trulliç sighed as he stretched his arms above his head, then gave a great yawn. He'd not slept properly all night but merely dozed, dipping into sleep between dreams of violence and chaos.

Atça was no longer worth his time. Trulliç could already feel the place where his mentor had once ruled with an iron fist dwindling.

It was good.

Trulliç looked down, finding Riyune there, as he expected. The ghost dog didn't climb up and share heat as often as the old dog had.

Or maybe he, too, had had a restless night, given the yawn Riyune now returned.

"Come," Trulliç said, standing. He quickly shed his sleeping tunic, putting on a nicely made off-white shirt that fit him perfectly across the shoulders, along with a sturdy pair of brown trousers.

Myrizhah had shaken her head at his request, but she'd gone ahead and cleaned the tunic he'd worn for his manhood journey, a symbol to remind him of how far he'd come. The tunic only came down to the tops of his thighs now, instead of hanging down to his knees. It still looked new. Though the linen was no longer stiff, the gold and green stripes looked fresh—the pale gold of the desert at first light mixed with the light green of the hills at the start of the rainy season.

Trulliç didn't go downstairs to meet with the war council who had probably already started to gather. Instead, he went up to the open top of the tower to bathe in the sunlight himself.

He felt himself grow stronger in the light, breathing in the dry scents of the desert mingled with the smoke of the cooking fires down below. He walked to the northeastern edge this time, casting his senses out, seeking the first of the emperor's attack.

For a brief moment, he thought he caught something. It was as light as a leaf blowing across a fence to land in a neighbor's yard before being quickly swept up.

He knew better than to think he'd imagined it.

Instead, Trulliç focused all his attention in that direction, seeking something, anything, that felt out of place.

The desert felt empty, though. He could sense a caravan up the main trade route, a little to the north.

Were these guards who were hiding? Or had he just been fooled?

Trulliç would go greet the council, then take a trip out to the border to make sure.

He was halfway across the open space, heading toward the stairs, when he felt the eastern border come alive.

The soldiers were here.

<hr>

Trulliç raced down the stairs and out the tower. There wasn't any more deliberation the council could do now. It was finally time to act. He flew over the sands to where his people had gathered. Many were just waking up, not ready to fight.

The star sisters saw his expression and knew, whether their charges were ready to go or not.

Loud hooting horns rang through camp. As they had practiced, people dropped whatever else they were holding and picked up their weapons. As one, they turned to face the east.

Trulliç swallowed around a dry throat. Many of these people were going to be killed today.

He would honor each and every one of their sacrifices the rest of his life.

"To arms! To arms!" came the unnecessary human call.

Nadeem appeared beside Trulliç. So did Riyune.

Levent came up quickly as well. He was dressed as a soldier for the first time. Trulliç couldn't afford to supply all his combatants with the fancy leather breast plates the emperor used. Instead, everyone had to buy their own.

Levent had worked a deal with a couple of leather merchants, who'd come up with their own version of a square badge, striped green and gold, that he wore proudly on one bicep. He had his own leather vest, with square pieces of leather staggered in rows, brigandine style. A thick leather apron covered the tops of his legs. Streaked with black coal, it looked as though it had come from a local smith. He had his own shield strapped to one arm, a tall wooden piece shaped like an arrowhead and rimmed with brass. He carried a sword in the other hand, curved like the men of the south.

Around his neck he wore a glass amulet given to him by Trulliç.

If there were to be any poems about today, Trulliç would start with Levent, standing brave and proud in mismatched armor, about to lead a horde instead of a well-trained unit.

Trulliç didn't take the time to talk to his company. They knew what they were up against. They knew the odds of survival.

They also knew that every man they killed would make the enemy stronger. So many of them carried ropes cut to short lengths to tie men up, or blunted swords.

Trulliç didn't trust the gleam in Nadeem's eye, as if she relished the upcoming brush with death. Hopefully she wouldn't fully embrace the goddess. Not yet.

With his head raised toward the sun like a flower, Trulliç gathered all his people together. He tasted the cool glass they all carried. He gave each piece a small boost of power, hoping to protect these souls.

They rose like a great storm and flew off quickly toward the eastern horizon.

The journey wasn't very far, just over a day's travel for a caravan.

However, the sight at the border gladdened his heart.

The emperor *had* underestimated Trulliç.

First off, the emperor had sailed his men down closer to Hayalevi to bring the fight here, rather than stop at Nusaybil to pick up a large contingent of star sisters.

And second, while the enemy soldiers were still far too many men to count, they were stymied at the border.

Hundreds of glass balls had risen out of the sand when the soldiers had tried to cross the border. The balls were arrayed on either side of the main column, as thick as a three foot wall. The balls were myriad sizes: some as small as a man's eye, while others were as bigger than a man's head. They floated at different levels in front of the soldiers, constantly shifting and threatening.

Trulliç deposited his army down on the desert side of the balls. "Check for star sisters slipping around the sides," he quietly instructed Levent before turning to slowly walk up to where the defenses stood. This also gave Levent and the others time to arrange themselves, getting ready to battle.

"How dare you challenge the emperor and his envoy!" a harsh voice called out as Trulliç drew near.

"You are no envoy," Trulliç countered. "You are an attacking force. If you came in peace, you wouldn't have disturbed my defenses."

It was mostly true. Only those with death in their hearts bothered the glass balls. Though the star sisters had rarely caused them to rise up, as they lived too closely to death.

"Let us through, so that we might negotiate," the soldier said.

Trulliç finally identified the man. Like Marius, he was shorter than the soldiers around him. He stood on bowed legs, his skin as dark as the desert people. However, he also had the features of the men from Lydae, with lighter eyes and hair.

"Negotiate what?" Trulliç asked. He knew these people were here to attack. What would they try to bargain for first?

"Your surrender!" the man said. He started laughing, and the soldiers nearest him also chuckled, as if he'd just told a joke.

Trulliç stepped back. "No," he said firmly. "The desert is mine. The emperor will have to come and take it from me himself if he wants it."

The soldiers seemed a little unsure about that. Maybe the emperor had assured them that Trulliç would be no threat.

How little they knew.

Riyune, who'd grown huge again, gave a warning growl. The soldiers closest to the dog paled.

The lead man looked to his left and his right before turning back to Trulliç. "All right," he said, sounding easy going as he strapped his shield to one arm then unsheathed his sword. "But it will be your widows mourning tonight, not ours."

He raised his sword and called out, "Attack! Attack!"

The call was taken up by others up and down the line.

Trulliç kept his ground though he trembled inside.

They were coming for him.

The glass balls quickly flew toward the soldiers running across the border. The men ended up swinging their swords wildly in the air as the glass balls attacked their heads. More than one soldier ended up injuring his neighbor as the glass balls swooped and turned.

As the balls got through the men's defenses, the soldiers started dropping to the ground, usually unconscious. If a soldier managed a lucky strike, the glass exploded, casting sharp slivers and slicing through the skin and armor of all the men nearby, some of which were fatal.

A group of more than two dozen men seemed determined to cut through all the balls to get to Trulliç. He kept retreating as he'd been instructed by Nadeem. His heart beat as hard as if he was doing all the fighting. He'd never been attacked this way, that slow pace backwards, as if treading through thick sand in a nightmare.

He suddenly appreciated what little wrestling training Nadeem had given him, trying to teach him how to be calm in a battle. He knew he'd never reach her expertise, but at least he could try.

Riyune had left his side, going to harry the invaders. His great speed startled them, and he crushed more than one with his weight.

He rarely bit, though Trulliç did see him take out the throat of a soldier who wouldn't turn away from Trulliç.

However, there were more men than defensive balls, something Trulliç had already known. He'd scattered the glass balls heavily up and down the battle line, leaving fewer to defend himself, hoping to protect his people.

Though the group focused on him had been halved, that still left over a dozen men on his trail. They each had the emperor's symbol glowing brightly in the center of their leather breastplates. They moved as a unit, connected through the emperor's magic. At least they were still running and not flying.

Fortunately, the soldiers fighting Trulliç's people weren't part of the emperor's elite and were more like regular men. This gave Trulliç's people more of a chance.

Finally, when the last of the glass balls dropped away, Trulliç stopped and stamped the ground with his foot. "Now!" he called. "I call on the shades of the star sisters to attack!"

Shadows rose all around him. They flowed toward the emperor's men like a dark wave.

The collision was silent, the men's voices already stolen from them by the dead.

The soldiers fought bravely. Trulliç would have to grant them that. They didn't freeze or run in fear. They stayed and tried to kill the dead, those dark souls who'd come for theirs.

As Trulliç watched, a few of the dark sisters lost the golden teardrop attached to their chest. Had they performed their final dance? Or had the emperor somehow reached out and sucked up what power remained to them?

Trulliç hoped they would manage to be reborn, leaving the goddess' court for good.

When the last man died, Trulliç turned his attention to the rest of the battle.

He didn't like what he saw.

Close to him, the battle raged fiercely. Clanging swords, grunting men, and the occasional breaking of bones filled his ears. The smell of gore washed over him, as awful as the first time. His stomach churned. He sent his winds, knocking away the foes, bowling them down so his people could disarm them.

Trulliç hurried up the line first, sinking soldiers to their knees in sand, blowing them over, and blinding them. He sent massive bolts of power through the linked groups, overwhelming their connection. The men fell apart and succumbed to the next wave from his people.

Past the line of soldiers, the star sisters fought, the dead with the living. Odd illusions wove in and out of the battling sisters, fantastic hawkmen, lithe goat women, and others.

Nadeem had told him of the great illusionary battles she'd once fought, partly as a precaution so the sisters wouldn't accidentally injure or kill each other. Maybe the old habits were deeply ingrained, so the attackers kept returning to their illusions.

Or perhaps the illusions fooled the shades, as he saw more than one of the dead star sisters fighting an illusion and not a physical foe.

Trulliç changed the ground under the feet of the star sisters, making the sand more slippery. It seemed to help. There wasn't much more he could do for them, however. While he disliked the emperor's soldiers, he felt bad killing the star sisters.

As his mother would say, his soft heart would always get him in trouble.

Trulliç turned and went back down the line, striking down foes where he could. He wasn't surprised to find that at least half the fallen soldiers were now bare chested. Whenever he found a breastplate beside a body, he cast it over the border. Let the emperor reclaim them there. He didn't want that foul magic in his kingdom.

Further down the line, Trulliç found Levent fighting. He gracefully slaughtered those who came to attack, his sword in constant motion, dancing to the right and left, twirling and punching. His face was covered in sweat and dirt, and blood spattered his leather armor.

The soldiers who came after him were the best. Trulliç aimed his winds carefully, trying to blow them away without striking Levent as well.

But he didn't aim well enough. A soldier stepped left, into the force, just as Trulliç started. The man got blown against Levent instead of away from him.

Before Trulliç could cast another wind, the man whirled and struck Levent, hitting his head hard enough that he dropped to his knees.

With a mighty *whoosh*, Trulliç swept away all those who were near, friend and foe alike. He hurried over and helped Levent rise up.

"Fool," Levent said through gritted teeth. "I had them."

Stung, Trulliç stepped back. "I was just trying to help."

"Go help those who need it," Levent said, shaking his head before leaping back into the fray.

"I will," Trulliç said, turning away. He really had been trying to help. He blasted the next soldiers who came near at least thirty feet in the air, dropping their broken bodies down onto the sand. Then he called up more glass, hurling molten balls at any who dared come near.

Trulliç heard the arrows before he saw them. He instinctively raised up a great glass globe around himself. The arrows dinged off the glass, sounding like winter hail. The cries of those outside of the globe were terrible to hear.

Trulliç rose up into the air above the next barrage of arrows, leaving those on the ground safely ensconced. Where were those archers?

There. Off in the distance. They stood behind a massive group of soldiers, all shielded. No one could reach the group.

Trulliç didn't bother getting closer. Instead, he sank the archers far into the sand, up to their chests. Those standing with shields started to sink as well.

"He's in the air!" came a loud cry.

A few of the archers had been hiding behind the main group, out of the way. They instantly shot arrows up at Trulliç.

Did they really think that mere arrows were going to hurt him? Or was this another feint?

Trulliç turned his well-protected back on the archers just in time.

A third group crept up behind him, intending to skewer him from behind.

"Blast all of you!" Trulliç said, growing angrier. Instead of glass globes he cast molten glass down on the group, burning the men alive. He made himself listen to their screams, not taking himself away.

He'd done that. He'd killed them. He could listen to them die.

The group who remained, Trulliç buried up to their necks in sand. They couldn't dig themselves out, couldn't escape. He knew his people could take care of them, knock them unconscious then dig them out and disarm them. He'd have to come back later to cast the armor aside.

When Trulliç returned to the main line, most of the fighting was over. His people had won this battle but at a great cost to themselves.

Still, the stragglers cheered as they saw Trulliç. The few star sisters who'd fought for the emperor had been all disarmed as well. Trulliç let Nadeem and the others deal with them.

It took Trulliç a moment to realize that Levent hadn't made it. Had he been too injured from Trulliç's mistake? Too angry? Trulliç would never forget how graceful the man moved in battle during his last few moments.

Trulliç would have to write a poem about him someday, once all the battles were over.

Trulliç had just gathered his people together, getting them ready to go back to Hayalevi, when he felt the start of the next incursion in Egreliki.

More troops had come.

He hurried as fast as he could, racing with the dead and the wounded back to Hayalevi. At least the sun remained high, powering him.

"To me! To me!" he called as soon as he set foot in Hayalevi.

The star sisters came rushing out. The loud ram's horns sounded again. A second group of citizens formed, this time all facing the northwest.

Riyune ran up to Trulliç as the group formed. The dog seemed unaffected by the previous battle, though blood still stained his muzzle. Nadeem came up to stand on his other side. Streaks of dried blood ran down her face. The star sisters who'd survived the first battle came up and joined her.

The group of people behind Trulliç swelled. Many of the desert people from the second battle had joined them.

Trulliç wanted to turn down their help, to tell them to stay in Hayalevi. They'd seen enough killing for one day.

But he couldn't. He needed them, all of them. He would be forever in their debt.

He closed his eyes briefly, refreshing himself with the deep, dusty smell of the desert.

Then it was time for the next battle.

CHAPTER EIGHT

NADEEM

NADEEM REMEMBERED HER DANCE FOR the goddess, how slow it had started and then how quickly it had progressed.

The battle at Egreliki had some of the same qualities. It took Trulliç more time than she expected to send them flying over the desert. Then again, he was tired, having already fought a battle that day, casting more magic than she'd ever seen him do before. Also, Egreliki was much farther away from Hayalevi than the first battleground.

Once they touched down, Nadeem felt herself speeding up. She enjoyed the dance, the thrusting, blocking, punching and kicking. She fought with her bare hands mostly, feeling as though the goddess had turned her entire body into a weapon, able to kill with divine grace.

The shadow sisters moved with her. She fought at their side. The emperor's specially trained guards were their primary target, as this group of invaders had no star sisters with them. The men, however, had the touch of the emperor, his magic seeping from their chests like yellow pus.

Nadeem breathed in the scent of sweat, her own and the soldiers in front of her. Their leather smelled, too, of dust and long days. The stench of the emperor's magic reminded Nadeem of a funeral pyre, that sickly sweet smell that came from burning flesh.

Her feet found the earth easily, never stumbling on the desert sand. It grounded her, reminding her of where she'd come from, where she was going. She'd always been a desert creature, shifting and flowing with the wind.

With her hands, she found her enemies. They fought with swords, foolishly thinking that bit of steel might save them. She used her knife on occasion, when a neck presented itself or a bare arm. Usually, though, she just used her hands to break noses, collarbones, arms, wrists, or necks.

She kicked, too, breaking legs, though that wasn't as common. Leg bones were much more difficult to break. Much easier to sweep a man's feet out from under him, then jump on his chest to break his ribs or kick him unconscious.

Through the length of the battle, Nadeem felt as though she floated in the embrace of the goddess. She didn't feel sorry for the men she killed. She wasn't angry at them, either, though she knew that Trulliç was upset at the deaths these men had committed, killing the pretty Zahra and leaving her broken body in the middle of the street.

Everything stayed at a comfortable distance.

The only time Nadeem had any qualms was when one of her shadow sisters passed, not through fulfilling her duty but because one of the emperor's men got ahold of her golden teardrop and sucked the animating force out of her.

Nadeem wasn't exactly sure how they were doing it. She suspected it was the emperor himself operating through the men, particularly given how their eyes burned and their tongues lolled out of their mouths.

She took extra care to kill those men. And possibly not as swiftly.

A group of them had surrounded one of the shadow sisters. She fought beautifully, but there were just too many of them, sucking at her strength.

Of course, it would take six of them to take down a single star sister.

Nadeem came up from behind. Her black blade, the one shaped

like a long *meslit* thorn, found her hand. She sliced through the armor of one of the men from behind, stabbing his kidneys and dropping him where he stood. The next, she sliced open the artery in his neck, blood spurting everywhere.

However, then the men turned away from the shadow sister and toward her. The deaths of their companions had seemed to enrage them more.

Belatedly, Nadeem recalled how the emperor lived on death, and his men were likely to do the same. Trulliç had told her. She hadn't remembered, though. It wasn't important to the goddess.

Too late now.

Nadeem fought. Blades found both her hands as she whirled, planting them in necks and sliding hides. Kicks found their targets as well—the soft parts of the body, like elbows and knees. The shadow sister tried to help, but she'd been drained by the men. Her eyes were lifeless, like black holes.

When only two remained, Nadeem found that she'd been cut. Blood flowed along her right arm. She didn't feel the pain. Knew she wouldn't, not until long after the battle.

After the battle. After the war.

Something lurched in Nadeem, possibly her frozen heart. For a moment, she stood on the battlefield with all her senses woken: the coppery smell of blood and iron, the panting of her own breath, the terrible sounds of dying all around her, how sore her bare feet were, covered in bruises, like her hands.

And these men were trying to kill her.

Nadeem growled as she sprang back into action. She forced her feet to move twice as fast as they had been. She was a desert creature. These men were monsters, here to despoil the quiet places, tear down the oasis, spoil the dates and sweet marsh plants that held in the water.

These were the men who marked the cheeks of the star sisters, forcing them into a singular life.

These were the men who had killed her people and her peace of mind.

Nadeem became a whirlwind between them, slicing them to ribbons.

When they'd both fallen, she found Trulliç standing next to her. She didn't cut him, though it was a close call as she'd mistaken him for an enemy at first.

"I thought I'd lost you," he said.

Or she thought that was what he'd said. Her ears seemed blocked by sand.

"Not yet," she assured him. She felt her face break into a grin. The movement felt strange, as if she hadn't smiled for a long while.

Then the goddess swept her up in her embrace again, and Nadeem rejoined the dance of killing.

<hr>

Nadeem fought desperately. The soldiers kept *coming*. It was as if more boats had pulled onto the shore and they'd raced from the piers and poured into the village of Egreliki. It surprised her that those pretty white walls hadn't been painted red with blood, given the number they'd killed.

Despite how the goddess had sustained her, Nadeem still knew she was fading. She moved with speed and diligence, striking down all those who would despoil her. But her feet no longer had the punch they once did. This last man didn't go down after she successfully kicked his knee to the side. At the start of the battle, that sort of strike would have dislocated the joint. Now she knew it was merely bruised, not broken, as the man straightened and came right toward her.

She had no shield, no sword. He had both. Her daggers bounced harmlessly away, not finding their targets. He even caught one with his sword, shattering the brittle obsidian.

And he kept coming.

His eyes burned with fury and his breath smelled of rotten eggs. A cut ran from his left temple down the side of his face, through his gray and white beard. The emperor's symbol on his chest glowed with a sickening yellow, like a diseased flower.

Nadeem tried to sweep his feet out from under him, but he hopped over her leg. At least that brought him close enough that she could bash him in the face.

He laughed at her, though his broken nose now poured blood. He licked at it, turning his teeth red and his breath more foul.

Nadeem blocked his next strike with her arm, then whirled, aiming for his head. He ducked.

Damn it! She was growing too slow.

Would this be her failed trial? The one that sent her to the golden court?

A loud growl came from behind her.

Nadeem spun with her next blow, unable to just look.

Riyune stood there. Like the soldier, the dog's mouth was covered in blood, even his teeth.

He growled again.

The soldier fought on as if he didn't hear or see the dog.

Nadeem stepped to the side as the soldier struck out first with his shield, trying to bash her, then with his sword, stabbing at her. He turned to follow her.

Riyune attacked.

He jumped in the air—an impossible height for a regular dog—firmly landing on the soldier's shoulders with all his weight. The soldier dropped flat on his face with a loud, "Oof."

Nadeem danced forward, kicking the man's head. She heard a loud *crack* when her foot connected.

Oops. She hadn't meant to kill him, just to knock him unconscious, so the desert people who were injured could then strip off his armor.

Maybe he'd made her angry, except she didn't feel anger. Or fear. Or any of those emotions that would tie her to this world again.

Just death.

She still took a deep breath. Maybe she did feel relief. She looked out over the other fights still going on at the foot of the path leading from Egreliki. More soldiers were bunched together, leaping down the rocks to join the battle.

"Thank you," Nadeem told Riyune. She took another deep breath.

There were too many soldiers, still pouring down. Had yet another ship docked at the nearby port? How could they stop them all?

Riyune seemed to be having the same thoughts. He looked at the soldiers, then back at Nadeem, his head cocked quizzically to the side.

"We need to stop them at the source," Nadeem said.

Riyune took a step closer to her, putting his back in arm's reach. Then he looked up at her and gave her a doggy grin, as if he found this fun.

"Let's go get them," Nadeem said, trusting that Riyune would understand and carry her to where the soldiers gathered.

She reached out her hand, touching his silken fur, the heat exploding through her as they raced away.

Nadeem had been correct. There were more ships. At least two more waiting their turn, crawling with soldiers like angry anthills. The ships were long, with a broad deck and two masts for sails. Over three hundred men at least waited their turn for battle in each ship.

The ships already docked were still emptying their cargo of men. The soldiers quick marched four across from the pier up the main market trail, heading across the foothills toward Egreliki.

Nadeem didn't know the name of this port town. Not much was here. But someone should have realized that the reason this place was chosen was because of how close it was to the desert. The emperor could keep pouring more and more men through this gap into the desert.

The mass of soldiers sent a tingle of fear through her. It wasn't enough to wake her fully to the world. She found herself shaking her hands, trying to shake off the emotion.

She felt tired, more tired than she'd ever felt before. Her arms shook though she tried to still them. Her legs felt wobbly, like spring reeds. Sharp spikes of pain pierced her chest from the effort her lungs had been making. The cuts on her arms and legs suddenly added to the cacophony of pain.

She had nothing left to sustain her except the sun and her will.

Riyune suddenly nosed at one of the bags tied to her wide leather pouch.

Ah! She'd forgotten. With shaking hands she slid the knot loose and stuck her fingers inside.

Warm sand caressed her skin. Suddenly, she saw everything much more clearly—the bouncing waves, the rocking boats, how beautiful the ocean sparkled in the sunlight.

Nadeem couldn't stop these soldiers on her own. Not even with the goddess' embrace and a pocketful of sand.

But she knew who could.

From high on the hill overlooking the ocean, Nadeem called the shadow sisters to her. They rose slowly, one at a time, probably finishing whatever personal battles they'd been engaged in before heeding her call.

When as many of the sisters had come as Nadeem could hope for, she pointed down at the pier.

"Stop the invaders," she said simply. "Let none of them come ashore and spoil this sacred land."

Though the nameless town and the pier weren't in Trulliç's territory, it didn't matter. She still felt as though the soldiers desecrated everything they touched.

A wave of happiness, possibly even joy, flowed through the dark sisters. Was it because they had a clear duty? Had they needed more direction?

No, that wasn't it. Barzhat's golden court was deep under her sea. Fighting near the water meant that they'd be closer to her.

If they'd been alive, the shadow sisters might have actually have expressed joy.

Like a spring flood rolling from the top of a mountain, they flowed down the hill, aiming first for the soldiers on the road, then sweeping further down to the pier. The men in their path fell quickly.

Yes, some of the soldiers who were already on the road would reach the desert. And hopefully their deaths.

But no more would come. The source had been cut off.

How long would the sisters remain? How many of them would survive? Would this be their final dance for Barzhat? Or would the goddess ensure that this pier was always protected, always sending more shades to battle against the emperor?

Questions for later, for that indefinable *after* that Nadeem couldn't let herself think about.

Nadeem sat beside Trulliç at the end of the battle. They were both dirty, bloody, sweaty, and tired. The desert people who'd fought with them weren't in much better shape. The star sisters were the only ones still in motion, tying up soldiers who weren't dead, stripping them all of their armor.

As they cast the leather aside, Trulliç sent winds blowing past them, picking up the breastplates and carrying them far off the coast, sinking them deep in the endless ocean.

Riyune stayed with them. He'd shrunk down to normal size and sat watching the star sisters with great curiosity.

Nadeem knew better than to close her eyes in the warm sunlight. She might never wake up if she did. Her limbs felt heavy, as if Barzhat had tied weights to her wrists, her elbows, even her knees and ankles. Her chest hurt. She knew she'd find massive bruises over her entire body when she got back to Hayalevi.

Soft cloth had been wrapped around her right arm, protecting the long scratch she'd acquired there. She could feel her pulse in her bruised feet, hot and angry. Her fingers felt swollen and probably were, battered and abused.

Still, if she just sat there any longer, she would possibly never walk again.

With a groan, she forced herself to her feet. Trulliç looked up at her in a daze.

"Stay there," she told him. "I just need to move."

It took a few steps for her legs to stop shaking. The pain in her feet subsided to a dull roar. Every breath hurt her bruised ribs. She opened her mouth and stretched her jaw, not surprised to find that her face hurt, too.

Riyune appeared at her side, as if there to help.

"Let's go clean up," she said. That was what it felt like they were doing. Cleaning the sand from the taint of the soldiers. As the soldier's half-naked bodies were piled up, Trulliç sank them far under the earth in unmarked graves, clearing their blood from the sand.

The majority of the cleanup work had started in the center of the battle and worked its way to the right. Nadeem joined the smaller crew on the left.

"Ye got to turn 'em over first," a young man directed as she approached. "Use yer feet, if ya can. Then cut 'em at the shoulders. Like this." He walked over to the nearest corpse.

Nadeem didn't physically take a step back, though she wanted to. The face had been hollowed out by the emperor, when he'd sucked out the last dregs of the poor man's life. The corpse's eyes were as empty as a dried out skull's. The skin had blackened, as if had been burned from the inside, almost turned to ash.

The rest of the man's body wasn't much better. The skin had turned brittle, flaking off as though it were shale. Whatever muscles the soldier had once had were now shriveled. The leather breastplate, which maintained its shape, looked as though it had been built for a man three times the size of the corpse that remained.

This was the body of the enemy. Not a friend.

Still, Nadeem felt a slight wave of unease push its way through her distance.

The young man beside her waited to continue until Nadeem gave him a nod. "They ain't all this way. Some of 'ems worse." He gave a dry cackle, then he showed her his knife.

It was similar to the ones the star sisters used, made out of black obsidian. However, the blade had a curve to the very tip, like a knife used for gutting fish.

"Now, youse have to cut here, and here," the man said, indicating the tops of both shoulders. "These where the leather is weakest." He demonstrating, using the tip of the knife to catch hold of the leather, then sliding it across.

"Sometimes ya got to use your boot on 'em," he added when the second side didn't want to cut apart as easily. He stood with his foot firmly on the man's shoulder as he tugged at the leather with his knife.

When the armor had been severed, Nadeem thought she heard a soft *plop*, like the sound a desert mouse made when she landed.

"Now, don't go picking this stuff up with youse hands," the man added. "Just 'cause it's cut don't mean it won't burn." He held up his other hand. A cloth rag had been wrapped around the base of it. He tugged the rag up over his fingers, then carefully picked up the armor with just the tips of his fingers, holding it well away from his body. "Drop it quickly," he added, doing so as he spoke. "Trulliç can be a might impatient, and it won't do to blow away with the armor youse holding."

That almost made Nadeem smile. She knew that Trulliç wanted to return to Hayalevi, to assure those who'd remained behind that they'd survived. But he would stay to finish the job. Even the old Trulliç would have done that.

The young man watched Nadeem clear the breast plate off the next soldier, making sure she understood the job before he moved off on his own.

Riyune stayed beside her. Was he protecting her? Or merely curious?

He went to sniff each piece of armor after she'd dropped it. The young man had been right about not touching it—even after just a few moments with her hand protected she could still feel how it burned her flesh.

But Riyune didn't appear to have much of an opinion of the leather pieces she cut away. He just sniffed each then went to sit beside her again, watching her work.

The first few breastplates cut easily without her having to use her foot. The bodies were all caved in, as if they'd been left in the desert for months and the sun had dried them after the birds had eaten their eyes.

After a dozen or so bodies, Nadeem felt as though she was getting the hang of it, though her tired limbs complained every time she walked to the next body and didn't sit down to rest.

The next soldier groaned as she turned him over. Nadeem took a step back, alert.

Was the man still alive? How could that be? His skin looked as burned at the others.

Then his eyes opened.

No, not *his* eyes, not the eyes of the soldier. Someone, or some*thing*, stared out from the holes that had once held the soldier's eyes. The eyes weren't human but yellow, like a cat's, burning with unholy fire.

The jaw opened and closed, as if the creature possessing the body were trying to figure out how to make it work. With a rattling wheeze, the chest lifted and filled with air.

"What are you?" Nadeem asked. She had knives in both her hands. Her complaining body put all its issues on hold as the dance of death came closer.

Riyune stood beside her, frozen in place.

The eyes from the body glared out at her, as if judging her too unimportant to answer.

Before the possessed being caused the soldier to rise, Nadeem darted forward and started slicing open one of the shoulders of the breastplate.

"Stop," came a commanding voice.

Nadeem ignored it.

She glanced over her shoulder. Riyune remained where he was, as if caught in stone. The dog didn't even seem to be breathing.

Then she returned to her task. The magic holding the leather together was stronger than any she'd encountered that morning. She felt her blade dulling as she hacked at the shoulder piece, using all her waning strength to attack the leather.

"Stop!" the thing cried out.

"May your dance at Barzhat's court be endless," Nadeem replied as she finally sawed through the first shoulder.

"You'll never win," the corpse grated out, his voice sounding much weaker.

Nadeem snorted. "Neither will you," she said as she started cutting apart the second shoulder piece. "You can cast as many men as you'd like against the rocky shores of the desert. They'll all die. None of them will ever reach Hayalevi. Or the desert heart."

"You'll die, too," the voice promised, growing more silky but with all the strength of a whisper.

"Not before we kill you," Nadeem promised, ready to swear a blood oath right there and then.

"I will feast on your bodies," the voice—the emperor?—said.

"You're going to have to find them," Nadeem said as she started cutting apart the second shoulder of the leather breastplate. "Which means leaving your comfortable grave, stepping out into the sunlight, and tasting the sand of the desert."

She didn't know if Aunt Parayat would be pleased or appalled at the words Nadeem directed at what might be the emperor.

The jaw moved again, as if trying to spit, but no saliva was left in the burned out hulk.

"Fine," the voice eventually said. The fire in the eyes started to dim as Nadeem continued cutting apart the leather. "I'll be there at sunrise."

"Should we welcome you like a beggar? Or a dishonest guest?" Nadeem murmured. The stranger who appeared at your door for dinner was always invited in, as too often the stories told of it being a god or goddess in disguise.

"Look for me as you would your precious Barzhat," the voice rasped. "For I will bring death."

"Looking forward to dancing with you!" Nadeem called in a sing-song voice.

Aunt Parayat would definitely be appalled by Nadeem's casualness. However, Nadeem wasn't sure she really cared. She was still far too removed from her situation to be frightened.

When Nadeem finished cutting through the leather, the lights in the eyes winked out like a dead star. A ghastly scent rose up, like cabbage rotting in an oasis marsh. Nadeem stepped back, coughing.

A plume of greenish gas rose up from the body. It remained shapeless, hovering over the carcass like a hungry vulture.

Riyune suddenly unfroze. He gave her a sheepish look, as if

expecting her to be angry. Then the dog darted forward. He leaped into the air above the corpse, his mouth open wide.

Nadeem heard a great *whooshing* noise.

The dog landed on the other side of the corpse.

The poisonous cloud was gone.

Huh.

She was going to have to remember to tell Trulliç about that.

As well as the emperor's approach.

After she finished cleaning a few more bodies…

<hr>

Nadeem took a step back as Trulliç grew angry.

Maybe she should have come to see him as soon as she'd finished talking with the emperor. It hadn't seemed that important at the time.

Nothing did. Breaking her fast in the morning, winning a battle, threatening the emperor—they all bore the same weight in her world.

At least she'd told him while they were still in Egreliki and not after they'd returned to Hayalevi.

CHAPTER NINE

TRULLIÇ

TRULLIÇ STORMED INTO THE WAR council, still angry that Nadeem hadn't told him immediately about the emperor's "visit." He knew he shouldn't be angry with her. The embrace of the goddess kept her apart from the rest of the world.

Was it keeping her safe? He didn't think so. Not when talking to the emperor himself through a corpse brought so little response.

Then again, it wasn't as if he hadn't been wishing for some sort of numbness himself, or strong drink to take away the images of the last day. The scent of the bodies clung to him. Not even a strong desert wind could carry the stench away. He'd never forget the image of Zahra lying in the middle of the path, her shirt torn from her, her neck at an unforgiving angle.

There were too many dead for him to compose poems for each. Though maybe he would try. It would take him until the end of his days and beyond.

Levent. Zahra. The other men and women of his city and the surrounding towns. The star sisters.

And maybe Nadeem.

He worried about her. He wanted to worry more.

But he couldn't.

He had to prepare for the emperor's attack the following morning.

Trulliç let the council talk while he cleaned himself. He'd already healed his own wounds, wishing he could do the same for all his people. He did what he could by easing their hearts, sending the desert peace to their side, and cool breezes to help them sleep.

When he returned to his room, Riyune stood in the center of it, looking puzzled.

"What is it?" Trulliç asked, instantly on guard.

But Riyune just shook his head and ambled away, down the stairs.

Trulliç set a mage light against the ceiling, seeing if there were any extra shadows.

Everything looked normal enough.

Trulliç put on a clean shirt, marveling again that he had clothing that was made for him, that fit him, instead of the hand-me-downs that he'd had growing up. He wore a darker tunic made out of solid green, with the thinnest of gold stripes. His pants also fit him well.

The *chafiyek* he wore was dyed gold, embroidered with tiny leaves of green. He knew he could call up a glass mirror, silvered and dark, to study himself, though he wasn't sure he'd see the differences that the others sensed.

He still felt them in himself. Even during all the battles over the last few days, he'd never let his rage have the upper hand. He'd been angry, yes, particularly over some of the deaths. Searing mad at the emperor for attacking. He hadn't lost himself in the swirling emotions, though. He'd kept his head as well as he could and so much better than before.

Could Trulliç battle the *Padisha-i-Ghazi*, the great emperor, and not lose himself? How could he counter the emperor's magic? What other tricks would the emperor pull?

Trulliç shook his head. At least he wasn't alone. It was still a novel feeling for him. He'd been so alone, so isolated, all his years.

He took a deep breath, then let it go. That had been another thing to lay at Atça's feet. The older magician had kept Trulliç isolated so he'd never have support.

Trulliç felt a smile cross his face. Admittedly it was fleeting and shallow, but a smile nonetheless.

Though he might die in the morning, he wouldn't die completely alone. And that was honestly something he was thankful for.

"We are all in agreement that the emperor will probably attack just east of Gaadiwala," Aunt Parayat said. "There isn't a village there, but it's in a direct line south of Atayurtkah, the emperor's main city."

Trulliç nodded. That made sense to him. "And where will the second attack come from?" he asked.

Aunt Parayat gave him a smile that made him feel like a student again, as if he'd just answered his teacher's question correctly.

"Here," she said quietly. It was north of Egreliki, where Magnus and the others had first touched the desert.

Trulliç nodded. Any ships that hadn't been able to land at the port near Egreliki would likely go up the coast and pull in there. While there were many more ports down the coast, most of them were several days' journey from the port town into the desert. In addition, the route wasn't easy, most crossed the mountains. The trade routes stayed on the coast side of the mountains, not the desert side.

"How many should I send to fight there?" Trulliç asked. Just being in his city had revived him. Plus, getting the grime and blood of the battles off his skin had refreshed him as well.

"We seem to be at odds about that," Aunt Parayat said smoothly. "I say throw everyone who can still fight up there. Including as many star sisters as possible."

"And I think that the majority of the army should be with you," Myrizhah said. "You need protection. Not the nearby towns and villages." The two women glared at each other, one protecting the rest of her sisters, while the other thought of her son.

They all turned to look at Trulliç, even Nadeem, who sat removed from the circle, listening but not interacting.

"I need a small troop with me," Trulliç said. He held up his hand so that they'd let him continue. "Yes, the emperor will be traveling with men, but they're a distraction. They aren't really there to protect him. They're for dealing with nuisances."

"Why would you put so many up near Egreliki?" he asked Aunt Parayat. He knew she'd reasoned out something, but his tired brain was too exhausted to figure it out.

"If you lose, those people will be able to run," Aunt Parayat said quietly.

Deathly silence gripped the rest of the council.

Of course, they should be planning other outcomes. It only made sense.

Trulliç nodded. "She's right," he said after a moment. "The desert people—they'll continue on in the desert, as always. The emperor will persecute them, but he won't kill them. He needs them to provide the empire with the wealth of the desert, the spices, sweet *meslit* syrup, even the salt he likes."

Seydat and a couple others shook their heads but remained silent. They knew he spoke the truth, though he could tell that they wished he didn't.

"The star sisters deserve a chance to live," Trulliç continued. Then he paused and thought for a moment. "The other star sisters, the ones who served the emperor instead of coming here, would they let them live?"

Aunt Parayat shrugged. "There will be some persecutions, as you say. But most will be able to live. If they can escape the desert, they can always lie about being here. Remember, not that many joined us."

Trulliç didn't want to agree with her or to point out that most of the sisters who had come to fight for him were already dead.

"Later this afternoon, I will send those who wish to Ishmirli, in the west," Trulliç said. He hadn't fully regained his strength, but there was nothing else he could do. "After the sun sets, I'll set out with a smaller group to the spot where the emperor is most likely to arrive."

"Do you want us to prepare a grand tent? So you can welcome your honored guest?" Seydat asked in a joking tone.

"I'm not sure there's anything I can do to bring that thief respectfully out of the night," Trulliç replied seriously. "Although—a tent may make him behave. At least for a little while."

"No," Nadeem said.

Trulliç turned to look at her, astonished. She'd grown so much more quiet.

She'd also cleaned up, but instead of her usual black star sister outfit, she wore a long, off-white tunic, shapeless, gathered around her waist with her wide leather belt. She wore her *chafiyek* around her neck, the black and blue cloth matching her bruises. She seemed to have recovered physically by arriving in Hayalevi, but her eyes were still haunted.

Probably like Trulliç's were.

"Every footstep he takes across the sand will give him more power here," she said seriously.

"Why do you say that?" Trulliç asked, curious. "I rule here. The desert is mine."

"But it's part of his empire," Nadeem said. "He's claimed the sands before. He's going to try to do it again. Don't let him."

"I won't," Trulliç said. Sometimes he wasn't sure if he was speaking with Nadeem or if the goddess spoke through her.

"Good," Nadeem said, nodding. She sat back and passively looked at the group again.

"I don't want to leave the desert," Trulliç said. "I lose power when I do. I don't want the emperor to set foot on the sands. What, are we just supposed to battle each other from across the border?"

"No," Seydat said, her voice sounding as if it were far away. "You will take a tent with you. But it won't be an ordinary tent."

Trulliç listened to her plan, nodding in agreement.

The others added some refinements, but in the end, they were all in agreement.

It was time for someone other than the emperor to be devious.

Trulliç sat, nervous as a new bride, waiting for the emperor. He'd done everything he could to prepare the location.

Scholars agreed that the *Padisha-i-Ghazi* was not a land magician. The more fanciful ones claimed that he was an *every* land magician, able to preform his magic throughout the Tanesh empire.

No one wrote of the magic the emperor did practice, though Trulliç now understood that it had to do with the dead.

However, the war council had all agreed that since the emperor wasn't a land magician, there was a good chance that he could be fooled.

The pavilion that stretched out above Trulliç's head was pure white, about as large as the base of Trulliç's tower, and able to easily hold two dozen men. He didn't bother with any banners. Thick rugs woven out of fine red-and-gold wool covered the dirt ground. Many pillows were strewn across the floor, the best Seydat could find in the market of Hayalevi, in every color, not just green and gold.

The seat of honor sat empty, with the finest pillows piled up there.

A silver tea set sat in the center of the area, with a pot of water boiling over a small fire just behind Trulliç. He willed himself to be calm, taking deep lungfulls of the mint and cinnamon tea. He just had to wait a little longer.

All of the people Trulliç had brought with him were stretched out behind him, a solid line, standing on the far side of the desert border. It made Trulliç nervous to be away from the desert, however, he'd agreed that it would be for the best.

Riyune had stayed with Nadeem, back in the desert. Trulliç didn't blame the dog. Riyune, like Nadeem, was a desert creature. Plus, Riyune deserved the chance to run into the desert if the emperor killed Trulliç outright.

Nadeem hadn't liked being sent back to the line. Despite the distance between them, she'd still wanted to be there to protect Trulliç.

But Trulliç had insisted. He needed to meet with the emperor alone. Though he knew better than to see if they could possibly negotiate a peace, he really needed to be able to study the emperor without any distractions.

Before Trulliç had to kill the *Padisha-i-Ghazi*.

Sunlight breached the dunes to Trulliç's right. The pavilion came with flaps on all sides, instantly changing it from an open area to a shaded one.

Trulliç turned his head toward the rising sun, letting it bake his face for a few moments. He longed to just loll in the sunlight for the day. Maybe go out into the deep desert and bathe in the sand like a lizard, letting the heat refresh his blood, heal his body. He still felt stretched thin. He knew he'd been doing too much magic with too little rest.

Only one more hour to get through. Then he would either be able to relax, or he'd be dancing in Barzhat's court, probably for an eternity for the people he'd killed.

As the heat rose, Trulliç forced himself to stand. While he quite enjoyed the warm sunlight, he doubted that the emperor would as well.

When Trulliç finished lowering the thick canvas on the side of the pavilion facing the sun, he looked forward again.

A dark smudge appeared on the horizon.

Trulliç felt his breath catch. Was that the emperor?

The figures slowly resolved.

A large, two-humped camel walked at the head of the line, carrying an enormous man who rode under a parasol, protecting himself from the desert sun. A tall gaunt man walked beside the camel. They moved quickly, more quickly than a normal camel would, though they didn't appear to be running.

Beneath their feet, a cushion of clouds carried them along. That was how they moved so fast. They didn't travel on normal ground. No wonder Trulliç couldn't feel them at all.

Behind the pair stretched a long line of soldiers. Trulliç quickly counted. More men than he'd brought, but at least no star sisters. Or none that he could see. He shouldn't assume they weren't there, either hiding among the men or disguised in some other fashion.

If they'd been on the desert sand, Trulliç would have seen them. He would have felt their footsteps. But they were here, on the border, and Trulliç stood on the emperor's side.

The camel, its rider, and the groom strode closer. The groom's robes were done in the same red and gold as the leather armor of the soldiers. But the groom held no shield, and his sword was tied to his back.

Still, Trulliç couldn't dismiss the man as harmless. He worked for the emperor, despite his dark coloring proclaiming him as a desert person.

The man riding the camel had dipped his parasol to the front, so that Trulliç couldn't get a good look at him until he dismounted.

Trulliç took a deep breath and waited patiently, desert winds blowing softly at his back, begging him to return to the sands.

Soon, he promised.

He would return to the desert very soon.

The emperor was a tall, *huge* man. He easily stood a head above Trulliç, and Trulliç wasn't short. He was also twice as wide around as Trulliç. His face was full of fat flesh, doubled up on his cheeks and under his chin. No hair grew on his face or his head. He had golden skin without any wrinkles—surely due to magic, as the emperor was at least two hundred years old.

The great cloak of the emperor hung off his shoulders like a dark shroud. Trulliç examined it with fascination. It was made out of row after row of glittering black scales. Were there that many magicians and star sisters? Trulliç had never thought about it before. Or was the cloak made up of scales from both the living and the dead? A thick golden chain held the edges of the cloak at the emperor's neck. The cloak flowed from his broad shoulders down to the ground, like huge black wings.

Trulliç felt revolted by the cloak. Was that because the scales were made out of the afterbirth of a babe with power? Could he fight the emperor in his cloak? Trulliç didn't know.

The emperor didn't wear a shirt under his cloak. His golden skin and fat belly shone in the heat. His pants were made from the finest brown silk that shimmered with red and gold as he walked.

It struck Trulliç as odd that the emperor wore boots instead of sandals, as did some of the merchants Trulliç had met who'd come from Lydae. Wouldn't the emperor want to feel the earth beneath him? Or was this yet another sign that the emperor wasn't a land magician? That he didn't understand the power of the earth?

The emperor's aura was unlike any Trulliç had ever seen. Instead of being solid bands of color, it appeared like a wispy shroud, the colors red and black. It was much smaller than Trulliç had expected, given that the emperor had so much magic.

If Trulliç was honest with himself, the emperor looked like an over-fed baby. Trulliç had never met anyone so fat.

By comparison, Trulliç knew he appeared skeletal. The desert had changed his body, making him more gaunt, his flesh more dry. His skin wasn't soft, but roughened by winds and sand. Trulliç had the same dark coloring as his mother, though his hair was a lighter brown than most, courtesy of his Lydaen father. It still curled slightly when he didn't have it covered with a *chafiyek*.

"Greetings, *Padisha-i-Ghazi*," Trulliç called out as the emperor approached.

He didn't get down on his knees or abase himself on the ground before the emperor.

He did bow his head out of respect, as he would for any leader.

The emperor didn't seem to take offense, though. "Greetings, o king of the desert!" the emperor called out in a high, thin voice that seemed out of place with such a large man.

"Please, come take part in my humble hospitality," Trulliç said, keeping his head lowered as the smell of the emperor passed over him. He stayed frozen for just another moment, fighting his gag reflex.

The emperor reeked of rotting flesh and ashes. He stank as well, as if he'd not bathed in years.

Trulliç willed his eyes not to water as he looked up, finding that the emperor was waiting for him. "I hope that you find my meager offerings palatable," Trulliç said, indicating that the emperor should take the seat of honor.

"No, no, I couldn't possibly," the emperor demurred. He appeared to be studying Trulliç as closely as Trulliç examined him.

"Please, I insist. I know it isn't much, compared to what you're used to," Trulliç said. He found himself relaxing. This was part of the normal dance of life, the offering and refusing of hospitality.

"I wouldn't want to take all that you have," the emperor demurred.

Trulliç made himself keep a straight face instead of replying sarcastically, *I bet.*

After a few more rounds, Trulliç got the emperor settled, and he turned to the task of making tea. An expectant silence grew between them.

"I hadn't anticipated this," the emperor finally admitted. "Though I should have known that you would treat an enemy like an honored guest. You desert people are just strange that way."

Trulliç bit his lips together to keep from replying about how *you desert people* were still going to kill him.

"Hospitality means a lot to my people, yes," Trulliç finally replied as he finished pouring the emperor the first cup of tea.

"You know I can't be poisoned, right?" the emperor said as he took the cup.

Trulliç looked truly horrified. "Why would I do that?" he said. "I would never—that would be rude!"

The emperor chuckled. "Yes, I should have expected that as well. That you'd never poison a guest, even one you meant to kill later. You'd never abuse your precious laws of hospitality that way." He took a sip of tea. "That is quite soothing," he said.

Trulliç looked at the emperor curiously. "Where did your journeys start? Since you aren't of the desert people?" He doubted the emperor was from Lydae, though he did have a large enough nose for it, and the people from Lydae were notoriously tall.

"I was born in the Tanesh Empire, well, back before there was such a thing. Before I conquered all the lands," the emperor said, chuckling. "East of Atayurtkah, along the main trade route with Uluborlu."

"And your family?" Trulliç asked. He'd never known any of the histories to record such a thing. The emperor was always presented as timeless, and the times before the emperor as mere chaos and not worth learning about.

"Rug makers, actually," the emperor admitted. "We would have traded well for such a rug as this."

"Thank you," Trulliç said. "I will be certain to tell Seydat that."

"Your wife?" the emperor guessed.

"I have no wife, no children," Trulliç said. He didn't want to hide from the emperor, to give his enemy a possible lever to use against him.

He got a wide smile in return. "I have no wife or children either. Just a large empire to control. You have no idea how much work that takes, how much effort."

Trulliç shrugged. He was starting to get an idea how much work something like that was. Since founding Hayalevi, he'd had more people coming into the city every day. He'd had to raise houses for them, widen streets, build more fountains.

"Particularly when an upstart such as yourself comes along," the emperor continued. "Tell me, Trulliç, what am I going to do with you?"

Trulliç blinked, surprised. He'd assumed that the emperor wouldn't want to bring their conflict up. Then he realized that discussing business always came at the end of the meal, another part of the desert hospitality. Make sure your guest is fed first and feeling comfortable before you approached the hard topics.

"Let me have the desert," Trulliç said earnestly. "It's all I want. All I need. I don't need any of the rest of your territory. You would still be the emperor over everything else."

"But you see, that's the rub," the emperor said. He looked very sincere, his fat face solemn. "I already own the Qaenev desert. It's mine, and as much a part of my empire as the Kingdom of Lydae. You can't have it."

"It isn't yours," Trulliç contested. "It doesn't respond to your footsteps. It doesn't carry your name to the people there. You don't share their dreams."

"Are you sure?" the emperor asked. "Because I dare say it would, once I set foot there again. Why else would you meet me here, on these lands? Other than to deny my rightful place on your precious sands?"

The emperor kept his tone silky smooth, but his words had hard edges on them, digging at Trulliç.

Trulliç nodded to the emperor. He kept his own tone light as well. "The reason I didn't want you to set even a single foot in the desert is because you corrupt everything you touch."

"Really, is that how you feel?" the emperor asked. He seemed delighted rather than angry.

"I do," Trulliç said. "Seydat has instructions to burn everything from this meeting, including melting down the tea service. Nothing else will remove the taint."

"Wonderful!" the emperor said, clapping his hands, reminding Trulliç once again of a fat baby. "Wonderful. It's so refreshing to talk with someone who actually speaks their mind. I may have to pay one of my servants at the court to do so some days."

"I'm glad my hospitality meets with your approval," Trulliç said dryly. He knew he'd never have that worry—the people of the desert would be honest with him. It was part of their nature, part of his own. If you didn't honestly face the sands, the deceit would kill you, eventually. Mirages were deadly.

"Then, could you do one more thing for me, dear boy?" the emperor asked. He leaned closer to Trulliç, as if about to speak a great secret.

Trulliç didn't recoil, though he dearly wanted to. That stench the emperor carried with him was overwhelming when he drew close.

"If it is in my power to give an honored guest, I will," Trulliç said. That was all the rules of hospitality demanded. Nothing more.

"Could you try to attack me?" the emperor said. "I mean, it's been so long since any land magician was foolish enough to throw himself at my cloak. I'm wondering if it's lost its effectiveness."

Trulliç tilted his head to one side as he considered his options. Was that part of the disgusting smell the emperor had? Was it just the cloak turning him away?

No, the emperor's flesh really was that corrupt.

Then Trulliç turned his attention to the cloak. It didn't draw him in or repel him. "How is the cloak supposed to work?" he asked the emperor.

"You know, that's a remarkably intelligent question," the emperor said with a wide grin. "It's the same reaction that you would have, if you'd had a child. Your magic recognizes the relationship and won't let you attack."

Trulliç nodded. Few magicians had children, but Atça had told him that if they did, they couldn't use their magic on them.

It was one of the reasons why Atça had been able to strike Trulliç on occasion, until Trulliç grew too large to be smacked easily.

By Atça, at any rate. Myrizhah still had that right. And if Nadeem ever came back, she probably would as well.

"So it's just my magic that can't get through?" Trulliç asked.

"My boy, if you think you can skewer me with a plain knife, go right ahead," the emperor said. He pulled back his cloak along the sides and bared his fat belly.

"Do you mind?" Trulliç asked, pulling out the small bag he always carried with him, filled with enchanted sand.

"No! Not at all!" the emperor said. "Fascinating. You know that land boxes are forbidden, right?"

Trulliç shrugged. "It isn't a land box," he said seriously. "This is just sand. My sand."

The emperor blinked. For a brief moment, worry crossed his face. Then his broad smile came back, bigger than before. "Your sand. Of course, of course."

Trulliç knew the emperor didn't really understand. He wasn't a land magician. He couldn't feel the earth beneath him. He'd forbidden the showy pieces of magic, like a box.

He'd forgotten that magic infused every tiny grain of sand.

Trulliç drew out a handful of sand, lifted it up, then blew it toward the emperor.

He'd killed more than a half-dozen men that way, his sands swirling and choking them to death.

Atça had merely been the first.

The sand flew directly at the emperor's face. Then, as if it, too, was repelled by his rank odor, it turned away.

For a brief moment, Trulliç felt a spike of panic. Would the sand turn and attack him now? How could he combat his own land?

But the sand merely fanned out, then slid away, heading back to the desert from where it had come.

"Fascinating!" the emperor said, "absolutely fascinating! Thank you so much! I haven't had that close of an encounter for decades." He beamed at Trulliç. "It's also good to know that the cloak continues to perform it should."

"You're welcome," Trulliç said. He stood up, stretching. "But now it is time for my honored guest to be on his way back home."

"Oh, no, I wouldn't dream of it!" the emperor said. "Now is the time for you to die."

T rulliç found himself frozen in place. He couldn't move his feet forward or back. He couldn't even wiggle a pinky. He could barely breathe, his chest frozen as well. Ice filled his veins. Pain radiated out with every heartbeat. The smell of long rotted corpses floated over him.

The emperor floated up from his position on the floor, instead of forcing his extraordinary weight up. He threw a look of pity at Trulliç before finally finding his feet.

"You see, while you were offering me your *hospitality*—and really, such a poor thing as this barely rates the name—I was finding your true self," the emperor explained. "It isn't that hard to do. While it's true I don't have *land* magic, as all you magicians pride yourself on, I do have *people* magic. Which is much stronger in the end."

Trulliç struggled to speak. The words came slowly, drawn out, as he forced his mouth to move. "You're...wrong." Trulliç found his senses moved at a snail's pace as well. Still he forced them down, under the layers of dirt at his feet, down under the rocks there as well.

"Wrong? Wrong? My dear boy, look at us here. I'm still hale and hearty after you tried what I believe to be one of your best attacks on me, and you're here trussed up like the goose for a feast!" The emperor shook his head and walked all the way around Trulliç. "I don't think you're in a position to call me wrong."

"People...aren't...anything...without...land," Trulliç managed to get out. "Without…home." He continued to drive down, down, down, like a seagull plummeting from the cliffs into the ocean.

"You're mad, you know," the emperor said. "I plan on bringing all the prisoners from Lydae down to the desert. They'll be happy to settle here. The desert rats you're so fond of will have to just get used to living in the mountains. With snow."

If Trulliç could have shivered, he would have. Myrizhah had explained snow to him. So had Atça. It sounded awful.

Still, he continued. "Home…is…important. More than you know." There it was. The desert sand buried deep underneath the ground.

The emperor looked confused. Obviously, no one had ever started to free himself from the grasp of death before.

Trulliç couldn't stamp his foot on the ground as much as he might want to. He couldn't make a strong physical movement to bring his magic up.

The sand still rose, like an unstoppable flood. It pushed the fine rug up and away, toppling the tea service, even quenching the small fire still burning. It brushed against Trulliç's toes, giving him more strength.

It even ran across the tops of the emperor's boots, then surged higher.

The sands did recognize the emperor.

They didn't like him. They couldn't do much to him, but they could hold him.

The sand scrubbed away at the last of the magical ties that held Trulliç frozen, swirling around him like a mini whirlwind. The emperor looked astonished.

Of course, he didn't look worried. Trulliç was merely a desert magician. What could he do to the *Padisha-i-Ghazi*?

"Attack!" Trulliç shouted as the sands lifted him up from the ground. "Attack!

The emperor stayed where he was, sinking in the ever-rising sand. His eyes grew wide as he tried to move away and realized he couldn't.

Fire blasted all around the emperor, glazing the sand with its heat.

Trulliç heated the sand further, then cast it back at the emperor.

"How dare you, boy?" the emperor roared. He sounded angry.

He still wasn't afraid. Not yet.

"You will drown on my shore," Trulliç predicted. "Be carried away by the sand. The desert winds will scour away your stench. You and your kind will never walk here again. It is your turn to die."

"NO!" shouted the emperor. Great winds tore out from him, carrying noxious gas.

Trulliç trusted his own winds to keep him safe as he brought more and more sand up. There was a river of sand running deep underground, from the edge of the Qaenev to where Trulliç had set up his tent.

He'd spent much of the night digging, helped by his people, casting forth a huge tongue of sand, then covering it back up again.

The great cloak of the emperor billowed around him, pushing the sand back. While the entire area filled with piles of sand from below, the emperor kept rising on the heap instead of falling to the bottom and drowning. Trulliç used his winds to knock the pavilion to the side so that their heads wouldn't strike the canvas.

The emperor shot out gouts of flame and gas, trying to strike Trulliç, the sand, anything. Trulliç's winds protected him, and the sand didn't feel a thing.

From the start, Trulliç knew he'd never be able to rip the cloak from the neck of the emperor. Even if he managed to get that close to the emperor, the cloak's chain would be too strong, the links enforced with magic.

However, the scales were merely sewn on with thread. All the stories about the emperor recounted that.

As Nadeem had pointed out, the creatures of the desert would obey Trulliç if he called them, particularly surrounded by the sands as he was.

It was from them that he'd demanded an attack.

A hawk came shooting out of the sky. It pecked at one of the scales, then took off with it like a magpie with a shiny toy.

Other creatures came to Trulliç's call. The desert mice. Lizards. Vultures. Rabbits. Moles. All types of birds. Even the tiny dogs that lived in burrows under the sand and only came out at night.

One by one, they carried away scales of the great cloak.

The emperor roared and tried to fight them off with his hands, blasting them away with his magic as the sand held him tightly from the waist down.

Trulliç tried to catch the carcasses of those who died, burying them deep in the heart of the desert.

He would honor those tiny deaths as much as the deaths of the people who were surely dying around him, holding back the emperor's men.

Finally, the scale that had come from Trulliç's afterbirth was removed, perhaps by the surprisingly tall ibis that had flown in from the nearest oasis. The sands roared as the emperor's power was suddenly diminished.

Now, Trulliç took a second handful of sand and blew it directly into the emperor's face.

"I would see you die," Trulliç said as the emperor started to choke, "rather than sustain your life any longer, or to try to torment you. You are unnatural. Go to the grave that's been waiting for you, then may you dance an eternity in Barzhat's golden court for all the grievances you inflicted on people."

The emperor's golden skin grew red. His eyes bulged out of his fat cheeks. His tongue turned black and stuck out of his mouth as if seeking air. His fat fists flailed in the air, grasping for something, anything. He pounded his arms against the sand, then found he could no longer move them either.

More poisonous gas leaped up from the emperor, horrible noxious fumes that made Trulliç's eyes water even as the winds blew them away.

Great gooey blobs began to fall from the emperor's flesh as the sand took hold of his chest. They rolled down the pile of sand and started to spread out, like a toxic, sickly-yellow moat.

Trulliç found he couldn't clear them away, as they sank deeper into the sand every time he tried to pick them up. Instead, he put hard glass around them, capturing them like a deadly poison. He'd have to bury these capsules, too.

The emperor's mass finally seemed to melt into the sand holding him. It was as if a great stitched together man had bled out all the sand that had been inside him. He stopped moving, and a great sigh filled the area.

Trulliç dared to float a little closer. Was the emperor dead? Or was this just another trick?

Nothing moved, however, when Trulliç sent a small whirlwind down to ruffle the emperor's now flat cheeks. The skin had blackened, looking as desiccated as the corpses the emperor had created. He looked like a slug who'd exploded in the sunlight.

A ragged cry went up all around Trulliç. Some of the soldiers still fought on, but many seemed dazed, their connection with the emperor severed.

With a blubbing noise, the corpse of the *Padisha-i-Ghazi* started to sink into the sand.

Trulliç understood. The heart of the Qaenev wouldn't have such a tainted creature on its shores. The emperor sunk deep and deeper still, past the hidden trails of rock and sand and into the core of the earth herself, never to rise again.

CHAPTER TEN

NADEEM

NADEEM WAS SURPRISED AT HOW far back from Trulliç that Riyune wanted to be, and that he wanted her to come with him. She followed him down the line. He kept pausing and looking over his shoulder at her, as if making sure that she would come.

"What is it?" Nadeem asked as they skipped a few more people down. "Why are you doing this? Are you scared?"

She wasn't sure what Riyune looked like when he was afraid. She'd never seen the dog fearful, she didn't think.

And wasn't he a ghost now, anyway? Even in the dim predawn light he appeared to have his own white glow. What did he have to be frightened of?

"All right, fine, I'll follow you," she said when he stood up again, then looked over his shoulder at her after he'd taken a few more steps. They finally stopped near the end of the line of Trulliç's people, with the pavilion over one hundred yards away.

The star sisters were all more concentrated around the pavilion, intent on protecting Trulliç from the emperor's soldiers. However, Nadeem didn't feel demoted by being so far away from the center of the action. Not exactly. Unlike Trulliç, her wounds hadn't fully healed. Her right arm was still bandaged from the battle the day before. Her feet were one massive bruise. So was her left hand and her ribs. A dull, constant ache beat under her skin.

Was Riyune just trying to protect her? Surely, he knew that she was completely capable of taking care of herself in a fight, injured or not.

She watched with interest when the emperor came up. It appeared to her as if all his group moved on low white fog, traveling faster than a man could run. It wasn't anywhere near as quick as Trulliç could move; however, it was still quite fast.

The camel the groom led appeared placid enough, not a war camel, which surprised her. Surely the emperor would have creatures ready to take him into battle.

The soldiers spread out in a line that stretched out much farther than the line Nadeem stood in. Plus, they stood at least three deep.

An unevenly matched battle. What else was new?

At least the deception seemed to be working. The emperor really sat down to have tea with Trulliç. Of course, the hospitality of the desert people was renown throughout the empire. It only made sense that Trulliç would offer tea before a battle.

Nadeem stared at the dark figure of the emperor. She couldn't make out much about the *Padisha-i-Ghazi*, except for the general impression that he was extremely tall, as well as round. What would he be like in a fight?

The cloak fascinated her. It was his primary protection. He relied on it keep him safe from the magicians and star sisters. No one could attack the emperor while he wore that coat, no one with power. And like Trulliç, a pure physical attack would be near impossible to slide in under the emperor's magical defenses.

Was that the emperor's primary weakness? Like Trulliç's? That he relied on his magic too much?

Nadeem felt the edge of worry start to gnaw at her when Trulliç stood, then stopped moving. Angry murmurs went up and down the line. Nadeem wasn't standing close enough to anyone else to hear what they were saying.

What was happening? Was all their work to be for naught? Had the emperor already gotten the upper hand? Was he destroying Trulliç?

Nadeem breathed a huge sigh of relief when the sand started

spilling out of the ground like an errant geyser and Trulliç was able to move again.

That was the last that Nadeem could pay attention to the pavilion. Then she had her own fight to take care of. The soldiers in front of her weren't ordinary: they were part of the emperor's elite squad. They moved as a unit, attacking ferociously.

Fortunately, that was the only way Nadeem knew how to fight. She gladly stepped into the dance of the goddess, reaching that higher plane where all she knew was blocking, kicking, punching, thrusting.

Riyune helped as well, taking down any soldier who dared to turn his back to the huge dog. His muzzle grew red and the air around Nadeem rang with his constant growls.

After a timeless time, the soldier in front of Nadeem faltered. She slayed him quickly, then turned to the next.

He stood frozen, as did the men on either side of him.

Had Trulliç succeeded? Had he killed the emperor?

Nadeem bashed the first soldier in the head, knocking him down, unconscious. That at least appeared to shake the other three out of their shock. They turned to fight her, but their strength had fled.

So had their fearlessness. When Riyune came rushing in, growling, and attacked the one on the right, the one on the left ran away, leaving the line and heading back into the lands beyond the desert.

Nadeem came out of her dance with her hands and feet bloodied but not as hurt as they'd been the last time. Or maybe she couldn't tell, as everything still just hurt.

The others in the line started cheering loudly. Both the men and women were crying, giving tears to the desert, to Barzhat, for saving their lives.

Nadeem wanted to feel their happiness. She wanted to share in their joy. However, both her exhaustion as well the distance away from the living that the goddess had placed her at made it impossible.

She found herself sitting, with her butt in the desert and her legs stretched out in front of her, her ankles touching the border. She felt it was appropriate for her to sit in that spot, neither here nor there.

The battlefield would need to be cleaned up. Would they have to strip the leather armor from all the soldiers again? Since the emperor was now gone, there might be no need.

Where the pavilion had once stood, a huge mound of sand remained. Rocks were already flying to the area, to protect the hill that was as tall as two men standing on each other's shoulders. It was all that remained of the emperor.

What would Trulliç do now? This wasn't part of his lands. Maybe that was more appropriate, though he might be able to claim it, since he'd directed such a huge river of sand from across the border.

What would Riyune do, now that Trulliç no longer needed so much protection? Now that the emperor was gone? Would he just disappear back into the desert? She glanced around, but she didn't see the dog anywhere.

Nadeem felt as though something else was missing. Something else she needed to think about.

Finally, the question occurred to her.

What was *she* going to do, now that it was after the war?

As it turned out, they did need to "clean up" the battlefield. The emperor's symbol on the breast plates of the dead soldiers started to ooze a yellowish slime that, according to Trulliç, was toxic magic. They had to use the same precautions and not touch it.

Nadeem worked beside the others, slicing away the leather armor. At least this time, it cut like normal leather, so the work went faster. The sun burned down hot on her head, though it was still early, before midday. Trulliç had raised a burbling stream of water so people could refresh themselves, as well as clear off some of the dried blood.

The woman working beside Nadeem accidentally brushed her hand across the yellow goo and promptly started to scream as her hand burned. She was a young girl, not much older than Nadeem's twenty years. She wore a man's shirt, ragged with many patched holes, and hand-me-down brown pants that were tied around her waist with a rope. Her *chafiyek*, however, was new, beige with green and gold stripes, the ends of it decorated with tiny glass beads. Nadeem vaguely recalled seeing her fight. She spat and hissed like a cat, and was very effective with the short dagger she carried. She'd joked about using it on her older brothers, once.

Nadeem rushed over to the woman's side, grabbed her hand, then pushed the edge that burned down into the sand. She understood the sand would help neutralize the toxins.

"Trulliç!" Nadeem shouted.

The desert magician appeared instantly at her side. He lifted the woman's hand slightly above the ground, then poured more sand on it, a steady stream. The remains of the sticky yellow goo dripped off and were instantly swirled away by Trulliç's winds.

"That should be the last of it," Trulliç said as he gently rubbed a finger over the back of the woman's hand.

"Thank you," she whispered in a choked voice, her face still wet with tears.

"No, I should be thanking you for doing this dangerous work," Trulliç said. "And for fighting with me."

She gave him a crooked smile. "It was the right thing to do," she said honestly.

One of the star sisters came up and led the woman away. Nadeem knew that her hand would be bandaged and she would be well taken care of.

"Hi," Trulliç said to Nadeem, sounding shy.

She looked at him quizzically. Then she blinked, remembering.

This was after the war.

What was she going to do? How was she going to come back?

"Hi," she said. "I…I—"

Suddenly, Riyune appeared next to Trulliç. He glanced from Trulliç to Nadeem, then sat down on his butt, put his nose in the air, and issued a great, long howl.

The slightest tinge of fear raced through Nadeem. Riyune had *never* made a sound like that. Never.

He'd disappeared after the emperor had died at the end of the battle. Where had he been? And why was he howling like that?

Trulliç appeared just as bewildered. Then he stiffened, stood, and looked north, out beyond the edge of the desert.

"Something's coming," Trulliç said quietly. Then he shouted, "Everyone! Get behind the border! Something's coming!"

Trulliç's people had never strayed that far from the edge of the desert. Still, they all scurried across, making sure they were well and truly in the Qaenev so that Trulliç might be able to protect them from whatever it was that came.

For a fleeting moment, Nadeem thought about stubbornly staying on the exact border herself. Then she shook her head. Why would she do that? Was it just so she could feel something? Fear, perhaps?

It took a little while before Nadeem was able to see what Trulliç had been feeling. Large shapes appeared on the horizon, moving quickly toward them. Running. Four legs. Heads pointed directly at them while their hind legs moved the spine up and down.

The creatures shrank as they got closer, changing from the size of a large hut down to the size of a camel, then finally, to the size of a dog.

Blood hounds. Five of them.

They crossed into the desert without raising Trulliç's defenses at the border. Nadeem heard the sigh of relief as everyone else noted that the glass balls remained hidden under the sand. That indicated that either the hounds meant no harm. Or…

She didn't like to think about the possibility that their magic was so strong they just overwhelmed Trulliç's defenses.

They continued their sprint, rushing straight at Trulliç.

No. They split, running around Trulliç and continuing straight to Riyune, who finally stopped howling.

None of the dogs seemed winded by their strange flight. They didn't pant. Their short red-brown fur glistened in the bright sunlight. They didn't smell like dogs either, Nadeem decided. Instead, they smelled like baked dirt and old stone.

One by one, the dogs walked forward and silently touched noses with Riyune. Then sat down to wait in a line beside him.

Nadeem could see the resemblance now. The heads were different —Riyune had different coloring, ears, and muzzle—but the bodies were similarly shaped, with a large chest, a long spine, and powerful hind legs.

When the last finished his greeting, for Nadeem couldn't think of the action as being anything else, Riyune didn't join the others in the line. Instead, he lay down in front of Trulliç, legs straight out in front of him, hind legs curled under.

What did he want? Everyone knew that the blood hounds had been conjured by the emperor. Shouldn't they have just vanished? That was what the war council had speculated.

The dog at the start of the grew motionless, as still as a statue. The short, red-brown fur rippled across his back, changing to an ash-white color. Deep inside his chest, the dog trembled.

Fog seeped from the edges of the dog, making it hard to see. Trulliç took a step back, and he called a cackling ball of pure energy into his palm, holding it ready.

A loud *crack* echoed across the sand, like the sound of a spine breaking.

Nadeem felt herself take a quiet gasp when the figure of the dog *changed*.

The back of the dog rose and rose. Ash poured off the body, making a sound like shifting sand. The smell of sweet incense floated through the air.

The fog cleared away. A man stood there now. He was shorter than Trulliç, with black curly hair, dark skin and eyes, and a proudly hooked nose. He wore a loose shirt and pants, both the same reddish-brown color as the blood hound's fur.

"I am Nishal," the man announced, his voice deep and rough. "I was—I am—one of those who you refer to as the old kings."

Nadeem watched with wonder as the dogs, one by one, changed back into men, some old, some young, but none of them ancient. The survivors from the battle stood in an awestruck circle around them as these legends came back to life.

Riyune went last. Nadeem wasn't surprised when he turned out to be the oldest of the kings. He also appeared to be a man from Lydae, with pale skin. His hair was golden white and his eyes were searing blue. While he was about the same height as Trulliç, he was thin and wiry.

He gave her a smile and a wink.

"We knew you could do it," Riyune said to Trulliç as he stepped away from the pile of ashes that had contained his true form. "Well, at least I had faith in you. Even though you were being such an idiot early on."

Nadeem blinked, surprised. Why would Riyune bring that up? All the old kings laughed. The sound grated on her. She wasn't sure why.

"What happened to you?" Trulliç asked.

Of course, the poet would want to know the history behind the kings.

Even at her distance, Nadeem knew that wasn't the right question to ask. Maybe it was her training as a star sister that had taught her to not trust as easily.

But the six kings had once ruled the desert from their grand city of Osmerli. In fact, they'd ruled much of the Tanesh Empire before the emperor had come into power.

What did they plan on ruling now?

"Before the emperor, there was no thing as a land magician," Riyune said. "Magic was spread out. More people could do small magics."

Everyone surrounding the old kings gasped. No land magicians? More people had magic?

"Women were more capable at illusions," Riyune continued. "While men had stronger physical magic, to match their physical strength."

"And the star sisters?" Nadeem had to ask. "They weren't marked, were they?"

"They were not," Riyune confirmed. He nodded at her, as if he'd expected the question. "They still existed in small, secretive groups that always went around with their faces covered. You never knew if the woman standing beside you truly looked how she presented or not."

The star sisters in the crowd grew still, as shocked as Nadeem had been.

"That was one of the main reasons why the emperor created us," Riyune said. "His original plan was for us to kill any babe of power soon after they were born. But even though he controlled us, that sort of killing weakened the spell he'd put on us. It was so foreign to our natures to kill innocent children. That was when he invented his cloak. By making us protect pregnant mothers, he made the spell holding us stronger."

"And the star sisters?" Nadeem said.

Riyune nodded. "Yes. Even with the cloak, they'd gotten the closest to assassinating him more than once. That was when he introduced the ritual of carving a star into the cheek of a star sister at her coming of age ritual. So that a woman could never completely disguise herself and get that close to killing him again."

Nadeem couldn't help but shiver. The emperor had corrupted their most closely held rituals. By the time Nadeem was born, the star sisters considered the ceremony their own. When it never had been.

"How did he come to power?" Trulliç asked.

Nadeem could tell that he wished he had a scribe with him, to write down all of these stories, probably so he could cast them into poems someday. It made her both smile and shake her head at him.

"The six kings ruled over much of what became known as the Tanesh Empire. You know that was his original name, right? Tanil. But he erased his name, became just 'the emperor', as if he was the only one and that there would never be another."

Trulliç nodded as if he understood that already, how important the names of things were. Nadeem knew she'd never considered it. Then again, she wasn't a poet.

"I was a king of Lydae, while the other kings ruled the other parts of the land. We were loosely consolidated, each country with its own character, its own people and problems. Once a year, the six kings gathered in Osmerli, to celebrate our peoples, to talk together, to make plans for the following year, share resources and wisdom." Riyune sighed.

Nadeem could tell that the memory was painful for Riyune.

"Tanil had already become a minor warlord to the east, near the border with Uluborlu. We'd agreed to bring him to Osmerli so that we could negotiate with him, see if we could give him enough land to make him stop warring. While we had guards and soldiers, none of us had a large army. We weren't intent on conquering more people. Our neighboring nations traded freely with us."

Nadeem wasn't sure why she doubted what Riyune said. Maybe because she'd only lived during the reign of the emperor. There were no records, no poems or songs, but she didn't believe that everything was all sweetness and light in the times of the old kings.

"He came with a small group of elite soldiers. Behind him marched a huge army. Remember, there were no land magicians. We had no warning that they were coming. The emperor hid their steps from us."

Trulliç sighed. Nadeem knew he was still upset how the emperor had managed to hide his soldiers from him as well.

"Tyranel agreed to everything we suggested, bargaining hard for a few things, letting some things go. We kings congratulated each other for doing so well."

All the other kings looked angry.

"But Tyranel had tricked us into lowering our guards with him. Instead, he stole our wills from us with his magic, forced us into our hound forms, then attacked the city."

A sigh went through the former kings, some of their anger replaced with great sorrow.

Nadeem could only imagine the havoc the emperor raised on a defenseless population. He would have killed everyone who didn't flee, then chased the ones he didn't catch right away and slaughtered them as well. Everyone knew how the emperor treated the enemy, that he never took prisoners, but instead took their lives for his own.

"We didn't understand the nature of his magic at first. None of us knew that he lived on death. It wasn't a power granted to any other, as far as we could tell. He was unique. While he gave thanks to the gods as one should, it was perfunctory. He worshiped only himself, and power."

The people surrounding the old kings gave a sigh. They'd been taught that the emperor was always right, to give him praise. The rules about always thanking him at every meal were new, but few had questioned it. The emperor would take care of them.

Would they mourn the passing of the emperor? Nadeem supposed a few would. They didn't understand the evil of the man.

Maybe that was why Trulliç had left the large pile of sand, now covered with thick stones, at the edge of the desert. So that people would have a grave to visit.

"We tried many different plans over the decades to overthrow the emperor," Riyune said. "We finally understood that a desert magician would be our best hope, as the sands had never fully forgiven the emperor for his attack. They obeyed him, but very grudgingly. It took the death of thousands for him to have the power to force the sands to cover over Osmerli. It took him years to obliterate the city."

While the other people listening gasped, Nadeem just shook her head and sighed. She remembered Trulliç speculating that just because there were no poems about a great war, didn't mean that the emperor had had the power to kill the kings in a single battle.

"There were many desert magicians over the decades," Riyune said. "All of them died before they could come to full power, either killed by the emperor when he realized what exactly the child could do, or else overwhelmed by the desert itself the first time they walked the lands."

He speared Trulliç with a look. "It was with great luck that your mother bore you so far north. The emperor wasn't really looking in Lydae for a desert magician. Then you had your great journey here, always moving. The emperor lost track of you."

"Were you the blood hound who accompanied my mother?" Trulliç asked. "The one who changed the tin horseshoe to glass?"

"I was," Riyune said with a lopsided grin. It was a very doggy expression. "Slid the glass into your chubby hand, right after you were born."

"Was Atça part of your plan?" Trulliç asked, holding himself very still.

Nadeem knew that while Trulliç controlled his anger so much better now, his rage at his former mentor would never completely disappear.

"No, that just worked out well for us," Riyune said. "He kept you hidden, better than we could have. We left you with him. He didn't report your powers to the emperor until the very end."

Nadeem bit her lips together, though she wanted to say something, anything, to comfort Trulliç. It was difficult for him to hear that his hated mentor may have saved his life.

At least that appeared to get Trulliç to start thinking.

"So, what will you do now?" Trulliç said, finally asking the question that Nadeem may have started with.

Riyune blinked, as if the question surprised him. "Do? We intend to rule again. As we did before."

Quiet engulfed all the people standing and listening. Nadeem saw them all tense. Were they going to run backwards, away from the fight that was about to start? Or would they run forward, to try to protect their desert magician?

"No," Trulliç said. Though the word was spoken quietly, it carried great weight. "The desert is mine."

Riyune laughed. It wasn't a pleasant sound. "We gave it to you, boy. We can take it back."

Trulliç shook his head. "You may have given me the power at the beginning. But the desert has given herself to me. You cannot take the land away from a land magician."

What Trulliç didn't say, but what Nadeem heard anyway, was that Trulliç would die without the land, starve like a man without food or water.

"Are you sure?" Riyune asked slyly.

Nadeem watched in horror as Trulliç's color faded. The familiar sand beneath her feet suddenly felt as foreign as the rocks and dirt beyond the border.

"You will stop," Trulliç commanded them. Great balls of glass suddenly rose up out of the sand, surrounding the old kings.

"You can't make us," Riyune said. He sounded pleased, like an older child taunting a younger one.

Yes, the old kings may have had great wealth in their kingdom, and possibly there had been peaceful trade between them and the other kingdoms.

More likely, though, they always held the threat of invasion over the heads of their neighbors. And the terms of their trade would always favor the kings. The other nations were more like slave nations.

Winds suddenly tore through the area. The kings looked surprised. Trulliç called up a powerful ball of pure energy to his hands. The sands came back under his control. Nadeem felt herself taking a huge sigh of relief as the nourishing lands supported her again.

The kings looked at each other. They all began to shake themselves, swinging their arms from side to side. Mist covered them as their bodies changed. Nadeem winced at what sounded like bones breaking as the kings transformed back into blood hounds.

Or what Nadeem had always called a blood hound. These creatures looked like blood hounds but were different. They were larger than a regular dog. Long fangs grew from their upper snouts, a weapon to use bringing down prey. Their paws were much bigger as well, with sharper talons and longer dew claws.

They all focused their attention on Trulliç. He stood his ground.

The one in front—it must be Riyune, though he looked exactly like the other hounds—stamped his paw on the ground, making the sand ripple.

All the comfort slid out of the land again. The ball of magic in Trulliç's hands died. The winds were chased off.

Nadeem heard the word as loudly as Trulliç did, she was certain.

Run.

Why did they want for Trulliç to run? Was it just part of the chase for them? Or did they want him to leave the safety of the star sisters and others who might come to his aid?

Slowly, Trulliç nodded, as if he heard more than what Nadeem had.

"I will be back," Trulliç directed over his shoulder, at Nadeem.

For a moment, their eyes caught. Nadeem felt her heart beating normally in her chest again.

Then her distance from him and the rest of the world reasserted itself.

The war hadn't ended. Not yet.

Trulliç raced away, heading deep for the center of the desert, with the blood hounds hot on his heels.

While the rest of the group gathered together, muttering to themselves about what they'd just seen and heard, Nadeem turned her back on all of them and went to sit on the border again.

Neither here or there. Neither alive nor dead. Waiting still for the war to end.

CHAPTER ELEVEN

TRULLIÇ

TRULLIÇ FLEW ACROSS THE DESERT. He realized that he'd gone faster when he'd been carrying his people to the battle of Egreliki. He wasn't going slower because he was tired, though he was. A deep weariness had settled into his bones after the fight with the emperor, after fending off so much fire and power, absorbing so much of the emperor's poisonous magic.

He traveled more slowly because needed to think as he flew along.

The other kings had all, in one voice, told him to run.

Riyune had added in a quiet whisper that none of the others could hear, "It's the only way to save your life."

Though the old kings weren't land magicians, they still had great power over the desert, and possibly all the lands. Their magic was different, however.

Trulliç wished that they'd all met under different circumstances, that he could have welcomed them to Hayalevi as honored guests. He longed to hear their stories, learn their history, and sing their poetry. They could have spent a month together, sitting with scribes who recorded their every word, and still Trulliç would have wanted more.

The kings could take the desert from Trulliç, he knew, if they all worked together. He felt it slipping away behind him as the dogs chased him, gathering the land back to themselves. It wasn't as strong of a hold as Trulliç had as a land magician. With effort, he could recall it to himself. Plus, the land didn't sustain the old kings, support them as it did the desert magician.

However, Trulliç couldn't stop running. The hounds would tear him apart if he did. He couldn't defend himself from them. The desert didn't recognize them as an enemy, particularly not when they were in their blood hound form.

What could he do? Where could he run to? He couldn't get away. They'd chase him up the tallest mountain and across the deepest ocean. The desert was their home, though. He understood that the blood hounds were originally bred from the tiny dogs who lived under the sand. How or why they were created, he didn't know, though he longed to. What ritual did they undergo to gain the ability to change from man to dog? It wasn't something they were born with, that much Trulliç intuitively understood about the nature of their magic. His forms were wind and sand, but he was a desert magician. A strong enough magician of a copse of woods would be able to take the form of a tree, maybe even one or more of the creatures who lived there.

But that sort of speculation, that his mind naturally turned to, wasn't helping.

Where could he go? How could he stop the old kings? He hadn't prepared anything. Only through elaborate preparations had he been able to kill the emperor.

The satisfaction at ending the corrupt beast of the emperor was tainted now by the blood hounds chasing him.

Riyune believed Trulliç might have a chance, though, if he ran.

For a moment, up ahead, a dark shape loomed. Trulliç thought it was the cavern that led to the myth lands.

The dark spot turned out to be a sole dune, piled up by the winds.

It gave Trulliç an idea, though.

He was at his moment of greatest need, tired, his magic no longer at full strength despite the heat of the sun beating down on him. He was drained after these last few days, full of battles.

"Help!" he called out to the desert itself. "I swore a blood oath to stop the emperor from desecrating the desert. I have fulfilled my promise. Now, I need your aid to stop the old kings from destroying my lands."

Trulliç didn't know what else to call it. He knew the old kings weren't as corrupt as the emperor. But something about them didn't sit easily with him.

If Nadeem had been more of her old self, she probably would have asked about the intentions of the old kings first.

Too late.

"Please!" Trulliç called out. "I beg you. Help me now in my time of greatest need."

In the distance, a dark shape shimmered into existence.

It was the cavern, the one that had aided him during his first manhood journey. The place that was actually a conduit into the myth lands.

Would it allow the old kings inside? Trulliç nearly gave an exhausted giggle when he remembered that there were only places for four sleepers in the cavern. Maybe it wouldn't allow them all to come in? Though since they were in dog form, maybe it would.

It might be a trap as well. There was only one way in and out of the cavern itself.

It didn't feel like a trap, however. The cavern valued integrity. That was why it showed its hidden jewels to all travelers. Those who desecrated the spot would be left to die in the center of the desert without water.

Trulliç directed his flying legs toward the cavern. It still looked as though it was made out of a haphazardly placed heap of rocks, with thin shale covering the top.

However, even as he grew closer, he couldn't see the guard stone just inside the door. Just endless black, like a starless sky.

Cold winds blew out from inside the cavern. They carried the scent of ash and bone. Trulliç couldn't smell the water from the burbling stream the cavern carried.

He still firmly believed that this wasn't a trap. It was still the same cavern.

And it was his only hope.

Without pausing, Trulliç let the darkness swallow him.

W here was the guard stone? Trulliç kept wondering. The cavern was no longer lit at all by the outside. Trulliç had thought that he'd be able to stop running as soon as he entered, but he plunged into the darkness and kept going, never striking a wall.

The cavern seemed endless. It reminded him of the one time he'd walked along one of the hallways in Atça's house, how it had grown dark and closed in on him.

Trulliç tried to call up a mage light. Normally, in the cavern, it was easy to do.

He could barely conjure a small flame in the center of his palm, and it went out as soon as he let go of it.

Where were the blood hounds? Trulliç couldn't hear them behind him. He couldn't hear anything, or really see anything.

And he was growing tired, more tired than he'd believed was possible.

He slowed, then slowed further, then finally stopped.

He listened to his own heart thudding hard in his ears. His breath came in harsh pants. The cool air instantly chilled his sweat, causing him to shiver.

Where was he? What was this place? He could barely see his hand in front of his face. Sand covered the floor, but he couldn't see any walls.

Finally, Trulliç turned around.

Though he'd run and run and *run*, the entrance to the cavern stood right behind him. The guard stone was still missing.

Trulliç took two cautious steps toward the doorway.

Stars streamed across the night sky. The sand glittered like broken glass.

It was the myth lands.

If he went out onto those sands, would he be able to come back?

Trulliç didn't know. But he believed that being in the myth lands would put him on more even territory with the old kings, if they'd followed him here. While Trulliç wouldn't have much desert magic here, the old kings wouldn't have much magic either.

Trulliç stepped out onto the cool sands. The myth lands always calmed him, even though this wasn't really his desert.

After Trulliç had taken a few steps, he looked back the way he'd come.

The cavern had already disappeared.

Six blood hounds stood there instead.

T rulliç watched, his fear turning into curiosity as the dogs stepped forward, then hesitated. Each one started to shake his paws, one by one, as if he'd stepped in something sticky.

They shook their heads. Then, one by one, they each transformed back to men.

It seemed that the myth lands wouldn't accept their dog forms, that they needed to be people here. Trulliç remembered how difficult it had been for Nadeem to perform her illusions when they'd come here. He'd had trouble doing his magic as well. The myth lands wanted its visitors to be in their true form.

However, the kings looked different here than they had back in the Qaenev. They no longer wore the same red-brown shirts and pants, clothes that Trulliç imagined had been part of the blood hound spell cast by the emperor.

Instead, they wore what Trulliç would call kingly garb. Even in the dim starlight, they sparkled. Riyune's was particularly fine, with a gold silk shirt, wide green pants, solid leather boots, and a long, black velvet sleeveless vest that flowed down to his ankles. A thin silver circlet sat on his head.

As they stepped forward, Trulliç gulped. He held himself very still, though his first instinct was to run again, far away and very fast. He shook himself and stood firm.

The creatures who approached him weren't men. Or rather, were no longer men. Instead, they looked like skeletons with skin tightly stretched over the bones. They had stringy hair, and the jeweled rings they wore hung loosely on their fingers. They walked forward awkwardly, as if their joints ground against each other.

What had happened to the kings? Or was this just their true form?

"You cannot escape," Riyune assured Trulliç. "We will destroy you here. You can haunt these lands forever."

Trulliç shook his head. "What happened to you?" he asked. He couldn't help himself.

Riyune gave a wheezy laugh. "We are ancient," he said. "Much older than you realize."

"Why else do you think the emperor was able to live as long as he did?" another of the kings said. "He'd stolen our magic from us."

"That was why you could be enslaved for so long," Trulliç said, nodding. "Because you would live that long."

Riyune gave a sharp shrug, the bones of his shoulders moving up and down. "The spells needed to be refreshed now and again. But essentially, yes."

Trulliç peered more carefully at Riyune. He did seem less solid than the others, here in the myth lands. "What happened to you? When you sacrificed yourself to seal the guard stone?"

Riyune barked a laugh. "There were always more than six women who carried babes of power. There were many shadows of us, fulfilling the contract with the emperor."

Trulliç gasped in horror. "Then your sacrifice wasn't real? The guard stone for the desert heart will crack soon?"

Riyune looked surprised, as if he hadn't thought about that. "Maybe," he said slowly. "But maybe not. When we ruled, Forit's temples were places of great honor. The people sacrificed to them regularly, which we think kept the guard stone strong. However, the emperor did away with all of her temples. It was why he was able to break the guard stone, as it was already weakened."

Trulliç nodded. If he survived this, he was going to have to make sure that all of the villages and towns of the desert started to honor Forit, as well as hire more priests and priestesses. Hopefully they would be able to spread the word throughout the former empire.

Trulliç studied the skeletons in front of him. While they were the ancient kings and they deserved to be recognized, he couldn't allow them to continue to live. Their old bones needed a rest.

"You must believe me when I tell you that I wish I could speak with you further," Trulliç said. "I would love to share tea with you, listen to your tales, hear about your world and your adventures. But I cannot allow you to leave here. You may not rejoin the land of the living."

The kings shared a look of disbelief. "How are you going to stop us?" Nishal said. He was obviously the youngest of the kings, his face more fleshy than the others. Perhaps he had more power as well.

Trulliç pulled out an obsidian knife. It wasn't Nadeem's, though it had the same weight and feel.

The kings grew still. Surely they weren't afraid that Trulliç thought he could hurt them with this?

Instead, Trulliç drew the blade across his left palm, making sure to cut deeply. The pain shot through his hand, feeling as though he'd stabbed himself. Blood instantly seeped out of the wound.

Trulliç went down on one knee, thrusting his palm against the desert sands. The agony made his eyes water, his arm burn. He breathed through his mouth, two large gulping breathes. Finally, he spoke.

"I swore to protect the desert from the emperor, that I would not allow him to desecrate the sands there. Now, I swear to protect the world from you and your kind. You belong in the myth worlds. I would give up my desert, stay here for all eternity as well, if that is what it takes to keep you here." Trulliç took another deep breath as he rose back up. "You *belong* here," he said again, feeling it more deeply in his bones. "You are creatures of myth and legend. Your time with the living passed, long ago."

The kings growled, sounding more like the hounds they changed into than men.

Trulliç put away his dagger. He hoped that Nadeem would understand. He shaped a curved sword out of pure light. It took effort to make it hold its shape, and Trulliç had so little energy left.

He planted his feet wide and took on a fighting stance, something he'd seen too many of his people do when the soldiers drew near.

"You cannot pass," Trulliç said. He knew that the cavern that led back to the world of men stood somewhere behind him. "You will stay here for eternity. And we will fight for that long if need be."

The kings looked at each other. Glittering swords shaped of moonlight and bone rose up in their hands.

Trulliç gulped. Of course, it would be six to one. That seemed to be the odds of his life.

Nevertheless, he nodded. Let them come.

He would never let them pass back to the land of the living.

T rulliç swore as he struck yet *another* sword down from the king he faced, and it didn't make any difference. Since the swords were conjured, it didn't matter if Trulliç broke his opponent's sword or forced it from his opponent's hand. The swords would magically appear again.

At least he'd managed to dispatch two of the kings and only four remained. The first had been a lucky shot. Trulliç had swung wildly as he spun around, and had managed to strike the neck of Nishal, sending his head flying.

Fortunately, the bodies of the kings didn't appear to be able to regrow their heads. The bones had dissolved into ashes. All that had remained was the thin circlet, tarnished and wan.

Was that where their power came from? Trulliç couldn't see it—the kings were too magical all over for him to be able to isolate one part of their magic from the other.

It gave him something to concentrate on, however.

The next king he dispatched, all he did was knock the crown off the king's head. The bones fell immediately, as if the strings that had been attached to them had been cut.

Now, however, the rest of the kings understood their vulnerability. They hung back, protecting themselves.

It made the fight easier, giving Trulliç a little breathing room. Plus, the kings now attacked one by one instead of two or three ganging up on Trulliç at the same time. Did they not trust each other?

Trulliç wished yet again that Nadeem was at his side. Or that they'd had more time before all of this had started, so that Trulliç could have learned better how to fight. He knew the basics, how to punch and block. He'd also picked up a lot of technique over the last few days, with all the battles he'd been in.

It wasn't the same, though, fighting with hands and feet versus using a sword. The reach was different. Trulliç easily bore a dozen cuts from when he'd overreached himself.

He faced another of the kings—his tired brain unable to cough up the name. It was the one with the tall ibis embroidered on the back of his long black robe. Trulliç remembered the ibis being the one who might have killed the emperor by removing the scale that had been created from Trulliç's afterbirth.

The king in front of him moved something like a bird, high on his toes, with long legs. He had a greater reach than Trulliç. He also made a weird bobbing motion with his head, as if trying to make sure it stayed protected, leaning back as he swung in with his sword.

Trulliç wanted to be patient, to study the king and find his vulnerabilities before Trulliç went for a hard attack. He couldn't, though. He was tiring fast.

With his left hand, Trulliç made a feint, as if about to throw a punch. Then he pretended to trip and took a few flailing steps.

This brought the bird-like king forward for the kill.

He didn't notice that Trulliç had swept around with his sword arm until far too late.

The king's feet flew out from under him and he landed flat on his back.

Trulliç leaped up, and with the flat of his blade knocked the king's crown off.

He didn't stay to watch the figure disappear. Two of the other kings attacked, one on either side. Trulliç fought them both, turning from one side to the other. He stumbled back, holding onto his own sword while he still landed on his butt. He sat there panting as the two kings strode toward him, menacingly.

Suddenly, Trulliç remembered the pocket of sand that he always carried with him. Would it help revive him here? He hurriedly reached his fingers into it.

Warm sand caressed his fingertips. Pure air filled his lungs. He caught the familiar scent of baking rock. The world took on harder lines and became less dreamlike.

With a roar, Trulliç jumped to his feet. He swung his blade to the right, taking the king there by surprise. With a real man, chopping through a neck was difficult. There were too many muscles and bones. With one of the old kings, however, the head wasn't attached with much of anything, the bones barely held together.

The head of the king toppled off, landing with a soft plop on the desert floor.

As Trulliç came to face the next king, Riyune came up from behind.

Before Trulliç could attack the king, Riyune slid his sword up, catching the silver circlet of his companion and flinging it out into the desert night.

Trulliç blinked, surprised.

Riyune was the last king standing.

He held up his arm with the sword, then opened his hand. The sword disappeared. Then Riyune opened his arms wide to show that he was unarmed.

Trulliç remembered at the beginning of the battle how Riyune had only attacked with the others, but how he'd also held back. Plus, Riyune had waited while the others had attacked Trulliç in ones and twos.

"Now what?" Trulliç asked, not lowering his own sword.

Riyune gave him a sad smile. "I, too, would love nothing more but to recount my history with you, to spend time reciting the old poems, and tell you of what had been but is no more."

A wave of relief washed over Trulliç. He was glad that his old companion felt that way. He'd always known that Riyune wasn't "his" dog, that Riyune was his own being. But they'd been together for many years. Trulliç had poured his heart out to his dog more than once, particularly when he'd been dealing with Atça.

"We don't have the time, I'm afraid," Riyune said. "The others are dead, finally. I was the first, and I shall be the last."

"What do you mean?" Trulliç asked. He didn't want to have to kill Riyune. Couldn't Riyune just live here, so that Trulliç could come and visit sometimes? Trulliç would need wise councilors in this new world where the emperor no longer ruled with an iron fist.

"You were right. We belong here, in the myth lands," Riyune said. He started slowly moving his hands back in from where he'd stretched them out. "We passed out of knowledge long ago. The emperor made sure of that. We have no place among the living."

Riyune placed his hands on either side of his head, near his silver circlet.

"Do you have to die?" Trulliç asked, cursing his soft heart and how his eyes were starting to tear up.

Riyune gave him a sad smile. "While I could live for many years here, honestly, it would be too lonely. And the temptation would be too much for me to come back and to rule." He paused, then added, "When you made the oath to stay here, to give up the desert in order to ensure its safety, I knew I had to make sure the others remained here as well. You've grown up nicely. I think you'll rule as well, if not better, than we would have."

"Thank you," Trulliç said. While he never would have heard those words from Atça, hearing them from Riyune meant just as much, healing a part of his soul.

Riyune gave a laughing bark. "Though you'll always be a boy in my heart," he said. With a swift movement, he lifted his crown off his head. His eyes grew wide, startled, and suddenly younger. "I gift this to you," he whispered as the strength left his body and he collapsed.

Trulliç ran to the side of the old king, but all that remained was ash with a few slivers of bone. Tears sprang from his eyes for his old friend and companion, though he knew that they'd never been as close as Trulliç would have liked.

How could they be? Riyune had been planning on taking Trulliç's desert from him since the very beginning.

Trulliç felt hollow by the time his tears dried. He also felt lighter and more carefree than he had before, possibly for the first time in his life.

The emperor was well and truly dead. The blood hounds were no more. Just memories and ghosts remained.

Winds that Trulliç hadn't felt had blown away all the remains of what had been Riyune while Trulliç had been crying. Only one of the delicate circlets remained, made of tarnished silver wire.

Trulliç slowly reached for it. His fingers felt the magic of it, as though running water flowed over his skin.

He did not put the crown on his head, however. It wasn't for him. And while Riyune had turned out to be an honorable man, Trulliç still felt as though Riyune followed the god Serril, a trickster to the end.

Instead, Trulliç stood, closed his eyes, and announced his intention. "Let me place this on the guard stone for Forit's heart," he said out loud. "Let the ancient magic wrapped in this crown protect the lands forever."

When Trulliç opened his eyes, there in the distance he saw a dark cavern, the twin of the one that had brought him here, with rocks haphazardly piled one on top of another.

However, for this cavern, the great, gray guard stone stood just outside the entrance to the cavern, completely blocking the way.

Dark storm clouds covered the streaming stars, casting the place in a dull light. The stench of old blood filled the area, making Trulliç's stomach queasy. Whatever was trapped in the cavern sickened him.

The knife that had killed Riyune the first time, or a shadow of the dog, still lay undisturbed on the ground in front of the guard stone. When Trulliç had placed the body of the dog on the stone, using Riyune's sacrifice to close the hole Marius had made, the center of the guard stone had grown cloudy, like a fog patiently hiding whatever lay beneath.

With steady hand, Trulliç lifted up the circlet and pressed it *into* the stone. The circlet resisted at first, sending tendrils of magic dancing up along Trulliç's fingers, around his wrists and arms, wanting to stay with him.

Trulliç pressed the silver more firmly against the stone, unafraid that it would break.

Slowly, the stone gave way, accepting the circle of silver into itself, taking the magic as its own.

When Trulliç stepped back, the cloudy parts of the guard stone had cleared away. The stone itself had grown glossy and black, looking much more solid than it had before, as though it had been carved and polished from a single piece of onyx instead of rough gray stone.

In the center of the guard stone lay a single circle of silver.

No one knew what Forit's symbol had been before the emperor had destroyed all her temples. Most of the gods and goddesses were represented with straight lines, while Onnet had the shape of a horseshoe.

Maybe Forit's symbol could be a circle to show her unending love and how her death led to more life which in turn always led to more death. The circle always turning, never finished.

Trulliç resolved to create yet another poem, now that the war was truly over.

Night had fallen by the time Trulliç returned to the true desert. The instant he set foot on the sands, he knew that the cavern had deposited him close to where he'd first run into it. The sands around him knew his name, but they no longer answered to him, the ties having been broken by the old kings.

Slowly at first, then more quickly, Trulliç gathered the sands back together, bringing all of the desert back to him. The cavern had refreshed him, given him time to sleep and heal along with delightful water to drink. It had shared more dreams with him this time, showing how the gods had been the ones to build the rocks around Forit's heart, then how the old kings themselves had crafted the cavern, calling a shadow of the original to them to act as a conduit.

It offered to bury the emperor's staff deep in the myth world for him, along with the deadly yellow poison that had poured off the emperor. Evidently the emperor had melted some of the bodies of the dead, rendered them for their fat, then used it to power his corpulent body.

Trulliç gladly took the cavern up on its offer, knowing that those powers would be safe in the land of the myths.

When Trulliç arrived at the edge of the desert, he found all his people still there, holding vigil. They'd felt the shifting sands when he'd returned, but they wouldn't allow themselves to believe that it was true until they'd seen him.

Trulliç spent more time than he liked reassuring people that the old kings were really gone, as was the emperor. No, he didn't know what was happening in the rest of the empire. He was going to be sure to hear about it, though. He would send out runners in the morning to go fetch the news, heralds telling the tales of the great battles the desert magician had been in, and how the emperor was now dead.

Finally, Trulliç was able to gather his people together and bring them back to the shining star of the desert, his city, Hayalevi.

Nadeem stayed by his side, silent and reserved as always. He didn't know what they were going to do, now that the war was truly over. Surely, she'd come back to him? Remove the distance between them?

But Nadeem hadn't recovered by the next day, or the one after that.

It took Trulliç a week of trying different things before he finally knew what he should do.

He was yet again at the end of his rope, in his hour of need.

So, he took Nadeem out into the desert and called the cavern once more.

CHAPTER TWELVE

NADEEM

NADEEM WANTED TO REJOIN THE world. However, she didn't know how. She couldn't pay attention to Trulliç no matter how much he might dote on her. She wanted to miss Riyune—he'd been there as long as she'd known Trulliç—but she couldn't. She found herself pricking her fingers with the tip of her knife blade just to make her feel.

When Trulliç saw the blood she drew, he told her it was enough.

But what could he do? The war had ended. He still was the desert magician. Would he be the last of his kind? When the last of the land magicians died, would the magic they held seep back into the earth? What would the world change into if more people had magic again?

Nadeem didn't know, and though she wanted to be excited about the prospect, she felt as though it was just too much effort.

News was slowly trickling into Hayalevi. It would take months, possibly years, before they heard from northern Lydae. But everyone had noticed the blood hounds disappearing. The emperor's symbol had supposedly fallen from buildings with his passing. People dreamed of stars shooting across the sky, usually a sign of great deaths.

Still, Nadeem felt nothing.

She knew about the star sisters calling an emergency meeting of all the *kabils*. The women had a right to know their heritage. Nadeem told them everything she could from her dream that Riyune had given her, of the old kings, how the star sisters went about completely covered with just their eyes showing so that none knew their faces. They could become anyone they wanted to be.

Would there be more star sisters like her, who chose to mangle the mark on their cheek? Would they change, as she had? Become creatures of the sea, or trees, or even mountains and sand?

She refused to go with them, however. She still belonged here, in the desert.

Though here was still not *here*.

It didn't surprise her when Trulliç asked her to accompany him out to the desert. A tiny thrill went through her, there and gone.

Was he going to try to kill her? Bury her deep in the sands? Free her?

But no, nothing as deadly as that.

He carried them swiftly across the sands. She traveled easily with him, enjoying the night breezes blowing through her short hair, which she hadn't bothered to cut in some time. It was starting to tickle the edges of her ears. She knew that before, she would have already been annoyed enough to cut it.

Now, it was just one more thing that might bring her closer to feeling.

A dark shape formed on the horizon. With a quiet gasp, Nadeem realized that Trulliç was taking them toward the cavern.

Did he expect her to find her cure there? Would the waters there soothe her heart, as they had always soothed her skin?

She found herself suddenly curious, poised again on the edge of being alive.

And then hanging there, as always, never able to take those full steps in again.

The cavern seemed much as it always did. The sound of the burbling water soothed her, and the coolness of it indeed did make her heart feel less heavy. They stretched out and slept on the shelves, with Nadeem up higher than Trulliç. That just felt right, though she knew that she probably no longer needed to defend him.

When she awoke, the stars streamed across the sky, lighting the cavern with an eerie glow.

The last time she'd been here, she'd gone to ask the goddess for a boon.

Was that what Trulliç was about to do?

When Nadeem stepped onto the sands, she suddenly felt the weight in her chest. It had been a part of her for so long that she didn't feel it as separate from herself, but as much a part of her as her bones.

Trulliç let Nadeem lead the way. She did, but didn't, know the direction. Away from Forit's heart, that much she knew. But where had she found the goddess the first time?

Winds carried sweet scents to them as they walked. Trulliç kept lifting his head up and looking around, as if expecting to see someone there, maybe a ghost.

Would the old kings remain to haunt the myth lands? Nadeem hoped not. She wanted them to be dancing in Barzhat's court, able to be reborn again finally. Though they would dance for a long, long while, she knew. Not because they were particularly bad men, but because they'd lived for so long, they were likely to have done many bad deeds over the course of their lives.

Finally, they reached the area that Nadeem knew, the hollowed-out spot where the shadow sisters had come to watch her dance. Trulliç appeared to recognize it as well from her description of the place.

Trulliç led Nadeem to the center of the arena, holding her hand tightly. He kissed her temple, tears making his eyes glitter. He squeezed her hand one last time, then he left her there and went to sit on the side of the bowl to watch.

Nadeem wasn't sure exactly what he expected of her. But the last time she'd been here, she'd danced for the goddess.

She started as she had the first time, her palms pressed together as she bowed her head low to the north. Then she started to dance again, those slow practice steps, blocking, sweeping away legs and arms, punching and kicking. A dance she knew so well.

When she finished, she immediately started again, a flowing river of steps.

Slowly, Nadeem started to speed up. She didn't allow herself to hurry, to rush to the end.

This might be the last time she danced for Trulliç. She needed to give him time to say goodbye.

She kept moving faster, though, until her hands and feet were blurred. She jumped high into the air when she kicked, higher than she'd ever jumped before. Her breath came hard and fast. Her fingers and toes tingled as she danced, the blood pumping hard.

Finally, she felt the teardrop buried deep in her chest start to move. She couldn't resist the temptation to look down.

It was rising out of her skin, like a monstrous growth.

She couldn't afford to stumble. If she did, the goddess might never take back her gift.

Faster now, Nadeem danced with all her heart. She wanted to return to the desert, to really feel the sand beneath her feet again. She danced for the coming dawn, to be able to revel in all its glory. She danced for the coming heat of the sun, how slickly it would make her sweat. She danced for the coolness of the water in the oasis, how it would soothe her burning throat.

She danced as she had never danced before, giving all of her life to the goddess so that she might enjoy this one last bit.

The teardrop in her chest rose up until just the tip of it was still connected, a single thin piece of skin looped through the top of it.

Nadeem pushed herself to go faster. This was for the goddess she loved, who she would welcome forever at every meal. This was for her shadow sisters, who had protected the docks from the invading soldiers. This was for all the good men and women who had died defeating the emperor.

But Nadeem was only human. She could only push her body so

far, though it had accommodated her much further than she'd thought possible.

She faltered in the same place she had the first time, by swinging out her leg then not drawing it back far enough. She didn't land solidly.

The next step, instead of bringing her foot out in front of her, she brought it too close to her first, misplaced leg. She tripped and had to stumble forward a few jarring feet.

The teardrop hanging from her chest broke free with the last jolt, a searing pain that went straight from her chest to her belly.

Her gift from the goddess dropped onto the sand at her feet, disappearing as it struck the ground.

The world rushed back into Nadeem. She felt everything—her sore feet, the stitch in her side, how her arms trembled and her back sweat. She smelled the sweet scent of incense and desert rock, already tasting the mint tea that Myrizhah would have ready for her. Her eyes cleared and the night became brighter.

At the front of the arena, Nadeem thought she saw the goddess again. Or a shadowy form of her, with two legs and four arms, her black face and her blue face arranged side by side.

Nadeem felt welcomed by the goddess, who seemed pleased to see her and possibly slightly sad to see her go.

But she would return, she knew.

Everyone, even the old gods, died.

The goddess vanished, and Nadeem found herself swaying. She collapsed onto her knees and found herself weeping. All the tears she hadn't shed for the last few days came pouring out of her. She mourned for all the dead, Riyune included. She mourned for how much she'd hurt herself and Trulliç as well. She mourned for the days she'd lost.

As her tears slowed, she found Trulliç kneeling beside her. He kept himself apart from her, though she could tell how much he longed to take her into his arms, a solid rock who would always be there for her.

And she cried a little more for him as well, leaning against his solid bulk.

When all her tears were spent, Nadeem finally nodded.
"Let's go home."

Nadeem stood at the top of Trulliç's tower, leaning against the balcony, looking out over the desert. Stars filled the night sky. She thought she smelled the ocean sometimes on the strong breeze, but the rest of the time it was just the dust from the nearby hills, the roasted chicken one of the nearby families was cooking, and the warm smell of the nearby palms and dates.

It had been three nights since they'd come back from the lands of myth, since Nadeem had fully returned from the dead.

It was still hard sometimes to be in the land of the living. Nadeem found her senses raw, like a newborn baby. She had raced to her room and cried more often than she ever had in her entire life. Not necessarily from sad things, though the ceremonies they'd had recently to commemorate the dead had certainly counted.

Joyous things made her cry as well, like being with Trulliç in bed, watching the sun rise, seeing a flower bloom in the oasis, or even tasting a sweet fig.

Nadeem had never thought that she'd have a home, not really. She'd believed that she would always be moving, roaming the empire, doing the bidding of the emperor himself as one of the special star sisters. Kardeş would be her main place of operation, where she'd recover between jobs. But it wouldn't truly be a home.

Hayalevi was closer to what she thought about as a home. She had her own building now. Trulliç had raised it for her. It was next to his tower, close to Seydat's house. It had its own bathing room where she could pump up water and have it shower down on her head. It also had its own cooking hearth, so she could prepare meals.

It wasn't very large, not any bigger than the tent Aunt Parayat stayed in at Kardeş. But Nadeem was already starting to make it hers. A small basket of carded wool and a drop spindle now sat in one corner. Trulliç had already offered to buy her a loom at the market.

Her bed had a quilt on it that had been specially made for her, with patterns of stars sewn into it.

Everything Nadeem could have asked for was here. A kind lover who was also her friend, who made her laugh as well as made her think. She could take him in a fair fight, though he was getting better at wrestling.

She had many people to work with, star sisters who were looking for a new path. They did but didn't want to follow hers—she knew that few would completely turn their backs on the sisters as she had.

Then again, few had a broken blood oath in their past.

Still, Nadeem found herself drawn up to the top of Trulliç's tower, casting longing eyes at the horizon.

Trulliç came up from behind her. They both wore merely sheets out of courtesy, though Nadeem would have gone naked. Trulliç wanted to approve, but he was still shocked at the core with how free she was with her body.

At least he understood her mood instinctively, that she needed a friend and not a lover. He kissed her bare shoulder but didn't put his hands on her. Instead, he stood next to her, leaning beside her and looking out over the desert.

"Trulliç," Nadeem started. Then she stopped again. She didn't know what exactly she wanted to say, let alone how to say it. "I promised you before that I'd be honest with you."

Trulliç smiled and nodded but continued to stare out at his desert.

"I'm grateful for everything you've done, everything you've given me. Even the poems you've composed for me," she added. She'd been delighted when he showed her the start of his first composition, detailing the amazing work that a star sister and a land magician could do when they worked together.

Trulliç nodded again. His smiled grew wider.

"But I need…I need…I don't know what," Nadeem said with a heavy sigh, feeling defeated.

"Do you want me to tell you what I think you need?" Trulliç asked, looking over at her.

Strange. He didn't seem the least bit afraid of talking with her honestly. That was something that Nadeem was truly grateful for.

Though she hadn't had that many relationships, no one had ever been as open and honest as Trulliç had been, both about his feelings as well as his own needs.

"I think your feet are telling you to dance away. You thought you'd travel, and now, though you have a comfortable home, it isn't enough."

Nadeem stared at him in astonishment. That was exactly how she felt. "I don't want you to think I'm not grateful for all that you've done for me," she said, wanting to reassure him.

Trulliç gave a short chuckle. "I know you're grateful. I actually had a bet with myself how long it would take you to realize that you needed to go travel for a while. I'm surprised that you lasted this many days."

"Really?" Nadeem asked, surprised.

Trulliç shrugged. "The bet was somewhere between two days and two months," he admitted. "But I knew you'd leave, sooner or later."

Nadeem nodded.

Trulliç reached over and took her hand gently between his. His skin felt rough as always. It was as warm as a rock kissed by the sunlight.

"I also think you'll always come back," he said, stroking the back of her hand with a single finger. "Or at least, that's my hope."

Nadeem smiled at him, her heart feeling lighter. "I will always come back," she promised solemnly. "I am a desert creature, like yourself. Sand swims in my blood, just like it does in yours."

"You know that I would like to travel with you someday," Trulliç said. "But right now…"

"I know. You couldn't possibly leave." The empire was still coming to grips with the death of the emperor. Most places could run themselves, and though the emperor was gone, their daily life hadn't changed that much.

Though they no longer gave thanks at every meal for the emperor. That order had been rescinded. None of villagers Nadeem had talked with seemed to mind.

Still, representatives from the major cities came pouring into Hayalevi every day to meet with the desert magician. Ambassadors and governors' assistants. They met with each other as well, signing new trade agreements and peace treaties.

There were still barbarians north of Lydae who would threaten her borders. Trulliç had no troops to offer, however. The emperor's soldiers were on their own. Some of them had banded together, offering their services to the larger warlords and kings.

Their magical armor had disintegrated over the weeks, the toxic yellow goo dripping off and needing to be buried.

Many of the soldiers actually were able to go home finally. Towns absorbed the returning brothers and fathers as well as they could.

Some of the coastal towns had actually asked for more soldiers to be sent their way, the ones who wanted to become seamen. There were always rumors that the endless ocean wasn't, in fact, endless, that there were other continents to find and explore.

So Trulliç couldn't leave Hayalevi, not yet. Not while so much still needed to be settled in the new world. Maybe in a year or two, though.

"You don't need my blessing," Trulliç said. "I want you to feel free to come and go as you please."

"Really?" Nadeem asked. She remembered her encounter with Levent, who would have tried to hold onto her with both hands if she'd ever dallied with him again.

"Really," Trulliç said. He took both of her hands in his now. "I want you to be free to fly and dance and fight as you need to. And to return to me, when you will."

"Is that what you want?" Nadeem asked, her heart already singing, plans forming about what sort of pack she'd take, where she'd travel to first.

"Of course not!" Trulliç said, laughing. "I'd always prefer for you to be by my side. But that would kill you, the free spirit inside of you. I'd much rather that you be free and happy, and return to my side willfully, rather than try to trap you and cage you."

Nadeem pulled Trulliç in for a deep kiss of affection. "Thank you," she said, knowing that by setting her free, he'd just captured her heart completely.

"We have all the world and all the time to explore these ties between us," Trulliç quoted. "But for now, fly."

Nadeem nodded, settling herself against his chest but still looking out over the desert spread out below them.

In the morning, she'd be gone, only to return to him time and time again, blown there by the desert wind.

GODS AND GODDESSES

Barzhat

The goddess of death lives beneath the great inner sea of the Tanesh empire. She sits in judgment of the dead on her throne encrusted with pearls and shells. In front of her is a huge golden court, full of souls dancing.

Every bad deed a person commits while they are living is weighed by Barzhat after they die. She creates a black vest covered with golden weights, each shaped like a teardrop. You must dance before Barzhat until all the weights fall from the vest. Only then will Barzhat give you the final kiss of true death, cleansing your soul for rebirth.

A common curse: May you dance forever in the goddess' court.

The star sister Manisat picked up an *ağrikat* shell on the shore of the Barzhat Sea. When she raised the shell to her ear, she heard the sad sighs of the goddess Barzhat and realized how lonely the goddess was. Manisat had made her way to the goddess' golden court while she'd still been alive and had promised the goddess that the star sisters wouldn't merely venerate her, but love her. They would welcome the goddess at all their feasts, big and small. A bowl was always left empty at every meal, a welcome place for the goddess.

Barzhat tests the sisters sometimes, coming for dinner as a stranger. They must show her hospitality or she will make them dance. However, in return for a star sister's devotion, Barzhat will grant her a single boon during her lifetime, if her need is great enough.

Though cutting across the Barzhat Sea would make travel from one end of the empire to the other faster, no one sails across it regularly. Men can only travel on the waters at her indulgence. Sailors must always be on the lookout when in her territory. If the waters are clear and blue, they can travel freely. If the waters turn black, they run. Otherwise, the goddess takes them down into her golden court where they must dance for centuries.

The goddess is always depicted with two faces, one blue and one black. The blue face is used for judgment. The black face is used for death. She is often called fickle, and is temperamental, as are all artists. She is often shown with four dancing legs and twelve arms, each holding a different weapon.

Symbol: Feet. Also represented by a single line toward the bottom of the space, ___

Colors: Blue and Black.

Innis

The god of fertility lives in the court of the gods. He is forever mourning his beautiful wife, Forist, whom he killed in the great battle with the darkness, and from whom all humanity came. He is known as a dark, somber god. Brining a new life into the world isn't to be done lightly.

Symbol: The spear. Represented by a single horizontal line —
Colors: Red

Serrat/Serril

The goddess/god of desolate places lives in the desert.

Like Barzhat, Serrat/Serril has two faces, a female and a male face. The male aspect (Serril) is worshiped by the land magicians, while the female aspect (Serrat) is honored by the star sisters.

Serrat/Serril is known as a trickster god. He/she leads men and caravans astray in the desert by creating fake oases. He/she also tricks sailors by making Barzhat's waters seem calm.

Yet, Serrat/Serril just wants to be loved.

Originally, Serrat/Serril lived in the court of the gods. However, the gods banished the god/goddess after he brought magic to man. Serril, in his male form, made a bet with the goddess Onnet, that a mighty human hunter could out shoot the goddess and her bow. In order for the hunter to win, Serril gave the human magic.

As Serrat, the goddess has a birthmark in the form of a star on her left cheek, which is why the star sisters carve one in theirs. However, she isn't much loved by them. (They love Berzhat instead.)

Symbol: Z

Colors: White (for Serrat) and black (for Serril)

Enkat

The goddess of rain lives in the court of the gods. She dances for the gods and goddess until the sweat pours from her and drips down from her hair to the earth as rain.

In the desert lands, Enkat is often portrayed as a female form with no face, just hair streaming down everywhere.

Symbol: Represented by three vertical lines. | | |

Colors: Brown and green

Xannil

The god of the sun lives in the court of the gods. In the north, Xannil is often portrayed as a fair-haired, happy god. In the south, he's shown as a darker, sullen, sadistic god. He is married to Enket. Stories tell of how jealous he gets. When he's in a rage, he hides her or sends her away so there's no rain. In addition, Xannil is also jealous of Enket's brother, Innis, the god of fertility. They are forever trying to best each other in drinking contests and wrestling matches, often with disastrous results. Serrat/Serril is usually called to come and fix whatever has been broken.

Symbol: Three horizontal lines.
Color: Yellow

Onnet

The goddess of childbirth and the hunt lives in the court of the gods, though she is often away, traveling, hunting.

Onnet is often portrayed as a crone, though she can take the form of a golden goddess as well. She aids women in childbirth and through their pregnancy. She has a magical bow and can shoot down any prey, no matter how far away. She also uses her bow and magical arrows to bring couples together. There are many stories of young men and women who are great hunters and shoot an arrow into the air, vowing to marry the person who finds it, who after many trials does turn out to be their one true love.

Symbol: Omega. Often represented by a horseshoe.
Color: Orange and green

Creation Myth

In the beginning, there were just the gods and goddesses and no light. Darkness reached everywhere. The gods and goddesses fought with each other all the time just to bring some sort of activity to their endless nights.

So Xannil, the god of the sun, created the first light, which the darkness stole away. He created a second light, which the darkness stole again.

After the third light had been stolen, the gods declared war against the darkness. The darkness divided itself into many beings to fight the gods. The battles raged across the heavens for eons.

Forit, Innis' wife and the fairest of the gods, sang such a beautiful song that the darkness revealed its heart. Innis pierced the heart with his great spear, killing the darkness.

However, the only way Forit could draw out the heart of the darkness was by binding it with her own. When Innis killed the heart of the darkness, he killed his own wife as well.

Forit's body fell from the court of the gods and became the earth. Her teeth became the mountains, her fingers became the many rivers, and the place where her heart had been became the desert.

As the gods and goddesses grieved the loss of the fairest of them all, their tears fell on her prone body.

Forit's freckles, the only imperfection about her, became humanity. The darker freckles became the people of the south, the lighter blemishes became the people of the north.

There are some myths that her heart, still bound with the heart of darkness, lives in the center of the desert.

ABOUT THE AUTHOR

Leah Cutter writes page-turning fiction in exotic locations, such as a magical New Orleans, the ancient Orient, Hungary, the Oregon coast, rural Kentucky, Seattle, Minneapolis, and many others.

She writes literary, fantasy, mystery, science fiction, and horror fiction. Her short fiction has been published in magazines like *Alfred Hitchcock's Mystery Magazine* and *Talebones*, anthologies like Fiction River, and on the web. Her long fiction has been published both by New York publishers as well as small presses.

Find Leah's books on Knotted Road Press at (www.KnottedRoadPress.com)

Follow her blog at www.LeahCutter.com.

Reviews

It's true. Reviews help me sell more books. If you've enjoyed this story, please consider leaving a review of it on your favorite site.

Come someplace new…

Are you a traveler? Do you enjoy exploring strange new worlds, new cultures, new people?

Journey into the various lands envisioned by Leah Cutter.

Sign up for my newsletter and I'll start you on your travels with a free copy of my book, *The Island Sampler*.

I will never spam you or use your email for nefarious purposes. You
can also unsubscribe at any time.

http://www.LeahCutter.com/newsletter/

ABOUT KNOTTED ROAD PRESS

Knotted Road Press fiction specializes in dynamic writing set in mysterious, exotic locations.

Knotted Road Press non-fiction publishes autobiographies, business books, cookbooks, and how-to books with unique voices.

Knotted Road Press creates DRM-free ebooks as well as high-quality print books for readers around the world.

With authors in a variety of genres including literary, poetry, mystery, fantasy, and science fiction, Knotted Road Press has something for everyone.

Knotted Road Press
www.KnottedRoadPress.com